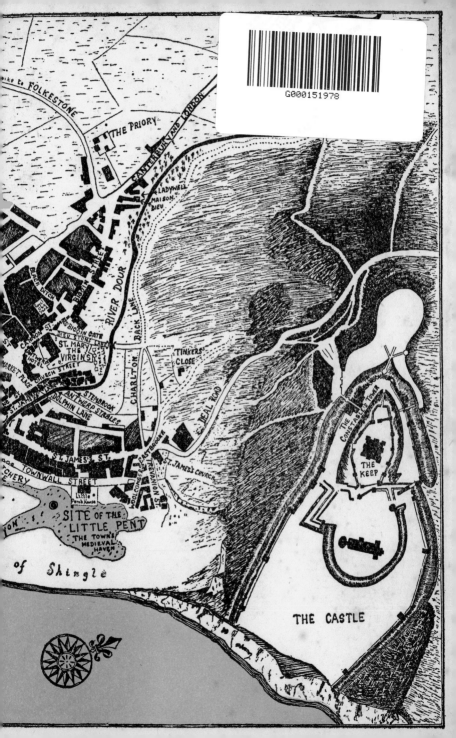

DOVER HARBOUR

miller

DOVER HARBOUR

BY

THOMAS ARMSTRONG

COLLINS
48 PALL MALL LONDON
1942

FIRST IMPRESSION   JUNE, 1942
SECOND   ,,   OCTOBER, 1942

AUTHOR'S FOREWORD

From the days of the Saxon Reeves, when the haven of Dover was no more than the small river which crept into the sea between the Eastern and Western Heights, until the present time, when the Bay of Dover is enclosed into a mighty harbour by a great breakwater and an Admiralty Pier, in all a massive line of masonry two and a half miles in length, the municipal records of the town have been preserved with admirably few exceptions. It should therefore be stated, lest charge be made of vilifying the dead, that the holders of ancient and colourful offices in Town and Port administration mentioned within the covers of this book do not refer to the individuals, worthy or otherwise, who took part in local government between the years 1789-1809. All characters, save those of national importance, are imaginary.

Fidelity in the chronological sequence of history has been adhered to, but perhaps it would be wise to remark that, when Admiral Villeneuve turned the combined fleet to the southard on the 13th of August, 1805, it is assumed as not being beyond the bounds of possibility that the Spanish Governor of Corunna dispatched a courier to the Tyrant of Europe with advice of the French seaman's interpretation of orders which, so ambiguously phrased against calamity befalling, would always provide a loophole of escape for the Imperial strategist who had framed them.

Navigational hazards, courses and bearings are taken from charts and sailing directions of the period.

CONTENTS

Part I

1789-1798

CHAPTER ONE

I

FOR TWO DAYS, beneath lowering grey skies, a westerly gale had howled about the eaves of the old buildings of the ancient Cinque Port of Dover. But now, on the third day, the storm had gone as quickly as it had come. The noon sun was shining brightly, and the Market Place was redolent with the fragrant aroma of wood-burning fires, the smoke from a medley of chimneys drifting leisurely in the light spring airs which had succeeded the fierce wind.

The Market Place appeared unusually quiet even for a day close to the beginning of the week. It was true that diligences and chaises passed regularly to and fro over the cobble-stones, and that there were many stirrings of life about each of the considerable number of inns in the vicinity of the square. But this was Dover, the principal port of embarkation for the Continent, a town which, though small, must possess conveyances and hostelries in abundance if it were to cater effectively for the crowds of strangers who used the packets.

Nevertheless the Market Place was strangely silent, though the reason was not far to seek ; in old St. Mary's, a few paces along Cannon Street, that reason could be found. There, in the church wherein at other times Jurats of Dover elected their Mayor, and free-men, less regularly, polled for parliamentary candidates, two influential families of the Cinque Port now held memorial service for the dead.

For six years, since the Treaty of Versailles had brought the war with France and the American Colonists to a conclusion, the minute bell of St. Mary the Virgin's, high above the departed Peter Monin's clock, had tolled its solemn note at eleven o'clock in the morning of each April Fool's Day.

Their conduct might have been foolhardy, but that was the day on which two younger sons of the banking house of Rochefort and three younger sons of the shipowning and merchanting house of Fagg had courageously died. Not by act of war had these young men perished, but rather in one of noble succour when a fine ship, caught by a sudden squall, had been cast on to the marl reef below Archcliffe Point.

9

On this sportive day, two surviving brothers paid respect to the memory of those who had borne their names.

Some few minutes before, the final trickle of sand having run out of the half-hour glass, the Rector of St. Mary the Virgin's had rounded off his address, and the throng, the last prayer over, began to rise from moth-eaten hassocks. Shortly there was a movement along the aisle and the clatter of the lodesmen coming down from the pilots' gallery at the west end, and soon the congregation began to emerge from the damp and mouldy church, headed through the low arched doorway by the adult members of the families most concerned, two gentlemen and three ladies.

Once on the new Yorkshire stone pavement outside, many stayed for a few minutes in narrow Cannon Street, for life in the old town was taken easily. Most of Dover's leading townsmen were there—amongst them the Mayor, a crowd of Jurats, the Clerk to the Paving Commissioners, sundry notaries, the Collector of Customs, the Agent Victualler, representatives of the Town Guilds, the Loadmanage men, Captains of Mail Packets, the Town Clerk, Members of the Fellowship of the Passage—indeed all who held themselves high in the counsels of the port and harbour.

It was perhaps strange that one of the principals taking part in the recent service did not appear at all disposed to linger. Glancing dourly at the bright sky, John Fagg nodded to his companion.

" Now," he growled, his steely eyes angry, " if the ladies will pardon my abrupt departure, I propose ascertaining whether a thirty-foot cutter can be scraped over the harbour bar. A nice haven we've got, damned if we ain't."

A man around thirty, the merchant-shipper was about middle height, square of shoulders and of jaw, and at the moment looked quite capable of putting his thoughts into far stronger language. Alone amongst that sober-hued assembly he was clad in a coloured coat, a long green one which came down to his grey worsted stockings, and he was singular, too, in that he wore his own hair plain, not so much for better cleanliness but rather because he felt that some gesture was needed against Mr. Pitt's tax on hair powder.

" Yes," he repeated himself, " a damned fine harbour we've got."

Mr. Henry Rochefort smiled. " Maybe 'twould be as well if the Mayor and Jurats began to consider the appointment of an assistant Water Bailiff, eh, John ? "

The duty of the last-named official, since the Middle Ages, had been the embarkation and disembarkation of travellers to and from the Passage Ships which, through lack of depth inshore, had too often been compelled to anchor outside the haven.

John Fagg snorted, but more immediate things concerned him now.
" Seen anything of the Clerk of the Cheque, Henry ? " he asked
levelly.

The Banker, as perhaps was fitting in a gentleman of his profession,
wore that indication of wealth, a fine wig. This curled creation of
horsehair was nodded gently.

" The old trouble, John ? " he inquired, a little indifferently.

Mr. Rochefort was a tall man whose height and presence were
indeed amplified by his sparse figure and austere face. He was swarthy
complexioned, dark-eyed and commanding, but rather pinched of
nostril. Always he held himself as though mindful of his proud
Huguenot ancestry.

" Egad, and you'll be experiencing a little anxiety if the time
should come when you see one of your boxes of guineas perched
precariously on the shoulder of a man stumbling through the surf,"
John Fagg retorted dryly, referring to Mr. Rochefort's many activities
in specie. " It makes all the difference when——" He broke off
abruptly, seeing the gentleman he sought standing in the Norman
porch.

" You'll excuse me," he said brusquely to the three ladies, and
forthwith, without more ado, pushed his way through the press of
local dignitaries.

" How monstrous uncivil of him," commented Mrs. Fagg, but the
eyes beneath the black straw bonnet were not unkind. She knew a
great deal of the exasperations under which her husband suffered.

" The harbour again, Polly ? " asked Mrs. Rochefort sympathetically.

The hands of the banker's wife were thrust deep into a large muff,
and though her clothing was substantial she looked chilled. She was
one of those few women who could justly be termed beautiful, sweet-
faced with it, too, albeit she was perhaps too pallid. In point of fact,
she had never been quite well since the birth of her little daughter.

Mrs. Fagg nodded. " Whenever we have a storm from the west
'tis always the same. And . . ." she smiled, " whenever a gale comes
from that quarter, John's temper rises with it."

" Fie, fie," Mrs. Rochefort laughed outright. " John's temper . . .
John's temper. The only thing I can say, my dear, is that the Harbour
Commissioners can account themselves fortunate they do not have to
deal with another gentleman I could name."

" Oh, come, my love," Henry Rochefort objected, fondly squeezing
his wife's arm as he turned to John Fagg's young sister. " By heaven,
Susan," he asked, " do you believe this of me ? "

Susan Fagg had been the baby of a large family and was not yet
out of her teens. She was a fair-haired young woman, blue-eyed, with

pointed chin, and it was indicative of her character that, despite the intimacy of the Rocheforts and the Faggs, she blushed vividly at the jocular question. It may be, too, that she was somewhat in awe of her brother's friend—he had that effect on stronger-willed people than herself.

" Oh, sir," she began confusedly. " I . . . I——"

Unluckily Mr. Rochefort, being still more heavily playful, succeeded only in frightening her further.

" Prithee, my dear Susan, are you such an ingrate that you decline me your support ? " he demanded crisply.

Thereupon, seeing the state of affairs, the banker's wife promptly drew attention to herself.

" Henry," she said teasingly, " 'tis no use you trying to gain Susan as an ally. Like myself, Susan utterly refuses to uphold you. And as for Polly——"

Mrs. John Fagg laughingly shook her head. " No, Henry," she told him, " we ladies stand together. . . ."

Gratitude and unbounded relief were in Susan Fagg's eyes. Her lips gradually ceased to tremble and the high spots of colour in her cheeks slowly started to fade. Over-sensitive, she was always convinced that some time or other she must completely disgrace herself.

Until her brother returned she stood watching the graceful acrobatics of a flight of pigeons which, against a patch of vivid blue sky, circled, dived and climbed around the tower of St. Mary's. It was beautiful to see them. . . .

John Fagg was in much better spirits, as a broad wink evidenced. " I'm for the South Pier now," he announced. " And after that I intend to have a plain talk with the Clerk at the Council House."

It might be mentioned that Mr. Fagg, but a few moments before, had begun that plain talk within a hallowed porch. This had been very much to the annoyance of the sedate Clerk of the Cheque, who had been indulging in a pleasant piece of gossip with the Mayor.

" Well, Mr. Waade," John Fagg had observed grimly, " I have to thank you for the honour you have just done to the memory of my brothers. But more to the point is, when shall I be able to find you in that empty, echoing Council House of yours ? "

The building he spoke of was the place from which the Harbour Commissioners, through their Clerk of Cheque, directed the affairs of Dover Harbour, which had long been wrested from the hands of those, the townsfolk of Dover, most vitally interested in the port's prosperity.

This stinging shaft caused Mr. Waade's cherubic face to become plum-coloured.

" Empty . . . echoing ! " he stuttered. " I fail to comprehend, Mr. Fagg——"

John Fagg had turned his unwelcome attentions to the Mayor, whose office gave him a seat with the Commissioners. "And when do you propose opening your mouth about the rotten condition of the harbour ? " he demanded bitingly. " Or are you also another who seeks a private quay for himself ? "

" Damme, sir ! " roared the Mayor.

" Thirty years or more since we had a Mayor worth his salt," continued John Fagg savagely. " And that was old John Bazely. He did strive until he had the satisfaction of knowing that half of the Passing Tolls were allocated to Dover for the repair and improvement of the port. But since then, ugh ! "

The constitution of the Board left any Mayor hopelessly out-numbered, so the manner in which Mr. Fagg contrasted this fighting example with others less persevering was perhaps rather unfair. But it was true that many a Mayor had taken the easy course and, whilst feathering their nests in what way they might, had not troubled over-much about the greater good of the town.

" And as for the Harbour Commissioners themselves," he added scathingly, " nothing more than a company of country gentry who don't know the difference between a spring and a neap tide. But what's the use——" He turned his back on two gentlemen scarlet with mortification, and then rejoined his wife and friends, there to find his sister Susan beginning to breathe again.

" And how is the likeness coming along, Elizabeth ? " he later asked jovially. Mrs. Rochefort, on her proud husband's insistence, was in course of having her portrait painted.

She made a laughing rejoinder.

Presently the three ladies set off to change the dark clothes of mourning they had decided it proper to wear, and John Fagg stepped out towards the harbour. Henry Rochefort, at his usual quick though dignified gait, made for the Guildhall. It was the day for the sitting of the Court of Requests, and the bank had a number of small debts outstanding regarding which it was necessary to institute proceedings.

After parting from his wife and the Rocheforts, John Fagg walked briskly towards the western side of the Market Place, along which were the ruins of ancient St. Martin-le-Grand.

To his left hand, in the middle of the Market Place, was the old Guildhall, with the gloomy jail directly ahead, the Almshouse Hospital being farther beyond. Taking the shortest route to the harbour, he picked his path through the tortuities of Last Lane, a narrow street overshadowed by the buildings where once leather artificers had fashioned shoes for the monks of St. Martin's.

Then he came into busy Snargate Street, a slow curving thoroughfare following a line of overhanging cliffs which seemed ready at any time to fall and engulf the houses and business premises which lay on the landward side of the street. On the other side, too, were more residences and commercial establishments, and beyond these, seen through the fire-alleys, was the Pent, a far-reaching stretch of water.

A little down this important street, immediately by a wall-plaque which was the only indication that once Snar Gate had stood there, he encountered the Clerk of the Cheque, doubtless on his way to the Council House. Mr. Waade gave him but a frigid acknowledgment.

" And when," began John Fagg, without preamble, " are the ' eleven discreet men ' proposing to do something . . . *anything ?* " he demanded sarcastically.

By King James the First's Charter, the control of the port had been vested in that number of gentlemen, one of whom was to be the Mayor of Dover. Apart from this last not a single Dover-born man, during the one hundred and eighty-three years which had elapsed since then, had apparently ever been considered to have the necessary accomplishments.

" The Commissioners, my dear sir," Mr. Oliver Waade answered angrily, " have already given instructions for expenditure on certain harbour works. The sill of the Pent is to be lowered and——"

" New wine into old bottles," John Fagg commented bitterly. " What I want to know is when the Commissioners purpose a comprehensive scheme of harbour development."

" But what action can be taken against the forces of nature, may I inquire, Mr. Fagg ? " the Clerk blustered.

He did not receive direct answer.

" One simple policy have the Commissioners," growled the ship-owner. " Let the shingle come, they say, and we will draw ground rents from the property subsequently built upon it."

" That does not answer my question," the official was rash enough to say pertly.

John Fagg gave him a look. " You poor fool," he said quietly but none the less forcibly, " if you'd but keep your clap closed a minute whilst you thought a space you'd realise that in close on two hundred years no real effort has ever been made by the Commission to defeat the forces you gabble about."

Luckily this blistering observation was made within the quietude of Pent-side, into which the two gentlemen had turned shortly before reaching the unfinished Grand Shaft on Snargate Street.

" Mr. Fagg . . . sir," stuttered the Clerk. He was crimson with fury, his eyes were venomous, he had all the bearing of one who would like to, but dare not, say a host of scurrilous things.

" Well, attempt there's going to be soon," John Fagg interposed grimly. "Something is going to be done if I have to turn this town upside down."

Mr. Waade sniggered. "You'll find that the townsfolk lack any authority concerning the harbour," he said, not without relish.

The shipowner was at him like a shot. "And the Harbour Commissioners'll soon find that energy and faith can move mountains," he retorted dryly. "There *are* men hereabouts who aren't in the humour to sit complacently much longer, and once we start——"

"You and Henry Rochefort have always thought that whatever you set your minds on you'll accomplish," Mr. Waade said angrily. "But stubborn as you both hold yourselves to be, and hand-in-hand as ever you may work, you'll soon find that you're up against a legally constituted body that'll——"

"*Body*, aye ! " interrupted John Fagg, smiling suddenly. "And dead, forsooth," he threw over his shoulder.

Striding out, he proceeded briskly into the hustle and bustle of Custom House Quay, the wharf which fringed the Basin, the middle one of the harbour's three waterways.

The Pilots Look-out, towards the extremity of the South Pier, was a fine vantage point from which to look at either the town or to seaward. But John Fagg, his back against the stout flagpost, and his face towards the sun, did not seem aware of a spectacle which normally would have aroused his enthusiasm and envy : that of fine ships—the East Indiaman proceeding towards Dungeness, so close inshore that her passengers, on the short poop, on the stern walk, framed in the quarter windows, were distinctly visible, as was the fact that this merchant vessel was pierced for guns ; and the three-master, further towards the horizon, with her royals set flying, a magnificent sight under her press of sail.

He was vaguely eyeing the shipbuilding yards on the beach below Archcliffe Point and the ten-year-old earthworks of Townshend's Battery, so made in the days of the American War as to be agreeable to the latest methods of fortification.

"Aye, she's there all right, John," a voice aroused him from his reverie. "That's the *Martha*, sure enow."

This smaller vessel of the Fagg-owned ships was bringing coke, for subsequent transport into the interior of the county, where in the kilns it would later be used for drying hops.

It was low water and the Tidal Harbour was dried out, making it all the easier to see the bulky twelve-foot-high accumulation of shingle which the sea, in two days, had deposited between the pier-heads.

"And what depth is there on the bar at high water to-night, Dick ? " asked Mr. Fagg, knowing the answer already.

He made no comment when he received a confirmation which told him that the *Martha's* cargo would have to be transhipped into lighters, an unnecessary expense which would turn a fair profit into a slight loss. Indeed he appeared to be more interested in a flight of godwits, migrants returning, whose yearly advent had caused them to be called ' lambing birds,' harbingers of spring.

" Right, Dick," he murmured thoughtfully.

Mr. Richard Breton, the Harbourmaster, a pleasant-looking gentleman, looked his surprise, but John Fagg made no further observation, and did not seem disposed to linger. Of a truth the shipowner was in a most unusual daydream, so much so that, at the side of the Tidal Harbour, he found his feet entangled amidst the corks and fine mesh of the mackerel nests set out there to freshen.

Thereupon he took a greater hold of himself, avoiding the silver-gleaming fish which, thrown down on the very edge of the quay, were being auctioned.

His route took him through Crane Street, then half-way on the Cross Wall, both of which flanked the Tidal Harbour. Thence he covered a few yards of the busy Custom House Quay, cutting then into old Strond Street, until finally he emerged into Elizabeth Street.

To one side of this thoroughfare was the old Paradise Pent, once a prosperous haven but now a waste of shingle, ooze and reed ; on the other side were solid seventeenth-century buildings, for the most part used as commercial premises.

John Fagg entered the large property which was his warehouse. It would not have been quite accurate, but neither would it have been quite unfair, to describe the atmosphere within as completely akin to that he had attributed recently to the Council House. If not empty-echoing, there was not the hum of commercial enterprise as might have been the case.

The Fagg dinner was at half-past two o'clock in the afternoon. A quarter before the hour, Mr. Fagg gave a few final instructions to his two clerks.

Apart from his shipowning activities, John Fagg indulged in a limited though varied merchanting trade, as was evinced by the range of goods in the lower storehouse. There were tubs of tobacco from Bristol, boxes of bellows from King's Lynn, cases of clay pipes from Poole, and violin bellies from London. Bales of woollens from Yorkshire, glassware from Newcastle, haberdashery and Manchester goods.

" Very good, sir," the elder clerk replied promptly.

After nodding again, Mr. Fagg sought out his right-hand man, to give the last word before returning home.

"And see about them lighters for the *Martha*, Valentine," he
shouted when he glimpsed that worthy.

Christian names may sometimes be fitting, but of all that might
have been bestowed upon the ex-Navyman, Valentine was the least
appropriate. Valentine Pepper was short and nearly as broad ; he
had great cauliflower ears and a face tanned towards duskiness.
Above all he had a definite squint which, when his barrel chest
swelled with homeric laughter, caused him to look fantastic, and
which also, when he was angered, gave him an expression of the most
sinister. At the moment, too, his appearance was in no wise enhanced
by a colourful black eye.

'Captain' Pepper—he had forced the title on the town some years
before—hastily closed a cupboard door, so hastily that he caused the
unmistakable chink of a glass.

"What-o, me 'earty ! " he retorted unthinkingly.

"Valentine ! " roared Mr. Fagg.

"Sir," the boatswain replied with sudden dignity.

His employer reiterated the order, to receive a reply couched in
terms so concise as to make it evident that, whatever might be Captain
Pepper's private diversions, he was also exceedingly efficient.

"All arranged, sir," he said smartly. "Everything shipshape, and
twelve waggons chartered for when the stuff's ashore."

Mr. Fagg grunted, made a few more inquiries on other points, and
opened three letters which one of the clerks had brought in from the
post office.

He then indicated his intention of leaving but, before doing so,
glanced somewhat significantly at that lurid, half-closed eye.

"Her husband catch you, Valentine ? " he observed conversationally.

"Sir ! " Captain Pepper retorted bemusedly.

"Or was it her brother ? " persisted his employer.

Possessing a physiognomy hardly lending itself to histrionics, the
boatswain, attempting a pained expression, only succeeded in making
himself all the more grotesque. But his manner of utterance, after he
had solemnly cleared his throat, made it very clear that he felt he
was resting under a most unjust implication. Before making his regular
call at the Fountain the previous evening, he continued loftily, he had
been taking a meditative stroll in the vicinity of the Plain.

"The Plain ! " suddenly chuckled John Fagg, tickled by the sober
mention of this low-town area which harboured pushing schools and
the rest.

Captain Pepper, more hurried now, rapidly finished his tale. It
was an account of an encounter with a shapely female who apparently
had not known the nature of the district in which she found herself,

and who had responded to the boatswain's diplomatic warning with a well-delivered swing of her fist.

" But it's the last bloody time, keel-haul me if it ain't, sir," he ended energetically, becoming the petty officer. " No more blasted Covent Garden nuns for me. Me, I'm for a-settling down with a nice little woman."

Mr. Fagg guffawed. " Made your selection yet, Valentine ? " he asked.

Vividly and blasphemously his servant pointed out that as yet he had had little time. Getting spliced was a major article of war, and he was not going to board the first wench he espied. But when he saw the right piece of goods . . .

" I'll take 'er 'fore she knows the wind's out of 'er canvas," he roared. " Me 'an 'er'll be bubble and squeak afore she's run up 'er battle ensign. And what's more . . ."

His master was still smiling long after the warehouse was behind. Mr. Fagg took the other way out of Elizabeth Street, emerging into Limekiln Street at the corner where recently the Wesleyans had converted two dwelling-houses to make the first Dover Chapel for their denomination.

Soon he was in Snargate Street and once more passing the entrance to the Grand Military Shaft, nodding to several gentlemen or raising his hat to a number of ladies who passed into the bow-windowed houses margining the old thoroughfare. Further down he paused to examine the bills posted at the Playhouse, and later, on the opposite side, passed by Henry Rochefort's commodious Jacobean mansion.

Then he was nearing Severus's Gate and Bench Street, and thus not so very far from home.

2

Dover's bay was in a semicircular form, with Snargate Street, before which were the Basin and the Pent, forming the land boundary on the southern half. On the northern portion of the semicircle, in reality a continuation of Snargate Street, was Town Wall Street, where John Fagg's residence was sited.

Little Pent House was modern, stucco-faced, and had been built at the time of Polly Fagg's marriage. She had point-blank refused to live in the old family house, which had been available when John Fagg's father had died about the same time. At the front the house came flush with the shingle sidewalk, but at the back, extending some little distance towards the lofty bank of shingle which hereabouts

touched the land after traversing Dover's bay, there was as beautiful
a garden as could be found in the town.

Mrs. Fagg was very proud of her house, as well she might be, for,
from the hall in white and gilt to the dormer windows of the servants'
bedrooms, the appointments were perfection.

Early that same evening the family were in the parlour, a cosy
elliptical-shaped room at the rear of the house, with three windows
overlooking the garden. Between the centre and right-hand windows
John Fagg had insisted that his pedestal writing-table should be placed,
thus securing for himself, when doing a little work at home, a view
which had always enchanted him. It was of the pier-heads, seen
through the one fortunate break in that tall barrier of shingle.

" Yes," he remarked, putting down the quill, " I didn't think she
looked too well."

Mrs. Fagg had been expressing her concern about Mrs. Rochefort,
but now she came to more personal matters.

" You'll be off early in the morning, dear ? " she said. " Gravesend, Rochester and Faversham isn't it this time ? "

These were the havens from which Fagg bottoms ran between
London River and the ports of the Baltic or North of England.

" 'Tis, love," grunted John Fagg. " And a nice damned shipowner
I look, having to set out on my horse to have a look at my biggest
ships now and then."

Mrs. Fagg, who was sitting in a wheel-back chair darning socks
before the dancing sea-coal fire in the Adam grate, vigorously remarked on the absurdity of it.

" But pray, John, what can be done about it ? " she asked.

Her husband, however, had decided to let the unprofitable topic
rest for a while. In any case, his attention had been captured by the
sight of his children.

" What's Charles doing ? " he laughed, throwing up the right-hand
window.

His two little daughters were playing at the extreme end of the
garden, but through the low trees beyond them he could see his son
busily occupied in the Canyon.

This deep cut, so christened by young Charles, extended from the
bottom of the garden to the very edge of the sea, passing through
the towering bank of shingle on its way. Had it not been for this
natural gorge, John Fagg would have had a far more restricted view
whilst glancing up when the suitable word eluded him, and certainly
would not have had that delightful vista, the pier-heads seen beyond
the end of his son's ' Canyon.'

" Charles," he shouted, after appreciatively remarking on the
lovely scent of wallflowers which was now permeating the room.

His small daughters, with as much speed as their hampering skirts permitted, made a bee-line for the house. But young Charles first put down the shovel he had been using, then set up a stick to mark the spot he had reached in his engineering scheme.

Susan Fagg had come into the room, and her brother, seeing her, gave her an affectionate hug. John Fagg had always been exceptionally fond of a sister who, though she was nearly grown up now, he would probably always regard as the family baby of his young manhood.

"Charles," she said laughingly, "proposes connecting the Little Pent with the sea."

"He does, does he?" John Fagg laughed. "And if he succeeds, some day or other we'll find the sea washing round the garden walls. Well, Cinque Port ships used to anchor there once, you know."

So they once did. Beyond the garden walls was just that same sort of expanse—waste, mud and reeds—which could be seen at the other side of the town, at Paradise Pent, close by the warehouse. All that represented the story of Dover's havens, of one refuge after another coming to disuse.

Charles was now shouting up. "Papa," he called out, "will you be avail . . . available shortly?"

With extreme gravity Mr. Fagg leaned out to speak to his son, a small boy brown of face and of grey eyes very steady.

"Within twenty minutes, m'lad," he said. "I trust that length of time will not prove inconvenient."

Charles thought. "It will be ad . . . admirable, Papa," he remarked at length.

"Right," Mr. Fagg was starting to say but, a smile playing at the corner of his mouth, adroitly changed the word into the more dignified "indubitably."

The forehead craned back below became a little perplexed.

"Indub . . . indub——" Charles Fagg began uncertainly.

"Indubitably, my boy," his father said momentously.

His son tried again. "Indubitab . . . indubitab . . . ," he muttered, until at last it came. "Indubitably," he said precisely, a smile of gratification breaking out.

"Indubitably," Mr. Fagg confirmed, and began to grin only when he saw that small figure trotting off down the garden.

Both Mrs. Fagg and Susan were laughing helplessly, though the former did make one attempt to be severe.

"Really, John," she expostulated.

"But 'tis so funny, Polly," giggled her sister-in-law. "I'm sure I'm hard put to it when Charles brings out one of his jaw-breakers."

There was a patter of feet over the tiled floor of the hall, and with the advent of the two little girls any further discussion was cut short.

Minnie and Lou, scooped on to their father's lap, made sufficient noise, with their shrill laughter and delirious squealings, for that.

Soon the light of the April evening began to fade. Keziah Hart, the martinet who had charge of the children, first came for the two girls. Later, getting near the time when a taper would be brought round for the wall-lights, she was heard in the garden.

" Master Charles," she screamed, " be you coming . . . if——"

Mr. John Fagg, though both his wife and sister denied it, swore that he heard his son reply with the new word.

3

Before midsummer there occurred the event which was to have such striking effect upon all mankind. John Fagg received intimation of this when, in his fast-sailing Folkestone-built cutter *Emma*, he put into Ostend.

Of the legitimate business which Mr. Fagg did, both as a shipowner and merchant, a substantial portion was transacted with the Low Countries and with the ports of Northern France, and it was his practice, twice a year, to visit consular officials, agents and so forth, from the Scheldt down to Havre. Which explains why, in early June, he sailed for Rotterdam, taking with him the seven-year-old Charles, who often before had accompanied his father to Calais and Boulogne but never before had been favoured with such an extensive trip.

So the excited young gentleman saw Rotterdam, Antwerp and Ostend. At this last port Mr. Fagg heard such confused account of happenings in France that he decided there and then to leave, to omit his calls both at Dunkirk and Calais, and to reach Boulogne with as much dispatch as wind and tide would permit. Boulogne was a town with which he did as much business as any other two added together.

He found the French port seething, with a strange new flag, the tricolour, flying everywhere. The well-worn, long-uncared-for planks of the quayside were piled dangerously heavily with baggage in care of servants whose manner ranged between the extremes of fearfulness and truculence. Everywhere, keeping close together, were well-dressed groups of those who, pending the restoration of order, had decided to take a sojourn abroad.

The *Emma* was secured alongside the poor wooden jetty, and was lucky to have got the berth, for soon lying outside were a dozen or more sundry craft, each reaping a handsome revenue in passage money, and none profiting more than those ruffians the local watermen who, between the muddy verge of the shore and these vessels, were either ferrying or carrying the exalted travellers.

Mr. Fagg's fine cutter was to sail on the evening tide, but before then she took in her cargo—flagons of olive oil, wines, small casks of French vinegar, threescore demi-pieces of linens, cambrics and lawns, and, very openly, a small quantity of brandy. Meantime her owner completed his various matters in the town precincts, not the least of which resulted in the less open re-embarkation, when brimming with the best brandy, of the many dozen stone jars which he had caused to be placed empty in the secret double-bottom before leaving Dover. These handy containers would serve as ballast for the return journey and the profit on this little venture would be quite worth while, even to the gentleman who was the biggest free-trader between Hastings and Margate.

Whilst his father busied himself thus, young Charles occupied himself in his own fashion, his first trip being to the Tour d'Odre, where lazy water lapped quietly against the lichen-covered rock foundations. There Charles stripped to the buff, and in the sun-warmed water bathed with a swarm of chattering urchins who welcomed him vociferously, and whose acquaintance he had first made two years before.

Later his fellow swimmers and dog-paddlers decided, as one man, to see off their friend, the *citoyen-anglais*—they had already adopted the current phrase. Indeed they went further than that, for the greater body of them followed Charles as he squeezed through the crowd of passengers who appeared to fill every available inch of deck space in the *Emma*. Mr. Fagg, urgently beseeched or haughtily directed, had proved not at all averse to earning a quite considerable and unexpected bag of clinking *louis d'or*.

" And where the devil have you been ? " he demanded, espying his son.

Young Charles, rubbing the side of his grimy nose with an even dirtier hand, pondered the question.

" First, Papa," he started to enumerate gravely, " I had a swim with Henri and Jacques and Pierre and——"

Mr. Fagg, despite a previous anxiety, was at some pains to conceal the amusement he felt at hearing his small boy preparing to account in a statement which he could see was destined to be both meticulous and lengthy.

" Dammit," he growled, " can't you see the ebb's begun ? "

Young Charles made no reply. Instead he glanced over the side at a small pulling boat which was tied to a buoy. The bight of the securing rope hung limp in the water, a positive sign that the tide was as yet slack.

" And get rid of that mob," bellowed Mr. Fagg, thus covertly discomfited.

"Yes, Papa," young Charles replied meekly, and forthwith went off into a shrill and vehement torrent of the local dialect.

"How he's picked up . . ." grunted Mr. Fagg, and glared when he caught sight of the grinning face of his skipper.

"A rare 'un is that," chuckled Captain Maxton.

By now the last of Charles's ragged friends were ashore and soon, a slight gurgle announcing that the tide was beginning to flow, warps were cast off, sail was made and the gaff set.

The *Emma* began to move towards the open sea.

The sun was rim down and the breeze gentle. The *Emma* had little or no heel, and the tiny sea ripples sucked and slapped melodiously under her bow as, that soft zephyr favouring, she headed to pass well to the weather side of the Ripraps shoal. Beyond there, her passage taking her between this danger to mariners and another, the always hidden sands of Gunman's Land, she altered course a point and a half, her new slant keeping the South Foreland dead ahead.

Young Charles, for some considerable time, had been thoroughly interrogating a number of noble passengers. Now he made his way to his father. Mr. Fagg, having finished the checking of the manifest in the fuggy cuddy, was on deck again, enjoying a pipe of tobacco which also had been gained without the payment of duty.

"Well, m'lad?" he said, when he saw who was approaching.

"Very well, Papa," replied young Charles unthinkingly. He wore an air of indecision. Evidently he came to the conclusion that the most satisfactory way to resolve his uncertainty was to try out the suitable leading question.

"From now on, Papa," he announced gravely, "all men are equal."

"They are, are they?" grunted Mr. Fagg. "And do you believe that, m'lad?"

Young Charles reflected awhile. "No, Papa," he eventually said stoutly. "But that was what they were saying in Boulogne. Though," he continued artlessly, "all the gentlemen I've asked aboard here haven't agreed."

His father guffawed. "Have you been asking *them*?" he spluttered.

He received an unwinking gaze. "Well, they're Frenchies too, Papa."

Mr. Fagg chuckled so heartily that the pipe nearly fell out of his mouth. "I'm damned, damned if I ain't," he roared, and forthwith sought to unburden himself to Captain Maxton of this gem.

More than five hours had now passed, and half the crossing had been accomplished. In the afterglow the white cliffs of Dover began to stand out clear. From the deck of the *Emma*, now bowling along under the influence of the usual fresh evening breeze, it was possible to see the coastline from the low promontory of Dungeness to the South Foreland.

From Dover to Folkestone the land kept high, but from the latter village, without pier or shelter and with its boats drawn up the shingle beach, that lofty line started to fall. On that line were ports once famous in the annals of English history, but ports which now were no more or at best sadly declined. There were Rye and Winchelsea, mud-choked and forsaken ; Hythe nothing more than a small pleasure resort ; Lympne, to which oared galleys had once sailed, now a village tucked away in the green folds of the Kentish hills ; and old Romney, in whose churchyard the oaken ships guarding England had aforetime cast anchor. And there was Dymchurch Wall, which had gained all the scotted acres of the vast Romney Marsh, but which was only, so many nautical men held, an unnatural obstacle preventing the un-hindered spreading of the sea, thereby causing the ills which had so blighted the proud Cinque Ports.

"Aye," Captain Maxton said sadly, as though reading his employer's thoughts, "and methinks old Dover's going the same way. I reckon 'twill not be long before the Ropewalk is cluttered up with them new-fangled Margate bathing-machines."

Mr. Fagg eyed him grimly. " Will it ? " he said succinctly. " Well, we'll see."

Some nine or ten miles on the lee bow the two great stretches of the Goodwins were beginning to be uncovered, though only for an infinitely small proportion of their far-reaching extent.

" *Swallowed* in a tide ? " gasped young Charles Fagg, who had been having a long yarn with the leading hand.

" Them bloody Goodwins, Master Charles," that seafaring man replied huskily, and went on, to the joy of his small listener, to recall tragic events which, winter after winter, took place in that dreaded place.

Dover was coming up quick. From the sea it was easy, admirably so, to see the valley at the foot of which lay the huddled red roofs of the town, delightfully confined between those high cliffs ; the Western Heights to the left, above Shakespeare Cliff, and to the right, perched on the complementary eminence, the Keep of the Castle, with its countless towers, Pharos and castellated walls.

Inshore and westwards of the South Pier there now showed the flat rocks of the King's Foundation, relic of a monarch who, knowing his country's need in this outpost nearest the Continent, had expended £80,000 all in vain effort.

" Well, King Hal tried it, you know, Mr. Fagg," Captain Maxton said obstinately. " And many more than him for that matter."

" Henry was unlucky," John Fagg observed stubbornly, and went on to explain how the Foundation, built up only to low-water level at the time, had, in combination with a south-west gale sweeping up the Channel, merely acted as a trap for the shingle which, in consequence, had formed itself into a great bank across the bay.

Dusk was coming, and ahead lights were beginning to twinkle through bull's-eye window-glass. On the old lighthouse of Dungeness the sea-coal in the grate at the summit had been fired, its yellow blaze just discernible through the black smoke which as yet had not died down.

The *Emma* dropped anchor off Archcliffe Point, where were the ruins of Our Lady of Pity, another foundation which a medieval nobleman had raised in praise of being saved from the sea. There she would have to wait until an hour before high water, when she might with reasonable care be taken through the pier heads.

" A damned nice haven," muttered John Fagg.

Charles, who had been listening to an eerie account of Jamaica Land, a spit on the North Goodwin where the first hand swore he had landed, heard his father make this strange observation.

Later he made professional inquiry as to the reason.

4

There was always a certain amount of hustle and bustle on the eighth of September each year, when in the old church of St. Mary the Virgin the Jurats of the town elected their chief magistrat for the following twelve months. For some weeks prior to this date local dignitaries were often seen in solemn conclave, there were many informal meetings in the Antwerp Hotel, and altogether all those indications of manœuvre which formed the political background of these activities.

These various exertions, it must be stressed, were purely a masculine prerogative, and the ladies had sufficient wisdom to avoid interference with their menfolk. Nor had they, it must be allowed, any desire to intrude into such dull affairs.

So it followed, in the same year in which reports of mob violence came from France, when considerable numbers of enthusiastic English Whigs crossed from Dover to Calais, that Mrs. Rochefort entertained her best friend in her charming Snargate Street house.

They were in the little drawing-room, a room divided from the drawing-room proper by wide, double doors.

" A shocking affair, really I think 'twas," Mrs. Fagg was saying emphatically.

" And together *all* night, too," added Mrs. Rochefort. " The law *should* be altered, Polly."

They were discussing the case of a girl who, after being caught in some misdemeanour, had from sundown to sunrise been locked in one of the Castle cells with two soldiers who themselves had been crimed.

" Of course we have to preserve law and order after all, Elizabeth," Mrs. Fagg said sagely. " And there isn't anywhere else where a woman could be jailed."

Mrs. Rochefort began to speak rather hazily on the agitation in recent years for prison reform, but her friend's thoughts were more on the girl who had spent the night in such circumstances.

"But with *two* men," Mrs. Fagg interposed significantly. "Really one can only pray for the best, but that female creature will be lucky if jail fever is the only outcome of . . ."

Mrs. Rochfort grimaced a little wildly, and simultaneously coughed to amplify her warning. There are some things not decent for a young unmarried woman to hear, and in the deep bay window with its pleasant view of the shipping in the Pent, Susan Fagg was sitting, her slim fingers netting a pair of white gloves.

Adroitly Mrs. Fagg moved on to safer ground, made some very ordinary comment concerning the hat she herself was trimming, and then drew her sister-in-law into the conversation. Or rather was speaking to that embarrassed young lady when her hostess's sudden exclamation drove any other thought from her mind.

" What is't, Elizabeth ? " she asked solicitously.

Mrs. Rochefort, slightly amused even as she did so, had hastily placed on her satinwood work-table the piece of petit-point on which she had been engaged, and was standing up rubbing her arm ruefully.

"A most exquisite shooting pain," she laughed. " What with recurring bouts of this and . . ." she lightly touched her bosom, " the other . . ."

Mrs. Fagg was uncommonly diverted by the allusion to the second ailment. Her friend was having slight discomfort in the breast, and Doctor Crouch had diagnosed that this might be the aftermath of the birth of the baby. But the learned gentleman, infinitely delicately, had hinted that probably the real reason was the style of corsets fashionable ladies wore for the upthrust of their breasts.

"Well, . . ." John Fagg's wife's smile was just a little Rabelaisian, " if you must be *à la mode*, Elizabeth."

Mrs. Rochefort twinkled at that, and was remarking that both shared the same staymaker when another spasm seized her, so severe this time that she turned very pale, much to the concern of the two ladies.

" 'Tis no more than a trifle," she said, when the sharp agony had ceased.

" Methinks it seemed a cruel trifle," Susan Fagg ventured shyly.

"Oh no, my dear," Mrs. Rochefort, recovered, laughed gaily, and made to dismiss the subject, though before doing so she made them both promise not to mention the matter to her husband. "You know what Henry is," she smiled fondly, "even if my little finger aches."

Yes, they knew what Henry Rochefort thought of his wife. How he always worried whenever the least thing ailed her, how he was so utterly devoted that it verily seemed that any suffering of hers gave to him, not merely mental, but indeed an equivalent physical pain.

"All an ado about nothing," Mrs. Rochefort ended lightly.

The pedlar had called that morning and, to distract her visitors, she brought out the broadsides, caricatures and pamphlets she had purchased. There were fairy-tales for the children, some ghost stories for herself, and for her husband murder trials, dying speeches and confessions. Last of all was a selection of ballads and love songs.

"For George," she told them, eyes dancing. "I'm sure, so far as ballads are concerned, he has a pretty conceit of himself. Or . . ." she added quizzically, "he had some six months ago. By now he may have changed, of course."

George Rochefort was Mr. Henry Rochefort's young brother, a youth not quite twenty. Shortly before the sixth anniversary of the quick death of the brothers intervening between himself and his stern elder brother, he had left Dover and, to learn further aspects of the banking profession, was to be away for two years. This period he was to divide between London, Paris, Antwerp, and then London again.

"I always thought," said Susan Fagg, blushing furiously, "that he had a very pretty voice."

"As to that," replied George Rochefort's sister-in-law, smiling, though most lovingly, at the recollection of him, "I'm afraid that I was rather of the mind that he liked himself in the role of singer."

"And what is his present role ? " laughed Mrs. Fagg. "How fares he with the ladies and gentlemen of the drama ? "

Mrs. Rochefort threw up her hands and rolled her eyes drolly.

"La, la ! " she giggled. "My dear, you are completely *outré*. The Drama is all behind."

"And what is George's latest, Elizabeth ? " tittered Mrs. Fagg.

Mrs. Rochefort's lips were twitching. "Music and the Opera, my dear," she said, essaying to be impressive despite her merriment.

The two ladies were highly tickled about all this, and laughed uproariously. As for John Fagg's young sister, all one could see of her was the top of her white satin cap as she bent low and industriously over her task.

About that time a servant girl came in with the news that Teakettle Tom had arrived. Her mistress produced from a reticule the penny which would buy enough Ladywell water for a brew.

" I always have it," she explained. " The wells about here . . ."
She shrugged distastefully, meantime glancing at the lantern clock.

The Ladywell Spring was in the wall of the Maison Dieu, and most
ladies living in the same district similarly acquired their water for the
making of tea. The backs of the houses in Snargate Street were on
Pentside, and so admirably placed for the disposal of nightsoil and
filth. But it was suspected, and there was unpleasant evidence in
support, that the water of the Pent percolated back to foul the wells
at the rear of the houses.

" One can't be too careful," agreed Mrs. Fagg, and from that,
whilst Mrs. Rochefort was taking from the commode a silver tea-caddy,
went on to speak of the coming autumn and the precautions she was
taking to guard the children against the putrid fevers of that season.

Soon the tea was ready and with it, as the ladies daintily handled
the fine India china, more talk, mainly of a domestic nature. The cook
who was now asking thirteen instead of the amply sufficient twelve
guineas a year ; the roasting fowls which Mrs. Fagg was buying at
9d. each against the 10d. Mrs. Rochefort was paying ; the merits
of a brown cambric muslin for morning wear, and so on.

In the midst of this orgy on family concerns Susan Fagg, cup in
hand, returned to her curved window stool. Her low bodice showed
a figure immature but definitely budding ; the manner in which she
held her tight but long-flowing skirts indicating her displeasure
regarding something.

Despite their preoccupations the two older ladies found time to
exchange significant glances.

Then Mrs. Rochefort's two-year-old daughter was brought in by
Martha Teddiman, and all else was forgotten with her advent.

" Lovey," cried Mrs. Fagg.

" Such sweetness," Susan Fagg said ecstatically.

The days when children, for their good, had received harsh treatment, when they were taken to executions to teach them something
of the world, when after seeing a felon dangled they were, the better
to impress the lesson, themselves whipped on the return home, were
fast passing.

So, now that indulgence was quickly becoming the mode, it was
perfectly proper for Mrs. Rochefort to sun herself in the child worship
which was being accorded to her pretty daughter.

" Isn't she the divinest creature, Martha ? " crooned Susan Fagg.

Martha Teddiman, a trim-figured and capable-looking young
woman, differed decidedly, though nevertheless her rather sharp face
was soft with affection.

" She can be a very Peter-grievous little girl, Miss Susan," she
declared sternly.

Miss Caroline Rochefort, seated on her mother's lap, stared wonderingly, her hand so far into her mouth that the fat-creased wrist seemed in danger, shortly, of disappearing also.

And then, suddenly, young Miss Rochefort favoured the company with a radiant smile. It was the same enchanting smile with which she was to cause, later in life, so much havoc in so many male hearts.

CHAPTER TWO

I

By the next summer the lodgings of Dover were becoming crowded with French folk, traffic with the Continent was rapidly falling off, and Englishmen more and more were seriously discussing the trend of events abroad.

On a hot Saturday in June, the Rocheforts and the Faggs took an outing to the Chalybeate Springs at Foord. It was Mr. Rochefort's fancy that draughts of the ferruginous water might prove of some benefit to his wife's disorder, about which he was becoming vaguely alarmed.

At the village the party left Mr. Rochefort's roomy barouche. The path up the valley was along the course of a fast-flowing stream which the two boys were enjoying themselves in jumping. All the children were there that afternoon, Charles Fagg with his two small sisters, Minnie and Lou, and Louis Rochefort with Caroline.

" Bet you can't jump it here, Charles," said Mr. Rochefort's heir. Louis Rochefort was a year older and a head taller than Charles. He was amusingly like his father in appearance, indeed the spit and image of the banker.

" Can you ? " Charles riposted blandly.

" Can you ? " demanded Louis, sensing disbelief.

The little river had widened at that point. Charles examined the jump appraisingly, and then shook his head.

" No, I can't," he admitted. " And neither can you." ·

Louis jeered. " Ur . . ." he said scornfully. But did not venture the crossing, a fact which the calm Charles noticed but at the same time did not comment upon.

The small Caroline was giving a certain amount of trouble to her ' Aunt ' Susan. She wanted to play with the big boys, she stated firmly. She did not want to play with either Minnie or Lou, she reiterated even more emphatically.

" A little madam, isn't she ? " laughed her mother.   " Caroline dear . . ."

Miss Caroline set up a howl of protest, made a dash towards Louis and Charles, was caught by the laughing Susan, and finally brought back, Mr. Rochefort's eyes all the while showing delight in his high-spirited little daughter.

They were now at the turn of the valley, and ahead was the famed Cherry Orchard, a lovely turf-covered amphitheatre beyond the confines of which could be seen the sugar-loaf pikes of the hills in the vicinity of Folkestone.

" Isn't it beautiful, Elizabeth ? " sighed Mrs. Fagg. " I can't think why we don't come here more oft."

" And music in these heavenly surroundings," replied her friend.

An old man was playing a fiddle, and playing it reasonably well, too. On the green, young women displaying coloured petticoats and young farmers with clean smocks over their clothes were dancing and tripping to the lively air, whilst at the side their graver elders were sipping tea or smoking.

" And what about a bite to eat?" said John Fagg, rubbing his hands.

The repast was most enjoyable, good plain food and plenty of it, but, with the last piece of fruit-cake bolted, the two boys set off further up the valley to Castle Hill, where once the Romans had had a summer camp.

Whilst they were gone, and the girls occupied elsewhere, Mr. Rochefort and Mr. Fagg spoke of more serious matters, and their wives indulged in a little gossip.

" Aye," John Fagg agreed, " 'tis very different nowadays."   He was speaking of the late war with the American Colonies and with France, during which things had come to a sad pass. " Food bad to get it was, and . . ."

" Trade disastrous," said Mr. Rochefort gravely.   " Well, the blessings of peace have changed all that, praise be. Since the Treaty of Versailles agriculture has boomed in the country, trade has reached to unparalleled heights of prosperity and should reach even greater heights if the peace of Europe is not again disturbed. And after all, though the disorders in France are most unfortunate, they will not do that."

Trade might be good, but to a man owning a score of ships most of which were too large to use the port of their registry, conditions could be vastly improved.

" Aye, generally speaking, business may be good," John Fagg admitted guardedly. " But . . ." he shook his head.

For the last few moments Mrs. Fagg had talked a deal more than her friend, with Mrs. Rochefort progressively contenting herself with fewer words in reply, until eventually she merely moved her head in agreement or dissent as the case warranted.

Mrs. Fagg, seeing this unfortunate state of affairs, soon took the appropriate action, after first giving Mrs. Rochefort the quietest signal.

" I vow," she said, rising and shivering most artistically, " that I'm a little chilled; I'm sure we ought to be moving."

Mr. Rochefort, thinking of a similar effect on his wife, was most apologetic and contrite, immediately recalling the boys and dissuading the little girls from the efforts which, in the fond belief that they were dancing, they were making on the green.

In Foord, Mr. Rochefort did not forget the real purpose of that afternoon's trip. The party were halted at the stone trough into which was delivered the healing water.

" Iron held in solution, I am told," he said learnedly, " by . . . er . . . carbonic acid."

An old woman, who earned a few coppers by loaning tumblers to those who wished to drink the objectionable liquid, added to that. Her range of information varied from the results of using the water for the boiling of cabbages, it preserving the full green colour, to the marvellous cures for which it had been responsible.

" There, my dearest," said Mr. Rochefort. " So you see."

In the glass was a substance, brownly yellow, full of sediment, a horribly distasteful-looking concoction.

" Ugh . . . ugh . . ." gasped young Charles Fagg, who had risked a drop.

Miss Caroline Rochefort was dancing excitedly. " Let me try, Charles," she screeched. " Let me try."

Mrs. Rochefort was hesitantly eyeing the tumbler her husband had given her.

" Go on, Mamma," laughed Louis Rochefort, seeing nothing untoward in the ghastly smile his mother gave him.

" Come, my dear," Mr. Rochefort said cajolingly.

" I don't . . . I . . ." she murmured uncertainly.

Her husband persuaded her, teased her, brought all his wiles to bear, and in the doing of these things showed the love and affection he had for her.

Bravely, even with a light jest before doing so, she drank off the bitter brew.

Dover was but a mile ahead now. The way back had been between thick hedges with here and there a few elms to give shade to the narrow road. Glimpsed occasionally to either side were fields, sometimes in pasture, sometimes in tillage, the latter of a richness the result of ploughing-in silver-gleaming sprats brought when the supply was plentiful. A fine nourishing manure they made, too.

Mrs. Rochefort, it appeared, did not want the pleasant afternoon yet to end. She suggested that a walk up the grassy slope to the right, which gained the lip of Shakespeare Cliff, would be very enjoyable.

" But, my dear," Mrs. Fagg smiled roguishly, " you'll have to keep me company, for I intend to move at a very serene pace."

" And I will keep the children out of mischief," Susan Fagg promised, a wealth of understanding in her tone.

John Fagg and his friend had already begun the stiff climb as Mrs. Rochefort gave the two women a glance of affection.

" Thank . . . thank you both," she said mistily.

A few minutes later, whilst Mrs. Fagg held her head, she was sick in a secluded corner of a meadow.

After that she was much better, and was able to tell her friend of the lump she could feel in her breast.

" Does it hurt abominably, Elizabeth ? "

" It doesn't pain me at all."

" Then . . . then it can't be . . ." Polly Fagg hesitated to mention the dread word.

" No . . . no it can't be that," Elizabeth Rochefort said. " And . . . and I'm so relieved, Polly." Her lips were a little tremulous.

Mrs. Fagg squeezed her arm consolingly, and the two ladies started to mount the green slope, half-way up which Susan Fagg was teaching three little girls to make daisy chains.

The view from the height was magnificent. Across the sea, remarkably clear, rose the hills above Boulogne and the steeple of Notre Dame of Calais ; between them, standing out bold, the grim Cap Gris Nez. To the left, in noble grandeur, white cliffs stretched to the South Foreland, and on the opposite hand there crept into the sea, endlessly it seemed, the low point of Dungeness, on its extremity the new lighthouse, three-quarters built, with the old lighthouse some distance behind, still another proof of the sea's action along that coast.

But, whilst the warm breeze wafted his brown hair, it was not at this fine prospect that John Fagg was staring. Oblivious to all this he stood, oblivious even to a tall-sparred Botany Bay convict-ship which, her long tack having brought her near to the slate-blue marl reef below, was going about with seaman-like precision. His glance was unwaveringly on his native town and on the harbour which lay before it.

" I own eighteen well-found vessels, Henry," he said suddenly, " and there isn't a bottom amongst them of a burthen of over three hundred tons that I can bring into my own haven. And all because of that sort of disgrace."

He pointed down to the desolate area inshore of the Tidal Harbour and Basin, nearby his own warehouse in Elizabeth Street, a miserable expanse which had obviously once been the site of some large pool— Paradise Pent, to which, with the outer waterway of Paradise Harbour, the mariners of Dover had moved when the Little Pent in front of his own house had become useless.

" And unless a stand is made, Henry," he continued soberly, " the Basin and the present Pent, maybe even the Tidal Harbour, will share that same fate."

For a space the banker thoughtfully eyed those three stretches of water which lay disposed behind the great bank of shingle ; the outer-most, the Tidal Harbour, was entered through the pier-heads, then came the Basin, and finally, also entered through lock-gates, the Pent, whose narrow upper neck reached almost as far as Town Wall Street.

Then Mr. Rochefort made strange comment.

" John," he said earnestly, " you work hard, I know. But do you get equivalent return for all the labour you devote to your shipping affairs ? "

Mr. Fagg's grey eyes showed his astonishment, but he laughed all the same. " Harkee, Henry," he grinned, " though maybe I couldn't quite match guinea against your guinea——"

Mr. Rochefort brushed this aside. " You're well-to-do, John," he agreed lightly. " But . . ." he tapped his companion's shoulder, " 'tis because of the one hundred per cent and more profit you make out of your ' free-trade ' ventures. And . . ." he waggled a long first finger, " 'tis out of that profit that you make good the deficiencies of your legitimate business."

John Fagg sighed. " Surely enow it costs me a pretty penny to keep my fleet going, subsidising it you might say. Nevertheless . . ." his voice strengthened, " if the harbour here was satisfactory——"

His friend interrupted with a suggestion. It was brought out so rapidly that one might almost have suspected that the speaker, aware of the reception it would receive, preferred to get it out before second thoughts could prevent the utterance.

" My advice, John," he said quickly, " is that you either sell off your larger ships or remove your centre of operations to the Port of London. I myself often consider the advisability of establishing an office in the metropolis, retaining my interests here only so far as they deal with bullion transactions or prompt Continental news-dispatches for money market activities."

John Fagg's look of amazement was ludicrous.

B

" Me ! " he ejaculated. " Me leave Dover ? "

" Why not ? " demanded the banker.

" Because me and my family have always been connected with the town, and wouldn't forsake it in its time of need," the shipper said decisively.

" But that's quixotic, John," Henry Rochefort objected sharply. " You must realise that the necessities of business come first."

John Fagg thereupon stated that there were some things outside capital and centage. For centuries Faggs had sailed Cinque Port ships, and had sallied out and fought England's enemies ; they had relieved Thames-bound Papal ships of Bulls which their king had found inconvenient to receive ; and at other times had descended to the depths, when trade was bad, of embarking on a few profitable days of piracy.

Despite these last humorous allusions, Henry Rochefort, always prone to discover a slight when surely none was intended, seemed to read a note of censure in his companion's words.

" I take it you mean that the Rocheforts have not been over here long enough to understand your traditions ? " he observed caustically. From that he went off into a rodomontade. The Rocheforts, he said, had been in Dover since the days of the revocation of the Edict of Nantes, and that was over a hundred years.

" Nay, Henry," John Fagg commented, quite unmoved.

Henry Rochefort did not show any immediate sign of being mollified, so perhaps it was fortunate that his wife and Mrs. Fagg came into view just then.

Later, however, at the very end of the afternoon, when the three ladies were in the drawing-room of his Snargate Street residence, he drew John Fagg into the dining-room. His face was not easy, for he always found apology difficult, just as invariably as, when he came to realise there was need for apology, he forced himself to act.

" John," he began stiltedly. " I must express my regret for the manner in which——"

John Fagg silenced him. " Say no more, Henry," he said heartily. " 'Tis only that I am devilish troubled about the harbour, and 'tis for men like us, Dover men mind you . . ." he smiled at that, " to struggle until we rally the townsfolk into one unanimous whole. For too long there have been two cliques in the town——"

" But you, and your family, have always belonged to what might be termed the govenring clique," the banker interposed.

Slowly John Fagg shook his head and then, very deliberately, began to outline his views. He was coming to the conclusion, he remarked, that the dominant faction was really composed of attorneys, officials and such like who gradually had elbowed out the traders who brought what prosperity there was to the port.

" Sooner or later the ' linen drapers ' must come into the picture,"
the shipowner went on. " Only then, when we have a united front,
can we hope to have any chance of stirring the Harbour Commissioners
into effective action. Meantime . . ."

He began to pace as he stated the first plank in his immediate
policy. The Harbour Commissioners, he said succinctly, had formed
the habit of taking the easy course.

" We must strive to discourage any building on the shingle and
mud thrown up by the action of the sea," he added forcefully. " Only
too delighted are the Commissioners to increase their revenues from
freeholds so gained. But . . ." he turned sharply, " if we can resist
them in that, they will be compelled to fall back on their proper
function—that of making a fine harbour whose dues would give them
all the funds they needed for its fitting upkeep."

Outside there was the faint tinkle of crockery. Henry Rochefort
moved his head slightly, but John Fagg had not yet finished. He was
staring at the few vessels which were lying alongside the wharf of the
Pent.

" Have you reflected, Henry," he said quietly, " that Dover is
the only seaport 'twixt Harwich and Portsmouth, and that is another
reason why the haven should be made of the first order. This is the
spearhead of the country, and . . ." he nodded significantly, " the
Continent is very near."

Henry Rochefort really laughed at that. " So you think it should
be a—a national harbour, shall we call it ? " he guffawed. " Well, if
'twas that, at last the Government would do the paying."

" So they would," John Fagg grinned. " Though I don't know
that I was contemplating the money side."

The banker had got all over his stiffness by now. Not being a
humorous man, he flogged this droll theme—that his friend's new and
great conception had been conceived with but the one thought in
mind. And that, of course, as he later carefully explained to the
ladies, was the provision of a suitable home anchorage for all the Fagg
ships.

Glad that the unpleasantness of a little earlier had passed, John
Fagg took his part in the lively talk, and good-naturedly laughed off
all such attacks on himself.

But Polly Fagg's gaiety was somewhat forced. She had a queer
feeling that Henry should not thus lightly treat a thing so close to
John's heart.

2

Both John Fagg and Henry Rochefort, against the usual Dover custom, had their business premises away from their homes. The Fagg shipping office and warehouse were in Elizabeth Street overlooking the rank, and sometimes stinking, vegetation which covered Paradise Pent, and Mr. Rochefort's bank was in Snargate Street-over-the-Wall, a thoroughfare gained after passing over the lock-gates separating the Basin and the Pent.

Snargate Street-over-the-Wall was narrow, and its buildings stood upon the foundations which aforetime divided these two sheets of water, their backs indeed going vertically down to the deeps, their lower limits covered with green moss and clinging seaweed. It was one of the busiest streets in the town, and throughout the day merchants and shippers and their clerks were ever passing up and down the restricted pavements.

The Rochefort bank, as were also the two rival banking houses, was situated towards the middle of this rather short street. Its door was impressive with great iron studs and a heavy knocker, the whole set in a massive rectangle of stone in the cross-piece of which was a date, 1627, when these premises were erected.

On either side of the door were small-paned, bow windows which were carried, only a thin band separating them, to the full height of the second story.

The public portion of the bank extended the whole width of the building, across which, a few paces inside the door, was a counter. Behind this comparatively low room was Mr. Rochefort's private office ; and another room, principally used to house the bullion safes. Here also were stacked the brass-bound export boxes whose use provided Mr. Rochefort with the greater part of his income.

The strong-room of the bank was a scene of extreme activity, and more than once Matthew Godspenny, very circumspectly, wiped his forehead. It was definitely hot before the weigh-scales in the window, through which the afternoon sun shone both directly and indirectly as its rays were reflected upwards from the Basin.

" Finding it swelky, Mr. Godspenny ? " the second occupant of the room, a counter clerk, was imprudent enough to ask. The task on which he was engaged was the packing in kegs, two thousand to each, of eight-real pieces, beautiful coins on one side of which were the arms of Spain and on the other two hemispheres flanked by the Pillars of Hercules.

With nice deliberation, on hearing this very innocent question,

Mr. Rochefort's senior clerk put down the grocer's scoop with which he had been dropping coins into a weigh-pan.

" You desire to know whether or not I find it close ? " he asked precisely. " Or . . ." he continued, his mildness of manner belied by the glint which had appeared in his deep-set eyes, " you wish to ascertain my views concerning various items set out in there ? " He gravely indicated a single folded sheet which was received twice weekly at the bank.

The flustered clerk, who knew the individual with whom he was dealing, made it very clear that he did not wish to gossip on any matter which might be found in the thin newspaper.

Thereupon Mr. Godspenny, a slow nod and a half bow putting an end to this fruitless discussion, continued his activities with that currency indispensable to trade and commerce, the piece-of-eight. Ever since the trade of the world had increased, these trade dollars, made of the silver which only Mexican mines could supply in sufficient quantity, had reigned supreme.

Meantime Mr. Rochefort, who had been called to the counter earlier, was now saying good-bye to his distinguished and unexpected visitor.

" Certainly, Sir Walter, only too glad," he was declaring. "And any other time you may want any service of me then I beg of you to name it."

Sir Walter Plumbley was a bucolic, seemingly good-humoured nonentity who until a month before had been unheard of in Dover, when it became public property that the responsible powers in the metropolis had elected him to the Board of Harbour Commission.

His only claim to fame was that he had once drawn a fabulous fortune from a lucky speculation in the Lottery.

" That's mortal amiable of you, sir," he observed warmly, very pleased by the tribute to his presence.

It had come to the notice of the authorities, most belatedly alas, that for many years hardly a single Commissioner had put in regular attendance at the meetings of the Board. Their remedy had been the appointment of Sir Walter Plumbley. The onerous nature of the office had been handsomely described to this flattered gentleman. It was subsequently felt that he would be most assiduous in discharging his duties, thereby stifling any more criticism on this particular score.

" So we can rely on you seeing to those disbursements, Mr. Rochefort ? " he asked searchingly.

This referred to certain payments which the Commissioners, reluctantly, were compelled to make. But minor repairs to the harbour were essential if a greater and more disastrous outlay, through further neglect, was to be avoided.

"Unquestionably, Sir Walter." Mr. Rochefort bowed.

Sir Walter rumbled into speech. "I understand that latterly there's been grumbling amongst the nautical men," he said. "But, good God, when we've completed these present details . . ."

The improvements which Mr. Oliver Waade had spoken of more than a year before had hung fire, but now estimates were to hand ; the apron of the Pent gate was to be lowered two feet, and two new sluices were to be built in the Cross Wall.

Mr. Rochefort laughed. "Unfortunately, Sir Walter, some people in this world are never satisfied."

"True, true, Mr. Rochefort," the new Commissioner agreed sagely. "But damme, when we've done this . . . they'll be able to get bigger craft into the . . . er . . . Pent, and with the new sluice gates we'll be better able to scour away the shingle which collects at the harbour bar."

There was further talk on these lines, quasi-informative, regarding the age-old method by which it had ever been hoped the harbour entrance might be freed from the curse of shingle. How the flowing tide went into the Pent, and how the gates of the Pent were closed at high water, thus retaining thousands of tons of water ; how this water, between high tide and the following low tide, was added to by the Dour, which ran into the upper neck of the Pent ; and how at low water the immense volume was released, to rush into the Basin and then to thunder into the Tidal Harbour, where at last, narrowed between the piers, it struck the obstruction to navigation which had collected between the heads, theoretically sweeping it away.

"To be sure, Sir Walter, to be sure," said Mr. Rochefort, springing to the door of the private office as he saw in his caller the desire to leave.

But Sir Walter had still another thing in mind, this time of a more personal nature.

"Fagg," he said, "er . . . John Fagg . . . heard a lot about the fellow, an' I'd like to have a word with him. Where can I . . . ?"

With somewhat of an air, Sir Walter mentioned the names of a number of Kentish gentry whom from time to time he had met socially. These gentlemen . . . friends, he observed ripely, had often boasted of the elegant returns they had received from fairly modest interests in the 'free-trader's' operations. Now that he had some more solid connection with the town, he was proposing to take up a slight invest-ment himself.

"Damme," he chuckled, "if every landed proprietor, magistrate, M.P. and parson betwixt here and Canterbury can share in Mr. Fagg's well-conceived runs, than I'm hanged to know why I shouldn't. I have it in mind to put . . ." he winked eloquently, "two hundred guineas into Mr. Fagg's hand an' see what he can do with 'em for me. But first, where can I find this wizard ? "

Mr. Rochefort had news of Mr. Fagg, but in any case felt it politic to draw this very influential contact as close to himself as he could.

" He's away, is he ? " muttered the baronet.

" But as I say, Sir Walter," smiled Mr. Rochefort, " if you would care to entrust the matter to me I would gladly arrange that you had a share in the ventures you spoke of . . . er . . . to the amount you mentioned. Mr. Fagg is by way of being a friend of mine, you know."

Sir Walter puffed a little, then admitted that he had rather thought of taking a view himself of the redoubtable individual who had proved himself such a thorn in the sides of the Revenue Officers, but finally placed the affair in the banker's capable hands.

" As for the money," he grunted, " I'll have a draft sent you for——"

Mr. Rochefort, with all the consideration the wealthy accord to those even more wealthy, waived aside the question of payment. " 'Twill do any time," he declared.

" Prodigiously accommodating of you, sir," Sir Walter avowed genially, though he would have been outraged had any other suggestion been offered.

In due course, step by step, the two gentlemen reached the side-walk. There at length farewells were made.

In high good humour Mr. Rochforte returned to the bank.

Umber clouds were stealing across the evening sky, and the light in the Rochefort strong-room was beginning to dim. It had been a very busy afternoon at the bank, with neither the banker nor his staff taking off more than half an hour for a meal. But now, neatly stacked, were the kegs—secured safely, each wired and affixed with a great oval wax-impressed seal, awaiting dispatch.

Mr. Rochefort moved to the window, and there took out his gold watch.

" Mmmmm," he murmured. " Getting near the time now. You saw Mr. Fagg yourself, Mr. Godspenny ? "

The senior clerk had gone into the bank proper and there, after some manipulation of the tedious flint and steel, had succeeded in lighting a candle. But young Louis Rochefort, who as a special treat had been allowed to come down for an hour of so that evening, answered the question himself.

" Yes, Papa," he said smartly, " the Emma will be alongside half an hour before the turn. Captain Maxton already has his orders for the delivery as well as for the gold he had to pick up in Antwerp on the return."

"Good," nodded the banker.

His son, so soon showing the promise of being as good a man of finance as his father, had an inquiry to make.

"Did any news dispatches come in to-day, Papa?"

"One from Paris, Louis."

Louis Rochefort wanted to know all about that and, having heard, was avid for more. A highly technical discussion followed on the broader aspects of exchange and international finance, with narrower reference to dealing in a market which was in a state of dangerous fluidity.

"That is why, my boy, the most extreme caution regarding French securities is necessary. "When . . ." the banker continued, "movements are wide, the essential factor to remember . . ."

Louis Rochefort was nodding sagaciously, an action which did not pass unnoticed by his fond parent, when Mr. Godspenny came in, the light of the taper he held emphasising his cadaverous features. The clerk had lighted the candles on the table and those in the sconces at the side of the fireplace by the time his employer addressed him.

"Methinks, Mr. Godspenny," laughed Mr. Rochefort, "that in this young man we have a very shrewd critic of our commercial practices. What do you say?"

It seemed that the senior clerk had a warm spot in his heart for the young gentleman. Certainly he spoke exceedingly well of him, a fact which brought a subdued smile of gratification to the face of the subject of the conversation. Indeed so pleased was Louis that, just as the fenders of the *Emma* touched the landing-steps, he was advancing the proposition that the bank should itself own, rather than charter, a fast cutter to further the many money-market operations in which his father indulged to such profit. Thereafter there was no time for idle talk.

In the yellow illumination from the lantern which lazily swayed at the *Emma's* mast, the precious kegs were carried down the slippery steps at the rear of the bank, and quickly stowed aboard.

"Cast off, Jonas," Captain Pepper bawled to Captain Maxton. As always, he saw Fagg ships off to sea.

But Mr. Godspenny thought otherwise. He pointed out that as yet no receipt had been received for a most valuable cargo. Without a signature the *Emma*, he gently suggested, might not be permitted to leave.

"Regular attorney, ain't you?" grunted Captain Pepper.

"You decline to conform to the usual custom, *Mr.* Pepper?" Mr. Godspenny asked politely.

"Hark you," a growl came from the squat figure, "have I so said?"

"So far," Mr. Godspenny remarked, even more courteously, "you have merely erroneously described me——"

"Bloody sea-lawyer," chuntered Valentine Pepper, laboriously penning his name.

Mr. Rochefort and his son were walking away, with Louis catechising his father as to where the responsibility lay, in the event of the House being without acknowledgment of receipt, should the *Emma* be lost before she cleared the liberties of Dover, which was the distance a horseman could ride into the sea before he failed to touch bottom with his spear.

Soon the vessel was slowly moving, her masts just discernible against the night sky, her wake a phosphorescence on the dark waters.

3

However young Louis Rochefort concerned himself with such weighty matters as the day-to-day quotations for various securities, there could be no doubt that he took a full share in whatever boyish diversions might be going.

In those hot summer weeks which passed whilst Mr. Rochefort watched the Continental money markets so closely, Louis Rochefort and Charles Fagg busied themselves, in the Island, with the erection of a bridge over the Dour. Dover's river reached the town's boundary at Buckland Bridge, a mile and a half out on the London Road, and from there, winding through the pretty village of Charlton, it came down the valley, finally entering the town itself and joining into the Pent after passing under Town Wall Street at Butchery Gate, somewhat nearer Mr. John Fagg's house than Severus's Gate.

Immediately after passing under Town Wall Street the Dour divided, its main stream, which was not very big after all, going for a spell straight through the shingle before it took a quick turn which brought it in a run directly into the upper end of the Pent. The other limb of the river, in itself little more than a broad trickle, crept alongside Town Wall Street, just outside where the town wall had once been, before joining the main stream close by the entrance into the Pent.

The patch of ground which was in the loop formed by the dividing Dour was called The Island. It was a favourite playground for the children, who could consider themselves fortunate that this apparently fine site, on the same side of the street as Little Pent House, had not been utilised for building purposes.

But, as Charles was conveying whilst balancing a piece of pickled oak which was to provide one of the supports for the bridge projected across the main channel, the Dour had an uneasy reputation.

> " Drop a spade into the Dour,
> An' the water's all o'er,"

he was saying, wordly wise, quoting the words of a Master of the Maison Dieu who, well over two hundred and fifty years before, had been instructed by an imperious Tudor Monarch to report on the state of Dover Harbour, with particular reference to the back-scouring potentialities of which the Dour, then adding to the volume of water in Paradise Pent, formed an integral part.

" I don't believe it," scoffed Louis Rochefort. " Watch me throw this in. And then you'll see *nothing* happens. All silly old tales."

The Fagg sheepdog, who had been snoozing comfortably head between paws, whilst the humans spent themselves in useless toil, now cocked an eye, the green one, intently watching her young master.

Charles would not have this. " The river *has* changed its course lots of times, Louis," he persisted. " That's why the mariners who used the Little Pent in front of our house had to move over to the other side when the river left there to go along the bottom of the cliffs to Archcliffe Point."

" Well, you'll see now," Mr. Henry Rochefort's son remarked firmly.

Soon a succession of Norman-squared Caen stones were splashing into the river, and soon it became evident that the Dour, whatever its aforetime wandering propensities, was not going to find a new bed on this occasion.

This exhaustive experiment over, the two young gentlemen continued with renewed zest on the bridge-building, until the baulks they had manhandled from their secret store had been used up. Replenishments in mind they began, with Nell in excited attendance, to scrunch past the posts of Mr. Beverley's Ropewalk, a portion of the great area on the top of the barrier of shingle which had so transformed Dover's haven in times gone by.

Half a dozen sweating men were laying a six-inch hempen hawser, and the boys were interestedly standing by the massive spinning wheel when Mr. Beverley himself came out of the Ropeworks. He found himself most deferentially greeted.

" And what are you young gentlemen after ? " he inquired suspiciously.

Very promptly Charles replied that Mr. Beverley was quite mistaken.

" But," he added disarmingly, " if to-morrow you could spare us two or three fathoms of old tarred rope, we———"

William Beverley guffawed, told them to be off, and promised he would see what could be done.

The cache, in which had been hidden, during the winter, the timber from many a ship which had come to grief, was well down towards Amherst's Battery at the beginning of the North Pier. But before the builders arrived at this carefully prepared hide-out there was a diversion which momentarily caused them to forget the great engineering feat upon which they were engaged.

It was Caroline who, her feet heavy in the yielding shingle surface, came stumbling towards them, her skirts hoisted high in her determined little fists, the lacy ends of her pantalets soiled and dirtied as the result of her games on the Ropewalk.

" Louis and Charles," she squeaked, " there's a 'normous shark with lots of little teeth and the fishermen are hanging it up to dry and . . ." she gulped a breath, ". . . then they're going to eat it as if 'twas beef and 'tis dark coloured above and under its tummy 'tis white and——"

The two young gentlemen were in no mood thus to have explained to them, and by a very little girl, something which they loftily, and not too truthfully, declared they had seen before.

" Seen thousands of them," observed her brother.

" A ground shark," added Charles Fagg competently.

Nevertheless the two boys lost no time in making in the direction pointed out. Caroline, apparently in no way subdued by her reception, half ran and half walked between them, chattering as hard as ever she could.

Beyond the heaps of soles, turbot, brills, smeardabs, plaice and flounders which littered the market beach, was the twelve-foot monster.

" There ! " said Miss Rochefort triumphantly.

" Caroline ! " Miss Susan Fagg reproved her. " Do you know you've frightened me to death. I couldn't think what had happened to you."

Susan Fagg, called 'aunt' by the Rochefort children too, looked very charming in her red-spotted print dress, her face shaded from the hot sun by a broad-brimmed hat.

" I'm sorry, Aunt Susan dear," Caroline said, giving that young woman a wheedling smile. " And . . ." there was now just some faint hint of mischief in her demure little face as she continued artlessly, " and I'm so sorry I fetched Louis and Charles because . . . because . . ."

Most artistically Mr. Henry Rochefort's small daughter waited until she saw that Minnie and Lou Fagg, with more importantly still, Charles and her brother Louis, had returned from their inspection of the savage denizen of the deep.

"Because," she went on innocently, after that necessary pause, "Louis and Charles have seen thousands of them before. *Thousands*."

Susan Fagg, worried though she had been at the child's absence, couldn't help laughing at that.

"Oh, Caroline," she giggled. "How can you say such a monstrous thing?"

Louis Rochefort understood all too well. "If you say any more, Caroline," he began, darkly threatening.

Minnie and Lou were jumping delightedly.

"Do, Caroline," they urged her.

But it seemed that Miss Rochefort had had her fun. She merely ended the matter by thrusting out her red tongue and wrinkling her small nose, the gesture unmistakably intended for Charles and her flustered brother.

Then a move was made up the Ropewalk. There were lots of interesting things along there, some of which the children began to collect, their finds signalised by shrill screams of delight.

"Look!" shouted Minnie Fagg, holding up the stinking corpse of a spotted dog-fish.

"Minnie!" said Miss Fagg, horrified. "Put it down at once."

But she really was genuinely upset when Louis and Charles found the body of a guillemot caught fast in a mackerel net.

"They dive into the water after the fish," her nephew Charles was explaining, "and they never see the net——"

Death often seems to have a fascination for the young, and the children had scampered to look at the find. In solemn deliberation they were gazing down until Susan Fagg, her face averted, shooed them away from this disturbing spectacle.

"Horrible of you," she said severely. "So horrid."

But there was more pleasant treasure-trove about: starfish, curious fossils, maritime plants and lovely sea ling.

The two boys were in the lead and, whether by chance or design it is not possible to say, they took a route which brought them near the Island. Of course the bridge had to be inspected, and of course Aunt Susan said just the right thing.

"'Tis wonderful, Louis and Charles," she declared. "And I vow that when it is finished you must 'low me be the first to cross on it."

Then the party went farther towards the sea, now with Charles and Louis, talking bridge construction, devotedly walking on either side of this intelligent grown-up.

It was delightful along the marge of the sea, and even more delightful when, at that one break in the high bank of shingle, they turned into Charles's Canyon, with its view of his father's house.

There was a pool and they made paper boats. And all of them, including Aunt Susan, who took off her cotton stockings after making sure that no one was about, paddled in the shallow water.

Minnie set up an awful yell when, just before it was time for them all to go home, she trod on something.

" Aunt Susan ! " she screamed.

" 'Tis only a sandray," Louis Rochefort said scornfully.

" It's bitten me," wailed Minnie Fagg.

" You've only stepped on those nasty sharp things, Minnie," Charles comforted her.

The sandray, with its black spots and keen spines along the edges of the fins, received a critical examination. The back and tail, beautifully shagreened, caused Caroline to make a remark which, at the mere mention of the name, brought a flush of rich colour into Susan Fagg's cheeks.

" Uncle George loves pretty colours like that," Mr. Rochefort's daughter said. " I wish we could show it to him."

" I wish we could show him the bridge," was Charles's contribution.

Whatever might be the sedate and severe Henry Rochefort's views on his temperamental brother, there could be no doubt that the young folk now speaking of him were exceedingly fond of George Rochefort.

There was quite an argument as to whether the sandray might be saved for his inspection, and whether the bridge might still be in existence when he eventually returned.

" Of course it might smell then, but——" Caroline was saying hotly.

Susan Fagg was laughing at them. " The . . . the question we have to decide, my dears," she smiled, " is . . . is when Uncle George will be coming back."

There was further controversy about this. It was finally and firmly clinched by Louis Rochefort, a young gentleman quite likely to be accurate on business affairs.

" Before next spring," he said decidedly. " Papa told Mamma so yesterday, just after he had opened the foreign mail."

" And that," Susan Fagg pronounced lightly, " is quite a long time, isn't it ? Such, such a long time."

The gathering at length determined that Uncle George would not be seen for another eight or nine months.

" And Uncle George sent you his love, Aunt Susan," Louis Rocheford proffered.

" And to Charles," Caroline amended firmly. " And to Minnie and Lou," she continued kindly, though a shade late.

It was very little, nothing more than a conventional expression of goodwill, as she knew well. But Susan Fagg's heart started to throb madly and there was some aching ecstasy in her soul.

Fortunately Louis began again to talk about his uncle. Uncle George, he said, had the previous year, before leaving London, made friends with a gentleman called Wordsworth, and Uncle George, apart from other things which had annoyed Papa, often wrote about Mr. Wordsworth's work.

" 'Tis silly poetry," he jeered.

" I don't think poetry is silly, Louis," Miss Fagg said, both accusingly and defensively.

It seemed that Louis' papa did not agree with her.

" But," Louis Rochefort announced knowingly, " Papa said that he'd rather have Uncle George waste his time with poetry than trifle with the . . . the rubbish he is doing."

Miss Susan Fagg wanted to know all about that, though she signified her desire in a roundabout manner. In any event she found that the precise nature of George Rochefort's preoccupations were a little obscure.

After which Louis Rochefort and Charles Fagg, drawing aside from the weaker vessels, began a secretive conversation in which ' free-trade ' figured prominently. The former appeared well versed in the finances of the traffic, and the latter in all the cute tricks of the smuggling trade.

4

Summer had gone, and then the golden days of autumn. Now winter had come again, and another five weeks ahead was Christmas, with its tradition of gifts and hospitality, the time when a lady would appreciate some exquisite French linen or lace, and a gentleman a supply of fine wine or brandies of the same origin. In short, it was the time of the year when John Fagg was extremely busy in those ventures outside the law.

On a foggy day in late November, when not a breath of air stirred and when the visibility on the sea was limited to half a cable's length or so, one such run was to take place. As was usual with the biggest ' trader ' for thirty or more miles either way, the operation was conceived on the grand scale.

Shortly before leaving his warehouse in Elizabeth Street, Mr. Fagg checked over the final preparations.

" That's everything, then, Valentine," he said briskly. " The inns have all been warned to have their hidey-holes ready, and you've sent a messenger to Lord Poynte's steward telling him to see that the doors of the big barn in the wood on the south-east of the park are left open?"

Captain Pepper rumbled into laughter. "An' 'ad answer, too, sir. His Lordship's pussonally going to ensure that all's in order for the stowage of the goods."

Mr. Fagg smiled, for Lord Poynte's enthusiasm was well known. But his smile did not persist, for just now there were matters of greater moment, and laughter could wait until after. He made inquiries about the waggons, the pack-horses, and the hundred men, farm labourers and sundry, who would each earn a guinea for their night's work.

"And there's the usual dozen scallywags amongst 'em," commented Captain Pepper. "But . . ." his squint became distinctly alarming, "I told 'em . . . *no firearms.*"

His master nodded agreement. Terrorism and brutality, even murder, were the rule rather than the exception amongst the smuggling bands, but Mr. Fagg would have nothing of that. Indeed this was a sound policy, even in a seaport town where magistrates and officials of the place alike were implicated in the trade. For though it was one of the most difficult things in the world for the Excise authorities to obtain a conviction, there could be one fatal factor. That was when the runners employed force.

"Now about our mode of operation, Valentine," Mr. Fagg said, and went on to outline his plan. At half after midnight the boats would come in off Archcliffe Point, and the landing would be made on the beach below Mr. Crundall's shipbuilding slips, or rather more towards the base of Shakespeare Cliff.

Captain Pepper whistled significantly at this choice, so very near the town, but winked appreciatively when he heard where the decoys were to work—on the other side of Dover, beyond the Castle, half-way in fact to St. Margaret's Bay.

"And the goods when loaded up are to be taken towards Limekiln Street, and then straight up the track to the Western Heights," Mr. Fagg continued equably.

His henchman's next whistle died in his throat. Captain Pepper gaped, so astounded was he.

"Into Limekiln Street!" he ejaculated. "'Sdeath, that means going 'long Crane Street, right i' front of the King's Head, and then 'long the Cross Wall——"

Mr. Fagg shook his head, and declared an alternative route which, on hearing it, reduced Captain Pepper to speechless admiration.

"From the beach directly 'longside Paradise Pent," he said eventually, when at last the sheer ingeniousness of this idea caused him to roar with delight.

"Pork and molasses!" he spluttered. "Talk about cutting-out under the enemy's wery teeth!"

"Chancy, you're thinking, Valentine?" John Fagg inquired.

Running close to the wind it certainly was, and the boatswain made no attempt to deny it. But he had sublime belief in his employer. In truth he could hardly have held other opinion, for John Fagg's tactical skill had resulted in a long series of victories over the Preventivemen, until the upholders of the law had virtually become demoralised.

"Aye, maybe so, sir," he chuckled. "But . . ." he clapped his fat thigh in glee, "we've allus hobbl'd an' bannocked 'em so far an' I concludes we'll keep on boffling 'em.

John Fagg smiled. "I warrant we shall, Valentine," he commented easily.

The project was quite simple, and in that lay the advantage. Mr. Fagg, whose office window looked over the waste of Paradise Pent, had a few days before seen some urchins playing on the farther verge. A reconnaissance late one night had enabled him to prove to his own satisfaction that the outer edges of Paradise Pent had, with the weathering of the years, become hard—hard enough for the passage of laden wagons.

Long after Mr. Fagg had left for home Captain Pepper's great face was wreathed in a grin.

Invariably the Fagg household was abed by ten o'clock, but on certain evenings, when profitable transactions were afoot, this unspoken rule was broken. The state of the tide was, of course, the controlling factor.

But soon after St. Mary the Virgin's had struck eleven times Mrs. Fagg, yawning, intimated her intention of retiring, putting down the *Gentleman's Magazine* with which she had been sleepily toying.

"I'll come up with you, love," said John Fagg, giving her an affectionate chuck under the chin.

The night air, laden with fog, had brought a chill everywhere, and as soon as she reached the bedroom Mrs. Fagg lost no time in getting into the four-poster bed. But once there, with the bedclothes well up to her chin, she settled herself for a few minutes' conversation with her husband, who, from a closet at the side of the fireplace, had taken out the old black coat, black woollen neckcloth, black knee-breeches and top-boots with turn-downs he was wont to wear on these swift occasions.

"I suppose nobody except Pepper knows about this new route alongside Paradise Pent?" she asked.

Mr. Fagg grunted. "Not a soul, and nobody'd believe it if they'd heard. Besides, we haven't any sneak informers in this town."

Had it been otherwise his record might have been substantially different. For three years he had not lost a cargo in a trade in which one successful run out of three left a clear margin of profit.

" Howsomever, take care all the same, dear," Polly Fagg remarked, more to keep the conversation going than from any sense of apprehension.

A few minutes later her husband tiptoed down the broad stairs, his hand sliding over the rail of the wrought-iron balustrade.

Outside the house he turned southward along Town Wall Street. It was raw and dark, nor were there any street-lamps, though these had been promised every year during the twelve years which had elapsed since the Paving Commissioners came into office.

But, despite the fog-laden gloom, he kept sharp look-out for the watchmen who guarded the streets and lanes within the wards.

In a quarter of an hour, taking a careful route, he had joined Captain Pepper on the beach below Archcliffe Fort.

" They're coming in now, sir," whispered that worthy.

" Right," John Fagg said softly.

Once again the renowned ' free-trader ' was to maintain his schedule. With oars muffled the fleet of boats came gliding in, their reception efficiently prepared for. Vague shapes moved about in seeming disorder, but the quiet commands given proved beyond doubt that there was perfect order.

In unending stream "porters" carried ashore small casks of brandy, ready slung, and equally steadily a line of laden pack-horses moved out.

At the foot of the cliff was a marl ridge, a blue-grey clay which, with exposure, had become as hard as stone. On this were stacked cases of every description, and by it, in the shaded rays of a dark lantern, Captain Pepper marked off the goods before they were lifted on to the wagons which, axles well greased, came alongside silently.

Within two hours all was accomplished. The last farm wagon and the last ' rider ' had gone, and John Fagg was sharing a flagon of genuine Hollands with his principal subordinates.

In little over that time, one of Dover's most respected jurats was in a warm and comfortable bed.

Some three nights later, when a stormy south-westerly wind was rattling the windows along Pent-side and the rising sea was beginning to thud against the South Pier, Henry Rochefort disclosed to his wife a secret which was the subject of no little speculation in the town.

" Yes," he marvelled, " John told me this afternoon. They took the goods through Paradise Pent . . . . or rather on the edge of it just beneath the cliff."

The banker was arranging a wine table more conveniently to his elbow and, after receiving a smiling refusal in response to his gesture towards the decanter, began to pour a glass for himself.

"But, Henry, didn't the horses and the carts sink?" Elizabeth Rochefort asked.

"No, my dear," he laughed. "You can be sure that John would not make a mistake like that. An exceedingly fly 'un is John."

With that he dismissed the theme and began to speak, with some acerbity, on the letter he had received from his brother.

"You know, my dear," he observed trenchantly, "there are times when I think George lacks any balance whatever. These . . . these ridiculous notions he has acquired lately."

"I shouldn't distress yourself, Henry," his wife remarked consolingly. "You know what George is."

Impatiently he crumpled the letter and threw it into the fire.

"I know that when he returns I shall speak plainly, very plainly, to him," he said crisply. "And now," he smiled at her, "something more pleasant, my love."

Despite this seeming throwing-aside of a care, his manner for the remainder of that evening revealed his preoccupation, so much so that Mrs. Rochefort, shortly before retiring, anxiously asked if anything else worried him. She received a reply which at first astonished her considerably.

"No, no," he assured her. "But 'tis just that I have been thinking of that strip of ground . . . for ground it is . . . at the edge of Paradise Pent."

"I don't understand, Henry," she said curiously.

He told her that there was need for more houses in the Pier District, especially near the Look-out on the South Pier, and that the Loadmanagemen were urgently demanding the provision of such accommodation.

An expression of real concern came into his wife's drawn face.

"You mean you have thought of buying that land . . . as a speculation . . . so that houses for the pilots may be built on't?" she asked.

He laughed at her perspicacity, and teased her for her new interest in his business affairs.

"My love . . . " he was beginning, much amused.

"But is that your project, Henry?" she inquired impulsively.

His profession, as he told her, was not one in which hurried decisions were made. Such a proposition must be seriously considered, it must receive grave attention. . . .

"Don't do it, Henry," she said suddenly.

He looked his astonishment, and even more showed his amazement when she told him her reason.

"True, John is my friend, my dear," he agreed. "But if I have money to lay out then I must place it where I consider it will be most profitable and advantageous. After all, Elizabeth, that is my duty as a banker."

"But you know John's views about building on reclaimed land," she urged earnestly.

"Of course, my dear, but that does not necessarily mean that I agree with him."

"Henry . . ." she began.

He sprang to her, for he could see that she was overmuch disturbed by this petty matter. In the soothing of her, in the consoling of her, he soon came to forget the issue on which they had differed.

CHAPTER THREE

I

The chill March afternoon was drawing to an end, and a soft after-light brought added beauty to the massive tower of the Cathedral Church of Canterbury, caressing one side to a warm glory and etching the other to a noble line clear cut against the rapidly greying sky.

Past the Butter Market, through the overhung streets of the medieval city, a stage-coach creaked and lumbered behind its three pairs of horses as Bell Harry began to toll for prayers. Their iron-shod wheels ground over the Guernsey pebbles which formed the year-old new carriage-way, and the swelling leather-covered roof hardly seemed to clear the projecting second stories of the half-timbered buildings. At each sharp corner the driver, glancing down and backwards from his height, directed a volley of lurid abuse embracing Paving Commissioners from Land's End to John o' Groats as the mettlesome leaders, a postilion on the near-beast, pulling wide and yet crabwise at the end of the long trace, failed to keep the ponderous red-painted near wheel clear of that crazy innovation of Scottish granite, the kerb stone.

The exodus at the Rose Inn had been nigh to complete, and on the final stage to the sea only two passengers remained. One of these was a middle-aged gentleman, obviously nodding. His bearing indicated the one desire there and then to fold his arms, sink his many chins, and forthwith compose himself either to sleep or to reflect on certain business matters to be accomplished on Dover's market day of the morrow.

His travelling companion, however, was in a different humour, and seemed in no wise fatigued by a journey which had begun, from the White Bear in Piccadilly, at the cold hour of four in the morning. He was a striking young man, lofty of brow, whose hair, raven black beneath its powder, was left untied. His brown eyes were at once soft and yet strangely arrogant, and as for the rest, in so far as could be judged from his seated position and the long-tailed full coat which enveloped him down to his high boots, he was tall and slenderly proportioned.

"But, my dear Mr. Baker," he began as the coach entered the Dover turnpike, "you must admit that even the famous Mr. William Pitt may be wrong."

Mr. Jephrez Baker, the proprietor of the candle manufactory in Market Street, Dover, spoke most testily.

"Maybe he can, young man," he snapped, "though as yet it hasn't come to my ears that he's made up his mind. He's like me and your brother Henry and a lot more others in that he's suspending judgment. Right enough at the beginning of the Revolution over there he believed that something good would come of it and——"

"That the . . . the Frenchies, once they had largely taken authority from the King, would be blessed with a democratic form of constitution more in keeping with English fancy, eh, Mr. Baker?" George Rochefort's mobile mouth, as he put this mocking question, curved in amusement.

The candle-maker scowled. "I'm withholding judgment yet," he observed doggedly, "an' you can go on arguing as long as you like."

The smile slowly died from the younger man's striking face, to be replaced by an expression of sternness. He took from his lap the slim duodecimo volume which was resting there and, almost with a studied air, tossed it to the far side of the leather, studded seat.

"Mr. Baker," he began gravely, "if I may be permitted, there are some few observations I hold myself under an obligation to make."

Meditatively he stared through the oval window at his elbow. Only when the round course of Barham came near, with the light-painted posts of the race-track showing beyond the bare hedgerow, did he put his thoughts into words. Then, as they passed through the vast reaching Down on which Men of Kent and Kentishmen had gathered whenever they felt the land of their birth to be in peril from foreign invader, he started to speak on certain vile blemishes of the social order.

"Have you, Mr. Baker," he said, his voice deep, "ever seen a score of pitiable creatures languishing hopelessly in the stinking little chamber which constitutes a debtors' prison? Have you ever reflected that self-styled Christian shipmasters still reap unholy profit from the miseries of the poor slaves battened down beneath——"

To this last Mr. Baker reacted at once, his yawn breaking off sharply.

" Now you're not going to charge me with indifference to that," he quickly vowed. " I'm all with Mr. Wilberforce in seeing *that* scandal is stopped, and many's the time I've said so in the Antwerp of an evening. And I'm sure that in time——"

Young Mr. Rochefort laughed, quite tickled. " In time, eh ? And just what do you mean by time, sir ? A year, two years, a decade, or what ? "

" These things can't be done in a minute," expostulated the candle-maker. " Parliament moves slowly, y'know."

For a space Mr. Rochefort smiled rather queerly. Then, so suddenly, his eyes took on a bright intensity as he leaned forward peremptorily to prod his fellow traveller's ample knee.

" But have you ever considered that if that laggardly body of which, sir, you speak with such veneration were to be swept away, then it would indeed be possible to substitute an order of government under whose beneficial auspices the affairs of mankind might be allowed to progress ? I need not, I hope, point out that we have recently witnessed glorious example, and that surely we English may follow that inspired lead."

Mr. Baker gaped. " You speak very strongly, young man," he commented.

The Dover banker's younger brother had a lovely voice.

" Liberty, equality, fraternity," he said melodiously. And then quickly and passionately : " And soon, pray God, the caps of liberty will be amongst us."

These words, coupled with a lurch as a wheel of the vehicle mounted an enormous stone and then squelched down into a muddy hole, caused the older gentleman to start violently.

" You mean that some of them French maniacs be coming here ? " he ejaculated.

Young Mr. Rochefort eyed him pityingly. " I mean, sir," he explained condescendingly, " that there are also Englishmen who are willing to hazard much for a conception they hold dear."

As he digested this, various emotions traced themselves across Mr. Baker's homely face. Then he pointed a warning finger.

" What you want to realise, young man——"

" I think I can decide for myself, sir," interposed George Rochefort cuttingly.

Mr. Baker's gloved knuckles thumped against the padded up-holstery.

"And I can decide some things too," he shouted. "And I've decided that I am wearied of your outpourings. So I'll thank you not to pester me for what remains of this journey."

"Pester ! " said young Mr. Rochefort furiously.

"Yes, pester," roared the candle manufacturer, so irritated that he spilt some of the precious contents from the tortoiseshell snuff-box which he had, with some difficulty, extricated from within his voluminous outer clothing.

Mr. George Rochefort got himself in hand, as was evinced by the indifferent manner in which he examined a fine chased watch. After which he leaned across for the slim book, recollected then that full dusk had come, and finally bowed stiffly to his companion.

"I deeply regret the error of having addressed myself to you, sir," he said frigidly.

The only reply he received was a glare following close after a sneezing bout.

The coach rolled on, now with the lamps bringing an extra sheen to the brown rumps of the straining wheelers. Soon came the sixty-eighth milestone, and Buckland Bridge, with its corn and paper-making mills. To the left twinkling rush-lights in the cottages of the lovely village of Charlton, and a little farther on the tollgate, and the rotting clothes and poor remains of a malefactor hanging from the gibbet near the Black Horse, Dover's official place of execution.

Now came the outskirts of the town, the old Priory on the right, and at the top of Biggin Street the Maison Dieu, where once Knight Templars and hospitallers lodged when coming in or going out of the kingdom, but now, as signified the red-brick Elizabethan mansion close by in which the Agent Victualler lived, devoted to more mundane purposes.

In crooked Cannon Street, where houses erected in the days of the Commonwealth made a crazy building line, the coach rumbled into the yard of the Royal Oak Inn, a hostelry adjacent to which were the Royal Oak Rooms, elegant premises used for meetings, balls, banquets and such like.

George Rochefort descended, flexed his travel-weary limbs, and then from the basket behind gathered his valise.

"And, young man," a familiar voice came from out of the gloom, "you'd do well not to let your brother Henry hear any of that nonsense of yours. If he does he'll never leave you alone until Domesday."

"And you, sir," George Rochefort countered curtly, "will please understand that I find it insupportable to receive unsolicited advice."

With that he left the fuming candle-maker and walked briskly into a town he had not seen for close on two years.

He diagonally crossed the Market Place, from the Antwerp Hotel corner to Captain Valentine Pepper's favourite Fountain Inn, whose light-washed walls stood out from the darker buildings around it. The distance was short from there to the water-front, and soon he had covered King Street, with its houses made with the stone looted from the ruins of St. Martin-le-Grand, and Bench Street, with its ancient buildings and tower, porched and portcullised, just vaguely discernible against the night sky.

At the end of Bench Street, where was Severus's Gate, he did not immediately turn right, along Snargate Street, but went a few paces in the other direction, and there stood, before the Island, in Town Wall Street.

But it was not at the divide of the Dour, with its quietly flowing waters, nor at the seemingly desirable building site, that he was looking. His glance was higher than that, higher even than the great bank of shingle which loomed beyond.

Nine leagues across the heaving black water lay France, the home of the new order.

2

Dover had a market twice weekly, on Wednesday and Saturday. It was on the midweek day following the one of George Rochefort's return that Susan Fagg woke up with such a sense of excitement, after a night in which she had hardly slept at all.

Glad that the rain had ceased, she continued luxuriously to lie abed, staring dreamily at a French agricultural print on the wall, all the time thinking of the plan which, for so long now, she had so daringly cherished.

She would first give him a charming little smile, she thought. And then, when it had dawned on him that this cool young woman was the girl . . .

John Fagg's sister giggled as she pictured his expression, his look of admiration as he saw sauntering towards him a ravishing creature. . . .

" No more of this silliness, Susan Fagg," she told herself severely, her every fibre thrilled with the thing she was conjecturing.

She slipped out of bed, opened the window, and as hurriedly withdrew when she saw that, near Mr. Beverley's Ropeworks, there was one of the carts used by the Paving Commissioners for collecting suitably sized stone.

Then there were preparations to be made, perhaps only preliminary ones, but important all the same. The hair beneath the lacy cap on which she had spent a full hour before retiring ; the sparkling cold water with which to rinse her eyes, and the lavender scent with which she would lightly massage her cheeks.

For the first time in her life Susan Fagg had decided to be really bold.

There was a pleasant smell of breakfast in the dining-room and an atmosphere most congenial, apart from the slight disturbance made by Charles shortly before he, with his sisters, departed with their books to the academy for the young kept by a noble French *emigré* and his wife.

"But I don't see why," he grumbled, rising from his wheel-back chair, " I shouldn't go to boarding-school at Canterbury the same time as Louis does."

His mother, who had just severely told Lou to fetch a clean hand-kerchief, was not of the same opinion.

" Louis is nearly a year and a half older than you are, love," she said.

" That——" began Charles scornfully.

" We shall be late, Charles," interposed his sister Minnie.

Her father, sanding a letter at his writing-table, now took a hand in the discussion, after first glancing along that loved view of his, through his son's Canyon to the pier-heads. For some weeks John Fagg had been in high humour, for it seemed evident that the Harbour Commissioners, even if not yet fully alive to their responsibilities, were at least doing a little towards the improvement of their charge. Following some deepening of the Pent, they were now employed in rebuilding seventy feet of the North Pier, damaged during a gale of two months before.

" So you think you're as good as Louis, eh, Charles?" he laughed.

Thereupon, methodically and very fairly, Charles started to enumerate the manly pastimes in which he and his friend at times competed, counting off respective debits and credits on his fingers.

Before the balance could be struck Mr. Fagg observed that he would have to think it over when the time came.

That did not completely satisfy the young man.

" You'll give it your . . . your mature consideration, Papa?" he asked earnestly.

" I will," his father remarked gravely.

" Of course, when the time comes," added young Charles, very reasonably.

Immediately Mr. Fagg exploded with laughter, but turned it off very brilliantly by his attentions to his sister.

" You're extremely chatsome this morning, Susan love," he roared.

" Singing and laughing and what not. What's the matter with you, girl ? "

The audacity of which Susan, earlier that morning, had persuaded herself she was capable, wilted a little. Certainly she blushed most vividly.

" You are ridiculous, John . . ." she was beginning very uncertainly, when fortunately the entrance of the children's nurse created a diversion.

Keziah Hart was a bustling body whose husband, a sergeant of artillery, had been killed, nearly a decade earlier, in the last ineffectual assault on Gibraltar, when a great French and Spanish fleet, aided by massive floating batteries and every device of modern warfare, had been destroyed by red-hot shot and the no less fiery courage of its intrepid defenders who, for three years, had held out against every attack.

She eyed the children austerely. " Now be you all ready ? " she demanded. Every morning she took them to school, a shepherding to which Charles had the greatest objection. At a discussion between himself and his father, however, he had heard that women often dislike to relinquish these loving duties, and that Keziah would be hurt if she learnt his views. Thereafter Charles had complained no more, but the understanding was that on his next birthday, his tenth, he alone should be entrusted with the care of Minnie and Lou.

" Ridiculous, eh ? " laughed John Fagg, affectionately slapping his sister's bottom.

Susan smiled at him, made a cheeky rejoinder and, in short, now that a critical moment had passed, recaptured all her daring.

" I think, Polly," she said carelessly, though her colour was still high, a fact which her shrewd sister-in-law had noticed all along, " that I'll walk on to the market before you." And from that, just so little incoherently, she went on to speak of a few personal errands she wanted to do. There was ribbon to be matched at . . .

Mrs. Fagg, with a face quite impassive, declared that she would miss the market altogether that morning. Susan could get those things she needed, she said. Briskly she related the household necessities that were required.

Shortly before eleven o'clock Susan glanced finally at herself in the mirror and, as a last afterthought, rummaged once more in her Tunbridgeware trinket-box.

She then descended to the white and cream-foiled hall but, at the front door, frowned when she saw that Town Wall Street was still thick in mud. Impatiently she seated herself on a gilt chair, and there

put on the iron pattens which, although they would largely save her
shoes from being soiled, would give her a slightly awkward gait.

Soon, however, she was outside, and was walking towards Severus's
Gate, a demure figure in a cambric bonnet and a glossy, wadded silk
mode coat, her hands comfortable in a pretty muff to match.

Still she was not satisfied. In Bench Street, first hurriedly glancing
to see that nobody witnessed her strange action, she stepped into the
recess before the portcullis of the old tower. There she discarded the
pattens with their iron ring which clanked as she walked.

Then she strolled daintily into King Street. That led into the
busy Market Place.

The Guildhall was an ancient building supported on carved wooden
pillars, underneath which, and flowing farther into the Market Place,
were the stalls and booths forming the market. In plentiful show were
the provisions of every kind brought in from neighbouring districts,
and from Calais and Boulogne there also came a chattering throng of
fish women and produce sellers, with fish and vegetables, game, fruit
and poultry. There was always a babel of strange tongues, the French
traders transacting business in a mixture of broken English and
French, and the Kentish dealers, as the result of this twice-weekly
intercourse with strangers, made a point of being amusingly bi-
lingual too.

Susan Fagg, who had been talking to a most striking young woman,
parted from her with a very real sense of relief. Kate Warren, the
daughter of the Collector of Customs, always made her feel most
childish, though Miss Warren, at twenty-one, was only two years older
than herself.

" 'Bye, Susan," said this odious female—that was how John Fagg's
sister couldn't resist describing her—whom the young men of the
town appeared to find so delightful.

" Good-bye, Kate," she smiled.

Miss Warren nodded graciously in dismissal—and that was how
Susan felt she had been dispensed with—and then waved saucily
towards two beaux who were making a bee-line for her.

" Affected creature," thought Susan, actually tossing her head
before glancing at the fourth stage of St. Mary the Virgin's tower, a
few score yards along Cannon Street. From where she was feigning
to examine laces set out for inspection she was unable to see the
clock, but at the same height on the southern side the sundial told
her that already she had spent an hour employed in an objective
which, even as she thought of it, caused her to colour.

It was just then that, chancing to turn about to walk along the
face of the Guildhall towards the irregular roofs, variety of chimneys

and many bow windows which filled the opposite side of the Market Place, she saw a tall and well-dressed figure wearing a broad black hat.

And Miss Susan Fagg, the bold one, at that sight very nearly lost her nerve.

Indeed, after seeing that George Rochefort had entered the printing-office situated there, she was so overwrought that an importuning travelling draper had wrapped up for her two yards of a quite impossible bonnet ribbon before she was able to reassert herself and put the impudent fellow in his place.

With this triumph behind her, Susan Fagg, her very air of the most determined, sauntered gracefully in a certain direction.

At the previous Saturday's market, Valentine Pepper had chanced to see a ruddy-cheeked young woman who, her arms through the handles of two great wicker-work baskets, had been bringing in butter and eggs for sale.

A big-built wench she was and, having a definite quest, Captain Pepper had decided on another inspection. This, very much in the cold-blooded manner of a horse buyer looking over a mare's points, he was now doing at the midweek market.

" Plenty o' chest and bedding," he muttered. " But," he grimaced fearfully, thinking of his compact little house, " she'd fill the bloody ship." Turning away disappointedly, he began to steer a steady course for the Fountain.

All this had been very much to the amusement of George Rochefort, who, though not knowing what important matter was about, had likened Pepper's open appraisal of the young woman to former incidents in the age-old history of the same Market Place, those of putting up Spanish prisoners of war for auction.

George Rochefort had had a busy morning, though his round of visits had in no wise been connected with the bank in which from now he would be expected to take over some considerable responsi-bilities. His calls had been of a personal nature, and the errand on which he had engaged himself had met with a mixed reception. His final talk, however, with the grimed young fellow who worked for Mr. Adcock the printer, of whom he had chanced to hear earlier on, had been as satisfactory as the rest put together.

As he emerged on to the pavement, he was reflecting that Stephen Hammond would prove an invaluable aide, when his thoughts were disturbed by a laughing inquiry.

" And how are you, Mr. Rochefort ? " a young woman asked archly.

Promptly doffing his hat, George Rochefort made an appropriate answer, meantime fully taking in the pleasing appearance presented by the daughter of the Collector of Customs.

"And you, Miss Warren?" he smiled. "Though assuredly," he said admiringly, "I had hardly need to ask that."

"Fie, fie, Mr. Rochefort," tittered Kate Warren, looking through her sweeping lashes. "I declare that such compliments from a gentleman travelled so much as yourself are enough to confuse any simple maiden."

Laughing, gossiping and chatting they stood there, the noise of the market to one side of them, and to the other the heavy thudding of Mr. Matthew Adcock's printing-press. Eventually Miss Warren, when the church clock boomed the hour, emitted a shrill little scream of mock dismay, protesting she must needs home and that quickly. And George Rochefort, who was mightily enjoying the badinage with this saucy female, vowed he would run through any man who tried to prevent him seeing her to her father's residence.

"*Would* you, Mr. Rochefort?" she asked coyly.

"I warrant you I would," he smilingly assented.

They were not able to cross the road all at once. First came the mail-coach, the armed guard blowing a horn and the driver sending his long whip-lash hissing through the air, a greater danger to the general public than to the fine animals he lightly flicked. And after that a long string of led horses, a very usual sight in the town which was the principal port for exportation of English beasts to the Continent.

Thus it was that the second glimpse which Susan Fagg had of George Rochefort showed him offering his arm to a young woman she already disliked, and from this moment positively hated. But somehow, though she never knew quite how, she forced herself to act as she had intended, or act as near that as her trembling limbs would allow her.

"Why, George," she lisped, or so, regrettably, it sounded. "It *is* George, isn't it?"

George Rochefort, even as he admitted his identity, could not prevent a broad grin escaping him.

"'Tis, Susan," he laughed.

Susan Fagg delicately extended her hand. "So, so charming to see you once again, George," she mouthed.

He guffawed outright, but immediately cut short any further display of his amusement when, in her blue eyes, he saw that tragic look of hurt.

"Susan," he began awkwardly, and then, hardly knowing what else to say, he asked her to give his regards to her brother and sister-in-law, and begged her to tell them that very shortly he would be paying his respects.

" Yes . . . yes, I will," Susan Fagg said strickenly, her face drained of any flush at all.

Then, suddenly, she turned and left them. Into King Street she blundered, in Bench Street she never saw the pattens which still lay before the portcullis of the old tower, and at the Albion Library in Snargate Street she blindly accepted the first book offered her.

She must have reached her bedroom, but she scarcely knew how she got there, her only impulse being to lock and bar her door.

For some time she sobbed on the bed where she had thrown herself, but at last, her face streaked with tears and her eyes sadly reddened, she got up shakily, and for some moments stood by the window, her head leant against her upraised arm.

" I . . . I won't give him up," she said. " I *won't*."

Courage seemed to be returning to her now, a courage finer than that with which she had so gallantly set out that morning.

" I won't give him up," she murmured.

And then she began, hopelessly, to cry again.

3

The King's Head was situated on Crane Street, the short thoroughfare which linked the Cross Wall with Townshend's Battery and the Pilots Look-out on the South Pier. Immediately before the old hostelry, but a few paces across the dusty road, was the Tidal Harbour, and to half left could be seen the lock-gates which connected that outer refuge with the Basin, itself in turn similarly communicating with the Pent.

On that sunny July day, at five o'clock in the afternoon, the establishment was charged with the aftermath of beefsteak, boiled fowl, and their accompaniments. The 'ordinary' had been served an hour before, and the gentlemen in the private apartment on the upper floor had signified they required no more.

When the remaining pieces of the earthenware dinner service had been removed and the door at last closed, the host of this gathering picked up the two-pronged fork which he had specially retained. Quite unnecessarily, for the heads of his guests were all turned towards him, he smartly rapped the polished board.

" Methinks," said he, " that we may now bring ourselves to the business on which we are met."

Rising, George Rochefort recalled to them the day it was, that second anniversary of an occurrence which Charles James Fox had spoken of as being " the greatest event that ever happened in the world ; and how much the best." And, the politician's words quoted, he invited them to fill up, to drink a bumper toast.

" Gentlemen," he said solemnly, his glass raised, " to the storming of the Bastille, two years ago to this very day."

A number of thirsty young men emptied brimming measures in that room whose walls were at once marred by cheap twopenny prints and beautified by two-hundred-years-old carved panels in which, delicately chased, were the initials of the original landlord and his wife.

" Drop of nice stuff, George," commented a red-faced youth who was licking his lips appreciatively. " Now if I'd a piece of laced mutton for to-night who was as kind——"

The age was coarse, and the suggestion nothing to be remarked upon in a company of males. Such an interposition, however, when weighty debate was afoot, was most unfortunate, as young Mr. Rochefort made no bones in frankly stating.

James Foord, the Agent Victualler's eldest son, accepted the rebuke good-naturedly, but his apology was delivered flippantly and in terms which obviously made wince the soul of one who had pretension to being a gifted orator.

" Sorry, George," he grinned. " And now that I've said that get on with your chin-wagging."

" Chin-wagging . . ." began George Rochefort, and then, for he was an ardent believer in the hard drive to the desired objective, he put aside the powerful retort he was contemplating.

" Let me," he said, " recall the stirring lines of the broadsheets the newsmen were selling a year ago.

> " Mark the Aera EIGHTY-NINE
> Must in future ANNALS shine,
> France from SLAVERY set free,
> By asserting Liberty,
> While, with Patriotic zeal,
> They destroyed the curs'd Bastille."

" Aye, an' they sold plenty of 'em too," James Foord commented. " But as I've always said, when a thing's a novelty——"

" An' 'twas that all right, James," another young man agreed conversationally.

" I can well remember what my old father said when——" a third young fellow joined in.

The two-pronged fork rang out an imperative summons.

" Gentlemen." George Rochefort's tone was ironically silky. " Perhaps if I may be permitted to proceed . . ."

A roar of good-humoured banter assured him that the man who had given such a fine spread must surely be allowed self-indulgence, and so long as the supply of liquor held out . . .

When the hubbub at last died George Rochefort began on the peroration he had so carefully drafted. His face was rather pale at the beginning, for he had had some difficulty in restraining a rising temper ; but at the end he looked animated and eager, carried away by the very torrent of his own declamation.

" Fifteen years ago, in the House of Commons," he commenced, measuring his words with quiet though telling emphasis, " Mr. Wilkes . . . er . . . " he smiled slightly, " *ventured* to suggest that even the meanest mechanic and the poorest day-labourer had important rights in themselves. But to-day, gentlemen, *I* venture to say more than that." From this young Mr. Rochefort, in growing volume, went on to speak of the inalienable rights of all men, whatever might be their degree, though, as he soberly admitted, this must inevitably create class war unless reason should prevail.

In the midst of developing this proposition he was challenged on two hands.

" Nonsense, George," one of his hearers remarked. " I'm with Mr. Burke, and be hanged to your agitators. Representation should only be given to the men with a stake in the welfare of the country, and that means to those who possess property in the land."

" That submission, sir——" the speaker was beginning coldly.

" In any case," another young man chimed in with an objection perhaps more true than he himself was aware, " the lower orders have not the education to enable them to express a political opinion. When they have, if ever——"

" Hear, hear," came a roar of approval, with the thick bases of glasses drumming on the table.

James Foord introduced a further dissentient note by going off into a sustained guffaw.

" George looks as if he ain't getting that unanimous support to which I'll be bound he feels entitled," he chuckled. " Never mind, George my boy," he bawled, " if I'm not with you yet at least I'm not against you."

He was vehemently tackled by a pale-faced young man who was sitting on the right of the host of the afternoon.

" That's one o' the indications of a wishy-washy mind, Foord," Stephen Hammond said sarcastically.

" What do you mean ? " demanded the Agent Victualler's son.

The pale eyes grew colder. " Just this," Stephen Hammond said sharply, his fist, the thumb ball of which was stained with the lamp-black and oil which betrayed his daily occupation, raised as if to come down emphatically on the table.

" Gentlemen ! " thundered George Rochefort, first silencing his henchman the printer, and then bitingly assailing those who would make a bear-garden of what should have been grave affairs properly and decently conducted.

But the general body of those present, having scented fun, would not hear him. There were sly jokes, outright jesting, and an increasing tendency to boisterousness until, in the end, George Rochefort told the shallow pates where they might take themselves.

When a more fitting atmosphere had been established, when the scoffers had gone, the gathering had been halved in number.

But how much better the few with clear vision than the multitude who cannot see whither they go.

" For this, my friends," George Rochefort said gravely, speaking of the attitude of those who had gone, " is but a sample of what we, in our efforts towards our . . . our noble ends . . . must expect progressively to meet as the days and months move on."

James Foord chuckled, his easy-going face wreathed in delight. As yet, as his interjections had shown, he had not fully grasped the implications behind his host's flowery phrases.

" Nothing better I like than a good skarmish," he remarked jovially.

By now the sun was passing behind the Western Heights, its line near to the Bredenstone ; the Castle, mellowed by the light, had taken on a less sombre hue, and Snargate Street, beneath its overhanging cliff, was being shrouded in a deepening gloom.

" Great causes, James," George Rochefort commented sardonically, " are not best gained by brawling."

The landlord was growing impatient, and now the masts, cordage, and spars of the vessels in the Basin were long shadowed on the glassy water.

" And so to the task which lies before us, gentlemen," said George Rochefort quietly. " Our path will be hard and bitter, as it must be to those who challenge a pluto-democracy. But challenge it we will, my friends."

He was to repeat those words later when, after threading through the throng making for the Ship Inn—a packet was in and most folk of importance stayed there—he and his companions turned into Strond Street, a road built on the site where once was a canal for the conveyance of water for the purpose of clearing the entrance to old Paradise Pent.

From one to the other of them he stared searchingly.

" Yes," he smiled strangely, " but challenge it we will, God helping us."

Rather bemused in mind, his friends, the weather lately having been hot, hastened their steps through the garbage and stinking filth which fouled the narrow streets of the town.

CHAPTER FOUR

I

IMMEDIATELY after passing over Buckland Bridge in the direction of Dover one had reached the town boundary, and it was the custom, when travellers of importance were arriving, that they should be greeted at this delightful rural retreat. In the view of most of his countrymen there could have been few more distinguished visitors than the Prime Minister, nor could there have been, in Kentish eyes, any office more notable than that of the Lord Warden of the Cinque Ports.

Thus it was only natural that when Mr. Pitt, whose political genius had first caused him to be Prime Minister of the land at the tender age of twenty-four, came down to the seaport to be installed Lord Warden, the townsfolk gathered on the near side of the Bridge gave him a royal reception, and as for the rest, the seven thousand inhabitants of Dover made a holiday of the day.

Whilst the Town Clerk read from a rustling piece of parchment the address of welcome, Mr. Pitt remained seated in his carriage. He was a somewhat haughty-looking gentleman, slimly built, whose most striking features were a pair of highly intelligent eyes and a nose which was long and definitely pointed. Those thoughtful eyes rested observantly on Mr. Stratton, but now and then their owner's attention wandered a little, and he would take in the Mayor's 'badge of his place,' the gown of the Chamberlain to the Corporation, or even the elaborately frogged coat worn by Sir Walter Plumbley, that Commissioner of Harbour who was beginning to find some enjoyment from the authority of the office he had undertaken.

Meantime John Fagg, a gleam of fun about him, was conducting a whispered conversation with the Rector of St. Mary the Virgin's, the Reverend Nathaniel Woodgate. The clergyman was attired in the usual knee breeches and black coat of his calling, and though his garments were shabby, they were neatly darned where necessary and his white stock was spotless.

"Knocked the sexton up, and then took the stuff in," said John Fagg. "Tubs in the vestry and stone jars in the vault."

There had been a run the previous night, and an act of indiscretion on the part of a body of over-confident riders had necessitated stowage in Doctor Woodgate's church. That, as most places of worship and churchyards for miles round, had often been used before for similar purpose, and the rector of St. Mary's, who brewed as good brandy punch as could be savoured within the same mentioned area, was obviously trying to indicate, discreetly, that he had no objection to the course which had been taken. But his face revealed a certain embarrassment, and the cause was not far to seek. Quite close to his other elbow was Mr. Howgate, and Mr. Howgate was the Revenue Officer.

" All right, Doctor ? " Mr. Fagg remarked, rhetorically rather than inquiringly.

" Quite, quite," said the parson, the words coming out faintly beneath the healthy clearing of his throat. " And now," he glanced hurriedly about him, espied Mr. Jeffrey Braems, Notary and Register of the Harbour, and forthwith made this legal light the excuse for abruptly leaving a disconcerting companion.

John Fagg's expression was still amused when, over that brief intervening space, his twinkling eyes met those of the Exciseman.

" Pleasant day, Mr. Howgate," he said genially.

The Revenue Officer, a gentleman in the fifties, gave the impression that he took life easily. Perhaps in his earlier days he had endeavoured to be the terror of the freetrader, but the eight years he had spent in Dover must have proved the last straw. Still he had a little spirit left.

" Following a pleasant . . . night, Mr. Fagg," he observed significantly.

John Fagg nodded. "As good a night as I've known, Mr. Howgate," he agreed blandly.

There ensued some innocuous sparring between two gentlemen who, apart from their own professional differences, held one another in high regard, until a hush fell over the assembly as the future Lord Warden rose.

Mr. Pitt said little in reply to Mr. Stratton's pompously delivered phrases, for the installation, which for hundreds of years had taken place at Devil's Drop on the Western Heights, would serve as a better opportunity.

Then, at the huskily shouted command of the Town Sergeant, the procession began to move, the ruling clique of the town well in the van, and the less superior, the ' linen drapers and such like,' in their appropriate station further to the rear.

*   *   *   *   *   *   *   *

The Bredenstone was the more proper name for Devil's Drop, though the latter designation was in more general use, the superstitious believing that the mass of stone, which emerged at such a curious angle from the ground, had been dropped there by the lord of hell. In point of fact, as had been recognised by antiquarians since the days when Queen Elizabeth's gay cavalcade wound over the same Heights whilst bells rang out and cannon roared in the town below, the Devil's Drop was relic of a pharos. This, together with the fine pharos still remaining at the other side of the valley, on Castle Hill, had been used by the Romans as twin beacons to guide their galleys into the haven after nightfall.

It was at this time-hallowed spot that the Barons of the Cinque Ports installed their Lord Warden.

The ceremony although short was impressive, but it was towards its conclusion, when Mr. Pitt's upraised hand vainly attempted to stem the prolonged thunder of cheering which greeted him, that the real moment of that day came. It had been understandable that at the beginning there would be the chaos inseparable from a mammoth social change. But in seven weeks more, three years would have elapsed since the common folk of France had their will with the Bastille and yet the turbulence across the narrow sea was increasing rather than declining. There was war too, the ruffianly Assembly having opened hostilities against Austria and Prussia, neighbours whom report declared feared mightily the example set over the French border. Many hoped that Mr. Pitt would clear up these perplexities.

The new Constable of Dover Castle and Lord Warden of the Cinque Ports, however, spoke far more of the honour which had been accorded him than of the grey shadow overseas.

" My friends," he said warmly, " on this day I am privileged to take up an ancient office which, since the times of Edward the Confessor, has been one to which any Englishman. . . ." He went on to talk of the virtue of tradition, of the proud birthright of race. . . .

Meantime a group of young people, to whom the polished delivery of an eminent statesman meant little, had escaped from their elders, and were occupying themselves in the ways they most enjoyed, none of which were likely to improve either the boys' wide white collars and frilly white cuffs or the long high-waisted summer dresses which the little girls were wearing.

The Western Heights made an admirable playground for any children possessing imagination. The block-houses made splendid make-belief homes, and to one of these Jack Woodgate, as father of the family, was returning after an arduous day at business, to be fondly greeted by his wife, Minnie Fagg, and his only daughter, Lou Fagg.

" And how is your head, dear ? " the devoted husband inquired.

Minnie sighed deeply. " A little better, my love," she murmured plaintively.

" Ah ! " said Mr. Woodgate sternly, his glance going to his little daughter.

Mrs. Woodgate nodded faintly. " I'm afraid, dear, that she has been so, so tiresome."

The man of affairs, something menacing in the very manner of his doing it, placed an imaginary hat on a hall table as exemplified by an old ammunition box. The full development of this interesting situation was, however, frustrated by the small girl playing the part of the daughter. " I'm not going to be slapped again," she announced shrilly.

" Lou ! " said her sister furiously.

" I'm not," Lou Fagg retorted mutinously. " And 'tis my turn to be mother now."

" You're not old enough to have a little girl," tittered the eight-year-old Minnie. " Is she, Jack ? "

" Not till she has taken a man," Jack Woodgate commented stolidly. The son of the Rector of St. Mary the Virgin's was a good-natured boy, and would have infinitely preferred to be joining in at the maritime exercises taking place nearby. Now he thought he had an opportunity for escape.

But his attempt was vain. Minnie seeming to have some sort of pleasure in laying hands on her sister's flesh, the proceedings grew so stormy that the noise must have been heard by the older ones.

The Heights, less than ten years before, during the French and American War, had been utilised for military purposes and, here and there, were fascinating finds.

Louis Rochefort was passionately fond of the many grass-covered trenches, in which he would stand popping off a Brown Bess, as represented by a stick, at the hordes of fierce charging infantry. It was whilst searching for some of these half-hidden depths that he tumbled into one such, coming out filthied and, what made his sister laugh immoderately, clutching one side of his nether garments—the buttons on his short coat, to which his long trousers were formerly attached, having been wrenched off.

" Oh, you do look funny, Louis," giggled Caroline. " Charles, look at him."

" Boom ! Boom ! " roared Charles Fagg. " Come on there, show a leg. Heave addy vaddy vo. Show a leg, show a leg, show a leg."

" Charles ! " screamed his friend's sister. " Look at Louis."

There were a number of heavy guns there, overgrown with vegetation, and behind one of these young Charles Fagg, fair hair moist and slightly curling through his exertions, was conducting a spirited

engagement with a French line-of-the-battle ship. His crew, as far
as could be seen, consisted of a number of Leicester and Lincoln sheep
who were industriously cropping.

"Boom ! Boom ! " the weapon resounded, but the gun captain
appeared far from satisfied with the speed of loading. "Show a leg
there, you goddam sons o' Satin," he snarled.

The gun team, a novelty brought into the Southdown country with
the idea of improving the breed, made little response. On the other
hand Miss Rochefort, scenting better diversion, forgot her brother's
predicament and took up position as number two.

"Aye, aye, sir," she reported smartly. "Are they striking yet,
sir ? "

Her senior officer shaded his eyes in the direction of the graves of
the victims of the 1666 plague. Swaying with the heavily rolling ship,
he stared unwaveringly over battle-racked waters.

"Not yet, my lad," he rapped. "But by God them Frenchies
shall, or me name's not Valentine Pep—Charles Fagg," he amended
hastily.

The battle continued to rage, and it seemed that the stubborn
Frogs would never yield, despite Louis Rochefort's persistently declaiming that the enemy had long disappeared beneath the waves. The
land arm made more appeal to him, though, with his trousers dipping
at one side and hitched high at the other, he hardly presented a martial
figure.

"You can't pretend at ships on land," by way of a change he
protested. "Let's man the trenches and——"

His sister screamed agonisingly, bravely bit back an anguished cry
and, her hand on her heart, staggered realistically.

"They've got me, blast 'em," she groaned.

She was being gently eased down to the deck when a storm of
huzzas told them that the new Lord Warden had completed his quiet
but stirring address.

It was true that Mr. Pitt Had not dwelt on matters which primarily
concerned those who lived in another country. Nevertheless, in his
final words, there was a hint of warning.

"And that is why, my friends," he said gravely, "I feel myself
especially honoured in receiving the appointment to the command
of this glorious strip of coast. Unhappily I cannot foresee that
the coming months will be as halcyon as we find conditions to-day,
but I can believe, and so do wholly believe, that the men of this
county of Kent will ever, as always, do whatever may be their duty for
the state." He waited until the roar of applause died. "But, my
friends, let us pray that our path lies in peaceful ways, towards that

more complete fulfilment of those aims essential to the betterment of mankind."

He spoke a little more in similar vein. Then, having concluded, he parted from the select company about him and set out to drive to Walmer, the Castle of which was the Lord Warden's official residence.

"Very sound, my love," commented Henry Rochefort, offering his wife his arm. "But . . ." he shook his head, "a little perturbing notwithstanding."

Elizabeth Rochefort nodded. "I suppose so, dear," she said, a little vaguely.

The throng was streaming away now. Some, the more venturesome, were making for the steep track which wound precipitously down to Archcliffe Fort and Paradise Pent ; others sauntered across the green down towards the rotting scaffolding which surrounded the shaft whose purpose was, if ever finished, to permit the defenders of the port speedy communication between Snargate Street and the Heights. The work had been abandoned at the close of the American War.

From the cliff edge, higher than the roofs and chimneys, there was a splendid view of the Rochefort house, with its two neat curves of green-painted railings guarding the windows on either side of the hooded door.

"I fear so," Mr. Rochefort observed gravely.

Mrs. Rochefort was extremely ignorant of political affairs and she was, too, becoming a little fatigued. But animation came into her voice when, beyond a dip in the rolling pasture, she saw the tall figure of her brother-in-law. Clinging to George Rochefort's arm was the attractive daughter of the Collector of Customs.

"Henry," she said excitedly. "I thought George had discontinued his attentions to Miss Warren, but . . ." she smiled faintly, "methinks I was mistaken."

In the early days of his return to Dover, George Rochefort had continually been seen in the company of the young woman she mentioned, but for nearly a year now it had been supposed that the affair had ended.

All of Miss Warren's bosom friends knew, however, that, after hinting only most indirectly at the tremendous concept in which he was engaged, young Mr. Rochefort had intimated to Kate, some eleven months before, that for the nonce he would not be able to enjoy much of her sweet society.

Henry Rochefort, when his wife made that remark, smiled grimly. It did not escape him that, as his brother walked along, many curious heads were turned. Originally there had been lively speculation in the town as to the young man's pregnantly secret preoccupations, but most of that had now died down. Only the recollection remained, though that provided many a sly aside and amused laugh as the young fellow marched on.

" 'Twould be as well if you were right, Elizabeth," he commented summarily. "That young female may be witless in many respects, but at least I'll swear she knows on which side her bread is buttered."

Before she spoke, Mrs. Rochefort glanced over her shoulder. The Faggs, she saw, were out of earshot, and the children were romping in the grass.

" I had sometimes thought that Susan cared for George," she said affectionately. "And I would indeed love her for a sister-in-law. She is so soft and gentle, and . . . and I think George needs somebody like that rather than a wife who is . . . hard and un-yielding."

" Susan ! " ejaculated the banker. And then slowly, even regret-fully, demurred. " I like the gal all right, in truth I'm really fond of her despite that nonsensical shyness of hers. Nevertheless she's not the wife for George."

" But, Henry, why not ? "

Henry Rochefort's stern face grew a shade sterner. " Because, my love," he explained, " I suspect George of having strange ideas, ideas which should not be in a banker's head. For that reason he needs a wife who will not be too milch-hearted."

" It sounds horrible," his wife remarked indignantly.

" George's character is such——" the banker was beginning when he received a quiet word of warning.

With the arrival of the Faggs, the three ladies began to talk about dress as the party strolled leisurely along the winding course of the rough military road. Their attitude concerning their present attire was, quite openly, one of complaisance. All three were in the very latest fashion of long clinging dresses, turbans and cow shoes, and it was not to be expected that it had escaped them that a large number of the ladies of the district had presented themselves at the Bredenstone in hoops and high heels.

" But . . . " sighed Mrs. Fagg, merrily woebegone, smoothing the bombazine over her thighs, " if only, Elizabeth, I was more willowy."

Whilst the discussion on feminine gew-gaws went on, the gentlemen talked together, with John Fagg monopolising the conversation. The shipper was in high spirits, for on that afternoon's tide an East Indiaman of 800 tons burthen, drawing twenty feet, was to enter the harbour, the first ship of such size to do so since the days of his boyhood.

Already some of the larger craft of the Fagg fleet, which for years had operated from Thames River ports, had come back to their own haven.

The evening was spent at Little Pent House, but shortly before supper, for the second time since high water that afternoon, John Fagg, rather shamefacedly, suggested another stroll along to the Basin, where the *Johann Sluys* was lying. A little with the air of one prepared to humour the fancies of a child, Henry Rochefort declared an intention of accompanying his friend.

The East Indiaman was secured alongside Custom House Quay. She was a fine well-found ship whose every rope-end was coiled down or cheesed meticulously, whose every inch of decking was holystoned to immaculate whiteness, whose lofty, tapering spars stretched high towards the deepening sky.

" Aye," said John Fagg contentedly, breathing in the enchanting aroma of cordage and hemp, of sails and tar. " A grand sight this if ever there was one."

Secured astern of the Dutch ship was his *Margaret*, a fast-sailer of nearly five hundred tons whose life hitherto had been spent between Wapping and the Baltic ports. Now she was to be employed nearer home and closer under the eye of her proud owner. On the morrow she was to load with wool for Colchester, whence, after discharging, she was to cross London Estuary to Rochester. There she was to pick up a cargo of Fuller's earth for the clothing centres of the North via the Humber and the Aire and Calder Canal from Hull, and at the Yorkshire port she was to take in a consignment of pigs of lead, mill-stones, corn stones and kerseys for delivery to the capital.

" Are you chartering her out, John ? " the banker asked keenly. " Or are you shipping on your own account ? " Simultaneously he began to frown for, beyond a group of men, a Revenue Cutter's crew in their canvas tarpaulin petticoats, he perceived an individual to whom he had not chosen to speak for five years. A difference of opinion at a meeting of St. Mary the Virgin's vestry had been the cause.

Mr. Fagg, also, had seen Christopher Crundall, with whom was Mrs. Crundall, a comfortable, ample-bosomed lady. He was desirous of a little talk with this worthy, and it was evident that the boat-builder was even more anxious for a few words with a townsman whose many ships would soon be occupying the harbour.

" So you'll have plenty of fitting out to do for me now, Kit," John Fagg said jovially. " And as for the other thing you've mentioned, we'll have to wait and see. But if all goes well then you can do what you suggest."

Mr. Crundall was a most enterprising gentleman, and one who had long chafed under the disabilities of the harbour, nearby which were his building slips. But now, when at last it looked as if the haven would be regularly used by larger craft, it seemed to him that the aspirations of a lifetime might yet come true. His desire was, not only to build the cutters and coastwise hulls for which he had won some considerable repute, but to run down to the water vessels large enough to sail the seven seas.

"As soon as you give the word, John," he said energetically, " I'll start on a big slipway."

"That'll do, Kit," nodded John Fagg. " You know it's always been a sore point with me that I've had to put so much of my work outside the town."

The two gentlemen, with Mrs. Crundall putting a word in now and then, discussed this aspect awhile. Both were agreed that Dover, having no coal within the vicinity, would never have the manufactures which, mushroom-like, were springing up in the North, and that the towns-folk would always have to depend on the harbour for their livelihoods.

"And now, surely to God," the boat-builder said emphatically, " the Harbour Commissioners will see that the back-scour is kept up to standard. A mixture of luck and a morsel of enterprise on their part have given them a better haven than we've had for fifty years."

"Aye, to be sure," John Fagg murmured reflectively, his face momentarily clouding. Then he went on to ask about the boat which Mr. Crundall was building for Charles. It was to be that young man's birthday shortly.

Mrs. Crundall laughed. "You'd better not ask Crundall about that, Mr. Fagg," she declared.

"That young 'un," commented Christopher Crundall, spitting prodigiously and shaking his head ruefully.

It was not exactly that young Charles made a nuisance of himself at Mr. Crundall's premises below Archcliffe Point. Rather it was that he had an inquiring as well as decided mind.

"He climbed up to my office every day for a fortnight before he finally thrashed out the merits of carvel or clinker-built," the ship-wright confessed wryly. "But," he laughed, " I think he's got a certain amount of confidence in me now."

John Fagg chuckled. " He's had a check on you though, Kit," he grinned. " Day after day he's come to the warehouse and him an' Pepper have argued it out from keelson to thwart."

"He has, has he ? " Mr. Crundall roared, highly edified.

A constant stream of people were visiting the quay, and with the approach of nightfall there was coming more rowdiness. A drunken fight was taking place near the *Margaret's* berth, and three young girls, all far from sober, had been cajoled to climb aboard the Dutch ship.

Respectable folk were beginning to leave, and soon Mr. Fagg sought for and then rejoined Mr. Rochefort. The pair began to saunter away, with the former talking of his fleet, of what he proposed to do with it, and how he proposed to enlarge it, and with the latter regularly interposing well-argued warnings regarding that nature-borne element, the shingle, which so often in the past had ruined bright hopes.

" According to you," John Fagg once observed huffily, " I'd better put my money into anything but stout ships."

" Not at all, John," the banker objected testily. " I am merely intending to convey that to build your plans around Dover is short-sighted to say the least of it."

John Fagg snorted, though he knew full well that there was a good deal of truth in what his companion was saying. But, contrarily, he would not outright agree to that.

They were in Town Wall Street now. He paused to look over the Island, and at a river sluggish with summer drought.

" Maybe I'd better give up shipping and put up a few fine houses here," he grunted. " Though that boy of mine has some lines of doggerel about the risk of tampering with the old Dour."

" There ! " commented Mr. Rochefort.

" 'Twould be a good paying proposition, Henry," observed John Fagg, showing signs of inward amusement. " Not a view in the town like it—barring my own."

The banker eyed the site carefully and was somewhat thoughtful during the next hundred yards to his friend's house. Latterly stocks and shares had been extremely erratic and he was beginning to be of the mind that some of his investments might be more securely placed, even though the interest received was less. It was at this stage that he started to think of that other building site, which he had forgotten for some two years.

His thoughts were dwelling on Paradise Pent as he entered Little Pent House.

The supper had been a light one of minced chicken, ham, tongue, and apple tart. Both the gentlemen had rounded off the repast with a pot apiece of old ale, and the ladies had ventured on a little wine in a tumbler three-quarters filled with water.

" Aye, young Charles is a one," guffawed John Fagg.

Henry Rochefort had waxed restive under the long and lively account of Charles's determination on the best for his boat, and immediately, when the shipowner had made that observation, went off into a eulogy in which his son Louis was the central figure. He told tales illustrative of his son's acumen, of how Louis wanted nothing more than to get into the bank as soon as he could, of how Louis had a marvellous head for figures. . . .

"I think, dear," Mrs. Rochefort said gently, "that you have talked enough about him."

Henry Rochefort looked not so much annoyed as surprised, until his face cleared and he, too, laughed.

The gentlemen began to speak of more weighty issues. It was rumoured that the government were being alarmed regarding the possibility of French ideas obtaining any hold in England, and both the banker and the shipowner were wondering whether Mr. Pitt's words quietly foreshadowed a withdrawal from the liberal policy which he had sought to pursue.

"Myself, I see no alternative," Mr. Rochefort observed. "Assuming, of course, that our neighbours across the Channel do not speedily bring themselves back to a saner outlook."

"And that time alone will show," John Fagg murmured sententiously. Actually his thoughts were blissfully revolving about the splendid change which that modest alteration to the Pent had brought to the haven.

One string of the harp, against which Susan Fagg chanced to be sitting, was at that moment idly and unthinkingly plucked by that young woman. She was at once flustered by the attention which she had brought on herself, and even more overwrought when this action caused Mrs. Rochefort to ask her to play on the pianoforte which, as the result of a profitable landing one black night the previous February, her brother had caused to be brought back from London in that other enterprise he ran, 'Fagg's Dover and London Hoy, for Passengers and Goods.'

"Oh, I couldn't," she stammered.

"Come on, Susan love," her sister-in-law said soothingly.

"That pretty little minuet you played for my special benefit t'other evening," suggested John Fagg wheedlingly.

In the end she was persuaded. She was uncertain and shaky at first, but with the passing moments and the pile of music before her, she shortly regained some measure of confidence, and soon, in that delightful secret world of hers, she was lost to all of them. In that delicious fantasy the room changed to quite another one, to one which belonged solely to her and *him*. She could feel that he was sitting listening intently to her, she could even feel specks of his perfumed hair powder fall on her bare shoulder when, the last note dying, he bent over her with tender appreciation in his musical voice.

George Rochefort, so she dreamt and yearned, lightly pressed his lips against her cheek.

In that moment, hugging this fanciful vision to herself, with the soft wax lights near and her lips so thrillingly parted, Susan Fagg was a very lovely sight.

2

Boulogne Harbour dried out at low water, a natural phenomenon which was driving to frenzy the captains of two cutters which were lying useless in the mud. It would be some hours before these raking craft would be waterborne, and the news which had arrived from Paris only a few minutes before was of inestimable value to their respective owners, two rival groups of London bankers. There seemed, however, little that could be done about it. Nevertheless, had the two blaspheming seafaring men, one of whom in any event must necessarily lose a handsome bonus, glanced at the small boy, sitting some distance away on the jetty, they might have found a messenger who could have solved their problem for them.

Charles Fagg, who a little earlier had heard the news and had, in itself, thought nothing of it, was in a sorry state. His coat was dusty, his pantaloons were torn, there were traces of blood in his nostrils, and his right eye was puffed and closing. Not so far away from him were his aforetime friends Jacques and Pierre, their state little better than his own, apart from the one fact that their clothing was incapable of showing any damage. Ragged they had always been, but in the years since France had made glorious change their condition had declined to the veritable scarecrow.

It was very obvious that some form of hostilities had recently taken place between the two representatives of the French Republic and the single upholder of old Albion.

Painfully young Charles rose, and began to walk along the planking, approaching his enemies, drawing level, passing them, his head slowly turning all the while, his sound eye never wavering from them, his whole attitude menacing. Likewise Jacques and Pierre watched him, too, and it was one of them who broke the strained silence with an expressive epithet when he was a few yards past.

Charles turned like a shot. "*Dites encore un petit mot,*" he said encouragingly, his fists clenched.

The two young Frenchmen did not repeat their former blood-thirsty proposition—that the enslaved citizens of London should storm the King's Palace, slaying the guards with the same brutality as a Parisian mob had employed less than thirty-six hours before at the Tuilleries. Nor did they make further reflection on the value of monarchs in general. Only Pierre, when his antagonist was a full fifty yards away, hurled further abuse. Charles, completely aware

with whom the honours rested, ignored the gibes, and continued
majestically until out of sight.

In the town, which was still wildly excited by the news received,
he broke into a steady trot. His boat was some two miles down the
inlet, in a sort of small lagoon from which half a fathom of water
never departed.

His pace increased. Now that the day's great adventure was half
over he began to think of the hiding he would get when he reached
home that night.

It had been a great adventure, too. The previous night he had
told his mother that he proposed sailing the following day. He had
said he would be rising early, and would find his own breakfast in the
kitchen.

Mrs. Fagg had at once strenuously objected, relented a little, then,
receding eventually from her rock-like stand, delivered a long homily
on the merits of taking care and the dangers of the sea, and had, at
last, given grudging permission. She would, she said, tell Keziah to
put out sufficient food for him to take with him as well as see that a
few slices of sustaining beef were there for his breakfast.

As he ran along he was debating a teasing question. If he said
nothing about having been to France then all would be well, but he
would thus be prevented from regaling his father with the splendours
of the expedition he had made. On the other hand, if he told the full
story it must inevitably come out that his idea of an early breakfast
had been for two o'clock in the morning, and that shortly after that
hour he had left Dover in the middle of the dark night.

As he made sail he came to the considered conclusion that the
receipt of a thrashing would prove the better value.

The tides and races of the Channel are as uncertain as the most
temperamental maiden. But Charles had luck on that day, and long
before the light had started to fail he was on the west mark of the
Gull Stream, keeping St. Margaret's Church bearing a little to the
left of the third cliff between the South Foreland and Walmer Castle.
Far away to the northard, dimly seen, was the most easterly point of
England, the North Foreland, for the upkeep of whose light, if passing
round it, every British ship had to pay twopence, and every foreign
bottom fourpence, on each ton. In the mid-distance were the lovely
spires of Reculver over Minster, and nearer still was the town of Deal,
whose inhabitants largely supported themselves in supplying the needs
of vessels which, as many as three hundred sail at a time in bad
weather, sheltered in the Downs, the vast expanse of water between
the shore there and the Goodwins.

" Sunset," muttered Charles, half an hour later, when expertly eyeing the set of the workmanlike lugsail. At that hour the main gates of Dover Castle from time immemorial had been closed, and faintly he heard the thin note of the call.

Soon he was within the Tidal Harbour, passing alongside the *Matilda*, one of his father's craft which was taking in chalk for delivery to the glass manufacturers at Newcastle. Fortunately the gates to the Basin were opening, and he was able to go directly to the boat-dock ; there Louis Rochefort met him at the top of the green-slimed steps near Amherst's Battery, close by Captain Pepper's weather-boarded little house.

" Have you been, Charles ? " he asked, just a little sceptically.

Charles gave chapter and verse, and answered a series of searching questions. Louis at length professed himself satisfied.

These major preliminaries completed, Charles told of the gory fight. " I wasn't going to let them insult our king," he observed stoutly.

" I should think not," Louis agreed loyally. " Wish I'd been there."

" Because they've just deposed their own king——" Charles was saying when his friend snatched his arm.

" Because they've what ? " demanded Louis Rochefort.

Charles told him again, and had forthwith, to his astonishment, to reply to a further string of questions. The point on which Louis seized was that the harbour of Boulogne, when Charles left, was dried out.

" But why do you want to know all these——" he was starting to ask.

But Louis was flying over the shingle towards the Ropewalk. He darted behind the Ordnance Stores, turned into Snargate Street-over-the-Wall, ran past his father's business premises, then along Pent-side, and from there through one of the fire-alleys, then pell-mell into his home.

Mr. Rochefort, who had been indulging in a smoke in the dining-room, irritably put down his churchwarden pipe and marched into the hall, from where he heard Louis's voice in the little drawing-room.

" Your mother is not in good health, Louis," he said severely when he entered there. " And your clatter is not likely to——"

" Papa," Louis interrupted excitedly, " the French have deposed their king and the news can't have got over yet. It only reached Boulogne an hour before Charles left there——"

" Charles ! " ejaculated his father.

Concisely the full account was told him, and a few minutes after-

wards the cause of all the pother peered cautiously round the door.
Charles was feeling the effects of the long day, and he had not hurried
after his friend.

" Come in, Charles," Mrs. Rochefort welcomed him.

He smiled back and, still keeping his damaged eye remote from
Louis' mother, sidled into the room.

Mr. Rochefort's cross-examination was thorough, and by its conclusion, assuming the informant to be trusted, he found himself in
possession of information which would have gladdened the heart of
any financier.

Rapidly he assessed the premises. But still he hesitated, still
not too sure of the one link.

" Charles," he said suddenly. " You are positive of all this ? "

" Yes, Mr. Rochefort."

The banker's face gathered an expression which would have unnerved many a weak vessel.

" You are *quite* sure, Charles ? " he asked sternly.

Charles was becoming a little restive. He disliked this interrogation
and he did not understand the reason for it.

" Yes, sir," he replied, respectfully but very definitely.

Mr. Rochefort stared at him and the small boy looked unflinchingly
back. Perhaps it was the steadfastness of those grey eyes which decided
the banker. Assuredly from then he lost no time.

" My dear," he explained to his wife, " I must leave for London
at once. Louis——"

Louis was instructed to make all haste to Mr. Godspenny's house.
The senior clerk was to open up the bank and to await the arrival of
his master. A servant girl was to go to the Antwerp Stables, there to
order a post-chaise for her master.

" And I shall prepare you some food for the journey, Henry," Mrs.
Rochefort said determinedly, despite her husband's protests. " We
haven't had supper yet."

The household was all in a scurry with the mistress of the house,
in so far as she was able, doing all she could to facilitate the traveller's
departure. Meantime the banker's cool brain, even as he talked of
more ordinary things, was exploring the full possibilities of the operation he contemplated in the stock market. There had been a bad
harvest that year, an increase in the number of bankruptcies, and the
House of Rochefort, though in no wise seriously involved, was carrying
more paper than he liked.

" 'Tis shocking," said Mrs. Rochefort, just before her husband
kissed her farewell. She was referring to the deposition of the French
king. " What will they do next ? "

Henry Rochefort shook his head gravely. " I don't know, my love.

But I haven't liked the look of affairs for a long time. Well, my dear . . . "

Together they went into the hall ; there, Charles and their daughter had been in conversation for some time.

Caroline, lolling inelegantly on one of the tall Carolean chairs, dark hair framed delightfully against floral carved back, legs swinging, was extracting piecemeal details of the day's adventure. She was also seeking a trip with Charles, a proposition which horrified the young man.

" You can't go sailing in my boat," he told her, aghast.

" Because why, Charles ? " she inquired, unabashed.

" Because . . . because there isn't a cuddy in her," Charles retorted, so ending the matter.

Miss Rochefort was not impressed. On the contrary she indignantly protested that she had no wish to be a passenger. Her desire was to have some hand in the running of the boat.

" Girls can't help to sail boats," stuttered the young gentleman, horrified.

Caroline sighed. " I so wanted to go with you one day, Charles," she murmured sorrowfully. " 'Tis such a lovely boat."

She received a stony stare. " You can't go with me," she was told decidedly.

" Oh, but Charles." An entrancing smile broke out on a very young minx's winsome face. " Couldn't you . . . " she thoughtfully licked her thumb as she glanced at him admiringly, " couldn't you employ me as a learner, like milliners——"

" Sign you on as a cabin boy," he corrected her authoritatively, his seaman's soul in arms at her nonsensical term, but with no further engagement than that.

To his sharp alarm, she clasped her hands in unbelievable ecstasy. " Oh, Charles, as *cabin boy*," she whispered, brown eyes starry with joy.

" I didn't say . . . " Charles was beginning hotly when Mr. Rochefort came out.

In the bustle of his departure, and in being lifted up to receive her father's kiss, Caroline, just then, may have forgotten both her whim and the refusal which Charles had embarked on. Or perhaps it was that she was perfectly satisfied with the progress she had made.

Charles, despite his growing sleepiness, was beginning to be distinctly curious as to the reason for which Mr. Rochefort was rushing off to London. To his question he was vouchsafed a reply which, in its very simplicity, epitomised one facet of the art of large gain without commensurate toil or stress.

" Why is your papa going to London so hurriedly ? " he asked.

" So that he can sell things before other people can," Caroline replied promptly, prior to commiserating him on an eye which, as she simply and reverently put it, had been so nobly gained.

The adventurer yawned hugely, and then took a pace off the step. "Good-night, Charles," Miss Rochefort said sweetly. "And thank you so, so much, Charles."

John Fagg's son was at Severus's Gate before he began to wonder just how much he had conceded to the little girl he had recently left.

Some five weeks later, on a September evening, Mr. Henry Rochefort presented to his son Louis and to Charles Fagg an inscribed gold watch apiece, to be put aside until they were old enough to wear them.

It was in the same week that news had been received of the ghastly massacres which had taken place in France, when hundreds of the King's friends were put to death, and of the report of the invasion and conquest of Belgium by the country whose National Convention proclaimed a republic three days later.

About then the name of George Rochefort again began to be bandied in the drawing-rooms, hostelries and coffee-houses of the town.

3

The leaves of the elms in the upper valley of the Dour were starting to fall yellowly, and the changing russet hues of the oaks made lovely pictures against the deep freshness of the green firs. In the high grate of Mrs. Rochefort's bedroom a bright fire was burning, its leaping flames reflected in the fluted posts of the tester bed. The candles were lighted and, immediately beneath the wall lights most remote from the curtained bay window, Caroline Rochefort was sitting on a low stool. Her small fingers were busied with a neat little sampler on which she had already worked in her name and age as well as an accepted tenet of the Christian faith. She was now finishing off with a basket of fruit at the bottom.

"Are you ready, Mamma?" she called out.

"Not yet, dear," her mother's voice came from beyond a closet door.

The same question was being asked outside the bedroom door. There was still ample time before he and his wife would start out for the evening's amusement, but Henry Rochefort had formed the habit of slipping upstairs when he thought Mrs. Rochefort would be dressed.

Martha Teddiman, with a certainty of manner assuredly no other female in Dover dare have employed, told the master that her lady could not yet receive him. Passionately devoted to her mistress, she well knew how much Mrs. Rochefort delighted to display herself to her adoring husband when, and only when, the last detail of her toilette was finished.

" Ha, ha ! " Caroline crowed joyously. " So you see Martha won't let you in, Papa."

The banker laughingly retired, whilst Martha Teddiman, severely observing that little girls should be seen and not heard, returned to her loving ministrations.

The daughter of the house triumphantly ended off the embroidery of the sun-kissed side of a rosy apple and then, her task done, held the sampler away from her to give it critical examination. It was then that she really, for the first time, read the line on which letter by letter she had laboured so diligently. The sampler was, of course, to be a Christmas present for her mother, and Christmas presents being much nicer when they are surprises, she had a special arrangement to cover this difficulty.

" Mamma," she cried out, after wrinkling her brow over the carefully worked declaration of faith, " how do I know that my Redeemer liveth ? "

" Because, my dear . . . " her mother's voice was meant to be reproving, " because all good people and all good little girls know it."

Caroline digested this thoughtfully. "But, Mamma, if all good people know it why did you tell me to put on it : ' 19 Job 28 ' ? So that if we saw some persons reading that part we should know they were wicked ? "

To the young lady's annoyance her mother, as she had often noticed grown-up people did, made an affectation of being cross instead of answering the question. She did not press the matter further, merely sighing sufficiently gustily for the sound to reach the powdering-closet.

Henry Rochefort was taking his wife to the Playhouse that evening, where a respectable company was in residence. As a very special treat, Caroline had been allowed to stay up to see her mother dress.

Mrs. Rochefort, the high towering coiffure completed, and the hairdresser having bowed himself out, carefully slipped out of the powdering-coat and then, in the bedroom again, quickly closed the closet door to prevent a cloud of scented dust from spreading all over.

" Oh, Mamma," Miss Rochefort declared ecstatically, " you look lovely."

" Do I, dear ? " her mother smiled, lightly caressing her daughter's dark head.

The sampler was then displayed ; after a renewal of the oath of blindness Mrs. Rochefort praised the skilful craftsmanship, and agreed that it would make a charming gift for *someone*.

" But you haven't seen it, Mamma ? " Caroline observed warningly.

Mrs. Rochefort closed her eyes, a gesture which appeared to satisfy her daughter. " How can I see it ? " she asked solemnly.

This piece of make-believe over, Caroline, first requesting her mother not to look, thereupon hid the sampler in the drawer in which Mrs. Rochefort kept the sachets of lavender.

" There ! " she breathed, with such supreme gratification that her mother couldn't help laughing, couldn't indeed help cuddling her.

Below, the front door was closed with the bang which could be associated with only one person.

" That's Uncle George," Caroline clapped gleefully. Latterly she had not seen so much of that young man as she felt she was entitled to do.

Martha was fussing about, now stooping to the floor to make sure of the latchet of her mistress's shoes, then shaking out the buffon which, slipped beneath the low, square-cut, short-sleeved sarsenet gown, would give to Mrs. Rochefort's bosom the pouter-pigeon-like appearance which was so very desirable.

" Doesn't Mamma look beautiful, Martha ? " Caroline asked, still enraptured.

Martha Teddiman's face, even as she was tying a bow in the ribbon strings which fastened a long glove above the elbow, glowed with affection.

" Indeed she does, Miss Caroline," she warmly confirmed.

Mrs. Rochefort's shapely head was poised to one side, as though, in that thick-walled house where sounds did not carry too well, she was worriedly aware that some unhappy incident might shortly take place.

She was not wrong. Within moments, in uncontrollable fury, her husband's voice rang out.

It was a newspaper, hitherto unnoticed, which caused such quick reversal of Henry Rochefort's happy and anticipatory mood. Prior to hearing his brother enter the house, he had been reading parliamentary reports or, his eye growing more wrathful, glancing down columns full of the doings of the French National Assembly.

The banker's frilled shirt and figured-brocade waistcoat presented every indication that he was prepared for a pleasant evening's recreation, but now his expression most definitely belied the presumption.

" George ! " he shouted, throwing open the dining-room door.

His brother, who had read much in the tone of that command, reduced his quick step and forthwith began to saunter, a tiny smile of amusement at the corners of his mouth.

" Yes, Henry ? " he said courteously.

From the floor to which he had thrown it, Henry Rochefort snatched up *The Times* newspaper.

" Have you seen this ? " he demanded, thrusting it in the younger man's face.

George Rochefort smiled easily. " I have indeed," he retorted cynically. " Scanning that Tory sheet in the coffee-house, I found that reaction had set in apace, that——"

" Enough ! " thundered his brother. " Have you got windmills in your head ? Do you imagine that liberal measures can be permitted when elsewhere we see that every concession can be taken as a weakness ? Enough, I say."

But the young man showed no sign of being stayed. " I imagine many things, Henry," he said sarcastically, " but at the moment I only note that the House of Lords has postponed the bill for the suppression of the slave trade, and that Mr. Fox's motion for the removal of the disabilities of the Dissenters has been defeated."

" But have you read what Mr. Walpole has to say about all these matters I gather you find so fine ? " shouted Henry Rochefort. " Speaking of the murderers who——"

George Rochefort, now quite pale, did not waver.

" ' Brutal insolence, bloody ferocity,' were amongst the terms he used," he commented dryly. " Such description is hardly likely to bring this country into amity with France. But fear travels fast, my worthy brother, and unquestionably the influential clique who misgovern this isle have reason for anxiety."

" From such as yourself," snapped Henry Rochefort. " Or so I am given to understand."

George Rochefort, sitting cross-legged, idly stroked a silken calf.

" I must confess, Henry," he drawled, " that what your newsmongers tell you is not entirely without substance."

" It isn't, isn't it ? " raved Henry Rochefort, beside himself at being so defied. " Now listen to me."

Boiled down to its essentials, Henry Rochefort demanded that his brother should immediately discontinue activities which were certain to cause the Rochefort name to become the laughing-stock of the town, for there was nothing more in them than to provoke that, he admitted. Nevertheless, he did not propose having his name held to derision, and from that it followed that George must sever at once his connection with the ridiculous society whose object, it would appear, was to ape that of similar lunatic organisations in France.

" And I want your word on't now, George," he stormed.

George Rochefort rose, his face colourless but icily composed.

" You shall have my word, and 'tis this," he said decisively. " I shall continue to follow the course which my conscience has dictated to me. Neither you nor any man——"

"Damn you, you insolent jackanapes. I'll show you——"

". . . shall force me to abate by one jot the path——" George Rochefort was continuing levelly when his brother's wild swing met the side of his head and sent him thudding to the floor.

"Yes, get on your feet again," bawled the banker. "And I'll give you the lesson you sadly need."

George Rochefort, a livid mark on his temple showing where he had struck against the wine-cooler, was scrambling up, now in his face a rage every bit as demoniacal as that of his brother.

"I'll kill you for this," he shouted. "I'll——"

"Kill me, will you? Kill your own brother, you say you'll kill your own brother," screamed Henry Rochefort.

Vicious blows were exchanged, there was the dull thud of bone on flesh, and the ever-increasingly laboured breathing of two combatants who in their struggle were whirling about the room, overturning chairs, bringing lovely ornaments to trampled ruin on the floor.

The door flew open and there, halted, her expression deathly, was Henry Rochefort's wife. For but a moment she so remained, horror in her dark eyes. Then she ran forward to pull at them, at last to separate them, when, hate in George Rochefort's look and a dawning shame in that of his brother, the two men stood.

"Henry . . . and George," she said strickenly. "How could you?"

Her husband, his limbs shaky with the recent stress and his soul sick with the realisation of his own lack of control, walked over to a gilt mirror and there attempted to arrange his disordered dress.

Mrs. Rochefort had taken her brother-in-law's arm, and was gently leading him away.

"I want to speak to Henry, George," she said sadly.

There was a hurt in her voice, some poignancy, which struck deep into George Rochefort. He tried to speak but failed.

Over the carved wood balustrade, close by the walnut tallboy on the landing, Louis Rochefort's face loomed whitely for a brief space until it was sharply jerked away as Martha Teddiman, holding Caroline by the other hand, whisked him off to his bedroom. And outside the dining-room door stood two servant girls and the cook, the last still panting with the effort of her run up the kitchen steps.

Mrs. Rochefort, her orders given quietly, sent them all away and then returned to her husband. He was sitting on one of the dining-room chairs, his elbows on the gate-table, his head in his hands.

"Henry," Elizabeth Rochefort murmured tenderly.

He looked up at last, some awful regret and contrition in him.

"I . . I can only ask your pardon, my dear," he said humbly.

" And express my sorrow that you have married a man possessed with a demon, for that is what I am."

Mrs. Rochefort's eyes were filling. " But the most tender and loving husband in the world," she told him softly.

They talked, at first with pregnant intervals, and then with a greater ease.

" 'Twas my fault, I know," Henry Rochefort miserably admitted. " But then . . . " he smiled faintly, " it always is."

She did not deny his words, but neither did she confirm them. Instead she repeated so movingly a catch-phrase of their more youthful days, one which, remembered by him, had often staved away a display of rage and temper.

" *One and two and three and* . . . " she said wistfully, her thoughts going back to those thrilling times.

" *One and two and three and* . . . " he repeated slowly.

It had happened at a rout when, in an annexe off the ballroom, she had been teaching him a step. A passing gentleman, careless of the sword which stuck out dangerously through his tails, had caught the pretty Miss Elizabeth Gay's gown, ripping it disastrously. And Henry Rochefort, made furious by his future wife's dismay, had rounded on the fellow with such vehemence as to bring a stupefied assembly to a standstill, thereby but adding to Miss Gay's plight. Subsequently the charming Elizabeth had declared that a life with such a husband would be intolerable, but being humbly beseeched, had gladly, so gladly, listened to her adorer's fervent plea. He had sworn that for the future, whenever he felt in danger of losing himself, he would say just those few words which would possibly, giving space for reflection, restrain him from the impulse which was a very part of his nature.

" If I'd only remembered them this night, my love," Henry Rochefort said soberly, thinking how much better it might have been had he reasoned calmly with George.

" I know," smiled Mrs. Rochefort. " But think no more of it now. Only, dear," she added earnestly, " you must not for ever hold this against George."

He took her hand and kissed it, in just the same manner in which, more than a decade before, he had sealed the compact.

Neither felt in the mood for the Playhouse that evening. And afterwards, with the firelight flickering on their faces, they talked together in that peaceful atmosphere which so often is the aftermath of the storm.

" But you know, my love," he said once, " George is being infernally irritating, with all this gibberish about Voltaire and Rousseau and the rights of man."

Elizabeth Rochefort spoke softly. " I realise full well he is, my dear, but we must remember that he is quite young yet, with all the impetuosity of his youth and temperament."

Henry Rochefort stirred. " You mean permit him to continue with all this nonsense in which he seems to have involved himself? "

" Yes, Henry." Her voice seemed remote.

For some time Henry Rochefort reflected, his keen eyes unseeingly on the smoke which curled up the chimney. Then he pulled himself out of the chair.

" For you and you alone would I do that, Elizabeth," he said fondly. "And for you I will, my love. Perhaps, if now and then I have a little tempered discussion with him, he will surely be weaned from this foolish but nevertheless unsavoury path."

Mrs. Rochefort's affection for her husband was reflected in her eyes. She knew, and none better, how his proud spirit must be galled by her brother-in-law's tendencies, and what this concession must have meant to him.

From then the banker's mood improved. It seemed that he, contemplating a line of action utterly alien to his dominant character, came to think that he, who rarely failed in any undertaking, must unquestionably succeed equally well in this novel course.

" The velvet-gloved method, my love," he explained shortly before his wife retired. " There are more ways of dealing with a frisky young horse than the over-abundant use of the whip. Would that I had months ago thought more clearly on this matter."

Thus it was that Henry Rochefort decided on this infinitely more subtle fashion of handling his young brother and, in furtherance, amply apologised for his conduct when George, incredibly late, arrived home that night.

George Rochefort accepted the expression of regret in the same spirit in which it was given. Notwithstanding, he declared in unequivocal terms that nothing on God's good earth could halt or stay his march along the thorny path he had so gladly undertaken.

As to a more precise definition of the path, that became more clearly known by the turn of the year, when the freemen of Dover in common assembly, being disturbed by tidings from abroad, decided to renew their engagement of 1783 for the defence of the Town and Port.

4

The Antwerp Hotel was the hostelry principally used by the leading townsmen of Dover, and generally on winter evenings its snug parlour was full. But on the night the freemen met, the cosy room, with only four gentlemen in it, looked extremely deserted. This quartet of die-hard Whigs, following the lead of the brilliant Charles James Fox in believing that an accommodation with France could be arranged, asserted they saw little reason for attending the Guildhall meeting.

"Not that I agree with this 'Edict of Fraternity' the Assembly have broadcast," Mr. Nicholas Stokes, the Clerk of the Passage, declared stridently. He was a bluff gentleman, ruddy cheeked, who gave the impression that he would feel more comfortable in a fight than in debating the finer points of political expediency.

Mr. Edward Hexstall, a builder who was also the Town Surveyor and Land Surveyor to the Harbour Commissioners, softly agreed as to this. Neither he nor the loquacious Post-master, Mr. Jonathan Dawkes, was of the opinion that the world could be better if all kings and ministers were torn from their places.

"Nor do we want the help the Frenchies offer to accomplish that end," grunted Mr. Robert Spisour, the Water Bailiff.

Mr. Nicholas Stokes rumbled into a powerful affirmation, and with that the little gathering sank into a long silence.

They had much to think of. The French had already overrun Belgium, were threatening to invade Holland, and had declared their intention of making Antwerp a great naval base, an action in itself a challenge to the greatest sea-power in the world. The reign of terror had also begun, and a bloodthirsty trio, Marat, Danton and Robespierre, were in course of impeaching Louis of France.

"Ah, well," sighed Mr. Hexstall. The builder had been speaking with some regret of a speech by Mr. Burke. That famous Whig leader dissented greatly from Mr. Fox's views, and in unmistakable terms had expressed his horror and abomination of doings across the sea.

"Aye," Mr. Spisour commented dourly.

The inn was now beginning to resound with the influx of some of those who had attended the meeting of the Volunteers of the American War. With their arrival Mr. Stokes and his companions were compelled to brace themselves, for they rightly judged that any display of uncertainty on their side would be most inadvisable. Argument there would be, they knew. And argument there was.

It was quiet little James Warren, the Collector of Customs, how-

ever, who caused the greatest sensation of the evening. It turned out
that Mr. Warren's youngest son had attended a gathering called by
Mr. Henry Rochefort's brother George.

" George Rochefort has *made* contact with the Jacobin Club in
Amiens ? " ejaculated Mr. Hugo Stratton, the Town Clerk, for once
omitting to purse his lips.

Never before had the subdued Mr. Warren been favoured with
such an attentive audience. Glowing with the pride of success, the
Collector of Customs told them what his boy had learnt prior to
telling George Rochefort all he thought of him.

" Forming a Correspondence Club *here* in Dover ? " The severe-
faced Mr. Jeffrey Braems, a notary who was Register of Dover Harbour,
looked as though he could hardly believe his ears when he received
further confirmation.

Both Mr. Warren and his son had good memories. The Collector
of Customs gave proof of that. The Declaration of Principals, already
drafted by young Mr. Rochefort, had been bound with a broad
tricolour ribbon, he said. He could even remember many of the
clauses.

" ' That all men are by nature equal, free and independent of
each other,' " he quoted, and caused a roar of laughter when he
remarked that, at this stage, there had been violent controversy
between George Rochefort and his henchman—a printer who worked
for old Matthew Adcock—as to whether ' free ' and ' independent,'
being synonyms, should both be used.

" There was another clause," choked the delighted Mr. Warren,
wiping streaming eyes. " ' That all government, abstractly considered,
being in itself an evil . . .' "

" But what's the numskull arter ? " chuckled Jeremy Nethersole.
Captain Nethersole, a seaman if ever there was one, commanded one
of the Mail Packets.

Mr. Warren achieved his greatest moment. " ' Our ultimate object
that same triumph which our French comrades have already so
magnificently attained,' " he replied solemnly.

A hush of stupefaction followed, and then a howl of glee, during
which further examples of George Rochefort's thoughts and designs
were, alas, lost.

Nevertheless the Collector of Customs subsequently told Mr. Oliver
Waade two of them. " A body of intelligent men prepared to martyr
themselves if necessary " was one, and " Better a handful of resolute
men than any number of waverers " was the other gem.

Had it not been for a dire calamity which fell on the haven the
next day, coupled with the swift rush of events abroad, there could
have been no doubt that the town would have hummed exclusively

with the report of the idiotic George Rochefort's conspirator-like doings.

The wind continued to rise, and at dawn the incoming herring boats had difficulty in making the harbour. By the time light vehicles were beginning to speed to London with the catch, a half-gale was blowing, and before the remaining fish were salted or hooked into frames for curing, great seas were rolling in from the west. And, before darkness descended on the town, the forecastle guns of a dozen merchantmen were booming out their doleful signals of distress.

Within a night and day the entrance to the harbour was choked with shingle and, when the storm subsided, it was found that not a craft above 50 tons could enter or leave the port at high water.

There was one hope. In eight days the spring tides would come. For a week the nautical men of Dover waited for the greater head of water they would bring.

  * * * * * * * *

Within a quarter of an hour it would be low water, and within minutes much would be resolved. The Tidal Harbour was dried out but, behind the lock-gates, a great volume of water was impounded in the Basin and the Pent. Soon would come the moment for its release.

" Let's run to the North Pier, Louis," said Charles Fagg. " Then we can watch what happens."

The level of the Pent, fed by the Dour, had been four feet higher than that of the Basin, but some half-hour before, the sluice gates at the beginning of Snargate Street-over-the-Wall had been opened, and now, when the lock-gates had also been brought back, the two expanses were as one, with the gates in the Cross Wall alone keeping an immense weight of water from the Tidal Harbour.

Standing by the lower lock-gates, Mr. Richard Breton examined his watch, then nodded abruptly.

From the end of the North Pier Charles Fagg could see his father amidst a crowd of Dover dignitaries. There was Mr. Waade at the elbow of Sir Walter Plumbley, and Louis's father. . . .

" They're opening, Charles," Louis Rochefort told him excitedly.

Cascades of foaming water appeared at each of the sluices, and with the gradual withdrawing of the lock-gates a low frothy wave began to advance across the sands and shingle of the Tidal Harbour, to be followed by a roar as the gates opened wider to permit the full flush to thunder from the Basin.

" Won't be long, Nicholas," Captain Nethersole remarked grimly to Mr. Stokes, Clerk of the Passage.

Seawards, between and beyond the pier-heads, was the massive bank of shingle which, for over a week, had prevented navigation. To his left, now narrowed between the piers, was the advancing mound, throwing up great splathers as it struck each vertical timber.

" Now . . ." muttered the Clerk of the Passage.

As yet the flowing water had made no impression on the barrier, though it had reached half-way to the mark of high-tide of ordinary springs. Many an anxious eye was being cast behind, for all depended on how much more pressure remained in the Basin and Pent.

" I suppose, Mr. Waade," Sir Walter Plumbley observed knowingly, " that little will happen until the uppermost limit of the obstacle between the pier-heads is reached and then . . . ah ! "

The rising water began to sweep over the shingle bank and, for a brief spell, it seemed as though success had been attained. The hope proved illusory, for the back pressure was spent, and the speed of scour was rapidly declining.

Mr. Breton, breathless with his run, was staring at the marks on the North Pier opposite.

" Taken about five foot off it," the Harbour Master murmured. " And that means there's still eight foot left."

Captain Nethersole began to speak of other days in Dover's history, when ships were smaller. In a voice which would have defeated any gale he roared that, in those days, the inhabitants were summoned and, bringing shovels, made the haven to be once more of service. But that, he added, could not be effectively done in these present times.

" Anyhow," he ended, growling deeply as he caught sight of Sir Walter Plumbley, " I reckon we've now another authority who are responsible."

He found his shoulder sharply tapped.

" You feel that way about it, Jeremy ? " John Fagg asked brusquely.

" I do, John," Captain Nethersole bellowed, staring.

" Then I'll bear it in mind," the shipowner observed queerly.

Many overheard his intriguing remark, and more than twoscore pairs of eyes watched a stocky figure as, shoulders squared determinedly, John Fagg began to walk down the pier.

The Harbour Master laboured to do whatever might be done in amelioration, but at the end of the third tide, having repeated thrice the same scouring operation, he had to confess himself beaten, with no more than a foot more taken off that tremendous obstacle to show for his work.

The harbour of Dover was back in its condition of a year before.

5

The day was dull and Mr. John Fagg's private room at the warehouse overlooking Paradise Pent was gloomy, but not a whit more gloomy than the faces of the four gentlemen present there. It was, however, speedily shown that the news which Captain Maxton had a few minutes before brought in from Boulogne was not the cause of the dismay.

"So they've guillotined the French King, have they?" muttered Mr. Crundall.

"Chopped his 'ead off, eh?" Captain Pepper grunted, after emptying his glass of moonshine brandy.

"That's what they've done, Valentine," nodded the skipper of the *Emma*. "An' what's more I'm damned if they don't sound delighted with what they've been a doing."

There was a little idle talk on the topic between the three of them, with John Fagg still standing at the window, glancing unseeingly towards Paradise Pent and the spot where Limekiln Street filtered out at the margin of the desolate waste.

He turned at last and spoke to the boatbuilder.

"Well, Kit," he remarked dourly, "it seems very much as if we've been wasting a lot of time."

Mr. Crundall swore violently. "Aye," he agreed. "An' damn me if I hadn't looked forrard like a child to putting a 700-ton ship into the water."

"What's been done afore can be done again," roared Captain Pepper.

"The Harbour Commissioners'll do no more after this," snorted Captain Maxton. "Now they'll take up their old attitude, and that means they'll continue to regard the bar as being as much inborn as sin."

"Any point, John," asked Mr. Crundall, "i' having a word with Sir Walter Plumbley?"

John Fagg laughed shortly. "What do you think, Kit?"

The shipowner began to pace restlessly, his mind active, his jaw pugnacious. It was, however, a chance remark of Mr. Crundall which brought his thoughts to quick life. That worthy philosophically observed that he was sorry both for himself and for John Fagg.

"Thankee, Kit, for your kind words of consolation," said John Fagg, smiling queerly. "And the same to you, too, though I can plainly see that you ain't particularly concerned about what's happened."

The boat-builder's eyes nearly popped out of his head. "Not concerned!" he growled. "You leave me to speak for myself."

Within a few moments Mr. Crundall was near to rage as John Fagg tantalisingly outlined the impotence of the traders of Dover. It would appear, Mr. Fagg concluded blandly, that the townsfolk of Dover must suffer their ills with as good spirit as they might, for, having no control over the thing which brought in their livelihoods, there was nothing else that could be done.

"We can raise hell with the Harbour Commissioners, can't we?" snapped the boat-builder. "For that's my humour."

"Mmmm," murmured John Fagg. "But there's a surer fashion of bringing the Commissioners to heel."

"What mean you, John?" Christopher Crundall growled.

"Listen," said the shipowner.

He spoke of the Harbour Commissioners and of the policy adopted for generations. The revenue of the Commissioners, he said, was derived from three sources. The first resulted from a half-share in the Passing Tolls and was like to be taken away altogether unless the harbour was considerably improved; the second came from the harbour dues, a rapidly shrinking source; and the third was provided by receipts for ground rents.

"But where has their ground come from?" he demanded. "From shingle thrown up by the sea, which they have seldom attempted to move as was their bounden duty. They preferred to let it stay, allowed its consolidation into firm land, subsequently deriving the major part of their income from its use for building purposes."

"Surely so," pondered Mr. Crundall, on whom a vague light was beginning to break.

John Fagg, keyed up by his deep disappointment, drove home point after point to demonstrate his belief as to how the Commissioners, indirectly, should be dealt with. It was, of course, not possible, he explained, to mulct the Commissioners of the valuable ground rents they already enjoyed, but it might be possible to prevent them from adding further to this same source.

"The Commissioners may be lessors of reclaimed ground," he said significantly, "but if there are no lessees coming forward, then where are they? In such cases the Commissioners must perforce seek extra income from the other two sources, and that means they must inevitably find the money for the substantial improvement of the harbour, not merely for its grudging repair, as they do to-day."

"And how would we stop folk from building on reclaimed land?" asked Mr. Crundall.

"Who leases it?" countered John Fagg.

His audience scratched their heads awhile. Finally it came to them that the folk who were thus defeating Dover's own interests were the people of the town itself.

"That's why we must educate 'em," said Mr. Fagg grimly. "We've got to make 'em see that sooner or later it means ruin to 'em. Ram it down their gizzards until they see the light."

Mr. Crundall, if shrewd, was a slow-thinking man. It was only when it dawned on him that all the houses in the vicinity of Strond Street, and all the big district between Round Tower Street and Beach Street, had been built on the site of Dover's former haven, Paradise, that he saw the full force of the argument which he had heard.

"Why . . . " he jerked his head towards Paradise Pent, " good ships have floated in all them places," he said aghast.

"Aye," growled John Fagg, " and the Tidal Harbour, the Basin and the Pent'll all go the same way if we don't watch it."

"We'll watch it, then," grunted Mr. Crundall, turning up the collar of his heavy coat.

New arrangements would have to be made, for none of John Fagg's larger ships would now be entering Dover Harbour. The shipowner, with the departure of the boat-builder, was settling down to the sad business when his wife called. Mrs. Fagg had heard the rumour of the murder of the King of France, in the upper warehouse had had this confirmed by both Valentine Pepper and Captain Maxton, and now sought further details from her husband.

"'Tis . . . 'tis terrible, John," she said, her eyes welling.

"Aye . . . " John Fagg agreed slowly.

It was then that Polly Fagg realised that her husband had greater troubles of his own, and it was then that she, being convinced that he still intended to carry on the fight, made one of the shrewdest observations of her married life.

"John," she began anxiously, " I know that sooner or later you mean to rouse the townsfolk about the harbour, but . . . but . . . " she hesitated.

The shipowner was eyeing her wonderingly. " Go on, my love," he said encouragingly.

"But . . . but, John, I shouldn't rely on Henry Rochefort helping you," she blurted out.

To her astonishment he was neither resentful nor surprised. Quietly he observed that for long he had been aware that Henry had little interest in such problems. It would have been fine, he continued regretfully, if Henry had been by his side, for the banker was one who would never be beaten.

"Though that, in Henry's case, is sometimes carried too far," John Fagg commented wryly, a faint smile breaking over his troubled face. " Still," he resumed more cheerfully, " if he isn't with me, at least he's not against me."

" Oh, he's *not* that," Polly Fagg agreed emphatically.   Any other suggestion, as her expression showed, would have been preposterous.

A little more talk and Mrs. Fagg went on her way, her destination being Snargate Street.   She had not seen Elizabeth Rochefort for a full three days, and most unusual that was.

Already in the street, as later she told Mrs. Rochefort, were manifestations of the sorrow decent people felt regarding the murder across the sea.   Quite a sprinkling of folk were wearing mourning, and a notice was posted at the Playhouse to the effect that the performance would not take place that night.

" How very wicked of them," Elizabeth Rochefort said, when she heard the dreadful tidings.

" 'Tis, my dear," nodded Polly Fagg.   " Now . . . now are you quite sure you want to go downstairs ? "   To her concern she had found her friend, not in her customary wing-chair in the little drawing-room, but lying down on the Stuart day-bed in her bedroom.

Mrs. Rochefort, who looked strained and wan, laughed that off gaily.   She wanted to know, she insisted, all about the new book of poems, bought by Susan, which Mrs. Fagg had chanced upon in Little Pent House.

" 'Tis very sad, Polly," she remarked, a little emotionally.   " But . . . but——"

Mrs. Fagg shook her head decidedly.   " You're right, my dear," she agreed, " I don't think George has the slightest interest in her."

For a while they talked of this poignant state of affairs ; of the young men who would have made a match with pretty Susan and at none of whom she would look ; and of George's goings-on which, now so long sustained, were causing his sister-in-law no little worry.

Mrs. Fagg, walking home later, was reflecting on these things when, meeting Mrs. Nethersole, she heard from that feather-brained little woman further sensational news.

Aliens before being permitted to land, she was told by Captain Nethersole's wife, had to state in writing their object for so doing, and those desiring to depart inland from the town had also to obtain a passport.

Three weeks later Dover's bellman was stentoriously proclaiming that the French Republic had announced a state of war with England.

Consequent upon this declaration there arose one of the greatest crises in the history of the country.   There were bankruptcies by the hundred, with an ensuing wave of panic.   And assuredly it seemed that the banking system would never survive the storm.

CHAPTER FIVE

I

THE issue by the Government of £5,000,000 in Treasury Bills saved the situation, but many anxious moments had to pass before businessmen and financiers began to breathe freely again. Altogether the war opened under most unfavourable conditions. The bad harvest of the previous year had caused a serious rise of thirteen shillings a quarter in wheat, and the economic collapse, due in the main to the overtrading of the country banks and the immensity of investments in the new industrial development, had but added to the strain.

Home events, as Captain Pepper made clear one evening in the Fountain Inn, were the cause of the severe shock the country received, not the outbreak of war with a land under the rule of a body of ragamuffins.

" Them," he declared forcefully, " we'll gollop 'em when we starts. True . . ." he laughed insultingly, his squint directed towards an ex-sergeant of foot, " we've nohow more'n 30,000 lobsters against the army of 'alf a million the Frenchies 'ave in the field, but . . ."

Every inmate of the parlour knew to what Valentine Pepper was broadly hinting—the 153 line-of-the-battle ships which could flaunt the battle ensign of old England, the ships which would win the war howsoever the army failed.

Hardly a soul thought otherwise, and most certainly not Mr. Henry Rochefort, though the banker, during that anxious time, never ceased to reproach himself for what he considered a previous neglect, in a matter distinctly apart from warfare.

One afternoon in March he made a remark to this effect.

" I should have placed a larger proportion of the bank's funds more directly under my control, George," he fumed. " And that is what I intend doing henceforth."

George Rochefort glanced up in some perplexity. He was not too good at figures and was in a little difficulty. The first war loan of £4,500,000 at 3 per cent had been issued, and he was endeavouring to ascertain the yield, the public being invited to buy at 72.

" But we have not been seriously involved, Henry," he protested.

" Nevertheless we hold canal and other shares, which in these days of fright are not acceptable as security," his elder brother said angrily. " No, for the future I shall seek other sources for investment, sources more directly under my eye."

" Of what description, Henry ? " George asked curiously.

Hands beneath his tails, Henry Rochefort marched over to the window, and there stood eyeing the Basin.

" Of . . . of a more local nature," he replied tersely.

Against Custom House Quay, opposite the Custom House, was a black-painted Revenue cutter, her bulwarks red, with her host of white-painted gigs and galleys hoisted high. But it was not at this lovely-lined craft that Henry Rochefort was glancing. Rather was he looking more towards the Cross Wall, his active mind busy as he steadily stared at the fringe of Paradise Pent, seen fleetingly through the alleys to the right of the Plain.

" Local nature ? " queried George Rochefort.

" Local nature," his brother retorted, mouth resolute.

Scratching his chin irritably, George returned to his task. Twice out of three times he had proved the interest to work out at £4 3s. 4d. per cent, but as yet he was doubtful as to the accuracy of this figure.

Meantime Henry Rochefort, as so he did for many months, continued to think of that idea which, more than once in the last three years, had come into his head.

Henry Rochefort was not the only one who did a great deal of reflecting during that first summer of the war. John Fagg, from spring days when 20,000 men were landed at Ostend, brooded continually, though his thoughts had no relation to finance or investment. Often in the evening he would stroll over the Ropewalk, past Amherst's Battery, now in course of being leisurely rebuilt, and then on to the North Pier, where he would sit.

One golden September evening Mr. Breton found him so and, following some small talk on the war and a more critical discussion on the rig of a Fagg ship which passed out London-bound with corn and malt, the Harbour-master, to his mild surprise, had a strange question put to him. In short, John Fagg asked Richard Breton if there were extant any of the early plans and proposals for the improvement of the harbour.

" Well . . . " the Harbour-master observed dubiously, " I'll search if you like, John."

" Thankee, Dick," Mr. Fagg commented briefly but, rather to the disappointment of his companion, said no more than that before departing for home.

Mr. Fagg, by way of change, made for Little Pent House by Snargate Street-over-the-Wall. Coming along Townwall Street he witnessed an incident which caused him no small amusement. The stables, Mrs. Fagg not liking them built on to the house, were on the

D

opposite side of the street, and towards them, in an attitude betokening trouble for someone, Keziah Hart was stamping.

" Where be you, Master Charles ? " she said shrilly, peering into the sweet-smelling place. " Do you know 'tis boblight already ? "

Charles, who, after ingratiating himself with a corporal of the garrison, had spent an enchanting two hours in the depths of the defence galleries at the Castle, had called in on his way home to see his father's latest acquisition, a four-year-old sorrel named Bob.

" I'm coming, Keziah," he hastily shouted, leaving the stall and shortly appearing to disclose a face which intent could hardly have made more filthy.

Keziah Hart, taking a long breath, told him what she thought of him, and what she proposed to do with him.

" I'll wash myself well, Keziah," Charles, extremely hurriedly, told her.

" And I'll be there to see you wash yourself, Master Charles," Keziah said grimly. " Don't you think you can best me, you little guttergrub."

With that she grasped one of his ears and, thus leading him, saw him safely inside.

John Fagg's grin died only when, a minute later, he encountered his sister. Susan, he thought, looked ill and despondent.

" Is anything the matter, love ? " he asked her affectionately.

" No, John," she laughed brightly, a brightness so unreal above the apathy which had, he was sure, enshrouded her for a long while.

He was not to know that Susan Fagg was terrified, terrified. The Government had become alarmed of late, and the Traitorous Correspondence Bill had become law ; already a Scottish advocate and a Scottish clergyman had been transported for life. Though she knew little of what George Rochefort was doing, though indeed she had not spoken to him for months, she was convinced that this measure was aimed at such as he.

Fear or no, within a month the most glorious radiancy came into her life.

2

Afterwards Susan Fagg never quite knew how, one dark autumn night, she came to be holding George Rochefort's arm, whilst in the other hand he swung the horn lantern with which he would light her home from the top of Biggin Street.

It had all happened so quickly, though the earlier part of the evening, from arriving at Mr. Foorde's Elizabethan house, she remembered perfectly. The Agent-Victualler's sons and daughters were giving a party and the usual thing it turned out to be—an elegant spread of confectioneries and beverages in the low-timbered dining-room, dancing in the drawing-room, and couples regularly stealing away to the big greenhouse. That was until Mr. Francis Stone called in to give most fearful news to his friends the Foordes.

By the time George Rochefort arrived, which was but shortly afterwards, most of the ladies were steadily weeping, with more than one gentleman distinctly affected.

" Mr. Stone ! " wailed Mrs. Foorde, when first she heard.

The paper manufacturer, back from a business trip to London, was on the way out to the Mill House at Buckland. The Metropolis, late on the evening before he left, was mourning the brutal death of the Queen of France. Having seen a copy of the *St. James's Chronicle*, he was able to give most melancholy details of the execution scene— Marie Antoinette's black-girdled white lawn dress, her small hands tied tightly together, the kennel-like cell from which she had been taken, and the hair shorn so that the cruel blade of the guillotine might fairly strike the slender neck.

Into this atmosphere of grief walked George Rochefort, late through working overtime at the Bank. The subsidies with which England was assisting the Allies were entailing no mean devotion on the part of the financial institutions of the country.

It was James Foorde, son of the Agent-Victualler, who beat half a dozen other young men with his question, completely forgetting that he was insulting a guest in his father's house.

" Well, George," he observed bitterly, " your fine Republicans of France first murdered their lawful king and——"

" I seem to recollect an earlier example much nearer home," George Rochefort retorted witheringly.

The reply incensed more than young Mr. Foorde, and Henry Rochefort's brother found himself assailed on every hand, amongst his denunciators being quite a few red-eyed ladies of the town. Miss Warren in particular was viciously direct. She did not, she said, wish ever to set eye on him again.

" You can . . . " she sobbed moistly, " join your murderous friends in Paris."

Very pale, George Rochefort held his ground . . . and more. After bowing, and most composedly informing her that, of course, he must accept her decision, he spoke more generally to the gathering. The substance of his remarks was to the effect that the death of the *soi-disant* Queen of France was perhaps to be deplored, but he felt himself under the necessity of pointing out one unchallengeable truism.

" And that is," he began, deliberately dabbing his lips with a fine cambric handkerchief, " that the passing of one woman, whoever she may be, is little to set against the boon gained from a new and beneficent order and society."

With anguish in her heart Susan Fagg heard the growl of anger which went up, with pride in her heart she watched George Rochefort dauntlessly face his aggressors. There was fierce controversy, and with the controversy and its slow petering out, many seemed likely to forget the tragic cause of the dispute. The older ladies had recovered somewhat, and the young ones, with a greater resilience, were obviously once again thinking of the delight of country dances in the drawing-room.

" After all," pouted the second Hexstall girl, daughter of the builder and Town Surveyor, " though we must give consequence to this sad event, I don't quite see why this pleasant evening should . . . "

Susan Fagg, blue eyes still on George Rochefort, murmured something in reply. George, in the picture again, had stalked up to Mr. Foorde and, stiffly, was inquiring whether the Agent-Victualler would prefer him to withdraw from the house.

From then, until she was in the refreshing air outside, Susan no more than vaguely remembered what she did. But she had one deep conviction. It was that George, after receiving Mr. Foorde's embarrassed assurance, meant to stay, meant to brave it out, perhaps even, though she felt monstrous guilty as she thought it, gloried in so doing. From that proud spirit of his she must save him . . . and now.

" Susan ! " said George Rochefort, catching sight of her and of her sharp distress.

Her heart thumping, she whispered to him that she was not feeling very well and that she intended to go home.

" Would . . . would you, George . . . " she felt that she was nearly choking, " see me there ? "

" Of a surety, my dear," he smiled kindly. " If you will get your things. . . ."

In such manner it came about that Susan Fagg found herself holding George Rochefort's arm close by the Maison Dieu.

For a while, walking down Biggin Street, George Rochefort did not speak at all, beyond asking her if she felt a little better, and it was only when she remarked timidly on the night that he came to greater animation.

> " Above yon eastern hill, where darkness broods," he began,
> " O'er all its vanished dells, and lawns, and woods . . ."

As so often when endeavouring to speak low, the dry throat of excitement brings out the voice startlingly loud. It was divine, so

Susan Fagg thought, that she herself could quietly whisper the lines with him.

"Where but a mass of shade the sight can trace . . ."

she went on with him, and knew from the first word that he must have heard.

George Rochefort, greatly diverted, held the lantern aloft and, in its soft light, glanced down at the crimson-stained face.

"My dear Susan," he laughed, "veritably I little dreamed I had with me a young woman capable of correcting me should I misquote William's——"

Susan became more confused than ever. "No, no, George," she told him incoherently. "'Twas only that I chanced to find the poem in a little book I . . . I came across. Of course I . . . I knew you were acquainted with Mr. Wordsworth."

"Your honesty does you credit, Susan," he smiled. "So much so that I must loan you one or two little books as well as tell you something of a friend who thinks as I do, and in whose judgment I have the most implicit faith."

Lightly he told her that they must make a detour to Snargate Street for that immediate purpose.

So Susan Fagg came to be, a few minutes later, in Henry Rochefort's house, with George Rochefort making a selection from a number of slim volumes which he took from the Queen Anne bureau-bookcase in the little drawing-room.

"Mmmm . . . this, I think," he remarked, "and . . . yes, perhaps this, but . . . " his tone changed pregnantly, "not this, I fear, Susan."

In the drawing-room proper, beyond the double-doors, there was the hum of voices, and it was very evident that Mr. and Mrs. Rochefort had company that evening. Susan was in the midst of wondering just what she would say if Mrs. Rochefort came, when George spoke so strangely.

"Not this," he repeated. "And methinks . . . " he laughed now, "'twould be as well if I removed it from here, for if my good brother Henry laid hand on't, I suggest this may represent how he would hold it."

It was Mr. Thomas Paine's *Rights of Man*, a volume which, with its "universal liberty of conscience" and what not, was creating a goodly amount of alarm in government circles, though a small band of intelligent men held it to be a powerful reply to Mr. Burke's *Reflections on the French Republic*. George Rochefort, amusingly illustrating his brother's attitude, delicately held the book between finger and thumb, away from him, wrinkling his nose as though the thing stank.

" Oh, George," Susan gulped unhappily, trying to smile.

She vaguely remembered the uproar in Dover the previous year when Mr. Paine, crossing to Calais, had suffered many indignities under the guise of Custom House regulations. And part of the condemnation directed against Mr. Paine's pervert social philosophy she recollected too.

" George," she said timidly, her eyes pools of dread, " you will take care, won't you ? "

George Rochefort was but human, and for long he had been the target for the wit of many a buffoon. It was, perhaps, balm to his soul that for once he was treated so very seriously, even if only by a girl.

" Take care, m'dear." He shrugged, smiling quizzically. " I fear, Susan . . . " he was suddenly grave and just as suddenly back to common sense. " But no more of this, for these momentous issues are not for young women."

As if finally to close the subject, he took her arm and drew her into the hall. The drawing-room door was slightly ajar, and through the gap could be seen the long-cased lacquer clock and the red lacquer cabinet, with Mrs. Hugo Stratton making quite a stir whilst she adjusted a face screen to ward off the heat from a face which never was other than empurpled and blotchy.

Thankfully Susan Fagg slipped by unobserved and, with the closing of the front door, she and George were in Snargate Street again.

Shortly afterwards, at Little Pent House, that young man was, in a brotherly fashion, wishing her happy dreams.

" And thank you so much for the books," Susan murmured shyly, now being in the full light.

George Rochefort said that that was nothing and, having discharged the duty he had undertaken, briefly though pleasantly bade her good-night.

To the loving heart a small gesture means much. Thrilled to her depths, clasping three thin volumes against her breast, Susan Fagg went directly to her room.

Earlier, in April, troops had been landed at Toulon, far too few for their purpose, and by the end of the year, when ill-news was coming from the Low Countries of the progress of the Army, it became necessary to evacuate them, the Navy successfully performing the difficult feat.

In the House of Commons Mr. Burke, in challenge to the followers of Mr. Fox, flung down a Birmingham-made dagger " as a sample of the fruits to be obtained by an alliance with France," ' a piece of business' intending to portray that the Frenchies would as soon as not stab a friend in the back if it suited their purpose.

The Navy's long arm had enabled the senior service to seize outlying French colonies, but the lack of any heartening news elsewhere, after ten months of hostilities, caused some heart-burning. In Dover Castle a great meeting was held to consider ways and means of equipping the Cinque Ports Fencibles and Volunteers. £6,000 was raised, of which Mr. Pitt himself contributed £1,000.

The war continued to drift on.

3

Winter months meant for the children dancing lessons at the Royal Oak Rooms, opposite St. Mary the Virgin's. There the Comtesse de Vaise, who would not have been a widow had not her husband, dressed in women's clothes, suffered discovery through receiving a familiarity from a lusty guard when on the very threshold of freedom, gave lessons once a week.

" Why should we have to come here ? " grumbled Louis Rochefort.

" Don't know," scowled Charles Fagg, malevolently glancing at one of the Jelly girls.

The truth was that the boys detested these Tuesday afternoons when, in best suits and with faces shining with cleanliness, they were escorted to the Rooms, where the lessons were given in the big ante-room, the one first reached after passing through the fine entrance in Cannon Street.

" And if the Comtesse makes me partner that awful Jellybag again . . . " Charles went on ill-temperedly.

There was so much fun awaiting him outside. Bob had to be shod, and there was the riding of the sorrel to the forge near the junction of the Dover and Folkestone roads, close by the Maison Dieu.

" Or that spicy Spisour," groaned Louis Rochefort. " And . . . " seeing Jack Woodgate approach, added threateningly to that young gentleman, " I don't want you to tell me any more about how our fleets are blockading Brest and Rochefort or wherever 'tis they are."

" How did you know that I . . . " the Rector's puzzled son was beginning.

" You never talk about anything else," Louis scoffed.

Mammas and elder sisters were disposed on the red upholstered sofas which lined the ante-room, and the Comtesse was making her usual round. When she clapped her hands, however, it would mean collecting in the middle of the floor, but until then a little fun might be snatched. Sliding down the broad banister rail of the grand staircase was splendid sport, or exploring the maze of deserted rooms which abutted on the Black Ditch, an unsavoury and desolate alley.

Though the boys had so much distaste for the afternoon's instruction, the girls were very different. They extracted a great deal of enjoyment from pretty dresses and the knowledge that, beneath this same roof, real grown-up ladies and gentlemen danced together at balls.

"I wish I was old, Grandmamma," Lou Fagg observed wistfully.

Mrs. Fagg's mother, a pleasant-looking old woman in the fifties, rather ruefully made the only retort, and then turned to Minnie and the other delightful little creature.

"You don't wish you were old, do you, Caroline?" she inquired in a rich Northumberland accent. She hailed from Newcastle, where John Fagg first met his wife when, in his young manhood, he had gone up to the Black Indies to arrange a coal contract.

Caroline Rochefort's forehead puckered. On the one hand she passionately wanted to attend assemblies and such like, but on the other hand she had a wicked craving lavishly to use coloured chalks for the embellishment of the marble face of His Majesty George III whose bust stood on a pedestal in a niche.

"'Twould be nice if one could be both old and young at the same time," she propounded earnestly.

Lou agreed, Minnie dissented, and their grandmother was smiling over the wrangling when Madame la Comtesse, having passed the right sort of word with every remunerative parent, began to clap her hands.

"Attention, attention," she called. "Children, children."

The onlookers settled themselves to watch the proceedings, though at first, in the general commotion, there was little of interest. But when all the young people had been gathered together Madame was able to begin.

Two of the boys were skulking, there was no question on that, nor was there any doubt that Madame intended to have no nonsense.

"Louis . . . and Charles," she said severely. "You know your partners . . . they are the same as last week, and no more foolishness, pliss!"

"I told you so," hissed Louis Rochefort, scarlet with mortification as he eyed the simpering spicy Spisour, whom Madame was leading to him.

Charles, no less enraged, found himself facing the Jellybag, the daughter of Mr. Jelly the Chamberlain, a girl who had, he was convinced, the silliest moonface in the world.

" Charles ! " the martinet continued. " What . . . do . . . you . . . do . . . now ? "

Fronting the giggling Miss Jelly, Charles made an ungracious leg, was told to do it again, and was made to repeat the performance until Madame was satisfied.

" Now you ask this lady to dance . . . how, Charles ? "

Taking a deep breath, Charles complied.

" May I be honoured with your hand, Miss Jelly ? " he snarled.

" You are too kind, sir," that young lady was tittering when Madame, drawing herself to her full height, extended a stern hand in dismissal. For his impertinence, Charles must be punished. He must leave the floor, she said.

Which Charles did, to be joined incredibly quickly on the bottom step of the grand staircase by Louis, who had misbehaved himself in similar style.

Whilst the culprits were thus sitting in happy disgrace, Charles's mother came in from Cannon Street. She was in no small distress.

" What is the matter, Mrs. Fagg ? " Mrs. Stokes, making room for her, asked anxiously.

Tears were starting in Polly Fagg's eyes.

" 'Tis Elizabeth . . . Mrs. Rochefort," she replied miserably.

Several ladies made kind inquiry as to the state of the banker's wife, but there was a shocked hush when Mrs. Fagg, fresh from Henry Rochefort's house, told them the grievous news. Despite a breast which had gradually grown smaller there could be no doubt that Mrs. Rochefort had the malignancy feared by all women.

" A Cancer ! " Mrs. Christopher Crundall said pityingly. " Oh, the poor creature."

" And what is to be done, Mrs. Fagg ? " Mrs. Jeffrey Braems asked.

Sniffing back her misery Polly Fagg told them that Dr. Crouch had sent a horseman with a message to a Tunbridge Wells colleague. Later, should consultation suggest the knife, a London surgeon would be called upon.

" Mr. Rochefort, how is he taking it ? " Mrs. Paul Elam, the wife of the Master of Lodesmen, inquired sympathetically.

Mrs. Fagg shook her head despairingly. " Don't ask, Mrs. Elam," she said simply.

The dancing lessons were over, and the young people, restraint past, amused themselves in their own way. Caroline Rochefort and Lou Fagg, in particular, had a game they always played. It took place in the big white and gilt ballroom into which, when unobserved, they slipped.

Inside there Lou became Miss Fagg, and Caroline both the Master of Ceremonies and a Mr. Rochefort. The game opened by the Master

of Ceremonies approaching Miss Fagg with the request that he might
be permitted to present a certain Mr. Rochefort to her, this being a
gentleman who greatly desired to make her acquaintance.

"Allow me, Miss Fagg," the Master of Ceremonies observed in a
squeaky-throated voice, "to present to you Mr. Rochefort."

"O fie, sir," Miss Fagg replied faintly, coyly averting her head and
screening her face behind a fan—her hand.

Apparently Mr. Rochefort was a raffish gallant who seized every
opportunity. Immediately he suggested the splitting of a bottle of
wine and a subsequent withdrawal to the conservatory.

"Sir!" Miss Fagg drew up in outraged maidenhood.

Mr. Rochefort's brows met diabolically. "You spurn me, wench?"
he demanded harshly.

"Spurn you, sir?" the lady said haughtily. "Nay, rather is it
that I mislike your manner."

"You mislike my manner, eh?" Mr. Rochefort laughed evilly.

Miss Fagg had reached the swooning stage when Mrs. Fagg, very
tearful now, called for them.

The boys had long gone, Louis to the bank, and Charles home to
change. This done, Charles, on the yellowish-red back of the good-
natured Bob, cantered up to the top of Biggin Street. The shoeing
completed, again down Biggin Street he came, to call at the Antwerp
Stables, premises quite separate from the inn of the same name.

Keeping Bob's stern portion alone visible through the arched
entrance, he grasped a swinging rope and peremptorily rang the
travellers' bell.

Jim Page, the ostler, a tiny fellow who vowed he had once been a
jockey but of whom it was affirmed locally that his greatest equestrian
feat had been to ride postilion, came hurrying along the cobbled
passage.

"Coming, sir; coming, sir," he shouted briskly. "Dreckly-
minute, sir."

His expression changed considerably when he saw a small boy on
a largish horse.

"Respectable bait for both man and beast, I presume," Charles
Fagg observed civilly.

"Respectable bait . . ." Jim Page choked . . . and darted.

But Bob and his rider were flying across the Market Place.

4

Henry Rochefort and his wife were sitting before the fire. In the wide grate a log crackled slightly, the only sound in that room since Caroline, twenty minutes or so before, had tumbled in impetuously to give her mother another sticky kiss.

The banker, marvelling at the composure he could see in his wife's transparent face, stirred uneasily.

" Oh, my love," he began desperately, " would that I could myself bear for you the torture and . . . "

Clumsily, for the glands in her arm were agonisingly swollen, she reached and touched him.

" I have all the endurance of any man, Henry," she told him gently, " so pray say no more on that. And . . . " a faint colour came into her cheeks, " now that I am so sure that you will love me no less when . . . " she was blushing now, " when I am mutilated and disfigured, then I am affrighted of nothing."

He had no need to reassure her on this score, for amply had he done so. Indeed, with the unspeakable horror of the morrow obsessing him, he hardly heard her and, without answering, forthwith began to broach, nay to urge, that she should submit to that other thing Dr. Crouch had advised.

" 'Twould be much better, my love, for you not to see anything . . . of the surgeon's manipulation . . . and——"

Deeply was she moved by his concern, but she would not yield on this. Blindfolded she would not be, nor, if that also were brought up again, would she be bound.

" If that is your will, Elizabeth," Henry Rochefort was sighing when, not unduly heavily, a door slammed.

The noise was not loud, but the banker's nerves were taut, his brain a tangle of raw sinews. Uttering a muffled expletive, he bounded from the room before his wife could restrain him, and a luckless servant received the full blast of his ungovernable temper.

" What the devil do you mean, my girl," he shouted, " by standing there ? . . . and send that young man about his business . . . do you hear me ? DO YOU HEAR ME ? "

The trembling creature pushed away her soldier lover and closed the door which had been responsible for the sharp draught of air.

" If this happens again . . . " her master bawled, and with that unfinished threat, his forehead beaded in sweat, he went back to his wife.

She saw all that was in his face, his knowledge that, in this hour of her greatest trial, he had been unable to discipline himself.

" I understand, Henry," she smiled consolingly. " Please, please, do not fret, my love."

" You understand so much, Elizabeth," he replied brokenly, staring mistily at the leaping flames. " No one in my life has ever known me as do you."

She smiled again. " I have tried, Henry."

" And have succeeded, my dearest," Henry Rochefort said huskily.

Slowly the minutes of that dread evening dragged along.

5

The Rochefort house was gruesomely silent that morning, as so thought Mrs. John Fagg when, her own face pallid, she came down the staircase. The servants had been sent out and the children, who were to spend the day at Little Pent House, had been fetched by Keziah Hart more than an hour before.

From the breakfast-room, in which the removal of the cancerous breast was to take place, there came a subdued undertone. Henry Rochefort and Dr. Crouch had made all the necessary preparations. A chair had been placed near, and with its straight back at right-angles to, the broad bay window. On the table, drawn conveniently to the side, there were kitchen bowls containing steaming hot water, with narrow rolls of linen, a sponge and other requisites, not least of which was a bucket which stood on the floor.

Mrs. Fagg shuddered when, through the half-open door, she perceived these grim arrangements and, knowing that the famous surgeon was due, quietly crossed the hall and entered the little drawing-room.

At the very moment when the Antwerp Stables hackney-coach jingled to a stop by the house, Dr. Crouch was endeavouring to console the husband of his patient on a matter which was causing Mr. Rochefort desperate apprehension. The physician was saying that, in his view, Mrs. Rochefort would no doubt swoon immediately she was opened.

" Pray God it may be so," Henry Rochefort murmured fervently.

Dr. Crouch gravely nodded assent. " Mark you, Mr. Rochefort," he added, " in any event Mr. Nussey has the reputation for carrying out his operations with the most amazing deftness and celerity. One of the most up-to-date men in his profession, he believes . . . Ah ! "

The banker hurried to answer the summons.

The instrument case had been placed conveniently and, after

glancing over the provisions effected, Mr. Nussey made inquiry about the patient, to be informed that she awaited his pleasure.

When Mrs. Rochefort came in supported between her husband and Martha Teddiman, both of whom were as pale as she, the surgeon was towelling off. To the barely concealed astonishment of Dr. Crouch, he had, meanwhile, scrupulously washed his hands.

The preliminaries were rapidly disposed of immediately the distraught husband had left the room, the patient being instructed how she should hold herself when the time came.

Out of sight behind, Mr. Nussey, who was evidently a most particular gentleman, scrutinised the instruments he had rinsed.

" You are sure, Mrs. Rochefort," he once observed, " that you will not take a tumbler of potent wine ? "

She moistened dry lips before replying. " No, sir," she said, her voice low but controlled. " And you need not fear that . . . that you will have difficulty with me."

For a trice the surgeon eyed her keenly, and then he bowed. " I have no fear of that, madam," he pronounced sincerely. " But perhaps you would permit your woman to hold your hand ? When I am ready, that is."

He was not long. An almost imperceptible nod to the local doctor, and a quiet request to Martha Teddiman that she should expose her mistress.

" Yes, sir," breathed that very faithful servant, now ashen-cheeked as she removed a cashmere wrap, fumbling-fingered as she unfastened the gown beneath.

" Now, ma'am," Mr. Nussey observed leisurely, concealing from her a bright-gleaming piece of steel.

Before the words were out of his mouth he had begun.

As the sharp scalpel burnt deep, a tremor passed through the emaciated body ; Mrs. Rochefort's head lolled, her eyes closed, and outwardly it seemed that she had fainted, though all the while Martha Teddiman could feel the ever-tightening grasp of a deathly cold hand.

With incredible speed the surgeon worked . . . until his purpose was done. Then followed the dressing and the final bandaging.

Mr. Nussey stood off. " I have finished, madam," he said, for the first time the strain showing in him.

Henry Rochefort's wife raised a face which appeared to consist of nothing more than a pair of agonised eyes.

"You . . . have . . . finished . . . sir ? " she asked wearily.

" 'Tis over, ma'am," he replied compassionately. " And never, ma'am, in my experience have I encountered such courage and——"

Elizabeth Rochefort's senses at last left her.

A long splash of blood had stained Mr. Nussey's bottle-green coat, and this he was sponging off when Mr. Rochefort returned from his wife's room.

" My dear sir," he said sharply, breaking into the banker's impassioned demands. " I can only say that we must hope for the best."

" But Dr. Crouch informs me your view is that the operation has been successful," Henry Rochefort retorted shrilly.

The surgeon, after sternly requesting that the husband of his patient should control himself more fittingly, then began to enumerate certain fears. Foremost, there was always to be apprehended the after-effects of shock.

" But if the operation has been successful . . . " persisted the banker.

Mr. Nussey's expression boded no good for a loquacious colleague who, in an effort to console, had said more than properly belonged to the physician's province.

" The operation in itself may have been successful——" he started off again, but once more was interrupted.

" Then why . . . " demanded Henry Rochefort, his eyes beginning to smoulder, " do you make reservations, sir ? I insist upon knowing precisely what expectation——"

Crisply breaking in, the surgeon observed that Mrs. Rochefort's strength had been wholly drained, wherein lay the danger of the hours ahead. Beyond that, he said, he would be failing in his duty if he did not warn Mr. Rochefort that the grievous disorder was often of a recurrent nature.

" A successful operation," sneered the banker, his voice quivering with anger.

Containing himself, Mr. Nussey stated his emphatic conviction that within the next decade or so the origin and satisfactory treatment of the scourge of cancer would be known. But . . .

" But I have to admit that as yet——"

The bag of guineas which Henry Rochefort threw violently on to the table slipped over the edge and fell to the floor.

" There is your fee for your *successful* ministrations, sir," he shouted.

Mr. Nussey's eyes were glinting as he stooped. But carefully he stuffed away the money, and indeed reached the door before he replied.

" And now, Mr. Rochefort, one warning for you, sir," he reverted grimly. " I fully understand the anxiety which presses so hardly on you, but no man may lose himself as you do without bringing upon his head the most harrowing tribulation." His voice deepened.

"Whether it be now or in the future," he was continuing, when peremptorily he was ordered out.

"Begone, damn you," Henry Rochefort bawled.

Soon he went up to his wife's room.

6

It had been arranged that the Rochefort children should return home during the course of the afternoon, but shortly before two o'clock Martha Teddiman, after speaking to Dr. Crouch, sent for Mrs. Fagg.

On her arrival it was decided that Louis and Caroline were to stay overnight at Town Wall Street.

But an hour before midnight George Rochefort was frantically using the door-knocker at Little Pent House ; his nephew and niece were aroused from their slumber, to be hastily dressed and taken to Snargate Street.

It had proved impossible to stop their mother's bleeding.

From talkativeness to restlessness she had speeded. Now she was sinking fast.

Tears streaming, Louis Rochefort came from his mother's bedroom, to be taken in hand by Polly Fagg.

Behind, Caroline parted for ever from her beloved mother.

"Mamma, darling," she choked. "You musn't leave us, you mustn't."

After poignant effort Mrs. Rochefort touched her daughter's dark hair.

"My blessing," she uttered painfully, "you know what you promised me."

The little girl nodded blindly. "Yes . . . yes, Mamma, and I will be brave and . . . and I will look after Papa."

"Then kiss me, my dear," her mother whispered.

Half a dozen candles illuminated the chamber, their living flames creating gently swaying shadows on the walls, their colour tinting deeper the yellow parchment hue into which Mrs. Rochefort's cheeks had changed.

"My little daughter," Elizabeth Rochefort murmured wistfully, when the child had so pluckily gone.

Before her husband came back she spoke to the broken-hearted Martha ; of Louis, a self-centred boy who, though he would be stricken by his mother's death, would recover soon, and of Caroline, a strange mixture of softness and pride.

" You will guard my little girl, Martha ? " she asked, knowing the answer all the time. " She is one who will all the more easily bruise by reason of her spirit."

Tears were pouring down Martha Teddiman's face. " I will always watch over her, ma'am," she gulped. "And over the master, too."

Mrs. Rochefort's glance rested affectionately on her abigail.

" Never, Martha, has a woman had more faithful friend than you have been to me," she said fervently.

" Nor a servant a mistress more . . . more . . . more . . ."

From the gloom at the other side of the big poster bed Dr. Crouch appeared, to bend under the tester and feel his patient's pulse, thin and rapid now. He lightly touched Martha Teddiman's shoulder, and that devoted creature, after pressing her lips to her mistress's clammy hand, went from the room, head bent, great sobs racking her when she reached the shadowed landing beyond.

" My dear love," Henry Rochefort muttered, his face a tragic mask.

" Henry," his wife murmured, very low.

For a while she rested, and then, on some fleeting accretion of strength, began to talk to him, ever trying to comfort him.

" And, my dear," she once said, " you are a fine man and might wish to marry again."

He heard her out, allowed her to tell him her sole thought was for his happiness. Then he slowly shook his head.

" I have had the purest of gold, my love," he told her passionately, " so why should I contemplate the base counterfeit ? I shall never marry again, my dear one."

Her sunken eyes were shining with love for him and with longing.

" Henry," she whispered.

Now *he* began to speak, of that evil in him of which she was so aware, and of its consequences, from which she had ever tried to ward him.

" But . . . " his jaw tightened, " I swear to you that, whatsoever it may do elsewhere, I will never allow it to shadow the lives of our children. That, my darling, is my promise to you."

The minutes of the dark hours were flying now, the earthly communion of two true-loving souls drawing to its inexorable end. She was giving long sighs, hardly seeming to breathe in between.

The screech of the Pent lock-gate, opening, aroused her. For a moment, as though not knowing him, she looked into her husband's face. And then her lips parted, and sweetly came her last words.

" Henry, my love," she said softly.

" Elizabeth, my angel," he huskily replied.

There was a quick convulsion and, taking that idolized picture with her, the gentle spirit of Elizabeth Rochefort sped lightly with the flowing of the tide.

For a full hour Henry Rochefort, all unconscious of the women who were performing the essential offices, had knelt at the side of the bed. After that he rose stiffly and, swaying uncertainly, he stared down at the blanched cheeks of his dear departed.

Then, to the profound horror of all who heard him, he began to swear, wildly and viciously. Venomously he cursed his fellow men and, without a break, brought his bitter tongue to the castigation of the creator of man.

They thought him insane, they who slunk past him in that chamber of death.

As grey dawn broke, the banker gave the impression of one so shocked as to be not far from deranged.

7

It was a Dover custom that ladies should act as pall-bearers at funerals of their own sex.

Mrs. Fagg, having conformed to local tradition, was in a grievous state of distress when her husband brought her home that afternoon.

Fortunately, before she again began unrestrained weeping, Keziah came into the parlour to report that Miss Minnie was a little feverish.

" I'll . . . I'll get a St. James's Powder, Keziah," Polly Fagg replied miserably. Rising unsteadily, smelling-salts still grasped in one hand, she sought for her keys and then, one slow step at a time, mounted the stairs to the landing, there opening the corner cupboard which was used as a medicine cabinet.

Rejoining her husband, she spoke of that other harrowing happening of which Martha Teddiman had told her. The first thing Henry Rochefort had done on returning from the funeral, Martha said, was to remove his wife's portrait from the dining-room and take it up to the room in which she had died.

" Afterwards," Mrs. Fagg said unhappily, " he locked the door and came down to us, and you know what his face looked like then . . . frozen and . . . I shall never forget that sight of him."

Her husband observed that Henry Rochefort gave the impression of being bent on withdrawing from all friendly intercourse, but expressed the hope that the banker would shortly rouse himself.

The days and weeks continued to pass, with little of outstanding interest in any of them. Around the town there was some desultory drilling by the Volunteers, and Mr. Pitt, in February, announced that the strength of the kingdom now amounted to 140,000 men. Extraordinarily enough, the mighty coalition of England, Prussia, Austria, Holland, Spain and Sardinia, which assailed France on every side, made little progress, and British forces on the Continent were thrown back into Holland.

When the elms were starting to burst into leaf, however, Martha Teddiman determined to speak to her master. It was her duty, she felt.

" Yes, Martha," Henry Rochefort answered drearily.

He was sitting at the dining-room table, on which was spread a large map of Dover. Upon this, when Martha knocked at the door, he was carefully pencilling.

" 'Tis about this house and about Miss Caroline and Master Louis, sir," she said resolutely. " Unless there's alteration 'tis enough to blight their young lives."

Visibly Henry Rochefort winced as she went on, for she left nothing to the imagination. For the sake of that boy and girl, she told him plainly, he must take a grip on himself.

" That's what I have to say, Mr. Rochefort," Martha ended doggedly.

His expression somehow defeated, he stared from the map before him to the houses beneath the cliff on the opposite side of Snargate Street.

" So already I have failed," he murmured sadly.

Martha Teddiman, still facing him squarely, put that into its proper perspective. It was only to be expected that he should have been broken by the dear mistress's passing, but now he should honour the memory of the dead by giving his love and attention to the children that sweet lady had borne him.

Henry Rochefort, rising, rested his hand on her forearm. " You have done well to speak to me as you have, Martha," he said quietly. " And . . . and sincerely do I thank you."

Whilst she was with him there was a domestic matter he wanted to settle. It was one which had dismayed him for some time, one for which only latterly, here to hand, had he seen the solution. As months succeeded months in the last stages of Elizabeth Rochefort's malignant complaint, Martha had taken more and more off her mistress's frail shoulders, so unobtrusively that, at this day, the running of the household continued without sign other than that of the major change.

" So if you would keep on, Martha, I should feel infinitely grateful," he said anxiously.

The thought of bringing in a female relative to sit in Elizabeth's place nauseated him ; nor could he abide the idea of a paid house-keeper, a stranger to the old house.

The determined Martha lost some of her iron composure. " Gladly I will, sir . . . gladly." Her mouth was not too sure, and she was fingering for the corner of her apron.

Nor did Henry Rochefort forget the lesson she had given him. When, later, George Rochefort arrived home from the St. James's Street gaming-rooms, bringing along with him a spotty-faced youth suspected, untruly so, of suffering from Drury Lane ague, the two young men discovered Henry Rochefort with his daughter on his knee and his son stretched on the rug before the fire.

It was really Caroline who was being entertained. George Roche-fort's dark eyes, he being quickly moved, misted when he realised that his brother was labouredly telling a fragile and charming fairy story to his little niece.

It was a heart-rending spectacle, he thought—that unhappy father striving so awkwardly but valiantly to close the gap in the lives of a motherless boy and girl.

CHAPTER SIX

I

THE close-season for free-trading, naturally enough, was during the summer months. After the Sunday morning's service succeeding the day on which the town had been gladdened by Lord Howe's glorious First of June victory off Brest, John Fagg, taking a walk before dinner, had little thought of the coming winter's illicit trading.

He had with him his daughters and Caroline. Caroline's father, who also had heard Dr. Woodgate's sermon, had not, however, accompanied the shipowner as once he would have done. In point of fact John and Polly Fagg had seen little of Henry Rochefort since his wife died.

Leaving Mrs. Fagg at Little Pent House, and there collecting Nell, John Fagg continued along Town Wall Street in the direction of Eastbrooke. This was the old approach to Dover's earliest haven, before the temperamental Dour changed its course.

Near the old church of St. James's, the party encountered Mr. Paul Elam, Master of the Lodesmen or, to employ the more modern designation which was coming into use, Master of Trinity House at Dover.

" Good day to you, Mr. Fagg," he said promptly, in a voice definitely too light for his physique.

In his official capacity the Master of the Lodesmen often received certain information a thought in advance of his fellow jurats and freemen. At the sight of the shipowner his sly eyes had lighted up maliciously.

But first he began to speak of the lamentable manner in which the Duke of York's army was being chased into Hanover. He propounded the view that Robespierre's way of dealing with unsuccessful generals had much to do with this.

" Wheesh ! " he whistled, illustrating the sound of a falling blade and adding to the picture by striking the back of his own flabby neck with the side of his hand.

" Tends to make 'em energetic," agreed John Fagg.

He and the Master were now walking down Woolcomber Street, at the end of which, brilliant blue and smooth, was the sea. Minnie and Lou, with their companion a pathetic figure in her bonnet and dress of mourning, were already on the shingle.

Mr. Elam coughed. " I dare say, Mr. Fagg, that you will be interested in a little piece of news I can give you . . . regarding Mr. Howgate."

At the mention of the Revenue Officer, John Fagg's grey eyes developed a greater awareness. Mr. Howgate, he heard, was retiring in the early autumn, and was to be replaced by a gentleman named Toke, one who in the vigorous exercise of his present office had won much praise.

" Toke, eh ? " the shipowner murmured reflectively. " And from where does he hail, Mr. Elam ? "

The new Revenue Officer came from Falmouth, where he had proved himself the terror of the smugglers, more than half a dozen of whom he had caused to swing.

" A most deadly reputation he has, Mr. Fagg," Mr. Elam continued to elaborate. " I assure you that the Cornish——"

" Then, Mr. Elam," John Fagg smiled blandly, " we Men of Kent must hope that our seafarers uphold the good name of this county."

With that he gave his attention to a Thames barge, of sails lovely and colourful in their dressing of fish-oil and ochre.

Piqued beyond expression, the Master of the Lodesmen decided that, instead of struggling back through the shingle, he would retrace his steps. Which he did.

John Fagg continued beneath that cloudless sky, to his left the dazzling sea, before him a sun whose heat was pleasantly tempered by the slight easterly breeze, his thoughts dwelling on the problem of the harbour, not on the menace which Mr. Elam had so graphically indicated Mr. Howgate's successor to be.

Some considerable distance ahead were the girls, with Nell still further beyond happily nosing the base of the first of Mr. Beverley's far-stretching series of posts.

Lou was talking about Jack Woodgate. Jack, she said, terribly wanted to go into the Navy, but so far his Papa had not been able to find a Captain who would take him.

" You have to have a Captain or an Admiral," she observed wisely.

Caroline declared that she would like to go into the Navy herself.

" Soft-eyed snowballs in Injer an' bawdy baskets in every goddam port—every port," she amended hastily, now beginning to learn that *everything* Captain Pepper said was best not repeated.

Minnie, however, had more complex ambitions, ambitions which had something to do with the delightful walk from the Western Heights to the limit of Shakespeare's Cliff. The path was a favourite saunter for Dover people, and the dells off it sought by couples courting inclined. Which aspect interested her she did not say.

* * * * * * * *

The pleasant walk to which the youthful Minnie had referred was beloved greatly by her Aunt Susan. Securing a sheltered retreat, one could give unmolested attention to a book, or gaze dreamily out to sea if one so desired.

Some few weeks after Mr. Elam's unsatisfactory conversation, Susan Fagg heard St. Mary the Virgin's strike a half after five. Church time being near, she hurriedly rose and, brushing off a few grasses which clung to her poppy-coloured taffeta dress, started for home. She was soon once more on the twisting path, but hardly had she attained it when she very nearly bumped into George Rochefort.

" My dear girl," smiled that young gentleman, cushioning the collision by grasping her shoulders.

Once only since the night of the party at the Agent Victualler's house had she spoken to him. That had been when they chanced to meet briefly in the Albion Library, where he had passed a humorous allusion to her progress in one of the arts.

Overwhelmed by the unexpectedness of it, Susan stammered out an apology, ever aware of a painful blush which would creep as far down as her neck, she knew it wretchedly.

" I . . . I wasn't looking, George," she confessed.

Their ways, for a space, were in the same direction, and so together they continued, Susan striving desperately to recall those witty and brilliant sayings she was able to conjure up in the night, and George, as always, easily conversational.

Before leaving Shakespeare's Cliff, however, he seemed disposed to linger. At the base of the ' sublime and awful precipice ' the tide could be seen distinctly sweeping eastward, carrying along with it shingle and sand, whilst far towards the western extent of the bay the garden of Little Pent House, with its hollyhocks, geraniums, carnations and forget-me-nots, made a delightful splash of colour amidst the monotonous yellow expanse of the Ropewalk. Between these extremes was Captain Pepper's little house, with its owner, having eaten a solitary meal and having washed the pots in the well-ordered little galley, now enjoying a pipe of tobacco close by his flag-staff, at the head of which the Jack was gallantly flying.

" One that gathers samphire ; dreadful trade ! "

George Rochefort murmured.

The practice mentioned by the immortal bard in his tragedy of King Lear continued to that day. Poverty-stricken folk, for the sake of the few pence they might acquire, were lowered down the cliff, there to pluck from the crannies the herb which made an extremely fine pickle.

" Pray recite more of it, George," Susan suggested daringly.

He shrugged, protested, and then, nothing loath, gave her of his best.

" Here is the cliff," he declaimed stylishly, " whose high and bending head
Looks fearfully on the confin'd deep,—
How dizzy 'tis to cast one's eye so low !
The crows and choughs that wing the midway air,
Show scarce so gross as beetles. Half-way down
Hangs one that gathers samphire ; dreadful trade ! "

Coming to seek her approving glance, George Rochefort met only the nape of her neck. In truth, she had not wanted him to discern how deeply moved she was.

" What ails you, Susan ? " he asked distantly.

There being no escape, she had to tell him. " Your voice, 'tis so lovely," she faltered, again mantling richly.

Recovered in a flash, he became excessive charming, and for her advantage again began to quote snatches of this, snatches of that, Herrick and Jonson, Milton and Marvell, and " dear William," of course.

" George ! " Time and again Susan Fagg, in an ecstasy at being so with him, repeated his name in simple wonder at his heavenly fluency.

"And . . . and Susan," George Rochefort suddenly said, delightfully teasingly, "tell me what it is you find so pleasing about my voice ? "

Susan Fagg's radiant expression had, immediately before, faded. A couple were approaching, and she felt horribly concerned for George. To meet Kate Warren face to face must be such, such embarrassment for him.

But his attentions to her, and the manner of them, drove all unpleasant thought from her mind. She quite forgot about young Mr. James Foord and the detestable Kate.

"I . . . I only know," she whispered, fleetingly meeting his eye, " that 'tis lovely."

He laughed extravagantly, took her arm, bent over and bantered her, and found time to give only the briefest of acknowledgment to the passing pair.

Considering that James Foord hoped to make Miss Warren his wife, he was not too tactful in the observation he made.

"Well, Kate," he said heavily, " if Rochefort had wanted to tell you that there's more than one fish in the sea he couldn't have arranged it better."

He glanced over his shoulder, to see George Rochefort in the same possessive attitude.

"Kept it dark too, eh, Kate ? " he marvelled.

Miss Warren made acid reply and took no little working round.

When that reconciliation was accomplished, Susan Fagg was walking home alone, with George Rochefort dropping quickly down the steep slope to Paradise Pent, a slightly more convenient route to his home. The blue eyes of John Fagg's sister were a little clouded, for she could not understand why George, after being so wonderful, should part from her in such an ordinary fashion.

Puzzling, she began to hurry. She had one consolation, however. Now that the reign of terror was over, now that the wicked Robespierre had been sent to the guillotine, England must come to terms with France.

Mr. Stokes had said so at John's a few nights before, and Mr. Stokes was only echoing the sentiments of the powerful Mr. Fox.

And if that came to be then George would be safe, oh, so safe.

2

Valentine Pepper had all the sailorman's love of the green countryside and, when it happened that one of John Fagg's carters sustained a slight accident, he seized the opportunity of delivering to Mr. Stone's paper mills at Buckland the last load of a consignment of linen rags brought from London in a Fagg bottom.

This done, Captain Pepper re-entered the mill, to discover the Master standing by a vat from which a man was lifting up thin coats of pulp by dipping a square wood frame stringed closely with fine wires.

" That'll be the lot, I'm thinking, Mr. Stone, sir," he remarked expectantly.

Mr. Francis Stone, who could also take a dram any time, nodded in response and, before leaving, gave a word of instruction to another man at a big screw-press. There the sheets of pulp, after being separated by felts, were squeezed prior to being hung on lines for drying, with sizing, re-pressing, and re-drying to follow.

Some ten minutes later Captain Pepper, wiping his mouth with the back of his hand, emerged into the mossy, cobbled yard.

Coming out of the Mill-house he saw Martha Teddiman and Henry Rochefort's daughter. It chanced that their call, too, had concerned refreshment—a glass of milk for the little girl.

" Miss Caroline," he beamed. " An' to think that e'en a'most I might 'ave missed you."

Martha's expression on encountering the roystering Valentine was sadly different from that of her young charge, and became even more sour and severe when Caroline started to beg for a ride back in the wagon.

" Oh but, Martha dear——" that young female, in protest, began coaxingly but, finding artful persuasion of no avail, became most praiseworthily resigned. She was leg-tired, it was true, but not too badly, and she thought she would be able to walk home if that was Martha's desire.

" So shall we start, Martha dearest ? " she asked bravely.

That worthy woman hesitated. " Are you nation weary, Miss Caroline ? " she said anxiously.

Miss Rochefort's eyes blinked, but only momentarily. Then she was as courageous as ever.

" Only the teeniest piece, Martha," she confessed. " 'Tis nothing an' . . . an' I can rest when we get back."

The bare thought of riding back to Dover with *that man* was horrifying to Martha Teddiman, but in the midst of worrying over the problem, the man himself took a hand. Very much ' Captain ' Pepper, he swept off his hat a second time and, with nice dignity, addressed himself to the housekeeper. He knew well, he said austerely, that a wagon was no suitable conveyance for two ladies and, that being so, would be delighted if he might be permitted later to return for them in a vehicle more proper.

"May I, miss," he inquired earnestly, "be 'onoured thus far, for 'onour I should 'steem it to be." His glance over the trim Martha was no less proper either and Martha Teddiman, impressed despite herself, began vaguely to think that scandalous report has often more of malignity in it than of truth.

It was Caroline's tired little sigh which determined the issue and, a decision reached, Captain Pepper immediately lifted the banker's daughter on to the front of the cart.

"And now if I may be allowed to assist you up, miss," he subsequently observed, extremely deferentially, meantime courteously relieving Mistress Teddiman of the heavy basket of fruit she carried.

So circumspect was his behaviour that Martha, blushing only slightly, gave him her hand whilst she mounted, although by the time she had seated herself she was fiery red. Out of the corner of her eye she had espied this smooth-tongued cavalier, and though she was not positive on it the almost incredible thought had entered her head that the scoundrel, behind her back, had been deliberately examining a pair of ankles necessarily generously displayed.

If that were so, however, the boatswain appeared of no mind to risk the taking of further liberties and, after grasping the reins, cluclucked the big horse into motion.

"I trust the 'opping has been pleasant, miss," he once remarked gravely.

Caroline and Martha had been some two miles beyond Buckland, at the fine estate of one of the East Kent planters, a customer of Henry Rochefort's bank.

"It has been most enjoyable, Captain Pepper," Martha Teddiman replied, bridling slightly under the attention she was receiving.

After expressing his gratification Captain Pepper, who had handed the reins over to Miss Caroline, now had to hear a demand from that rapidly improving young creature. It was for a model of a 74 sail-of-the-line, the possession of one of which made a number of Dover boys consider themselves highly fortunate.

"A puffect replica from truck to sheathing", Caroline declared enviously. "Not a single spur missing and not a muzzle what ain't polished until it shines like a——"

Captain Pepper's sudden, noisy and powerful bout of coughing drowned whatever regrettable simile Miss Rochefort might have been about to employ, and thereafter the boatswain, after dilating self-pityingly on a weakness not too apparent in a deep chest, consulted the older lady on a wish which might be considered strange when emanating from a female.

Martha, her judgment appealed to, found herself conversing freely with a man vastly different from what she had believed him to be. And, gratified by his patent desire not to go against her will, she agreed that Miss Caroline might have such a boat.

"Oooh!" that young lady gasped. "When?"

Captain Pepper, who for the third time had been asking the housekeeper if she were quite comfortable, jerked his head towards the excited little thing, and following that smiled confidentially at Miss Teddiman.

"When shall it be, eh, Martha?" he chuckled indulgently. "You knows I take pride i' making——"

His words died, and he swallowed hard under the glare from a basilisk pair of eyes.

"What——" he was beginning feebly.

All the softness had gone out of Mistress Teddiman. "Who gave you leave to make yourself free of my name?" she demanded witheringly.

Captain Pepper, swallowing again, made a half-hearted attempt to take the offensive but, being frostily silenced, fell into confusion. For a while he was exceeding dismal, hardly seeming to listen to Caroline's story of Louis' preparations for going away to school, which was to take place at the middle of the month. Only when the narrow, richly scaled arches of St. Mary the Virgin's tower came into sight did he offer Martha Teddiman any explanation.

"You see, miss," he said, very moved, "Martha was my mother's name, an' I 'ave ever thought it the most beautiful a female can possess. I ax your pardon, miss, but that be my excuse. Well . . ."

He continued very melancholy and subdued through the town but, pulling up in style at Mr. Rochefort's house in Snargate Street, became a little more animated. That short journey, he said, had proved to be one of the happiest of his life, despite a misfortune the outcome of a tongue he would now gladly cut off.

Martha, stirred by his grief for a dead mother and, it must be allowed, rather flattered by the glance he then gave her, hurried Caroline into the house, meantime Captain Pepper's eyes roved speculatively over neat waist and interesting bosom, taking all in and more.

With these delights gone from sight, he began to drive towards Elizabeth Street, a broad smile of appreciation breaking out. He liked a wench of spirit for it was all the more salty to tame 'em, and he accepted it as beyond doubt that Martha was a woman of that quality.

The afternoon was drawing to a close and Captain Pepper, for the fifteenth consecutive day, had a special job to do. After seeing that all was well at the warehouse, he slipped back to the Market Place, there for a quick call at the Fountain.

" Where's the Admiral of the Blue ? " he bawled, on entering the inn.

The host came hurrying out in his blue apron and, without putting a question, set about making this regular customer's favourite mixture.

" An' if you christen that 'ere brandy," Valentine Pepper roared, still mightily pleased with himself.

The Sir Cloudesley, a concoction of small beer, brandy, sugar and lemon, named after a famous admiral, was drunk with relish, was repeated, and then Captain Pepper was off.

Exactly two hours before high water he had a task to perform, that of dropping into the sea, one hundred yards off Archcliffe Point, a number of red-painted pieces of cork obtained from Mr. Philip Virgile, the cork-cutter. Meanwhile John Fagg, on the South Pier, watched the course taken by the bobbing little objects, jotting down the results, his endeavour the creation of data relative to the currents surging round the pierheads. The tests were to be continued for another fifteen days, that is, thirty days in all.

* * * * * * * *

So long had John Fagg been poring over the reports of previous engineers on Dover Harbour that the fire in the parlour had nearly gone out and a maid, hastily called in by the master, was vigorously using bellows to fan the dying embers into flames.

" I think that'll do now, Mary," Mr. Fagg was saying as his wife, fresh from her gingerbread making, came in.

When the door closed Mrs. Fagg mentioned a matter which had been puzzling her for a day—and that was a long time for Polly Fagg.

" What is the Habeas Corpus Act, John ? " she asked. " And why has it been suspended ? "

The shipper, who had been looking into the garden where, beyond the coral-coloured berries of a holly-tree, he could see his sister Susan in the gazebo, smiled at the question.

" The Habeas Corpus Act, m'dear," he told her quizzically, " is part of the Englishman's charter of liberty, but its enactments have been suspended so that the government are better able to clamp into duress those who want a greater liberty."

Mrs. Fagg accepted this, as well as her husband's further communication, for what it might be worth. John Fagg, as he bluntly observed, believed that the government were making a mountain out of a molehill, declaring that their action only served to give some semblance of reality to movements of negligible importance.

" Because a few buffle-headed windbags . . . " he was continuing,
when Mrs. Fagg, who must have been leading to this, brought up
George Rochefort's name.

" Secretly courting our Susan ! " ejaculated John Fagg, after he
had heard her out.

" That's the ridiculous tale that keeps coming to me," Polly Fagg
nodded solemnly.

Engrossed in a subject of far greater import, John Fagg speedily
dismissed the nonsensical rumour. He was far more interested in the
old papers Mr. Breton had obtained, with no little difficulty, for him.

" This plan, Polly, of Mr. Digges in Queen Elizabeth's days," he
began eagerly, putting aside the last of Valentine Pepper's flotation
tests. Of all the many schemes propounded, none had gripped him
more than this ancient report, one which, so magnificent was it in
concept, suggested the complete enclosure of Dover Bay.

There was a chatter of voices from the hall. The daughters of the
house, who had been playing hide and fox, abandoned their game
to join their brother and Louis Rochefort in watching the gar-
dener and coachman carrying a mahogany bureau upstairs. This
piece of furniture came from the dining-room, where Mrs. Fagg had
long wearied of the sight of it. It was, at the earnest request of Charles,
to be placed in his room, and abnormally anxious did he seem about
its safe transport.

" Mind the corner, William," he called out more than once, when
he perceived the probability of mishap.

Charles's bedroom was over the parlour, and of the same shape,
elliptical. The bureau was carefully placed between the left-hand and
central windows, and once there its new owner cleared the room of
his sisters, cleared it indeed of a companion who would be leaving for
boarding school on the morrow.

" Why me . . . ? " Louis Rochefort grumbled indignantly. Nevertheless his friend was adamant.

It was evident that Charles had a most special reason for gloating
over the ownership of the bureau, one which made him almost
forget that he would not, for a year yet, be accompanying Louis to
school.

The reason Louis was to learn when, a few minutes later, Charles
mysteriously beckoned him into the bedroom. It appeared that it all
concerned a secret drawer, one so remarkable that even Louis, these
days bearing himself as cognizant of his pending advanced status, was
impressed.

" Now turn round, Louis," Charles said firmly. Within a moment
he was to demonstrate how a piece of paper, placed on the bureau,
could be made to disappear.

A stamp on the floor and the vibration set up was sufficient to operate a small spring. There was a slight click, and that folded sheet vanished completely.

" Phew ! " Louis whistled, immensely diverted. " Show me, Charles . . . no, let me find out for myself."

Supremely confident in the efficacy of the device, Charles allowed the attempt to be made, and Louis Rochefort, being of stern stuff, persevered for long.

" Give it up, Louis ? " he was eventually asked.

Louis scowled, had a further sustained shot, but finally had to confess himself beaten. But before Charles would reveal the drawer's secret, Louis had to take the oath.

" Swear you'll never tell anybody, Louis," Charles demanded.

Louis crossed his heart and then spat profusely into his palm.

" Swear it," he agreed concisely.

Then, and then only, was he permitted to share the great mystery.

3

On Market Days the Corn-market was held in the Royal Oak Inn and, on a raw afternoon when the young people of the town were putting finishing touches to Guy Fawkes's bonfires, Henry Rochefort came from this assembly of farmers and merchants, an expression of thorough annoyance on his hollow face. The fact was that he had been attempting to collect sums due to him since the financial collapse of nearly two years before, but neither money nor one single concrete proposal for settlement had he received. That, indeed, was sufficient to give any man of finance cause for reflection.

Crossing Cannon Street, he entered the Antwerp Hotel, where the Master of Lodesmen greeted him, promptly inviting the banker to a gin toddy, hot, with sugar, for the warding off of the possible effects of chill and damp.

" Thank you, Mr. Elam," Henry Rochefort nodded, accepting the offer and settling his long frame on to the time-polished bench. " 'Tis coarse weather indeed."

A huge fire crackled brightly in the wide grate, and the innkeeper's pretty daughters, carrying out their errands, continued to squeeze through the press ; the air was blue with tobacco smoke, and ever there was the encouraging chink of glassware.

"Aye," Mr. Elam declared sententiously, " 'tis hard enow to swallow, but them Frenchies are surely extending their sway over yonder, an' amazing it be, Mr. Rochefort." He went on to speak of the new and unbelievable turn the war was taking, and of the signs which seemed to indicate that the coalition against France would not last much longer.

Still preoccupied with unsatisfactory business perplexities, the banker was giving but cursory attention, until his companion, forsaking the international field, began to speak of certain needs of the pilots.

" Over four years we've been agitating for houses nearer the Look-out station," Mr. Elam remarked disgustedly.

Mr. Rochefort, his dark eyes a deal keener all the same, casually observed that special provision could hardly be made for the one or two pilots who might require such accommodation.

" One or two ! " the Master of Lodesmen said forcefully. " There's over fifteen out of our fifty clamouring for convenient residences, and you know what our men earn."

The banker was digesting this plain admission that the pilots were well able to pay handsome rentals for houses which suited their professional needs, when John Fagg came up to him.

" Ah, Henry," the shipowner laughed, face lighting up, " nearly a stranger, eh ? "

" Business . . . and other matters——" Henry Rochefort began stiltedly.

" Sure enough they're bad, damned bad," John Fagg agreed sympathetically. " Still . . . well, Nicholas, what's ado with you ? "

Mr. Stokes, the Clerk of the Passage, a mischievous smile playing about the corners of his mouth, had joined the three gentlemen. Surreptitiously jerking a thumb over his shoulder, he pointed out a group further down the long room.

In the centre of a circle of local personalities was the new Revenue Officer. Mr. Ralph Toke was a long-chinned gentleman, fussily brisk of movement.

" So you got him all right, Mr. Toke ? " gravely commented the Clerk of the Cheque. This was in reference to a smuggler the chase for whom the Revenue Officer had been retailing.

" Nay, Mr. Waade," Captain Jeremy Nethersole broke in, " didn't you hear Mr. Toke say as how the villain was hung at Bodmin ? "

It might be remarked that though the Clerk of the Cheque and Captain Nethersole whole-heartedly disliked one another, the ranks were always closed against the Excise authorities and their hirelings.

Clement Foxley, senior assistant to the retired Mr. Howgate, had brought his new superior officer into the Antwerp. Now, at the approach of a certain renowned gentleman, he cautiously drew Mr. Toke's attention.

" This is Mr. Fagg, sir," he whispered. " Coming d'reckly here."

The situation must have had its possibilities, for not a soul in the parlour but intently watched the meeting of John Fagg and Ralph Toke.

"Your reputation has preceded you," the 'free-trader' began amiably. "I vow every smuggler around these ports must already be a-shivering in his boots."

"Maybe as yet it is a trifle early for that, Mr. Fagg," the Revenue Officer remarked significantly.

John Fagg's keen eyes crinkled. "Then I may take it, Mr. Toke, that you think that that time will eventually arise?"

The Revenue Officer's hard glance bored back. "That, sir, is my belief," he said bombastically. "My very profound belief, sir."

The shipowner chuckled. "In which case you will prove a welcome benefactor to the port, for I assure you that a little extra amusement would be monstrous welcome."

"Amusement, Mr. Fagg?" Mr. Toke snapped.

"Amusement, Mr. Toke," John Fagg observed easily.

There wasn't a face but had a grin on it, not a gentleman there who wasn't hard put to contain himself.

As if aware of the derision in the atmosphere, the Revenue Officer paled resentfully, but always his eyes remained on the man about whom Clement Foxley had bountifully apprised him.

He smiled thinly. "As to that, Mr. Fagg," he told the shipowner, deadly emphasis on every syllable, "I will do my utmost to see you have the kind of amusement you desire."

John Fagg deliberately nodded his comprehension. "Spoken very fair, Mr. Toke," he remarked equably.

When the Revenue Officer and his sly-looking assistant took themselves off, the roar of glee which went up was loud enough to endanger the timbered roof.

* * * * * * * *

Valentine Pepper did not forget his promise to Miss Caroline.

One rough evening, shortly before Christmas, following a day in which dark low-lying clouds, Folkestone girls, had been sailing over the town, he put on his coat, his purpose to effect delivery of the craft.

"Howsomedever," he muttered, draining off a glass.

Outside, the wind howled and, just a little across the Ropewalk, the seas thundered in, each receding one leaving in its wake the sucking roar of the churned pebbles.

"Howsomedever," the Captain murmured again. Since the drive back from Buckland he had not seen Martha Teddiman. To leave a woman wondering might be very sound practice, but it took a second glass to restore an optimism which for an hour or more had been declining.

The door closed behind him, the boatswain, buffeted about, staggered until he gained the lee of the buildings in Snargate Street-over-the-Wall. From there, apart from the crossing of the lock-gate bridge, he had an easier passage.

His step thus far had been supremely audacious but, now that Mr. Rochefort's residence was nearing, it began to shed some of its former confidence until, along Pent-side, close by the fire-alley adjoining the house, the amorous captain came to a halt.

"Hmmm . . ." he mumbled. "Well . . . I suppose . . . hmmm."

Indecision had so gripped him that in the end he repaired to the Market Place where, in the Fountain, he took a couple of fortifiers, and then a third.

The moral fibre thus strengthened he returned to the banker's house and, on the knocker of the back door, rapped out a challenging summons.

Shortly, a servant girl appeared. To her the boatswain stated his will.

"Tell Mistress Teddiman that Captain Pepper 'opes as it willn't be illconvenient for 'er to 'ave a word with 'im," he said jauntily, preparing a pleasant smile in readiness for Martha's appearance.

The wench disappeared and the caller, with the thought of escaping the now driving rain, was stepping into the rear hall when a voice brought him sharply to.

"Merciful goodness ! And what do you think a boot-scraper be for ? " the housekeeper demanded.

Captain Pepper's smile vanished and most of his courage with it. In truth he was stammering some sort of excuse whilst she ranted on.

"Spandling the filth of Pent-side into a gentleman's mansion," she said scathingly. " What with pedlars, an' beggars, an' now sailors——"

Disconcerted he might be but, assailed on one tender spot, he protested strongly. The model went down with a bang on to a polished side-table, and its maker bluntly started to inform Mistress Teddiman that if she cared to do captain's inspection of his cottage——

"Hearts alive, go round *your* house ! " Martha trilled lightly at the idea—until she saw what he had done with an object wrapped in sacking. "Take that disgustingly dirty bundle off there," she ordered him furiously, immediately examining the waxed surface for scratches.

Already the gallant Valentine was sweating prodigiously, but just as much bent on carrying out his purpose. Somehow or other he succeeded in entering the housekeeper's snug little room, just off the hall. There, recovering his showmanship, he whisked the cover off the model.

" An' what do you think Miss Caroline will say to that 'ere ? " he asked triumphantly.

The tiny ship was truly beautiful, a wonderful model of the same 74 in which the boatswain had served when Admiral Rodney's squadron, in the last war, had destroyed the French fleet off St. Lucia, a battle in which Captain Pepper had lost the toes of his right foot, so ending his service. A seaman who could not use bare feet equally as well as hands was of scant use in His Majesty's ships.

" She'll love it, Captain Pepper," Martha Teddiman conceded, becoming more human at the sight of the exquisite craftsmanship, evidence of the many hours given to it.

Valentine Pepper brightened a shade. " Better not let Master Louis see 'er first, miss," he suggested, still a little tentative.

Martha laughed grudgingly at that. She was fingering the finely carved figure-head, and eyeing in wonderment taut shrouds and sheave-blocks hardly larger than a grain of rice.

Greatly emboldened, Captain Pepper dwelt on the well-cut sails, coming daringly close to the housekeeper to point out the neat stitching.

All unnoticing that Martha had sniffed, all unaware that she was in full blast of his spirit-laden breath, he ventured on a more personal matter.

" Sewing," he began lugubriously, " 'tis very well for the making of a little boat but . . . " charged with his own eloquence, he did not perceive the danger signal in her eyes, " but . . . but, miss," he continued, emotionally, " an 'ouse without a mistress, a man without——"

Martha Teddiman sprang back as though in peril of contamination from some foul disease, her stiffly outstretched arm a sign-post to the door.

" You are under the influence of liquor," she denounced him shrilly. " Go, you drunken wretch."

The boatswain, cut short in his vibrant appeal, was so flabbergasted that he, unluckily, could only think of the palpable foolishness of the statement.

" Me, pickled ! " he said outraged. " No amount o' liquor can make me so, an' there ain't a man in all the Cinque Ports that I can't sup under the table."

Martha, changing her tactics, was nodding, regularly and gently. " So there . . . isn't a man," she went on, ever nodding, " that . . . you . . . can't——"

" Not one," boasted the unhappy boatswain.

" Not one," repeated Martha Teddiman, luring him to his doom.

E

Too late had Valentine Pepper perceived her drift.

"What I was saying, miss," he started off hurriedly, "was nothing more than a manner o' speech——"

Manner of speech or no his stay was not prolonged. In the downpour he gritted his teeth—Valentine Pepper, he swore violently, would show that he was no warrior dismayed by the failure of the first assault. "Impossible" was a word the Navy did not recognise an' God rot 'em who thought otherwise.

4

Exactly two years to the day after the outbreak of war, John Fagg received a note from the Agent-Victualler. Mr. Foord presented his compliments, and requested the shipowner to call at the Maison Dieu at his early convenience.

The same afternoon Mr. Fagg walked up to the old place where once had lodged both outward-bound Crusaders and incoming pilgrims whose destination was the Shrine of Thomas à Becket at Canterbury.

"'Day to you," Mr. Foord greeted him. "Well, I hear that shortly you're going to bring out a great scheme for the improvement of the harbour."

John Fagg made a smiling response in reply to the jest, and then the two gentlemen got down to business, government business it turned out to be. There was great distress in the industrial areas of the north, near to famine conditions indeed, and it was considered imperative that supplies of wheat should be transferred there with as little delay as possible.

"Aye," the shipowner remarked laconically, after noting the quantities it was proposed to send from Dover. "I'll put you two-three vessels on the job. But . . ." he shook his head.

Mr. Foord, taking the point, did likewise. "I quite agree, Mr. Fagg," he observed soberly. "If food conditions worsen here I'm afraid we may have a deal of trouble too."

A short but definitely gloomy conversation ensued, ranging from the spread of French ideas, which caused servants to be demanding tea twice a day, to the discontent which seemed to be coming to a head in Ireland, a source of danger to a country already engaged in war.

"And the Navy is mortal short of men," the Agent-Victualler said. "Consider the bounties they're now paying to obtain ordinary seamen."

"Up to thirty guineas apiece in some localities," the shipowner agreed.

On this disquieting note the two gentlemen parted.

John Fagg, however, was not long with his thoughts. Fifty yards beyond Ladywell, whose water was so prized for tea-making, he came across his sister Susan with whom was her friend, the daughter of a linen manufacturer of Maidstone, who was staying at Little Pent House.

" Well, Alice," he laughed, " enjoying our Dover air ? "

Miss Vanderhey was a pleasant-looking creature, though her face had something of the heaviness characteristic of her family, one whose ancestors generations before had escaped to England from the Duke of Alba's persecution of the Low Countries.

" I vow, Mr. Fagg," she pouted, affecting to shiver mightily, " that never have I experienced such exquisite cold in my life."

" Why, Alice," giggled Susan Fagg, " only this morning——"

John Fagg solemnly warned his sister not to tell tales out of school, and in this pleasing fashion, the gentleman teasing the two young women, the trio continued down Biggin Street.

On Town Wall Street, opposite the Island, the shipowner's keen eyes picked up his elder daughter who, with another girl and two boys, were talking together, huddled close in the angle of the remnants of the old town wall.

It was an ordinary and most innocent spectacle—two little girls each about eleven years old and two boys somewhat older. But John Fagg's raillery at once ceased and his strong mouth grew stern.

" Minnie," he shouted peremptorily.

Below, the tittering stopped abruptly and, in pretended surprise, Minnie Fagg glanced up. Her father's unmistakable gesture left her with no room for doubt.

" Papa . . . " she nevertheless protested hopefully, " can't I stay out just——"

" You've heard me, girl." The shipowner said no more than that, but it was sufficient. Minnie Fagg lost no time in obeying her papa.

The other small girl, a pale-faced little thing who was the daughter of Mr. Stone at Buckland, evidently thought it advisable to keep her face hidden. Later, too, Mr. Stone's child apparently concluded that, if she returned home by way of the town, her adventures might reach the ears of her parents.

Though it was much longer, she decided to walk along the Ropewalk and gain the Western Heights after passing Archcliffe Fort.

She was scurrying over the southernmost fringe of Paradise Pent, thinking all danger past, when she very nearly ran into a gentleman well acquainted with her father. Vaguely she wondered what Mr. Rochefort was doing in that deserted place.

5

From the Rochefort bank in Snargate Street-over-the-Wall to
Council House Street there could be only one route suitable for
any business man who held himself to be of some dignity in the
town. Nevertheless, when Mr. Henry Rochefort, on an evening in
early April, left the bank he perceptibly hesitated on the pavement
outside, his obvious inclination to turn left down Snargate Street-over-
the-Wall and thence to skirt the Basin on the very proper Custom
House Quay. But in the end the advantages of precaution conquered
and, though his expression indicated some chafing at so doing, he
turned right and proceeded quickly up the street to the Ropewalk.

Once at the top, with a stinging wind in his face, he floundered
through the shingle which lay to the seaward side of the Basin, passing
between Amherst's Battery, nearly refurbished now, and a large ruined
property, the Buildings, where a hundred years before had resided the
very shrewd individual who farmed the Customs.

In this evasive fashion the banker attained the swingbridge which
surmounted the lock-gates separating the Tidal Harbour from the
Basin and, grasping the handrail firmly, passed over into the Cross
Wall, in which decent thoroughfare he was able to reduce the speed
of a nervous gait which had propelled him rapidly through the concealing dusk.

Within two minutes he was in Council House Street, and then in
the wainscoted entrance hall of the building from which the Harbour
Commissioners directed their enterprises.

Mr. Waade, the Clerk of the Cheque, received him in an oak-
panelled room adjoining that in which the 'eleven discreet men,' or
a small portion of their number, sat at irregular intervals.

"Take a chair, my dear Mr. Rochefort," he said gushingly. "This
one you'll find pleasantly near the fire, and I warrant we need a good
one yet."

"Thank you," his caller observed.

Mr. Waade was bustling about. He offered a little drop of something warming, and chuckled as he did so.

"The product of one of . . . er . . . " his eyes darted to his
visitor, "Mr. Fagg's runs, or so I understand. Though," he admitted
largely, "I did not purchase it directly from that gentleman. I'm
afraid that Mr. Fagg does not regard myself with any approval."

"Is that so?" commented the banker non-committally.

For the moment the Clerk thought it expedient to leave the topic
of John Fagg. After expressing profound regret at Mr. Rochefort's
refusal of a tot, he spoke of other matters which were of grave concern

to any Englishman. Prussia and Spain had acknowledged the Directory, and Holland, after being overrun, had been forced to become the ally of her conqueror.

"Which means that the strong Dutch fleet will now be ranged against us," he declared pontifically. "Howsoever——"

Mr. Rochefort, who was staring beyond Red Pump Square to the harbour mouth seen faintly in the gathering gloom, stirred so suddenly that the Clerk had the galling thought that his measured pronouncements were receiving scant attention. But, immediately reassuring himself, he went on again.

"—Howsoever, I am supremely confident, my dear sir, that even though we are now left only with Austria and Sardinia as our friends, we shall see this struggle through to its fitting end."

Henry Rochefort turned sharply from that fading view of the pier-heads.

"I should feel obliged, Mr. Clerk," he said curtly, "if you would proceed with the matter which is the purpose of my call."

"Certainly, Mr. Rochefort," Mr. Waade observed hurriedly.

"Is everything prepared for my hand?" the banker demanded.

"Decidedly so, sir," the Clerk retorted with some dignity.

"Then let us complete the affair forthwith," Henry Rochefort said, stripping off his gloves.

Mr. Waade's discomfiture was passing for, with a thrill of restrained glee, he was now beginning to realise that it was his own crafty allusion to John Fagg which was responsible for the banker's testiness. Contrarily, some annoyance remained with the Clerk, and this he relieved by opening the door and bawling for candles.

In the soft light he untied a piece of pink ribbon.

"Yes, Mr. Rochefort, the agreement *is* prepared," he smiled.

He began to speak of that parcel of land, aforetime known as Paradise Pent, lying between Archcliffe Fort and Elizabeth Street. Meantime his first finger ran over the crackling parchment on which Mr. Braems's engrosser had worked with a loving hand.

The tenor of the impressive document was to the effect that His Majesty's Commissioners for Dover Harbour, for the consideration and under the conditions stated therein, granted to Henry Rochefort, Esq., Banker and Freeman of the Ancient Cinque Port of Dover, the sole right to build, or otherwise sub-lease for building purposes, on that reclaimed land heretofore stated.

"You . . . ah . . . find that quite satisfactory, Mr. Rochefort?" Mr. Waade asked blandly, indeed almost giving a sly wink.

He received a look of cold appraisement. The banker, in that detached scrutiny, made it plain that he was of no mind to indulge in any intrigue. The effect on the Clerk was instantaneous. He at once became exceedingly voluble and through his patent attempt to curry favour immediately made a more disastrous mistake.

"Of course, Mr. Rochefort," he said hastily, "you may be sure that no whisper of this transaction will escape my lips."

Henry Rochefort's dark brows beetled. "What the devil do you mean, sir?" he demanded.

The Clerk wilted a little under the fierce regard, though in his voice he strove to maintain a tone of airiness.

"When you first saw Sir Walter on this matter, sir," he objected, "I understood that you impressed on him the need for secrecy."

"And is not that the usual basis of commercial practice?" thundered the banker.

"Assuredly, my dear sir. I was merely confirming——"

Henry Rochefort did not reply at once. He had securely placed into an inner pocket the bulky parchment, and was buttoning his coat preparatory to departure when he did.

"Then keep that excellent custom in mind, Mr. Clerk," he said curtly.

Soon he was in the darkness of Council House Street, and soon, too, the Clerk of the Cheque, despite the sharp rebuff he had received, was smiling at his own thoughts.

Rubbing his hands, Mr. Waade began to reflect pleasurably on the happy chance which had placed two determined men on opposite sides, for that was how he conceived the relationship which, sooner or later, must come to exist between John Fagg and the gentleman who had just left.

CHAPTER SEVEN

I

THE boat-dock was in the form of a narrow arm off the Basin, and ran from the rear of Captain Pepper's cottage to within twenty paces of the steps at the back of Mr. Rochefort's bank.

In it were many small craft, and round it was one of the favourite playgrounds of the Fagg and Rochefort children and their friends. From here it was that Charles Fagg, accompanied by Louis Rochefort when that youth arrived home for the summer holidays, set off in his boat, and here also it was that the boys did most of their swimming.

One hot afternoon about a fortnight after Charlton Fair, Charles and Louis arrived at the boat-dock steps, their intention to join Jack Woodgate in a cooling dip. That young man, whose hopes of getting into the Navy seemed as remote as ever, had already been in the water for quite half an hour. Methodically, to and fro, he was ploughing across the Basin, between the end of the boat-dock and Custom House Quay.

As the swimmer drew nearer Charles Fagg hailed him.

" What is't this time, Jack ? " he shouted.

Young Mr. Woodgate, treading water, gyrated slowly until he faced his inquirer, upon which he removed from between his teeth a gleaming knife.

" Wrecked three miles off shore, Charles," he gasped cheerfully.

" South seas, eh ? " commented Mr. Fagg. " Any sharks attack you ? "

Jack Woodgate gave details of three encounters ; one man-killer driven off, and two, of wickedly flailing tails, dispatched after gory battles.

It proved that the sole survivor of the frigate's disaster was now only a cable's length from salvation.

" But what about the current against you ? " Charles asked sternly.

From the surface of the water came a wail of protest, and following that a heated argument broke out on the issue. A compromise was finally achieved, and Jack Woodgate, three more crossings necessary to bring him to the atoll, set off again with renewed resolution.

Louis, who had stripped off his shirt, was pulling down his breeches whilst keeping a wary eye on Minnie Fagg who, with her unpleasant friend from Buckland, was sauntering much too near and glancing far too often for his liking.

" Ready, Charles ? " he asked. " Minnie and that awful . . . "

" Right," said Minnie's brother.

Two gleaming white bodies neatly cleft the water, and the two boys raced down the dock.

On the steps behind Mr. Rochefort's bank, two girls were enjoying themselves in their own respective ways. Lou Fagg, with a contrivance of bobbins and some coloured cottons, was busy in the fabrication of a material for the embellishment of her third-best doll, whilst Caroline Rochefort, lying flat on the slimy bottom landing, was making a last adjustment to the fine ship Captain Pepper had modelled for her.

Lou giggled suddenly. " Oooh, Martha will be cross when you go in, Caroline. Your panties are drefful dirtied."

" Panties ! " Caroline said scornfully. " Who cares about panties when a sail-of-the-line has got its . . . her sailing orders ? "

The *Orion*, with one important reservation, was ready for the great adventure. Her mistress, cocking an eye, seamanlike, at a flossy white cloud drifting across the blue sky, frowned a little. She never could remember when the mighty warship had to carry lee helm. However, that must be ascertained beyond doubt.

"Charles!" she shouted, scrambling up.   "*Charles!*" she screamed.

He was down the Basin, near the Cross Wall, supporting himself comfortably on the cable of one of the smaller packets.

"That baby sister of mine," grinned Louis Rochefort, "with her boats and oaths an' what not."

"Better than Minnie's ideas," Charles observed briefly, preparatory to paddling a little nearer Mr. Rochefort's bank to impart the directions obviously so desired.

Happy days they were for the youngsters. Picnics and outings, with never a thought to such things as the Treasonable Practices Act or the Seditious Meetings Bill, either of which might make sad difference in both the Rochefort and Fagg families.

The weeks passed, with Charles Fagg's excitement increasing. But at last the morning came when he was to go away to school.

Charles rose very early, for he had much to do and many calls to make. First and foremost he had to say good-bye to Jim Page at the Antwerp Stables, not forgetting a present of sugar to each of the thirty post-horses in the stalls.

Then he had to take Nell for a special ramble, her last with him for nearly three months, with a sorry ending-up when he had to inform the sagacious creature of his pending departure.

Breakfast over, he changed into his new school clothes and later, glancing at himself in the chimney mirror in the drawing-room, was caught by Keziah Hart, who chanced to look in at the door. The stern Keziah, it may be said, was a trifle weepy-eyed that day.

"Vanity, Master Charles——" she began.

Being somewhat shamefaced, Charles carried that off by energetically rotating her round the hall, much to the endangerment of the cream and white fluted pedestals on each of which stood an urn.

"Master Charles," she gasped.

Lou joined in by taking firm hold of Charles's queue, and the proceedings were showing every indication of becoming more noisy when the mistress of the house came out of the parlour. Mrs. Fagg speedily put the culprit in his place.

After that, Captain Pepper rolled in. With him Charles had a grave talk on the care of his skiff during the winter months. An operation of some magnitude had recently taken place, the craft being re-rigged with jib and spritsail.

"You can trust 'er to me, Master Charles," the boatswain stoutly promised. "And . . . and——"

His embarrassment was due to the parting gift he had brought, one of the most splendid and ferocious knives Charles had ever seen.

" By heaven ! " Charles's eyes nearly popped out of his head with pleasure as, after opening the dangerous blade, he balanced the fearsome weapon in his hand.

Valentine Pepper's honest face was wreathed in delight.

" You like 'er, Master Charles ? "

" Like her ? " In sheer joy Charles tossed the knife, to catch the haft neatly as it came down.

Happy as if he had found a bag of yellow *Georges*, Captain Pepper made off for Elizabeth Street. More than this single ground for jubilation had Valentine Pepper, for Martha, besieged without respite, gave token of partial capitulation.

Quite a crowd saw off the special coach at the Royal Oak yard, for eleven Dover boys were travelling to school.

" What a knife, Charles ! " Jack Woodgate said, awed by the implement.

" Fine, isn't it ? " grinned its proud owner, continuing to throw it up whilst congratulating the pent-up Jack on another matter. Dr. Woodgate, after vain search far afield, had the previous night discovered that Lord Poynte possessed a cousin in the Navy, a full-blooded serving Captain. His Lordship, in racing parlance, had picturesquely declared that young Jack should have his wish, demned if he shouldn't.

" Charles ! " screamed Mrs. Fagg, terrified by her son's trick.

Her husband restrained her. " The lad's got a good eye, Polly," he remarked, adding that if Charles missed just once he'd get the lesson he needed and wouldn't do it again.

Mr. Rochefort was there with Caroline, and Louis, pushing through the throng, brought tremendous news.

" Charles," he said excitedly, " I've heard that Bow Street Runners have come to the town."

Susan Fagg, hearing this, went deathly pale. Latterly, to her frantic joy, she quite often saw George. Sometimes he would stroll with her on Sunday afternoons, sometimes he would call at Little Pent House with a book of verse. Even amongst his wavering associates, George Rochefort was desperately lonely, and her adoration, her belief in him, were balm to his soul.

" All aboard, young gentlemen." The guard blew his horn, and the youths who had gathered about Louis Rochefort, after having kissed their relatives, began to climb in.

There was a high-pitched cheer as the coach lumbered into Cannon Street.

The old familiar sights passed. Biggin Street with the forge and the Maison Dieu at the top ; The Black Horse Tavern with its gibbet opposite and the toll-gate ; the village of Lyddon and the Half-way House.

Denn Hill and then Barham Down, where for centuries prior to the threat of Philip of Spain's Armada freemen had gathered whenever a blazing cask of pitch was chain-hoisted at the beacon and where, even now, there was a respectable number of military tents.

Charles Fagg drew a deep breath as the racecourse came into sight. Behind was his childhood *emigré* school and a year at a tutorial establishment ; ahead was a great seat of learning.

" By heaven, Louis," he said, again using the new oath, " I'm enjoying myself."

Delight in that day was his, but for his Aunt Susan it was one of sheer dread, with no lightening in the days and months ahead.

In Paisley there had been serious riots, inspired by an organisation whose head described himself as Citizen-President. The government, determined to stamp out such evils, had sent their trained emissaries wherever there were reports that subversion was raising its ugly head.

2

Susan Fagg, from her childhood, had always lived in a realm of her own fancies, keeping her lovely little secrets huddled to herself, dreaming dreams in which she figured in great romantic parts.

But never, in all her years, had the fragile fibres and ephemeral yarns of her imagination suffered change into the warp and woof of solid fabric. Never, that is, until one gloomy Saturday afternoon in November when the market stall-holders, mindful of journeys home through hock-deep mud and the long darkness, began to pack up their wares.

First in the Market Place there was a stir of interest, with one head after another turning in the direction of Market Street. Down that narrow way, passing the coach-builder's, the wheelwright's sawpit, and then Mr. Baker's candle factory, came a small group of young men, trundling along with them a handcart on which stood, planted in a sawn-down barrel, a green shrub.

Susan Fagg was peering into the shop windows within the colonnade which extended from St. Mary the Virgin's to the Antwerp Hotel corner. Aroused by the tumult, she glanced towards the Market Place and so witnessed the opening stages of an incident which was to bring that shadow existence of hers nearer to reality than ever before.

Amongst the crowd in the Market Place there were three or four soberly-dressed men, strangers to the town, and there could have been no doubt that these gentlemen, had they been able to hear more clearly, would have stopped the proceedings at the inception. Only those near to George Rochefort and his score or so of apprehensive companions could have sworn, beyond question, to the words which were being sung. Following the example set in another part of the country, where a tree of liberty also had been planted, the remaining members of the Dover Corresponding Society were roaring the tune of " God Save the King " though wording it differently.

" God Damn the King " the Bow Street Runners would have heard had they been within earshot.

When the cart creaked to a standstill near the pillars of the Guildhall the symbolic ceremony began. The tree was lifted down carefully and then Stephen Hammond, requesting order, held up one of his lamp-black soiled hands.

" You will ask," he began shrilly, trying to throw his voice above the prevailing disorder, " why we march into this old Market Place of Dover. . . ."

Despite the chill air, upper windows round the Place were being thrown open ; on the south side felons in the jail were fighting for sight-seeing opportunities through the bars, with their fellow companions in misfortune, the debtors in the miserable chambers overhead, no less interested. From every side lane the curious were running, with every passing minute the dimensions of the crowd grew larger.

" . . . this tree, this emblem of our belief . . . " the printer's assistant yelled.

Badinage and catcalls were drowning his delivery, and soon he could not be heard at all. It was evident that he would not be allowed nicely to work up to the introduction of his leader, the real speaker of the afternoon.

" 'Tis no good, George," he admitted weakly. " Better if we disperse an'——"

The pressure of the throng had pushed the thin ranks of the Society against the stone staircase leading to the Guildhall. Now George Rochefort, seeing his henchman shilly-shally, quickly ascended three or four steps and, his tall figure erect, turned about to face his audience.

" Friends . . . citizen-friends of Dover," he shouted. " We, being——"

A howl of laughter cut him short awhile, but slowly the commotion subsided. In a brief interlude George Rochefort spoke of the war with Republican France, of the manner in which it was being muddled through, of expedition after expedition which had come to grief.

" But why, citizen-friends," he asked passionately, " why should we be at war with the French ? Why should we permit an evil state which in its consequences has brought food to famine prices, until the spectre of starvation is beginning to stalk the land ? Why, I say——"

George Rochefort was no small dandy. Just then a husky-voiced keel-bully from the Plain district bellowed that the fine gentleman's clothing would keep him and his family for a month.

The spark had been fired. It was not that the keel-bully and his friends agreed or disagreed with what had been said. Probably they, like so many of their better-placed countrymen, were divided on the merits of the war with France. It was rather that they felt some vague form of resentment, and manifestation of that feeling followed.

Aftermath of the market, bruised produce, lay on the cobbles of the Market Place, and such missiles were seized upon with alacrity. The members of the Dover Corresponding Society received a thorough pelting ; fruit squelched on the wall behind its founder's head, and once George Rochefort took a fast-flying apple on the temple. That hurt abominably, he felt very sick.

He was sitting on the step when Susan Fagg reached him, prepared, if needs be, to face death at the side of the man she loved.

It did not work out like that, after all. But she, a refined young lady, had pushed through an unpleasant crowd and she, who always had lived a life sheltered from coarseness and brutality, had done what she set out to do.

So perhaps one of her dreams had really come true.

The Market Place, and all that had happened there, seemed to be of another world and of another age. The candles had been lighted in the drawing-room of Little Pent House, the fire burned cheerfully, and the earlier contretemps, when George Rochefort entered the house, was now a fast fading memory.

Keziah Hart, when Miss Susan brought Mr. George in, had made just the most unfortunate remark she could have done.

" Warm water, Miss Susan ? To be sure," she had said, and to that added, on perceiving the ugly bruise on George Rochefort's forehead, " you haven't been fighting, have you, Mr. George ? " And she put the question very puritanically.

George Rochefort, the crude misunderstanding irritating him beyond endurance, had replied caustically to that.

" Well," retaliated Keziah imperturbably, " the only thing I can say, Mr. George, is that it looks as if you 'ad been fighting . . . or *brawling* as you appears to favour that word."

But all that was past, and now Susan Fagg and George Rochefort sat alone, the house quiet and peaceful. Susan's two nieces were still in Snargate Street at Caroline's, and her brother and sister-in-law had gone for the evening to Mr. Crundall's.

George Rochefort was discoursing freely when he chanced to notice that Susan was staring steadily into the fire, her hands involuntarily clasping and unclasping.

"And what," he said, breaking off his theme, "worries you, m'dear?"

She started at the sudden question and, being so startled, perhaps said far more than in other circumstances she would. Whilst from time to time he nodded assent, she incoherently voiced her anxieties for his safety, speaking of the Bow Street Runners and of the constant sedition trials, with the savage sentences imposed.

"I . . . I fear, fear monstrously for you, George," she told him tremblingly.

"My dear Susan," he shrugged lightly, "the life I lead is but the penalty for my convictions."

"But, George," she said imploringly, "I am positive you are in the utmost danger."

He gravely admitted that he supposed his life hung by the proverbial thread, and was enlarging on this when the faintest of sounds caught his attention. Tears, very slowly, were beginning to run down his pretty companion's cheeks.

"My dear Susan," he observed resolutely, "I see my clumsiness has distressed you, though at least . . . " he smiled wryly, "I perceive I have one friend who would mourn if——"

"Don't, oh don't, George," she begged him desperately.

"One friend who . . . " he murmured.

The unkind might have asserted that he was extracting a measure of gratification from this intimate scene, but if that were the case, he assuredly did not dally when Susan, wholly, broke down. Promptly he went across to her and, slipping down to one knee, took her hand and patted it kindly between his own.

"Come, my dear," he said consolingly.

There could be many an explanation of what took place then. It may be that he was deeply stirred by her agitation and no less moved by the heroic part he felt himself to be playing; it may be that never before had he seen eyes so blue, or ever smelled a lavender scent so fragrant. Possibly it was that, though unaware of his own weakness, he intuitively knew that she, never failing him, would provide him with the audience for which he ever craved.

"Susan, my dear," he began gently, "will you be my wife?"

Unbelievingly she stared at him, her lips slowly parting. Then some lovely radiance came into her and, not replying to his question, she said the thing that was always in her thoughts.

"I . . . I love you, George," she whispered.

"Of course, my dearest," he remarked a little later as he paced the room, " I should not wish to ask John for your hand yet, nor can we be married until I have emerged safely from my present hazardous course."

She was watching him adoringly. " I want only to do as you wish, George," she said simply.

More talk in similar vein and then he had to go. It was essential that he should find a more secret place for the meetings of the Society and . . .

With firm step, his carriage upright, he left her. But some paces along Town Wall Street he hesitated. The night was unpleasant, and he was neither in the mood for the society of Stephen Hammond nor did he wish to encounter his brother if he went home.

" George ! " All the happiness a woman may know was in Susan Fagg's eyes when she greeted him again.

Afterwards she played the piano, as once she had prayed she might to this chosen lover. It was still another dream which had come true.

3

The weather towards the end of the year became persistently bad, and, on the day Charles Fagg was due to return home after his first term at school, the violent south-east wind began to back. The great anchorage of the Downs, with this shift, was a death-trap for any craft attempting to shelter there and, nearer home, a fine ship off Shakespeare Cliff dragged her anchor, to become a total loss when forced on to the blue marl reef over which the grey seas boiled.

Her crew were clinging in the rigging and, it being impossible to launch a boat from the steep-to beach, an attempt at rescue was made from the haven.

Once again the shallow bar of Dover Harbour was to take its toll of human life—five gallant Kentishmen perished there whilst striving to bring aid.

John Fagg, his mouth grim, was walking homewards along the Cross Wall when the bodies were being recovered.

" A very cruel business, Mr. Fagg," Mr. Templeman, the wool-stapler, remarked, falling into step.

Mr. Templeman's premises were up an alley off Cannon Street, but at the moment he was making for the Poorhouse in St. James's Street, a thoroughfare behind, and parallel with, Town Wall Street.

" 'Tis, Harry," John Fagg agreed curtly.

Poverty had become so widespread that the Poorhouse was full to overflowing and Mr. Templeman, who supplied the authorities with the raw material to keep the inmates employed, was on his way thither to look after his interests. It might be remarked, too, that Mr. Templeman was Mayor of Dover, an office which also invested him with the Coronership of the port and liberties.

" And what verdict will you bring in, Harry? " John Fagg asked suddenly. " Accidental death ? "

The woolstapler, puzzled a little, said he supposed that that would be so, and in return heard what course he should take. The Harbour Commissioners, Mr. Fagg observed forcibly, were the responsible parties. It was through their palpable neglect that five decent men had lost their lives.

" But I can't charge them——" the woolstapler protested.

" Of a surety you can't," the shipowner declared dourly.

Mr. Templeman, though slow-thinking, decided it was wisdom to leave the matter there, and began to speak of other things. He grumbled about trade and about the government ; why, he asked plaintively, had loyalist troops been landed at Quiberon Bay when only a month later their remainder had had to be evacuated by the navy ; why, in September, had General Doyle and his 4,000 men been put ashore in the Isle d'Yeu, for no better purpose, it appeared, than to provide a re-embarkation exercise shortly afterwards.

" Muddle, muddle, muddle," he growled. " Reverse, reverse, and still reverse."

John Fagg commented briefly and, Little Pent House being near, informed Mr. Templeman that the Wall Passage was the quickest route into St. James's Street.

From the dining-room of her residence Mrs. Fagg, who had been glancing over the party-like decorations of the table, chanced to glimpse her husband's set face.

She sighed. " I wish this awful tragedy hadn't happened just as Charles was due, Susan. Really, 'twill cast a cloud . . . "

Susan nodded sympathetically. She knew how her brother felt on the harbour question.

Mrs. Fagg was not the only parent in Dover who desired for a son a joyous homecoming, but Henry Rochefort, in those few minutes before the boy arrived, believed it his duty to speak plainly to his brother.

" George," he began gravely, " you must realise that if you persist you will be risking transportation or worse."

George Rochefort was at the window, staring down Snargate Street.

" I imagine, Henry, that of the twain transportation is a far more distasteful prospect," he observed flippantly, without turning.

With an effort the banker checked himself. He spoke of families such as the Rocheforts, the many families who in generations gone by had sought, and had been given, refuge in England.

"Such as we," he resumed earnestly, "must take especial care that we contribute equally, nay more——"

"High moral grounds, eh?" George Rochefort remarked cynically.

Only the sound of Caroline's excited voice prevented the brothers from quarrelling. She, with Minnie and Lou, had been to greet Louis and Charles.

Neither, of course, would permit himself to be officially met by any adult member of his family.

4

In the first few months following the day of its inception, the membership of the Dover Corresponding Society had grown apace. But after the outbreak of war the secretary had noted down a regular diminution which varied proportionately to the fear excited by certain statutes the government had placed on the book.

But, as the founder of the Society had once remarked, "Better a handful of resolute men than any number of waverers."

Nevertheless it was not surprising that, in the February of the following year, three weeks after a Mr. Stone, in London, had been charged with conspiracy to high treason, the members who assembled in the crypt beneath the old tower in Bench Street were both few in number as well as deficient in courage of the most glorious quality.

"'Tis very well you talking, George . . ." one of them began queasily.

"Excellent, my dear fellow," George Rochefort observed cuttingly. "Then may I take it that now I can proceed with this matter?"

The "matter" concerned the printing of handbills for distribution to the soldiers in the garrison and on the Heights. Their projected form was to be of such nature as to give the objector ample grounds for his protest.

"Proceed nothing . . . so far as I have to do with it," growled a beefy young man. "It don't smell over sweet to me and I'll thank you to erase my name from that membership list which Hammond keeps."

It was very evident that the Society had reached a crucial point in its existence. Another young man, supported by five more, made a demand, not for the mere removal of his name, but for the immediate destruction of the records themselvs.

"Aye, that's what we want," the cry was taken up.

It was a strange scene which followed, that fierce fight taking place in candle-light beneath the groined stone roof, that struggle which eddied round the massive central pillar which supported the venerable arches.

When it was over, and they were gone, George Rochefort rose shakily, his nostrils oozing blood and his clothing filthied from the uneven floor.

" They have had their way, Stephen," he gasped, " but that shall not deter us from our purpose."

Stephen Hammond was knuckling his smoked eyes, and at the same time stamping on the smouldering ashes of the documents of the Dover Corresponding Society.

" No," he coughed. " But . . . but you'll have to try to do the printing, George. You've seen me oft enough at work, and I can loan you a key——"

" Et tu, Brute ! " George Rochefort declaimed accusingly.

The printer's assistant, in a wordy reply, protested against the overt insinuation. It was only, he said, that he was dependent for his livelihood on Matthew Adcock, and if the illiterate old fool found out that he, Stephen Hammond, had set up a seditious handbill . . .

" And 'tis seditious, George," he continued shrilly. " If 'tis printed like that fellow in Lancashire did it, 'tis seditious all right."

He was referring to a Manchester printer's apprentice who, after distributing Tom Paine's *Rights of Man* to the troops stationed in the neighbouring barracks, had bethought himself to do some composition on his own account.

George Rochefort's dark eyes gleamed hotly, though his pride was too much for him ever to think of making an appeal.

" I will see to this business myself," he announced icily. " It only remains for me to request you to lock up in your heart all that which has already taken place. You see, my friend . . . " he smiled faintly, " from now on I travel alone, only my own life in forfeit."

Instead of accepting this courageous decision at its face value, Stephen Hammond, employing that mordant tongue of his, remarked that Rochefort all along would have done better had he not dramatised himself perpetually.

" I tell you," he said sarcastically, " your reiteration of deadly perils put mortal fear into the members of the Society long before there was foundation for't. I'll agree that now——"

" I require neither your agreement nor your dissent," George Rochefort interrupted, trembling with fury.

Little more was said before they left the undercroft, a chamber which, those members who had used it wisely holding their tongues, was not to be re-discovered for many decades.

After scrambling into the adjoining length of cellarage the blocks

of stone were replaced, and the way out cautiously reconnoitred.
Shortly, in the blackness, the two young men entered Bench Street.

5

Snow had fallen without intermission for a full day, but on the next
night it ceased.

Where streets were as yet unlighted, it was obligatory on dwellers
therein to keep a candle burning in the window, and by the occasional
illumination from these it was possible to see that the old footprints in
the snow were now depressions rather than sharply defined shapes,
and that there were scarcely any newly made. George Rochefort,
hurrying along King Street, thence keeping directly on that side of
the Market Place, was relieved that few were abroad. Nevertheless,
before opening Mr. Matthew Adcock's door, he glanced about him.

He stiffened slightly as he perceived a figure dimly outlined
beneath the one lamp in the Market Place, that at the arched entrance
to the Antwerp Stables. Squeezing back into the doorway he waited
but, in a while, reassured, he entered the printing office, bolting and
barring the door behind him.

" There ! " he muttered, drawing off his gloves.

With hands that were cold, he was awkward in manipulating flint
and tinder, but eventually he succeeded in lighting a candle, carefully
screening its rays from the window on the street side.

The room was long, with a broad alcove, looking over St. James's
Lane, at the further end. In the recess was a font of type, set up on
an easel-like board, and this, together with the hand-press, was the
only prominent feature in the workshop. On the walls were hung
recent playbills and several announcements of sales, and elsewhere
were tables piled with printed matter ready for delivery.

" No time to lose," he murmured, teeth already beginning to
chatter.

He went into the alcove and, dripping a blob of hot wax on to
the wooden box, firmly fixed the candle so that the light fell on the
divisions containing type. Slipping out of his coat, he took from an
inner pocket a crumpled broadsheet, carefully smoothing it out.

Now he was ready, with the composing stick in his left hand. Each
letter of the first line came out of the upper case, that holding capital
letters.

" T," he said softly, and then, when it was found and placed in
the composing stick, he looked for the next, " O." This done, he
had painfully completed a short word and now he had to search for
the separating blank.

So he continued until the caption was completed, when mainly he used the small letters in the lower case. As he proceeded he grew more dexterous and once, when emptying into the galley the lines which had filled the composing stick, he smiled.

"Of a certainty if brother Henry could prevent my receiving a handsome competence in the practice of banking, I might at least earn a sufficiency——"

His body went rigid. There was a queer growling noise, and then a dull thud. An uncanny and protracted silence followed, though in fact it could not have been more than three seconds before the taut hearer realised that the sound which had so affected his senses was nothing more than a weight of snow sliding off the roof.

"Must be thawing, damme," he ejaculated inconsequently, taking in a gulping breath.

But from now on he acted with a greater urgency. The galley filled, he made the forme. Then came the preparation for printing.

He shifted the light, as he moved glancing anxiously at the window, white with its coating of soft adhesive snow. Placing the candle down he hurriedly looked about him, at last discovering a heavy ledger which reasonably masked the rays which reached towards the front aspect of the building.

He got to work again, wetting suitably sized paper and finding a pair of soft, undressed sheepskin balls which, after being applied to the ink-block, were beaten on the face of the type in the forme.

"Nearly ready," he said to himself, scrutinising the press, with its rolling carriage and long handle operating the screw.

Placing one foot on the angled ground-board and giving the correct double pull on the handle, he made a proof.

Exultantly he looked over it.

TO THE BRITISH ARMY

Comrades,

Are not the sailors proving that not only can they think, but that soon they will ACT ? And ACT FOR THEMSELVES full as well, or better, than when under the tyranny of the officers.

Can you think a parliament, speaking like fathers and brothers, would treat you as you are treated ?

Are you so well cloathed as soldiers used to be ? Ask the old pensioners at Chelsea College, whether horse or foot.

The power is All Your Own.

BE SOBER. BE READY.

" The proper note," he murmured. " First cause discontent and then——"

He glanced sharply, first at the door and then at the window. Unmistakably there had been a sound. Tensely he waited, his heart pounding.

As the seconds passed he decided he must have been mistaken, but nevertheless he crept into the gloom beyond the screen afforded by the ledger and, his head sideway and his eyes alert, listened by the door. But he heard nothing more.

Now work began in real earnest until, as St. Mary's struck the midnight hour, he lighted another candle from the dying flame of the old, and forthwith began to count the strewn sheets so tediously made.

" Three score . . . and ten . . . four score . . . and——"

Quickly he turned and rigidly remained as he was, half bent, his eyes narrowed on the door, the nearby candle almost scorching his hair, one side of his face vividly illuminated, the other in deep shade.

There was a faint noise as though a hand was gently trying the knob. Then a vague mumble, and at last a tap.

" Who's out of bed at this hour ? " he heard someone ask.

In a fever, George Rochefort looked about him, first at the door to the cellar and then, more intently, at the window at the rear. He began to make quick preparations, first speedily donning his heavy coat, and then losing more time than he had gained by searching for a hat he found he had never taken off.

" Who's there ? " came the demand.

Tucking beneath his arm the dangerous broadsheets, he snuffed the candle, threw up the sash of that window, and had got one long leg outside when he recollected an omission. He perceptibly hesitated, his dominant impulse to escape. Let a faithless associate explain it away as best he could. . . .

" I . . . I must not leave it," he said, however, between clenched teeth.

Nerving himself to re-enter, he groped through the black workshop, and at last pocketed the big key, only a panel of wood separating him from those in the Market Place. There *were* more than one, his acute senses told him long before he dropped silently into St. James's Lane.

In the days when Dover's main harbour had been the Little Pent, this narrow street had been used by the Norman Kings as the principal landing-quay for the material from which was built the Keep and various towers of the Castle. Here, where great blocks of stone had been man-handled ashore, George Rochefort pressed close into a shallow recess.

To his right, some forty or fifty paces down, he thought he could see a lurking figure. Step by step, he edged in the opposite direction towards the lower corner of Dolphin Lane, at the far end of which was the lantern at the entrance to the Antwerp Stables.

Immediately without the ring of light he saw a quick movement.

George Rochefort began to think desperately. Before him, at the other side of the lane, was the barrier formed by the dark and swollen Dour. Down-stream his path for flight was already barred. But up-water was Stembrooke, with its tannery and narrow alleys, and that way gave a hope of security.

He ran across Dolphin Lane, hearing a shout from the top even as he did so.

It was an eerie chase, with the footsteps of all made silent by the carpet of snow. In the labyrinth of stinking Stembrooke he fought to get clear, but always he was headed back, ever compelled to double on his tracks.

There was more shouting now, and his breathing became more difficult. He knew that relentlessly he was being penned into a more restricted area.

" God ! " he gasped, now back at the lower end of Dolphin Lane.

From right and left they were coming, not yet visible but their voices carrying clearly.

Cold sweat broke out from him, knowing so surely he was irrevocably caught. But, though his brain was working hazily, his instinct was to prevent their laying hands on him whilst he was engaged in ignominious flight. He would walk back to them with dignity.

Another paralysing chill shivered him as he remembered the broadsheets still tucked tightly beneath his arm. Panic-stricken, seeing no other hiding-place, he thrust the incriminating pamphlets into a drift of snow.

Then, pausing only partially to recover his breath, he started to saunter down St. James's Lane.

A minute later they were about him. Five men whose voices, as suited their purpose, varied astonishingly from the softly inquiring to the harshest and most uncivil.

" A strange hour to be abroad, sir," one remarked evenly.

A lantern was thrust near to his pallid face.

" Young Mr. Rochefort, I believe," another observed blandly.

He stared imperiously at them. " Pray, what is your business with me, if any ? " he demanded haughtily.

A small, smooth-faced man smiled easily. " Why, young sir," he asked, " should we have business with you ? "

Quite what happened then he knew not. But one of them appeared to slip and clutched at him for support. Then he was jostled between them, and even in his wild rage he comprehended they sought a bundle of leaves, the edges of which must have fluttered as he had run.

" Well, sirs ? " he inquired ironically.

After that they became less considerate, just as their manner became more disappointed. They hectored him, threatened him, worked to break his will, and utterly failed. In the end they had to let him go.

" Good-night, gentlemen," he said cuttingly in parting.

He was answered by a rough oath from the one carrying the lantern. But, as he turned into the Market Place, he could see them stooping, see the lantern moving along as they began to search.

From then, as George Rochefort passed the Guildhall, his first relief began to be replaced by a growing foreboding. Against Lester's Saddlery, on the corner of Queen Street, he half hesitated, but finally went on. Only near the old tower in Bench Street did he decide to go back and attempt the recovery of those dangerous sheets.

Driven by his dread, he quickly regained Dolphin Lane. With a throb of hope he saw that the Bow Street gentry were now busily occupied close to Mr. Bullack's tannery.

In that quaint overhung street named after the decorated rings on the long-vanished mooring posts, he began to seek an elusive drift, chancing on the one he wanted just as that slowly swinging light started to move nearer, silent step by silent step.

" Got them," he half sobbed, his arm immersed to the elbow.

He heard a hoarse shout, but was off. The passage clear, his long raking strides soon put the pursuers far behind, and in minutes only he was on Pent-side, quietly opening a back door with a key his brother did not know he possessed.

When he was within, he removed his high-boots, and then proceeded cautiously into the dining-room, where he saw gladly that the red glow of a fire remained.

On his knees he began to burn, a few at a time, those addresses he had impressed for the soldiers of the British Army. They were still damp and, charring rather than flaming, took long to disappear.

It was in one of the intervals of waiting that he came to realize the degrading and cowardly thing he was doing. From the few dozen broadsheets which remained he glanced at those other evidences of fear and evasion, his trembling hands and discreetly stockinged feet.

" Craven ! " he murmured bitterly. " Methinks I should have been the last to have decried Stephen Hammond. A craven," he repeated contemptuously.

His eyes blazed as he rose, purpose in every movement. He stuffed into his pockets the pamphlets which had escaped destruction, and then made again for the rear of the house and for his boots and coat.

Soon he was once more on Pent-side. Three long hours passed before he returned.

George Rochefort, in that time of his further absence, visited the quarters of the Castle Garrison, and then struggled through clinging snow to the temporary barracks on the Western Heights. Near the one he was challenged, and on the other, close by the Bredenstone, a bullet whistled past his head.

He distributed the broadsheets, leaving them where they might be found, not in places where they were certain to be seen.

That this was not the style of the man who dares all he knew well enough in his own self-accusing soul. Even as he stripped off his clothes in his bedroom, his mobile mouth bitterly revealed the knowledge which goaded him beyond endurance. And then, in the midst of his scathing denunication of himself, he was violently sick.

6

For a week or more after George Rochefort's escapade there was a hue and cry for the miscreant who had dared to attempt the subversion of the armed forces of the Crown, with the bellman calling a reward for information which would lead to the apprehension of the rogue. But by early spring, when the war had taken an even more unfavourable turn, such talk died down. Strangely enough, apart from a few lynx-eyed officials who continued to take interest in every movement Henry Rochefort's brother made, not a soul in Dover ever pointed the finger of suspicion at Susan Fagg's lover.

By this time, also, John Fagg had thoroughly digested the many reports he had obtained on the haven. Thereupon he broached to his wife the idea of a social evening at Little Pent House. To this, four gentlemen, with their respective wives, were to be invited.

Despite certain catering difficulties, Polly Fagg hailed the suggestion enthusiastically. She ever took a keen pride in being hostess.

" 'Twill be delightful, John," she agreed, her mind already busy on the spread she would endeavour to set. "Now I'm sure to see both Mrs. Stokes and Mrs. Nethersole at the market to-day, and if I don't happen to meet Mrs. Breton or Mrs. Crundall I'll pay 'em a call very shortly."

John Fagg nodded his satisfaction. For a long time he had been testing out leading jurats and, quite apart from technical matters in connection with the haven, he was convinced that the husbands of the four ladies mentioned were of the right metal.

"Slowly I'm going to do it, Polly," he said resolutely, "but equally surely I intend to build up a party which will fight the Commissioners to the last ditch."

Eagerly the shipowner awaited the night of this special party, and in high spirits was he when the morning of the day came.

The same forenoon, Dover had a taste of that rising popular feeling which hitherto its townsfolk believed belonged only to the densely populated manufacturing areas of the kingdom.

Mr. Fagg's *Emma* was alongside Custom House Quay loading from the Royal Victualling Yard foodstuffs for the relief of distress in the north, when an angry mob swarmed over from the Plain District. The lumpers and keel-bullies, their ragged women among them, made short commons of the few men engaged in the work and, before John Fagg could reach the scene, a considerable value of goods had either been looted or wickedly tippled into the Basin.

A duty of one shilling per chauldron was imposed on coal entering the haven, the proceeds being passed over to the Paving Commissioners, and Mr. Fagg was busy with Mr. Warren on a customs reckoning when the trouble began.

"And what . . ." John Fagg was asking angrily, after speaking of corrupt practices and the deplorable condition of the streets of the town, "do they do with the money?"

The mild little Collector of Customs was doing his utmost to defend the close ranks of officialdom when his attention was drawn to the clatter of wood staffs and the growing uproar.

"Hearts alive, Mr. Fagg!" he ejaculated. "What . . ."

When the shipowner reached his skipper, it was all over. Though bleeding from a nasty cut, Captain Maxton was not vindictive.

"*Their* bellies are empty as well, Mr. Fagg," he commented, wincing slightly as he fingered the wound.

"Aye . . . aye . . ." his employer said slowly. "Nevertheless . . ." Mr. Fagg shook his head ; law and order, and the rights of ownership could not be so defied.

The attack caused a sensation and was fully discussed that evening at Little Pent House. Mr. Crundall, in particular, took a most gloomy view.

"Proves the country is at sixes and sevens," he observed dismally, "and in the very middle of a war that ain't going at all happily. 'Tis all very well Jeremy claiming that an English vessel o' war is a match for any two of the Frenchies', but now that Spain has declared war on us——"

The crux of the matter was that the fleets of France, Holland, and now Spain, if combined, outnumbered those of his own country. All depended, the boat-builder persisted stubbornly, on whether the squadrons blockading the Texel, Brest, Toulon, Ferrol and Cartagena could prevent the enemy effecting such concentration.

Captain Nethersole and Mr. Stokes, Clerk of the Passage, spoke simultaneously.

" Nonsense, Kit," Jeremy Nethersole began, " even if any of 'em do get out——"

" 'Tis ridiculous, this conflict," Mr. Stokes started at the same time. " Why should we——"

A battle royal followed. Captain Nethersole was an ardent Tory, whilst Nicholas Stokes, as ever, adhered to his political leaders. If Mr. Fox and Mr. Sheridan still pleaded for peace with France, that was good enough for the Clerk of the Passage.

· The argument became so heated that in the end the ladies intervened, though not until the supper table was reached did the two gentlemen really subside.

After that, in the drawing-room again, John Fagg casually brought up the subject which formed the basic purpose for the gathering. Quickly he outlined the position as he saw it.

Mr. Stokes nodded agreement. " I'm with you there, John," he once said. " The policy of the Harbour Commissioners has always been to push seaward, leasing off the reclaimed land behind."

The " law of eastward drift " was mentioned by Captain Nethersole, and from that, John Fagg producing his charts and plans, a highly technical conversation took place.

" 'Tis possible, John, yes, I think that is quite possible," Mr. Breton thoughtfully remarked at one stage, in reference to an observation of the shipowner regarding the true tideway.

The four gentlemen, smoking away, each with a glass close at hand, were becoming more and more interested in the novel suggestions which were being propounded to them.

About this time, Mrs. Stokes, much to the ill-concealed satisfaction of the mistress of the house, was speaking warmly of the pleasing appearance of the drawing-room, newly decorated, biscuit coloured, foiled in white.

" So very genteel and tasteful, my dear," she declared.

Polly Fagg's head waggled. " Oh, really no," she laughed, " really no. Though . . . " here her expression switched to the more serious, " I must confess that I thought 'twas not . . . not entirely inelegant."

Both Mrs. Breton and Mrs. Crundall volubly assured her that she was far too modest, with the boat-builder's wife avowing, so taken was she by the room, that she intended to persuade Crundall to pull out the dismal panelling which marred so many of her own rooms.

The other guest, fluffy Mrs. Nethersole, chatting gaily with Susan Fagg, was sitting on a settee in one of the recesses, immediately below a gilt mirror. Susan was on the piano stool, the light of the nearby torchère falling on a pretty face which, perhaps vaguely, had changed a little. Her happiness in George and her fear for him had been responsible for that.

Captain Nethersole's good lady was dying with curiosity, but nothing she hinted at brought her any further forward, and it was not until John Fagg's sister chanced to leave the room that she was able to be more direct. Then, smiling fleetingly and rather meaninglessly towards the gentlemen, she changed her seat and established herself by her hostess.

" Dear Susan," she opened fondly. " Such a lovely nature, hasn't she ? A dear girl indeed."

It was not long, however, before she was down to essentials. She had, she said, several times lately seen the sweet creature with Mr. Henry Rochefort's brother. Were they betoken, she asked. And, whether or not they were, did Mrs. Fagg think it was *quite* wise.

Polly Fagg's expression became somewhat disturbed. Secretly her thoughts were very much on the same lines, but loyally she supported her husband. John, individualistic always, still maintained his belief that George Rochefort's romantic nonsense was so much wind, and better treated as such.

So the evening passed, ending in a fashion which gave John Fagg the utmost satisfaction. A master mariner, the Clerk of the Passage, a boat-builder, and the Harbour-master had pledged themselves in the evolution of a scheme for harbour development.

" We're not engineers, but we do know something of old Dover," grunted Mr. Stokes.

" Which is more than that——" Captain Nethersole, remembering the presence of ladies, pulled himself up sharp, and then spoke more mildly of Sir Walter Plumbley.

Mr. Crundall cheerfully observed that they had set themselves a task which would occupy their spare hours for anything up to a couple of years. And Mr. Breton rounded it all off by saying that he would do everything he could, though his participation, for obvious reasons, must not be disclosed.

" And when we've got our suggestions ready, John ? " the Harbour-master finally asked.

" Put 'em before the Harbour Commissioners," the shipowner promptly replied. " Give 'em the first chance so that we're in the right whatever we do later."

John Fagg was in high humour when he lighted the lanterns for his departing guests that night.

Shortly after this, one of those scarifying waves passed through government circles. It was held by many well-informed officials that the French might very soon stage an attack on the sea-girt isle.

It was recognised, too, amongst those close groups, that the country was ill-prepared. In consequence there began to be a great beating of the drum. Politicians, all in a hustle and bustle, delivered passionate exhortations—volunteers were called for in immense numbers, though how they could be armed was skilfully glossed over.

There was an orgy of departmental preparation and, within a month, the realm was fully prepared—on paper.

7

Mr. Henry Rochefort was appointed Director of Stock for Dover. It was his duty, unpaid, to make a return of all horses and vehicles in the area ; his mission to enrol as pioneers all smiths, carpenters and wheelwrights ; to arrange for a company of expert horsemen as messengers and guides ; to prepare lists of boys who would, if the worst came to the worst, assist in the removal of women and children.

A most thankless task it proved to be, more especially as the authorities in London, almost by every mail, bethought themselves to vary their instructions.

" If this, Mr. Garroway, is a sample of the manner in which our affairs are conducted," the banker snapped, throwing down a quill, " 'tis small wonder the country is in its present condition."

David Garroway, George Rochefort's friend, was spending a few days at Snargate Street preparatory to being inducted into the living of a pretty village near Tenterden, some thirty miles away. He was a sweet-faced young man, one very different in appearance from the usual hard-drinking, fox-hunting, country parson.

He was making a sympathetic rejoinder when, following a tap at the door, Mr. Godspenny came in from the specie room.

Apparently his master knew what was wanted. The bank was engaged in most lucrative operations with Hamburg, the exchange being such that a clear profit of $8\frac{3}{4}$ per cent was being made by shipping gold to the Hanseatic port.

" Yes, yes," Mr. Rochefort rapped. " I will be with you within five minutes, Mr. Godspenny."

The clerk inclined gravely. " Very good, sir," he said quietly.

Actually Henry Rochefort wished to resume a conversation he had begun with Mr. Garroway the night before.

" I want to talk to you about George, Mr. Garroway," he started earnestly. " You know something of his ideas, I suppose ? "

" I do, sir," David Garroway replied ruefully.

Unhappily the discussion had not gone far when George Rochefort came in. At the time Henry Rochefort was quoting, as illustration of his brother's stupidity, a fatuous and most ill-balanced comment on Mr. Pitt.

" Damme, Mr. Garroway," the banker fumed, " 'twas Mr. Pitt, the man George so maligns, who was responsible for the Reform Bill of 1783, and for——"

A dispute at once broke out between the two brothers. As it appeared their differences would speedily attain uncontrollable proportions, the young clergyman decided to intervene.

" George," he began sternly, " I should suggest you suspend judgment until you read up your history. Mr. Pitt——"

" Mr. Pitt ! " George Rochefort interposed flamingly. " May our liberties never be swallowed in a Pitt."

Fortunately Mr. Garroway was of an equable temperament. Unruffled, he spoke of the Prime Minister. Mr. Pitt, he said, was a man of wide vision, as witness his interest in Adam Smith's *Wealth of Nations*, the repeal of old-time legislation against the Romanists, his willingness to concede a considerable measure of self-government to the great colony of Canada, and his advanced views on free trade.

" You would do well to reflect on these things, George," David Garroway subsequently observed when he and his friend, arm-in-arm, were strolling towards the coffee-house in Market Place.

George Rochefort smiled slightly. " My dear David," he drawled, " I fear that I cannot expect a clerk in Holy Orders to understand these complexities. The Church and the rulers of this land invariably march hand in hand, whereas in France it has been seen . . ."

A crowd of men were about the Guildhall staircase, one or two going up in turn. The Navy's need was so enormous that it had proved necessary again to put the press-gang into operation, and that evening the Mayor was issuing notes of protection to those who might properly claim them.

From this spectacle David Garroway turned.

" Perhaps, George," he began soberly, " I don't understand much that I might, but there is one thing upon which I am very sure."

So intense did he sound that George Rochefort laughed. " And what, O philosopher, may that be ? " he inquired lightly.

Sparingly, but effectively, the young parson declared his belief. In the early days, he admitted it, the war with France had been one largely of politico-social differences.

" But now, George," he ended, " it is very different. To-day 'tis a war of conquest, with the Directory taking up the old policies of the Bourbons."

"War cannot remain static," George Rochefort responded quickly. "A country to defend itself must needs oft go beyond its own frontiers."

"But has France brought her vaunted freedom, or any freedom forsooth, to the countries she has conquered?" David Garroway asked shrewdly.

For once George Rochefort was plainly quite nonplussed. Then, though not with exactly his old vim, he made an airy retort. After which, changing the subject, he spoke of taking David on to Little Pent House to make the acquaintance of his Susan.

"A dear little creature, you'll find her," he laughed. "Not particularly intelligent or well-versed, but charming notwithstanding."

There was an even greater expression of shock, of anxiety, on David Garroway's face as he glanced at his friend.

CHAPTER EIGHT

I

By now it had become "Martha" and "Valentine," and never did a man walk so jauntily as Captain Pepper did one evening in midsummer. At long last he had persuaded Mistress Teddiman to look over his house and, whilst he was showing her the place, Captain Pepper had determined to pop the question.

Contrary to his usual custom, the boatswain left the warehouse before the clerks and, when in Elizabeth Street, turned towards the Cross Wall, passing alongside Paradise Pent which, incidentally, looked very much the same as ever.

His cottage, when he entered it, smelt very savoury, and, once there, he soon settled down to a repast of German Duck—there was nothing he relished better than half a sheep's head boiled with onions.

The pots and dishes had all been washed and put away when Mistress Teddiman arrived. She was exactly a quarter of an hour late, but feminine coyness, the thought of keeping Valentine Pepper on tenterhooks, could not be ascribed as being the reason for her belated appearance.

"Martha, you 'adn't ought to have done this to me," Captain Pepper beamed welcomingly. "I've been in a frape these last ten minutes an' no mistake. But come in, m'dear."

Still hovering hesitantly, Martha nervously tittered, quite unlike herself. Truth to tell she was mightily apprehensive. After all she would be alone in a house with a man, and although she had arranged one safeguard . . .

"Do you think as I ought," she asked timidly.

Captain Pepper looked his complete bewilderment. "That's what you come for, ain't it, Martha?" he ejaculated.

After taking a deep breath she at last entered, her manner much as if she were beneath the roof of one of those places of debauch in foreign parts, ever poised for swift escape if he made a false move.

A huge chuckle of pleasure shook the boatswain. "And now, Martha, I'll show you as shipshape——" He glanced in some astonishment at the door which his companion, instead of closing, had pushed back as far as it would go.

He winked wickedly. "I reckon 'twill be more snug if we shut that, eh?" he grinned broadly.

Martha Teddiman recoiled at the suggestion. "No . . . no," she said hurriedly, "'tis very sweltry to-night an' . . . an' . . ."

Thrusting a couple of fingers beneath his wig, Captain Pepper began to scratch the back of his neck, meantime eyeing her in some perplexity.

"True, 'tis a bit 'ot," he agreed. "But . . ." he left it at that. There was no accounting for a woman's whim . . . and maybe she had guessed what he was going to ask her and was perhaps excited about it. He cheered up on that.

"Now you be a-going to do Sunday morning inspection afore divisions," he told her jovially.

The cottage was really delightful, with not a speck of dust to be found. The kitchen, or galley as Martha noticed he termed it, was immaculate, and the two tiny bedrooms, though she took care not to go beyond the doorway of either, were charming. The parlour was a low and comfortable room, its walls covered with panelling from the saloon of an East Indiaman which had come to grief off the Brakes Sand by Sandwich, its line of small windows made from the stern of an old flagship.

"Couldn't improve this much, could you, my dear?" Valentine Pepper remarked proudly.

"You lack a cannon," Martha Teddiman retorted deprecatingly.

She was recovering, and moreover was very much impressed by all the evidence she had seen of a sailorman's handiwork.

Captain Pepper guffawed as he knelt down to remove a floorboard. He was beginning to know Miss Teddiman, and already he had concluded that she was not ill-pleased by what he had shown her.

Now, though in a roundabout manner, he got down to business.

From between the baulks he produced a leathern bag. Untying the neck, he showed her many gleaming guineas.

"Sixty-five of 'em there, m'dear," he announced with pride. "No skinflint me, but I likes to save as well."

"My sentiments, too, Captain Pepper," Martha Teddiman affirmed warmly, more impressed than ever by the gold.

Captain Pepper coughed. "You'll be 'aving a tidy few put by, I reckon?" he murmured casually.

That very nearly undid all the good. Martha's eyes flashed suspicion, and he had no small difficulty in coaxing her round. When he had accomplished this hard feat he mentioned why he preferred to keep his money close at hand. The financial collapse of three years before, it seemed, had not been forgotten.

"With all due respex to Mr. Rochefort . . . no banks for me," he grunted, hiding away his savings. "Specially now, for I'm sartin things ain't too rosy and there'll be trouble agin you'll see."

Martha coldly stated that she did not care to discuss her master's affairs, and thereupon Valentine Pepper, being convinced that she was deliberately holding him off, proceeded with his suit.

"Me," he began, "I'm no dangler. Me, as soon as I get my answer, 'tis a dilly from Jim Page's stables and a 'eigh-'o tally-'o."

Her eyes opened extremely wide, Martha made a remark. "I don't quite follow you, Captain Pepper," she said demurely.

He made it plainer. He wanted "a bright face t'other side of the table at brekfus," he wanted "a cosy supper for two of an evening," and aye, he wanted a loving woman abed with him of a night.

Martha Teddiman's cheeks were scarlet, she hardly knew which way to turn.

"So you've beguiled me here," she choked, "so that you can make . . . make indelicate——"

"Nay, Martha——" Captain Pepper expostulated. He had a conviction that something had gone wrong, but what he could not imagine.

By now Mistress Teddiman's rage had got the upper hand. That she, a decent woman, should be so insulted by a . . .

"I suppose," she said shrilly, "that when you got me here you thought . . . thought I . . . I——"

Captain Pepper made a worse hash of it by *mentioning* the very thing she dare not say.

"'Pon my word, Martha," he said solemnly, "I'd no thought, strike me dead if I 'ad, of axing you to go to bed with me now, though . . ." the humour of it sharply seized him, "if you feels that way, Martha," he chuckled roguishly, "I wouldn't say no if——"

Mizmazed, Martha Teddiman ran to the door, immediately outside which she met Miss Caroline. That young lady was extremely surprised when she learnt she would not be allowed to see her great friend, the boatswain, when she had arrived exactly as she had been told to do, that is on the half-hour.

But soon Henry Rochefort's daughter had forgotten all this and, whilst Martha, tight-lipped, hurried on, she began to talk gleefully of the boys, who shortly would be home for the summer holidays.

As for Valentine Pepper, he was for long completely bemused, nor did the solution come to him at once. When it did, he was in the parlour of the Fountain Inn where, to the amazement of the company, who were discussing a young French general called Bonaparte, he suddenly exclaimed most irrelevantly :

" That be it, Valentine. For the future you'll 'ave to mind your P's and Q's with 'er."

There was a roar of mirth, during which Captain Pepper put down his glass with fine deliberation, and at once rose.

His most evil squint roamed over the gathering. " Did I 'ear laughter at the expense of a 'foretime petty officer o' the R'yal Navy ? " he demanded.

With striking unanimity he was assured his ears had deceived him.

2

Summer holidays for the boys meant just those delights which never cloyed : sailing, swimming, picnics, cricket, fishing, and as many more of such simple pleasures as could be crowded into the long days. Charles Fagg, besides these diversions, spent hours at the Antwerp Stables, grooming the post-horses and, joy divine, exercising them. He had, as Mr. Page confidentially informed Captain Pepper, " a very nice seat on an 'oss."

For Jack Woodgate the early days of August were days which hardly seemed true. But in due course *the* morning came, and, at the Royal Oak yard, his brand-new sea-chest was lifted on to the stage-coach and, scarce able to contain himself in the uniform he wore, he left Dover for the first time in his life, the great world and Chatham Dockyard awaiting him.

" Well . . . " sighed Lou Fagg as the coach rolled out of sight after passing the Maison Dieu. Latterly sighing had formed her manifestation of growing up.

But the exciting departure of a familiar friend does leave a certain sense of flatness, and the crowd of young people who had given Jack such a tremendous send-off wandered rather disconsolately towards the harbour.

" Let's go see Mr. Crundall," suggested Caroline Rochefort.
" He's got a new barrel of apples."

The big boys quite ignored her, but it was noticeable that there
was a mass move towards the shipbuilding slips near Archcliffe Point.

There the party first examined the cutter nearing completion on
the beach, then the shed where pulling boats were built, and finally
a number of chosen emissaries mounted the outside wooden steps to
Mr. Crundall's office overhead.

" Well ? " the boat-builder asked blankly. He had his own way of
extracting amusement from such calls.

" Jack's gone now, Mr. Crundall," Charles Fagg said pleasantly.

" He has, has he ? " Mr. Crundall still gave no change.

" He was monstrous obliged to you for the half-guinea you kindly
gave him, sir," Louis Rochefort observed with extreme courtesy.

" He was, was he ? " the boat-builder remarked, just a little moved
now. In point of fact the fruit or sweets which could so often be found
on the premises were kept there for the sole pleasure of giving them
away. He and Mrs. Crundall, not blessed themselves, were passionately
fond of children.

" 'Twill be mighty useful for him, sir," the second Nethersole boy
added sententiously.

Meantime Miss Rochefort was steadfastly and longingly gazing
at a barrel, her position such that Mr. Crundall must sooner or later
see her.

As shortly he did. " You come for your elevenses, young lady ? "
he chuckled, highly tickled by her antics.

Her innermost thoughts so obviously revealed, Caroline affected a
very proper confusion. She frankly confessed that never in her
whole life had she tasted apples so sweet and so juicy.

" But, Mr. Crundall, there are such, such a lot of us," she said
nobly. " You couldn't give all of us . . . "

Mr. Crundall slapped his knee joyously and very soon began the
distribution of the rosiest and largest apples possible to set eyes on,
with supplies for those who still waited hopefully outside.

On the beach, low down by the softly rippling sea, the company
sat down, cheeks bulging, steadily champing away.

" Wonder how they ever got those enormous stones there ? "
someone asked.

It was low water and directly before them were the massive
remnants of the King's Foundation.

" Charles'll know," the Chamberlain's daughter said admiringly.

Whereas Charles winced when the Jellybag's moist eye caught his,
Caroline glanced scornfully at that girl, and continued to regard her
unwaveringly until long after the story of the gigantic boulders began.

F

"When King Henry VIII decided to build the Foundation," the narrator started off, his enunciation distinctly blurred by a mouth too full.

Not more than half a dozen of the young people went off in search of other amusement, though amongst these was Charles's sister, Minnie, who climbed up on to the South Pier. There, lately, sentries had been regularly posted.

"This John Young . . ." Charles continued, "proved by using nuts and eggshells that great weights could be lifted by buoyancy and then carried along by the sea. The stones came from Folkestone, where at low water barrels and pipes of wood were fastened to them and later, when the water rose, the whole lot was towed here."

Louis Rochefort wanted to know what King Henry gave to the ingenious gentleman and, on hearing the amount of the life pension, expressed the view that Mr. Young was a most indifferent business man.

More tales followed, some new, some very old favourites. There was the story of Spanish seamen being sold in the Market Place at £100 apiece and of their being placed in the jail until their friends paid—a highly profitable scheme for the then mayor until the Privy Council in London became cognizant of his little game. And there was the account of King Henry leaving Dover in the darkness of night for the Field of the Cloth of Gold, with that romantic picture of the bluff monarch standing on the tall poop of a lovely ship, two hundred flaming torches lighting the historic scene.

The sunny minutes passed, with an audience sprawled in various attitudes on the shingle.

"Time for dinner," Louis Rochefort said as St. Mary the Virgin's struck again. Scrambling up he flung a healthy-sized pebble down the beach where, some fifty yards away, it whizzed perilously close to Mr. Ralph Toke and a subordinate, who had been examining a charred heap of snuff and tobacco. Such seized goods, when at the subsequent auction no bid equalled the duty on them, were always publicly burnt.

The Revenue Officer's angry eyes searched for the culprit, but all he saw was a small group whose innocence of mien could hardly have been improved upon.

"How did your papa get on last winter?" Louis afterwards grinningly asked, surreptitiously jerking his head towards Mr. Toke.

Charles had any amount of confidence in his father. Louis Rochefort was given to understand that the Revenue Officer had proved but a negligible factor, however Mr. Toke might have bragged when first he came to the town.

This conclusion did not entirely meet the case. John Fagg, long before the coming autumn's campaign, had decided he must exercise the utmost caution in all he did.

3

One crisp afternoon in mid-October, John Fagg was at the warehouse working out the account of a coal voyage. " Price coal purchased," he muttered. " Keel dues at Newcastle, Trinity House duties, trimming, an' beer for keelmen. Then——"

This collier was regularly employed between the Northumbrian port and London. At the capital its owner had to allow also for the King's Duty, the charges payable towards the upkeep of the Nore Light, and the selling commission of one-half of one per cent.

" Incidental charges," he mumbled. " Victuals, clearing at Gravesend, pilotage and candles. Then wages——"

At this stage Captain Nethersole presented himself.

" How are you, John ? " he roared. " Will you be at home to-night ? " He went on to explain that he had been puzzling over a new method for scouring the harbour bar and would like to talk about it.

" I'll be very pleased, Jeremy," John Fagg said heartily. " An' bring Mrs. Nethersole along wi' you, though . . . " he was perfectly solemn, " you mustn't stay too long."

The discourteous proviso did not evoke any resentment, nevertheless Captain Nethersole's reply was rather extraordinary.

" You an' Mrs. F. going to bed early ? "

" That's it, Jeremy," the shipowner twinkled, " we're going to bed early. Methinks a good long rest'll brighten things up."

Captain Nethersole winked broadly and remarked, *sotto voce*, that his *spirits* were low, too.

Towards the end of these ambiguous exchanges there was a shrill scream in the distance. The woman's voice was almost immediately drowned by an angry uproar.

" Press gang," Captain Nethersole vouchsafed laconically. Two men, he added, had already been taken in the Market Place and a rare fight there had been when a rescue was attempted.

Both gentlemen agreed that it was a sorry business, but the Navy needed more recruits and there was no disputing that soon old England, unless change came quickly, would find herself in a most awkward position, with the last of her allies broken.

" This Bonaparte," the seaman growled, " is overrunning Austria and Sardinia as rapid as you like, an' if they both fall before him——"

" We maybe shall have need for all the gamekeepers an' licence-holders that Mr. Pitt is suggesting should enrol in the supplementary militia," John Fagg commented succinctly.

"Aye, shouldn't wonder, John," Captain Nethersole grunted as he made for the door.

When he was alone Mr. Fagg again got down to his figures. There was common wear and tear on the ship to be provided for, and interest on its value, each of these taking five pounds per cent, to which had to be added insurance at one pound per cent per month.

"Mmmm . . ." the shipowner muttered at last, pushing aside the papers and rising to pace the room. Within the last few minutes he had proved that heightening costs had largely offset the additional gain he had expected from the steadily increasing war demand for coal.

"Well . . ." he murmured in conclusion, and with that proceeded with more pressing matters.

In such wise the afternoon passed.

The graveyard of St. James's Church, beneath the Castle Hill, was the scene of that night's run. There, in the blackness of the night, a single lantern cast its yellow light over crazy-leaning tombstones and on the soft carpet of grass and the pale gold of fallen leaves.

"Keep moving, my lads," John Fagg said quietly.

In continuous procession they came up from the sea, treading silently along the boards which the 'free-trader' had caused to be laid over the betraying shingle, their passage seldom heard unless, further inshore, one chanced to step on a twig, or acorn, or fir cone.

"Four hundred dollops passed," the checker, one of Mr. Fagg's clerks, murmured without looking from the book in which he made the tally.

"Very good," the shipowner observed evenly.

He was standing on a rickety, box-like tomb, staring beyond the Ropewalk and harbour to the southward where, past Archcliffe Point, down towards the base of Shakespeare's Cliff, he could see many moving lights. From there also came many a shout as Valentine Pepper and his half-score of self-chosen dare-devils acted decoy, giving Mr. Toke and the Preventivemen plenty of exertion at least.

"Five hundred, sir," the report came.

Still they came up from the boats, looming into the light and then vanishing quickly into the darkness towards the waiting carts. Some portaged casks of brandy, ready slung, but the majority bore dollops of tea, *ex* Scheveningen, canvas-sewn packages each containing forty pounds nett weight.

"Ah ! . . ." the shipowner ejaculated.

From a third of the way up the more accessible slope of Shakespeare's Cliff a blue light thrice swung widely, and then fell in an arc towards the beach as Captain Pepper, having done all he could, got rid of the lantern and began to think of his own safety.

John Fagg dropped off the tombstone and, after inquiring how much tea still remained, made a quick calculation. He reckoned he had eight minutes left.

" Right," he said briskly, " bring the lot up, and then . . . every man away."

Down to the sea he next went, until thigh deep he was standing by the nearest boat. Sixty casks of brandy were as yet waterborne.

" Can't do them," he decided. " We'll have to sink 'em here, old Diddlum, and recover later."

" Aye, aye, Mr. Fagg," came the confident response from the inky gloom.

The free-trader gave final instructions. " Small sinkers," he ordered. " Twelve foot o' line with cork markers. Let 'em go half a cable out."

Only the spirits of the dead were in the quiet churchyard of St. James's when Mr. Toke and his men arrived. But there was a trail of tea from a punctured dollop, and a two-way track of planks as evidence of a large and carefully-planned run.

" Looks like Fagg again, sir," Clement Foxley panted.

The enraged Revenue Officer made no reply. There still might be stragglers about and if one of these could be taken it might be possible to pin on to Fagg . . .

" Matson, Barley, Cutson and Broome," he snapped. " You four will take——"

There was a startled oath and a yell of terror. Before Mr. Toke knew what was about, his men were flying in every direction, with a mortally affeared Assistant diving straight into a tombstone as well.

There was, perhaps, excuse. It was, after all, a graveyard at dead o' night, and a piece of white-painted canvas cut in the shape of a human, suspended from a low branch and weighted at the bottom, can be a most alarming sight when, in such circumstances, it is swayed eerily by a puff of wind.

Ten minutes passed before Ralph Toke collected together the men under his command.

4

For some months a dispute had been raging between the pilots of Dover and Deal as to the ground each covered. Dover pilots, so the Deal men swore, had been seen well to the eastward of the South Foreland, and the Deal lodesmen, their Dover colleagues took oath on it, had been observed soliciting Thames-bound ships as far west as the Red Fall at Folkestone.

To settle the dispute the Court of Loadmanage was summoned for the last day of the year. The full meeting, according to custom, was held in the little church of St. James's.

At the end of the sitting Mr. Henry Rochefort might have been seen leaving the church in company with Mr. Paul Elam, Master of Lodesmen.

" A touch of frost about, Mr. Elam," the banker commented.

The two gentlemen were passing Little Pent House at that moment, with Butchery Gate, the Island, and Severus's Gate ahead.

Mr. Rochefort's presence at the Court of Loadmanage had had no connection with the differences of the pilots of Dover and Deal. There had been a subsidiary dispute, a local one. The Dover pilots, who paid into a common fund amounts according to their status and employment, had been demanding from their Master an account of his stewardship. Mr. Rochefort, as banker to the fellowship, had been requested to attend.

" And indeed quite sharp for this time of the year, Mr. Rochefort," Mr. Elam remarked in that light-coloured voice of his.

Considering the season, it was a foolish submission, but then the Master of Lodesmen was still shaken by the aspersions which had been passed on his probity, a point-blank refusal on his part to produce evidence of disbursements being the cause of that.

Mr. Rochefort had already formed an opinion as to the honesty of his companion and, beyond the civilities, did not attempt to further the conversation. Nevertheless, one piece of news to which Paul Elam happened to refer did cause him to take considerable notice.

" A new road to Dover, Mr. Elam ! " the banker exclaimed. " By Limekiln Street, you say ? "

It was most singular that the Master of Lodesmen, who once before had spoken to Henry Rochefort of the pilots' need for houses near the Look-out, should now give him information which, if true, would substantially increase the value of Paradise Pent as building land.

" Quite settled it is, Mr. Rochefort," Mr. Elam declared, after disclosing that the government, for military reasons, were paying a major part of the cost.

The banker, both then and for some hours later, before he set out to bring home his daughter from a New Year's Eve party, was extremely thoughtful. He did not at all like the financial outlook, being sure there was much disorder amongst the country banks and in the paper circulation, and already he was withdrawing as much coin as possible from London. The growing invasion scare had made the money markets wildly erratic, and the vast outpourings of coin and bullion to Continental allies had aggravated a most difficult situation.

Henry Rochefort eventually determined to sound Edward Hexstall that night. The war, judging by the present, might last for years, and he was now virtually resolved gradually to bring certain bank matters on to a footing he had long believed to be desirable.

It had been a lovely party, with spillikins, riddles, conundrums and every other jolly game imaginable. But it was drawing towards nine o'clock now and the small children were becoming querulous.

Henry Rochefort brought his conversation with Mr. Hexstall to a close . . . nearly. It had dwelt on the issue of Spanish dollars, the use of which had been forced on the country by the never-ending demand for silver for an immensely valuable Eastern trade.

" 'Tis most strange, Mr. Rochefort," Mr. Hexstall smiled agreeably. " I mean our use of the coinage of a country with which we are at war."

The banker was looking around for his daughter. He had already sighted Lou Fagg, and to be sure that very faithful friend was near to Caroline.

" And how is business with you, Mr. Hexstall ? " he inquired conversationally. " I suppose present-day costs make the price of building quite prohibitive ? "

Edward Hexstall, who acted as Surveyor to several local authorities, was also the most prominent builder in the district.

" Not at all, Mr. Rochefort," he reacted warmly. " 'Tis true the cost of materials has advanced, but nothing like one would have expected."

" Not so much, for example, as the price of the essential foods ? " the banker remarked, beckoning his girl.

The Town Surveyor was no fool. " May I ask, Mr. Rochefort, if you contemplate any building ? "

Henry Rochefort gave him to understand, in confidence, that the possibility existed. And Mr. Hexstall, in reply, vowed that he would most certainly respect that confidence, and would gladly await the banker's further word.

5

Miss Caroline Rochefort had a most secretive appointment with a gentleman, one so important that she had decided both to wear her best clothes and to play truant.

The escape from home, in her new winter coat and latest bonnet, was the less easy of these. Martha *would* fuss before she left.

Ultimately Miss Rochefort carried out her purpose by the simplest device. After breakfast she hurried to her pleasant bedroom overlooking the Pent. Taking from the clothes-press the desired clothes, she rapidly changed.

"There!" she exclaimed, eyeing herself with satisfaction.

Next came the cautious descent of the stairs and then the making sure that Martha was in the small room off the hall.

Caroline's next move, if crude, promised to be effective. There was a flight of stone steps to the basement kitchens. Immediately behind the door which gained the hall was a shelf on which were various stock utensils, not least of which were metal strainers and a number of pans. A good push set them falling; there was a most infernal noise as these articles clattered to the bottom.

"For goodness' sake," Martha Teddiman gasped, darting from the housekeeper's apartment.

The excitement below was not less intense and when the daughter of the house glanced down, after re-entering the hall from the little drawing-room, she saw that Martha had joined cook and two of the girls.

"Martha, dear," she cooed, "I'm going now."

The housekeeper seemed half inclined to come upstairs, but a vehement reassurance checked her.

"Well, Miss Caroline," she said, "if you're sure you've covered up your throat an'——"

Miss Rochefort, calling out a gay good-bye, skipped for the front door, and soon was walking along Snargate Street.

Captain Pepper duly awaited her outside the Albion Library. The bow window of the establishment was filled with those delightful cards which formed the object of the meeting. There were Valentines in silver and in gold, with arrows, hearts, lovers' knots, and charmingly sentimental greetings.

"'Tis what she'd like I'm sure," Captain Pepper beamed, "an' if you'd go an' buy that one, Miss Caroline——"

"We must see what else they've got," he was firmly told.

Captain Pepper's face fell. "Me go in there an' ax to look at——"

His small companion eyed him coldly. "You want dear Martha to have the very nicest, don't you?"

"I does," the boatswain agreed wretchedly. "But . . ."

The little madam would not hear his excuses and, miserably, Captain Pepper trailed into the premises.

It was to be a very proper shopping call. Miss Rochefort, graciously acknowledging the assistant who came forward at the tinkle of the bell, seated herself.

"May we," she asked politely, "see some more of your selexshun of Valentines?"

Half an hour later Valentine Pepper was sweating profusely, though faint hope was beginning to dawn in him. The counter, it was true, was bestrewn with discarded cards, but Miss Caroline retained one at least. On this she consulted him.

" You couldn't find a better nor that, Miss Caroline," the boatswain urged eagerly.

At last the choice was made and a suitable withdrawal made.

" Did I act well ? " Captain Pepper was asked after the small lady had minced out.

" You did, miss," he groaned in reply, his sole thought the need for a call at the Fountain.

Arrangements were then discussed as to how Martha should receive her Valentine and, this settled, Captain Pepper decided to proceed towards the Market Place.

" So you're a-coming my way, Miss Caroline ? " he said.

That lady, perceptibly starting, gave him her attention, but he perceived the nature of the shop at which she had been looking. There he purchased two halfpenny sticks of Spanish for her.

" Oooh, thank you so, so much, Captain Pepper," she danced delightedly, prior to silencing herself with the sweetmeat.

The pair proceeded along Bench Street, and then into King Street.

" You still along of me, Miss Caroline," Captain Pepper chuckled. " I reckon you must know where I be a-going."

Miss Rochefort said nothing, but her darkly-ringed mouth opened in a smile which disclosed sadly stained teeth.

At the top of King Street Captain Pepper crossed the road, his companion following faithfully. Before he reached the Fountain Inn the boatswain was beginning to glance down somewhat uneasily.

" Well, now, Miss Caroline . . . " he mumbled. " An' . . . an' where be your destiny ? "

A melting pair of brown eyes were fixed on him. " I can't go home yet," their owner said piteously. " Not till school comes out."

" Then . . . " Captain Pepper observed desperately, " you'd better come with me."

Miss Rochefort enjoyed the Fountain where, with little regard for her fine coat, she sat on a table soiled with sticky circles. She had two lemonades and, respectively from three gentlemen who made a great fuss about her, a mouthful of mulled ale, a sip of punch, and a pull at a churchwarden pipe.

There was much talk in the warm room. It was widely rumoured that the French were massing troops on the northern coasts of France.

They little knew, those in the Fountain who agreed or disagreed on the prospect of invasion, that on the same day, St. Valentine's Day, a serious attempt at invasion had been foiled.

The Spanish fleet, slipping out of Cadiz to effect juncture with the

French fleet, the joint purpose the carriage of an invading force to
England, had been caught off Cape St. Vincent by Sir John Jervis and
Commodore Horatio Nelson.   Fourteen English sail-of-the-line gave
the thrashing of their lives to the twenty-seven of the enemy.

The news, when it arrived five days later, had a heartening effect
on a people who were growing despondent. It was to prove, however,
the solitary flash of light in a remorselessly deepening gloom.

*   *   *   *   *   *   *   *

Before the rejoicings for the battle of St. Vincent had faded, the
French made another attempt at invasion, this time in Fishguard Bay.
The effort failed and although there might be an amusing side to this
venture there was another far more disturbing, one which definitely
proved that the old chivalrous days of warfare had gone ; that the
new conception of the art of war, as brought into being by the French,
was the attainment of victory by whatever dastardly means might
best serve.

" Ugh ! " John Fagg growled contemptuously, glaring over the
newspaper.

The red cloaks of the Welsh women lining the hills around Fishguard had signally disconcerted the French commander-in-chief, he
at first believing that an army was drawn up for his reception. The
shipowner had laughed at a mistake which had been invaluable to the
scanty number of defenders, but after that his expression grew grim.
Papers, seized from the staff of the invading force, containing orders
for the conduct of the campaign, were the reason for his anger.

" Well, George," he said scathingly, " your friends across the water
appear to believe that the waging of war is best accomplished by doing
so on women and children."

George Rochefort paled perceptibly at the unexpected thrust.

" If you will kindly explain yourself, John," he retorted, at once
in arms.

John Fagg threw over the single sheet.

This occurred in the drawing-room of Little Pent House, the two
men being alone. The mistress of the house, together with her sister-
in-law, were in the dining-room giving last touches to the supper table.

" Well ? " the shipowner demanded. " Small wonder, ain't it,
that they've subjugated half the Continent if they've used those bestial
methods ? "

For the quick conquest of any country, so were the instructions of
the French staff, it was necessary to ' destroy all public utilities ' and
' to spread terror amongst the population.' Thereby, it was pronounced, the prospects of success would be immeasurably enhanced.

" It . . . it may be, John," George Rochefort began, whiter than ever, "that even the regrettable wrong done to the minority may result more quickly to the greater good of the majority."

"There isn't a decent Englishman who would countenance such brutal precept," John Fagg declared bluntly. "Nor, I hope, one who wouldn't fight to the last drop of his blood against those who supported it."

That attack on Fishguard, and the knowledge of the preparations in progress on the northern coasts of France, had many repercussions. Already the deficiency of gold and silver, brought about by the immensity of the subsidies to the Allies, had caused a profound weakening of the financial structure, and now the scare of invasion created a further strain on the central institution. Every bank in the country had been withdrawing coin from the Bank of England, and there could be only one end to the drain.

Two days later the Bank suspended cash payments.

Past midnight for three days candles burned in Mr. Rochefort's bank on Snargate Street-over-the-Wall. On the morning of the fourth day the senior partner called for the chief clerk.

"Mr. Godspenny," Henry Rochefort said wearily. "I want you to find Mr. Edward Hexstall. Present him with my compliments and ask him to make it in his way to come here at once."

"Yes, sir," Matthew Godspenny replied promptly.

The House of Rochefort was in no manner seriously involved. But Henry Rochefort had had a nasty fright.

In due course the Town Surveyor was ushered in. He was asked to furnish plans and submit estimates for the erection of twenty residences on Paradise Pent.

6

During her long history England has suffered many vicissitudes, but never had her people been so stunned as in April of that year. It seemed unbelievable, it was surely the end.

When the news reached Dover a number of gentlemen in the Antwerp Hotel were maliciously displaying one of Mr. Gillray's masterpieces to Mr. Jonathan Dawkes the Postmaster and Mr. Robert Spisour the Water Bailiff, ardent Whigs both.

The cartoon was brilliant. Mr. Pitt was revealed in the brawny clutch of Mr. Fox, the latter unmistakably a fiendish Republican. The Prime Minister, subsequently and most audaciously, was shown to have turned the tables.

"What I say is this," blustered the unhappy Water Bailiff.

Then the incredible information came.

" Mutinied ! " Mr. Stratton the Town Clerk gasped. " The fleet at the Nore has mutinied ! "

After that a queer silence descended over the room, descended over the port, hung like a pall over the kingdom.

That afternoon George Rochefort was taking Susan for a walk over that part of the Western Heights not yet closed off by the military. Quite a number of people remained up there despite the counter-attraction of a small packet which was landing French prisoners-of-war. The day being fairly clear, many hoped to glimpse the large forces on the coast little more than twenty miles opposite.

" George, dearest," Susan Fagg began, lovingly glancing at him, " are you very worried about something ? "

Sharply he pulled himself out of the brown study into which he had sunk.

" Worried . . . worried ? No, my love," he laughed lightly. " 'Tis only that the prevailing atmosphere is hardly conducive to gaiety."

" You mean everybody talking about invasion, George ? "

" I suppose so," he replied, suddenly irritable.

They were slowly sauntering back, she holding on to his arm. For a while after that neither spoke.

Then, carefully avoiding mention of those doings which disturbed her, she started to chat, as brightly as she could, on other matters, inconsequential little matters. Nor did she so much as look at a notice, a new notice it was, on a post by the side of the military road. She knew what its purport was, as did every soul in the coastal areas of Kent. The Commissary General of the Southern District had issued instructions regarding the civilian use of the turnpikes in the event of a French landing. These, it declared in heavy type, must strictly be kept clear for military traffic.

She thought she was persuading him from his gloom when, at the sound of an unpleasant voice, her heart sank. The young man she knew by sight, and she had a vague idea that he was one of those who attended the earlier meetings of the Society her dear love had formed.

" Harkee, Rochefort," this horrible creature jeered viciously. " Congratulations to you and all your renegade friends."

" What the devil do you mean, sir ? " George Rochefort demanded violently.

" I mean, sir," thundered the young man, oblivious of the female who was trying to draw him away, " that you have succeeded in planting your rotten principles amongst those who can do our . . . no, *my* country most harm. You will be pleased to learn, I doubt not, that the fleet has mutinied."

"The fleet . . . has mutinied," Henry Rochefort's brother murmured slowly.

"Yes, you dirty——"

They were fighting now, a fierce fight in which, though Susan's lover was a good stone lighter, he came out victor, but a sorry sight.

"I ask your pardon, my love," he said shamefacedly.

"Oh, George, you are hurt." Tears were fast welling in her blue eyes.

Thereafter he stated bitterly that she would be better without him, and thereupon she said she could not exist without him.

"I could not, George, dear," she sobbed. "Please, George, do not allow anything . . . *anything* to part us."

He was staring at Paradise Pent, upon which he remarked, freshly deposited there, timber and bricks, all the evidence of Henry's intention.

"I fear, m'dear," he observed soberly, "that soon the name of Rochefort will stink in your brother's nostrils."

So strange was his tone that Susan Fagg looked up in perplexity. "But, George, dearest," she asked wonderingly, "why should John——"

He smiled humourlessly. "'Tis better, my dear, that you do not know now. I protest you will soon enough."

George Rochefort was right. On the morrow, as John Fagg walked along Elizabeth Street, he at once saw the preparations. Before the end of the week he learnt who was responsible.

"Henry Rochefort!" his wife gasped when she heard.

Polly Fagg dropped into a chair. Her husband's back was towards her; he had walked to the right-hand parlour window and, though his head was facing the pier-heads, he was in such fury that he saw little of a view of which he never tired.

7

Most of John Fagg's anger had passed with the night, and only regret remained. Once more he looked across Elizabeth Street, then sighing faintly he bestirred himself and called in Captain Pepper.

"I'm going along to the bank, Valentine," he said quietly. "You'll send out a boat to the *Annie* with instructions."

Captain Pepper deftly squirted tobacco juice into a spittoon. "Aye, aye, sir," he responded smartly.

The *Annie* was in ballast off Archcliffe Point, back from a trip in which she had brought Yorkshire woollens down to London. She was now to go on to Arundel, and there load up with beech pit rails for delivery to Newcastle.

"We'll have to put another on the same service too, Valentine," Mr. Fagg continued. "The armaments works are clamouring for coal and the collieries are hard put to keep up with the demand."

There were two or three other minor matters to attend to, and then, these completed, he left the warehouse.

Strond Street, with its fine residential houses of the Stuart period, was quiet as usual, but Snargate Street-over-the-Wall was, as always in business hours, fairly thronged. Most of those going about their affairs there, whether merchants or clerks, glanced curiously at John Fagg, for the news had speedily got about concerning the project which must inevitably cause a deep rift between the shipowner and Henry Rochefort.

Matthew Godspenny, behind the counter of the bank, greeted the familiar caller. Yes, Mr. Rochefort was in his room, and yes, certainly, he would tell Mr. Rochefort that Mr. Fagg was there. Promptly he abandoned the latest War Loan offer which the junior partner had calculated yielded £6 6s. 10d. per cent.

"Good-morning, Henry," John Fagg said gravely, when the door closed.

"Good-morning, John," the banker replied.

It was a strange meeting. John Fagg standing instead of relaxing into a chair, and Henry Rochefort rising formally rather than giving a careless and friendly little nod.

"I am informed that you are building houses on Paradise Pent," John Fagg asked quietly. "Is that correct?"

There was just the least appearance of dismay in the banker's mien, as if he realised that earlier he should have disclosed what he proposed doing, instead of leaving himself open to be charged as though he had committed a crime.

He did not prevaricate. "Quite correct, John," he said clearly.

The shipowner made no attempt to argue. He was concerned only with giving a warning couched in the most unmistakable terms.

"You know my views about building on reclaimed land, and my views on the folly of thus strengthening the hand of the Harbour Commissioners," he opened crisply. "And so I won't trouble you with them again. But I do intend to tell you, here and now, that I shall continue to fight them, and to fight such as you, until the time that I succeed in my aim."

"Such as me . . ." Henry Rochefort said sharply, for he had read into those words something of contempt.

"That's what I said, Henry," his caller confirmed imperturbably.

For a short space it appeared as if the banker would not be able to curb a temper that was gradually rising. And, though he did so, the strain at first was apparent. But he did succeed, eventually, in moderately putting forward his own point of view.

"This isn't a matter of mere gain," retorted John Fagg.

Mr. Rochefort did not pursue that aspect. He went on, emphatically, to express the firm conviction that Dover Harbour, from the very nature of the disabilities under which it suffered, could have no prosperous future. Had he thought otherwise, he admitted it freely, he might have felt differently about building.

"But if the harbour becomes useless, then not only will the Passage be lost but the town as well, for we can look to nothing else here," John Fagg persisted. "Then where will you be with your property?"

The banker laughed. "That will be a long time ahead," he observed. "And . . ." his dark eyes glowed with pride, "I am sure that Louis, in his time, would see that advantageous disposal was made long before others realised that their investments might be in jeopardy."

Mr. Fagg picked up his hat. "We see things differently, sadly so. But . . ." he could not resist the taunt, "I suppose us Faggs must have a greater interest in this stretch of coast than any newcomers."

"Newcomers!" snapped Henry Rochefort. "Like all you Kent men you can never forget that——"

"Or it may be," John Fagg soliloquised maddeningly, "that bankers have nothing more than specks o' gold sluggishly oozing in their veins."

Henry Rochefort laughed harshly. "Enough of them to build what property I like and where I choose."

"But this setback in Limekiln Street'll not stop me from fighting the Harbour Commissioners, and that's my purpose," the shipowner countered grimly.

The banker, his hands resting on a stack of the new £1 and £2 notes the Bank of England had issued, leaned over the table.

"And I'll still go on building where I will, my friend," he retaliated sarcastically. "Which means, if I might so point out to you, increased revenue for the Commissioners."

John Fagg's shoulder was towards him and so he did not see the impish flash which passed through those steady and shrewd grey eyes. Certainly it was all gone when the shipowner turned.

"And maybe I'll do a little building soon, *my friend*," he growled.

"You'll build?" Henry Rochefort inquired ironically.

It would seem that the jibe, small as it was, caused John Fagg, there and then, to determine on a course which he hardly meant.

"Yes, I'll build," he roared. "I'll put up one or two eleg⸗

houses with a view second to none in the town, even though I'll not receive the ten per cent you'll demand for the guineas you lay out."

" You will, will you ? " shouted the banker.

As he passed through the doorway the shipowner's smile was not nice, of a quality such as made the banker bent on thwarting, even anticipating, whatever it was his erstwhile friend contemplated.

For a while Mr. Rochefort sat thinking, and then rose to look at a plan hanging on the wall, one which Mr. Hexstall had made of the town.

The land inshore of the Basin and Pent to the cliff behind Snargate Street was fully occupied ; Paradise Pent he had acquired himself, and to the southward of the Tidal Harbour there were only Mr. Crundall's shipbuilding yards and lowly habitations, no locality fitting for the erection of good quality residences.

" A view second to none in the town," he puzzled, repeating those words which, relative to John Fagg's pride in the situation of Little Pent House, he had often heard before. That gave him the clue.

" Town Wall Street," he said quickly, excited now.

Then, with a thrill, he found the site, along Town Wall Street towards Severus's Gate, the same place on which aforetime he had heard John Fagg vaguely speak about building.

" The Island ! " he said triumphantly, staring at that place where the Dour divided after passing under Butchery Gate.

He began to consider the possibilities. To give direct access from Town Wall Street it would be a simple matter to fill in the shallow branch of the Dour, diverting the water to the other. Yes. . . .

Henry Rochefort was quite aware that the man whom he intended to humiliate was one who could act quickly.

His destination was the Council House. This time there was no necessity for undue discretion, and the tall and dignified banker turned left as he emerged through the bank's portals.

Ten days later the agreement was signed whereby Henry Rochefort became the lessee of that area of land bounded to the one side by Severus's Gate and the foundations of the old town wall and to the other by the outer channel of the Dour from Butchery Gate to the Pent.

The Clerk of the Cheque received, on this occasion, an unmistakable hint from Mr. Rochefort and, much as Mr. Waade disliked the banker, he acted very promptly upon the half suggestion, being exceedingly conscious of the intimacy which was growing between Sir Walter and Mr. Rochefort.

Thus it was that, speedily, the news was brought to John Fagg of the march which Henry Rochefort had stolen on him.

In public the shipowner fumed a great deal, but in private his tude was peculiarly different.

"Charles," he said, as much as two months later, "what was that piece of poetry you used to say about the river yonder?"

Charles Fagg was fifteen now, but he had not forgotten the bridge-building efforts of his childhood, nor those lines of a former Master of the Maison Dieu.

He grinned.

"Drop a spade into the Dour,
An' the water's a' o'er."

His father nodded several times. "Aye, to be sure, my boy," John Fagg remarked smoothly. "Aye, to be sure."

But after that he said no more. Nor would he, on Mrs. Fagg's curiosity rising, give any explanation for the inquiry he had made.

8

Gradually it became known that the mutiny at the Nore had not arisen through the sowing of abominable foreign doctrines. Instead it was that the men of the fleet had genuine grievances which, had the Board of Admiralty been wiser, should long before have been rectified. Woefully wrong-headed, indeed criminally foolish, had been the method used to seek redress, but there could be no possible question as to the loyalty of the mutineers.

And how nobly was this demonstrated in the early autumn of that year when the men under Admiral Duncan . . . the same men who had so strikingly drawn attention to victuals not fit to eat, to pay which was hardly worth the name, to a treatment often too tyrannous, to a blockading service which took superhuman toll of their bodies . . . proved their deathless devotion at Camperdown.

There, by their courage and matchless seamanship, they once again won victory in a conflict which, with that of St. Vincent eight months before, was the present salvation of their country. The Dutch fleet, escaping from the Texel and bearing a force for the overrunning of Ireland, was annihilated.

In Dover, the eight bells in the tower of St. Mary the Virgin's rang out a joyous thanksgiving.

But, before Dr. Woodgate preached his next sermon in the old church, the devastating news came that the Austrian Emperor had been compelled to capitulate. By the Treaty of Campo Formio, Belgium and Lombardy were finally surrendered to the insatiable French.

"One morsel of brightness and then a cruel knock-back," sighed Mrs. Jelly, wife of the Chamberlain.

" 'Tis terrible," agreed Mrs. Nicholas Stokes. " What with food at such wicked prices an' . . . "

The two ladies had met on the Cross Wall, where both had been buying fish. They were not friends, far from it, but trouble makes many a strange bedfellow.

" This General Bonaparte must surely be a wizard," Mrs. Jelly remarked lugubriously. " Whatever he attempts——"

There was a slight diversion as a phaeton and pair came by from the direction of Council House Street.

" My ! " ejaculated the Clerk of the Passage's good lady, eyeing the filthied vehicle in which, furious-faced, sat Sir Walter Plumbley. The Harbour Commissioner had had a most unpleasant experience but a minute or so before when a crowd from the Plain district, enraged that a few mean wooden habitations, on reclaimed land, were being pulled down to clear the area for leasing purposes, had made an attack on him. His horses had been held whilst the mob, empty bellies making them quite careless of the consequences, pelted him with every handful of foul refuse on which they could lay hands.

" Outrageous ! " declared the well-informed, quick-witted Mrs. Jelly. With lips tightened she stated her opinion of the scum who could thus treat a real gentleman.

" They've lived down there for a score years, haven't they ? " Mrs. Stokes demanded, immediately aggressive.

Here was difference, wide difference and, it might justly be said, the view of officialdom on the one hand and that of the less well-entrenched section of the community on the other.

Had it not been that Mr. John Fagg passed then, there seemed every probability that the two ladies would have pursued that particular difference. As it was the shipowner's grim visage gave them an even better theme.

" I protest," tittered Mrs. Jelly, " that Mr. Fagg barely spoke civil to us. One wonders just what must have so mortified him."

If Mrs. Jelly was quick-witted, then Mrs. Stokes was as sharp as they make 'em. She knew what John Fagg's business at the Council House had been that day and she rightly guessed the shipowner had received from Sir Walter and Mr. Waade a bland refusal to consider the harbour improvement scheme upon which he and her husband, with the faithful co-operation of Mr. Breton, Captain Nethersole, and Mr. Crundall, had laboured for eighteen months.

" And pray what, Mrs. Jelly, do you imagine has put Mr. Fagg out of humour ? " she whipped back.

From then Mrs. Jelly began to be evasive, for Jelly would hardly be pleased if she passed on information Mr. Waade had confidentially given him.

Mrs. Stokes's expression portrayed her thoughts on these weak outpourings and her tongue that she was in no danger of being deceived.

"Fie, Mrs. Jelly," she said scornfully, "you know perfectly well why Mr. Fagg is like to be in a passion. Oh, yes, Mrs. Jelly, I swear you are well enough acquainted with what is taking place an' 'tis shame on you."

"And for why, Mrs. Stokes?" snapped the Chamberlain's wife.

"Because," she heard in stern reply, "there should not be two factions on the question of the haven."

That was exactly what John Fagg was thinking as he walked with quick step along Snargate Street, past Henry Rochefort's house and then Severus's Gate. Means must be found to force home to the people of Dover just what was in jeopardy if the harbour were permitted to fall to the lowly estate of Rye's, of . . .

In his abstraction the shipowner very nearly came to grief over the handle of a wheelbarrow. Pulled up short, he saw that the inshore branch of the Dour was being filled with rubble and that building operations would soon begin on the Island.

At that sight his dourness fleetingly passed; a glint came into his eyes, and a tiny smile played about his mouth. Then he continued home.

"Well?" Polly Fagg asked, coming into the hall to meet him, her glance going to the rolled plan he carried.

He shook his head. "Sir Walter very kindly advised me of a piece of Dover's history," he said wryly. "By King James's Charter, so he apprised me, all authority in the haven is vested in the Commissioners, who feel themselves entirely capable of conducting its affairs."

"Oh, John," Mrs. Fagg murmured, shocked. "And after all the labour you've all given to it. 'Tis cruel."

It was not a very happy evening, what with this blow to ardent hope and the dark shadow stealing from across the seas. Of this last the worried mistress of the house tried to elicit her husband's views.

"I don't know, my dear," John Fagg said quietly. "But I fear that troublous days lie ahead of us."

In grey November the Directory proclaimed that "England and the French Republic cannot both continue to exist." The brilliant young Citizen-General Bonaparte was appointed to the *Armée de l'Angleterre*.

CHAPTER NINE

I

IN the Channel ports of France and in the shipyards of the Batavian Republic flat-bottomed boats were being built by the hundred, with French agents everywhere purchasing or chartering trading vessels to participate in the great venture. And, day by day, news was passed into England of the horrors with which that peaceful country would soon be assailed. Instead, however, of fear being raised by these terrifying premises, the country found all the spirit she needed.

During that winter, volunteers throughout the land flocked in large numbers to the colours, and in every town meetings were held towards the providing of funds for clothing and accoutrements.

In Dover . . . where, one hundred and fifty-six years before, a handful of jurats had climbed the towering cliff to effect for the Parliamentarians the seizure of the Castle, afterwards successfully held against every Stuart assault by that passionate devotee of freedom, Sir Algernon Sydney . . . such a meeting was cried, belled, and advertised.

The Town meeting was held at Tinker's Close, on the lower slopes of Castle Hill off the Deal Road, and never in the memory of man had there been such a gathering within the liberties, and never had such wildly enthusiastic shouting rent the heavens.

" Harkee to that, Martha," grinned Captain Pepper, eyes aglow. " Did you ever 'ear——"

Mistress Teddiman was on his arm and the boatswain broke off abruptly to deliver a powerful jab in the ribs of a gentleman who, because of the press of folk, could hardly help squeezing against the lady whom the gallant Valentine held in tremendously high regard.

" Did he a 'urt you, love ? " Captain Pepper inquired fondly, his menacing squint still on a luckless individual who appeared to be in some pain.

Martha blushed. " No, Valentine," she said softly. " And I'm sure he didn't . . . sssh."

One of the members of Parliament for Dover began to speak again.

" My friends, what London can do to prepare herself, so can we no less."

From that he started to read extracts from a pamphlet, " Hints for the defence of the Capital." Blockhouses in each square ; barricadoes for every street and a bell to summon inhabitants to their posts ; corner houses to be supplied with grenades ; fire engines to be placed in proper positions.

"All these defensive measures may be taken and more," the gentleman was concluding, when another storm of cheering drowned his words.

"And more, Martha," Captain Pepper declared hoarsely. "Cutlasses an' bayonets an' Spanish knives an'——"

"Valentine ! " begged Miss Teddiman, closing her eyes in horror, to open them quickly when a roar of applause greeted the Mayor.

Mr. William Beverley, prior to appealing for contributions, took a different line.

"There may be a number about 'ere," he shouted, "who prefer to turn a windlass drawing a raft filled with the Frenchies——"

A gale of laughter went off. Not a soul but knew of Mr. Gillray's latest cartoon in which he so cruelly depicted Mr. Fox and Mr. Sheridan thus assisting in the enemy's descent on these shores.

"And . . ." the ropemaker's upheld hand requested silence, "there may be some few, some very few, who would stab us in the back."

Now was hissing and a mass booing, during which Captain Pepper assured the quivering Martha that he was positive the Mayor was not referring to Mr. George.

Following further exhortation, Mr. Beverley spoke of the need for masters to equip their employees for the defence of places of business, and for the inhabitants of the various wards to form themselves into armed associations.

"'Tis my privilege now," he then resumed, "to inform you of the promises already received."

For a small and poor town the list was imposing and, comparatively speaking, was not shamed by the Defence Fund opened at the Bank of England to which the King had donated £20,000, Cabinet Ministers £2,000 and Bishops £1,000 each, with, as contrast, a hundred guineas from the boys of Merchant Taylors' School, this at the sacrifice of avoiding the tuck shop. Regiments had given a day's pay, and seamen and marines ten shillings from their humble pittances.

"Aye," Captain Pepper observed a little over half an hour later when Martha informed him that her master had given two hundred guineas, "an' Mr. Fagg's put all our big craft at the disposal o' the government."

They were on the westerly summit of Castle Hill, from which the boatswain had hoped to glimpse the new-fangled telegraph which the Admiralty had placed at Walmer. He was staring longingly at a vessel cruising towards Cap Gris Nez.

"*Sirius*, 36-gun," he muttered. "Well I remember . . . well——"

"You done your share, Valentine," Martha comforted him.

He came out of his daydream, chuckling. Wait till she saw him in his uniform, with belt, pouch and sling, and . . .

" You've joined the Volunteers ? " she gasped.

" All the lot of us at Elizabeth Street went along of the master," he said proudly.

And, on this martial note, he once again asked for the reply to a question he had put to her a week before.

" I can't, Valentine," Martha Teddiman said unhappily. " I can't wed you."

Until she told him why, he looked like a dog unfairly thrashed. Then he brightened. " I'll wait for you, love," he muttered, blinking all the same. " And for just so long as it needs, God rot my bl——"

" Valentine ! " Mistress Teddiman said sharply.

Captain Pepper, who had already learnt he must keep close watch on what he said, hurriedly swallowed a line of language which, had he uttered it, must surely have damned him for ever with her.

" And you understand, Valentine ? " she asked wistfully.

Of course he understood, bellowing to cheer her up. Nor, declared he, would he have her do otherwise.

" 'Twouldn't be you if you abandoned ship," he roared.

So down the hill they went again, Captain Pepper with an even more possessive hold on her. She was sad because of her refusal, but glad in that she was keeping her word to a beloved and long-dead mistress. She would stay with Miss Caroline and guard her until . . .

" An' 'ow's Mr. George ? " the Captain inquired.

Martha's face was very concerned. He was ill, she thought, dreadfully ill.

" Hmph ! " snorted the boatswain.

Luckily there was diversion. The Cornwall Militia had marched into the town that morning and now, in the gathering dusk, came the Militia of Glamorgan.

When the tramp of feet died away they walked back through streets strangely deserted. It was rumoured that a hot-press was in the neighbourhood, and a hot-press had little regard either for notes of protection or that powerful legal instrument, the apprentice's indentures.

Later, there was supper which Captain Pepper, as Miss Teddiman's future husband, took in the housekeeper's small room.

After that, good-night, a smacking kiss, and their separate ways.

" Good-night, Valentine."

" Good-night, Martha m'dear."

Captain Pepper rolled off into the darkness ; Martha Teddiman went upstairs to cry.

2

Mr. Secretary-at-War Dundas spoke of " putting arms into the hands of the people " and, though the weapons were by no means yet available, the spirit was there amongst a large section of the community.

On the day when Mr. Pitt's niece, the Lady Hester Stanhope, was to present colours to the Dover Volunteers in the presence of the Kentish Light Horse and the Cinque Ports Cavalry, George Rochefort decided to drive Susan over to see the new light-house at Dungeness. He wanted to get away from it all, from the orgy of martial prepara- tion, from people who could talk of nothing else but the long list of puppet republics which the French were setting up, or the rumble of gunfire which that morning had come over the sea.

" 'Tis lovely," sighed John Fagg's sister, taking in the beauty of the sweet countryside ; the hedge hawthorns in full bloom, lilac and laburnum out everywhere, the meadows pleasant with cowslips.

Beyond the little village of Lydd, at a cottage towards the shore, the horse was baited, and backstays, for the easier passage to Dungeness, were borrowed.

" There, m'dear," George Rochefort said, rising after fastening the leathern thongs about her ankles, and then giving her a hand.

So into the yellow wilderness, the foot-boards, snow-shoe like, assisting them over the loose and slippery surface of a shingle desert which, formed by the prevailing winds, had taken up long curving ridges not dissimilar from those in a ploughed field. Here and there, from the region of a thin cluster of rushes, a migratory bird would rise from this breeding-ground of great sea swallows, Shrewsbury terns, pies and sunderlings.

" Why are you so silent, George ? " Susan asked, just as they approached the light-house.

" Silent . . . silent ! " He smiled obscurely. " I am not silent, m'dear."

Nevertheless that was how he continued all day.

In the glass-enclosed room at the top of the new conception they wondered at the seventeen Argand lamps each with its twenty-inch silver-plated reflector, and, at the bottom again, viewed the one patch of green the proud keeper displayed to them—a tiny garden protected by planks, old wreckage, and spread sailcloth.

Then back to Lydd, near which George Rochefort was aroused from his apathy by the sight of a long furrow laid with horse-hair traps for the ensnaring of timid little wheatears.

" The cruelty of man," he muttered. " Still . . . "

"George, dear," whispered Susan Fagg, "please do not be so unhappy."

"There is little in the world to make for happiness," he said sombrely.

His restlessness drove him back home and, that same evening, they walked up Castle Hill through a town now agog with the news that the gunfire of the morning had been caused by the Navy's attack on Ostend. The canal lock-gates there, after successful assault, had been blown up, thereby making infinitely harder the concentration in French ports of the small boats which were being built in Dutch shipyards.

"If . . . if one could be sure that we were engaged in righteous cause, Susan," George Rochefort murmured sadly, "then how glorious indeed would be the opposition which our sailors never fail to put up."

He stared across the gently moving sea. A couple of frigates, as did their sisters over thousands of leagues of sea, in every condition of weather, were maintaining an unrelaxing watch over enemy ports, their purpose to foil that dangerous combination of fleets which might bring overwhelming force against the strained squadrons of the island empire.

"'Tis strange," he thought aloud, " that the future of the British race depends utterly on a few ships and on the band of sorely tried men who man them. Though . . . " his voice fell low, " whether or not it would be better if we succumbed to the French . . . "

On the way down to Little Pent House George Rochefort saw an aged and tattered handbill fluttering from the trunk of a tree.

"100 GUINEAS REWARD" it read, the date being of more than two years before, some three days after a small number of seditious pamphlets had been distributed where they might possibly be found.

"Was I right or were they, Susan ? " he asked broodingly, his eyes running over the blurred print which declared that, out of their subsistence, 420 non-commissioned officers and men would gladly pay the aforementioned sum for information which would bring to justice the person or persons who had infamously attempted to corrupt the loyalty of the Royal Artillery quartered at Dover.

"Please, oh please, George," Susan Fagg begged him, " do not distress yourself more."

He took her arm. " One way or another, my perplexities must shortly resolve themselves, m'dear," he told her tonelessly. " Then, my love, I must follow my convictions, whatever they may be, to the end."

Within a month the plans for the final subjugation of England became slightly more vague. The French General Humbert, it was true, landed in Connaught with a small force and a large number of ells of green and white ribbon for the making of Irish patriot cockades, whilst the invasion preparations in Holland and France continued apace.

But the armies behind the ports began to dwindle, and many weeks passed before the reason was known.

The French, rather than attempt the direct and more conclusive assault upon the coast of an obstinate enemy, had preferred to move to the Levant. General Bonaparte, without the formality of declaring war upon the Sultan of Turkey, overran Egypt, his ultimate objective the striking at England's wealth in India where already, harnessing treachery and treason to the military arm, he had instituted wide intrigue.

At home Mr. Coleridge penned his *Fears in Solitude*, a copy of which the proprietor of the Albion Library obtained, having a standing order in such matters.

The poet was greatly perturbed concerning the horrors which might fall upon his native land :

> " My God, it is a melancholy thing
> For such a man, who would full fain preserve
> His soul in calmness, yet perforce must feel
> For all his human brethren—O my God !
> It weighs upon the heart, that he must think
> What uproar and what strife may now be stirring
> This way or that way o'er these silent hills—
> Invasion, and the thunder and the shout,
> And all the crash of onset ; fear and rage,
> And undetermined conflict—even now,
> Even now, perchance, and in his native isle."

Mr. George Rochefort, a valued customer of the library, duly received his copy.

3

John Fagg had long come to the conclusion that the obstructive, so-called governing clique, as well as the Harbour Commissioners, must be utterly defeated if his own dreams for the haven were ever to come to fruition.

Towards this end, in his own style, he opened a campaign to interest the ' linen drapers ' and those tradesmen not directly concerned with shipping matters.

One Thursday afternoon, there being the excuse of a consignment of goods for London, he called upon Mr. Jephrez Baker, the tallow-chandler, in Market Street.

" 'Afternoon, John," Mr. Baker greeted him dolefully. " Well, woeful tidings from Ireland, ben't they ? "

That turbulent country had risen in arms, with report of atrocious doings which a Paris mob in their heyday would have been hard put to emulate.

" Aye, 'tis bad, Mr. Baker," John Fagg agreed soberly.

Discussing the lamentable state of affairs the two gentlemen began to walk down the long and very odoriferous room, passing women who, piece of smooth board and razor affixed to their knees, were cutting wick-lengths of Smyrna cotton from large balls, these lengths subsequently being fastened on to rods for dipping, 72 to each rod.

" Invasion here . . . India . . . Ireland . . . Egypt . . . " Mr. Baker said explosively. " And on top of it all there's now a 10 per cent income tax. I tell you, John, we're in very desperate straits."

The tallow-chandler had an extremely good business, despite his gloom. Six coppers, from daybreak to nightfall, boiled sheep and bullocks' offal for the manufacture of the very best candles. A dozen men were employed in dipping, that is immersing into the hot tallow, the lengths of cut cotton, hanging up the rods to allow each coating of fat to harden, the process being repeated until the candle was built up to the required thickness.

" Income tax ! " John Fagg observed mournfully. " Be glad that you have to pay it, Mr. Baker, and hope that for long you may continue so to do."

" Eh ? " At such strange sentiments the tallow-chandler grunted his astonishment.

What the shipowner next said was a thought involved, but his companion unquestionably gathered that he was being asked whether, when the harbour became impossible through silting, he would retire from business or start afresh in some more convenient locality.

Jephrez Baker's jaw dropped. " Retire ! Start afresh elsewhere ! " he ejaculated. " I don't follow you, John."

Nodding towards a cask of imported Russian tallow, John Fagg, instead of explaining, put another question. He desired to know whether the local butchers' fats, which their boys, it being a killing-day, were bringing in that very afternoon, would be sufficient if it came to the pinch.

" Though even if they were," he rounded off by finding the flaw in his own argument, " you wouldn't be able to export your finished goods, I'm afraid."

" Hey ! What's this all about ? " the older man demanded, thoroughly roused by now.

Briefly John Fagg spoke of the harbour. There was little to say on that sorry subject, he said. When the haven became useless it would be useless, and nothing one way or the other might profitably be added to that.

" But, John . . . " expostulated the mightily disturbed Mr. Baker, taking a prodigious pinch from the same tortoiseshell snuff-box he had carried when travelling back to Dover with George Rochefort years before, " you'll not have to leave it like this. I want to know——"

The shipowner, during a lull in the bout of sneezing which followed, firmly stated his disinclination to be drawn further. He much preferred, he observed, to see the print Mr. Baker had mentioned in the Antwerp the previous night. It was a copy by an enterprising London publisher, he explained, of the French print, ' It is but a step,' which showed the Straits of Dover, with the *Armée de l'Angleterre* waiting near Boulogne to take the short stride.

" I know what it is well enow," Jephrez Baker remarked irascibly, producing the treasure.

Nothing would mollify the tallow-chandler, nor could anything prevent his reverting to the subject which had upset him.

" Start fresh elsewhere," he growled, retailing at some length his family's connection with the candle manufactory, one which had begun in Queen Bess's reign when the municipality gave over the enterprise into private hands.

" And what about your ships, John ? " he ended ill-humouredly. " Starting afresh elsewhere with them, eh ? "

" I hope not, Mr. Baker," John Fagg replied calmly. " Not if I can help it."

More and more did the tallow-chandler's eyes grow choleric as he heard of the fight which a small number of Dover worthies proposed to make for the saving of the harbour.

" Why not me as well, Fagg ? " he choked. " If you an' Nethersole, an' Stokes, an' Crundall——"

John Fagg expressed a degree of surprise that Mr. Baker should wish to enter into what would be a stern struggle against the powerful Harbour Commissioners and others.

" You feel surprised, do you, Fagg ? " shouted the incensed Mr. Baker. " Let me warn you that if I'm not asked to attend the next meeting you have on this issue I'll see you're a demned sight more surprised."

Gravely, seeing how the candle-maker felt, John Fagg promised that this should be done, and gravely he parted from the now triumphant Mr. Baker.

Crossing the Market Place towards King Street, the shipowner was beginning to smile broadly over the events of the last hour when he chanced to catch the eye of Mr. Ralph Toke. Most erroneously the Revenue Officer believed he was the object of this mirth.

"Yes, you can laugh, Mr Fagg," he snapped, eyes narrowing. "But my turn will come, I can assure you."

"And I assure you, Mr. Toke——"

"Mark my words, Mr. Fagg," the Revenue Officer interposed venomously, "my turn will come."

What with this, and Mr. Baker's burning zeal to pit himself against the Commissioners of Harbour, John Fagg really had something to keep him grinning as he walked home.

4

During a summer afternoon a sharp shower is really the most horrible visitation, but fortunately the downpour is often brief.

When the rain ceased Caroline Rochefort and Lou Fagg, who had run hurriedly for shelter into Caroline's home, immediately discontinued the game of battledore and shuttlecock with which they had been whiling away the time. They had something very much more amusing on their programme.

"Where are they drilling, Lou?" Caroline clapped excitedly.

Lou giggled. "On the Ropewalk near Mr. Beverley's works."

Some two months before it had been decided that the younger generation should fit themselves, by drill and manœuvre, for the sterner part they might later have to play in the defence of their country. Youths and the older boys were attached to the Volunteer associations, but their juniors were formed into companies, self-officered, who received instruction twice a week from a Chelsea Hospital veteran.

"They're there, Caroline," Lou Fagg whispered. "Let's hurry."

The fingers of mothers and sisters had been exceedingly busy, and very proudly did the boys' Company hold themselves in their blue jackets trimmed with yellow, with mitre-shaped caps each with its tuft of horsehair in the front. In fine style, behind their own drum and fife, they marched up the firm centre of the Ropewalk.

"Par . . . ty . . . HALT," rang out the treble voice of the Colonel. "RIGHT . . . TURN."

"A very fine body of men," Miss Caroline Rochefort remarked loudly and admiringly to her friend.

Up to this moment Colonel Breton, the twelve-year-old son of the Harbour-master, had not realised there was an audience. Seldom has a pleasant-faced lad so suspiciously eyed a pair of nice-looking young girls. Unhappily for him he decided to treat their presence with contempt, whereas, being no match for Miss Rochefort, he would have done infinitely better had he chased her off there and then.

" The Company," he now shouted sternly, " will prepare to receive the enemy. Remember, men——"

" Good God, Lou, the Frenchies are here ! " Miss Rochefort, greatly agitated, spun on her heel to glimpse the savage invaders.

" I can't see them, Caroline," cried her distraught companion. " Oh, what shall we do, dear me, dear me ? "

She received a glance of scorn. " Calm yourself, child," Miss Rochefort said cuttingly. " Are there not gallant soldiers here, soldiers well disciplined and finely armed ? "

Disciplined or no, the ranks of soldiery very nearly broke there and then, for the company had been touched on its sorest spot, its weapons. These consisted of small wooden gunstocks with mopsticks for barrels, the latter being given a metallic appearance by the plentiful usage of both blacklead and elbow-grease.

" Who asked you to come here ? " Colonel Breton stormed. " Coming interfering——"

" Silly idiot females," a private cut in on his senior officer. " What you want to do, Jim——"

" You don't call me ' Jim ' on parade, Volunteer Bullack," bawled the infuriated commanding officer.

Whilst the dispute ran its course a horseman began to come from the direction of the sea. Charles Fagg had been walking in the brine one of the Antwerp horses afflicted with a stiffness and now, on his way back to the Market Place, he decided to watch the young 'uns.

Knowing Louis' sister from her babyhood, he soon guessed precisely what mischief was afoot. Indeed, he arrived at the very moment when a humble member of the Company, for long grievously tried by a hypnotic eye, burst into hysterical laughter when Miss Rochefort rounded off her act by making one of the most grotesque grimaces possible to imagine.

" Charles," Colonel Breton appealed desperately, " Caroline Rochefort and your Lou——"

Miss Rochefort shook her head regretfully. " I fear me, Charles, that here is an officer whose men are quite out of hand, *quite.*"

Flushed with her success, she attempted further heights. She observed to Lou that that young lady's brother held himself remarkably well on a horse, and was indeed a part of the creature.

" Do not mistake me about it, Charles," she told him graciously. " Never have I seen——"

" So Colonel Breton's men are quite out of hand, eh ? " Charles Fagg commented expressionlessly.

He bent to have a quiet aside with the irate officer, an act which Miss Rochefort viewed with just a shade of disquiet. She, too, knew Charles well, and she knew you could never be quite sure where you were with him.

" Charles," she began hastily. " I hope that——"

" 'Tis a sad affair when men get out of hand," Charles Fagg observed solemnly.

Sweet revenge in his gleam, Colonel Breton gave a brisk order. The Company at attention, he advised them of information he had received of the two French spies who were in the town disguised in girls' clothes.

" Charles, you beast," Miss Rochefort said passionately, picking up her skirts in prudent anticipation. " tell him we're not——"

" Fix bayonets," yelled Colonel Breton. " CHARGE."

The highly delighted Company sped down the Ropewalk in pursuit of two very young ladies in frantic retreat. The chase surged beyond the Ordnance Stores, through busy Snargate Street-over-the-Wall, to the very door of Mr. Henry Rochefort's house into which, in the nick of time only, Caroline and her friend had darted.

Colonel Breton, having a gorgeous inspiration, placed guards around the residence. The two girls, willy-nilly, spent the remainder of that lovely day indoors.

5

The summer evenings were beginning to shorten. In Henry Rochefort's own chair his brother sat, in almost the same huddled position as that in which he had been two hours earlier when Matthew Godspenny had wished him good-night.

George Rochefort's face was pale and drawn, as indeed it had been ever since he had called at the post office whilst on his way home. There he had collected two letters, one from David Garroway containing arguments of which he was already sickly aware, the other from a friend of Paris days. So, with all the uncertainties of many aching weeks resolved by the reading of these and the thought of food nauseous, he had returned to the bank for the solitude he craved.

Then, as St. Mary's boomed, he rose painfully and, in the window overlooking the gold-shot water of the Basin, he once again ran his reddened eyes down those lines which, he knew it truly now, would change irrevocably the course of his life.

" My dear George," he read,

> " I fere that I have been more than remiss in not writing you
> these last two years or more, but . . ."

He skipped the next few lines of apology, and came to that part
which he had examined time and time again.

> " Our mutual friend, W. W., is mightily put about by the Frenchies'
> latest piece of aggression, the invasion of poor, harmless, peace-loving
> Switzerland, and has ruffed out a quite respectable sonnet expressing
> his feelings on't, a draft of which I enclose. Whether he will publish
> it . . ."

" *Respectable*, damn his mercantile soul," George Rochefort said
vehemently. " 'Tis of the essence divine, howsoever unwittingly
William may have finally brought home to me my folly."

He stared mistily out of the window, at Custom House Quay, and
at the Cross Wall. These two thoroughfares, normally an evening
parade, were unusually deserted, having no more than two or three
couples strolling along them, and these obviously soldiers with sweethearts clinging.

His lips began to frame the words, for now he knew them by
heart :

> " For high-souled maid, what sorrow would it be
> That mountain floods should thunder as before,
> And ocean bellow from his rocky shore,
> And neither awful voice be heard by thee ? "

From Custom House Quay came the regular tramp of well-drilled
feet as a naval officer, together with a score or so of seamen, marched
round the corner of the Royal Victualling Yard and along the frontage
of the Revenue Office.

" A hot-press," murmured George Rochefort. " Small wonder
there's so few abroad. Well . . . " he laughed mirthlessly.

As he watched, some strange purpose invested his dark eyes,
remaining there long after those stalwart tars had disappeared beyond
the Ship Inn at the further end of the Quay.

Shortly he opened the door of the bank and, lest there might be
other gangs at work in the vicinity, first glanced cautiously along
Snargate Street-over-the-Wall. Then, his expression visionary, he
hastened over the lock-gate and took the quick cut into Pent-side.

The Rochefort household in Snargate Street was not an unhappy
one. Henry Rochefort, wholly devoted to his children and ever

mindful of their well-being, had done his utmost to ensure that. But the sad loss of the mistress of the house and the long-sustained difference in opinion of the two brothers could not be without effect.

Thus it was that Louis Rochefort, on entering the hall, was palpably astonished to hear from upstairs the sound of merry whistling, and more than spellbound when he saw his uncle.

George Rochefort wore a prominently striped cut-away coat embroidered in gold and silver, with a no less heavily striped yellow and green waistcoat trimmed with figured gold lace. His nether limbs, down to the ankles, were covered in maroon-coloured pantaloons instead of the usual cloth breeches and silk stockings.

" Phew ! " Louis gasped.

His uncle heard, but boisterously welcomed him into the bedroom, remarking that he had certain gifts to make.

" My new set of ebony-backed brushes and my silver-mounted razor," he laughed, apologising because the latter article had been in slight use.

Louis Rochefort was too dumfounded to do little more than divide his attentions between these prized presents and his uncle's zebra-like clothes. Never before had he seen a fashion that had come into being about the time when Henry Rochefort's brother, returning from the Continent some seven years before, had stayed a few days in London. It was a fashion which, from its very extremism, had died nearly as quickly as the tailor had made the garments.

" But . . . " he protested at last, " that's your best razor, I know, Uncle."

George Rochefort chaffed him gaily. Louis would soon be a soldier of His Majesty, and if he wished to present himself smartly on parade he would need a keen edge to remove the stiff morning stubble. No, he would hear no more objections.

" You're rising seventeen, eh, Louis ? " he quizzed, busily rummaging in a drawer. " And that's a man's age in these days. As for me . . ." he shrugged, " my old wood-hafted blade will serve admirably."

A few minutes afterwards, Martha Teddiman, fresh from her tucking-in and final cosseting of the daughter of the house, met her master's young brother at the top of the stairs. Her speech contained many pauses.

" No, Mr. George, I'm sure Miss Caroline isn't asleep yet . . . " she said wonderingly, her astounded gaze passing from one feature to another of his extravagant attire. " No, I'm sure . . ." she meandered mechanically, taking him all in.

After a pleasantry, he went into his niece's bedroom, leaving the housekeeper still gaping.

" Oooh, Uncle George," Caroline sat up delightedly, seeing her visitor, " you are a tremendous beau. Are you going to see Aunt Susan ? "

George Rochefort settled himself on the edge of the bed, gave his niece a hug and a kiss and, with a great air of secrecy, took from a small square of velvet a handsome ruby ring.

Caroline, quite speechless for once in her young life, saw him try the ring on her small fingers.

She swallowed. " For . . . for Aunt Susan ? " she asked breathlessly, the pink ribbons of her pretty sleeping cap hardly moving.

He first observed that he had thought of presenting to Miss Fagg his diamond ring, the one he invariably wore. As for this bauble, it was true that it would always be too large for Miss Rochefort, but when she grew up a crown piece to a jeweller . . .

" For me ? " screeched his niece.

Withholding, he first teased her, but afterwards admitted that the ring was to be her own. But, whilst the deliriously happy young miss bounced up and down on the bed, he added that, though she might keep it now, she was not to wear it until she came of age.

" But . . . " though Miss Rochefort frowned her tone was dulcet in its cajolery, " I shall have to wait ten years yet, Uncle George."

Seeing her roguishness, he could not resist cuddling her again. Later, however, they compromised on this issue. Caroline might publicly wear his gift on her eighteenth birthday.

" I wish I was that now, Uncle George," she said longingly, looking up from the shoulder against which she was nestling. " An' going to assemblies and balls and . . . "

Some of the animation and forced gaiety which had been in the young man's face began to ebb.

" Don't wish the years on, Caroline, my love," he warned her sadly.

The girl was looking at him searchingly, then anxiously she asked why he was so troubled.

He tried to smile. " I was ever a troublesome gentleman, my dear," he said ruefully.

Now he threw off his dejection. Soon he must leave her, he declared, or Aunt Susan would be growing jealous. And, in his new liveliness, his niece forgot the despair which had drawn her quick attention.

" But before you go, Uncle George, you must take me in to supper," she demanded gleefully.

" To supper, Caroline ? " he asked, at first not comprehending.

" To supper, Mr. Rochefort," she simpered, in an instant becoming the silly young lady of current fashion.

G

He guffawed and into supper they went, the gentleman solemnly lifting his feet in measured tread upon the red Turkey carpet at the side of the bed, the lady's small feet likewise keeping time beneath the bedclothes.

" 'Tis prodigious close to-night, Mr. Rochefort," Miss Rochefort remarked agreeably. Her arm was tucked into her uncle's and her hand was resting on his sleeve.

Her admirer deferentially suggested that, after the collation, he might be permitted to escort her into the refreshing atmosphere of the garden, whereupon Miss Rochefort reluctantly removed her glance from the red-gleaming jewel on her finger.

" La, la, sir," she minxed him, her demurely downcast eyes nevertheless not missing the distinguished gentleman who was bowing to her.

The escort sighed. " Lackaday me," he commented gallantly, " there's another from the hungry horde who seek your favour, my fair lady."

" And he the noble Mr. Pitt," Caroline informed him naïvely, meantime curtsying to the great statesman, a feat not without its difficulties within the confines of a bed.

In this wise the pantomime went on, until simultaneously both burst into laughter.

When George Rochefort left the room it was with the memory of a soft pair of arms about his neck, with the memory of a loving little creature showing him without stint all the affection she bore for him.

As was so often the case in the evening, Henry Rochefort was diligently working on a mass of bank papers when his brother entered the little drawing-room.

Brother looked at brother, the elder's eyes roving over the younger.

" Well ? " Henry Rochefort asked, his inspection completed. " And what may your business be to-night in a foppish habit that will draw attention to you from every quarter ? "

George Rochefort was so stung that momentarily he forgot entirely the humility of his purpose.

" And was not that how the French aristocrats robed themselves for the tumbrils ? " he inquired bitingly.

The banker looked as astonished as any man who doubts his own senses.

" Maybe," he remarked curtly. " Though I'll confess I think that such expression of admiration comes strangely from your lips, George."

" 'Tis no expression of admiration, Henry," George Rochefort said, his voice deepening. " Only the visible symbol that I . . . that I, Henry, have come to the end of a long road."

Henry Rochefort, whilst his brother paced to and fro, sat back, sardonically awaiting the younger man's pleasure.

He had to wait an unconscionably long while before George turned sharply in the midst of his perambulations.

"Henry," he began ringingly, "on this evening I come to tell you that I acknowledge the wrong I have been doing these last years. It has been grievous, and I own it, and I will pay for it. Pay for it with every sinew in my body, pay for it with every tortured nerve, pay for it——"

Mildly interposing into the full flood, the banker asked for a more informative definition of the wrong his brother had in mind.

"My . . . my opposition to the order of government in this country," was the rather deflated reply.

"You feel that you have been in error from the beginning?"

George Rochefort announced that he could not admit that. He propounded, however, that though there was theoretically much in the tenets of the Revolution which England could in time, and no doubt would, copy to advantage, the rulers of France had long departed from those precepts on which their *régime* had originally been founded.

"Now they lust for conquest," he trenchantly denounced them, "with the veil of new thought under which they seek to cloak their aspirations wearing thinner with every moon. They seek world domination and . . ." he made a wry face, "I am a true Briton after all."

Henry Rochefort, despite the spate of grandiloquence, had been thawing for some moments. Now, brotherly affection in his expression, he started to rise.

"Your words do you credit, George," he observed warmly. "And right glad am I to hear them."

A smile of ineffable sweetness came to George Rochefort's mobile mouth. "You'll give me your hand then, Henry?" he asked emotionally.

Hand grasped in hand they stood, until George Rochefort, for the sake of his very manhood, had to turn away.

"I shall ever remember this reconciliation of ours, Henry," he said, shoulder towards his brother. "As . . . as I hope you ever will."

"Come, my lad," Henry Rochefort was beginning kindly.

But George Rochefort, in one of those extraordinary changes of which he was capable, had braced himself afresh.

"And now," he announced gaily, "I must be off to show my magnificence to Susan. I verily believe the dear creature will swoon when she sees me."

The door closed, and with its closing the banker resumed his work. But somehow debit, credit and vital differences of exchange seemed to elude his keen brain; somehow, even as he looked down the columns of figures before him, a vague sense of uneasiness came to pervade him.

He was half resolved to walk abroad in search of his brother when a light scampering of feet drew his attention.

"Caroline, my dear," he said, but not sternly.

That young lady, full of her news, perched herself on his knee.

"Uncle George has given me his lovely ruby ring, Papa," she exclaimed excitedly. "And when I am eighteen . . ."

Henry Rochefort's thoughts were racing and involuntarily he rose, sliding her from his lap.

"What is the matter, Papa?" she asked.

He smiled, picked her up, and swung her in his immeasurable relief. Through the window, on the far side of the Pent, he had espied the strikingly clad figure of his brother walking along the Ropewalk.

By taking that route, George Rochefort was wisely eliminating any risk of walking into the press-gang which his brother knew was operating in the town.

Mr. Rochefort, thus freed of a nonsensical foreboding, forgot his work and indulged in a pleasant half-hour with his entrancing little daughter.

6

In the late evening light, the garden behind Mr. John Fagg's residence looked as lovely as a simple English garden can do. The tall clumps of hollyhocks were motionless, and the honeysuckle and sweet peas permeated the barely moving air with their charming scent.

But the mistress of the house for once was unmindful of the campanulas, the double dahlias and the delightful smell which always grew more insistent towards nightfall. Carrying a few pinks and carnations, she hurried into the house to find her husband.

"John," she said worriedly, "I've just met George going to join Susan in the gazebo and I thought he was really queer."

John Fagg, speaking with a pipe in his mouth, answered rather indistinctly. The purport, however, was that he considered George a queer fellow altogether, though harmless at bottom.

"He assuredly thanked me in a very queer manner for what he called my continued kindness to him," his wife persisted.

"Maybe he's decided to remove himself away from all human society," was her husband's illuminating observation.

Mrs. Fagg laughed at the drollery. "No, but really, John——"

The shipowner grunted, a mannerism which might have meant

that he had little patience for the subject. Actually, he was definitely of the opinion that his sister would have been wise to have accepted long ago a suitor from one of the more normal young men who were attracted by her. Now, at twenty-six, Susan was in danger of becoming a tabby.

The gazebo was peaceful, and to it there was creeping that astringent odour smelt when outflowing salt-water leaves bare mosses and seaweed, and a continuous lullaby as tiny ripples died sweetly against the smooth shingle of the beach.

Susan Fagg could not clearly gather her lover's meaning.

"But, George, dear, Mr. Wordsworth must have altered extraordinarily,"she said, puzzled. " I remember not so many years ago——"

George Rochefort began promptly.

" ' Rejoice, brave land, though pride's perverted ire
Rouse hell's own aid, and wrap thy fields in fire :
Lo, from the flames a great and glorious birth ;
As if a new-made heaven were hailing a new earth ! '

" That was how William wrote then, my love."

John Fagg's sister, in pretty conceit, repeated her observation about Mr. Wordsworth's change of heart, whereupon George Rochefort tersely remarked that he had thought he had made it intelligible enough that both William and himself now saw events in a different light.

To hide her hurt she bent her head, her first thought the keeping from him of her distress, and the second the kissing of the sparkling diamond in the ring he had given her.

" George, dearest," she said tremulously, " I am sorry, so——"

" 'Tis noble to declare undauntedly one's belief, yea perhaps even more noble if one stands alone, dear Susan, but . . . " now taking in her apology, he flashed her a smile, " little goose," he murmured, and then, almost as if there had been no break, slipped back effortlessly into the theme he had so admirably developed earlier.

" But . . . " impulsively he sprang up from the rustic seat, " 'tis indeed glorious, after having held those same beliefs, publicly to avow one has been in error."

She adoringly followed his movements and, lips parted, visualised him, not as the high-souled outcast from society, but as her dear lover in the uniform of His Majesty the King.

" So handsome," she whispered. "Oh, George, my dear one, how proud I shall be when I see you as an officer of militia, or ensign of——"

" Hard as my chosen path will be I shall not hesitate. Publicly, in a guise drawing the attention of all—— *Militia,* my dear gel, an officer of militia ! " He knelt on one knee before her, taking hold of her hands.

" No, my dearest," he said strangely, " you will not see me thus. Nor parish soldier will I be."

Then, as awful apprehension began to efface the tenderness for him that was in her, he explained. The fault had been his, he declared, and he it was who must expiate that fault. But not tamely, for that wise, the vulgar misunderstanding, would bring only intolerable laughter about his ears.

" It must be an expiation glorious in its sublimity, my sweet. An act that shall silence every tongue, a sacrifice which shall live through the annals of time."

Susan Fagg could bear no more. She went to him, to cling to him, to stammer incoherencies.

" You're frightening me, George," she told him with quivering lips.

St. Mary the Virgin's began to strike. When the tenth reverberation had died away he spoke quietly, discarding the impassioned utterance which, through the long minutes previously, had climbed steadily to its peak.

" Now is the hour, my love," he said simply, gently putting away her trembling hands.

In the silent air of the languorous evening there came clearly a man's voice raised in full-bodied protest, and then a woman's piercing shriek.

George Rochefort smiled faintly. " Yes, this is the hour and . . . and I must be gone."

" George ! " she gasped, so queer had he become.

He softly silenced her, comforting her so sweetly but so sorrowfully.

" And now I must leave you, sweetheart," he said soothingly. " And you must promise, dearest, to wait here until I am gone."

" George——" she began beseechingly.

" You will promise, my angel ? " he repeated insistently.

She gathered the confused impression that he wished to retain a last picture of her framed in the twilight setting of this lovely garden.

" Good-night, my love," he murmured.

He did not take her in his arms and press his lips against hers. Instead, as if it were an act of pure dedication, he held her shoulders and, so deliberately, stooped to kiss her forehead.

Then he was gone, striding head erect with never a backward glance.

When his footsteps died away Susan Fagg rose from the seat

to which, with his going, she had sunk. Stumblingly she went up the path and, once in the house, infused more life into her uncertain limbs.

In her bedroom she began to recover a little, for this was not the first of such scenes through which she had passed and, as before, there would come another day.

" Pray God it may be so," she whispered.

Somewhere, in the far distance, there was an angry shouting.

Perhaps that sound brought to life the subconscious thought which had been born a little before. The hairbrush which she had been mechanically using fell with a soft thud. Unheeding she stood, her cheeks draining until they seemed wax-like.

And then she snatched up a dark cloak and ran : ran wildly down the stairs, ran wildly into her brother and sister-in-law.

" George . . . George . . . " she screamed, before she flew away.

" Susan . . . Susan, love," shouted Polly Fagg. " Oh, whatever is the matter with the girl, John ? "

For so stocky a man, John Fagg was not long before he was in pursuit.

Mr. Hereward Smith, Lieutenant of the Royal Navy, was a soured man of fifty-four who, lacking patronage or influence, had spent over twenty years in the gunrooms of His Majesty's ships. Discharged at the conclusion of the war with America, he had been commissioned back into the service with the opening of hostilities with the French Republic.

It was not surprising that My Lords recruited from such disappointed men the officers needed to carry out the necessary brutalities inherent in the impressing of men, and it followed equally well that all men, when the press was at work, took every possible precaution to prevent themselves from being taken by the pinning elbow grip.

From which it may be understood how Mr. Hereward Smith, marching at the side of his men along St. James's Street, found himself out of tongue when he realised that he was being accosted, being sought out, by a young man, a civilian, who emerged from one of the Passages leading to Town Wall Street.

" Damned if I ain't dreaming," he ejaculated. " Me, one of the hottest press officers the meanest government on earth so poorly requites."

His previous thoughts, concerning his miserable lodgings and a wife's shrewishness brought about by perpetual poverty, sped in the shock of the novel circumstances.

" Cut my bowels out," he cogitated, eyeing the zany who carried a gold-knobbed stick and who wore a narrowing top-hat.

George Rochefort bowed gracefully. " Am I to understand, sir," he asked gravely, " that you are desirous of drawing public attention to the merits of service in His Majesty's Navy ? "

This was taking place close by the carved door of the Red Lion Inn, the house of call for coaches bound for Deal and Thanet. It was a locality which, at that hour, was definitely busier than the Market Place.

So it was not merely the elderly Mr. Smith who was bemused by the inquiry. Every creature amongst the many occupying the bench beneath the projecting upper story of the hostelry gaped in stupefaction over their tankards.

" That, in short, you would, sir, not entirely look with disfavour upon one who desired entrance into that noble body of seafarers whom I am sure, sir, you yourself so heroically represent," George Rochefort continued courteously.

" Disfavour . . . heroically represent ! " The naval officer's leathery cheeks went turkey red and, from the saying of those few words, his attitude changed. It was as though, from being dazed, he came to the conclusion that he was being mocked by this pert young cock of the walk.

His voice thundered out, and at the hoarse command the petty officer in charge of the party halted his men.

" You shall know the 'tween decks of a ship-of-the-line, my fine feathered bird," he roared. " You shall know——"

" My good fellow," drawled George Rochefort, " have you not gathered that my presence here indicates that I am perfectly willing——"

" *Good fellow !* " choked Mr. Hereward Smith of the Royal Navy. " Before you're another twelve hours older——"

George Rochefort was deathly pale, but his restless and unfathomable spirit drove him on to still further indiscretion.

Meanwhile there was assembling a crowd of such dimensions as would have gratified any man who wished to take his bow in grand style.

The news of young Mr. George Rochefort's astounding conduct spread quickly, and already the inns as far away as the Market Place were being denuded of custom. Through the Passages and the Lanes people came hurrying, to form a circle so dense that the stout driver of the Margate stage-coach discontinued all attempt to maintain his schedule.

But it was the domestics in the Red Lion who, throwing up the sash windows of that overhanging upper story, had the most comprehensive view of all. They it was who saw a young woman, her pretty face distorted with her fears, using her poor strength to force through the throng. Light was rapidly fading but they recognised her albeit.

" 'Tis Mr. John Fagg's sister . . . Miss Susan Fagg . . . " one after another they took up the cry, many of them now in imminent danger of falling on to the sea of heads below, so precariously were they leaning out.

" And there's Mr. Fagg 'imself," said another, a sharp-eyed one, who had perceived the shipper dive into the outskirts of the crowd, his powerful shoulders and strongly wielded elbows clearing the path he wanted.

Mr. Hereward Smith of the Royal Navy, midst the hubbub, bawled the order to march. Catcalls and cheers vied with one another, and there came a great roar when young Mr. Rochefort, now closely guarded between the files of seamen, took off his high hat and waved it jauntily.

" George . . . George . . . " Susan Fagg cried desperately, that bonny face of hers shapeless in its grief and shame. " George . . . oh, George," she sobbed.

Summoning her tottering legs for one final effort, she reached him before the man on the captive's right realised what was about.

" George . . . how . . . could . . . you . . . " Tears streaming, she was broken now.

" Susan, my love," he began. And then recalled to her how his last vision of her must be as she was in that garden. His dear one must go, must hasten home. . . .

" What the hell ! " bellowed Lieutenant Smith. " March, blast you, and see that female is put aside."

Susan Fagg was too stunned to hear that, and all she knew then was that she was crying out her heart on her brother's broad chest.

" What the devil do you mean by making this exhibition of yourself, my girl ? " John Fagg asked furiously, but that was when he first grasped her and, so bemazed then, she did not remember that.

" Damn him," the shipowner swore viciously, drawing his sister from the stream of humanity eagerly thronging up the street in pursuit.

Nor did she recollect that indictment of her beloved.

But always, for the rest of her life, she never lost a picture of St. James's Street. The receding crowd with its broken step and, faintly heard, the regular beat of disciplined feet ; the thoroughfare itself stretching away until it became merged into Castle Hill, a bulky shape which, there being no delineation in the half light, had added to its stature by being capped by a castellated crown, the skyline of the walls and towers of the old Castle.

And ever down the years, she could recall the proudly held head of her lover above those, whether the jostled guards or the curious, who, close-packed, hemmed him in.

7

On the first day of August the forces under Rear-Admiral Sir Horatio Nelson destroyed the French fleet at Aboukir Bay, thereby preventing General Bonaparte, should he have so desired, from returning with his forces to Europe ; the following month saw the end of the Irish rebellion, with the French, who had endeavoured to aid the revolutionaries, entering Dublin—as prisoners of war.

In October Sir John Borlase's squadron obtained a decisive sea victory over still another French expeditionary force whose destination was Ireland, the possession of which by an enemy would be a pike at the throat of Britain. And from further afield came news of General Wellesley's brilliant successes in India.

In the first month of the new year Mr. Pitt succeeded in forming a second coalition against the French—it surely seemed that England, Russia, Turkey, Austria, and the Two Sicilies, united in a common determination, would speedily end a condition of menace which otherwise must forever prevent the progress and happiness of all mankind.

It is comforting and heartening when, after losing allies one by one, after solitarily sustaining the attacks of a powerful enemy, partners once more come forward to lend a hand. Altogether there showed the first gleam of light in a sky which, for six years, had steadily darkened. As a consequence the highly gratified nation, be it in so little, began to relax the heroic efforts it had been making.

There was small wisdom in that.

Part II

1799-1804

CHAPTER ONE

I

SUNDAY morning service was nearly over in St. Mary the Virgin's, and Dr. Woodgate was ending a most peculiar sermon.

"So let us pray, my friends," he said solemnly. "Let us pray for the soul of the poor creature who, by this hour on the morrow, will have taken the journey to his Heavenly Father."

The church was packed. In their own private pews were John Fagg and Henry Rochefort, both in the uniform of the Volunteers, with them as many members of their households as could be spared from domestic duties. And on the highly decorated seats behind the communion table, upon one of which King Charles, with true humility, had once declined to sit, believing that they were ". . . above the Majesty of Heaven!" was the Mayor and a full assembly of jurats, now sliding from fringed velvet cushions to kneel in an attitude of devotion.

"Let us pray," the Rector repeated, when the shuffle of movement had died. "Let us pray, not only for a wretched felon from whose eyes the light of day must soon for ever fade, but for those men whose sworn evidence has sent him to the gallows. . . ."

There was a fleeting stirring throughout the building—the Doctor was going strong, so many a one thought.

"Let us pray that their evidence was true evidence," Dr. Woodgate continued inexorably. "Let us pray that . . . "

Susan Fagg was praying, praying devoutly for George. There was an expression of especial rapture on her face, for only two days before she had received a beautiful letter from her lover and her heart was full of joy.

". . . for it would be infamous if a man's life were sworn away by false testimony," the Rector went on sternly.

Mrs. John Fagg shivered. She looked pale and troubled, her thoughts too mixed to allow of any reasoned prayer.

"And now to God the Father . . . "

Soon the congregation were streaming into Cannon Street, amongst

them Martha Teddiman on her devoted Valentine's arm, he as proud
as a peacock to have her so.

Then, as invariably after divine service, the Volunteers and
Fencibles collected their weapons from the church porch and put in a
short but brisk drill in the Market Place. Most of their females and
children stayed to watch, taking up a sheltered point of vantage to
escape the keen March wind.

The glance of Mrs. Fagg kept wandering to the semicircular
archway of the prison, with its shattered doorway and scarifying token
shackles hanging to either side.

" I . . . I think I'll go home, Susan," she said miserably.

As she did, taking Minnie with her and leaving Lou with her aunt.

There had been vast disturbance in the town since a member of
a Folkestone smuggling galley had been caught red-handed by the
Revenue Officer who, on the grounds that the luckless fellow was in
possession of a lethal weapon, demanded the death sentence when the
case came up for hearing.

. Mr. Spisour, the Water Bailiff, who was again Mayor that year,
could, through his office, pass that penalty, but being extremely reluctant to do so, adjourned the proceedings, the better to find suitable
excuse to offset the watertight evidence provided by Mr. Toke.

That night, entirely misunderstanding Mr. Spisour's beneficent
intentions, the jail was stormed by a Folkestone mob quite undeterred
by the reading of the Riot Act. The prisoner was released, nor was he
apprehended for a fortnight.

. Dragoons brought him back for trial, and this time the Mayor
very promptly dismissed the charge. Equally promptly the thin-lipped
Revenue Officer forwarded an account and his complaint to London,
upon which the case was referred back to Dover's chief magistrate, with
the plain intimation that the Mayor must, on certain pains and
penalties, pronounce a verdict in accordance with the law and the
testimony given.

The drilling over, John Fagg, with his sister and younger daughter,
took a smart walk along the South Pier and then, with faces tingling
pleasantly, they made back for home and dinner.

Susan, who had a very lively imagination, believed that she had
seen, in a window of the Bridewell where he was now held, the pitiable
being who was soon to die.

" John," she asked worriedly, " do you really think he had a
pistol ? "

They were passing between Severus's and Butchery Gates, before
the two houses Henry Rochefort had erected on the Island. John
Fagg did not even glance at this site. For a winter and more, especially

after storm, he had done so, but since Christmas he had decided that, whatever the Dour had been once, it had now taken to more sedate ways.

" Mr. Toke and his hireling Clement Foxley both gave oath on't," he replied to his sister's question, his expression changing to the forbidding.

He would not speak any more on the matter.

Then came dinner. A fine piece of sirloin it was, but for the first time there was not the usual pudding. Mrs. Fagg, being as patriotic as any of her friends, had followed the example set by the Privy Council. For the future the inmates of Little Pent House were not to eat puddings and such-like containing flour.

*   *   *   *   *   *   *   *

An enormous concourse of spectators began to move out of the Market Place into narrow Cannon Street, thence straight along towards the Maison Dieu.

At the head of the procession was a cart. It contained Dr. Wood-gate, a coffin and the man who was destined to be placed in that wooden box.

Around the death-wagon, in which the Reverend Nathaniel Woodgate, wearing his robes as Chaplain to the Commonalty, gabbled to the palsied victim extracts from a prayer-book, the mob eddied, jostling one another in their efforts to press closer.

Slowly the cortège moved on, past the forge at the top of Biggin Street and then along the London Road as far as the toll-gate near the Black Horse Tavern, opposite which was the gallows.

Now munching jaws became stilled and mouths gaped open. Excitement grew apace and once, when it became known that the executioner was missing, a wild shout went up.

Four hours it was before another hangman could be found.

Again the mob was at fever-heat, straining on tiptoe not to miss a thing.

Dr. Woodgate delivered the last solemn exhortation, and an ashen-faced creature began his dismal ditty, the last words of the psalm barely escaping his dry lips when he was skilfully turned off.

" And that, Foxley," Mr. Ralph Toke observed with quiet satisfaction, " is only the first."

" Yes, sir," Clement Foxley very promptly answered.

" We shall find others," the Revenue Officer went on. " Bigger fish, I trust, Foxley. Perhaps *the* big fish."

The silent crowd opened to let them pass.

There was company that evening at Little Pent House, with music, some singing, and the passing round of a most amusing set of caricatures.

But Polly Fagg, on whom recent events had weighed heavily, was glad when their friends were gone. Immediately she spoke to her husband on fears he had not, until then, known she had.

When she had come to a watery-eyed finish John Fagg, after attempting to console her, laughed heartily.

" Forsooth, my dear, I should have thought you would have had more faith in me," he exclaimed ruefully.

" But Mr. Toke means to catch you, whatever unscrupulous means he uses," Mrs. Fagg urged.

" Yes, he's unscrupulous all right," John Fagg agreed, all the twinkle vanishing from his grey eyes. " He'll manufacture evidence, I'll vow, but I'll take care he don't succeed against me."

" You will take care, John ? " Polly Fagg said anxiously.

He assured her that he would and, more than that, he told her that nowadays, whenever a run was made, he always provided a back door for escape.

" Sometimes two of 'em, Polly," the freetrader ended, his smile coming back. " 'Tis a little expensive but then 'tis a form, so it now seems, of *life* insurance after all."

At that joke he began to laugh heartily.

2

In due course April Fool's Day came round again, with once more a Fagg and a Rochefort, despite strained relationship, holding in St. Mary's joint memorial service for the dead. For sixteen consecutive years had honour been done to the memory of five gallant young men, but a freak phenomenon in early summer was to have results which put an end to this orderly sequence.

It was somewhat close on that evening before the disaster occurred, and many of the townsfolk were out seeking a breath of air ; sitting gossiping on the piers, on the Western Heights, on the grassy slopes of Castle Hill.

There was much to talk about, too. Conditions in England might still be deplorable, but surely the war was at last taking a turn. General Bonaparte remained out in the East, but in his onslaught on Syria the sailors of Sir Sydney Smith's fleet had, at Acre, given the ever-victorious Frenchman his first rebuff on land.

" A general wins time after time, until the dangerous conviction springs up that he's infallible," Mr. Hugo Stratton remarked oracularly. " But he's only human after all."

"Aye, to be sure," said Mr. Jeffrey Braems, expressing agreement with the Town Clerk. "The only thing to do," the Notary to the Harbour Commissioners went on, "is to keep plugging away . . . er . . . assiduously striving."

This discussion took place on the South Pier, and, only a stone's throw away, on the North Pier, Mr. Nicholas Stokes, with no little delight, was speaking of the resolute fashion in which an Austro-Russian army was driving the French out of Italy.

"Aye, to be sure," agreed Mr. Crundall. "When—well, I'm damned."

He stared at a heavy-timbered, clinker-built little boat whose pronounced rake on stem and stern parts was exceedingly familiar to him. In it, Lou Fagg reclined elegantly, and another young lady, to wit Miss Caroline Rochefort, tugged away at the oars, doing her utmost to feather correctly.

"An' she pulls a very fair stroke," chuckled Captain Nethersole,

"Methinks if Charles learns of it . . " guffawed Mr. Stokes.

Miss Rochefort, red-faced with her exertions but with a very complete air of satisfaction about her, triumphantly proceeded across the Tidal Harbour, thence in fine style through the lock-gates into the Basin.

Their smiles gradually dying, the gentlemen seemed about to resume their interrupted conversation. But Mrs. Nethersole, who was with this party, was mightily weary of the topic. She brought it to a conclusion by a most graphic description of how she could always tell for sure when a thunderstorm was in the offing.

"A tightness across my temples," she said, rolling her eyes gravely. "And a feeling all around me . . . " Her waggling fingers moved in a mysterious halo about her head.

Subsequently she declared her belief that such a storm was imminent. Captain Nethersole's wife was right, too.

About three o'clock in the morning there was a rumbling or two and, before the quarter after, a tremendous peal.

Shortly came the rain, torrential rain, and, nine miles away, over the high ridge of Barham Down, there was a cloudburst.

A spate of water came down the channel of the Dour, its force so violent that, when it reached the arched culvert at Butchery Gate, the surface of Town Wall Street was thrown up.

It was John Fagg's elder daughter who was the first at Little Pent House to remark the amazing happening. Always frightened of lightning, Minnie Fagg had burrowed beneath the bedclothes but, when the reports grew less frequent, she ventured out of bed. Never had she heard such rain in her life.

She looked down into the street, to find a street no more, but a river lashed white with myriads of vicious raindrops, the central gutter lost to sight and hopelessly inadequate to deal with the volume.

From that she proceeded stealthily to the landing, her idea to view the Ropewalk.

One glance was sufficient and she was flying to her parents' bedroom.

" Papa," she gasped, " 'tis just like being in Noah's Ark.   The sea is all round the garden and poor Mamma's tulips are all broken——"

" The sea about the garden ! " ejaculated her father, out of bed in a trice, running as he was in nightshirt and nightcap, barefooted.

In less than three minutes John Fagg had ascertained just what had taken place.   The Little Pent, Dover's earliest haven, was aflood— but not with its old salt-charged element.

The Dour had changed course.   Perhaps cherishing resentment at the tampering which had robbed it of one of its channels, it now looked another way, its waters, instead of feeding the Pent, steadily moving easterly.

Like a Biblical flood the Little Pent increased hour by hour, until at last the overflow started to escape into the sea.

The Clerk of the Cheque was not long before he was on the scene. Forthwith he sent by horsemen urgent messages to his superiors the ' eleven discreet men.'

Four Commissioners of Harbour, including Sir Walter Plumbley, duly made an appearance.

3

For once the press of business on the Harbour Commissioners was sufficiently large to cause it to be necessary for the members present to lie in Dover for that night.

The disaster which had deprived the Pent of its supply from the Dour had made a difference, averaged, of over five thousand tons in the weight of discharge for scouring away the accumulations on the harbour bar.   In effect, until the position could be completely recti- fied, the haven was grievously afflicted.

On that day notaries and civil engineers came to and fro along Council House Street.   But it was not until late in the afternoon that real news came from Town Wall Street—the one hundred and twenty men working there had, after three days of feverish energy, at last opened up a channel through the close-packed filling which blocked the inshore limb of the river.   Now no longer was it possible to step directly from Town Wall Street to the pair of houses on the Island, and already a thin stream of water was beginning to flow down to the Pent.

The other operation, too, was proceeding well. Before the end of the week, it was confidently expected, the Dour would have been sealed off from its new course through the Little Pent to the sea.

This satisfactory outcome arrived at, the Commissioners adjourned to the Antwerp Hotel for supper, their Notary receiving instructions to present himself at that hostelry at nine o'clock the same evening.

There being no question whatever upon whose shoulders the responsibility for the calamity rested, the Commissioners of Dover Harbour decided it was expedient forthwith to protect themselves.

*　　*　　*　　*　　*　　*　　*　　*

Both Mr. Braems and the Clerk of the Cheque had been closeted together until the small hours, but despite a tendency to yawn Mr. Waade looked particularly cheerful the next morning as he strutted down Snargate Street-over-the-Wall. He had a certain amount of pleasure in anticipating the events of the next quarter of an hour or so.

Henry Rochefort received him at once.

Feeling not unlike the cat with the mouse, Mr. Waade did not immediately bring himself to the grave business which was the subject of his call. He first applauded the subjugation of Southern India by the annexation of Mysore and the Carnatic.

"It will teach the Frenchies, my dear Mr. Rochefort," he said sagely, "that however they may intrigue in India or elsewhere, the final advantage——"

"Your business, sir?" snapped the banker.

Dissembling his delight in a mild glance of reproval, Mr. Waade took time over his preparations. He rubbed his spectacles with a silk kerchief, was finicky in fixing the gold wires over his ears, and in general made his presence felt. At last, opening an impressively-big folder of parchment, he cleared his throat.

"But, my dear Mr. Rochefort," he first said, peering over his spectacles, "I must tell you how deeply . . . how *very* deeply, I deplore the nature of my errand."

"Damme, sir, will you proceed," shouted Henry Rochefort.

The Clerk bowed low, his bent head hiding his joy in the moment.

"Assuredly, sir," he replied stiffly.

Shortly, sonorous phrases and terms rolled out from between his fleshy lips, with here and there interspersed a word or two in quaint medieval Latin. The document was indeed a faithful copy of one extant in the Middle Ages, with all the pains and penalties of those harsh and far-away times.

"Strike off my right hand!" ejaculated Henry Rochefort. "Come, sir, let us have no more of this nonsensical fantasy."

" Fantasy, sir ? " the Clerk retorted coldly. " Allow me to inform you that the act in question has never been repealed. Under a statute of the eleventh century, shortly after an Abbott of Buckland had similarly inned the Dour, it was empowered——"

" If you say another word," the banker warned him passionately.

But the Clerk of the Cheque would not be stayed. Indeed he added greatly to his offence by emitting a faint gurgle as he wagged a finger playfully.

" And I must remind you, Mr. Rochefort," he said with a pretty relish, " that . . . sir . . . sir ! " he choked.

Like a cat and mouse it had been before, but now a terrier with a rat best illustrated the scene of violence. With firm grip on the Clerk's stock Henry Rochefort shook his victim so heartily that Mr. Waade's spectacles became awry, until he yelped in very terror.

" And now, sir, the import of this document, *at once*," the banker, pale with passion, demanded.

He did not have it so quickly, for the Clerk was wheezing and coughing for a while. But when Mr. Waade had partially recovered, that gentleman, thinking only of putting himself out of reach of a man he swore was a lunatic, proceeded with nervous dispatch.

" So that is it," said Henry Rochefort.

Essentially the substance of the communication was simple. Unless the banker forthwith engaged himself to reimburse the Commissioners for whatever sum might be expended on the satisfactory restoration of the inflow to the Pent, and other consequent damage, the Commissioners would immediately set the law in motion.

" And . . . and 'tis going to cost you a pretty penny, sir," the Clerk ventured, presuming further by attempting to console the owner of a couple of houses to which access was now far from easy and which were, in any case, dangerously undermined.

Henry Rochefort's composure was returning. He smiled mirthlessly at that petty effort.

" And I can tell you, my dear Mr. Waade," he said venomously, " that this affair in due course shall cost another pretty dear. For, hell take him," a flush of fury held him momentarily, " all this is the result of a knavish trick played on me."

" A knavish trick ! " ejaculated the Clerk, for the nonce curiosity gaining on the desire to remove himself.

But the banker had no intention of satisfying a gentleman who was well known to be as gossipy as any old woman. All he wanted to do then was to see as soon as possible the man he believed responsible for the position in which he found himself. There was only one question he had to put to the Clerk.

" Is Sir Walter still in the town ? " he demanded abruptly.

Answered, he bluntly dismissed the instrument who carried out the
desires of the Harbour Commissioners, those gentry with whom he
must establish a closer relationship if he were to carry out a design
he had made within the last hour.

That done Henry Rochefort made for the Antwerp Hotel.

Sir Walter Plumbley found it most amusing. He chuckled, slapped
his thigh, and winked perpetually. And Henry Rochefort, fully
mindful of the necessity for not offending, made it in his way to treat
the misfortune lightly, too.

" Of course, y'know, Rochefort," guffawed Sir Walter, " we've *got*
to make you pay for the damage."

Henry Rochefort forced a smile. " As I will, Sir Walter. But
that is but one minor aspect of this sorry affair, and I would like, if
it is your pleasure, to explain myself."

Sir Walter belched and now, with chin sunk deep, was patting his
chest.

" Proceed, my dear sir," he said invitingly.

The banker's desires were very modest, though their conclusion
was reached only after a discourse of some length. They were to the
effect that he would feel mightily obliged if the Harbour Commissioners
would receive him. His purpose then, he said, would be to tender his
regrets for the recent untoward incident.

Sir Walter Plumbley blew out his cheeks. " Hardly see any
necessity for you to do that, Rochefort," he grunted. " So long as you
put the damage all right then that's all we need to worry you about."

Mr. Rochefort protested. He felt apology was needed ; and having
caused considerable inconvenience to the Commissioners, he would
not be completely satisfied until he had made a personal appearance
before them.

" Well, if you're so insistent, Rochefort," Sir Walter conceded.

With that characteristic austerity of his adding emphasis to his
words, the banker in a dignified little speech thanked Sir Walter for
his good offices.

So it was that Henry Rochefort prepared the path for his long-term
assault upon John Fagg and the haven which the shipowner held dear.
His short-term policy was another thing, quite separate, but one
which, he was sure, would strike Fagg nearly as hard.

Hot with resolve he left the Antwerp Hotel. Immediately, just
over the way against the ruins of St. Martin-le-Grand, he walked
straight into his former friend.

Not a soul in the busy Market Place but did not loiter to witness
the outcome of the meeting of the two men.

To their disappointment, however, no act of violence took place, and neither the voice of John Fagg nor Henry Rochefort's was raised.

"I have to thank you for all this," the banker began. He intended to avoid drawing public attention to himself, for he realised that by so doing the whole town would guess how he had been fooled.

John Fagg did not attempt evasion. "You have," he remarked equably. "And 'tis but a fitting penalty, though nevertheless I'm not without dismay about it."

"How so?" Henry Rochefort asked unbelievingly.

With that expression of disbelief still persisting he heard John Fagg speak self-accusingly of the irrevocable damage which might have been done to the harbour.

"That's one reason why I'm sorry, Rochefort," continued the shipowner. "The other is because I think we should both be better employed than in squabbling. This is a time of war when personal differences should be sunk."

The banker laughed harshly. "I'm with you in that, but," his dark eyes glittered, "do you imagine in your foolishness that by this belated contrition——"

"Not contrition, Rochefort," John Fagg retorted flatly, "far be it from that. A fight suits me all right, but I was conveying that I'd sooner wait until the bigger fight is over, until we've beaten the Frenchies."

Henry Rochefort's quick brain was working apace. In his heart he agreed with what had been said. In such a course, too, the minor blow he intended would come as a more bitter pill in the palmy days of peace, a far more devastating laceration to Fagg's pride.

"That will suit me well," he said, "and so, my ingenious fellow, until the tumult of war passes from the land you may have no fear. But after that you may be sure I shall teach you the lesson you need."

John Fagg's eyes glinted. "Thinking of doing a little more building then?" he asked artlessly.

That observation, so unconcernedly delivered, very nearly caused the banker to lose his self-possession. But he was not unaware that there were a number of highly interested spectators.

"As to that, Fagg," he smiled strangely, "you shall in due course see."

It would seem that John Fagg had wearied of a situation which he was beginning to feel not dissimilar to a childish feud. In a few pungent sentences he brought Henry Rochefort back sharply from the unnamed vengeance to be exacted in days of peace ahead.

"If that's the stand you're taking, then you needn't send Godspenny around again to Elizabeth Street to inquire if you can charter the *Emma*," he said crisply.

"I have no doubt that other equally good cutters are available," the banker replied angrily.

"Maybe so," the shipowner grunted. "But if we're playing baby games, then you can't have mine."

Furiously, Henry Rochefort turned on his heel. He fired a parting shot though.

John Fagg, he snapped, would live to rue the day on which he had tricked the banker into leasing a site called the Island.

4

By the time the Little Pent reverted more or less to its old appearance the townsfolk of Dover had fresh stimulation from the arrival of large numbers of Russian soldiers. It was widely rumoured that these troops, in co-operation with a British force, would shortly essay the restoration of the Netherlands, thereby threatening the northern frontier of the French Republic.

Two or three days after the last of the savage Muscovites had been landed, Louis Rochefort and Charles Fagg returned home from school, the former for good, the latter to return for still another year.

Schooldays behind, Louis Rochefort was very much the man of the world, and very much the indulgent uncle to his twelve-year-old sister.

"Really, my dear," he smiled when, for the second time, Caroline casually mentioned the Playhouse. That evening there was to be a performance of *The School for Scandal*, a play she longed to see.

"Yes," Mr. Rochefort answered gravely in response to a question his son put to him, "undoubtedly large numbers of forged Spanish dollars are being circulated."

"Silver-plate, I suppose," Louis said keenly.

This conversation took place over the dinner table, and continued mainly financial, ending with a discussion as to when Louis should take a stool in the bank. The young man, it seemed, had no wish for a protracted summer holiday, and proposed to begin his duties forthwith.

"Shall we say Monday of next week?" Henry Rochefort suggested proudly, highly delighted with this son of his.

The suggestion was agreed upon and then, in a flash it appeared, Louis Rochefort entered into the adult world of responsibilities.

Caroline sighed. "Now he'll be able to take ladies to balls and concerts an' . . . an' *theatres*."

Her brother burst into a grin whilst Henry Rochefort, as always striving to keep pace with his children, smiled widely though perhaps a little vaguely. The banker felt certain that his daughter was up to something, but had no intention of revealing that he had not the least idea what it was.

" So you think that Louis will shortly be escorting the fair sex to assemblies and what not, eh, Caroline ? " he asked, laughing heartily.

" She wants me to take her to the Playhouse," guffawed the schemer's brother.

As it happened, Mr. Rochefort had to drive out that evening to see a hop-planter who was indebted to him in a considerable sum. The banker, too, held a number of £50 shares in the Playhouse, so there would be no difficulty about seats. Therefore Miss Rochefort had her way.

Caroline's one regret was that she could not be handed out of the carriage at the Playhouse in grand style, but, as that house of entertainment was only a few score yards along the opposite side of Snargate Street, the thought was perhaps best not broached.

However, she made the most of the short walk. Hastily bolting the remains of a succulent confection before leaving home, she took her brother's arm with fine dignity as they set forth. Females never admitting to pockets, she carried in the other hand a pretty purse, three pebbles in it, with which she toyed with a sufficiency of airs and graces.

" This is fun, Louis," she giggled, the haughty mask of her face slipping momentarily.

Louis Rochefort, one cheek bulging, made indistinct reply, but his knowing wink showed that, for the moment at least, he was back to younger days and quite forgetful of his coming importance.

Indeed, after the performance, on their way homewards in the darkness, he became distinctly boyish.

There was to be, he said, a grand rally of the Volunteers of Kent on the first of August—at Lord Rodney's Maidstone seat. He was in a great stew as to whether the tailor would be able to have his uniform ready by then.

Quite a large contingent from Dover, with wives, children and sweethearts, made the journey to Moat House, where a dinner for close on six thousand men had been prepared.

The timbered park, with a narrow sheet of water before the mansion, looked delightful on the bright summer day. There were tents and marquees, with flags lazily drooping everywhere, and the nature of the ground made an admirable amphitheatre for the spectators.

In the early afternoon serious business began. One by one, keeping perfect step, heads erect and carriage resolute, the Volunteer companies of Kent came towards the house, approaching by a hump-backed ridge over the unrippled water of a stream.

"Watch for Papa," Lou Fagg said excitedly. "Aunt Susan, are you watching for Papa?"

Susan Fagg made a smiling rejoinder and, squeezing the arm of her friend, Alice Vanderhey, passed a teasing observation which caused that young woman to blush both prettily and prodigiously.

"Your Aunt Susan," laughed Polly Fagg, ceasing an effort to glimpse Minnie, "is helping Alice to look for the Maidstone company, my love."

Miss Vanderhey was to wed, on the following Wednesday, a gentleman in that gallant band, and Susan, one of the bridesmaids, was of course staying over for the ceremony.

"I protest, Polly," the victim cried indignantly, reddening still more.

"Take no notice of her, Alice," Susan comforted her.

A band started up a martial tune and Mrs. Fagg, eagerly turning to watch the march past, forgot to deliver another bantering remark, forgot even about her elder daughter. Minnie Fagg, it may be said, was having the time of her life amongst so many males. Pleading urgently not to go back to school, her mother and father had assented to her wish, and Minnie, not sixteen yet, felt herself quite the grown-up, though in a very different sense from that experienced by Louis Rochefort.

"Don't they look beau-tiful!" Caroline Rochefort exclaimed, intent on the splendour of cocked hats, white breeches, and cut-away red coats with brightly contrasting facings.

The companies, in perfect squares, were advancing along the green-turfed frontage of the house, the swords of the officers, upraised in salute as each section swung past the dais, glistening in the strong light.

All about were the fair lands of Kent, to the southard the blue hills which tumbled into Sussex, to the eastward rolling downs, lush green meadows and gleaming cattle; stately homes, with shady groves and smooth lawns, snug farmhouses and thatched cottages; mellowed brick oast-houses and fruitful acres soon to be in full golden corn; sun-drenched villages, their ragstone, flint and timber peeping amidst the dark foliage of woods, and peaceful churchyards with spreading yews and tombstone slabs in aged but shining Bethersden marble. A glorious heritage, indeed.

5

Horn-blowing at nine in the morning on a September day meant that, in the church of St. Mary the Virgin's, the Common Councilmen were assembled for the appointment of the Mayor.

That year Mr. Joseph Denne, a colourless individual, though
nevertheless one of the elect through his office of Clerk to the Paving
Commission, received the highest honour jurats and freemen could
bestow on him.

Mr. Denne, by way of appreciation, delivered himself of a few
well-worn platitudes, avowing an unshakable determination to do
whatsoever might be within his power to forward the affairs of the
town and port.

"Then we may accept it, sir, that as a Harbour Commissioner
you'll think of the haven now and then?" John Fagg asked brusquely.

This ill-timed inquiry quite disturbed the even flow of the proceedings. Messrs. Hugo Stratton, Oliver Waade, Edward Hexstall, Robert
Spisour, Jeffrey Braems, Henry Rochefort, Paul Elam and Ralph
Jelly, in their varying manner, asserted that the shipowner was out
of order. On the other hand, Messrs. Jeremy Nethersole, Christopher
Crundall and Nicholas Stokes fiercely affirmed that a civil question
required a civil answer, with Mr. Richard Breton taking sides to the
extent of nodding judicially.

"No, I've had answer enough already," John Fagg observed
laconically, addressing himself to his supporters. Plainly he could see
that as yet there was far too much conflict of opinion, or rather that
the hostility of a powerful clique was in no wise abated.

"But . . ." he added in prophecy, "as sure as God made them
rosy apples we can smell just now, you'll all, sooner or later, realise
your duty."

With no more than that he began to march off between the lines
of laden fruit baskets and neatly bundled sheaves. Sunday next was
Harvest Thanksgiving, and the musty odours of the old church had
been splendidly replaced by the scents from the produce of field,
orchard and garden.

Mr. Fagg had not taken more than three paces when his attention
was arrested, like that of many an other, by the meek voice of Mr.
Philip Virgile.

"I've been conversing a time or two lately with Jephrez Baker,"
the cork-manufacturer announced apologetically.

Following this most uninformative beginning he looked about him,
as though hopeful that what he had said would be sufficient. Unfortunately the gentleman whose name he had mentioned was absent
that morning and, there being no help for it, Mr. Virgile, willy-nilly,
had to proceed. His further remarks were equally obscure.

"Mr. Baker has put things into my head," he confessed solemnly.
"An'——"

The ripple of laughter which succeeded this unlucky statement
entirely unnerved the cork-cutter, who in addition to incoherently

voicing his fears, spoke far too freely of the family business. How, he asked, could he obtain his bark from France, Spain and Italy after the war if vessels were unable to enter the port.

" Mr. Baker put that question to me an' . . . an' I was flabbergasted," he said defiantly. " Of course I've oft heard of the dispute about the condition of the harbour but never until now has it come home to roost so clearly. . . . "

" 'Twould affect, may ruin, every soul in the town," John Fagg remarked sympathetically, dissembling his delight about the proselyting Mr. Baker was obviously doing.

A friendly ally at hand, Mr. Virgile opened up even more. He spoke of the cork spencers he was making for seafarers, and of the limited numbers of cork-cutters, through scanty supplies of raw material, he now employed. But the war would not last for ever and, when it was over, he looked forward to building up his business to its old proportions, with perhaps fifty hands, on a piece-rate per gross corks cut. He had three boys . . .

" To be sure, Mr. Virgile," Nicholas Stokes agreed, deeply understanding. " And very natural too. But——"

" Aye, we know what the ' but ' means, Nicholas," Captain Nethersole sighed lustily. " If there ain't a haven . . . "

About now there seemed every indication that two widely differing parties would break into open quarrel, and certainly Christopher Crundall and Henry Rochefort exchanged many heated words.

" Nonsense," the banker exclaimed.

" What know you——" the boatbuilder shouted.

Dr. Woodgate, who was immensely enjoying the disputation, then belatedly recollected who he was and where he was. Extra sternly he reminded them that *this* was the House of God, an admonition which should have closed the subject. However, in the more orderly atmosphere which followed, Mr. Francis Stone, a gentleman much in the company of the official fraternity, expressed a desire to be further enlightened on the question of the haven.

" Nay, Francis," laughed Mr. Oliver Waade.

The paper-maker brushed aside the Clerk of the Cheque's raillery. His business, he observed succinctly, received its rags through the haven and dispatched the finished product by the same cheap and convenient route.

Susan Fagg, looking most attractive in a marmelouc cap and cloak, was at the church door in Cannon Street when the Common Councilmen emerged. She saw her brother in close conversation with Mr. Stone of Buckland and, as she slipped into the church with her great bunches of Michaelmas daisies and chrysanthemums, she encountered

George's brother Henry who, despite his annoyance concerning the events of the last minutes, greeted her most kindly. Henry Rochefort might hold a bitter grudge against one man but, to his credit, he would not extend it to that man's family.

In the quiet building Susan started deftly to arrange the offering, her thoughts ever on her dear love.

Outside the church, dusty, fatigued, but straightening up smartly on reaching the end of their journey, the 27th Regiment of the Line marched into the town, the forerunners of further reinforcements. The good news which had been coming from overseas was thought to be proving illusory, and already were signs of a tightening in the plans of defence. Swarms of labourers toiled in the throwing-up of fresh mounds and ramparts, and miners, directed by engineers and surveyors, started to excavate rock for the provision of further souterrains and casemates.

The Dover Volunteers, whose drilling had sunk to three times a week, now began to meet twice each day.

*   *   *   *   *   *   *   *

Day after day the Volunteers snatched an hour from shop, counting house, or works, masters and men vieing with one another to reach a high degree of proficiency.

Snargate Street-over-the-Wall being too narrow, Mr. Henry Rochefort, for drilling purposes, used to march off his staff at eleven o'clock on the dot to a smooth stretch alongside the boat-dock.

One morning in October, the second Thursday it was, the little company, fully three minutes after the eleventh reverberation of old Peter Monin's clock had died away, were still outside the bank awaiting orders. Matthew Godspenny, as great a stickler for punctuality in matters of warfare as in those of civil life, decided that this was a sorry disciplinary example.

" The precise time, sir," he began aloofly, on entering Mr. Rochefort's room, " is close upon four minutes after——"

" Very good, Mr. Godspenny," the banker broke in tartly, " I will be with you in . . . better still, take the section yourself."

Shortly afterwards, the sing-song voice of the chief clerk rang out in command, and his highly tickled subordinates, albeit keeping their grins very much to themselves, stepped out in the direction of Captain Pepper's cottage at the seaward end of the street.

Henry Rochefort was extremely busy that morning. The rising number of forged coins, and the increasing skill of the forgers, were creating an acute problem, and to add to this there had been a bad harvest and much report of commercial instability from a great Hanseatic port.

" These various bills for the B. of E., Papa ? " his son called out.

The banker was examining a news-advice which had been so important that his London agent had sent it down by horseman through the night. The *La Lutine*, 32 guns, Captain L. Skynner, Royal Navy, had been lost off Terschelling in the recent heavy N.N.W. gale. She had been carrying a fortune in *louis d'or* and Spanish dollars to the Low Countries, for those British troops whose position by now was, incidentally, becoming desperate.

" Er . . . they'll discount them at 5 per cent per annum not exceeding sixty-one days," he replied.

Louis dealt competently with his task, after which, there still being ample time before the post office would decline packages for the night mail, he went off with his father.

" Why are the government so dilatory in issuing weapons, Papa ? " he asked, frowning at the sight of Mr. William Beverley's ill-equipped men. " Surely 'tis most unbusinesslike after all these years."

Henry Rochefort sighed, thinking of various portents. " And dangerous, I fear, my boy."

Markets are often sound pointers, and many ill-tidings were soon to come. The British force in Holland, compelled to withdraw, were allowed to do so only on the humiliating condition that 8,000 French and Batavian prisoners in England should be released. The conduct of Russia, too, was another shock, her crazy Tsar deciding that she must withdraw from the Coalition, this taking place not long after the subservient Directory, terrified by the charges of mismanagement levelled at them by one who was their servant, made effort at placating General Bonaparte, on his return from the East, by appointing him First Consul.

By then, after being in the bank no more than six months, Louis Rochefort had become of very real assistance to his father.

Of this Mr. Henry Rochefort spoke one evening when Sir Walter Plumbley had condescended to take a glass of wine in the Snargate Street mansion.

The Harbour Commissioner nodded profoundly. " Not surprised to hear that, Rochefort," he remarked sagaciously. " I've got an eye for a sharp lad, y'know, an', by George, you need to have your wits about you these days."

Which from every point of view, and most certainly from the financial, was absolutely true. There had been a series of grave failures at Hamburg, with the exchange falling 14 per cent below par and gold touching 85s. an ounce.

" Indeed so, Sir Walter," the banker agreed just a little irritably. A number of London bankers were, in the circumstances, making substantial profits by the smuggling of coin, but Henry Rochefort refused to enter into the traffic, believing that it was against the interests of his country. Still his slight irascibility was but human nature, for it must have been galling to know that others of his profession, those with fewer scruples, were working to such advantage.

"And now, Rochefort," the Harbour Commissioner began weightily, "pray let me have for consideration your submissions on the mattter you spoke to me on."

This was with regard to the receipts for harbour dues which, owing to the slowly deteriorating condition of the haven, were on a steadily downward trend. Henry Rochefort, a few days before, had ventured to suggest to Sir Walter Plumbley a very simple remedy for this growing ill.

"In short, Rochefort," that gentleman now observed when the banker had concluded, "y'mean squeeze more out of the existing lessees, saving . . . " he winked, " the lessee o' Paradise Pent."

Mr. Rochefort duly paid tribute to that piece of wit, though he cautiously dissented from the use of the word "squeeze." It was, he declared, rather a question of upward adjustment to a basis more compatible . . .

Sir Walter was grunting about " the splitting of hairs " when his host's son came in. Louis Rochefort, between his long hours at the bank, drilling with the Volunteers, reviews and military church parades, was collecting subscriptions for a bridge proposed to be erected at Severus's Gate, and altogether tremendously busy.

"I swear he never has a minute," his sister Caroline laughingly told Lou one day at Little Pent House. "Or rather," she amended, loosely knowing that there was some distinction between the two, " he knows exactly each minute what he has to do."

Lou had been reading a story of rich pashas and, giggling, she inferred that she knew just what Louis's industry would make him.

"The wealthiest man in Dover, with hundreds of servants, an' dozens of wives——"

Her friend's face fell, for this far-fetched flight of fancy possessed delicious scope for development. But fact is fact, and she had heard Louis advocating a London office when peace came and, from his attitude to young women, she was sure that he would always put the bank first.

"But we can still pretend, Lou," she said, greatly relieved by this solution.

The two girls were doubled in mirth when the mistress of the house came up from the kitchen. For once Mrs. Fagg was vile-tempered, the cause being half a dozen heavy and unpalatable loaves which had just come out of the oven. Recently the government, striving to ameliorate a gravely critical shortage, had passed the Brown Bread Act. This, besides forbidding the sale of bread either new or pure white wheaten, insisted that it should be made half of rye.

"And, pray, what are you making all this silly noise for?" she asked crossly.

"Oh, Mamma," her daughter gasped, quite exhausted by merriment.

"Oh, Mrs. Fagg," Caroline Rochefort murmured, tears of joy streaming.

A ludicrous story in which Louis Rochefort, Mayor of Dover, was entering St. Mary's for Sunday morning service at the very moment when the last of an immense line of children was emerging from his residence in Snargate Street, was not to be told.

The long-protracted struggle with France was having its effect on well-to-do and poor alike, not the less so because it seemed that, with General Bonaparte now the leader of a military despotism, the war might be said to be beginning all afresh.

So, whilst information trickled over of the French commandeering Batavian barges for the carriage of cavalry horses, the wealthy grumbled about taxation and the poor about their privations. Nor could there be any doubt but that these last were very real. Bread was the staff of life and, out of earnings which did not average more than half a guinea a week, the labouring classes, against the fourpence for which they would have bought a quartern loaf at the time of the outbreak of the Revolution, were now compelled to pay one shilling and tenpence for a much inferior article.

It was perhaps God's mercy that wheat fell in price before irrevocable mischief was done.

CHAPTER TWO

I

Towards the middle of the year there were two public ceremonies largely attended by the townsfolk. The first, a necessity arising from the cruel ravages of war, was the consecration of a new burial ground outside the Castle walls.

It was a very solemn affair, on leaving which it was most inappropriate that Susan Fagg should have been softly trilling a three-year-old song which, in the renewed threat of recent months, had taken on a fresh lease of country-wide popularity. Its sentiments came

222 DOVER HARBOUR

strange from her gentle lips, but in extenuation of that it had a most
taking air.

> " We'll fight for our right to the island,
> We'll give them enough of the island,
> Invaders should just, bite at the dust,
> But not a bit more of the island."

" You *are* happy, Aunt Susan," Lou Fagg said affectionately.

Her aunt just nodded gaily. She had had another letter from
George in which he had told her that he hoped to be home from the
Mediterranean by the end of the year. And now she had decided to
mark off the days before his return instead of, on the morrow, adding
another day to the one year, nine months and four days since she had
parted from him.

" She's thinking of Caroline's uncle," her niece Minnie announced
quite unnecessarily, meantime taking a frank interest in a pitiable
debtor who was being dragged to jail.

There was a slight squabble between the two girls, during which
Lou, flushing to the roots of her fair hair, confessed that if she had a
sailor lover in far-away blue seas she would often think of him.

" Oft," she repeated firmly, quashing her elder sister.

Coincidences cannot be commonplace if they are to be worthy of
their reputation and it chanced that, just as Lou was speaking so
poetically about blue waters, a young gentleman, fresh from that same
sea, was approaching.

Susan Fagg, stretching to secure a lovely piece of pear-blossom,
saw him first.

" Jack," she gasped. " *Jack Woodgate*, I do swear."

In nigh on four years the son of the rector of St. Mary the Virgin's
had changed. He was taller and more squarely set, and his deeply
bronzed face had taken on itself lines of youthful authority.

" Jack ! " Minnie Fagg cried, eyeing him admiringly. " 'Tis
indeed delightful to see you, Jack. Only yesterday was I thinking
that it surely seemed like as if never again should we . . . "

" Hullo, Jack," Lou murmured shyly.

" Hullo, Lou," he smiled warmly.

But he was still the same old Jack Woodgate, even to the outgrown
coat and the short sleeves disclosing a good three inches of wrist. Just
the same serious lad who, in dogged pursuit of a career he could never
have been sure of attaining, fitted himself for every hazard of that
career by swimming across the Basin an immense number of times.

" When did you return, Jack ? " Susan Fagg asked excitedly.

" Do you think we've changed greatly, Jack ? " Minnie inquired
coyly, fingering one of his brass buttons whilst he answered her aunt.

Mr. Woodgate, Midshipman of the Royal Navy, dealt factually with that. Solemnly scanning the ladies in turn, he made report. Aunt Susan, he said, still using the name of childhood, was thinner of face but beyond that there was not the least difference. Minnie was much taller but apart from that he did not see any alteration, and as for Lou . . .

" I do declare, Jack," John Fagg's elder daughter pouted crossly, " that you are the most ungallant sailor I ever heard of."

" And as for Lou," the forthright young gentleman went on unheedingly, " I'll take my oath that she is much more presentable than she used to be."

Lou, blushing under the unwavering scrutiny, now found that she had something of which to complain.

" So I was mortal repulsive when I was smaller ? " she demanded, her colour still heightening.

Mr. Woodgate straightened up that misconception. She had been far from repulsive, he asserted, but never had struck him as being pretty.

Minnie, very much on the high horse, went off in search of some friends. And Susan Fagg, so funny did she think it all, was hardly able to hold herself in.

" But now you find Lou is, Jack ? " she laughed and laughed.

Again he made appraisal. " I vow she is most amazingly pretty, Aunt Susan," he declared, very humanly this time.

Lou's nose was in the air. " Thank you kindly, sir," she replied huffily.

" I say . . . " the blunt-spoken youth began somewhat apologetically.

Miss Lou Fagg gave him no more than the back of her bonnet at which to look.

There was one thing above all which Susan wanted to know. Had Jack seen her lover; surely when they were in the same fleet . . .

No, Mr. Woodgate had seen nothing of Mr. George Rochefort, but he believed that Mr. George's ship would be ordered home soon. Sailing with nothing more than a sheath of copper between her and eternity . . . it was time she was relieved.

" Jack ! " Miss Susan Fagg's hand went to her heart, she being alarmed by the parlous state of her dear one's vessel.

That gentleman, vaguely perturbed by Lou's scornful " frightening Aunt Susan so," hurriedly explained an expression arising from the thrifty Lord St. Vincent's tenure at the Admiralty.

" 'Tis true we put in much sea-time whereas the Frenchies stay in harbour," he boasted. " But . . . "

He quoted his beloved Sir Horatio. " Their fleet suffers more in a fortnight than ours in a year."

Miss Lou Fagg, on this, gave him a disdainful little nod of approval.

With an old friend at home again there was new pleasure in familiar pastimes. When Charles arrived back from school he and Jack spent the hot days in the old sports of sailing and swimming and picnicking, with Louis Rochefort joining in whenever he could spare the time. The older boys listened entranced to the young sailor's talk of battles and sudden death, of foreign lands and of foreign ways, of many things.

" 'Tis no lie, Charles," Jack Woodgate sighed enviously. " There is a post-captain who reached his rank after being only a month at sea. Would that I had such influence."

" How old was he, Jack ? "

" Fifteen," Midshipman Woodgate remarked glumly.

Louis Rochefort testified that similar abuses existed in the Army, and referred to an article in *The Times* of some three years before.

" Youths of fourteen with commissions in the Guards," he said conclusively. " ' Baby officers ' and ' sickly colonels ' the writer described 'em."

" Well . . . " young Mr. Woodgate commented regretfully.

It was time then to go to Severus's Gate, where the second public ceremony of that summer was to take place. Surrounded by a considerable concourse the Port-Agent for Prisoners of War laid the foundation stone of a bridge which was to span the Dour, thus giving quick access from Bench Street to the Ropewalk. The bridge was to be built in brick which Fagg vessels had brought from Grays in Essex, and the constructors, with a dread example before them, took every precaution to ensure the bed of the river should not be interfered with.

Mrs. Fagg was there with her husband and, after smilingly noting that her daughter Lou and Jack Woodgate were in animated conversation, she saw Henry Rochefort, with whom was his daughter. Caroline was wearing a pretty spotted dress, and on her head was a bonnet which was really fetching.

" John," she said suddenly, " just look at that girl. She's a picture, isn't she ? "

" A bonnie little lass," the shipowner heartily agreed, glancing at a very lovely profile.

" She's uncommonly like her mother," Polly Fagg continued. " Though . . . " She hardly knew how to word her thoughts. It was rather that she thought Caroline would never be quite the beauty Elizabeth had been, but that Elizabeth's daughter had a vivacity which her very dear friend had never had.

Miss Rochefort was having a great day, and that afternoon she gave a most stately tea party in the big drawing-room.

The earliest of all to arrive were her most intimate companions, and it was then that she decided she must conform to the tradition of her darling mother.

"But 'tis most awkward, Martha," she gesticulated. "Tea without Ladywell water——" She closed her eyes in sharp disgust at the very idea.

Martha Teddiman, who had been gaping at her young mistress's antics, very nearly made a most unfortunate disclosure. A small foot pressed on her own prevented that.

"But, Miss Caroline," she had begun, "Old Teakettle Tom——"

"The wretched creature," Miss Rochefort interposed in fine pet. "On this very afternoon . . . still . . ." she sighed delicately.

It would be most improper for a hostess not to be present to receive her friends, one gathered she said, and Lou Fagg, on whom the glance from a pair of distressed brown eyes had fallen, immediately offered to go to the Maison Dieu.

Caroline brightened instantly. "*How* delightful of you, Lou," she murmured charmingly, taking care not to look at Martha who, with arms akimbo, was watching her grimly. "But, my dear, I fear 'twould be too heavy for you an'——"

Again her disappointed eyes roved, this time to dwell a little on Jack Woodgate.

"I'll go with Lou, Caroline," that simple soul remarked with alacrity.

"But really, Jack . . ." Miss Rochefort seemed rather aghast, "do you think I ought to let you?"

"Don't be silly, Caroline," grunted the young sailor.

From then the hostess of the afternoon began to mature until, by the middle of tea, she was a matron of not less than forty.

Being such, she was entitled to view that very young couple, Lou and Jack, with a benign and indulgent smile flickering about her lips.

Charles Fagg, much amused, had been watching this comedy for some little while. Now, across the Harbour-master's son, he solicitously inquired as to whether Miss Rochefort had toothache.

"Toothache, Mr. Fagg . . . Charles?" His hostess lost some of her formality when she came fully out of her fantasy.

On hearing that she was in no pain, Charles gravely expressed his pleasure, in response to which Caroline thanked him profusely for his regard for her.

"Not at all, Caroline," he replied pleasantly, at the same time taking certain unseen precautions. He knew what might be done within the concealing cover of a table.

Miss Rochefort ended the matter by bowing graciously, and then resumed her conversation with another friend.

Very soon afterwards 'Colonel' Breton gave a sharp yelp of pain.

H

" Ugh," he shouted. " Somebody's kicked me."

His hostess turned a most innocent and shocked face. It was impossible, her expression declared, that such horseplay could occur at one of her elegant functions.

" Somebody has *kicked* you ? " she asked unbelievingly.

' Colonel ' Breton, his face growing redder and redder, was staring menacingly at the elder Braems boy, a sworn enemy.

" An' I know who did it," he said threateningly, rising forthwith.

Louis Rochefort and others of the older males put an end to the heated dispute. But there was quite a bit of disorder.

During the disturbance the eyes of Charles Fagg and Caroline Rochefort chanced to meet. One of the young gentleman's closed in sober triumph, whereupon that very young lady, mouth beginning to twitch, hastily but haughtily turned away.

2

The Commissioners of Harbour decided, with one reservation, to advance by a quarter the annual rents of all lessees on their estate. If further evidence of falling revenue was needed, a glance at the haven day by day provided all the corroboration necessary.

In short, the number of vessels entering and leaving, as proved by the figures of Mr. Warren, the Collector of Customs, was steadily declining. And, as any one with a pair of eyes might have remarked, hardly any but the most desultory and scamped attempts at repair were being effected in those parts of the haven vitally needing attention.

John Fagg called together an informal gathering at Elizabeth Street to discuss the depressing situation.

" Aye," grunted Christopher Crundall, " 'tis a gloomy outlook."

" What with this on our doorstep and the war news," Mr. Francis Stone commented lugubriously.

The distressing information was at hand that the First Consul, after transgressing all military canons by crossing the St. Bernard Pass incredibly swiftly, had struck, at Marengo, so hard against the Austrians that all Italy had fallen into his hands.

" Discouragement after discouragement," the paper manufacturer resumed, his voice melancholy.

With canny foresight, Mr. Fagg led the discussion into safer channels. None knew better than he how his two staunch allies, Jeremy Nethersole and Nicholas Stokes, Tory and Whig, must inevitably exchange bitter words if the war continued as a topic.

" Now, gentlemen," he began briskly, " there's the question of the Passing Tolls to consider."

Then there was argument and an immediate split of opinion, with a concensus of opinion against the shipowner and Mr. Virgile, his sole supporter. Mr. Jephrez Baker was particularly vehement.

"I see no wisdom in attempting to secure money which the Harbour Commissioners would handle," the tallow-chandler snapped.

It was John Fagg's belief that, if the townsfolk themselves, by petition, could obtain for the haven a greater share of the Tolls, they would be in a much better position, should the receipts not be used for their rightful purpose, to charge the Commissioners with dereliction of duty.

But he was no mean tactician, and he realised the perils which come from lack of unanimity. Therefore the question of the Passing Tolls, he suggested, should be deferred for discussion until the time appeared more opportune.

That ended the proceedings in so far as they concerned the haven, and the seven gentlemen could give more attention to their pipes and glasses.

"I hear there's a goodly amount o' coin being smuggled abroad by the Folkestone cutters," Mr. Breton observed, stroking a shaven head. For greater comfort he had taken off his wig which, incidentally, since the law now forbade it, was not as beforehand powdered with flour.

At this, several pairs of eyes were turned on John Fagg, but the shipowner's caustic references to those who profit to their country's detriment made his position clear and brought the talk to the more honourable aspects of illicit venture.

"Autumn'll be coming round again," chuckled the Clerk of the Passage, looking up from his labours.

He was cutting a piece of Flushing tobacco—a cleverly disguised article made in the form of a rope, rum-washed hemp being laid over a highly-dutiable core

"'Twill, Nicholas," guffawed Captain Nethersole. "Eh, John?"

Four months later, on the eve of Dover Fair, seven weeks after an angered country heard of still another disastrous expedition, that of Sir James Pulteney at Ferrol, the shipowner found himself in the tightest corner of his life.

Singularly enough, at the very moment when John Fagg received information that the Dragoons were closing in, the sail-of-the-line upon whose watch-bill George Rochefort's name was entered, passed within half a mile of the South Pier.

Apart from the poor illumination from a purser's dip, it was dark in that cramped and evil-smelling place below the water-line.

Seaman George Rochefort, in effort to expel a little of the foul air, worked vigorously on the hand-pump and, this done, wryly took a sip of tainted water before completing the missive upon which he was engaged.

Smiling a little he continued with his task, that of writing to a young married woman in Maidstone.

" Alice . . . Alice . . . damme ! " He frowned momentarily until her new surname came to him and then, laughing afresh, he addressed the letter.

He stowed the folded sheet into his ditty box and thereupon, a sense of excitement gripping him, made for the upper deck, ducking beneath the lines of hammocks vaguely outlined by the rays from a magazine lantern.

The night was dark and only faintly could he see the black line of high land and the great fortification of the Castle on its loftiest point.

In the town of his birth there were strange happenings that night, with Dragoons, at first guarding all roads of egress, now beginning to move in a lessening arc towards the foreshore.

Ralph Toke had suffered many humiliations before he had been granted, on this occasion, the aid of the armed forces of the Crown.

The Colonel of Dragoons had no more love for the servants of Revenue and Excise than had any man, gentleman or humblest labourer. But a written instruction from London, and on none other could he have been compelled to act, forced on him a most distasteful task.

" Very well, Mr. Toke," he had said icily that afternoon.

Thus it was arranged and, as six bells sounded sweetly in the vessel over whose broad bulwarks George Rochefort was leaning, the Dragoons began to move.

The landing of the goods took place on the beach opposite Trevanion Street, by the old fishermen's church of St. James's.

John Fagg was not caught wholly unawares. Three flaming bundles of straw told him what was afoot. They showed, almost simultaneously, from the vicinity of the Bredenstone, from the plague-graveyard above Archcliffe Fort, from the Deal road, high above Tinker's Close.

The free-trader acted with all that decision of which he was capable. Fortunately, through the nature of the cargo, he had no wagons to trouble about.

With amazing dispatch the coach-houses of a number of convenient residences were quietly opened up for the bestowal within of a precious cargo, and as the wooden cross-bar of the Water Bailiff's stable was placed into position, John Fagg received report from faithful subordinates.

" That's the lot then," he said gravely, wiping sweat off his forehead with the back of his hand.

Then came final orders. Lie low or gain their homes if that

seemed practicable was the command for those who were not horsemen.

Came faintly the sound of the iron-shod feet of the soldiers' beasts. The Dragoons flew across the Market Place, then along King Street and Bench Street, the company dividing at Severus's Gate, part turning towards the Pier district, the remainder spurring along Town Wall Street.

Putting Mr. Spisour's house behind him, John Fagg dived on to the Ropewalk as the thunder of horsemen began to increase.

Turning to face east he smiled a little. Around the base of the great Castle cliff a string of one hundred and thirty ' riders,' led by a cat-eyed individual who knew every rock, cranny and track, was making by this most ingenious route for St. Margaret's Bay and, after many a detour, for home.

John Fagg did likewise.

Nowadays, whenever John was out o' night on ' business,' Polly Fagg never slept well, and always she kept a candle burning.

She was wide awake when her husband returned. He was breathing somewhat heavily.

" A fairly near call to-night, my dear," he told her in response to anxious inquiry.

" Everything is all right, John ? " she persisted.

He was telling her that, by George, he would soon be ashamed of her when, at the front door, there came a hammering on the panels.

" John," Mrs. Fagg said faintly.

Never, assure her as he would, had he seen this competent wife of his in such a pother. He must go at once and ascertain what was to do, she declared tremblingly.

" An honest citizen doesn't waken all at once," twinkled John Fagg, leisurely discarding a dark hat and drawing on an article of nightwear.

It was this disconcerting sock-like nightcap which Clement Foxley, as he delivered his message, saw in the dim light cast by the lantern he held aloft.

" An' what," John Fagg yawned widely, " is the Revenue Officer's need of me at this ungodly hour ? "

A set of stained teeth were bared in a smile. The shipowner learnt that Valentine Pepper and eighteen men had been caught, red-handed, running brandy. As attempt at arrest had been met by force, the offence had become of a capital nature. An information was to be sworn against them, for which purpose the Mayor—and the Town Clerk, to allow of no mistake—were at that moment being dragged out of bed.

Returning to the bedroom the free-trader dallied for that interval which otherwise he would have taken in dressing, meanwhile acquainting his wife with the circumstances.

"You are sure 'tis all right, John?" Mrs. Fagg asked again, though her husband's calm had gone far towards soothing her.

"Sure, m'dear," he laughed. "You can take it, Polly, my love, that one of the life-policies I've been paying out for is coming in very handy after all."

Leaving his wife to reflect on this mysterious observation, the ship-owner went downstairs.

The scene was strange. A wagon, piled with casks, standing on Custom House Quay. Mr. Toke and his men, with Mr. Oliver Waade, the Mayor, and Mr. Hugo Stratton, the Town Clerk, pressed about a yard entrance, a few paces into which Valentine Pepper stood watch before his confederates, a menacing baulk of timber in his strong hands.

"Well, gentlemen," John Fagg smiled easily.

"Well, Mr. Fagg," the Revenue Officer smiled too, his eyes gleefully malicious.

There was no real reason, the circumstances being as he and his master alone knew them, for Valentine Pepper to betray any anxiety. Nevertheless instinctive fear of Mr. Toke's dark methods was causing the boatswain to take every precaution.

A hoarse warning came from him as Clement Foxley and three men, trying to take advantage of this diversion, sidled a pace or two nearer.

"Keep your distance," he growled. "Think I'll allow you villains to plant a weppin on me?"

"Weapon or no, Mr. Fagg," gloated Ralph Toke, "he's employed violence and to this I've already called the attention of His Worship an' Mr. Stratton."

After a warm bed it was chill out there and Mr. Waade shivered transiently. Whereupon Mr. Stratton, blowing out his cheeks anticipatively, recalled that it was the custom, whenever a seizure of liquor had been made, to broach a tub for the inward gratification of all.

"Though," the frozen Clerk of the Cheque chimed in pointedly, "I doubt if Mr. Toke has come across the practice since he came to these parts."

The Revenue Officer swallowed this unpalatable hometruth as well as he might and, whilst one of the men was sent for a cask, he gave his testimony before God.

"I, Ralph Toke, being His Majesty's Officer of Revenue for . . .

apprehended the same Valentine Pepper together with . . . tubs of spirituous liquor upon which no duty . . . So help me——"

From the darkness there came a cry of astonishment and dismay.

" What ! " the Revenue Officer shouted wildly in reply.

Now the lanterns were about the wagon where Ralph Toke, fury and inconceivable mortification joined in him, desperately searched through the remainder of the load.

Hugo Stratton, strange in him, burst into a quite unlawyerlike bellow.

" Vinegar, begad ! " Mr. Waade chuckled, taking a sniff himself. " Mr. Stratton, damme me if this ain't the most comic——"

" Comic ! " screeched the Revenue Officer, now lost to all reason. " Fagg has played a trick on the majesty of the law an'——"

The shipowner, grave as a judge, inquired of the Town Clerk as to the illegality or otherwise of a man carrying on his business at whatever hour he considered fit.

" Carrying on his business . . . " Mr. Stratton, a thick-necked man, wheezed and choked.

Ralph Toke, white as death, his lips a thin line, ordered Clement Foxley to assemble the men.

Soon Custom House Quay was silent again.

Parting company at Severus's Gate, John Fagg had a last word with the Mayor and Town Clerk. He suggested that neither should be surprised at whatever he might find in his stable the morn.

It was Mr. Waade's turn now. He laughed so much that Mr. Stratton felt impelled to clap him on the back.

As dawn was breaking three highly respected gentlemen of Dover, bitterly opposed in other instances, parted from one another with a strong sense of fellowship.

Once more John Fagg had made a successful run.

3

Shortly before Christmas, in the last week of the last term of Charles Fagg's schooldays, an unprecedented south-westerly gale swept up the Channel. Within forty-eight hours eleven ships had been cast away on the South Sand of the Goodwins and three more in the spume-misted waters over the barely hidden Bunt Head, that western tip of the North Sand. Within this short space more than two hundred lives were lost.

The harbour of Dover suffered desolating damage, and altogether, in the closing days of the year, the outlook, both close to the Cinque Port and further away, was singularly unpropitious, for in Germany the French had earlier, at Hohenlinden, won the victory which crushed remaining continental resistance.

England, late in the eighth year of the war, once more found herself struggling alone.

In France immense numbers of flat-bottomed boats were being laid down.

Invasion tactics had changed. Formerly the enemy had sought to effect conquest by the landing, from sail-of-the-line, of comparatively small bodies of troops.

Now warships were not thought of. Innumerable boats, transporting tens of thousands of war-seasoned soldiers, were the latest concept for the subjugation of a proud people.

With England still poorly prepared, apart from her navy, and with only 198,000 men in arms, including Volunteers, that Christmas of 1800 was not a pleasant one.

Charles might be a tall, nicely-built, well-formed young gentleman, but Keziah Hart, maybe overcome on seeing him, gave him an old-time buffet about the head.

His sisters reacted to his arrival in their several ways, and his mother, after kissing him fondly, promptly took him into the drawing-room. Mrs. Fagg, latterly, had had the sofas covered with striped silk and of these she was extremely proud.

The son of the house, with a twinkle at the back of his grey eyes, made no comment on the attractive change. Instead, ignoring many indirect allusions, he presented his mother with a parcel containing a dress length of Chamberry, made on Canterbury looms at the factory belonging to the father of a school friend.

" Charles ! " exclaimed Polly Fagg, delightedly fingering the elegant cotton.

She was giving him another hug when Lou brought in Shep, the pup whose birth, eight months before, had caused dear old Nell's death.

" Lou, be very careful that Shep doesn't——" Mrs. Fagg began, alarmed about her new furnishings.

The young sheepdog, one glance only at the newcomer, gave a frantic leap, and from that continued to lick, slobber, jump, until at last the mistress of the house demanded his instant removal.

" And now, Charles," that lady continued when the menace had been withdrawn, " sit down with me." She patted the upholstery invitingly. " Sit down on the *sofa*, dear."

Gravely her unobservant son did as she wished. Meanwhile Minnie expostulated hotly about a party at which they were all expected that evening, appealing on one particular aspect to her brother, surely a man of affairs now.

" I do declare," Mrs. Fagg said vehemently, " to hear you talk, Minnie, one would think you were grown up instead of being little more than a child yourself."

" Still, Mother," Mr. Charles Fagg dissented, " 'tis hardly fun playing baby games with little girls an'——"

Mrs. John Fagg put her foot down, hard. She was not going to have Mrs. Jelly offended and they would all accept the very kind invitation which had been given them.

" Very good, ma'am," Charles grinned. And grinned even more when, after rising to go upstairs, he bent down to whisper. " I do avow, Mrs. Fagg, that you have the most excellent taste when it comes to the decoration of a genteel home."

" Charles ! " his mother shouted and, seeing herself so scored off, started to laugh.

But, two at a time, he was flying up the stairs and, in his bedroom, went to one of the windows to look at old haunts.

The wind had backed to the eastward and, with the new drift, the aftermath of storm and destruction was being collected along the full width of the bay.

For a while he remained there, drinking in a scene he ever loved, whatever might be the prevailing weather. And after that he began to unpack, briskly putting his clothes in their appointed places, his books in the bureau he had once begged for his own.

" Ah ! " he smiled, fumbling for the hidden catch of the hidey-hole.

Much amused, he started to lift out the cherished possessions of youth—a few sea-shells, a tangled fishing-line, a box which in old days had held worms.

" Really, Charles," he laughed.

But, aged as he might be, he did test the efficacy of that secret drawer.

Placing a slim schoolbook in position, he gave a sharp heel-tap on the floor and, heigh-ho, it was gone.

Then he went downstairs, there to greet his father and his aunt, a firm handshake for the one and an affectionate kiss for the other.

The family, united again, sat down to dinner.

The Jellys' party was the usual sort of affair and, of course, rhymed charades played their part.

" Now try to guess this one," the Jellybag said competently, giving the good-looking Charles Fagg a fleeting though fascinating smile.

She started to read from a slip of paper.

> " Divided I'm a gentleman
> In public deeds and powers.
> United I'm a monster who
> That gentleman devours."

The spy fever was once more in the ascendant, the capture of a number of these French emissaries having fanned the public temper. After many extraordinary suggestions the answer was provided, one with the topical flavour of A-GENT.

" And now methinks . . . " Miss Jelly smiled archly. " I propose we play forfeits."

In due course Mr. Charles Fagg was under the injunction to choose a lady and take her to the parlour and there kiss her.

Studiously avoiding the invitation in his hostess's eye, he quickly scanned the line of females of his own age, sighing inwardly. Then he chanced on Caroline's flushed face—Caroline liked parties, he remembered. A pretty little thing, she would save him some tedious moments.

" I think," he laughed carelessly, " that Caroline will serve admirably."

Miss Rochefort, two extra-high spots of colour in her cheeks, marched with dignity to the parlour.

" And what, m'dear," he asked kindly, " have you been doing with yourself lately ? "

" I suck my toes monstrous often, Charles," she confessed.

He eyed her and then, in a flash, knew what it was. " My apologies, m'dear," he grinned. " I'm afraid——"

" How dare you ? " she said passionately. " Do you know how old I am ? "

Thinking of Lou, he hazarded " thirteen," to receive from the termagant the truth. " Nearly, *very* nearly, fourteen," Miss Rochefort announced witheringly.

She really was a pretty little thing, he again thought, and, he grinned anew, certainly the moments had not been tedious.

" You must forgive me, Caroline," he smiled. " And now I suppose . . . " He put his arm about her slim shoulders.

" I won't allow you to kiss me, Charles," she declared tempestuously.

Never has a young man been so surprised as Charles Fagg when, bending down to settle the forfeit, his face was slapped just as hard as a blazing-eyed young creature could slap it. And never has a grown man of just eighteen been so confused, not because of a stinging cheek, but by reason of a pair of lips so soft and fragrant and sweet.

Caroline was strangely white. " Will . . . will you be so good as to take me back, please," she asked him, her voice very low.

" I'm mighty sorry, Caroline," he muttered awkwardly. " I've been——"

He was cut short by a miss who, unbelievingly quickly, recovered her spirit.

" And never, *never* speak to me again," Miss Rochefort said stormily, fire in her brown eyes.

Often in the past had Charles, after some trick or difference, made Caroline laugh when he had caught her glance.

But for the remainder of that evening she never so much as looked his way. All he saw was a young lady of thirteen, *very* nearly fourteen, for whose favour grown men of his own age sought with no little fervour.

4

To lie outright to her brother and dear Polly, never did Susan Fagg think she would be able to do it, *never*. It was a wicked thing to do, and never did heart beat so loud as did hers when, one of Alice's letters in her hand and the other tucked away in her bag, she entered Little Pent House.

Luckily it was close on candle-lighting time and, what with this and the counter interest of the haversacks and belts and other trappings which, it being his purpose to join the Volunteers forthwith, had been delivered for her nephew Charles's inspection, no one noticed her agitation whilst she explained.

Her sister-in-law, indeed, twitted her about her excitement, and chided her on the grounds that she was out of breath with hurrying overmuch.

" Calm yourself, Susan love," Mrs. Fagg laughed. " Goodness me, one would think you were going away for a lifetime."

Later, of course, the letter was handed round. Her dear James, wrote Alice, was to go to a regiment of regulars for a musketry course, and, though she asked pardon for this short notice, she begged her dear Susan to keep her company during her husband's absence.

" The day after to-morrow by the first coach," John Fagg observed. " Mmmm . . . " he murmured, and then remarked that Charles had better go along to the Royal Oak Coach Office and book a seat in the stage for his aunt. On the morrow, he reminded his wife, the Dover Volunteers and the Essex Militia were to combine in a *feu de joie* to celebrate the union of Great Britain and Ireland, and if many spectators stayed overnight even the usual cheap squeeze into the basket would be at a premium.

Mrs. Fagg smilingly folded the sheet. " I'm sure Alice is extremely agreeable," she commented. " Of course I always said she was a nice girl. The very first occasion I set eyes on her . . ."

The former Miss Vanderhey, at the conclusion of a gossipy letter, during the course of which she mentioned seeing Mr. George Roche-fort's parson friend, David Garroway, " whom I found most pleasant," sent much love to all, " especially to dearest Polly who cosseted me so, so delightfully when I stayed under her hospitable roof ! "

When Susan had gone to her room Polly Fagg declared that the little change would do the girl good.

" 'Tis all very well her living in George, but I vow she'd be better if she was . . . was a little nearer earth than heaven."

Her husband nodded. " Aye," he agreed reflectively, " an' she hasn't had a lot of real happiness with George if it comes to that."

John Fagg little knew how soon even that measure of happiness was to be cruelly snatched from his sister.

*   *   *   *   *   *   *   *

On that cold winter's morning Susan Fagg necessarily had to dress by the light of her candle and then, barely tasting her breakfast, she went upstairs again.

Fearing paper currency she had hoarded away a few guineas, saved from her ribbon-money, and from this small fund she took out what would be sufficient.

" Ready, Aunt Susan ? " Charles called from the hall.

" Yes . . . yes, Charles," she cried, frantically putting away Alice's other letter, the one which she had perused so many times.

" . . . so, my dear," Alice had penned impulsively, " you will take the same stage and at Ashford you will, I vouch for it, receive the most delishus surprise of your life. The gallant sailor who has writ me from Chatham—shall I or shall I not inscribe his name. . . ."

When her nephew bounded up she was engrossed over a second purse into which she was placing counterfeit coins, in prudent precaution against any highwayman who might be on the road.

" It's stopped snowing, Aunt Susan," he told her. " An' methinks the fall has only been slight, so you are not like to be unduly de-layed."

Prompt on the hour the throbbing Miss Susan Fagg of Dover left for her assignation.

The countryside was clothed in a coating of virginal white on that morning she journeyed to her lover, but Susan Fagg saw little of it. Everything seemed in strange blur—the houses at Folkestone, the winter-grey sea between that village and Hythe, the farm buildings about the winding turnpike which from there left the coast directly behind.

Only when the stage crossed the graceful, four-arched stone bridge at Ashford did she more fully realise her surroundings.

She saw George at once, in the doorway of the Saracen's Head, and remarked, too, that his uniform clothing, the blue jacket, red waistcoat and white trousers of the King's Navy, were sadly worn and in need of repair. But after that everything went misty again.

"George," she said faintly, burying her face in his breast as he took her in his arms.

"My dearest Susan," he murmured fondly, finger raising her chin.

"Oh, George," she sobbed, "it has been such an age, such, such an age."

"Come, my angel," he laughed, "'Twon't do, my dear."

He must have picked up her valise, must have armed her into the hostelry, must have given her a glass of lemon-sweet spirits . . . for she came to vivid life in the calash which awaited his orders, with her valise still there, and a most comforting glow stealing over her.

Now she could look properly at him, could stroke a cheek which was deeply bronzed. And, pity filming her own blue eyes, she saw that his face, thinned beyond what it had ever been, bore all the traces of the hard life he led.

"Have you suffered terribly, George?" she asked miserably.

A muscular arm tightened about her. "'Twas hell at first, my love," he admitted freely. "And even now, accustomed as I be to all its ills, 'tis no life I would recommend, but——"

He did not continue immediately and she had to prompt him.

"But, George?" she reminded him.

"'Tis a man's life," he resumed eloquently, "and 'tis a privilege to be numbered amongst those who alone stand between a tyrant and his boundless ambition. Whether our lot is the bloody hand-to-hand struggle which is the portion of a boarding party, the serving of a breech-loader when most of our mutilated messmates lie about in a welter of tangled sinew and sticky-red——"

"George, George, please," Susan Fagg's eyes closed in horror at the picture he was conjuring up.

Mightily contrite was he, and many round oaths did he deliver at himself for his clumsiness.

"You see, m'dear," he said apologetically, lightly kissing her paled cheek, "what may be a commonplace to me . . ."

Then he made her laugh by asking her opinion of his fine queue,

" the hall-mark of the real seaman," as he proudly declared it, and from that they spoke of more personal things, of themselves, their friends, and of Dover, which place he hoped to see again as soon as he was granted the more proper absence due him.

" And . . . and then, George ? " she whispered, eyes starry.

He pursed his lips, teasing her with the delay. "Yes . . . yes, I think so, my sweet," he remarked at length.

He could hardly, he added, pointing to the patched Russian duck of his trousers, have presented himself in Dover in this condition.

" 'Twould assuredly be a sorry anticlimax to a leave-taking which was not, after all," he smiled slightly, " entirely lacking in drama."

" Don't speak of that dreadful night, dearest," Susan beseeched him. " And," she went on, now shyly, " I . . . I prefer this."

" Secretive and abandoned little creature, eh, m'dear ? " he rallied her.

Her cheeks stained deep. " Such an . . . an adorable secret for me to keep," she owned in rich confusion.

The calash sped on, a fairylike vehicle, she thought, which passed silently over the soft cushion of the snow, with only now and then a crinkly sound as a few ice-pressed pieces were thrown back from the horses' shoes.

They were drawing nearer to a noble monument, a lofty church tower which stood out from the white landscape.

" Tenterden," George Rochefort said softly. " Where, my angel," his dark eyes were on her, " I have secured the accommodation we need."

She could not look at him, and barely did he hear her inaudible " Yes, George."

Then came the quiet little town, with its timbered Market House patterned into exquisite perfection by the light crystal dusting the east wind had brought in the night.

The host of the White Lion who, humble uniform or no, knew a gentleman when he saw one, took them up to their room.

" And right glad am I to have you an' your lady, sir," he observed welcomingly. " We'd be in a sad plight, sir, if 'twasn't for the Navy."

" We but do our duty, my worthy fellow," George Rochefort conceded modestly.

Up the crazily winding stairs, past a pleasantly ticking clock on the landing, then into a room in which a cheerful wood fire burnt.

" Oh, George," Susan murmured, when the bedroom door closed.

" You love me a lot, eh, my sweet ? " He took her in arms which had grown so strong, bruised her lips with all the force of a man whose arduous profession has largely denied him the company of decent women.

She could only nod, for her limbs were weak.

Then he released her so suddenly, and so quickly became the lover than whom, she could swear, no other could be more understanding or considerate.

He would allow her a quarter of an hour . . . no, he glanced out at the long-cased clock, ten minutes must suffice. Surely that was ample space for any female to prepare herself for . . .

" Oh, George." She smiled dewily at his banter.

" Ten minutes exactly, m'dear," he repeated firmly.

A third of that time Susan Fagg spent on her knees by the side of the four-poster, the rest a breath-taking scamper. But seldom has a woman looked more pallidly radiant than she when, precisely as he had said, she found her lover awaiting her at the foot of the stairs.

5

It was an eventful first quarter.

Mr. Addington became Prime Minister, Mr. Pitt resigning from office because the King had intimated the refusal of the royal authority to a bill promised to the Irish Catholics for the relief of their political disabilities. The new Premier, the rumour went, was a gentleman who desired peace on any terms, though for the moment he threw dust into the eyes of those desirous of carrying on the war to its logical conclusion.

In the Near East, Sir Ralph Abercrombie defeated the French at Alexandria, there being two outcomes of this fine victory ; the first that Egypt was immediately restored to the Turks, the second that dissension in England grew more pronounced, one party declaring that a unique opportunity for compromise was provided, the other that it was an incentive to still more resolute effort against a man who was not far removed from being the dictator of Europe.

At home the food situation remained precarious, and the government announced bounties for the importation of grain.

Whilst in the North the mad ruler of Russia, at the instigation of the First Consul, persuaded Denmark and Sweden to ally themselves in an Armed Neutrality for the purpose of denying British trade to the Baltic.

" We should take the sternest of measures," Mr. Henry Rochefort burningly declared one evening in the parlour of the Antwerp.

The banker was not only a fiery advocate of the policy of no parley with the enemy, but also was particularly incensed by the recent news of the seizure of many an English vessel by the naval forces of the Danes.

" The Swedes and Danes may have acted against us under duress,"
he continued emphatically, " but diplomatic exchanges will not serve
us. Action is demanded, and only through ruthless action shall we
gain the respect which will bring in staunch allies."

Very hot indeed was Henry Rochefort. " Action ! " he repeated,
bringing the edge of his fist down hard on to a table.

Mr. Jephrez Baker rose tempestuously, rum and water trickling
down him from a glass which had overturned.

" Action your blasted self, sir," he roared, his eyes pink with quick
choler, as he straddled and eased his sodden breeches at the fork.
" What the devil . . . "

A highly-amused audience heard the ensuing argument—the
banker moving from profuse apology to swift irascibility as his early
protestations of regret failed to mollify the testy tallow-chandler.

Christopher Crundall, his grin dying slowly, then heard the rest
of Captain Nethersole's tale relating to the Sea Fencibles' reluctance
to devote all the time they might to manning the off-shore guard-boats,
though they unhesitatingly declared their position should the invader
be announced.

" Aye," nodded the boatbuilder when Jeremy's vehemence
slackened.

Just then the hoofs of the four horses of the mail beat out a tattoo
on the cobbles, the high-hung body of the coach darkening the windows
of the room.

" John's late," Kit Crundall remarked, glad to dispose of a tedious
subject. " I wonder where he's got to ? "

The shipowner, as it happened, had received a message from Dick
Breton and now, at the Harbour-master's snug house on the corner of
the Cross Wall and Custom House Quay, was hearing most interesting
news.

As the result of the damage caused by the violent storm of the
previous December, the Harbour Commissioners, so Mr. Breton told
him in confidence, were calling in as consultant the famous engineer,
Mr. Rennie, partner in the renowned firm of Rennie and Walker.

" Then, Dick," the shipowner said delightedly, " when Mr.
Rennie presents himself down here I'm going to get into touch with
him."

He rubbed his hands gleefully. This, he observed, was just what
was wanted. When the Commissioners received report . . .

" They've had plenty in times past, John," the Harbour-master
remarked soberly.

But this time, so John Fagg vowed, it should be different.

The topic exhausted and the shipowner leaving, Richard Breton
made sympathetic reference to Mr. Fagg's mother-in-law, expressing

agreement with his companion's intention to send Mrs. Fagg by road to Newcastle instead of by sea as he would have done in the fairer weather of summer.

Polly Fagg, who was leaving the next morning, was in a sad state that evening. She was worried about her mother's illness, she was convinced that her family could not manage in her absence, and she was both despondent and apprehensive about a journey which would take over a week, the exact time being dependent on the condition of the roads.

" Cheer up, my love," John Fagg said consolingly.

His wife made fresh effort to check her growing tendency to tears.

6

Having for some weeks debated the question, having examined it from every angle, the new ministry reluctantly determined on active steps against the Danes.

Their orders received, the Admiralty acted with all expedition.

The wooden walls of England began to move east.

Captain Riou of H.M.S. *Amazon*, 38 guns, was instructed to buoy the Channel of the Outer Deep before Copenhagen, in preparation for the passage of the fleet under Admiral Sir Hyde Parker and Vice-Admiral Lord Nelson, last-minute correspondence with the Danish commander of Cronberg Castle, at the entrance to the Sound, having demonstrated that his government, for fear of the consequences other-wise, still remained of hostile disposition.

On the evening of the day on which, in Dover, no memorial service, for the second time, was held for certain gallant young men, the British fleet anchored off Draco.

On the morning following April Fool's Day, Lord Nelson's flag-ship hoisted the signal to weigh and engage the Danish line, the action beginning at five minutes after ten, and continuing for four hours, the slaughter on both sides being severe.

During the afternoon, the Danish forces having been largely sunk, burnt, or dispersed, Lord Nelson, for humanity's sake, sent a flag of truce ashore.

His Royal Highness the Prince Royal of Denmark, receiving the magnanimous offer, consented that negotiations should be set in train for an armistice.

His country, as a result, withdrew from the association of Armed Neutrality, and the First Consul's schemings earned a sharp check.

The towns of the United Kingdom were beflagged in celebration of the Glorious Victory.

CHAPTER THREE

I

DURING the absence of Polly Fagg, her sister-in-law was thoroughly enjoying herself. It was not that Susan was other than extremely fond of her brother's wife but rather that, whilst the mistress of Little Pent House was away, she was able to indulge in housekeeping to her heart's content. And that, of course, meant, even as she looked after John's well-being, she was seeing herself doing the same for George when at lovely last they were together in their own home. Mistress Susan had ever been one who dreamed a lot and one, too, who had always delighted to keep her intimate little secrets, a storehouse of joy to which only she had access.

But there are some secrets which may not easily be hidden, and Keziah Hart, her soul at once deeply shocked and contrarily her heart aching for the plight she guessed beyond doubt the master's sister was in, longed for the return of the mistress of the house.

Susan's face, as that shrewd and horrified observer noticed, had become fuller of late, and even now revealed indication of becoming puffy. Nevertheless the young woman appeared to be in the highest of spirits, appeared indeed unconscious of what ailed her.

" Yes, Keziah dear," she was saying gaily at the front door, meantime drawing on her glove, " I'll call at the Bazaar for you, and I'll get you those red buttons at the draper's, and . . . "

It was the week-end market, two days after the news of the victory of Copenhagen had reached the now excited and jubilant town.

" . . . and everything, every single thing," Susan laughed. " So you needn't stand there with that distrustful expression."

Keziah had a flash of despairing inspiration, one which she was convinced must force the poor creature into the open. She put on a definitely unreal smile, and made the remark as casually as she was able.

The lady she mentioned was the fashionable staymaker whose premises were in Upper Snargate Street, close by Severus's Gate.

Her eyes intent, she made the suggestion.

" And for goodness' sake see Madame Tupper while you're out, Miss Susan," she said volubly. " 'Tis nearly two months since you said you'd get measured for another pair, and she's one who always takes her time in making them."

The shaft had no effect whatsoever. Instead of Miss Susan showing confusion she merely pouted, vowing that she positively hated

Madame's stuffy parlour, and then declaring that it was full time she departed on her errands.

Keziah lingered at the door to watch a receding figure which, far more decorously than was wont, proceeded towards Butchery Gate.

" The poor little innocent," she wailed, for it had just come to her why there was such unconcern about what was taking place in a slim body. " To think, to think . . . And if," in a flash she changed to a consuming ferocity, " I could lay my hands on that monster who must have forced himself on her when she was away at Maidstone I'd . . . I'd . . . "

But surreptitiously, lest any of the servants whom she ruled with an iron hand should see her weakness, she brought a corner of her lilac apron to her eyes. Then, blinking back her emotion, she miserably closed the door.

Dover Market had changed greatly. The French traders, with their fruit and game, were no longer there, and the space beneath the Guildhall was nearly sufficient to contain the scanty array of stalls which formerly had stretched so far into the Market Place as to leave barely room for the passage of a coach along the boundary formed by the kerb edge. What there was on offer, too, made a remarkably poor show when judged by long-forgotten days of plenty, materials displayed being of the shoddiest description, with foodstuffs often of that greyness denoting inferior quality.

All the same there was gathered in the Market Place as large a crowd as ever had been seen in the palmy days of peace. It was a jolly assembly, celebrating in the best manner it could the stirring episode of Copenhagen, with the gentlemen often slipping into the inns, and their womenfolk happily occupied in gossiping and whatnot with their own kind. There was one such group of ladies consisting of Mrs. Braems, Mrs. Waade and Mrs. Stone, who exchanged significant glances when a young woman left them.

" Well . . . " said Mrs. Waade, with a wealth of meaning.

Mrs. Hugo Stratton, who had been standing nearby with the Water Bailiff's wife, Mrs. Spisour, joined them. She, too, watched John Fagg's sister.

" Mmmm," she murmured for the benefit of all.

Mrs. Jeffrey Braems nodded understandingly, and smiled gently.

" So tragic . . . even for the wickedest gel," she remarked. " But," she tittered, " when 'tis Mr. Fagg's spoilt sister . . . "

The object of their attention, all unaware that the most virulent tongues in Dover were bandying her good name, had encountered two dear friends. With Martha Teddiman was Caroline, and it was very evident that Martha, doing her duty according to her lights, had brought her charge a-shopping for her instruction in those things a young lady should know.

It seemed that Caroline had little patience for housewifely training.

" Isn't it silly, Aunt Susan, " she said crossly, " having to be dragged out to buy *cabbages*? "

Martha, who had been glancing rather curiously at Miss Susan, heard the tail-end of this remark.

" When you're married, you feasy miss," she said severely, " you'll have to buy cabbages, much as you scorn them."

" Or her husband will have something to say, eh, Martha ? " laughed Susan.

" He truly will," Martha retorted vigorously.

Miss Rochefort achieved a vicious sneer. " Husbands ! " she commented scathingly, wrinkling her pretty nose. In point of fact, her ambitions vaulting, she had been in the boat-dock early that morning, when she was sure that Charles would be at the warehouse—it would have been *too* embarrassing had he caught her practising making sail in his skiff. She might have sadly grazed her hand on the snotter supporting the heel of the sprit, but it had been delicious fun. And, by contrast with her present weary doings . . .

Martha, though with the best of intention so far as it concerned Miss Caroline, was unwise enough to dilate on the desirability of any unmarried female thinking well of the married state, a statement which, her preoccupation about Miss Susan coming to mind, she immediately regretted.

Susan was laughing but her blue eyes took on a different sparkle when, near the Guildhall staircase, she glimpsed a young woman seeking to attract her notice. Hastily she excused herself, for the daughter of the Postmaster often brought her good news.

As soon as Mary Dawkes had told her of the letter which awaited her at the post office, the brightness which had transfigured Susan's face turned into an expression of puzzled inquiry.

" Not from George ? " she said.

Her rather high-pitched giggle preceding her explanation, Miss Dawkes vouchsafed that the hand was not that of Mr. Rochefort.

" Nor of your friend at Maidstone, Susan," she tittered.

" Then who can it be ? " John Fagg's sister wondered, searching her mind.

In due course, after enduring further elephantine teasing from Miss Dawkes, she elicited the name of the correspondent.

" 'Tis Jack Woodgate's inscription, for I know it well," the sharp young woman declared.

" *Jack Woodgate !* " Her very manner of mentioning him proved Susan's wide-eyed astonishment. " Maybe he has seen George and——" A disquieting thought struck her. Perhaps her dear George was ill, perhaps he was even dead.

She was palsied by this last thought, but soon she was hurrying along to the Letter Office in Lower Snargate Street.

Mr. Jonathan Dawkes took his pipe out of his mouth, the better to relieve himself of a few pretentious quips. It would be his personal function, if not official ordinance, he said, to inform Seaman Rochefort of Mistress Susan's carryings-on with a senior officer. Men have to stick together, the Postmaster observed sententiously, and now that it had come to his cognizance that Mistress Susan was barefacedly encouraging two beaux . . .

Mr. Dawkes, though prolix, was far from being an unkind man. Nor was he so enraptured with his own wit as to fail to see the distress of the young woman.

" 'Tis from Greenwich, my dear," he intimated, now soberly. " And the charge will be fivepence."

Susan's fingers, she being convinced of the worst, were shaking as she extricated from her purse the coppers for the portage.

" Thank . . . thank you, Mr. Dawkes," she said tremulously.

Watched curiously by the Postmaster, she tore the wafer with those same uncertain fingers, and unfolded the single sheet. She read but a line or so of the short note and then, as an anguished cry escaped her, she began to sway.

> Dere Miss Susan—she never noticed the formal opening—
>
> Being just returned from the glorious action of Copenhagen, and giving passage to many grievously wounded it is my sad duty to inform you that we had abord Mr. George Rochefort whom I chanced to see when doing rounds. The infirmaries being filled to capacity, he now lies . . .

" Miss Susan ! " the Postmaster cried anxiously, darting from behind the counter.

" I . . . I am all right, sir," she said faintly, once again staring in horror at what the son of the rector of St. Mary-the-Virgin's had writ.

> . . . where he was carried on our arrival here, and of which place I am also advising Mr. George's brother Mr. Henry Rochefort. A ball severed both legs above the knee and the Surjon instructs me that his condishon is exceeding grave.
>
> I fear me that this will prove sad news indeed, Miss Susan, but I judged you had better have this news than none at all.
>
> And would you have the goodness to give dere Lou my best respects.
>
> I have the honour to be, ma'am,
>
> Y[re] most humble and obed[nt] servant
>
> John Woodgate.

" A little brandy, my dear ? " Mr. Dawkes asked solicitously.

" No . . . no . . . " she whispered, her blue eyes dazed.

Before the alarmed Postmaster could press her further she had stumbled out. Her destination was Elizabeth Street—there she hoped to find her brother.

Towards its southerly end Pent-side, from being a narrow path for the use of foot-passengers only, broadened out considerably until, close by the lock-gate in Snargate Street-over-the-Wall, it made a convenient loading-place for those cargoes which were not of a nature to make the handling difficult.

About five o'clock of the same day on which John Fagg's sister had so blithely set out on her shopping expedition, the shipper's cutter *Emma* was lying alongside this natural wharf. Her bulwarks were level with the rough quayside, for the heavy showers traditionally characteristic of the month had brought the Dour into occasional spate and there was a big head of water in the Pent.

In such circumstances the proud *Emma's* cargo had been quickly stowed, and now young Mr. Charles Fagg was checking the manifest with the disgruntled Captain Maxton. It was a mixed consignment. Two hundred reams of brown paper from Mr. Stone's paper mill at Buckland, eight barrels of Mr. Virgile's corks, and four trusses of Mr. Bullack's saddle leather. There were a half-score packs of wool from Mr. Templeman's warehouse, and five great hawsers from Mr. Beverley's ropeworks at the other side of the Pent, each of the huge coils containing eighty fathoms to the thickness of a boy's calf.

Concluding checking these items, Charles Fagg rapidly completed a long list of sundries.

" All satisfactory, Captain Maxton," he nodded. " And a good trip for you. Where are you laying to-morrow night ? "

The *Emma's* destination was London River, and her captain, in bitter reply, strove to express humiliation in his own fashion. Captain Maxton had never quite got over the necessities of war which removed him and his speedy packet from the Passage.

" At Wapping, Mr. Charles," he said mincingly and mockingly. And then growled, " Among the quality tubs and snub-nosed barges that crowd into Little Barbary."

The younger man chuckled, made a laughing rejoinder, and then, as Mr. Breton's men were inserting stout bars into the capstan-like piece of machinery which opened the lock-gates to the Basin, he sprang across the gap on to the wharf.

A creaking of the turning part, the metallic clicking of the pawls, and a rattle of the rusty chains announced that they had begun.

" Forrard there ! " roared Captain Maxton. " Stand by to cast off. And not so handsomely, my lads. We want to leave here afore——"

Charles Fagg was raising his hand in farewell when his notice was drawn to his father's skipper. Captain Maxton's attention was riveted, not on the men working in the bows, but towards one of the fire alleys communicating with Snargate Street. Then he pointed imperatively.

"Mr. Charles," he shouted, "you'd better hasten up there, for——"

Already Charles Fagg was running towards a familiar figure. Spent with her fears and frantic exertions, his Aunt Susan was all but broken.

"Oh, Charles," she said weakly, "I must find your father . . . and . . ." She began to cry again, the steady monotonous cry of exhaustion.

"He's somewhere off Archcliffe Point showing Mr. Rennie the currents," Charles answered concernedly. "What is——"

The urgency of her need giving her fresh strength, desperately she tugged at her tall nephew's arm, turning up to him a face which was wet and blotchy.

"I must go to George at once, Charles," she said imploringly. "I can't wait for the London stage in the morning and I must go, I *must* go." Dumbly she held out a crumpled letter. "I must be with him," she whimpered. "I *must* be with him."

As Charles told her how impossible that was she gathered new energy.

"Charles," she began strangely evenly, only her clasped hands betraying her tension, "I won't cry any more, but I tell you that I mean to go to George at once, howsoever it be encompassed. If . . ." she paused, fighting off an emotion which seemed as though verily it would stifle her, "if you will not aid me, Charles, then I ask you not to attempt to dissuade me, for go I will."

Charles Fagg eyed her gravely, seeing in those few seconds not the old Aunt Susan who never seemed quite sure of what she did, but rather another woman, a soft woman beyond question, but one who, for the sake of a loved one, had gathered to herself a resolution beyond the ken of mere man.

He hesitated no more.

"I'll take you, then," he said decidedly. "And . . . and you must hope for the best, Aunt Susan."

By now the *Emma* was moving a little, her sweet side a good yard from the rough timbers of the wharf.

Whatever Captain Maxton's astonishment when he heard that he would be carrying two passengers, he acted with admirable promptitude. His master's sister, jumping that widening space, found herself caught in a pair of brawny arms, to be set down gently on the holy-stoned deck.

Meantime Charles Fagg, below, picked up a quill and hastily penned a brief note to his father.

Mr. Ralph Jelly it was who found himself destined to effect delivery of that missive. The Town Chamberlain, after calling at Rochefort's Bank in Snargate Street-over-the-Wall, heard himself uncompromisingly hailed near the lock-gates.

" Young fellow," he said severely, for the heavy marlinespike, to which a scrap of paper was secured by a twist of spun-yarn, had only just missed his foot, " you had better be more careful . . . "

Charles Fagg was glancing up.

" I should feel myself devilish pleased, Mr. Jelly, if you would see that that note is delivered to my father, and as soon as may be."

The Chamberlain stuttered, so angry was he. " Damme, what do you think I be, sirrah ? " he demanded.

He received the information that the contents of the letter were of grave urgency.

" And, sir," Charles Fagg ended grimly, " you will answer to me, and to my father, should it not safely and promptly reach its destination."

Mr. Jelly was already thickening about the neck, and there could have been little doubt that, had he been ten years older, he would have had a seizure.

" Answer to you . . . to you Faggs ! " he bellowed, shaking his fist.

It is, however, difficult to be completely crushing when the other party is gradually moving away. Thus, with many an oath, the outraged Chamberlain stooped to the ground.

The *Emma* was drifting over the smooth surface of the Basin. Shortly she passed the Cross Wall lock-gates and then was in the slightly more disturbed waters of the Tidal Harbour.

Beyond the Pier-heads her canvas ceased its desultory flapping and became without wrinkle from peak to tack, from throat to clew bellied out taut by the fresh wind. The water under her stern bubbled as, with the light-heartedness of a saucy girl, she sped briskly towards the chalk-white cliffs of the South Foreland.

2

The *Emma* threaded a course between the hundred or more outward-bound sail which had assembled in the Downs to await the escorting frigates of the inward-bound Mediterranean convoy whose snowy-white topsails had already been sighted off low-lying Dungeness, as was indicated by the Admiralty semaphore telegraph close by the Lord Warden's official residence, Walmer Castle.

The guardship, an old seventy-two gun ship-of-the-line whose open ports showed gleaming muzzles ready for instant action, dropped behind, and now, with more sea room, Captain Maxton brought round the head of the craft of which he was so proud. Steering N.N.E., the *Emma* raced along the seven-fathom line, her track bringing her directly between the Brakes and the North Goodwin Sand.

Sandwich, with its leading mark of St. Peter's Church, was falling abaft, and now Ramsgate, with its Purbec stone harbour built under the direction of Mr. John Smeaton—the object being, if possible, to provide a refuge when gales from S.E. to E.N.E. rendered the Downs' anchorage unsafe—showed as a white line square on the weather beam. From the bow, brought by the off-shore breeze, there came intermingled with the characteristic tang of the salt air the odour which, under similar conditions of wind, told the seafarer that he was within the vicinity of Broadstairs. And more than once, in time of fog, that hideous smell had been responsible for the safety of a good ship.

" Ugh . . . " spat Captain Maxton, " that cod-liver oil that they makes there."

" They tell me the trade is declining," Charles Fagg commented.

The skipper nodded. The vessels fitted out specially for Icelandic trade were, he said, moving north.

The setting sun, in its westerly transit, had left the sea horizon and now was sinking behind the land, its red rays, cut off starkly, causing a dull greyness to invest the great easterly stretching bastion of the North Foreland, the out-thrust arm around which all south-about craft for London River must turn.

Day was beginning to fade when Charles, the first time for the best part of an hour, spoke to a man no less quiet.

" Perhaps a little fresh air for my aunt," he said anxiously.

" Aye, aye, to be sure, Mr. Charles," Captain Maxton agreed warmly. " Fetch her up, an' . . . " Scenting the need for action, he broke off abruptly as his master's son, first grasping the forward edge of the little hatchway, clattered down the brass-edged steps to the tiny saloon. Glancing aloft at the spreading canvas, Captain Maxton gave seamanlike commands to avoid the two craft.

Making directly for her home port of Margate, running in on a long slant from the Kentish Knock, with foam curling about her cut-away bows, was a two-masted vessel, square-rigged, with a boom mainsail.

Despite his preoccupation with this and the crowded hoy which, beating out laboriously from the same haven, was almost stationary at a point on the *Emma's* bow, he could not resist guffawing. Jerking his thumb towards the brig, he bawled a witticism to the mate.

" There'll be a few extra shovels o' malt drunk in Margate to-night, eh ? "

The mate replied suitably. " Aye, aye, sir," he grinned. " Admiral Nelson knows 'ow to open up trade."

The town of Margate, apart from its cultivation of holiday-makers, did a considerable business with Memel and Riga, importing from there deals, hemp, tar and iron, products particularly valuable during a war. More than one of the fine ships owned by the burghers had been trapped in the Baltic, but the victory of Copenhagen, and Admiral Nelson's subsequent sweep, had freed them.

Soon Charles brought his young aunt on deck, marvelling at her new composure.

" You're not cold, Aunt Susan ? " he asked.

She shook her head, idly watching the close-by hoy which had now gone-about. Margate's entertainment industry had been largely developed through these craft, for they provided a rapid communication with the Metropolis, and the charge of half a crown per head, with an additional sixpence a hundredweight for baggage, for the single journey to the wool-quay station on the Thames, near the Custom House, was one few could deplore. In consequence the craft, bottoms of close on a hundred tons burden, always ran to capacity, being crowded with the quality and their servants indiscriminately packed together.

Whilst the *Emma* was skilfully piloted through the shoaling water behind the lengthy extending Margate Sand, Charles Fagg, holding Susan's arm as they paced to and fro within the restricted confine, tried to interest her in what manner he could devise.

Off the Redbury buoy he pointed to the Reculvers, hard abeam, and to the towers called ' The Sisters,' erected by an abbess of Faversham in memory of a sister lost and as thanks for herself saved from the sea.

" For generations, Aunt Susan, mariners held the edifice in such veneration that not one of 'em would pass without lowering their tops'ls," he told her.

She affectionately pressed his hand against her side.

" You're being so lovely and understanding with me, Charles," she said softly.

" Nonsense, Aunt Susan," he declared stoutly.

" And now, Charles dear," she started again quietly, " I should like to tell you something."

Seeing her insistence, he took her into the bows, and there seated her on a coiled rope. Night was falling fast, hiding the desolation which the vitriol works, with this dawn of an industrial age, had so quickly brought to Whitstable.

Turning on her finger the diamond ring her lover had given her, she began.

"I don't think George will live, Charles," she said remotely. "Nor do I think that . . ." she shuddered and closed her eyes, "he would wish to do, shattered and helpless as he would be. Can you think he would, he who was ever so full of life?"

"Aunt Susan!" He was masterful, trying to divert her from these grisly thoughts.

She was silent for a while, only once, almost inaudibly, passing an observation which brought a beam of piercing light on to George Rochefort's character.

"But he might wish to live, even so," she murmured. "And I . . ." her lips trembled, "would wish nothing better than to serve him for the rest of my life."

Her nephew told her very firmly that he would not allow her to continue in this strain. She must not anticipate the worst, only be prepared for it.

"And now methinks you should try to get a little sleep, Aunt Susan," he observed decidedly, as he got up.

She drew him down again. "I have but a few more words to say, Charles, dear," she said wistfully.

The *Emma* was nearing the East Swale where, when the tide began to turn, she would anchor off the Isle of Sheppey for the night.

"Only this, Charles," Susan resumed, her eyes luminous. "My dear one needs me, for whether dying . . ." she saw her nephew's quick protest, "or only grievously sick, he has the right of all for a loved one to be at his side. That is why I came, Charles, for that reason and to tell him of our coming child."

The twilight hid the dismay which flooded Charles Fagg's face.

"Your child, Aunt Susan?" he asked, horribly chilled.

Once she would have swooned of very embarrassment, but now she was never so calm and collected as she rose.

Bending, she kissed him fondly. "My child, Charles dear," she murmured gladly.

He saw her down to the little cuddy, and then returned on deck. Throughout the dark hours, covered with an old horse rug, he stretched there, sleeping occasionally but more often thinking of what the morrow would bring.

Charles Fagg was immensely disturbed on account of a pretty aunt who knew so little of the world.

Within an hour of daybreak the *Emma* began to move again. The morning was pearly clear, and far away across the estuary, on the Colchester side, two noble ships-of-the-line, leaving the Gunfleet buoy behind, were proceeding majestically through the King's Channel, symbols of the might of England despite all her travail.

" And . . . and she's worth fighting for, Mr. Charles," Captain Maxton muttered unexpectedly.

The gold of the rising eastern light brought glory to land and sea alike, richly colouring many a sleeping village, giving lovely sheen to the dancing surface of the maritime highway to far-flung Empire's capital.

Charles Fagg, drinking it in, drew a deep breath.

" She is, indeed, Samuel," he said devoutly.

Between Sheppey and the Isle of Grain, close off Sheerness, a big cat-built collier, in ballast, was lying anchored. Her delivery effected at Rochester, she soon would be leaving for one of the northern ports of the kingdom.

The *Emma* kept in the main stream, on her starboard hand Canvey Island and Shell Haven, with pretty East Tilbury on the curve ahead ; far away on her larboard beam, across and beyond Upner Castle and the wide tongue of land separating her from the Medway, was Chatham, with its great Sail Loft and Ropehouse, with its Smith's Forge wherein, in these days when every human effort was needed, more than fifty fires burned day and night.

There came into view the lush-green oval of Dartford Brent, on which many of the best cricketers in the land had performed prodigious feats. And at last Woolwich, with its Gun Park packed with cannon and mortar, its furnaces belching volumes of dense smoke, its vast testing range from which, even as the *Emma* passed, a group of engineers and officers of the Board of Ordnance were departing, breakfast their purpose, after having proved the quality of artillery since the crack of dawn.

Greenwich now lay around the sharp bend beyond the Bow River.

" Aye . . . well . . . " sighed Captain Maxton, thinking of the desolate female he carried.

Charles Fagg nodded. He was staring at the throng of bricklayers who, like so many busy ants, were adding largely to the number of small buildings in which, earth-banked to each end for safety, were stored supplies of fireworks and cartridges, bombs and grenadoes.

Soon the *Emma's* gear came down with a rattle, and her anchor splashed to reach good holding ground. The dumpy row-boat was being lowered over the stern when Charles went below, there to tap on the polished door of the cuddy.

" We're there, Aunt Susan," he called gently.

She was fully attired and had been so for the three hours she had sat on the narrow bunk awaiting the summons.

She glanced bravely at him. " I am quite ready, Charles," she said, her voice with only the merest falter in it.

He assisted her aloft and thence into the stern of the boat which, by now, had been brought alongside.

The blades of the oars began to dip neatly. With a long powerful stroke, smoothly feathering as was the pride of every Dover-born seaman, the mate of the *Emma* expertly pulled towards the flight of water-washed steps on the river's bank.

3

From the pleasant terrace Charles Fagg, leaning against a handsome stone balustrade, some little distance apart from a group of pensioners similarly employed, gazed over old Thames. The pale sun had passed its zenith, and already he had decided that shortly he would walk back across the smooth green turf to the lovely Wren building which, so gracious without, was so unsuited for its purpose within.

For a few minutes he stayed to watch the panorama. There was a big East Country ship, dwarfing all other craft, moving royally up to Wapping ; a number of wherries diagonally crossing the stream ; a barquentine whose three masts, hidden in the lower part by a warehouse close by at Blackwall, could as yet be seen only from crosstrees to truck as she warped out of a basin at Limehouse.

He remained a little longer in these pastoral surroundings, vastly interested in what was taking place in the mast-dock at Deptford, nearby on his left hand. There a tapering spar, a foremast for a new ship-of-the-line, was being raised by the ingenious tackle in which the dockyard specialised. Slowly the head went up and the broader heel of the mast went down, until the spar was half-way to the vertical, in readiness for the lowering and the stepping on the keelson.

Then Charles Fagg began to walk across the springy carpet.

At the spacious entrance he encountered the surgeon whom he had met earlier that morning.

" How is he, Mr. Martin ? " he asked.

This gentleman, whose sleeves were rolled up and whose right elbow bore generous traces of a gruesome task he had recently performed, was wiping his hands on his apron.

" My dear Mr. Fagg," he said impatiently in a rich brogue, and went on to relate the outrageous number of patients of whom he had charge. " But," he added, relenting somewhat, " I can tell you, young gentleman, that he won't last much longer."

" He's speeding, then ? " Charles remarked quietly.

By the manner in which the Irishman laughed, it almost appeared as if he took professional objection to the length of time George Rochefort had cheated the grim reaper.

" Damme ! " he grunted, " by every law of surgery he should have been dead long afore he left the Sound. The shock of the first wound in the foot, the shock of the subsequent mutilation, the shock when his raw stumps were plunged into a boiling compound . . . but there 'tis, Mr. Fagg, there 'tis ! " he ended airily.

After expressing no more thanks than he deemed necessary, Charles went slowly down the broad flagged corridor, at the far end to glance into a lengthy room.

For a space he stood irresolutely watching his Aunt Susan, wondering if he should go in, trying to decide whether a third would be an intruder into a company of two who should be alone in these precious ebbing hours of a man's life.

In the end he went outside again, to loiter once more amongst those who, with arm in sling or foot a mass of soiled bandages, or howsoever they were maimed or howsoever they were of vulgar tongue, could proudly number themselves in the roll of England's sea warriors, of that comparatively small band who so far, thanks to God's mercy, had saved a great and perhaps not wholly ignoble nation.

Charles Fagg, inobtrusively guarding his soft-hearted aunt, many a time returned to peer within that doorway. She, too, should not be alone when she found that the spirit of her lover was gone.

But, when evening was not far away, he was near the stately entrance gate on which, for some time, he had been keeping a watchful eye, believing that before nightfall his father would come, perhaps even Mr. Rochefort as well.

Charles was not wrong in either surmise.

John Fagg and Henry Rochefort, not five minutes separating the arrival of their sweat-marked beasts, appeared before sundown.

The room was filled with the sounds of semi-conscious ravings or agonised groanings, its airless atmosphere a stench of unhealthy tissue.

With the influx of the heroes of Copenhagen the sixteen beds forming the ward were hopelessly inadequate and now, between them, more than a score of straw-stuffed palliasses were laid on the floor.

John Fagg's sister, pale as death with nine-hours of unceasing vigil, was kneeling beside one such filthy mattress on which a hero of Copenhagen had been placed.

" Don't try to talk, dearest," she whispered.

She was wetting a cloth in a stone jar, wringing it out before she put it on his waxen forehead.

His blanched lips moved. " You must not try to rob me of that pleasure, my angel . . . my angel of mercy," George Rochefort said feebly, " I was . . . was always . . . "

He made a picture that would have stirred the heart of even the most indifferent stranger, let alone the heart of the woman who adored him. His long dark hair hung moistly over his brow, and his cheeks were long drained of any vestige of colour. Half-way down the palliasse there was an ugly up-swelling where a crude cage sought to take the weight of the coarse blanket from his gangrenous upper legs ; below that there was nothing, no ridge where his feet should have been.

His dark eyes closed, and for a while he dozed. When again he came back to conscious life his voice gathered a new power as he took up the story he had for long been telling, the tale of bloody battle in which he had not been backward in doing his brave share.

" When Admiral Nelson gave the order to close, my love," he renewed, " we closed in, holding our fire despite the punishment we were beginning to receive. 'Twas hell, Susan, but never a man amongst us so much as flinched . . . flinched——"

" Please don't try to talk so much, dear George," Susan pleaded anxiously.

But he would have his way, would tell her how, notwithstanding that first cruel wound in the foot, he continued to serve his smoking gun.

The fleeting accretion of energy passed, and once more his eyelids sunk with very weakness. He lay supine so long, he breathed so very faintly, that the giant with pain-racked eyes on the next palliasse thought he was departed.

But George Rochefort, perhaps with that same indomitable will which had kept him alive since he had received his hurt and which perhaps was the real kernel of his torn soul, brought himself out of the black abyss. There was something he knew he must say before he went if he was to go in any peace.

" A courageous fellow, ain't I, Susan dear ? " he said huskily, his mouth mocking as often it had been in other days.

Her hand, made uncertain by this new queerness, trembled as she stroked the lank black hair off his brow.

" Don't, George," she implored him.

" A hero, ain't I ? " he persisted, his eyes intent on her.

But he saw nothing but hurt in her, nothing but a dismay that he should unfairly scorn himself. And with that, his head relaxed, and slowly a glistening came into those expressive dark eyes.

" No, no, my love," he began painfully, all truth at last in him, " I am no hero, only a mountebank who has ever strutted before the footlights . . ." the tears were coming fast, " a poor creature who would now wish gallantly to proclaim that he fears not death but who . . . " he began to cough hollowly.

" For my sake, George . . . " Susan begged desperately.

The sands of life were running out fast, and a dread greyness was stealing into the sunken cheeks. He looked appealingly at the fragrant young woman so near him.

" I . . . I don't want to die, Susan," he whispered. " I don't want to leave you until I have more surely proved I am a man, if it be only by my bearing when but the shell of a human being."

She could not let him slip from life carrying such tormenting scar. Passionately she assured him of his courage, and passionately, even as she spoke, she prayed for help divine.

And God, in his goodness, came to her aid through the medium of a heavily knotted forearm which fumbled across the gap between her dearest's palliasse and the next. To Susan that rough-voiced, brutal-looking fellow was an emissary from heaven ; that man, whose feet projected beyond the coverings over his limbs, was the answer to her anguished plea.

" You were a man . . . all right, George, on that day . . . within range of . . . the floating batteries," he said painfully. " And, my lad, I shall . . . always be glad . . . to own you . . . as a shipmate o' mine."

A change showed on George Rochefort's face. He listened attentively to the familiar voice coming out of the growing void. Susan, sensing what he wanted, cradled him about the shoulders and, indescribably gentle, managed to raise him so that he could see.

" I did not fail, Aaron ? " he asked wistfully.

" You did not fail, my bond on't," came the solemn reply.

There was a refulgence about George Rochefort as he sank back, a new sureness in him as he spoke about their child.

" So you may tell him, my love . . . for he will be a boy I'll warrant . . . that his father was . . . was——"

" A brave and noble gentleman, George, my darling."

" And," he went on gladly, " you may tell him, notwithstanding my mummer's fashion of giving myself, I held it to be my duty to serve my country in her need."

" I . . . I will tell him."

Steadfastly he looked at her. " In this I do not lie, my very dear."

For a space, his cold hand clasped in hers, they remained before he spoke again.

" 'Tis only this day that I have really known you, Susan," he began dreamily. " And . . . " his dying eyes lit up, " on this day I love you infinitely more than I have ever done in my life."

" And I you, George," she said, heart-broken.

He smiled tenderly. " Don't grieve overmuch, my angel. Don't let this spoil your life."

As if in final benediction, the evening sun, in shaft of golden light, began to move over his hollow face.

She only just caught his last earthly words. "Susan, my own sweet darling," he whispered, but those halting words and the true love for her which she glimpsed so surely in his filming eyes were to be the consolation she held for her remaining days.

He sighed, just as a child might have done in sleep. And, with that soft exhalation and the creeping shadow which followed the rich glow, he was gone to the everlasting peace, perplexities and torments behind.

For how long Susan stayed kneeling she did not know, nor did she at first realise that it was her nephew who, after she had pressed her lips to the lofty forehead of her cooling dead, turned the rough blanket over the sightless eyes.

" Come, Aunt Susan," Charles Fagg said compassionately, his arm about her shoulders.

Slowly they proceeded towards the doorway which his father and Henry Rochefort had then reached, thence down the echoing corridor to the freshness of the evening air.

" Susan, my dear," John Fagg began lovingly, " I'm sad for you and . . . and I'm sorry, too, that I wasn't at hand before you . . . well, never mind about that now, m'dear," he added, kindly but abruptly.

Far too revelatory was that clumsy withdrawal. The implication was that when a young woman involves herself in such manner she surely must find many malicious tongues wagging to her disadvantage.

" I could not wait, John," she said simply.

Henry Rochefort laughed harshly. In the hour before leaving Dover a certain rumour had come to his ear, and here in the brighter light outside he had been scrutinising her closely.

" I fear, Fagg," he announced grimly, " that your sister had good reason for coming, however her hopes of a wedding ring and the fathering on to——"

A pulse in John Fagg's forehead was beating visibly, and his neck muscles seemed to swell. His intent evident, he took one pace forward, but then somehow checked himself.

" For this foul insinuation, Rochefort," he thundered, " I'll——"

" 'Tis true I should say, nevertheless," the banker persisted.

John Fagg whipped round. " Susan," his voice rang out, " throw the lie back into his teeth and then I'll teach him that the good name of Fagg women may not be treated lightly, by God I will."

Charles's thoughtful glance was passing from one to the other of them. He sensed in Henry Rochefort some expression of shame, as though the banker deeply regretted the impulse which had caused

I

him to make the charge at this time ; he saw his father move from
fierce anger to a state not far removed from supplication ; and he
came to think that there was sublime glory in the blue windows of his
aunt's sad eyes.

"Father . . . and Mr. Rochefort," he began gravely, his grasp
tightening about that slender figure, "Aunt Susan honoured me with
her confidence on the way hither, but I suggest that this is neither
the time nor the place——"

"Susan," John Fagg interrupted sternly, "are you with child ? "

Henry Rochefort, seeing her dignified nod of admission, could not
but feel deeply stirred. Indeed he tried to make amends.

"I think, Fagg," he said, nervously clearing his throat, "that
Charles is right, and that we should . . . er . . . you should defer . . . "

The shipowner took not the least notice of him. John Fagg had
always been passionately fond of his young sister, and bitterly was he
stricken by the fate which had befallen her.

"Susan," he muttered, shaking his head miserably.

She had played little part in all this but now, freeing herself from
her nephew, she went to her brother, thenceforth to become, this frail
creature, the one at whom they all wondered, a gallant female aware
of the faint movement within, aware of the glorious destiny awaiting her.

"George made me his wife at the beginning of the year, John,"
she said shiningly. "Mr. Garroway married us at his little church——"

"You were wed to George ? " John Fagg, still breathing heavily,
spoke as if he could not believe his senses. "But . . . but how, when
could . . . "

"Yes, John," she replied, so quietly and yet so joyously.

Distress and contrition filled her brother's face.

"Susan, m'dear," he groaned. "Why didn't you tell me and then
you would never have laid yourself open . . . open to . . . "

Not knowing how adequately to word his regret for the cruel
injustice he would have done her, he did the only thing possible. In
his loving embrace she rested awhile but, just as she was starting to
quiver, she raised her face. Now, that unreal composure was beginning
to leave her, and blessed nature was giving her relief.

"And . . . and, John," she said tremulously, "my few days with
him were . . . were the loveliest . . . and holiest hours of my life."

"I understand, my love," John Fagg murmured affectionately,
stroking her hair.

She began to sob and they were wise enough to let her be.

Before leaving Greenwich in the chaise, John Fagg had another
word with Henry Rochefort. The *Emma*, he told the banker, had
gone up-river but would pass by again in the early morning.

"An' if it please you," he said, "your brother's body may be conveyed to Dover in her."

"Do you imagine," Henry Rochefort replied contemptuously, "that I should allow you of all men——"

The shipper silenced him. The offer was not made, he explained bluntly, because he had found George to be a brother-in-law. Rather he made it because he would wish to do honour to a man, to any man, who had gallantly died in a noble cause, that of the fight for freedom.

"That brand of freedom, Rochefort, our British brand, which he did not discover all at once," John Fagg observed dourly. "But discover it he did, and I for one will not discount his sacrifice because he went about it in a theatri—— in a manner alien to my own temperament."

"It was part and parcel of him," the banker nodded, utterly quietened.

"Albeit I consider that to be nothing more than an unhappy defect, a weakness in him," John Fagg continued soberly. "And I believe that at the end, when he came to understand the nature of the tyranny we are against, he did the great thing his conscience dictated, however much we may deplore his crowd-drawing method."

"I think so too, Fagg," Henry Rochefort sighed.

A few words more, not one beyond those necessary, and the details were settled. These completed, the banker began to walk away, being in no humour to draw closer to a man whom in due course he intended to punish, for he would not swerve from that.

Thus the *Emma* carried out the sad errand.

4

Custom House Quay and the Cross Wall were thronged with curious spectators; the men working late in Mr. Crundall's shipbuilding yard, and those spread over the Ropewalk from Mr. Beverley's premises, desisted from their essential labours to watch awhile; the sentries in the Batteries were distinctly distracted from their duties, and the Loadmanage men from the keen lookout they should have kept. And, as far away as the Castle Hill and the Western Heights, everywhere were groups witnessing the return of one of Dover's heroic sons.

Susan Rochefort, standing at her bedroom window in her brother's house, saw that last journey of her loved one, too.

The tide was ebbing and the *Emma* perforce was compelled to anchor off Archcliffe Point.

At that distance it was not possible to see exactly what was happening out there, but later, when the spick-and-span Navy cutter came

back, rhythmically propelled by flashing oars, it became easier. The
close-packed ranks of humanity on both piers had the finest view of
all as the boat swept towards the Tidal Harbour.

They saw the tars and the diminutive midshipman in command ;
they saw the Admiralty-pattern coffin beneath a new white ensign
in which the flag in the upper canton wore the diagonal Red Cross
of St. Patrick, an addition marking the recent Union.

Now the cutter was heading for the steps opposite the King's
Head, where once had been given a dinner acclaiming the Fall of
the Bastille.

" Bows ! " piped a boyish voice.

The bowmen tossed their oars and, after boating them, stood up,
boat-hooks ready. One stroke more by the remaining oarsmen and
then :

" Way enough ! " came the youthful command.

Two banks of oars swung to the vertical, feathered and in line,
dripping blades glistening in the sun's yellow-red rays, their slim
lengths twistily reflected in the ruffled water to starboard.

The gliding craft began to lose way, its frothy-white bow wave
diminishing until it was nothing more than a tiny V-shaped ripple.

On the quayside there was a stilling of winking gilt buttons as
Mr. Hugo Stratton, officer in charge of a company of Dover Volunteers,
turned smartly in readiness to deliver the order which did homage to
the dead

Borne on the shoulders of his comrades-in-arms, solemn step by
solemn step, the honoured remains were brought up the slippery stone
flight.

" PRE—SENT . . . " In the deep hush Mr. Stratton's martial
voice carried far and wide.

So George Rochefort came back, every vantage point crowded
with the men and women belonging to the Cinque Port he had known
throughout his short span.

The nature of his departure for war had proved a topic which
had thrilled the town for weeks, and there could be no doubt that
his last homecoming would be a subject no less fertile.

Perhaps, though more derisively now, he might have appreciated
that, too.

CHAPTER FOUR

I

In the Market Place the drill competition between the Volunteers of the Snargate Street and Biggin Street wards had just ended.

"A very fair exhibition, my love," Captain Pepper allowed condescendingly, being totally convinced that Mr. John Fagg's company would have beaten both.

"I thought 'twas excellent, Valentine," Martha Teddiman said judicially, invitingly opening her arm so that it might be taken.

The evening being pleasant they decided to stroll along the bank of the Dour, and with this objective in mind made across the Market Place for Dolphin Lane, on the corner of which, just without the arch of the Antwerp Stables, Jim Page, the usual straw in his mouth, was airing his views to all and sundry. The crazy Tsar Paul of Russia having died, the head ostler was explaining why his successor, Alexander I, had determined to break with the French and come to terms with England.

"Not a doubt on't, an' I says . . ." Mr. Page was summing up when he glimpsed the approaching couple.

Civilities followed, during which the talkative ostler made himself most agreeable to Miss Teddiman whilst Harry Jenkins exchanged some good-humoured banter with Valentine Pepper, a gentleman whom he himself was amazingly like in build.

"An' mind you an' Mistress Teddiman keeps on moving when you get into them quiet parts up——" the squat-built Preventiveman was joking, when he caught Captain Pepper's frenzied warning.

Fortunately the lady did not hear this potential vulgarity, and anyhow there was a diversion as Mr. John Fagg's son, in passing, called a greeting. Charles, who had taken pains to keep up his French, was with an elderly *emigré* who had been in the town for close on ten years.

"A nice young gentleman," remarked Mr. Jenkins.

Valentine Pepper agreed with the Preventiveman on that, as indeed the pair agreed on many subjects, they being cronies rather, a friendship cemented through the medium of many convivial evenings in the Fountain. Only certain vocational differences separated them, these of course relative to the defiance of the law under the dark cover of night.

"If you be ready now, my dear?" Captain Pepper asked gallantly, and, this little interlude over, he and Martha continued into narrow

Dolphin Lane, thence hurrying past Stembroke from where came the stench of Mr. Bullack's tannery.

Above Dieu Stone Lane it was very delightful, the river running tunefully through green fields, its song vieing with those of the birds.

Martha Teddiman sighed, and her fond Valentine knew why.

" 'Tis so tragic," she murmured, blinking slightly. " Mr. George cut off in full vigour and Miss Susan . . . have you heard anything later, Valentine ? "

Captain Pepper, from glancing at a new corn-mill, one of many which were being built through the help of a subsidy from the Victualling Department, tried to console her. The master, he told her, was more cheerful about Miss Susan's state, and Doctor Crouch no longer proclaimed so positively that his patient would sink into a decline.

" Still . . . " Martha persisted, deeply distressed.

" Now come, love," the boatswain said coaxingly.

" But 'tis terrible, Valentine," she cried out miserably. " Mr. George gone an' Miss Susan without a loving husband during the months when . . . " Miss Teddiman flushed a little, " when she most needs one."

The subject of the coming child had never been directly broached between them, but of course Captain Pepper was perfectly aware that Mr. George had laid a keel afore he parted cable.

" Martha, ducky," he slipped a comforting arm about her waist.

Thereupon Miss Teddiman promptly burst into tears. " 'Tis awful, Valentine," she sobbed.

" Martha, m'dear," he said anxiously.

But nothing seemed to stop her, leastwise nothing until, desperate with racking his brain, he hit on the ideal solution. Laughter is the cure for many ills, and with joyous relief it came to him just how he could make her split her sides—well, smile perhaps. He went about it in a roundabout way. So much so that his first objective was successfully attained.

" Miss Susan," Martha Teddiman ejaculated, " could steal sheep on the Downs without fear of the consequences ? " She had stopped crying, and was gaping at him as though she thought he was demented.

Highly pleased with the successful outcome of his strategy, Captain Pepper guffawed.

" They couldn't dangle 'er, love," he explained.

" Dangle her ? " Martha's face was a picture of bewilderment.

The boatswain graphically illustrated. Head twisted down on to his shoulder, strangled tongue out-thrust, his eyes fixed into an unholy squint, he portrayed the felon's passing.

Martha Teddiman's fascinated glance remained on the macabre spectacle until she could bear no longer.

"Valentine," she asked faintly, "how concerns this Miss Susan?"

A last death-rattle and Captain Pepper, mightily delighted with the performance, broke into a broad grin.

"Being in 'er condition, the judge wouldn't order her to be swung," he roared. "'Tis called the Belly Plea, m'dear."

"The Belly Plea." Martha Teddiman actually repeated the indelicacy, so stunned was she.

"Aye, the Belly Plea," he chortled. "An' many's the time . . . the time——"

Seldom has change taken place so quickly in a woman's face, and seldom has a woman so speedily snatched away her arm.

"*Valentine Pepper*," she stormed, heaven's wrath in her.

Never had Captain Pepper thought so swiftly. The satisfaction vanished from his face as the sick conviction engulfed him that, according to standards long laid down for his conduct, he must have transgressed every goddam canon of decency.

"Martha," he swallowed, "you doesn't want to go off like brimstone 'fore——"

"*Valentine Pepper*," the verdict was about to be given, "this . . . is . . . not . . . the . . . first . . . occasion——"

"My poor mother once similarly misunderstood," Captain Pepper, sweating profusely, interrupted loudly. "Agnes Pepper, she says to 'erself when she discovered 'ow wrong she was——"

"You told me she was named——" Miss Teddiman broke in furiously.

"Martha Agnes Pepper," the boatswain resumed feverishly, his mien hunted. "And never, barring yourself, Martha, was there a female more refined. But she was one, too, who would face up to the fax o' the case."

"The facts?" Martha's curiosity momentarily threw her out of her stride.

"The fax," Captain Pepper advanced recklessly. "And them is that a manner o' speech wot comes proper from the lips of a gentleman like the Lord Chief Justice of England is good enough for lesser folk."

Martha's eyes widened. "Does he term it that?"

The accused felt that ground was being gained, and so both followed his rising star and changed his tactics. Loftily Miss Teddiman was informed that the words which she complained of came almost directly from the Latin tongue, one greatly used by those in the practice of the law.

"Well . . ." Martha Teddiman said dubiously, "but if I ever finds this be another of your Canterbury-tales . . ."

Deliberately putting aside a subject on which he had been cruelly maligned Captain Pepper began distantly to carry on a most impersonal conversation. Now that Lord Nelson had been appointed to the command of the coastal waters from Sussex to Suffolk, he commented, there would be a deal more action hereabouts and . . .

" Valentine ? " Martha murmured, a thought worriedly.

That gentleman relaxed in so much that he showed her a broadside smuggled over from France, one which, though he did not consider it policy then to advise her, he had brought especially for her benefit.

" Wicked miscreant ! " Martha Teddiman gasped.

The Corsican Bonaparte's handbill presented a charming prospect for John Bull and his family, the riches of whose centres of Sheffield, Birmingham, Liverpool and Bristol, amongst other items, would soon be in the possession of brave Frenchmen.

" The villain ! " Martha said angrily.

Her Valentine, despite the tiny squeeze she gave to his arm, did no more than nod austerely.

" Valentine, dear," she tried again, whispering softly.

Some two hours later the company in the parlour of the Fountain Inn were startled out of their wits by a wild bellow of laughter which came from a well-known figure occupying his accustomed seat on the corner settle.

Captain Pepper, three Sir Cloudesleys warming him nicely, was highly tickled by the deft manner in which he had got himself out of a very tight corner.

2

On one of the early days of August there was a mighty cannonading across the Channel, and soon the people of Dover were flocking to Castle Hill, from there to watch Lord Nelson's attempt to destroy the invasion flotilla which the French were in course of preparing outside Boulogne Harbour.

A most interesting sight it was but, in truth, Charles Fagg's grey eyes kept straying towards a privileged young lady who, within the Castle enclosure, was sitting on the scrolled carriage of Queen Elizabeth's Pocket Pistol, a great piece of brass ordnance which, it was affirmed, the burghers of Utrecht presented to the Virgin Queen.

" Er . . . what ? " He came to life hurriedly, finding that Louis Rochefort had had to address him twice.

" Now that you've come out of your daydream or whatever 'tis," Louis chaffed him, " may I inform you that I propose having a word with a certain Mr. Warren whom I see yonder."

" Sorry," Charles grinned. " No . . . " he added in response to his friend's inquiry, " I think I'll stay here. Or perhaps I'll saunter across and keep your little sister company."

The only comment Louis made was that Caroline never lacked company so far as he was aware. The Stone twins, young Breton, the Strattons—he humorously enumerated the young gentlemen who danced attendance on the miss.

However, Miss Rochefort was alone when Charles joined her after strolling across the same smooth stretch of grass along which, sixteen years before, the balloon of Mr. Jeffries and M. Blanchard had dragged before leaving the cliff for a voyage in which it ever continued to lose altitude whilst crossing the Channel.

" Hullo, Caroline," he smiled, saluting smartly.

She gave him a pleasant welcome, but not quite the same tempestuous greeting he would once have had. In point of fact, looking back through the days since the Jellys' party, their relationship had undergone a subtle change, one which he could not entirely fathom.

With this idea predominant Charles carefully settled himself down. He was in his Volunteer uniform—stove-pipe hat, vivid-coloured coat with its striking turnbacks, white waistcoat and light breeches which, for the length of the leg below the knee, buttoned to give a gaiter-like appearance.

" 'Tis remarkably clear, Charles," she said brightly, as a fresh thundering rumbled over the sea. " I vow that never before have I so clearly seen the French coast."

The view was indeed extraordinary. The British attacking force faintly visible, and the smoke which rolled from gun and battery, with behind all this stirring picture the white tents of the French army of invasion pitched on the hills about the French port.

" Or the weather more delightful, Caroline," Charles Fagg observed dryly.

She glanced at him. " Or the weather more delightful, Charles," she agreed serenely.

It being this kind of lifeless conversation, Charles continued it by speaking of the latest menace the French were contriving. The invention of an American named Fulton it was, a submarine boat which already, in Brest harbour, had dived to twenty feet, remaining under water many minutes.

" I heard Papa telling Louis about it," Miss Rochefort told him gently.

For a while Charles stared reflectively at the Castle—at the Constable's Tower with its embattled curtain and fine gateway ; at the Pharos with its material bonded together with salmon-coloured Roman mortar ; at the Well Tower beneath which was a four-hundred-feet deep well, an astonishing creation when one considered the tower was so near the cliff's edge.

"Caroline," he asked quietly, "are you for ever going to be terribly offended with me?"

She blushed vividly, but her eyes met his bravely. "I was monstrous hurt, Charles," she confessed.

"'Twas only a game, Caroline."

"But I asked you not, Charles."

He nodded slowly, turning over a few pieces of small change, coin of which there was becoming an increasing shortage.

"And I asked your pardon, Caroline," he reminded her, tossing and re-tossing a fourpenny piece. "And do again now."

She smiled at that. Of course she forgave him, she laughed, for often had she thought how foolish she had been to make such ado. For it was nothing, after all.

"Why, Caroline?" he inquired curiously.

She told him whilst he idly toyed with one of the popular Invasion Promissory Notes, wherein John Bull, ' for self, St. Vincent, Duncan, Nelson & Co., promised to pay Mr. Bonaparte or Bearer the sum of Two Pence when the Gallic flag should triumph over the British and the French should become masters of the sea.'

". . . so 'twas so silly of me," Miss Rochefort rounded off. "After all one does kiss an unconscionable number of boys at parties."

"I suppose so," her companion chuckled, over-heartily.

At the bottom of the hill an enterprising old lady was selling lemonade. Somewhat briefly he asked Caroline if she would care to have a cooling glass.

Miss Rochefort expressed herself as delighted, thereupon a move was made towards the refreshment.

From the high knoll on the bend there was an admirable view, not only of the sea but of a distant path which wound round the verge of the cliff.

On the narrow walk a couple were strolling, the one a captain in the Radnor Militia, the other, her arm in his, a young lady.

Charles Fagg, at this sight, came out of his preoccupation.

"Damme!" he ejaculated. "That looks mightily like Minnie."

Caroline was highly amused. But whether or not she used Minnie as excuse to relieve herself of laughter more closely identified with another incident it would be difficult to say.

Certainly her eyes continued to sparkle for quite a while. Really, she vowed, it was . . .

"Devilish diverting, eh?" Charles inquired astoundingly, just as if he had been reading her thoughts.

This time Miss Rochefort flushed most embarrassedly red. "If it was Minnie, you mean, Charles?" she asked confusedly.

Mr. Charles Fagg made a most non-committal noise in his throat.

Eleven days later the attack on Boulogne was resumed, this new operation taking place at night, the English boats going in with muffled oars.

There was heavy loss of life in this essay to cut out the Frenchies' craft, and on the following morning large numbers of wounded were brought into the harbour, the ladies of the town doing their utmost to mitigate the poor fellows' sufferings.

Mrs. John Fagg, who would normally have assisted her friends in their merciful ministrations, was otherwise occupied, for that same day her sister-in-law gave birth to a lusty child.

Mrs. George Rochefort's baby was a boy.

Shortly after this time many rumours began to circulate in the port, a port which, through gentlemen like John Fagg, succeeded in maintaining contact with the Continent in time of war.

It was said that the French were becoming weary of conflict.

That this was true was borne out in October of the same year.

3

The proposals for an armistice were brought over from France by General Lauriston, *Chef de Brigade* in the Republic's Artillery. This gentleman, as the packet came alongside Custom House Quay, held up a gold box containing the precious parchment, whilst ashore a mob from the Plain roared themselves hoarse with such cries as "LONG LIVE BONAPARTE," a demonstration about which a noble sailor subsequently spoke in unequivocal terms.

Lord Nelson, after saying that nobody rejoiced in the prospect of peace more than he, remarked that he would sooner burst than let a Frenchman know it. He would, his lordship added, "adhere to a peace whilst the French continued in due bonds, but whenever they overstep that, and usurp a power which would degrade Europe, then I trust we shall join Europe in crushing his ambition; then I would with pleasure go forth and risk my life for to pull down the overgrown detestable power of France."

But the minds of the crowd besieging the quay were of a different quality, and here, as elsewhere, citizens gave vent to their relief. Outgoing mail-coaches were decorated with laurel before they passed through the Market Place; the vessels in the Pent, the Basin, and the Tidal Harbour were dressed with flags; and the bells of St. Mary the Virgin's clashed out their joyful message for the remainder of the day.

In their various forms Rocheforts and Faggs reacted to the news.

Before General Lauriston had placed a foot ashore, Louis Rochefort was posting to London. Positively there would be a substantial rise in the price of stocks—the House of Rochefort, geographically better sited than any other financial institution in the country, was making the most of its advantageous position.

And Henry Rochefort, some little while after his daughter had gone out in the early evening, sat in his dining-room, his thoughts busied with a personal rather than a business matter.

" No, not yet," he muttered. " But 'twill come."

He had decided that an armistice is not an official peace. This being so he must not, on peril of breaking his word with one who was an enemy, proceed with certain plans directed against John Fagg.

He had waited long ; he could wait a little longer.

This decision reached, the busiest and loneliest man in Dover settled himself to work, still more work, on this eve of widespread rejoicing.

Little Pent House was ablaze with light that night, and it certainly seemed that all the young folk of the district were there.

Minnie, to the astonishment of her parents, produced a Captain Morgan Davies, a gentleman who was not a whit less than thirty-five.

" But . . . but, John, he's twice as old as the child," Mrs. Fagg remarked concernedly.

John Fagg was in high feather. He had great hopes on the outcome of the very extensive survey Mr. Rennie was making, and further to this he was looking forward to full peace, when he would once more have back in his own control the craft he had chartered to the government.

" He's not, Polly," he laughed. " Minnie has been grown up herself ever since she entered her teens, I warrant. Besides . . . " The shipowner, so lighthearted was he, went off into such hissing sing-song parody of the Radnor Militiaman's speech that Shep, who was examining Captain Davies's boots and pantaloons, promptly relinquished this critical scrutiny to fling himself on his master.

" Iss it not so, my——"

" Sssh, John." Mrs. Fagg was trying to quieten her exuberant husband when the sheepdog's playful onslaught saved her the necessity for further remonstrance.

Such a noise there was in the house that Miss Caroline Rochefort became excessively worried lest her baby cousin Horatio should be disturbed.

" Do you think, Aunt Susan," she said wheedlingly, " that I might see if he's awake, or crying, or——"

Susan Rochefort laughed. " We'll both go, my dear. But he'll be all right, and he must become used to the uproar there so often is here."

To Polly Fagg's astonishment, she had found that Susan had the most decided ideas regarding the rearing of the young. Horatio, his mother declared, should have the tenderest upbringing, but never should he be pampered. That was no way for him to become the man his father had been.

" Pray let's go then, Aunt Susan," Caroline urged eagerly.

Mrs. George rose smilingly. She still looked exceedingly delicate and her eyes were still tragically sad. But there was about her, who had always leaned on others, a new sureness since the advent of a son who must for so long depend on her and none other. She had been given responsibility, and she had risen to meet responsibility.

As it happened, Horatio was sound asleep, so his cousin's rhapsodizing, as she bent over the crib, had to be carried on in a hushed voice.

" Isn't he like Uncle George, Aunt Susan ? " Caroline whispered towards the end of her transports.

Soft happiness flowed into Susan Rochefort's face. " Methinks so, too, Caroline," she said joyously.

The door opened wider, and Lou came tiptoeing in. With her arrival, naturally there was more talk of the sleeping wonder.

" Do you think we should waken him, Aunt Susan, if . . . " Lou asked anxiously. " You see, Aunt Susan, if we wouldn't . . . "

It all came to this. Mamma had said that they might clear the drawing-room floor . . .

" To dance ? " Caroline's eyes danced, too. But then she shook her head decisively.

Mrs. George affectionately disposed of their fears. They should have their dance, she said firmly, and she would play the piano for them. No, nor would she hear argument on it.

From the hall, where he was indulging in a smoke, Charles saw them come down the wide staircase. In the middle his Aunt Susan in black, the girls in their pretty party dresses on either side. A most pleasant spectacle they made, too, he thought.

" I take it," he remarked solemnly, putting down the pipe, " that you have been inspecting a creature with a red and crab-like face——"

Miss Rochefort was so incensed that, even when Aunt Susan and Lou had gone into the drawing-room, where the gentlemen present started an heroic furniture shifting, she remained behind, the more forcefully to impress her views on Charles. Of course, before, when Horatio was only a few days old . . .

" You speak very much to the point, m'dear," Charles Fagg observed mildly.

" He's a delicious baby an' . . . "

Charles had taken her arm, Charles was slowly walking her down the hall, and Miss Rochefort felt a most amazing thrill from head to foot.

" . . . an' beautiful looking," she ended a little breathlessly.

On the way back from the door she risked a glance in a gilt mirror, and saw Charles's fair head towering above her, and her own nearly, very nearly, up to his uniformed shoulder and . . .

" You find we make a moderately presentable pair, Caroline ? " he asked casually.

Miss Rochefort, between crimsoning and thinking furiously that Charles had the habit of saying the most unexpected things, succeeded in informing him that, even if he had a pretty conceit of himself, she was far from being likewise.

Charles Fagg sighed deeply, and for full two lengths of the hall, whilst still keeping firm hold of her, said not a word. Coming up the third time he steered gradually until they squarely faced the mirror.

" No," he murmured reflectively. " Most assuredly I was wrong, though barring one thing 'twould be a perfect picture."

" How so, Charles ? " she asked.

In her disappointment she hardly realised that he had released her, hardly knew that, stepping to one side, he had left her standing before the silvered glass.

" A perfect picture," he said slowly.

Then she knew what he meant. " Charles ! " Her colour was coming and going.

In the drawing-room gentlemen were taking partners. The Virgile boy settled his fiddle comfortably beneath his chin, and then nodded, whereupon Mrs. George Rochefort struck up a lively air.

Charles Fagg bowed low. " May I have the honour of your hand, Miss Rochefort ? "

Miss Caroline Rochefort curtsied deeply. " You are most amiable, sir," she whispered.

For a palpitating moment before he gave her his arm, grey eyes looked into brown, lovely brown into steadfast grey.

4

Lord Nelson was not alone in his pessimism. Mr. Secretary-at-War Yorke stated that he would not give twelve months' purchase for any peace with France, and by France, as he said, " I mean the military despot of France."

Mr. Pitt, too, was far from happy. Two days before Guy Fawkes Day, after speaking in admiring terms of the Navy and of Britain's unique capacity for waging a world-wide war, and after paying heartfelt tribute to " the unparalleled exertions of the colonial possessions," he employed the ominous expression, " In time of peace, prepare for war," surely a strange utterance when the emissaries of two great powers were forging out the articles for a permanent and lasting adjustment of differences.

" 'Tis indeed extraordinary, Polly," John Fagg observed in the parlour a few evenings later. " A handful of eminent men crying from the wilderness as it were, whilst the rest . . . "

" I suppose, John," Mrs. Fagg murmured from her sewing, " that Mr. Addington himself would have peace, and in that spoke for many in the nation. Eight years is a wearying long time to be at war."

" 'Tis, my dear," the shipowner agreed. " But——"

He had the fixed belief that Bonaparte desired a cessation of hostilities for one purpose only, that of preparing to resume the war. If, in the interim, the First Consul could regain the French Colonies, build up the shattered French Navy, and . . .

" Aye, and bend the subject states o' Holland, Switzerland, and Italy until they're truly a part of France itself, ready to do whatsoever——"

Mrs. Fagg, with some deliberation, put down her needlework. She was looking forward to peace, she remarked emphatically, and not thinking of it as a prelude to still more war. There had been too much war . . .

" Egad ! " grunted her husband. " Methinks I'm becoming so that I can't express an opinion in my own house. Damned if I ain't more henpecked than poor old Pepper is."

Polly Fagg laughed until her eyes streamed, and so loudly that Susan, who had been absorbed in the *Mysteries of Udolpho*, came to earth to inquire what it was all about.

" John likens himself to——" Her sister-in-law rocked.

" You shall decide between us, Susan love," John Fagg chuckled.

In the midst of this promising domestic comedy the knocker on the front door resounded, and shortly afterwards Mr. Jeffrey Braems was ushered in. Apart from holding the office of Notary to the Harbour Commissioners, Mr. Braems was a lawyer in private practice, and as such had been entrusted by the elder Rochefort with the settlement of the late George Rochefort's estate.

His stay was neither protracted nor particularly harmonious.

" And so that is it, is it, Mr. Braems ? " the shipowner commented dourly.

It may have been either that he was becoming more touchy in reference to anything concerning Henry Rochefort, or that the lawyer added a savouring of patronage to the instructions he had received.

" Precisely, Mr. Fagg," bowed the severe-faced Mr. Braems. " The exact value of the late Mr. George Rochefort's partnership in the bank is now very much higher than it was at the time——"

" Why should my sister benefit additionally to this extent ? " John Fagg glinted.. " Her husband's property should be accounted as at the time of his death, according to the usual custom."

" Strictly, yes," nodded the notary. " But . . . " He went on to explain that Mr. Henry Rochefort felt that it would be unfair in the circumstances, when Mr. George had sacrificed his life so near to the conclusion of an exhausting war, to take advantage of the unduly depreciated figures ruling then.

" And further, Mr. Fagg, my client would wish . . . " here Mr. Braems smiled faintly, " to ensure that Mrs. George has a sufficiency for the support of herself and her child."

Despite the fact that John Fagg knew perfectly well that Jeffrey Braems disliked him intensely, he was far too angry even to suspect that a mischief-maker might be at work.

" My father, sir," he rapped, " left my sister not entirely without means, and whatever else she might need either for herself or her boy I am well able to provide myself, an' gladly."

With intention very obvious he made for his writing-table, thrusting aside the chair in which, when at home during the hours of daylight, he sat so often. Unlocking a drawer he brought out papers which the lawyer had left earlier.

" Take these, sir, and inform Mr. Rochefort that I am mortally obliged by his condescension to my sister but——"

" No . . . no, John," Susan interrupted him, palely determined. " I am George's widow and 'tis no matter of charity, though I will have no more than is lawful."

" Have you no pride, girl ? " demanded her brother.

Mrs. George Rochefort's blue eyes, even as her sister-in-law went hastily to her, were beginning to film with moisture.

" None, John," she faltered. " None at all when it concerns Horatio, and I will not for pride, even for your pride, John, rob him of what belonged to his dear father."

" Now, my love," Polly Fagg murmured consolingly.

The decision was for his sister alone, and John Fagg knew it. Indeed, after staring searchingly at her, he neither hesitated more nor attempted dissuasion.

Summarily, immediately he had been informed that George Rochefort's widow required no more than that to which she was legally entitled, the Notary of Dover Harbour was lighted to the door.

5

Whenever afterwards Polly Fagg thought of it a horribly cold shudder went down her back. She ever declared that, had she known at the time, when she stood on Custom House Quay watching the *Alices* and *Marys* and *Emmas* coming in, their hulls and main spars picked out with lanterns, she would have died there and then. To think that Mr. Toke was amongst a crowd of notabilities in the *Emma*, all unconscious that beneath his feet was one of the biggest cargoes of contraband ever brought into Dover—no, it just didn't bear thinking about.

It happened on the evening when the town, in the seventh month after the opening of armistice negotiations, celebrated the official Declaration of Peace.

Earlier that day, surest symbol of all to coast-wise dwellers that strife was over, Lord Nelson brought the fleet to anchorage in the Downs. A magnificent, gripping, perhaps even poignant sight, were those battle-scarred ships, mighty sail-of-the-line, graceful frigates, bombs and corvettes, under their lofty white canvas, in perfect station, each and all bearing themselves as though proudly conscious that a formidable task had not been ill done.

Whilst in the Antwerp, repairing thither from watching that impressive array of sea power, local dignitaries discussed—or rather exchanged shouts, for the eight bell-ringers in St. Mary the Virgin's were giving of their best—how the auspicious event might fittingly be marked.

All agreed there should be illuminations that night and, on this being decided, Mr. Jephrez Baker promised to donate five gross of his finest candles.

" Shouldn't do it if I didn't want to," he growled when the Mayor, Mr. Wade, Clerk of the Cheque, thanked him for the offer. In truth the Commissioners of Harbour and the ranks of officialdom had now no greater enemy than the tallow-chandler.

Just who suggested a grand procession of boats dressed in lights, gondola-like, was not quite clear, though certainly afterwards both Mr. Jonathan Dawkes and Mr. Joseph Denne claimed that honour.

However, be that as it may, the point upon which the town subsequently seized, crowing over it for days, was the plain fact that the novel scheme came from a group amongst whom was the Revenue Officer.

" Aye, the tide'll be suitable to-night," nodded Mr. Richard Breton, on being consulted by the Agent-Victualler.

Mr. Paul Elam's light voice made inquiry as to whether there would be enough craft to make a sufficiently impressive presentation. That was all right too. One belonging to so-and-so, another to Jeremy Nethersole, three of John Fagg's . . .

" And the *Emma* should make port early in the evening," Mr. John Fagg interposed. " So," he added most helpfully, " she can join in."

Whilst this was going on Mr. Henry Rochefort spoke in turn to Christopher Crundall and to Edward Hexstall. " . . . 'tis most inconvenient, this chartering," he ended to the first named.

" Yes, I suppose I could build you a cutter," the boat-builder submitted briefly. " I've made 'em afore."

" Then I should feel obliged if you would furnish me with a price," the banker said shortly, not too pleased by this independence. " I want a fast craft, one suited for the purposes in which I engage."

With the Town Surveyor Henry Rochefort's conversation was equally curt, even if this time it provoked a greater astonishment.

" Build *there* ? " ejaculated Mr. Hexstall.

" There, my dear sir," the banker confirmed, his dark eyes gleaming.

Meantime further details of the Venetian-like entrance had been arranged. In the first craft would be the Mayoral party. . . .

And most picturesque it was that night, the sable waters of the Basin reflecting the many lights in the ships which, one by one, drifted through the lock-gates after passing across the Tidal Harbour.

" Pheeew ! " slipped from Captain Pepper.

Martha did not notice his jumpiness, being too enthralled with the wonders of Custom House Quay. There were coloured stars, olive branches in lights, large P's for Peace, and transparent inscriptions declaiming Universal Happiness.

" There's the *Emma*, Charles," Caroline Rochefort declared mutinously. " And I protest 'twas simply horrid of you not to let me come in in her. 'Twould have been lovely."

" But very crowded, m'dear," Charles Fagg smiled, his eyes a thought anxious as he watched.

Just as it had been decided that the leading vessel should contain the representatives of local government, so it had been arranged that the last should bear those in government employ. Amongst the company in the *Emma* were such as the Collector of Customs, the Agent-Victualler and, last but not least, the Revenue Officer, with John Fagg jollying them all, including Mr. Toke, as much as you please.

As Captain Maxton's charge drew nearer the wharf, Valentine Pepper dabbed his beaded forehead again, upon which Martha, wondering if he were sickening for an ailment, made a worried inquiry.

"No, love. 'Tis only that excitement allus makes me 'ot, love," groaned her swain.

But all was well. The Mayor delivered himself of a most gallant speech, there were storms of cheering, and a final huzza, after which the inns began to fill to capacity.

In due course John Fagg made his way to Little Pent House, there to find that Captain Morgan Davies prayed for private talk with him. The militiaman not only asked for Minnie's hand but, being evidently of a thrifty disposition, suggested that the marriage should take place at a very early date, his regiment being under orders to return to Radnorshire, for disbanding, within the month.

"Of course Minnie is eighteen, John," Polly Fagg remarked when she and her husband later talked it over. "Still . . ."

John Fagg glanced shrewdly at her, but it was Keziah Hart who put many a thought into a concise phrase.

"Miss Minnie is best wed, ma'am," she promptly observed when her mistress told her the news.

The young lady's father asked why.

"Because," Keziah said darkly as she went out with a tray, "I've seen things."

Some little time after the door had closed, Polly Fagg broke into the silence, being very annoyed by her husband's faint smile. They had both often troubled about their elder daughter, she thought miserably, and it was far from nice of John to treat so light-heartedly . . .

"I fail to see anything amusing in it, John," she said very severely. "Really, no one would think you were her father. Really, to see you sitting there——"

"I wasn't thinking of Minnie, my dear," John Fagg, very hurriedly though perfectly truly, told her.

Eventually they decided it was wisdom to allow the chit her will.

*   *   *   *   *   *   *   *

In the early days of May Minnie left with her husband for her new home near Llandrinod Wells, and at the beginning of the next week John Fagg set out in the *Emma* to renew contacts in the Low Countries and ports of Northern France.

During his absence the Revenue Officer learnt of the trick which had been played on him.

At the Revenue Office on the corner of Strond Street and Custom House Quay, the morning after an evening in which a number of local gentlemen had congratulated Mr. Toke, most ambiguously, on his pilotage of as fine a consignment of duty-free liquor as ever had entered the haven, Clement Foxley's superior officer did not present a very pretty picture.

The instructions he issued were no more pretty either.

Whenever there was a Fagg run in which any contact was made with the personnel engaged, the order was to shoot and ask the questions afterwards.

"You understand, Foxley?" Mr. Toke said thinly. "*Shoot* first."

"Yes, sir."

It was the only course to adopt if the traffic was to be stopped, the Revenue Officer added harshly. The townsfolk, from the chief jurat to the lowliest keel-bully, were ever closely associated in defiance of the law, and never, in ordinary case, would the bench convict. Even when there was resistance, when a weapon was found, there was extreme difficulty . . .

"Aye, aye, sir," ventured Mr. Foxley. "They've never forgotten the hanging o' that Folkestone man."

"So shoot first and . . ." his senior laughed mirthlessly, "then we'll see that a weapon *is* found."

Later in the day the Revenue Officer pointed out to his subordinate that, though such method might at first sight seem improper, the end undoubtedly justified the means.

Whether the sly Clement Foxley accepted at its face value this fine-sounding submission is neither here nor there. He too, however, was anxious for promotion.

*   *   *   *   *   *   *   *

Quickly the town began to change as English folk bethought themselves pleasurably of Continental travel, and already, when John Fagg returned from his very extensive trip, the packets for Calais and Boulogne were crammed with tourists.

Mr. Breton, as the *Emma*, pending the opening of the gates to the Basin, dropped anchor in the Tidal Harbour, hurried out of the Harbour-master's House, still chewing a mouthful of prime spring lamb, so anxious was he to speak with the vessel's owner.

Seeing that urgent hand-waving, John Fagg had himself sculled over to the same flight of lichened steps up which the body of his brother-in-law had been carried.

"What's to do?" he asked, perturbed by Dick's long face.

His own expression darkened as he listened. The information that the South Pier was in a dangerous condition was bad enough, but the news that Mr. Rennie's scheme for harbour development had been turned down by the Commissioners was indeed a cruel blow.

"Howsomever, Mr. Rennie is still here, John, though he leaves this afternoon. If you're of humour to see him . . . he's at the Ship——"

Within five minutes John Fagg was closeted with the engineer who, though surpassingly understanding, could hardly disclose matters for which he had received a handsome fee from others.

"Well, I'm sorry about it, Mr. Rennie," John Fagg said quietly, "though I promise you . . ." his jaw was resolute, "that sooner or later I'll make the authorities here carry out their rightful obligations, rot me if I won't."

He stared out of the window. Along Crane Street, from the direction of Townshend's Battery, a small-wheeled wagon, laden with a cannon, was lumbering past the King's Head, its destination the foundry at the bottom of Snargate Street. Mr. Addington, a man of peace, was also a believer in disarmament. Throughout the country guns were being melted down, officers and artificers were being discharged from the dockyards, even hemp was being sold out of the Navy.

"Rot me if I won't, sir," he repeated inflexibly.

With that he became a little more cheerful. The two gentlemen talked of the 'true tideway' in relation to the haven, and John Fagg once raised a laugh when he spoke, maybe a trifle tentatively, of a vision he had, that of enclosing Dover's bay to make a grand harbour.

"I declare," Mr. Rennie smiled, "that you are indeed a progressive, Mr. Fagg. Methinks that soon you will be looking into the steam-propelled craft, the *Charlotte Dundas*, now in service on the Forth and Clyde Canal."

"*Service*," the shipowner laughed. "Still . . . " he shook his head, "one never knows."

There was more raillery on these lines and some outright fun bearing on a report in the London papers that, within the last week, a Frenchman had been caught making a military survey of Hull harbour.

"Maybe the poor fellow don't know the war is over," John Fagg chuckled as he held out his hand.

But his twinkle quickly died when he had left the engineer, as the host of the Ship Inn discovered.

From that moment the shipowner steadily pursued the policy of urging on all classes of townsfolk the plain truth that their prosperity depended ultimately on the state of the haven.

"When I've no custom ? " ejaculated the comfortable innkeeper, in much the same fashion as once Jephrez Baker had done.

Leaving him puzzling this very alarming question beneath the huge painted sign of the *Great Harry*, John Fagg made for Elizabeth Street, his thoughts gloomy, his spirits by no means lightened by the sight, at the far side of Paradise Pent, [of the long row of houses which Henry Rochefort had erected there.

For the next two months or more the shipowner was ceaselessly busy, travelling as never before through Kent, endeavouring to cope with all the economic confusion resulting from a change-over from war to peace, too busy even, during the days of the Parliamentary election, to register his vote at the polling station in St. Mary the Virgin's.

But always, despite his many preoccupations, he thought of the haven.

6

Charles Fagg's oval-shaped bedroom was remote from the Town Wall Street side of his father's house, and it was his invariable custom, on getting out of bed, to go over to the window and there inspect the portents of the weather. But on that sunny July morning, the day on which Henry Rochefort put into execution the short-term plan he had cherished for just over three years, the young man did not follow his usual practice. The previous evening, together with a few friends, he had driven out to a tavern in the country, and, once there, in talking and drinking deliciously cool ale, the hours had gone rapidly, with still eight miles for him to travel home. Which explains why it was that Charles slept late, and was in such a hurry to get downstairs the following morning.

Habit, however, dies hard, so it was that just after he had given a pull to the lapels of his coat, he turned from the mirror and glanced over the Ropewalk.

" Good God, what's afoot ? " he ejaculated.

It was not at the white mares' tails in the high ceiling of the blue sky nor at the faint wind eddies which dimmed the glassy surface of the sea that he was gazing. A number of labourers were in the Canyon, a cart along with them, a great shire horse between the shafts. The load was mainly composed of long wood stakes, pointed at one end, and on top was disposed a sledge-hammer and a few coils of new rope.

" What the devil ? " he muttered to himself, amazed.

Then he dallied no more but sought his breakfast. In the dining-room he found that what he had seen had been noticed there also. His mother and Aunt Susan were full of it.

" What can they be doing ? " asked Mrs. Fagg.

Lou made some sort of idiotic suggestion, but then, as her brother informed the family, between poking baby Horatio's fat cheek, that was the response one would expect from a feather-brained female.

" Oh, Charles," laughed his aunt.

" But egad ! " He rose, elevating his arm in the manner of the Roman salute. " I shall unravel the mystery, and that eftsoons. How deep the secret may be hidden you may trust me to bring it you——"

" Fool ! " Lou giggled.

They were all amused by his buffoonery, and in that, and in the banter which followed, the subject which had aroused their curiosity was all but forgotten.

Nevertheless it came back into Charles's mind as, after a parting sally, he left them to go to the warehouse. He decided to make a detour, to walk across to the Canyon.

There being no attempt at concealment on the part of those to whom he spoke, he quickly learnt what was in hand, soon knew the lengths to which a man's spitefulness may lead him and, sobered now, he went back home.

In the very midst of his short recapitulation, Mrs. Fagg sat down abruptly, second by second growing more concerned.

" Henry Rochefort is building there ? " she asked unbelievingly.

" He is, and there's no doubt on't. Nor any doubt," her son added grimly, " on his reason for doing it."

Within the range of her social and domestic activities, Mrs. Fagg was a brisk and competent woman at most times, but just then she looked quite dazed.

" But why, Charles, *why* ? " she demanded. " I know matters between your father and Henry Rochefort have come to a pretty pass, but why this building *here* ? "

As it happened, she had sunk into her husband's chair, into that chair in which, either at work or in leisure, John Fagg spent so many hours.

Charles twisted her around, set her looking along the Canyon towards the pier-heads beyond.

Stark illumination came to her. " He's doing it to spoil your father's view," she gasped.

Her son nodded gravely. " That's why he's doing it, Mother."

Mrs. Fagg did not speak straight off. When she did, it was to express sentiments which seemed strange from her lips, as though this was not the talkative, house-proud, and sometimes inconsequent Polly Fagg, but rather a stranger who could plumb greater depths.

" Henry Rochefort is doing an unutterably mean trick, Charles," she said slowly. " One which makes me feel very sad about him, for underneath it all, I feel sure, he really knows just how ignobly he is acting. You should know too . . ." she glanced at her son, " that he's not without a sense of justice either, and this despite the fact of the sorry relationship betwixt himself and your father."

Charles flushed a little. " I'll say for him that he's never tried to stop our friendship with Louis or . . . or Caroline," he admitted.

Mrs. Fagg sighed. " That's just it," she said. " A fine man ruined, but . . . " she shook her head, " since Elizabeth Rochefort died——"

She blinked at the memory of her friend, was indeed wiping her eyes when her son gave her a consoling squeeze.

" Whether he's got good qualities in him or no," Charles began, " the plain fact is that Mr. Rochefort, long after the heat of temper has gone, continues on whatever path he has decided on during the course of that same bout."

" I know," sniffed his mother.

When her distress had lessened she started to talk of Charles's father, of her anxiety about what he would do when he knew of the miserable revenge Henry Rochefort was putting into execution.

" He comes back this afternoon, too," she murmured. " Ah, well . . . " she sighed.

It was evident that John Fagg's wife, as she went about her household duties that morning, was a very worried woman.

As she had done for half a dozen times during that last hour, Polly Fagg again thought she could hear the sound of hoofs. Hurriedly she turned from the sight of Henry Rochefort with that rolled plan in his hand, and quickly went into the hall.

Her hand was on the knob of the drawing-room door when she saw her sister-in-law on the half-landing of the stairs.

" I . . . I think 'tis him this time, Susan," she murmured.

Susan Rochefort hastened down the lower flight, and then ran after her. Both women stood tensely watching from the window.

In the distance, between Severus's Gate and Butchery Gate, they saw coming along the street a familiar fat-bellied sorrel horse. Bob, as always when nearing home, had slightly increased his usual lethargic gait.

" 'Tis John," whispered his sister, drawing in her breath.

Mrs. Fagg's troubled eyes went again to the approaching animal and the square-built rider upon him, and then came back to her sister-in-law.

" Yes," she said simply.

It was perhaps understandable that John Fagg, wearied with a journey he detested, did not perceive the false brightness with which they greeted him.

" Polly, love," he laughed, giving her a smacking kiss, at the same time encircling Mrs. George Rochefort's slim waist.

" What sort of a journey have you had, dear ? " asked Mrs. Fagg a few minutes later when she was alone with him. Her sister-in-law, by prearrangement, had disappeared towards the seaward side of the house.

The shipowner embarked on a grumbling account, here and there leavened by the addition of some amusing incident which had befallen him, when Susan returned. That agitated lady gave a little warning signal, just the slightest shake of her head. Mr. Rochefort, that movement explained, was still there.

Realising the inevitability of it all, Mrs. Fagg nerved herself to tell her husband.

"John," she said quietly, "I want you to come with me."

His rollicking laugh broke off sharp. "What's the matter, Polly?" he asked imperatively, alarmed by the look of her.

The best she could do was to take his arm, draw him into the parlour, there dumbly to indicate the scene of activity, men toiling in the bright afternoon sun; and Henry Rochefort, too.

His eyes were narrowing, his mouth hardening with every tick of the clock.

"And what does that mean, Polly," he asked slowly.

She told him of Charles's inquiries, and of the surprisingly full measure of information which had been gleaned. Henry Rochefort's unlucky speculation on the Island had received wide publicity and, the banker swore, so should the counter-stroke.

"A beach house, he calls it," she gulped. "But he's building it two stories high."

John Fagg was a level-headed man but here was provocation of the most flagrant kind. Nevertheless he remained true to his nature, saying nothing, gazing steadfastly at a prospect which, as the weeks moved towards the autumn, would be blocked out, mortar-course by mortar-course.

"'Tis petty," he mused abstractedly. "Contemptibly petty."

"I know, dear," said his wife, immeasurably relieved by his comportment, "but we can't help it and we must make the best of it."

She began to bustle about in preparation for the meal, regaling him with details of the succulent repast. There were a couple of plump chickens. . . .

His voice was quite without expression when he interrupted her.

"I'm going out to see him," he remarked tonelessly.

Acutely more frightened by that seemingly complete lack of feeling, Polly Fagg rushed to him, all power of reasoning lost in the apprehension of the present and unknown.

"John," she said imploringly, "I'm terrified lest something dreadful should happen. Pray don't go now."

As he walked towards the door, she keeping anxious pace with him, he held her aside with his arm, never looking at her whilst he spoke.

"Don't fear, m'dear," he said. "I'm not a Henry Rochefort, and . . ." his eyes glinted, "hard words are the worst weapons I shall use."

He would say no more.

The extensive garden at the back of the house sloped gradually down towards its boundary, a hedge. Beyond this, and to the sides of the garden as well, was the wide waste of the Little Pent through whose centre, running at an angle to the sea, was that cut which Charles in his young days had named the Canyon.

Towards this, along a curving, brick-paved garden path, John Fagg steadily walked.

It was manifest that by a common impulse the men who should have been working made pretence only of doing so when they saw that determined figure approaching. They watched John Fagg reach the limit of his own property, they saw him stride behind the hedge until he came to the opening which gave access to the beach. Surreptitiously they eyed him when, after negotiating the slippery shingle, he stood silently behind one of the newly driven posts of the roped-in enclosure.

It was Henry Rochefort who, perhaps unnerved by an unwavering regard, broke into the strange quietude.

" So you see, Fagg," he opened jauntily, " I *was* thinking of doing a little more building. You may remember that was the question you put to me one June day quite a long time ago."

" I do," the shipowner agreed impassively.

The banker, even as he spoke, seemed to be goading himself on to the worst he could do.

" 'Twill be a pleasant retreat——" he began tauntingly.

" 'Twill be a memorial to a man lost to all sense of fitness and decency," interposed John Fagg, his voice cutting. " 'Twill be a thing which will bring a pang to a few, but to one it will surely come to be a cursed sight which he would fain forget, a pillar of stone which shall ever damn him in the eyes of his fellow men. Rochefort's Folly I name it, and Rochefort's Folly it will remain to your dying day. Yes, you've built all right——"

" And I'll build more," shouted Henry Rochefort. " I'll build in those places which will defeat still further your crazy ambitions for the port, and I'll go on building until . . . until . . . " he stammered in his fury.

" Punished you should be, Rochefort, and nothing would please me better than to inflict that punishment," the shipowner declared sternly. " But I have a finer task, one from which I will not be diverted for any personal satisfaction."

" The harbour ? " the banker sneered.

" The haven," he heard in solemn reply. " And that shall be my triumph over you."

Henry Rochefort was now by the stoop, driven there by the force of his anger and vehemence.

" I'll swear it never shall," he cried passionately. " For whatever you project I'll defeat you, however you plan——"

John Fagg was turning away. He had only a few more words to say.

" The mills of God grind slow but sure, Rochefort, but as surely as there is a God above, you will suffer grievously."

Still watched by a half-score pairs of gaping eyes he retraced his way across the deep and yielding shingle, mounted the three crudely constructed steps which gained the gap in the boundary line, passed behind that green hedge, marched along the brick path. And then he disappeared from sight.

CHAPTER FIVE

I

WITH full peace, after so many desolate years, Kentish folk settled themselves whole-heartedly to enjoy the summer.

For four friends in Dover, however, there could be little pleasure until a decision was reached as to the stand which was to be taken against all curiosity. The town, it may be said, still hummed with talk touching on Mr. Henry Rochefort's Folly—that name had stuck.

" So we ignore it," Louis frowned.

This special meeting of the two Faggs and the two Rocheforts had been brought about by Caroline, and took place on the beach immediately below Mr. Crundall's shed, outside which the ribs of Mr. Rochefort's new cutter were already in position.

" A demned silly idea, anyhow, for the money wasted in building materials could have been put out at decent interest," he added sourly, glancing about.

Louis Rochefort felt a trifle embarrassed in sitting there, by the edge of the sea, like so many children. After all, in two months he would be twenty-one ; only his fondness for his sister had persuaded him into such a setting, though otherwise he was in complete agreement with the conclusions arrived at.

" Louis, we also said we would not criticise Papa," Caroline reminded him firmly.

At this her brother cocked an eye, but Miss Rochefort discreetly warned him off. She would have hated, *positively* hated, Charles and Lou to know of the morning when she had marched up to her father and told him that never, never, would she enter the horrid rotunda.

Still less would she have liked them to hear of the painful scene when she was thrust into her bedroom, the intimation ringing in her ears that she would stay there until she apologised. But, even now, her eyes filled a little when she recollected how her papa, at dinner-time on the second day, came up to her full of remorse for what he had done.

" My love," he had said sadly, " I should never ask you to go against your loyalties, and never think, because Mr. Fagg and myself are at cross-purposes, I should ever wish you to give up your companions."

After that it had been so beautiful, with Papa talking of Mamma, and never so much as a mention of the Canyon, where loathsome people now crowded on Sunday afternoons.

Charles Fagg started to rise, for he and Louis were going out to Charlton Green to play cricket.

" That's finished, then," he remarked with relief. Neither he nor his sister, in the circumstances, had been able to say a great deal.

But Lou still wanted to hear more of her brother's short vacation in Paris, with Louis, who in November was proceeding to that capital for a few months' commercial training, not entirely disinterested either. As for Caroline, she was romantically intrigued by Charles's encounter in Boulogne with Jacques Perrier, a boy with whom, many years before, he had fought a bloody battle on the merits of storming Windsor Castle.

The first two items dealt with, Charles gave attention to the third, this arising out of one of his now constant trips to the French ports.

" Jacques ! Damme, 'tis Jacques, isn't it ? " he had asked dubiously on the quayside.

It was Jacques Perrier, a dark-haired young man with a thin face, intense eyes, and a knee shattered at Aboukir Bay where, as powder boy, he had served in the French fleet.

" M. Charles." He had stared, limping forward. " Comment vous portez-vous, M. Charles ? "

" Très bien," grinned Charles Fagg, wringing a calloused hand. " Et vous, Jacques ? "

The two young men had laughed, eyed one another, caught up the past years, then returned to the days of youthful bathing at the Tour d'Odre.

" And now, thank God, 'tis peace again," Charles had said.

A sensitive mouth had grown bitter. No, his companion declared, it was but an interlude ; had not the accursed Bonaparte made himself First Consul for life, and would the miscreant rest content with that?

" You think there'll be war again, Jacques ? " Charles Fagg had asked, nevertheless thoughtfully nodding.

Jacques Perrier had glanced over his shoulder. The agents of

Fouché, the renegade priest whom the despot had appointed Minister of Police, were everywhere, and a slip of the tongue . . . Yes, blood would soon flow again.   What, in his lust for power, cared the cursed Napoleon for such as he—he who wanted nothing better than a peaceful life a-fishing, but who must now live out his years with pain as a bedfellow?

" Oh, how monstrous tragic ! " was Caroline's reaction.

" I hope war doesn't come to spoil Canterbury Races in August," Lou said more practically.

Both girls were, of course, wildly thrilled by the thought of going to Barham Down for this tremendous social event.

Louis Rochefort, after the quartet had scrambled on to the South Pier, was teasing the girls, a morsel heavily, on the possibilities of hostilities when he spotted that his sister's hand was in his friend's.

" Ho, ho ! " he roared, mightily amused.

" Caroline and myself," Charles observed calmly, " have discovered a fondness one for the other, eh, m'dear ? "

Miss Rochefort blushed violently. " Yes, Charles," she murmured.

That young gentleman nodded gravely.   " To such purpose, Louis," he announced, " that I am proposing signing her on as my cabin boy."

" *Charles !* " Miss Rochefort screamed, ecstatic at the prospect. " You're going to teach me to sail your boat ?   Properly ? "

He eyed her at length.   " Properly, m'dear ? " he inquired judicially.

Miss Rochefort, dimpling, confessed she had some little familiarity with the skiff.

With no small disgust Mr. Charles Fagg coldly proclaimed that now he knew just what her protestations of affection were worth.

*   *   *   *   *   *   *   *

Canterbury Races and Louis' twenty-first celebrations were attractions immensely looked forward to.

" Of course it would do this now," Caroline said tempestuously. She was doubled up on a window stool in the little drawing-room, elbows on her knees, chin cupped in her hands, her scowl directed towards the rain splashes in the Pent.

Lou, who also had a new dress and new bonnet in readiness, agreed pettishly.   For weeks and weeks, she said, it had been unbearably hot.

" But now for three days it has done nothing but come down heavens-hard."

But, faced by this recrimination, the Clerk of the Weather relented. The morrow was fine and, under a pale, water-washed blue sky, the carriages of East Kent headed for Barham Down.

For the second race, to Charles Fagg's delight, he was offered a ride, though on reflection he concluded it was one of his lordship's whimseys, rather than Jim Page's testimony, which had gained him the honour.

"Damme if it won't be droll, your lad up on that sprawling-legged drummer o' mine," Lord Poynte choked to Mr. John Fagg.

This animal of ill-repute had been purchased out of the profit the noble gentleman had received from participation in one of the free-trader's 'runs,' and a sorry bargain he had proved to be. Lord Poynte, however, having a sense of humour entirely his own, had promptly christened the beast *Toke's Quality*.

"Farcical, begad," he bellowed. "An' 'tis to be hoped that thin-lipped Revenue Officer is present 'safternoon."

Nevertheless there was a more serious aspect to the matter. Lord Poynte had a wager that his animal would finish up with nose in front of Mr. Bynge's daisy-cutter *Bo-Boy*, whether or not they numbered ninth and tenth or were tailed off to the last pair.

"Fifty guineas," his lordship observed succinctly, and then, in a flow of language most inadvisable to repeat, proceeded to give riding instructions.

Toke's Quality must not be allowed his head or he would never stay the distance ; he must be kept on a tight rein until the home turn and his legs must be saved as much as possible.

"Hang on to the rails——"

"If it pleases your lordship, I think not all the way," Charles Fagg remarked civilly, pointing across to the Canterbury turnpike alongside which, and cambering away from it, the course ran for some distance.

"Eh ? " Lord Poynte grunted as he eyed the vehicles, wagons, two stage-coaches, even the mail which had pulled up to watch the sport, this much to the anger of a passenger in a chaise to the rear.

"'Twill be firmer going on that side nearer the road, your lordship. Whereas lower down by the rail 'twill be slushy and holding."

His lordship—who was being much amused by the fury of a gentle-man unable to proceed on his business by reason of a column in front, a steep gorse-covered bank to one side and a hedge to the other—perceived the drift. He slapped his thigh, thumped Charles on the back, and congratulated the young man's father.

"A cool customer this 'un, Fagg," he roared, highly delighted at the march he was going to steal.

The Ladies' Plate of that afternoon became a most thrilling contest.

"They'll soon be starting." Caroline Rochefort clapped her hands excitedly.

She, with her father and Lou, were three tiers up the New Stand, from which there was a magnificent view of the lovely Down upon which now not a single army tent was pitched ; a rough green acreage with here and there traces of the barrows of an earlier race.

"They're off ! " The shout went up, and then over the crowd, gentlemen in new civilian clothing and ladies all bedecked in their best, a silence fell.

By the bend on the far side the favourite was lying third, going easily, with a bunch behind, close astern of which was Lord Poynte's unfortunate purchase.

"Come on, old fellow," Charles Fagg cried encouragingly, pulling away from the rails, taking *Toke's Quality* wide, flashing along the hedgeside so near to the turnpike.

From then the story best belongs to the personalities in the stand.

"Like to make it a hundred yellow Georges, Bynge ? " Lord Poynte bawled from one end.

"Aye, an' double that," yelled a plucky gambler.

The wager went up again, to four hundred guineas, then to a round five—all before Charles made his effort.

"Look . . . look, Caroline ! " gasped Lou, her face white with tension.

Toke's Quality, by comparison with competitors in the mire, was flying. Shrewd racing men began to hedge : 10's came to 8's, dropped to 6's, tumbled to 4's.

Bo-Boy was out of the picture, and raking stride by raking stride, *Toke's Quality* was beating the favourite out of second place, with the leading horse rapidly cracking up.

"*Toke's Quality* . . . *Toke's Quality* . . . " the howl resounded.

At the final turn Charles cut for the rails, necessarily losing ground in doing so, but as he entered the straight he had three good lengths in hand of the favourite though, alas, no more the advantage of harder surface.

"Charles, Charles, Charles . . . " Caroline, in very agony, was dancing up and down, seeing all the time that precious distance diminishing.

A drumming in her ears, two horses thundering by, and then the shout, " Dead heat."

"Damme, a fine rider an' a sharp 'un," his lordship, crimson-faced, elbowed through the press to deliver his encomiums.

Round Charles Fagg, when he had dismounted, surged a throng, a throng from which went up a huge cheer when, after Lord Poynte had offered to present him with any beast in his stables barring three, he remarked that he had taken a fancy to the sadly maligned fellow who had recently carried him.

"Then *Toke's Quality's* yours, young fellow," roared his lordship.

Later, behind the stand, Charles displayed his acquisition to a number of friends and acquaintances.

The eldest Stratton made condescending comment, ' Colonel ' Breton was openly envious, the Stone twins produced a horsy jargon, the Stokes and Nethersole boys opened immediate negotiations for the loan . . .

" A deuced fine beast," Louis Rochefort exclaimed knowingly.

" So think I, Louis," Charles agreed gravely, unerringly catching the whip he had been tossing. " He carries well, eh ? "

Miss Caroline Rochefort, an affectionate little piece, had abundant quicksilver in her. She went off into a burlesque of that familiar trick of Charles's. Her eyes slightly veiled, her outstretched arm, even to the opening and closing of her hand, throwing up and rethrowing an imaginary whip, all with supreme conceit and surety.

" So think I, Louis," she drawled lazily.

Upon which Mr. Charles Fagg observed that, this slight on him, he could hardly, on the next day, examine her on the parts of a sail.

" Head . . . luff . . . leach . . . foot," she responded without hesitation. " Throat . . . peak . . . tack . . . clew."

" Mmmm . . . " murmured Charles, and then grinned wide.

Caroline's eyes sparkled. " Isn't it divine, Charles ? " she smiled. " To-day, to-morrow, all the days, so lovely."

" Mmmm," he murmured again.

Miss Rochefort required a deal more enthusiasm than that. Aloofly she spoke.

" And, *of course*, there's Louis' party, though 'tis a devilish time yet."

But that landmark in her brother's life came soon enough. Days of happiness pass all too quick.

In the afternoon of the great day when Louis Rochefort reached man's estate, his father's cutter, named by his sister, was launched from the shipbuilder's yard.

" A fine craft, Mr. Crundall," Charles Fagg said warmly, eyeing the green-painted cutter, the *Elizabeth Rochefort*, after she had gracefully taken to the sea.

" A tidy job, I'm thinking," nodded the builder.

Then there was a short trip in the craft, and after that the return to Snargate Street, where Martha Teddiman had done the young master all respect. The dining-room was gaily festooned, and on the table was everything one could imagine in the confectionery line.

Mr. Rochefort, at the right moment, made just the most suitably felicitous speech he could have done, though, and in this it was easy to tell the overwhelming pride he had in his son, his voice broke a little when he presented to Louis the engrossed piece of parchment which he had instructed Mr. Braems to prepare.

" Deed of partnership . . . " Louis Rochefort's eyes came up from the document to meet those of his father. " Papa ! " he stammered.

" You deserve it, my boy," the banker muttered emotionally. " And I've every . . . every confidence in you."

Not a note of discord was there, excepting a little later, when Henry Rochefort asked of Mr. Edward Hexstall what he thought of the First Consul's annexation of the continental half of the dominions of the King of Sardinia and of his sending 30,000 men to occupy the chief passes of the Alps.

" Well, Hextsall ? " he demanded.

The Town Surveyor, as so many of his persuasion would have done in those days of rising uneasiness, only blustered in reply.

" Methinks you Whiggamores would acquiesce if Bonaparte seized this country," the banker said caustically.

It was the beginning of a period in which the Whigs, for their assumed beliefs, were to suffer much castigation.

Meantime there was a great surprise. Martha whispered to Miss Caroline, and Miss Caroline in turn to Miss Lou. Thereupon the latter young lady, first glancing at her pale reflection in the pier-glass between the two windows of the drawing-room, went out on the arm of her friend.

" Hullo," Caroline smiled welcomingly.

Yes, it was Jack Woodgate, shorter of sleeve than ever.

" How so, so delighted we all are to see you, Jack," continued the young mistress of the house, for Lou, flushed divinely now, appeared quite incapable of speech.

" I came to see Lou," Mr. Woodgate remarked stolidly.

Miss Rochefort, for the remainder of that evening, ensured that he saw Lou, even to cheating the draw for the couples who, tied together with a handkerchief, negotiated the ascent of the Grand Military Shaft. This engineering feat, after years of fitful work on it, had been opened to the public a few days before.

Charles Fagg, it may be admitted, was equally dishonest. It was Caroline's shapely ankle which was secured to his when, breathless, they reached the top step leading on to the frowning cliff.

2

Since midsummer the talk in the town had been about the Folly and of the hostility between two men, but, as the oaks became more richly tinted and the orange leaves of the beeches started to fall, this

K

interest diminished and another, concerning one only of these gentlemen, took its place.

As the weather grew darker it came to be more and more
speculated as to whether Ralph Toke, discomfited so often at the
hands of John Fagg, would be able to revenge himself for the many
humiliations he had received. With lively anticipation the townsfolk
settled themselves for a contest they believed inevitable.

But, although the free-trader ran plenty of fine cargoes, not a single
incident arose, and soon it came to be laughingly bruited abroad that
the Revenue Officer, spirit broken by ill-success, was likely to go the
way of his predecessor, Mr. Howgate, taking the easy course.

Those of this view, however, were poor judges of character. Ralph
Toke might, for the moment, be lying low, but it was ominously so.
And only Clement Foxley was acquainted with the real why, wherefore,
and when.

" First, Foxley," his superior said one windy evening in October,
" we must, despite this present setback, ascertain whence the Faggs
draw their liquor."

The reversal to which he referred was the advices contained in a
number of reports from revenue cutters. These, for over a month
now, had been keeping close watch on the northern French ports,
with never a sight of Fagg craft in suspicious circumstances.

" They still carry on their illicit traffic," Mr. Toke continued
impassionedly. " But where," his fist emphasised on the table, " where,
where, do they load the goods from ? "

Foxley deemed it expedient neither to echo nor commiserate upon
his superior's query—Mr. Toke, for long, had been a most uncertain
factor.

" But," the Revenue Officer's eyes gleamed, " find out we shall
in the fullness of time, and then, when we are satisfied as to that,
when we are satisfied on every nicety, when we are satisfied that not
one thing has been left undone . . . "

In short, Mr. Ralph Toke was possessed of a certain quality of
patience. The pounce should be made only when the capture was a
surety, when there was no possible room for doubt.

At the Strond Street end of Elizabeth Street, some way separating
it from Mr. John Fagg's warehouse, was a residence which, though considerably dilapidated on the outside, was notably different within.

On the lower floor of these premises, Polly Fagg was examining
a number of bolts of muslin from one of which, shortly, she cut off a
dress length.

" 'Twill make Lou a most charming gown, I do declare," she said
to herself.

There was a valuable assortment of goods, both wet and dry, in the low room, many of them contributing to an odour which was far from unpleasant ; dollops of East India tea, cinnamon, condiments, Hollands, coffee beans, wines, brandy, tobacco, earthenware made on the Continent.

" Yes——," Mrs. Fagg murmured, now dividing her attention between lovely thread lace and the most delicate of silk.

In due course her inspection was over, and soon, two small packages under her arm, she was going towards her husband's private room at the warehouse, returning thither by a narrow, winding passage which, in its uneven course, went under the property of a ship's chandler and two storehouses belonging to the Victualling Office.

Towards the end, when standing at the bottom of a flight of steps, she waited awhile for, despite the thickness of the concealed door above, Mr. Templeman's voice, though muted, carried clearly to her.

The wool stapler was unquestionably in a violent temper.

" And when I see Jonathan Dawkes an' any more of that kidney," he roared, " I'll let 'em know what I think, so help me. If this is peace then damme I'd as soon we was at war again, an' to hell with their Charles James Fox."

Polly Fagg had not to wait long before her inquisitiveness concerning the threat to the Postmaster was explained.

Her husband, hearing her light tap, locked his outer door and then slid the panel to allow her in.

" Oh," he told her gravely, " the *Matilda* is very nigh loaded with packs for Rotterdam, an' Harry's just heard that Bonaparte's ordered the Dutch to impose a prohibitive tariff."

" On wool ? "

" On all English goods, Polly," the shipowner replied grimly.

" But why ? " he was indignantly asked.

John Fagg, who appeared to be very considerably disturbed, was not able to give her any satisfaction, and Mrs. Fagg, her own piece of business very gratifyingly accomplished, set off for home.

She went by way of Custom House Quay and regretted it, for the gale of three days before had not completely blown out and her skirts were whirled about most indecorously. Still, on that busy thoroughfare, she discovered far more diversions than she would have done either in Strond Street or Lower Snargate Street.

Alongside the wharf were four vessels, two of them her husband's ; the *Dover and London Hoy*, five or six travellers, some green-looking so soon, already aboard, and the *Matilda*, from whose hold Mr. Templeman's goods were being feverishly removed in hope that the tide might not be lost. Then the green-painted *Elizabeth Rochefort* which would, as she knew, be taking Louis over to France that same day. And last, but not least, there was Captain Nethersole's packet, her owner ashore, awaiting the appearance, from the Ship Inn, of his distinguished passenger.

"Though," Jeremy Nethersole shook his head, "methinks I ought to be fetching him back from Calais instead of carrying him there."

He was referring to Lord Whitworth, that noble gentleman being on his way to take up post in Paris as His Britannic Majesty's Ambassador to the French Republic.

"John is anxious too, Captain Nethersole," Mrs. Fagg observed wisely, and would have stayed chatting awhile had not the skipper of the packet chanced to mention the time of high water. Polly Fagg was deeply interested in the extraordinary amount of luggage which his lordship was taking for himself and his swarm of children, but above all she did not want to meet Henry Rochefort, who she felt sure would be seeing Louis off, and who might appear at any moment.

So she hurried into Snargate Street, her intention being to pass the banker's house as quickly as possible.

Polly Fagg did put the mansion behind her without any embarrassing encounter, despite the fact that she was compelled to walk slowly. A funeral, that of two men who had been drowned at the harbour's mouth on the first afternoon of the, recent storm, was proceeding for the service in St. Mary the Virgin's.

Had she been less preoccupied, she might have noticed that although on the faces of the mourners there was a proper sorrow, there was also something not far removed from suppressed anger.

Her husband's ceaseless campaigning was having its effect. Many of the Barons of the Cinque Port, high and low degree alike, were beginning to think more and more of their sorry haven and of those who held it to be of such small account.

3

Dover Fair came towards the end of the month in which Louis Rochefort went abroad, about which time the editorials of the London newspapers were criticising in sharp terms the First Consul's arbitrary demand that the Government should expel from England those princes of the royal house of France who had sought refuge there.

From then, progressively, the relations between the two nations deteriorated.

In the New Year the ruler of France, intimating the desire for a Colonial Empire, announced that " Europe is too small for me," a sentiment alarming sounding, though there could not be, on the face of it, more than dark suspicions about the pressure earlier put on Spain to cause her to cede Louisiana to him.

On the other hand, he himself became President of the Italian Republic and, in phraseology of a tenor unheard of in modern diplomatic exchanges, arrogantly made request that England should recognise the legality of his conquests in Italy and Switzerland.

The end of January, as Louis Rochefort wrote to his father, saw the French Government settling debts for 25 per cent in paper which, when negotiated, brought in 10 per cent.

The money markets of the world appeared in little illusion as to the future.

A bank, by common conception, is a place of austerity wherein little more than the turning of a ledger page should desecrate the holy silence. Certainly such premises should never sound as though they harboured a blacksmith's shop.

Nevertheless, on a frosty morning preceding St. Valentine's Day, shortly after the packet had come in from Calais, this lamentable illustration was not utterly wide of the mark. A most infernal row *was* coming from Mr. Rochefort's bank.

The reason for the apparently unseemly display was not far to seek. The shortage of coin in the country was growing more chronic, and banks everywhere were impelled themselves to attempt the amelioration of a situation which was causing havoc in many directions. If the Bank of England, said they, could countermark Spanish dollars with a bust of George III in armour, then so might they proceed on similar lines.

Operations were taking place in the specie room where, using a stout bench erected for the purpose, three clerks were working with chisels, dies and seven-pound hammers, on beautiful coins. And glorifying in this break from dull routine indeed they were.

One was stamping on to Spanish dollars the inscription, ' *Payable at Mr. Rochefort's Bank, Dover 4/9d.* '; another was cutting Mexican pillar dollars into three parts, these being valued at 1/8d. apiece, the small profit nicely covering the cost.

And a third, to obtain a smaller counter still, was dividing a pile of dollars into quarter portions.

" They say, Mr. Godspenny," quoth this last, after picking up a half-piece which had flown against the wainscoting, " that some clever people can get five quarters out of each piece."

" Five pieces, eh, out of each coin ? " The senior clerk nodded his head gently, always a dangerous sign. He was, of course, supervising the work.

" Five out of each," confirmed the luckless clerk.

" Five out of each," softly repeated Matthew Godspenny.

Whilst his more versed colleagues smothered grins, the unfortunate young man, greatly flattered by the attention he was receiving from one whom he held in great awe, gave chapter and verse as to how it might be done.

" 'Tis easy, I vow, Mr. Godspenny," he said, confidence ever rising.

The first thing to do, he vouchsafed, was to cut each coin into fifths. Then, taking each segment, he would file the straight sides until the two lines, at joining, made a right-angle. The piece so produced, he admitted it freely, would be a shade smaller than the more lawful portion. . . .

" But, I'd swear, Mr. Godspenny," he laughed heartily, " to pass many a one without a question being asked, I would truly."

That smile of his died quickly as the chief clerk's long arm shot out, as a pair of basilisk eyes were fixed on him.

" Your pockets, sir," Mr. Godspenny hissed.

" My . . . my pockets ? "

But turn them out he had to do, every pocket in his clothing, whilst the martinet, prying and poking to ensure the wretched culprit was not light-fingered as well, bitterly reproached himself for recommending to Mr. Rochefort one who had all the instincts of a felon.

" A forger . . . a counterfeiter," stammered the hapless youth.

Now the chief clerk, hands behind him, was rapidly pacing the narrow confines.

" To think that in this bank," he soliloquised aloud, as though the iron had entered into his soul, " where large sums——"

The individual who was impressing His Majesty's knight-like figure choked suddenly, but fortunately for him there came at this moment a sharp rap on the counter of the bank.

Mr. Godspenny, balefully eyeing the new offender, responded to the summons.

Without, there awaited an erect, well-built Frenchman whose age would be between twenty-five and thirty.

M. Armand Saval, it appeared, had just landed from France. He desired, he announced decidedly, to see the proprietor or a partner of the bank.

The chief clerk made the necessary inquiries.

Quite apart from the fact that M. Saval presented credentials welcome to any banker—a not inconsiderable sum in *louis d'or* and a substantial draft on London—Mr. Henry Rochefort found the gentleman most agreeable.

The Frenchman's manner was polished and, though obviously he came of a good family, he made no pretence of belonging to the *haute noblesse*. Dover harboured many *emigrés* and, such is the world, quite a few of them had pronounced themselves of a rank and distinction to which, it was afterwards discovered, they had little claim.

" Had it been otherwise, Mr. Rochefort . . ." the caller, smiling faintly, was gently fingering the lobe of his ear, " I am afraid I should have had ver' little of my modest fortune left."

" True, true, monsieur," Henry Rochefort nodded understandingly, thereafter hospitably indicating the decanter.

" And so, monsieur," he remarked subsequently, " you propose making a stay in Dover ? "

" That depends, Mr. Rochefort," was the stiff reply he received.

" Quite," frowned the banker, who felt he was not an unduly curious man.

Evidently M. Saval, then, was disinclined to explain himself further, but later, when Henry Rochefort was thinking his visitor had a most powerful handgrip, he decided he owed the banker something more.

" You see," he defined, less rigidly, " I am convinced that soon there will be war between our two countries, and I prefer to offer my services in the cause of liberty rather than be compelled to fight for a swollen tyrant. That is why, monsieur, I came here."

At this direct speech Henry Rochefort's expression became a little worried, for it confirmed much he believed himself and, above all, he was growing most concerned about Louis. Despite this preoccupation, however, he did not forget to express appreciation for the fine sentiments he had heard.

M. Saval, contrarily, appeared to regret his outburst, deprecating himself in a manner which did him no harm with the banker.

" Meantime, Mr. Rochefort," he smiled, " I shall amuse myself in my own fashion. A little riding, a little drawing and painting, perhaps . . ." he laughed outright, " a little pistol practice in readiness for all I have so gloomily outlined."

They parted company on excellent terms. Henry Rochefort, a lonely man himself, reflected that the young man would be a delightful companion of an evening, and was a little annoyed with himself for not suggesting such a meeting.

However, he soon found the opportunity to repair the omission. Within five minutes M. Saval returned, his purpose to inquire as to where superior lodgings might be had.

Matthew Godspenny, called into conference, guardedly stated that he knew of three.

The Frenchman chose the one in Trevanion Street. From there, close by St. James's beach, he would have sight of the loved land of his birth.

Late in March, messengers and couriers were passing almost hourly through the town, once again troops began to appear, and trenches were being dug in certain parts of the Ropewalk.

It was known that considerable military preparations were afoot in the ports of Holland and northern France, and that many dock facilities were being improved.

The French 5 per cent *Consolidés* were down to 56 and still falling, and it was reported that the vacillating Mr. Addington was exceedingly dismayed about the trend of events.

4

The First Consul might be massing forces along the coast bordering the English Channel, he might be enlarging the French havens for the more rapid dispatch of the boats carrying an army of invasion, and his latest piece of provocation might be the insolent requirement that certain English newspapers should be suppressed, but . . .

But it was spring and there was still peace, and the sun was shining, and the sea was blue, and the wind soft and caressing, and there yet was ahead all the summer before Caroline Rochefort would be leaving Dover for a whole year.

" 'Twill be awful, Charles," she murmured, her brown eyes momentarily shadowed. " I can't think why Papa wants me to."

Henry Rochefort had ever been grateful to Martha Teddiman, but he knew that the housekeeper was not qualified to instil into his daughter those greater refinements she should know. For that reason Caroline, at the end of September, was to go to Worcestershire, there to stay this unconscionable while at the stately house of a cousin of her father, a very genteel home indeed.

" 'Twill pass, m'dear," Charles said consolingly, giving her small hand an extra nice squeeze.

They were at the seaward end of Snargate Street-over-the-Wall by now and, after waving gaily and calling a greeting to Martha and Captain Pepper, descended the steps of the boat-dock, Shep naturally in busy attendance.

"A bonny pair, Martha, love," Valentine Pepper beamed, evidently highly pleased because Miss Caroline had insultingly described him as a mixture of Parbuckle and Turk's Head.

Shifting his pipe into the opposite corner of his mouth he began, whilst tending to the halliard of the Jack, to express his delight about the couple.

Martha, who was sitting against the base of the flagstaff, demurred considerably.

"I won't 'low that, Valentine," she said severely. "Though Mr. Charles is surely a young man now, Miss Caroline is only sixteen, and for that reason 'tis nothing more than a boy and girl affair. Calf love, I'd name it."

Captain Pepper, at the last moment recollecting that he must not spit, had very different views. Mr. Charles, he observed pugnaciously, was as fine a gentleman as you could find, and Miss Caroline as lovely a little lady. . . .

"And when she's full upgrown an' back from being made into a proper lady, Martha," he declared oracularly, making the point with his pipe stem, "you mark my words what'll happen. Them two'll be spliced afore we'll know what's what."

"I'm not saying that Mr. Charles isn't——"

Her swain was in full sail. "Moreover, Martha," he pronounced resolutely, "they'll not be spliced twenty-four hours before another similar ceremony will be a-taking place."

Miss Teddiman tossed her head. "As to that, Pepper . . ." she said distantly.

"Not twenty-four 'ours," rumbled the boatswain.

Her head bent low to hide a tiny smile of pleasure, Martha busied herself with her needlework.

"Perhaps, Valentine," she coolly suggested some minutes later, risking a coy glance, "*if* they do wed, then perhaps within the month——"

"Twenty-four 'ours, my girl," her future husband determinedly informed her. "And, love . . ." he gently touched her shoulder, more simple and humble now, "I'm looking forrard to it a mort, Martha, for 'tis lonesome without you."

His will not too brutally made known, Valentine Pepper limped with no little air towards the house, his purpose to put on the kettle.

From the Basin, Shep's barking continued as Mr. Charles's boat, Miss Caroline in supreme charge, drifted leisurely towards the Tidal Harbour. That young lady, on arrival at the boat-dock, had done everything, to making sail. She had shipped the rudder on to the pintles, put the tiller into the rudder head, seen that the poppets were secure . . .

"Ssssh, old boy," Charles Fagg admonished the highly elated sheepdog.

That was one thing which Caroline specially loved in Charles—he never fussed. He had taught her to sail and having done so had a confidence in her which gave her additional confidence in herself.

" 'Tis a funny thing, Caroline," Mr. Fagg remarked just outside the north pier-head, quite ignoring that she had taken it a little too fine and that the backwash from the timbers might easily have caused a minor disaster, " that Shep makes such an infernal row immediately he gets afloat."

The breeze was tumbling Miss Rochefort's ringlets, her glance was riveted ahead, and she was putting the tiller up.

" Only when we're in the harbour, Charles," she murmured, " as soon as he gets his sea-legs . . . "

Dover began to drop astern, with the South Foreland and St. Margaret's-at-Cliffe ahead.

Charles was reclining almost on his back, hands clasped behind his head, his attention divided between the sky and the rapt face of the boat's captain. Shep was sitting upright on the bottom boards, peering inquisitively over the gunwale first to the weather and then to the lee side, and giving tremendous tongue when, to his palpable amazement, he heard a familiar voice coming from over the dappled sea.

The *Margaret*, one of Mr. Fagg's craft now very largely engaged in carrying paving stones from Poole to London, was passing, and her captain's hail had rung out.

There were spirited interchanges before the larger vessel drew clear. Then the idyllic cruise was continued, the course being altered towards the King's Buildings at Deal.

Caroline, it could truly be said, had not merely become expert in the handling of a boat, but also she was in way of being well acquainted with the ten mile or more stretch of waters inshore of the North and South Goodwins. She knew the Gull Stream, between these last and the dangerous Brakes Sand, and she was familiar with the leading marks which gave courses for the avoidance of many perils.

" And how, m'dear," Charles's grin flashed out, " does one approach Deal without piling up on the shoal where the *Minerva* struck ? "

She had been staring that way, watching the rotating sails of Upper Deal Mill, clear-cut against the sky behind the town.

" Upper Deal Mill and Deal Castle in one, sir," she retorted smartly.

" Qur-wite correct, Rochefort," chuckled Charles, in most amazingly faithful mimicry of a pedant of Canterbury.

Miss Rochefort, proving herself an accomplished mariner by day, now wanted to know about the helps to navigation visible at night. The High and Low Lights of the South Foreland, Dungeness, the

North Foreland, the three triangularly-set lights of the Goodwin Light Vessel. . . .

" 'Twould be delicious to see them all, Charles . . . when 'tis dark, I mean," she hinted delicately.

Exude innocence she might, but nevertheless Charles Fagg eyed her suspiciously.

" And that means, m'dear ? " he twinkled.

" Yes, Charles," she laughed, nodding quickly. " Do bring me out . . . just a little way . . . some time when they all show."

And so it was arranged, there being no difficulty on the one important factor. Henry Rochefort's daughter had a way of getting out of her home by a route which would have caused Martha Teddimen, had she known of it, to have seven fits in rapid succession.

Charles, as he looked towards the eastward, was still smiling.

Promptly he was indignantly challenged, for it looked exactly as if he was amused by what might seem to be a youthful desire to look at a few lights winking across the dark waters.

" No, Caroline," he grinned. " I was thinking of Mr. Toke."

After that, of course, he had to reveal a secret which the Revenue Officer would gladly have given quite a few clinking guineas to know.

" You see, Caroline," Charles laughed, " the Frenchy and Dutch traders rendezvous with us on the Goodwins, and the transfer is effected there."

" *On* the Goodwins, Charles ? "

As a hand in the *Emma* had once, many years before, explained to him Jamaica Land on the North Goodwin Sand, so now he told her of the spit which, for a brief interval, dried out at low water.

" I'd love to go there too, Charles," Miss Rochefort said enviously. " 'Twould be marvellous to step on a place which is used to make Mr. Toke look so silly."

Then she began to giggle, all at the memory of a morning of the previous week when she had seen Charles, very solemnly, pull up in the busy Market Place to ask the Revenue Officer's opinion of the beast he was riding.

" Oh, Charles," she gurgled. " I'll never forget his face when you showed him *Toke's Quality*. 'Twas too enraged for words."

" Poor old Toke," Charles remarked easily, adding that he could swear Ralph Toke was now every whit as venomous towards Mr. Charles Fagg as he was to Mr. John of the same surname.

Very skilfully had Caroline brought round the boat for the homeward run, and then, as was the established custom, Charles took over the tiller.

Caroline, her legs tucked beneath her, settled herself before him, her head resting against his knees.

For a long time neither spoke until, when Dover's bay was drawing near, Caroline sighed.

" It has been lovely, Charles," she said dreamily.

Charles lightly ruffled her hair. " It has, m'dear," he smiled.

Their intimate silence deepened, and continued until, as was *his* established custom when he saw the pier-heads, Shep went into the bows, there to stand, barking again, hurling defiance at every swooping seagull and every rippling sea.

Then into the Tidal Harbour where, the flood only just having begun, Charles had to leave his boat.

Some little way beyond the rough ladder whereby they clambered to the top of the North Pier, a gentleman, easel erected, was drawing.

" 'Tis M. Saval, Charles," Caroline said, seeing him first. " I declare Papa is becoming terrible fond of him, for I believe he comes in again to-night."

As they drew near the Frenchman rose, doffing his hat gracefully.

" Ah, mademoiselle," he laughed. " I see that you have been enjoying yourself, whereas I——" He grimaced, nodding towards his work.

" Not gone too well, eh, monsieur? " Charles Fagg grinned, taking in the sketch.

On his attitude and about this remark Miss Rochefort subsequently rebuked him.

" The poor man," she said pityingly, as they scrunched across the shingle towards Snargate Street-over-the-Wall, " he knows perfectly that he has little of the art, but as he likes it 'twas most unkind to make fun of what he had done."

" Oh, come, I wasn't doing that," Charles chuckled. " Though hang it, Caroline, his idea of the Cross Wall and the lock-gates presented to me a picture a deal more resembling one of those infernal theorems of Euclid than anything else."

She was amused by this angular illustration of the artist's effort, but she nearly died with laughter at what Charles next said.

" 'Tis lucky that Jack wasn't with us," he observed gravely.

The thought of what the very plain-spoken Mr. Woodgate would have said sent them into howls of glee.

Then they had tea together in the little drawing-room, in most formal style, too. Martha, for reasons best known to herself, had arranged it so.

CHAPTER SIX

I

WITH each passing week the position grew more impossible and at the beginning of May the fleet, in the dead of night, slipped by the South Foreland, the passage of great ships-of-the-line revealed by no more than the top-lights of the repeating vessel, a frigate which, sailing through the lines from one division to another, transmitted the Admiral's signals.

On the sixteenth of the month England declared war on France.

Two days after, the townsfolk of Dover were treated to a spectacle not dissimilar from a pantomime, namely the farcical arrangements, entered into by the authorities on both sides of the Channel, to ensure that Lord Whitworth, the retiring Ambassador, and M. Andréossi, his opposite number in London, should be on the high seas at the same time, each having been sped from his port of embarkation by the same number of guns.

Enlivening all this might be, but it was only a matter of hours before ugly news was at hand, one item of which, the fact that three Dover packets had been seized in Calais, caused Mr. Nicholas Stokes, the Clerk of the Passage, to tip Mr. Robert Spisour, Water Bailiff, into the Basin. It was all a regrettable mistake too, for Mr. Spisour, Whig though he might be, was equally as much determined as the next to fight the French until their ambitious world despot was laid low, cost what it might.

"You damned hasty-tempered fool," the Water Bailiff gasped when he was fished out, and forthwith fluently informed the Clerk of the Passage as to what he thought of him.

It was characteristic of the mood of the nation that Mr. Spisour, who might reasonably have felt some loss of dignity in standing shivering, dripping wet, on Custom House Quay, thought first and foremost of the fact that his patriotism had been doubted, rather than of his condition and of the loss of a silver-buckled shoe.

But a really savage howl of wrath went up from the country when it became known that the First Consul, against all the laws of civilized dealings, had apprehended 10,000 English tourists, virulently intimating that in France they would stay until the war was over—as incidentally they did, and for eleven years that was.

These last tidings utterly distracted Henry Rochefort. Louis, he knew, had reached Boulogne, having been seen there, in the distance, by the skipper of the *Elizabeth Rochefort*, that craft being extricated from the hostile haven only by the skin of her captain's teeth.

"Louis over there," the banker groaned, pacing the front room of the bank.

The news spread rapidly. That night, after borrowing ten guineas from Captain Pepper and acquainting him of his design, a young man disappeared from Dover.

Within three days Charles Fagg was by way of being a hero, and on the afternoon of the fourth the Mayor's Sergeant came on official business to Elizabeth Street.

Mr. Pitt, he said, was at the Guildhall and, having expressed the desire to meet the young man who had effected the daring rescue of a friend, his Worship requested young Mr. Fagg's attendance at once.

So Charles met a gentleman whose never-flinching fight for his country and for the cause of freedom was destined to flame for ever amidst the annals of that country.

It was Caroline, however, who learnt something more, though little enough at that, of the manner in which her brother had been prised from the clutches of the monster.

She had just gone to bed when Martha's scream of delight aroused her and, after Louis, frantically implored, had run upstairs to hug her, she was peering down into the hall, being too scantily attired to descend herself. There she saw Charles backing towards the door, and her father following him up, wringing the embarrassed young man's hand.

"Good-night, Charles," she called out affectionately; "you must tell me more of it . . . soon, *very* soon."

Apparently Charles, glimpsing her flushed face round the edge of a walnut tallboy, knew the meaning of an expressive gesture she fleetingly made. Anyhow, after shaking off the banker, he forthwith turned into the fire-alley alongside the house.

Shortly, above his head, he heard a faint sound and very soon Miss Rochefort, a few more suitable clothes hurriedly donned, negotiated the outhouse roof beneath her bedroom window, to drop lightly beside him.

"You ever like to finish things, eh, Caroline?" he laughed.

She was all agog, and very disappointed with the dull account she received.

"You went to Boulogne . . . you found Jacques Perrier, who hates Napoleon, and he helped you . . . and you used three guineas for bribery to get Louis out . . . and then you came back," she said tempestuously. "'Tis ridiculous, Charles."

"'Tis true, Caroline," he smiled.

Had the surroundings been more appropriate she would have swept away from him in lofty disgust. As it was, attempting the same feat on her undignified return, she began uncontrollably to laugh whilst on a slippery, sloping roof.

" Ssssh, m'dear," Charles warned her.

Being quite spent by her paroxysm, she had no little difficulty in climbing into her room.

Then out came her mischievous face.

" Good-night, Charles," she said softly.

" Good-night, Caroline," he called up.

The next day, as has been said, Charles Fagg had the honour of being received by Mr. William Pitt.

*   *   *   *   *   *   *   *

For 60 million francs the First Consul sold Louisiana to provide himself with funds for the invasion attempt. In France conscription was put into force, with the standard height reduced to 5 feet 2 inches, and Bonaparte, never forgetful of the greatest project of all, wrought mightily for a temporary command of the sea, beginning by recalling his best ships from the French colonies. He sent out raiders to destroy British shipping, and the shipyards of his province of Holland were busy laying keels for ships which should be used finally to destroy a stubborn-necked people.

But England, this time, was not idle.

The day after the French Ambassador left Dover, the bellman went round the streets calling out the militia ; every day after that, at five in the morning and again at the same time in the afternoon, the bugle-horn sounded for the Volunteers' two-hour drill. The Italian Republic might subscribe 5 million francs for the purchase of two warships to carry the tricolour, but the East India Company gave 20 ships for the protection of the Thames, the Brethren of Trinity House funds for the building and manning of 10 frigates, and Lloyds voted £20,000 for the comfort of maimed warriors.

England was ablaze, wrathfully and grimly so.

Mr. Henry Rochefort, as example, denounced a friendly firm of rival bankers for guinea running. It was true it proved to be an error, but it also proved the spirit of the man.

" The evidence seemed plain, and in a similar belief I would do exactly the same," he announced stridently one evening when a few acquaintances had called at his request, his intention that they should discuss a town meeting to advance in what manner Dover might the interests of the country.

" We are engaged in a war for our existence, gentlemen," he added, glancing at the sentry now on duty outside the Grand Military Shaft. " And I would act no differently if . . . if 'twere my own son who was hindering the common cause."

There was a hearty round of applause, at the end of which the Town Clerk inquired of M. Saval—rather unnecessarily most thought—as to that gentleman's attitude to France.

" 'Tis my own country, monsieur," the distinguished-looking Frenchman replied curtly. " But never will I return thither until a Bourbon rules again."

This very fine sentiment earned, as it deserved, a roar of approval.

Yes, England was once more at war, but no longer apathetic on the merits of the conflict. The Ballot Act and the General Defence Act were passed ; not a voice was raised against the Levy en Masse, a bill which could be said to take freedom from every able-bodied man in the land.

Indeed Mr. Charles James Fox, speaking in the House on these measures, said that he did not look to " the regular army, but to the mass of the country ; acting, not in single regiments, but as a great mass of armed citizens, fighting for the preservation of their country and their families, and everything that is dear to them in life." So spoke Mr. Fox, who so often before had tilted against those who supported the war with France.

Day after day regiments, by forced marches, came into Dover, with the Militia of Oxford and Lancaster in the van of those who, from every corner of Britain, rallied to this bastion of liberty in fair Kent. Mr. Pitt, as Colonel of the Cinque Ports Volunteers, drilled his troops at Walmer every day and, between this, saw that, in his capacity of Lord Warden, the luggers of the same ports were armed with death-dealing 15-pounders.

Yes, the French might speedily overrun Hanover, but the Navy, on the stroke of the declaration of war, was already in war stations outside enemy ports from Holland to the Mediterranean, speedy frigates keeping close watch inshore, the great battle fleets in support behind.

The one country which stood between an autocrat's dream of world-wide domination and its bloody attainment was aroused as never before. Resolved, indeed, was the land to a man, and never was righteous flame more fanned than when, in July, *The Times* newspaper described the First Consul's inspection of the ports from Antwerp to Calais, with especial reference to an official dinner given at the last-named place.

There toasts were drunk, so the struggling ' Thunderer ' reported, " To the men who shall execute the vast project of placing French and English in their due and respective positions ; " " To the barrack-master who shall issue the first billets at Dover ; " " To the first review of the French troops in St. James's Park."

"Billets in Dover, eh?" rasped Mr. Jonathan Dawkes who, pike and all, had called in at the Antwerp for a pot of ale.

"An' you think that's the sort o' piece to oppose agin a musket, Mr. Dawkes?" Mr. Ralph Jelly observed sarcastically to the Postmaster, who ever had followed Mr. Fox and Mr. Sheridan through thick and thin.

That did it. No, it wasn't a quarrel between these two worthies.

Both joined together in heartily reviling the government. Who, they demanded, had failed to keep up stocks of seasoned timber in the dockyards, *even* naturally curved timbers, during the truce of—nay, the false peace of Amiens it was better to name it? Who had asked for volunteers and who, when the rush had become too great, had damped the enthusiasm of all by issuing a notice to the effect that further enrolments would not be authorised?

"Addington." The Prime Minister's name, in irate decry, rose to the raftered roof of the parlour.

The consensus of opinion was that the government, instead of worrying themselves silly about reports that an American inventor's plunging boat had, at a French port, remained under water for a clock hour and covered half a league in that time, four men being in it, should. . . .

"Put honest to goodness weapons in our hands," Mr. Thomas Bullack growled, "an' to hell with such nonsense. Then we'll take care o' Boney's Dover billets."

Not a soul spoke a word in support of the peace-loving gentleman who was the King's chief minister.

2

On a balmy day in late September a number of gentlemen, one lady with them, were riding over the Western Heights after visiting General John Moore at the new military school which had been founded at Shorncliffe.

More than once the company had paused to stare at Gris Nez, the great headland between Calais and Boulogne. Off this, a British squadron, under Admiral Saumarez, was attempting to cut out a flotilla of French boats *en route* from Dunkirk to Boulogne for the purpose of concentration at the latter port.

"Methinks 'tis now Lady Hester's turn," laughed a field officer, relieving Mr. Pitt of a spy-glass and handing it to that gentleman's niece.

"Quite becalmed," Mr. Pitt observed, and with that, there being little to see at the moment, gave his attention, as a move was made, to a discussion on the new attempts which the First Consul was making to stir up trouble again both in Ireland and India.

"Nor," interposed the Lord Warden, mentioning another sore point, "would I accept Spain's answer to our submissions relating to the repair of French ships in Spanish ports. I suspect, very strongly so, that there is an understanding there if not a secret treaty."

The general talk on these matters of high state was drawing to a conclusion when, approaching the Bredenstone, the sharp eyes of one of Mr. Pitt's secretaries recognised one of two riders who were nearing them.

"The young man, sir, who effected that most amazing rescue from Boulogne."

Another in the entourage laughed. "The Comte d'Hubiêres told me a dooced amusing tale about him t'other day. Apparently young Mr. Fagg speaks two descriptions of French equally well, the one a most cultured accent he has picked up here and the other the most diabolical patois as may be heard between Ambleteuse and Gravelines. The story goes . . . "

Charles was on his beloved *Toke's Quality* and Caroline was riding the skittish grey mare her father had bought for her sixteenth birthday.

"'Tis Mr. Pitt, Caroline."

"And Lady Hester, Charles." Miss Rochefort was eyeing with frank interest that very renowned young woman. "And, Charles, I believe they're going to stop."

As they did, with Lady Hester, who was rumoured to be a truly devastating creature when in the mood, making herself devilish agreeable, and all those very important gentlemen behaving most gallantly towards the pretty miss who sat her beast so well.

Mr. Pitt's thoughtful glance was resting, somewhat searchingly, on Charles; meantime he spoke concerning the prospect of a successful outcome to the naval operation which was taking place across the smooth waters of the Channel.

"I doubt it, sir," Charles Fagg remarked respectfully.

The Lord Warden wanted to know why and, in reply, heard of the local currents which must draw the French flotilla more and more within the protection of their powerful coastal batteries.

"The cliffs bristle with 'em, sir," Charles added ruefully.

"I gather you know that neighbourhood exceedingly well, Mr. Fagg," the right-honourable gentleman smiled.

Charles grinned. "I've been acquainted with it since I was very small, sir."

Thereupon Mr. Pitt dismissed entirely the subject, apart from remarking that it was only fitting that young Mr. Fagg should have a small memento for the very plucky piece of work he had done. He would feel obliged if Mr. Fagg would present himself at Walmer the morning of that day week.

" Isn't he lovely, Charles ? " Caroline said glowingly, when company had been parted. " And isn't it wonderful that you're going over to the Castle so that he . . . *Mr. Pitt*, Charles . . . can give you a souvenir ? "

" Demmed nice of him, Caroline," Charles agreed warmly.

Now they talked of more practical matters, for in the morning Caroline was to leave Dover, and a year's absence is a long time.

" 'Tis, m'dear," Charles murmured. He was staring down at seven ships which, anchored off Archcliffe Point, waited for the tide. Four of them were his father's and he knew the business upon which they were engaged. The threat of invasion looming nearer every hour, it had been decided that the Metropolis should be stocked with flour sufficient to cover a fortnight's consumption, with a further three weeks' supply left in the hands of the millers.

" But 'twill pass, Charles dear," Caroline said later in the dining-room of her father's house, into the window of which *Toke's Quality*, secured to the green railings outside, was peering inquisitively.

" Of course 'twill, m'dear," he laughed, trying to cheer her.

Colour was stealing into her cheeks. " Charles," she whispered, her face uplifted to his, " I know that you will be wishing me Godspeed in the morning, but don't you think we might say our real good-bye here ? "

His grey eyes were tender, his mouth a little whimsical.

" But once before did I attempt it, Caroline," he smiled. " And I swear that for two days I burned."

She dimpled at the recollection. " I won't slap it very hard this time, Charles," she promised him with nice forbearance.

So Charles Fagg, for the second time in his life, kissed Caroline Rochefort, and found her lips no less sweet, as ardently he reflected when slowly riding *Toke's Quality* to Town Wall Street.

Miss Rochefort herself, her heart going pit-a-pat and with a tendency to swallow now and then, went up to her room for a while before setting out for the bank to say good-bye to Mr. Godspenny and the clerks.

She did not stay long in Snargate Street-over-the-Wall. The government had concluded that it would be sound policy to pay the Army in coin rather than in paper, and Mr. Rochefort and his staff, the bank being one of those entrusted with specie for the purpose, were excessively busy.

Martha Teddiman was to journey as far as London with her young mistress, and a great crowd saw the travellers off. Captain Pepper was

there, Lou had brought Horatio for a last cuddle from his ' Aunt '
Caroline, and M. Saval, now becoming something of a friend of the
family, came along with Henry Rochefort.

" I declare, M. Charles," the Frenchman laughed upon kissing
Mr. Rochefort's daughter's hand before she took her seat in the
chaise, " that I must formally acquaint you that you have a rival
for the affections of this charming lady."

" Valentine ! " Miss Teddiman said sharply.   The boatswain,
unmistakably, had relieved himself of a scornful " Ugh."

The ladies were indulging in an orgy of kissing, whilst old Peter
Monin's clock ticked off the minutes.

" If it please you . . . " grinned Jim Page who, important as he
undoubtedly was in the Antwerp Stables, could shed his rank when
the driving of a favourite passenger became the question.

Soon the vehicle was speeding up Snargate Street, a small white
handkerchief waving valiantly.

Henry Rochefort's house was a deal more lonely that night.

3

Blithely, apart from the one regret, Charles Fagg rode over to
Walmer, where at the Lord Warden's official residence he handed
Toke's Quality to the care of a groom. A footman, whose hair was most
grandly done up in a hoop, announced him at the door of what he
took to be the room of one of the secretaries.

" Ah, Mr. Fagg," this gentleman said pleasantly, motioning him
to a chair.

Mr. Pitt, he added, was engaged at the moment.

It was perhaps something under a quarter of an hour before Charles
was ushered into the presence of the gentleman who, many months
before, in days of a queer peace, had written to Mr. Wilberforce,
" If he, Bonaparte, is to feel he is not to trample in succession on
every nation in Europe." Surely prophetic words.

Some two hours later Charles Fagg, his face strangely grave,
mounted *Toke's Quality*.

Soberly he rode home, never even perceiving, as he descended the
steep hill past Dover's Castle, a most interesting sight off Archcliffe
Point, that of a sloop, her sails riddled with shot-holes.

This craft, showing honourable signs of recent action, proceeded
down Channel, and Charles proceeded with his thoughts.

CHAPTER SEVEN

I

On that Saturday afternoon in October, during the week preceding that in which the Day of General Fast was to be held, Polly Fagg seemed not far removed from weeping.

"But, John," she protested, "you told me you believed 'twas against the interests of the country and that you wouldn't do any more whilst the war was on."

Her husband shifted uneasily. He was sitting before the fire, not in the chair from which the view had been so wantonly ruined by the round building Henry Rochefort had erected.

Mrs. Fagg, before she resumed, glanced at herself in the convex mirror and was relieved to find that as yet she showed nothing of the heartache which gripped her.

"An' I do declare," she continued, sniffing all the same, "that never was I so happy, and never could a woman have troubled less on hearing that our income must substantially decline."

Making light of her apprehensions, John Fagg put aside the newsheet which was resting on his lap, and went over to her, to put his arm about her plump shoulders.

"Come, Polly love," he said persuasively. "I'm not proposing running big cargoes in the old style, nothing more than small consignments easily brought in."

"Then you won't make much money," flashed his wife. "So why should you and Charles risk . . . risk dreadful penalties for little or nothing?"

The shipowner, momentarily nonplussed by this shrewd attack, got out of it the best way he could, muttering on "the need for not losing our connections."

"'Tis cruel, *cruel*," Polly Fagg cried desperately, and flew off into the hall where the flurry of her heel-taps on the tiled floor drew the attention of her sister-in-law.

Susan Rochefort, freed by Horatio's having a nap in the room overhead, was playing softly in the drawing-room, but at that quick step she hurried out, to find Polly trying to stifle her tears with a handkerchief.

"Polly!" she asked anxiously, "whatever is't?"

Quickly she drew her brother's wife into the drawing-room, closing the door behind them.

Then, between sobs, it came. "I'm frightened, Susan . . . frightened for John and Charles. They're . . . they purpose smuggling after all, an' though that wicked man Toke has been quiet for long, I'm sure, positive, that he's only waiting his opportunity to pounce."

" Polly, dear," Mrs. George said soothingly.

But, try all she could, it was a long time before the rising tide of her sister-in-law's distress began to subside. Mrs. John Fagg plainly was terrified.

Shortly after the outbreak of war, when it stood out crystal clear that all effort must be directed towards the one end if the nation was not to perish, John Fagg had decided that certain unlawful though lucrative business practices must cease. Forthwith, with a word of explanation, he returned to a number of Kentish gentry their sub-scriptions in these highly illicit ventures.

Lord Poynte, one of such, received his and, on doing so, expressed blasphemous approval of the motive behind Fagg's action. Incidentally Sir Walter Plumbley, who had at one time shared in these profits, had long been paid out, John Fagg being in no wise disposed to put guineas into the already well-lined pockets of a man who, however much his attitude might be ascribed to pomposity and stupidity, was nevertheless a real stumbling-block to any scheme of harbour improvement.

This course so very properly adopted, the shipowner was human enough to experience a glow of satisfaction when reflecting on the high moral stand he had taken, but later, facts being facts, he could not but keep thinking heavily that the loss of revenue thereby must necessitate a-looking after the pennies in a household which hitherto had not worried overmuch about these trifles.

However, Polly, as he expected, had not complained in the slightest when he mentioned the pending change in their circumstances. In truth, her manner had been quite the opposite and, though he was familiar with her frets on the dangers of smuggling, he had never until then fully realised just how much she had grown to hate it. Nor was her light-heartedness a mere flash in the pan. She continued astound-ingly gay until the day when, some spell after Charles had ridden over to Walmer to see Mr. Pitt, he perforce had to tell her of the less rigid position he was taking up on free-trading.

That came about as result of the talk he had with Charles when the young man returned from his visit to the Lord Warden.

In the early days of the war John Fagg had been plainly despondent on quite another matter. Then, when men's minds were devoted exclusively to the defence of their country against over-whelming attack, it appeared iniquitous to attempt the diversion of energies from that essential purpose. Later, however, he gradually reversed this opinion, honestly believing that, in this case, the wish was not father to the thought. The harbour, if improved, would not only be an asset to the town but it would be one also for the nation. Being so near to the French invasion ports, Dover's haven would be, if made worthy, of immense value to the national effort. . . .

On the afternoon of the day on which Charles responded to Mr. Pitt's command, John Fagg was thinking on these lines when his son came into the low, oak-panelled, private room at Elizabeth Street.

" Well ? " the shipowner smiled welcomingly, putting away a plan of the harbour at which he had been looking.

Speedily Charles disabused him of the idea that there was a gossipy sort of tale to be related.

" If 'tis convenient now, I would like to have a talk with you, Father," he opened quietly. " The matter, I need hardly say in advance, is highly confidential, and Mr. Pitt has my promise that it shall not be revealed save to those who must further the ends proposed by me."

From then Mr. Fagg's expression steadily moved from inquiry to gravity as he heard the story and all it portended. For close on ten minutes Charles spoke, his account neither emphasizing nor glossing over the difficulties ahead.

When he had done his father did not pronounce immediately. John Fagg, his fingers drumming on the desk, stared at the houses on the opposite side of Paradise Pent and at the scarred cliff behind them.

" You know, Charles," he murmured at last, eyes still far-focused, " we Faggs have always fought for our country in its need. Your great—I don't know how many times great—grandfather sailed out against the Armada, and before that——"

Charles Fagg nodded. " But thousands of men can bear arms and few, if Mr. Pitt is right, can do what I can."

" And you know how this may end, Charles ? " the shipowner asked sharply.

His son smiled grimly. " That aspect has occurred to me," he said.

" A grey morn and a high wall, with you dying with your back agin it," John Fagg commented briefly. " But . . . " now his own steady eyes squarely met another pair of grey eyes no less steady, " I take it, Charles, that you're decided on't ? "

" Yes," was the simple reply.

The older man, knowing resolution when he saw it, made no more difficulties, though perhaps the half-ashamed manner in which he shook his son's hand might have been set down to the emotion he was experiencing.

" Well now, Charles," he resumed briskly, " your plan, what is't ? "

On the way back, Charles had thought it out. His father, he suggested, should start smuggling again, or at least put up a façade of so doing. This would provide cover . . .

" There's a point there," Mr. Fagg interposed. The land, he went on, was united, every class in it, as never before. " And, Charles," he ended, " that means just one thing. Anybody who is suspect of a lack of enthusiasm for the common cause, or of failing whole-heartedly to put his shoulder to the wheel, is sure to have a most unpleasant time."

" I suppose so," Charles Fagg agreed soberly.

A listener, hearing the discussion which followed, would have learnt much about a governing rule of action which had contributed largely to a long record of free-trading good fortune. Such an eaves-dropper could not have failed to appreciate to what extent brilliant planning, not luck, had played its part in these successes.

" So 'tis this, then," Charles recapitulated shortly.

His mother could not, of course, be told. If not the complete chatterbox, she was always gossipy-inclined and, should Charles eventually come into disrepute, as well he might, she would be under an intolerable temptation if hard things were said about her unpatriotic son.

" And your position, Father ? " Charles continued. " On reflection I'm convinced that 'twill be infinitely better if you dissociate yourself, later on, from the smuggling, real or unreal, which I do."

It was hardly a glorious role, but John Fagg saw the advantages which subsequently would ensue if he himself were unsuspect.

" On t'other hand," Charles suddenly smiled, " your war-time scruples must not cause you to order me from beneath the roof of Little Pent House."

The shipowner chuckled. " I vow 'twould be more in keeping with me than to sit down complacent."

" Nor the latter," laughed his son. " I suggest something between the two."

There were still many more details to thrash out. Transportation to the French coast, the picking up of Charles for the return journeys. . . .

" Aye, Pepper's the one," John Fagg agreed. " And not a soul on this earth would ever get a word out of him, not if they used thumb-screws."

Charles was laughing heartily even as he asked what Valentine was doing.

" He's down at the Tidal Harbour," John Fagg answered, his glance sharp as he put the next question. " Any special hurry, Charles ? "

"Only that I'm taking my first trip to-night," Charles Fagg grinned, his hand on the knob.

"Then good hunting to you, lad," guffawed his father.

When the door closed, the merriment quickly faded from the ship-owner's face, to be replaced by the shadow of apprehension.

He went over to the window. From there he could see his tall son striding down Elizabeth Street.

John Fagg slowly, perhaps sadly, shook his head.

2

Throughout the kingdom the Day of General Fast was observed, and in every village, town and city, places of worship were packed with uniformed figures.

Nor was Dover less forward in humbly interceding for divine help. The old church of St. Mary the Virgin had a congregation greater than ever known ; martially attired jurats occupied every stall behind the altar ; freemen and more jurats, volunteers all, filled the body of the church ; the gallery groaned beneath its weight of pilots, to a man every lodesman a Fencible ; six deep at the back of the edifice stood another throng.

O God, Our Help in Ages Past. With impassioned fervour, on this day when a nation dedicated itself to God and its duty, that noble hymn thundered up and beyond the Saxon feuillage which decorated the capitals of some of St. Mary's columns.

Doctor Woodgate, furious that His Grace of Canterbury still refused permission for the clergy to take up arms, preached a sermon which was the most arresting the folk of the port had ever sat under.

"The vile apostate, Bonaparte," he began malignantly, and from that went on to relate examples of the specious promises of the Grand Subjugator.

Long after the sands had run out of his half-hour glass the Rector was still speaking in similar vein.

"Shall we," he once demanded, " be made the appendage of Continental despotism . . . ? "

It was the most notable address the good Doctor had ever delivered. From that not a soul dissented. The talk was of nothing but it as the vast assembly shuffled past a notice on the church door which reaffirmed the necessity for keeping the roads clear of encumbrances in case of a French descent.

After the service the Volunteers, in companies, took the oath of allegiance in the churchyard, and then dispersed for an hour and a half, there being a special drill in the afternoon.

"A most excellent address, Mr. Waade," Captain Hugo Stratton commented as, with the Clerk of the Cheque, he stepped out across the Market Place.

"The proper note," Mr. Waade agreed weightily.

The Town Clerk was eyeing the crowd which had collected beyond the Guildhall, on that side of the Market Place adjacent to the ruins of the old monastery of St. Martin-le-Grand.

"Shall we take a look, Mr. Stratton?" his companion anticipated him.

The two gentlemen turned towards the exhibition machine invented by Colonel Crichton of the Association for Promoting the Defence of the Forth, the alternative point at which it was believed Bonaparte would strike.

It consisted of a lengthy but lightly-built cart-like body which, when mounted on chaise or coach wheels and drawn by a pair of horses, could travel as much as seven miles in the hour over moderately rough country, conveying at the same time anything up to a dozen men with their arms and equipage. It was Colonel Crichton's belief that, if this device could be brought into extensive use, a large proportion of the foot could be given far greater mobility.

"Mmmm," murmured the Town Clerk, a very keen military man. "Decidedly the government's offer should appeal to the fish merchants and farmers." Premiums were offered to those who prepared wheel carriages on which Colonel Crichton's novel framework could be bolted.

"Money, my dear sir, always does appeal to farmers," Mr. Waade guffawed, and was about to expand this humorous opening when Hugo Stratton, who had developed an inordinate brusqueness of manner since receiving his commission, left him without so much as by your leave to speak to Louis Rochefort.

"Have you seen Charles Fagg lately, Rochefort?" the Town Clerk rasped.

"Not for three or four days, Mr. Stratton, and then he spoke vaguely of having to go to Rochester or——"

"*Captain*, if you please, Rochefort," Mr. Hugo Stratton snapped. "Missed three drills in succession he has, and you may inform him that the five shillings forfeit has been doubled," he boomed on. "Damme, don't he know we're at war? If not, maybe the disbursal of thirty shillings will impress it on him."

When the disciplinarian had betaken himself off, Henry Rochefort's son and M. Saval strolled towards King Street. Both were in uniform, though the Frenchman's was of a non-military character, he having offered his services as interpreter to the Port-Agent for Prisoners of War.

Grimacing disdainfully Armand Saval pulled an ear reflectively. " Ver' conscious of his rank, the worthy capitaine," he drawled.

Louis Rochefort was still ruffled. " Yes," he replied shortly.

A forthright rejoinder to the Town Clerk would, he felt, have been out of keeping in one of his profession. But he was irritably wishing he could have confounded the inflated loon with a retort which was crushing without being overt.

3

Parliament reopened in October, when the Secretary-at-War, in a statement, gave numerical evidence of the nation's effort.

More than half a million men—volunteers, regulars, and militia— were in arms out of a total population of 13,000,000. That seemed reasonably satisfactory, but in days of extreme crisis it was hardly good enough, and many were the grumbles directed at the government.

" Boney's going to see 'isself as Emperor o' the World unless there's quick i'provement," Harry Jenkins growled one dark November evening in the cosy parlour of the Fountain.

The squat-built Preventiveman shifted his haunches more comfortably prior to advancing a belief that Mr. Addington would have to go.

" Peace at any price, that 'un," he observed contemptuously.

Jim Page, putting down a pot and wiping his mouth, began to speak of the statesman who, increasingly, was in men's thoughts.

" Aye, he's still at Walmer," he said, spitting adroitly. " An' they say he willn't go up to Parliament till the wind settles in a quarter less dangerous."

" He'll have to go 'fore there's a change," someone else suggested.

The powers that be got it hot and strong. Why, it was asked, were the arsenals empty ? Why were the Dover Volunteers, seven out of every ten of them, armed with pikes, the remaining three hardly better equipped with firelocks of obsolete pattern ? It was true the demand for weapons was on an hitherto unknown scale, but why hadn't it been anticipated ?

" 'Tis all very well sheets far back in Lunnon calling Boney an obscure Corsican," Jim Page propounded sagely. " But he's got many a thousand experienced an' disciplined sojers less nor thirty miles from here, each of 'em with a modern weppin in 'is hand."

" An' us has got to meet 'em fust," the sexton of St. Mary the Virgin's, a weedy-looking individual, was unwise enough to remark.

Little Jim Page, a regular bantam cock, hotly took up the challenge, quite forgetting the stand he had taken a moment before.

"Frenchies!" he scoffed. "Why me an' Pepper an'——Valentine's late to-night," he interposed irrelevantly.

Captain Pepper had, at that moment, completed one of the strangest jobs of his life, one to which he had not, even yet, grown accustomed.

It consisted of taking half a dozen tubs of brandy from the secret store in the end house of Elizabeth Street and of conveying them furtively, in three journeys, to a boat in the Basin.

"Rot me," he ejaculated when the task that night was done, and the small cargo well covered, "if this ain't the most comic way o' running goods I ever 'eard tell of. I loads up 'ere, takes it out to sea, an' then brings it back agin."

Marvelling over the manner in which Mr. Charles was to acquire the reputation of a smuggler, Valentine Pepper rolled off to join his friends.

4

The invasion ports—Flushing, Ostende, Nieuport, Dunkirk, Gravelines, Calais, Wissant, Ambleteuse, Boulogne, Etaples—each and all resounded with the blows of shipwright's hammers; the chimneys of the arsenals of France belched smoke throughout the day, every day; ammunition was being produced in thousands of tons; tree-fellers were at work in every forest within a hundred and fifty miles of the northern coast; the road to the sea carried a steady stream of waggons—on this one, scantling, on that, rough-shaped timbers. Wood from the pine forests of Rouen for oars and masts. . . .

Every boatbuilder, carpenter and sawyer, between the ages of 15 and 60, conscripted to the stretch of coast from which the jump-off 'over the way' would be taken.

France, a nation mobilised body and soul for conquest.

The short winter's day was closing over Boulogne, chief port of concentration for the assault on England, and the feverish activities of thousands, soldiers and civilians, engaged in deepening and en-larging the harbour facilities, would soon be brought to a standstill by the coming dusk.

Enormous effort was being made everywhere. On the Pointe de Crêche and the Pointe de l'Heurte forts were being built in stone, with a third of wood facing the approach to the haven.

But it was mainly in preparations of an offensive nature that human bodies were being strained to the very utmost. Troops and labourers, toiling waist-deep in mud, were digging out the new basins which would allow, when finished, nearly a thousand boats to get away by the same tide.

" And then, comrade ? " a begrimed sergeant of artillery, who had been glad of the extra pay which the wielding of a shovel gave him, winked at the fair-haired young man with whom he had fallen into step whilst walking off the beaches.

" And then, eh ? " The tall young fellow grinned, showing a line of fine white teeth. He was dressed in a ragged barbel, a petticoat-like, brown-proofed fisherman's garment peculiar to both sides of the Channel.

" Shouldn't be long at this pace, I'm thinking," the artilleryman guffawed as he turned off towards the army lines.

Charles Fagg glanced about him before he made for the short high-street. The air still buzzed with the sound of many saws, there came still the regular thud of those who drove piles for the scores of new jetties. Two lines of carts continued to move creakingly along in endless chain, the one, midst a cracking of whips, bringing up the excavated earth, the other, braked wheels squealing, taking down low but heavy loads of rough-dressed stone.

" And now, damme, methinks something for the inner man," he muttered, a half smile breaking out as he watched a cutter, in charge of a lieutenant, go alongside the quay in most unseamanlike style. The French Navy, it was very evident, had not yet recovered from the loss of so many of its best officers in the Revolution, though it was equally apparent that strenuous efforts were being made to remedy these deficiencies in professional skill.

Outside the *Mairie* Charles paused to examine an order of the day, issued under the hand of Admiral Bruix. It had not been there when he was last in the port, ten days before.

> All Frenchmen are ready to march to punish a Government which is an enemy of the peace of the world, and especially an enemy to the glory and welfare of our country.
>
> To you your country first commits the care of satisfying her just vengeance.
>
> Redouble, therefore, your zeal ; multiply your services ; and the nation which oppresses the seas will be conquered by terror, before it experiences the fate of arms, and sinks beneath the blows of our heroes.
>
> BRUIX.

" O yes, O yes," Charles Fagg murmured. " Undoubtedly a formidable, if sadly misinformed, gentleman."

First he sought a wine shop and for the second call a hot, pleasantly smelling bakehouse. Then, holding on to a bottle and with a crisp warm roll tucked under his arm, he climbed the hill behind the town before taking a wide detour back to the narrow inlet.

Skirting batteries which he had already marked on a plan, he reached the edge of the cliff, and there, in a shallow depression, he wolfed the food and drink.

It was grey evening now, the cold was increasing, and he still had five hours of inactivity.

Shortly before eleven o'clock, stiff and frozen with the wait for the tide, and almost sick with the fatigue consequent upon three nights out of bed, he crept down to the verge of the tidal waters, his tired eyes ever alert.

It was inordinately black, and he did not all at once find the great humpbacked rock.

His hand against the side of his mouth, he cried the seven-whistlers, the note of the long-billed curlew heard at night.

" Ewe-ewe, ewe-ewe, ewe-ewe ! "

Soon came a cautious reply from the darkness.

" M. Charles ? "

" Jacques ! "

The boat crept further in, with Charles, as soon as he located her, wading through the icy water, then to spring himself aboard, to join a young man whose face was no more than a white blur.

"*Allons, Jacques,*" he whispered, gratitude expressed by a warm grip on the other's arm.

" *Très bien, monsieur,*" Jacques Perrier's teeth showed in one of his infrequent smiles.

The little craft disappeared into the inky night and, reaching the middle of the fairway, slipped down towards the sea, the motion steady at first but later, when an oily beam swell had its sport with her, like that of a gigantic see-saw.

Well clear of the land, course was altered towards those hidden and extensive sands which, some half-dozen or more heaving leagues away, flanked Britain's shore.

5

The demand for more vigorous measures of defence was reflected, not only throughout the country but in the House of Commons too. There the government, which seemed to devote itself solely to clinging to office, was roundly attacked. Mr. Pitt expressed his disquiet, whilst Mr. Fox—now a private in the Chertsey Volunteers—described the

Prime Minister and his cabinet as "nature's fools," for, whilst professing to know that the Peace of Amiens could not be lasting, having failed to make greater exertions towards the provision of more muskets and other accoutrements of war.

Every class in the land, from landed proprietor to the lowliest workman, chafed at this lack of direction, all being commonly joined in an enthusiasm and will to see this grim task through to the bitter end.

Even the Quakers, without openly departing from their usual refusal to pay taxes for purposes of war, evinced a belief in the nobility of the cause, there being tacit understanding that when the collectors called upon them the open cash-box should be available for the direct taking of the dues.

Mr. Sheridan, who for years, with Mr. Fox, had opposed the war with France, issued his Address to the People. It was one of the most stirring broadsheets ever printed—in it he wrote of the French being " by a strange Frenzy driven, fighting for Power, for Plunder, and Extended Rule."

From John o' Groats to Land's End, meetings were held to raise funds and to rally every manner of support to the war effort. The town of Deal offered to provide fifty gunboats, and in Dover, following on the suggestion first broached by Henry Rochefort, a town meeting was called for the Thursday preceding Christmas Day, its purpose the opening of a Dover Fund in friendly rivalry.

On that December day, when the Market Place was knee-deep in snow, Mr. Rochefort capped every subscription by announcing his intention of contributing one thousand guineas.

"Bravo, Rochefort!" clapped Sir Walter Plumbley, who now, so many had noticed, appeared to be on quite intimate terms with the banker.

"Phew, Jeremy!" whistled Mr. Nicholas Stokes, his breath showing as a thin streamer in the air.

Beneath the leaden sky the Market Place looked exceedingly picturesque, its roofs virgin white, the walls and windows of its buildings powdered with the same soft purity.

From the top step of the Guildhall staircase the Mayor, Mr. Jeffrey Braems, held up his hand to still the roar of applause which signalised Mr. Henry Rochefort's donation.

" Freemen of Dover," he shouted, his colourless voice not carrying over far.

He proceeded to inform his hearers that he proposed to read a declaration unanimously carried at a crowded meeting held in the London Stock Exchange. Mr. Henry Rochefort, he added, had been privileged to be amongst the five thousand inhabitants of London who had presented themselves at this gathering, and had been strikingly impressed by the conclusions arrived at, believing that these applied, not only to the citizens of the Metropolis, but to those who dwelt in every town and hamlet in the land.

The introduction ended, Mr. Braems began :

" The independence," he read out precisely, " and existence of the British Empire—the safety, the liberty, the life of every man in the kingdom are at stake. The events perhaps of a few months, certainly of a few years, are to determine whether we and our children are to continue free men . . . we fight for the independence of all nations . . . to strike terror into tyrants and to give courage and hope to the oppressed . . . every man should deem the sacrifice of his fortune and life as nothing more than his duty. . . .

" Upon our efforts will depend the triumph of liberty over despotism—of national independence over projects of universal empire —and finally of civilisation over barbarism."

Thunderous approval greeted the Mayor's ending, during which that legal luminary, first bending down and exchanging a few words with those about him, straightened himself up, his obvious intention being to declare the proceedings terminated.

However, a slight commotion in the throng drew the attention of all, and almost immediately it was seen that the scholarly proprietor of the Albion Library was forcing through the press, an expression of appropriately subdued excitement on his face and a sheet of paper in his gloved hand.

Thereafter, to the mystification of all, there were confabulations on the Guildhall staircase and, by the time the Mayor again spoke, his audience was agog.

" My friends," Mr. Braems shouted, somewhat hoarsely by now, " you will remember that not so long ago Mr. William Wordsworth stayed awhile in this district. Well, my friends, I have supreme pleasure in informing you that Mr. Wordsworth has lately written a battle cry for the Men of Kent. With your indulgence——"

" Let's be 'earing it," bellowed a rough-looking fellow from the Plain District.

" 'Twould be more useful if we 'ad some weppins put in our 'ands," one of his cronies bawled blood-thirstily.

This last wish earned such support that fully two minutes elapsed before the Mayor was able to carry out the agreeable duty, that of declaiming the poet's stirring words :

> " Vanguard of liberty, ye men of Kent,
> Ye children of a soil that doth advance
> Her haughty brow against the coast of France,
> Now is the time to prove your hardiment !
> To France be words of invitation sent !

They from their fields can see the countenance
Of your fierce war, may ken the glittering lance,
And hear you shouting forth your brave intent.
Left single, in bold parley, ye of yore,
Did from the Norman win a gallant wreath ;
Confirmed the charters that were yours before ;—
No parleying now ! In Britain is one breath ;
We are all with you now from shore to shore :
Ye men of Kent, 'tis victory or death ! "

Mr. Jeffrey Braems did not recite well. But, when he had done, the hush remained for a space.

Then never did such a rolling cheer rise in the old Market Place of Dover.

Mrs. Stokes, as her husband knew, was at Mrs. Nethersole's, and so the Clerk of the Passage continued along with Captain Nethersole, the two gentlemen discoursing on the recent meeting and on other matters, one of which was distinctly comical.

Tuesday evening of the previous week, Valentine Pepper had disgraced himself through an over long session at the Fountain, being so tipsy that his progress home had been, to say the least of it, erratic. The drunken stupor into which he had subsequently fallen had incapacitated him the whole of the next day, and it had been a definitely sheepish-looking individual who had presented himself at Elizabeth Street on the third morning.

" Known many a hard-headed 'un come to grief the same mode," Captain Nethersole declared. " Without apparent effect they goes on until one bright day—he'd do well to cut down his supping or he'll be a-counting the blue devils. Once they've reached that stage . . . "

Nicholas Stokes chuckled, but it seemed that the mention of the boatswain's libations brought another thought to the Clerk of the Passage.

" By the way, Jeremy," he asked casually, " how are you for liquor ? "

Better friends than ever now no political differences separated them, the pair had no secrets from each other. Captain Nethersole frankly granted that he could do with more brandy, though young Charles had brought him a demi-john within the week.

" Me, too," Mr. Stokes murmured thoughtfully.

Neither spoke again for the full length of Bench Street, but then it became plain that their thoughts were running in similar channels.

" But a bit of ' running ' can't hurt the country overmuch," Captain Nethersole observed, not very convincingly.

On this broad issue Mr. Stokes, with one qualification, expressed guarded agreement.

" Still, the lad shouldn't allow it to affect his drills, Jeremy."

Captain Nethersole did not directly dispute that. But, on the other hand, he was inclined to blame the Town Clerk for much of the unpleasantness that had arisen.

" Stratton had no right to suspend Charles from the company," he growled. " Just because the lad refused to pay that first thirty shillings for non-attendance——"

" Charles's point was that the crown forfeit was doubled in his absence," Mr. Stokes interposed.

" As 'twas, so he has room for complaint," the mail-captain was nodding as he used the scraper at the side of his front door.

The small parlour was invitingly warm, and there was a pleasant aroma of freshly brewed tea and lavishly buttered toast. Not only was Mrs. Stokes there, but also Mrs. John Fagg and Mrs. George Rochefort.

The mistress of the house, however, was in such a flutter.

" Jeremy," she twittered, " I feel all of a oo. Mrs. Fagg has brought with her the most iniquitous sheet I ever saw of. The Frenchies are coming over to invade . . . under the sea, and up in the air and . . . "

Whilst Captain Nethersole gallantly comforted his wife, Mr. Stokes examined the offending French production. It showed a great balloon, canopy kept inflated by a series of lamps beneath, on its platform many soldiers and . . .

He smiled. " Well, 'tis said that an American engineer has a plunging boat in one of their ports, and we do know that two balloonists once left here——"

" Jeremy ! " screeched Mrs. Nethersole. " So 'tis true."

Whilst Captain Nethersole did his best to reassure her, Mr. Stokes inquired of Mrs. Fagg how the French print came into her hands.

" Charles had torn his pocket and I thought I'd sew it up for him," Polly Fagg laughed. " And 'twas there I found it."

An easy tolerance towards free-trading was too much in the blood of both Jeremy Nethersole and Nicholas Stokes for them, at one jump, to regard it as an evil.

Each burst into loud laughter. Both thought they knew upon just what business young Charles had been concerned when that broadsheet came into his possession.

CHAPTER EIGHT

I

ON Twelfth Night three separate conversations took place, and although none of these appeared to have any bearing one on the other, outward signs are not always infallible. The exchanges to be related had, unquestionably, a common denominator, he being, of course, Charles Fagg. This gentleman had, it may be said, settled outstanding differences with Captain Stratton the previous day, his simple method being to resign from the Volunteers.

This news Dover heard with mixed feelings. The majority, red-hot patriots, roundly abused the young man, whilst even those who protested that he had suffered undue provocation felt very considerable doubt about such a step taken in the midst of crucial war.

By and large one was under the impression that John Fagg's son would soon become a highly unpopular figure in the town.

The deplorable condition of the country brought deepening burden upon financial houses, and bankers spent many hours beneath the sky rather than under their parlour roofs. Where loans had already been granted, the closest surveillance over the security was a vital necessity, and no new loans could be granted save after the keenest investigation.

When, for example, an accommodation was solicited from Mr. Henry Rochefort, he would ride and satisfy himself personally as to the number in a herd of cattle, or rough-estimate an acreage in barley, or look into the condition of buildings and the stock therein.

On the morning of Twelfth Night the banker had been over to Hythe on one such errand. His business completed, he chanced on an acquaintance who told him of a rumour which was circulating in that town.

"From Dover you say this illicit traffic is being done?" Mr. Rochefort inquired sharply, foot on the first step of the Swan's joss-block.

On receiving confirmation his brow knit and, before mounting his horse, he expressed himself very positively on the morals of those who, for gain, would so conduct themselves in such days.

"You may be sure, sir," he remarked grimly on leaving, "that I shall make it my affair to speak exceeding forthright to the Revenue Officer on my return."

With that decided intention he left Hythe. Henry Rochefort had much in him reminiscent of his brother George, not least of which was a singleness of purpose too often carried to the extreme.

Reaching the outskirts of Dover, the thought struck him that he might advantageously call at several houses of refreshment. Everyday matters of life were still greatly hampered by the rarity of small change, and Mr. Rochefort had come to the conclusion that the inns quite likely might have quantities of coin which would do something towards alleviating the situation.

He began with the Salutation, some way below the forge at the top of Biggin Street, and within the hour had the promise of seven or eight gallons' measuresworth of copper.

Well pleased with the outcome, the banker stabled his beast and, after a brief look into Snargate Street-over-the-Wall, walked home for dinner with Louis.

The meal over, Mr. Rochefort indulged in a half-pipe and then set out for St. Mary the Virgin's, a church whose parishioners had the unique privilege of appointing their own rector, with the corresponding disadvantage of finding the income for the benefice.

There was to be a meeting of the Vestry, the cost of living having risen so much that Doctor Woodgate had found it necessary to make application for an increment of £10 per annum.

When this knotty piece of business had been settled, Henry Rochefort walked briskly in the direction of the Basin.

The entrance to the Revenue Office was on Custom House Quay, with the rear of the building, in which was Mr. Toke's own room, overlooking quiet Strond Street.

Some minutes before Mr. Henry Rochefort bethought himself of the matter he had learnt in Hythe, the Revenue Officer was closeted with his chief subordinate. There could be little doubt that Mr. Toke considered Clement Foxley's information of the highest importance.

" Strange lights . . . in the vicinity of the North Sand Head," he muttered.

" Yes, sir."

Again the Revenue Officer stared at the chart, his finger-tip moving around the North and South Goodwin, finally hovering over the former, with its Bunt Head and two dotted patches drying out at low water, one of which was, as the cartographer had writ, ' By some called Jamaica Land.'

" I wonder," he murmured.

Clement Foxley coughed. " We proved whiles ago, sir, that the Fagg craft came in a southerly slant down the coast instead of more dreckly from t'other side."

" I wonder," Ralph Toke repeated, his eyes taking on a hard

gleam. " Methinks that may be the solution of many things which have mystified . . : Jamaica Land ! "

There still remained much to be explained, much to ascertain. If, as the Revenue Officer curtly stated, his assumption were correct, how did . . .

About then, Mr. Henry Rochefort marched into the sanded stone passage at the front and, entering an arched doorway on the right, found himself in a room in which half a dozen or so preventivemen were lolling. It was not a very cheerful apartment forsooth ; with its poor fire, gloomy air, and rows of handcuffs hanging on the wall, it bore no small resemblance to the hallway of the town jail.

With all the ardour of the earliest crusader, the banker made peremptory request that Mr. Toke should see him at once.

A third party, knowing the respective circumstances, would have discovered the interchanges of the two gentlemen as being not without humour. Henry Rochefort, too full of fire to realise that, whether or not there was truth in the incapacity he was charging to the Revenue Officer, he himself certainly had no standing whatever. And Ralph Toke, white with suppressed fury at being so dressed down, choking back much he would have liked to say had he not been aware that Henry Rochefort was not only friendly with such as Sir Walter Plumbley but also, through his visits to London, had the ear of many important officials there.

" This smuggling into Dover to which you refer, sir," the Revenue Officer did manage to say without revealing his all-consuming chagrin, " I venture to suggest 'tis only hearsay . . . unless, of course, you have a notion as to who may be implicated."

" If I had," the banker demanded furiously, " should I withhold such information from you ? And, speaking as to those concerned in't, am I to understand that you, a functionary entrusted with the guardianship of this coast, are quite devoid of any knowledge of what is obviously taking place under your nose ? "

Ralph Toke was not without cunning and, foolish as the admission might make him appear, he acted as though wholly ignorant. He knew Henry Rochefort would be without qualm if the finger of suspicion were pointed at John Fagg, but he feared, despite the banker's red heat, that the tale might be different if his incensed visitor heard that Charles Fagg was held to be solely culpable. After all, young Mr. Louis Rochefort had been saved from France by the same impertinent jackanapes, Hell take him, who tethered that ill-named animal of his to the Revenue Office staple whenever he rode down. . . .

" I am far from satisfied, Mr. Toke," Henry Rochefort observed blisteringly. " *Far* from satisfied with the lame answers you give me."

The banker was flaming with wrath and, in a torrent of words, declared his resolve. Either a most lamentable state of affairs was brought to a speedy end or . . .

" Mr. Rochefort, sir."

Ralph Toke, churned by resentment as he was, perceived to the hilt his own danger. Unless somehow he could appease his caller, the madman would think nothing of posting up to London with a complaint.

" Well ? " the banker bawled.

The Revenue Officer, his cheeks whiter than the chart to which his glance sometimes involuntarily strayed, controlled himself sufficiently to stave off disaster. He had, he admitted, recently acquired a promising clue to the method by which the malefactors were operating. Patience, however, was still needed, as he was of no mind to take premature action which would only have the effect of . . .

" And immediately, Mr. Rochefort, all my plans are laid I will gladly inform you," he said conciliatorily. " Indeed 'twill give me pleasure to keep you posted antecedent to that."

" Then I shall await hearing from you, sir," the banker said coldly, menace still strong in his dark eyes.

With that he curtly bade the Revenue Officer good-day, striding on to the quay where, seeing a small collier unloading, he made inquiry as to the consignee. Men of finance, necessarily, keep their ears very close to the ground.

The cargo, belonging to John Fagg, was of no concern to the House of Rochefort and, a worthy task rightly performed, Henry Rochefort turned towards the bank.

Meantime Ralph Toke, quivering with venom, looked again at Jamaica Land and the North Sand Head. This time, he knew it, there must be no mistake. The hunter was being hunted in turn.

Owing to the perils of the sea the price of coal invariably rose during the winter months and, following a period of gale, the black diamonds of the first incoming ship would always command a premium ranging as high as twenty per cent.

John Fagg profited from this last conclusion by adopting a most simple system. During the summer months he would well stock in, and, when the appropriate conditions were established in one of the dark months, would draw on this bulk to implement the overdue quantity received into the harbour.

Thus, on the day Henry Rochefort made his intention known to the Revenue Officer, Captain Pepper was along at his master's coal warehouse near St. James's Church. One hundred and thirty chauldron of coal had come into the haven that afternoon—Mr. Fagg would shortly dispose of close on four hundred chauldron, all at the advanced rate.

"Aye," Captain Pepper grunted.

He locked the door and, turning into Town Wall Street, proceeded at his usual gait until Little Pent House, and especially its kitchen windows, was drawing near.

Here he lagged perceptibly, being in two minds, the one to risk hurrying past, the other to shun all danger by crossing the street to Fox Passage, thence into St. James's Street beyond.

"But why should I be skeer'd of any woman?" he mumbled. "If that Keziah Hart does so much as to shout at me agin . . . I'll choke 'er luff that cruel 'ard——"

He turned hot at the recollection of the crowd which, a month before, had heard Sergeant Hart's widow tell him just what she thought of him. It had been in the Market Place on Wednesday's Market Day. . . .

"Harkee you!" Grim resolution was in Keziah's face as she darted along the side of the house.

At the screeched demand, at the sound of a voice he feared mightily, Valentine Pepper's heart sank into his boots.

"Death's 'ead on a mopstick," he muttered.

Of the plump Keziah that description was very wide of the mark, but it was the first which came into his head as, apprehension growing, he waited for the Fagg's nurse.

"I wouldn't have beleft it of you, Pepper," Keziah announced witheringly when still a dozen yards away.

The boatswain tried an ingratiating smile.

"Beleft what, Keziah?" he asked disarmingly.

Whilst completing the wiping on her apron of a pair of floury hands Mrs. Hart, in uninterrupted flow, expressed her views on a villain whose master was strong liquor. It was shame on him, he who only a little while ago had told her he would mend his ways. But if mending his ways meant . . .

"Being incapacitated for nigh on three days," she said scornfully, "then——"

"I weren't," Captain Pepper announced desperately. "'Twas that I were called away on business."

Triumphantly Mrs. Hart had him there. He needn't attempt to lie to her, she snapped, for she'd like him to know that he'd been seen in the town on the second evening. Down by the far side of the Basin it was—— She supposed he was staggering with a bucket to the King's Head for replenishments. . . .

Captain Pepper's expression, from being disconcerted, took on a penetrating alertness.

"Who said I were down there?" he demanded, squinting alarmingly.

Mrs. Hart didn't remember, didn't care, and dared him to put his evil eye on her. All she was concerned about was poor Martha. Did he know how much he was hurting a woman he'd been courting for over nine years?

Captain Pepper, pent up, really did groan dismally.

"I 'opes, Keziah," he began anxiously, "you'll not pisen 'er agin me."

Left with no possible room for doubt on Mrs. Hart's attitude towards him, Valentine Pepper miserably proceeded in the direction of Severus's Gate, with every step the sick conviction growing that it wouldn't be long afore he had lost Martha for good.

The whole trouble was that Mr. Charles could never say precisely when he would be returning, and often it was necessary to spend two or three nights cruising around the North Sand.

A bout of drunkenness provided ample cloak for these absences, but, as Captain Pepper's sorry mien revealed, a main of trouble was being piled up elsewhere.

Along Snargate Street there rolled a wagon bearing highly odoriferous tubs of refuse, on each of which householders paid twopence for the contents to be thrown into the Pent.

Charles Fagg, keeping well to windward of the noisome load, dodged into Snargate Street-over-the-Wall, his intention to go home by the Ropewalk, enjoying the enlivening breeze on the edge of the sea.

Near the bank, however, he encountered Louis Rochefort, and Louis, with all the gravity of a gentleman twice his years, requested Charles to step inside, there being a matter on which, so Henry Rochefort's son said, he felt it his duty to speak.

"At your service, Louis," Charles replied solemnly and, hiding a twinkle which was not so often in his eyes nowadays, dutifully followed the young banker.

Mr. Rochefort was out and to the senior partner's room Charles was conducted. There, with Louis ageing still more, Charles was invited to occupy the client's chair, the one which faced the bright western light beyond the Basin.

"I confess, Charles," young Mr. Rochefort began momentously, "that I have found little pleasure from contemplating this interview."

"Oh!" Mr. Charles Fagg observed non-committally.

Elbows on the table and finger-tips together, Louis explained. It pained him grievously, he indicated, to be compelled to speak thus to one whom he had known from boyhood, but . . .

" And the matter on which you propose speaking, what is't ? " Charles inquired ingenuously.

He may have smiled just so faintly. Perhaps that was the reason why Louis Rochefort, realising that his friend was amused rather than disturbed, speedily reverted to what he was, a young man only a year and a half older.

" Well, 'tis this, Charles," he said angrily. " In my opinion it is full time you put your country before a ridiculous vendetta with the Town Clerk."

Charles Fagg slowly shook his head. " I'm disappointed, terrible disappointed in you, Louis."

His hearer was so surprised that he frankly gaped.

" Disappointed in me ? " he ejaculated. " What signify you, Charles ? "

Fingering a quill on the table, and still keeping his face straight, Charles extracted all the fun he could from the situation.

" Would you disagree with me, Louis," he asked sententiously, " if I asserted that England to-day is fighting for the cause of freedom ? "

" Would I disagree ? Nay, hang me——"

" And for that of justice ? " Charles cut short the emphatic disclaimer.

" That most certainly too, Charles," Louis Rochefort declared incisively.

Much to his bewilderment the admission, so far as Charles was concerned, seemed to end the matter.

Quite two minutes elapsed before Louis Rochefort discovered Charles's meaning, that justice between individuals is just as important as justice between nations. The bone of contention, as the young banker then discerned, was Mr. Hugo Stratton's high-handed action.

" But thirty shillings, even if 'tis fifteen too many, is nothing after all," he expostulated.

" 'Tis the principle," Charles said self-righteously.

" But damme, Charles."

Assuming the dupe in this sort of argument to be no simple Simon, as the elder of the two young men certainly was not, there could be only one end to this play. Eventually being forced to admit that, strictly speaking, there are not varying degrees of justice, Louis Rochefort, belatedly deducing he was being fooled, promptly lost his temper. And in so doing made a number of allegations singularly unfortunate.

" No question on't," he stormed, " you are but using Stratton's action as excuse for your own ends. I can only hope that the guineas you earn will salve what conscience you may have. If not——"

Charles Fagg had risen, something in his eyes, something about a jaw which in the last months had grown harder, which silenced the other.

" Louis," he suggested gently, " methinks you have said enough."

Louis Rochefort laughed shortly. " I warrant there'll be much more said in Dover unless you speedily change your ways."

On this note of antagonism the two parted ; Charles, beneath the easy manner of his exit, a little touchy that this friend since childhood had assumed so much on so little, and Louis, on his dignity, inwardly swearing that Charles should be left to his own devices until he came to reality and common sense.

2

When Mrs. George Rochefort and her son, both dressed for out-doors, reached the bottom of the staircase, young Horatio made a dash for the front door.

" Wait for me, dear," Susan called firmly, smiling for all that at his eagerness.

Horatio, not yet three, pursed his lips reflectively, showed every sign of rebellion, but nevertheless did as he was bade. He was a nice-looking boy, with eyes and hair coloured similarly to his dead father, but with a sturdy body taking more after the Fagg side of his blood.

Seeing that his worst consisted of no more than showing a manly independence by removing the big key and peering through the keyhole, his mother went into the parlour.

Polly Fagg was still reading Minnie's letter.

" All the same, Susan," she resumed, effortlessly taking up a con-versation which had ended half an hour before, " I do think 'tis far too soon."

" But what can you do about it, Polly ? " her sister-in-law asked.

Mrs. Morgan Davies's first baby, a girl, had been born some five months before. Now Minnie wrote that another was on the way.

" No," Mrs. Fagg sighed prodigiously, " I suppose not."

By the noise now taking place in the hall one might well have imagined that its tiled floor was in course of being torn up. In fact the lively Horatio was indulging in a game with a gilt side-table, the feet of which, as he energetically pushed it before him, squealed excruciatingly.

" Horatio ! " his mother said severely, reaching him quickly.

The young gentleman eyed her warily, the top of his head no higher than the improvised vehicle behind which he stood.

" I was playing cart an' horse, Mamma," he chuckled.

His mother explained that horses never push carts, they always pull them.

Horatio digested this a long while, almost as far as the New Bridge by Severus's Gate. Then he pronounced.

" I'm a horse what pushes, Mamma," he observed determinedly.

Mrs. George laughed delightedly.

So she and her son continued their usual walk, being able, with the evenings becoming longer, to follow a regular routine. They would stroll down Snargate Street, through Pent-side and along Custom House Quay to the South Pier, on which they would go as far as was nowadays permitted, to the guardhouse, one of which stood on each pier. After that they would retrace their steps to the Market Place, and there watch the Volunteers drill.

For once, however, they did not get beyond the Basin. There, quite a throng were staring at two vessels newly arrived, a pair of the latest type of cutter, recently supplied to the Revenue Office on Mr. Ralph Toke's urgent representations.

" Fast craft, I'll swear," Mr. Richard Breton had observed something like an hour before. " Them that hopes to escape 'em," he shook his head, " 'ull have plenty on."

When Horatio had sufficiently eyed the boats and their red-flannel-shirted crews, and had asked so many questions that his mamma completely tied herself into knots, they perforce turned back lest the great event of the day should be missed.

The Market Place was already a scene of activity, and narrow Cannon Street was choc-a-bloc with those fetching weapons from the racks fitted in St. Mary the Virgin's. Some were fighting a way into the church and others, wielding eight-foot long pikes, were struggling out.

" Twenty muskets, *twenty*," growled Mr. Nicholas Stokes, speaking of the latest case sent down by the Ordnance Department.

" An' the old India pattern at that," Mr. Robert Spisour added disparagingly.

" Eight out of every dozen of us buy our own clothing," grumbled Mr. Edward Hexstall.

" An' as many our own weapons," Mr. Christopher Crundall remarked disgustedly.

" Not five score ball cartridges paid for by the government have been fired in this town sin' the war started." Mr. Ralph Jelly chimed in angrily.

It wasn't that those gentlemen begrudged any outlay. But whilst they, one and all, toiled to prepare themselves to receive the enemy, the government in London sat complacently. . . .

" I don't know about one and all," Mr. Jeffrey Braems criticized thinly, and went on to express his regret that the stocks, ducking stool, and pillory had been taken down.

John Fagg knew surely enough to whom the Register of the Harbour referred, though certainly Mr. Braems's scared face when the ship-owner, coming down the length of a pew, grasped his bony shoulder, revealed that the lawyer had not been aware who was within earshot.

"And pray, Mr. Braems, for whom would the stocks be used?" John Fagg demanded, his grey eyes like gimlets.

The Register temporised so palpably that the shipowner, laughing contemptuously, let him be.

Later, Mr. Francis Stone spoke plain words on the subject of Charles Fagg. Whatever were that young man's misdemeanours, his father could not be held accountable for them.

"Indeed," he wound up conclusively, "any of the clerks at Elizabeth Street will tell of how their master is sick to the soul with Mr. Charles's goings-on."

"But he's John's lad, eh, Mr. Stone?" Jonathan Dawkes commented wisely. "An' blood is blood after all. Consanguinity is the most omnipotorous——"

"An' when 'tis your own boy," Mr. Philip Virgile observed vaguely. "I know that ever since Mr. Baker put into my head that my business might come to naught because of the state of the haven . . ."

If the full drills were to be got in before the light failed there was scant time for gossip, and soon fusty old St. Mary's was silent again.

Every square yard of the cobbled Market Place, barring a narrow lane for coaches, was in use. Here some sections were contesting for the blue riband of the company; there a group, with many a sarcastic aside of "remember Agincourt," were practising the use of the ancient pike. The air was filled with the sounds of martial command.

"Com-pan-EEE!" yelled Captain Stratton.

This gentleman, to his credit it must be said, had been no more affronted by a recent order which democratically declared that 'officers should have no indulgences beyond those of the privates,' than Mr. Thomas Foord, the Agent-Victualler, had felt himself to be humiliated at drilling in the ranks with one of his juniors as his commanding officer.

Bonaparte, it was stated, had very nearly completed his plans for concentration at Boulogne. Well . . . the Barons of Dover prepared themselves with a will.

"An' wunnerfully disciplined they are, Miss Susan," Martha Teddiman agreed.

She had met Mrs. George and Horatio and, outside the Coffee

House across the road from the Fountain Inn, they were watching the display which was becoming a nightly entertainment for the ladies of the town.

" Tremendously improved too, Martha," Susan Rochefort added warmly.

Military affairs are all very well, but two females were not likely to be wholly enthralled in them. Horatio's progress had to be reviewed, with meticulous account from his mother as to how, with flannel and goose grease, she had dealt with a cold on his chest far more efficaciously than Dr. Crouch had done.

And then, of course, Martha Teddiman had to speak of her pet. In another three months, she glowed, Miss Caroline would be home.

" 'Twill be lovely, Martha," smiled Mrs. George.

Martha was full of Miss Caroline's doings. The master's cousin, she said proudly, had written saying her charge was the most charming creature in Worcestershire and how all the young men were flocking . . .

" Mamma," Horatio was hot with neglect and resentment, " I can't see the lobsters."

" The lobsters ! " Martha Teddiman laughed. " Hark at him, Miss Susan."

Mrs. George Rochefort smilingly hoisted the young gentleman, and was about to make a suitable reply when, out of the corner of her eye, she chanced to see further along the crowded pavement that horrible person, Clement Foxley. Mr. Foxley, she thought, was vastly absorbed in what was taking place somewhere on the opposite corner, and indeed gave the impression, as he stood near the printing office, of behaving quite furtively.

" Martha . . . " she was beginning, greatly interested.

It was young Horatio, however, who not only drew his mother's attention to the Fountain Inn but proved he was possessed of an acquaintanceship with Captain Valentine Pepper far closer than she had known.

" Rot me," Horatio squealed delightedly, " if that ain't me old friend the sea-crab. What O, ol' pumpkin 'ead . . . "

Mrs. George Rochefort never so much as wondered where her son had learnt this awful language. Her one idea, on seeing her brother's servant leaning drunkenly against the doorpost of the tavern, was to get Martha away as quickly as possible.

" 'Tis nearly over now, Martha," she said brightly. " I suppose you will be returning to Snargate Street ? "

" I . . . I suppose so, Miss Susan," was the wooden reply.

" Then you must take Horatio's hand, Martha," Mrs. George laughed gaily. " He dearly loves to be swung."

By the middle of King Street, Susan Rochefort's breathing was easier, and more and more she was thinking she must have been mistaken about Martha's manner.

On the Rectory corner, however, Martha gave way.

" I saw 'im, Miss Susan," she murmured brokenly, the first tears starting to form.

So affected was she that Mrs. George Rochefort insisted that she should go to Little Pent House for a while.

As the Volunteers broke ranks at the command of dismissal, Valentine Pepper decided it was time for home.

Steering a hazardous course, and treating himself from time to time to a snatch of ribald song, he made for Snargate Street-over-the-Wall, ever cautiously followed by a soberly clad figure not easily seen in the growing dark.

In this guise Captain Pepper reached his trim little house and there, by the very door, nearly fell over a dog which enthusiastically greeted him.

The boatswain rocked on his heels. " Nay, Shep m'lad," he bellowed, his tipsy roar of such proportions that it must have carried to the far side of the Basin.

Laughing in a maudlin way, he entered the kitchen. There, many a spark flew before he succeeded in making a light. Sharply outlined by the candle he held, and so perfectly seen by any beholder, he swayed considerably as he drew the curtains.

This done he locked the door.

" Well, Shep boy," he grinned, " be you waiting for your belly timber, eh ? "

With all the handiness of a sailor he deftly prepared himself a meal, and afterwards, when the sheepdog had cleaned up the platter, slapped his flanks affectionately and turned him out for home.

Bolted up again, Captain Pepper glanced at the long-cased clock, made a silent calculation, nodded, mended the fire and, after pulling off his boots, stretched himself in a chair.

The hours passed—seven o'clock, eight, nine, ten, eleven . . . midnight.

" Eight bells," he yawned.

Now it was action. A pot of porter from the barrel, the donning of extra heavy top-coating, the snuffing of the candle, and the silent opening and locking of the door.

Softly, with hardly more than an odd scrunch or two of the pebbles, he reached the boat-dock.

It was profoundly dark, far too black for him to see the form which watchfully crept in pursuit.

Clement Foxley witnessed it all. Near the Buildings, crouched behind the lock-gates, he saw a small boat glide into the Tidal Harbour ; on the North Pier head he strained to visualise that same craft as, cleverly negotiating the boom, it slipped out to sea.

Mr. Ralph Toke's senior assistant laughed soundlessly. Soon the evidence would be gathered which should encompass the bloody ruin of a young man.

3

If England had any doubt that Bonaparte fought for his own aggrandisement—and by now she had not—the despot's brutal murder of the Duc d'Enghien, on the flimsy pretext of a dangerous royalist conspiracy, would have disposed of that. And assuredly the unanswerable confirmation came shortly afterwards when Bonaparte, after ordering the Pope to present himself in Paris, was crowned as Napoleon I of France.

" *That* upstart a king ! " Mrs. John Fagg said disdainfully. " But I vow 'twill make him all the more to be feared."

" Jack says . . . " Mrs. Woodgate smiled happily.

This was outside the bakery on the corner of Grubbin's Lane and Bench Street. The two ladies had met there, and for once the wife of the Rector had done all the talking.

Jack had arrived home the previous morning, and Jack had slept nearly twice round the clock. " Of course he oft hasn't his clothes off for eight or nine days" was one of Mrs. Woodgate's pieces of news, itself a striking commentary on the stress undergone by officers and men of the Royal Navy.

It was Jack's opinion that Boney, before attempting invasion, would try to concentrate his Toulon and Brest fleets in the Channel. . . .

" And I'm not going to leave my house, compensation ticket or no," Mrs. Fagg proclaimed contemptuously.

" Nor me, Mrs. Fagg, however all the softies may run away from Eastbourne." Mrs. Woodgate, judging from the extreme shabbiness of her neat but old clothes, would have been hard put to raise the stage-money had she wished to escape, but there could not be any question as to the genuineness of her spirit.

Nevertheless, invasion scares were becoming more frequent, with the government adding fuel to the fire by issuing instructions for the burning of crops and the destruction of houses should the need arise.

" Nor am I going to have a valise packed ready at the side of the bed," Polly Fagg announced, supremely defiant of the French and their evil works.

" Invade *England* indeed," jeered the parson's wife. " If . . . if they came to the Rectory . . . I'd . . . I'd——"

The massacre which could be accomplished with a broomstick was fully dealt with, and then the two ladies, their redoubtable threats petering out, came to more material things. The appalling price of food ; the iniquitous cesses for rates ; whether or not to have windows blocked to save the tax on them. . . .

" We'll all soon be paying by bills on the Aldgate Pump," Mrs. Fagg laughed.

Still, there was one great consolation. At last the peace-at-any-price Addington was gone, and now at the head of affairs was a gentleman inflexible enough to cope with all the treachery and double-dealing of the new Emperor.

" Mr. Pitt won't stand any nonsense, Mrs. Fagg," Mrs. Woodgate said confidently.

It was evident that the country's joy in the political change was reflected by the ladies. Neither disputed for an instant that the Lord Warden of the Cinque Forts would be equal even to the tremendous emergency. Under his strong leadership a nation, which hitherto through the ineptitude of its rulers had grown sadly discouraged, was renewed. A fighting leader and a fighting people it was to be, a combination which should bring a militant autocracy tumbling about its Emperor's ears.

" As we shall, Mrs. Fagg," the Rector's wife said with an entire absence of flourish, a calm surety in her.

" Yes, m'dear, we shall," Polly Fagg agreed staunchly.

Both, if dimly, were aware of the gigantic task which lay ahead, a fight in which thirteen million Britons were engaged in life-and-death struggle against nearly five times that number. Yet, perhaps intuitively, they knew that, given resolution, they who wage war for right have a strength above mere numerical computation.

4

On that Sunday afternoon when the odours of roast meat and vegetables had died away, Little Pent House was peacefully hushed, its mistress taking her post-prandial rest in her bedroom, the servant girls out, and Mrs. George Rochefort departed on a walk during which she and Horatio would go round by the jail as was their weekly practice. Susan, a young widow with a modest income, always spared a crown piece or its equivalent for the poor creatures who stared so hopelessly from the barred windows, and this donation her small boy put into the collecting-box over which was painted in chipped white lettering, ' Pity the Poor Debtors.'

In the parlour Charles Fagg and his father were talking quietly.

" So you'll be going over again shortly, eh ? " the shipowner observed.

His son nodded. " Within the next few days."

At that John Fagg did not comment all at once, being inordinately interested in a smoke-ring which, made lovely by the sun streaming in, slowly ascended towards the ceiling.

" You know, Charles," he remarked pensively as the perfect circle started to eddy and break, " local feeling against you is growing apace, and I can't quite understand why Mr. Pitt couldn't give you some special appointment to save you this unnecessary unpleasantness. Suppose, for instance, he let it be known that you were engaged in important government work."

Charles Fagg, a half-smile on his lips, was glancing into the garden, along a path of which his sister Lou and Jack Woodgate were strolling arm in arm.

" Because, Father," he turned, " 'twould be devilish dangerous for me."

" Dangerous ? " ejaculated Mr. Fagg.

Fleetingly, Charles's old grin flashed out. " I'd call it that if I found a reception committee awaiting me one night at t'other side."

" Damme, Charles," the shipowner expostulated, " what's this tarnal nonsense ? "

" Fouché's agents over here," his son said laconically.

Only a brief interval elapsed before comprehension flooded into John Fagg's own grey eyes. He nodded understandingly and, taking out his pipe, whistled silently.

" I must be getting mismazed," he confessed ruefully, " for I'd never given a thought to that. An' are there many of the Frenchies' spies around these parts ? "

Downright dryly, Charles retorted that as to that the authorities themselves would like to be advised more accurately. But, he pointed out, one of such gentry having been caught red-handed at Deal during the last week, and two more near the Commander-in-Chief's headquarters at Canterbury within the month, the inference was plain enough.

" Aye, to be sure," John Fagg muttered, quite oblivious that his son's manner was more impatient than was warranted. " Well . . . " he sighed, " in that case there's nothing else for't."

" No," Charles said soberly, staring beyond the Canyon, wondering whether or not to sail his skiff on those pleasantly-lonely waters.

Soon, however, he went up to his room, and there made sure he was prepared for the next trip—French money, thin tracing paper, a slender notebook. . . .

After that a brisk walk to the seaward end of Snargate Street-over-the-Wall, and the delivery of the stand-by warning to Captain Pepper.

"Betwixt now and Thursday night, Valentine," he said crisply.

"When you gives the word, Mr. Charles," the boatswain replied stoutly.

They spent a half-hour together in the cottage checking over every detail, both for the outward journey and for that of the return. It was not until he was leaving that the younger man noticed that beneath his companion's jauntiness there was a suspicion of the forlorn.

"No, Mr. Charles, I ain't going to give over, nohow," the sea-dog growled when, after lying valiantly, the truth had been dragged out of him. "'Tis true that Martha don't seem to want to 'ave aught more to do with me, but . . . but 'aps 'twill be different some day when she knows what it 'as all been about."

"You'll be a hero, Valentine," Charles twinkled, seeing how it was.

Captain Pepper had not got over that by the time he was opening the door, no not even when he had reached his tidy gate.

"I know who'll be the 'ero, Mr. Charles," he roared. "I just paddle out part way whereas you goes on an'——"

"Softly, Valentine, 'twill be as well if you moderate your voice," Charles Fagg said quickly, jerking his head significantly.

At the sight of Harry Jenkins sitting placidly on a bollard at the edge of the Basin, Captain Pepper adroitly squirted tobacco juice for a good twelve feet.

"'im!" he grunted contumeliously, with a snap of his fingers dismissing both preventivemen and their service, being in no humour to be baulked from saying what he intended. "Whereas you," he rumbled on, "risks your neck for days on end an' gets no better reward 'ere than . . ."

Charles hastily made his adieu and set off for home by his favourite way.

It was interesting along the Ropewalk. New defences, ranging from ponderous stone-built forts to low earthen bulwarks, were springing into being. Short as the time had been since Mr. Pitt had taken office, the signs of his dynamic will were everywhere in evidence. It was an encouraging sight save to one who knew how paltry this effort was as compared with the frenzy of ordered preparation taking place across the water.

"Aye," Charles Fagg muttered grimly.

Lou and her sailor lover, as the bells of St. Mary-the-Virgin's sent their summons ringing over the evening air, were sauntering towards the house when, after skirting the Folly, he entered the bottom of the garden.

As he saw them Charles smiled. It was silly, perhaps, for a brother to think his sister looked sweet, but that was what he thought of Lou —in her pretty bonnet and gay little dress, prayer-book in one hand and the other resting on Jack's blue sleeve, with Jack himself a gallant figure in frock coat, white breeches and silk stockings, cocked hat tucked beneath his arm.

" Charles ! " Mr. Woodgate called out, his face lighting up.

It appeared that this well-seasoned naval officer had a problem. Less than two months before he had been commissioned as lieutenant and so, having surmounted the most crucial step in his career, his thoughts had gone to Lou.

" The point is, Charles," he began without preamble, " do you think we could live on my pay ? "

This, to digress, was the first intimation, officially, Charles had heard of the new relationship of the pair.

" You propose living with Lou, Jack ? " he inquired solemnly.

Miss Lou, blushing outrageously, was laughing helplessly all the same.

" Oh, Jack dearest," she giggled, " I vow you never change."

Her brother, still grave as a judge, felt it his duty to ask whether Mr. Woodgate's plans for the lady involved a circle of gold to fit on a finger.

" Taking a man . . . or a woman, I think you used to name it, Jack," he laughed, recollecting days of mock marriages in their youth.

Lieutenant Woodgate eyed him in some perplexity. " Taking a —oh, solemnisation of matrimony," he muttered and then, having a one-track mind, pursued his first inquiry.

" I'm afraid I'm hardly an authority on't," Charles grinned.

There was unconscious pathos in the sailor's next remark, in his patent relief as to how the tricky point might infallibly be solved.

" I'll ask Mamma, she'll know," he said simply.

The saint's bell was ringing out its solitary note, and worshipers must hasten if they were not to be late.

" 'Tis time we went, Jack," Lou protested, becoming all at once a firm little madame. " And," she smiled happily at her brother, " you'll come with us, Charles."

Charles Fagg shook his head. It wasn't that he feared meeting the townsfolk, but he was becoming somewhat weary, somewhat angry beneath it all, at the virtual ostracism he was suffering.

" Oh, please do, Charles," his sister persisted.

" Damme, why not ? " Jack Woodgate demanded.

His glance on the Folly, Charles was incuriously eyeing the white marks of saline effervescence which, the result of using salt-water for the mixing of the mortar, were appearing on the face of the cheaply constructed building. He was thinking of Jack who, having been a month in Dover, must be alive to what was being said. Maybe those, he meditated sardonically, who are in the front line of battle are always the most tolerant, leaving the backbiting to others more safely placed at home. Yes, Jack was a good fellow.

" I'll be glad to come with you, Jack and Lou," he said suddenly, a smile coming with the acceptance.

The head of the family, with his wife and sister, had already gone ahead. Soon three young people were walking along Town Wall Street, pretty Miss Lou Fagg between the two young men, holding on to her lover and adored brother.

5

For the six or so hours of darkness which followed twilight, Ralph Toke was not far removed from being out of his senses. During that short period many things might be resolved, perhaps much guesswork translated into proven fact.

Earlier that evening news had been sped to the Revenue Officer that Valentine Pepper was in the Fountain Inn, drinking heavily. Already it had been established that there was a very direct connection between the old navyman's carousals and a young man's reappearance in the town ; that, in short, the former indication was a positive sign that Charles Fagg would be back in Dover within a day or so.

" Drinking, eh ? " Mr. Toke had said, his eyes gleaming.

Forthwith he had laid his plans for final verification. Instructions had been rushed to coast watchers and to the lieutenants of the two revenue cutters, with nothing left undone which might have the effect of closing certain gaps in the chain of information.

As was anticipated, Pepper sneaked out of the harbour that night and now, as the eastern sky showed a vague lightening, Mr. Toke and Clement Foxley were stretched behind the low wooden parapet of the South Pier.

" I think there's supm coming, sir ? " Clement Foxley whispered.

The Revenue Officer's hands were shaking as he held the night-glass to his eye. On the next few seconds would depend so much. If Fagg was with Pepper then some weeks might elapse before he went a-trading again, but if not . . .

" 'Tis Pepper's boat methinks," his Assistant vouchsafed, breath bated.

Seldom could a man have so *willed* that there should be only one occupant of the craft as did Ralph Toke.

" An' he's alone, sir."

A faint shape came round within the ebon loom of the North Pier, hardly discernible, so skilfully was every advantage taken of the prevailing condition. It passed between the narrow heads before silently disappearing towards the far side of the Tidal Harbour, so cleverly brought in that an unsuspecting watcher might have rubbed his eyes and declared it was all an illusion.

The tremor in the Revenue Officer's voice betrayed his tension.

" Then," he muttered, " he'll go out again to-morrow night."

" Yes, sir."

Full comprehension of what this meant permeated Mr. Toke's soul.

" An' whether it be to-morrow or still another night, he'll meet Fagg," he said exultantly, stiffly rising.

The thought that young Fagg would shortly fall into a trap from which there would be no escape fired the Revenue Officer's brain, but he composed himself sufficiently to thank the sergeant of the guard for ensuring that the little boat, if she had been seen, was not challenged on entry.

" And *now*, Foxley," he remarked, restrained elation on his long-chinned face.

" We'll soon be teaching 'im that smuggling in the summer months ain't over-healthy, sir," Clement Foxley smirked.

At this reminder of young Fagg's crowning impudence, the Revenue Officer's expression swiftly changed to the ugly.

" Yes," he observed curtly, his rage rising again.

They began to walk towards the Cross Wall, and thence into Custom House Quay.

Keyed to a high pitch, the bliss of bed and rest did not enter into Ralph Toke's calculations. Whilst the strengthening blush of dawn changed the candles in the Revenue Office from the living to the pale, he sat awaiting the reports he knew would soon come, meantime giving Foxley certain orders. If the expected intimations were satisfactory the selected men were to be assembled at two of the clock in the afternoon. . . .

There was the sound of heavily-booted feet coming up the flagged passage, and then a light tap on the door.

" Yes," Mr. Toke barked, on seeing who it was.

The Acting Mate of one of the cutters brought intelligence. Pepper's craft, he said, had steered for the North Goodwin Sand, and there had run on to Jamaica Land. Once, when a lugger had chanced to pass by, Pepper had shown a signal. . . .

" A signal ?" the Revenue Officer snapped.

" Yes, sir," the seaman replied stolidly.

Clarified by probing questions here and there, little by little it all came out, until most of the pieces of the puzzle fitted into their due and proper places. And how simple it was, how easy to reach a solution compounded of conjecture in small part and certitude in large.

Young Fagg would go across to the other side and there, having made his purchases of contraband, would come back along with them in a French or Dutch free-trader. Contact being effected with Pepper, as much as possible of the goods would be transhipped on the Sand, the remainder probably being anchored there to await another night.

Mr. Toke's eyes flamed with triumph.

Old Peter Monin's clock struck two, and promptly Clement Foxley opened the door to the outer room, there to stand with beckoning finger.

" All correct, sir," he reported to the Revenue Officer when the shuffle had died and half a dozen embarrassed preventivemen were thumbing their hats along the side wall of the inner office.

Mr. Toke's hard eye roved over the company and, as prelude to detailing the dispositions he proposed for the night, he advised them in pungent phraseology of the fate any would suffer should blunder be made in carrying out his plan.

" And now," he ended grimly, after outlining his concept, " we come to the recognition signal, a lantern deliberately raised and lowered thrice.

" And that is precisely what Jenkins will do—*thrice*," he repeated emphatically.

Solemnly, in no wise realising he might seem droll to his inferiors, he grasped an imaginary lantern and for that number of times raised it aloft.

" Is that clear, Jenkins ? " he asked sharply.

As it happened, the violence of his manner had struck awe into them all, and the preventiveman could do no more than nod his complete understanding. Normally, when seen on a settle of the Fountain Inn during an evening's leave, Harry Jenkins was a jokesey fellow of a build not dissimilar from that of Captain Pepper. In this physical resemblance lay the beauty of Mr. Toke's scheme.

" Then, unhindered and unsuspected, we draw near to Fagg," the Revenue Officer rasped on, " either taking the miscreant from the vessel he is in, or seizing him immediately he lands on the spit."

A mention of Jamaica Land created a little stir. Respectfully tugging his forelock, Jenkins voiced a question which, judging by the alarm in their expressions, was already providing food for thought amongst his mates.

"Beggin' your pardon, Mr. Toke, sir," he said awkwardly, " but did I 'ear you say as 'ow we might 'ave to land on the Goodwin *ter-night*, sir ? "

"If necessary, my good fellow," the Revenue Officer replied curtly. "And why ? "

In a grown man it was hardly seemly for him to confess that he feared to tread on what was, after all, nothing more than coarse sand, albeit the graveyard of many a fine ship. Nevertheless Harry Jenkins blurted out some of his anxieties. They concerned the rotting timbers of lost vessels, and ghosts and spectres and other wraith-like apparitions.

"Pish ! " Ralph Toke retorted cuttingly, and at once came back to the real issue.

His project was, in truth, admirably conceived. Every minute from sundown the cottage at the end of Snargate Street-over-the-Wall would be kept under close observation, and subsequently, when Pepper was making for the harbour to execute his part in young Fagg's scheme, he was to be effectively put out of action.

"Smash in his head sufficiently hard to keep him quiescent for a week or more," the Revenue Officer observed ruthlessly.

The ex-boatswain disposed of, the preventivemen were to put to sea in three boats, the first a small one which Jenkins, in the rôle of Pepper, would sail, he being accompanied by Mr. Toke and Clement Foxley, both of whom would, when the time came, conceal themselves in the bows, their pistols cocked ready.

"You understand, Jenkins ? " the Revenue Officer demanded.

"Yes, sir. You an' Mr. Foxley 'ides well forrard."

Proceeding some distance behind this boat were to be the two revenue cutters, one of which was to run inshore of the Goodwins towards Bunt Head, the other to keep the ten-mile stretch of the submerged sands on her larboard hand, their purpose to prevent any retreat, to cut off the foreign craft once Fagg had been taken.

There was some further discussion—provision for alternate eventualities and such like—and the mention of various points of technical interest only. It was a period of spring tides, with a rise and fall of over sixteen feet, but Ralph Toke, determined to settle accounts once and for all, intended to guard against any potential adverse factor. The boom between the pier-heads, by arrangement with the Officer Commanding the Royal Engineers, was to be slackened until the bight sank a further half fathom, so permitting the cutters an ample margin.

"Very good, men," the Revenue Officer wound up harshly.

When the party had filed out he allowed a measure of his delight to escape him.

"And now, Clement," he said almost genially, "for our real plan,"

"Yes, sir!" his assistant answered dutifully, if curiously.

There was a strange gleam in the Revenue Officer's eyes as he glanced at Foxley.

"Do you recall an instruction I once gave you concerning the Faggs?" he asked abruptly. "'Twas about their apprehension."

"As regards shooting, sir? Shooting first and asking the questions arterwards."

"That, just that, Foxley." Mr. Toke's mouth was brutal as he nodded. "And do you remember that I also told you we would see the necessary weapon *was* found?"

There was nothing squeamish about Clement Foxley. Nevertheless he licked lips that seemed to be dry.

"Yes, sir," he replied throatily.

Without further word the Revenue Officer unlocked a cupboard, taking from it a plain-handled pistol of a type and quality very common.

"Follow me, Foxley," he said edgily.

His demeanour was so sinister that Clement Foxley perceptibly changed colour but, orders being orders, he reluctantly followed his senior into the deep cellars below the old building.

In a pregnant silence Mr. Toke put down the lantern, produced a cartouche box, charged the pan of the pistol and, with few seconds to spare before his companion would have bolted, fired the piece, filling the confined space with thunderous report.

"Do you see now, Foxley?" he demanded, his eyes wild-looking through the curling wisps of acrid smoke.

"Yes . . . sir" coughed his scared subordinate.

The Revenue Officer's smile was wolfish. "The pistol, as you see, has just been fired," he resumed malevolently. "You will take it and, when young Fagg is destroyed, you will place it on his body. That, Foxley, will be our justification."

Unquestionably, Clement Foxley's knees were knocking. But he managed, nevertheless, to put a finger on the one flaw.

"Jenkins, sir, he'll know different," he said tremulously.

The Revenue Officer had foreseen that possibility. In the excitement of the moment, when he, with a pistol in each hand, and Foxley had pulled the triggers, it would be easy to make the dull-witted Jenkins believe that one of the three shots came from the runagate Fagg.

A nefarious design arranged to the last trifle, the two men ascended from the gloom of the damp cellar to the lovely brightness of the day.

Slowly the sun moved westerly. Sweet peas and honeysuckle began to give off their fragrance, and the birds to think of closing songs for the day.

The breeze was beginning to blow more steadily, and a few larger clouds were coming into the mackerel sky.

One of the summer days so often found on that strip of proud coast was drawing to its pleasant end.

Part III

1804-1806

CHAPTER ONE

I

To Martha Teddiman's horror Miss Caroline, now surely a young lady of position, insisted on riding on the outside of the mail on the return to Dover. The housekeeper, who three days earlier had left Snargate Street for London, with purpose to chaperon her mistress from there homeward, had winced visibly at every stage, for it was at each of these that the miss chose to stretch her legs.

"Of all the wayward madams," she had groaned at Rochester, glimpsing through the window some lacy extremities as her charge descended from a lofty perch. "Why I ever consented for her not to take a chaise . . ."

Herself feeling the effects of the hours of jolting, Martha, by Canterbury, was in danger of becoming really cross with a dancing-eyed creature. "Well," she remarked, just so slightly tossing her head, "if *this* is how the master's grand relatives 'as taught you to behave . . ." She snorted in lieu of concluding and, to relieve her ire, signally disconcerted the quite harmless guard by the frostiness of the look she gave him.

Thereupon, apparently so affected by the reiterated condemnation, Miss Rochefort developed a spasm of travel-faintness, one which could be assuaged only by a draught of bitters.

The alarmed Martha, after negotiating backwards the three deep steps from the high-slung body of the vehicle, hurried into the Rose Inn, and soon emerged with the beneficial specific. It was accepted gratefully and drunk with avidity, whereupon the distressed female roundly expressed herself as divinely refreshed and, as evidence, gave Mistress Teddimen an outsize wink preparatory to climbing back to the high box beside the driver, a portly, flaming-nosed individual whom she had cajoled, from time to time, into allowing her to handle the four beasts.

"You . . . unforbidden . . . wicked girl !" the housekeeper gasped, shocked by this perfidiousness. "I shan't forget this behaviour, Miss Caroline, I can tell you."

Nor did she for, even whilst Caroline was again hugging her

346

father in the broad hall of the Snargate Street house, she preserved an icy look of disapproval.

"Papa, I'm monstrous glad to be home," Caroline said joyously. "'Tis lovely to see you all again and to smell boiling pitch and the tang of salt in the air. So divine, Papa, so truly marvellous."

Henry Rochefort was every whit as pleased. Taking her hands, he pushed her a little from him the better to see the elegant young lady she had become.

"No more the little girl, eh, Martha?" he declared fondly.

Caroline, releasing herself, pirouetted gaily, and then went into a wicked burlesque of a fashionable dame's social gait.

"And no more Italian masters for this, Papa," she laughed. "And . . ." she wrinkled her nose entrancingly, "no neat sewing and horrible embroidery. I *hate* neat sewing."

Martha Teddiman, seemingly still unreconciled, sniffed audibly as if bent on drawing attention to herself, as indeed she was.

Caroline Rochefort's brown eyes twinkled understandingly.

"Martha darling," she tried wheedlingly, "I'm so sorry I misbehaved myself. 'Twas so dreadful of me."

The housekeeper, back still stiff, allowed herself nothing more than to glance distantly at the supplicant. In the middle of a second dulcet appeal, during the course of which Martha was visibly relenting, a dignified tread announced the arrival of Louis Rochefort, on his face a faint jubilation which he was fighting manfully to suppress. He had, in point of fact, taken the Captain's second prize at the musketry competition.

"Ah, Caroline," he observed precisely, his efforts causing him to be more grave than he intended.

Sinking her chin, Miss Rochefort produced an amazingly fruity voice.

"Ah, my dear sir," she inquired weightily, "may I ask if 'tis still your view that further issue of paper will reduce B. of E. notes to common *assignats*?"

Just for so little the young banker's face was a picture of stupefaction. His sister, upon delivery of this searching question, had blown out her cheeks very much in the manner of Sir Walter Plumbley and was treating him to the same shrewd scrutiny employed by that witless gentleman.

Quickly it dawned upon him. "Caroline, you little devil!" he shouted, his grin breaking out before he soundly kissed her. And, even as her father had done, he drew off a pace admiringly to survey her. "Phew!" he ejaculated, "I foresee that shortly this poor house will ring to the tread of many martial feet. What say you, Martha?"

Martha, who had been watching the delightful reunion with

something approaching moist emotion, had evidently decided that her frolicsome young mistress had made amends. Certainly she unblushingly stated that it would have to be a fine soldier indeed who would be good enough for Miss Caroline.

" Oh, Martha dear," laughed that young lady, " I fear me that your heart is more concerned with a gentleman who belonged to another service. And," she ended teasingly, " how is dear Captain ——"

Her father coughing warningly and her brother nudging her, she perceived that for some unknown reason her query would be better left unfinished. It was time, she improvised on the spur of the moment, that she removed the stains of travel and changed into a more befitting dress. Then she was ravenously hungry and . . .

" We have delayed supper against your return, my love," Henry Rochefort said smilingly, squeezing her trim waist.

" And don't trouble to fal-di-la yourself so much," Louis Rochefort called up when she was passing the high window on the half-landing. " I'm sharp-set, my girl."

With Martha in attendance Caroline, after an absence of nearly a year, entered her old bedroom, there to stand at the window drinking in the scene—the Pent, the Ropewalk, and seabirds majestically riding up-wind without a movement of their graceful white-tipped wings. Her glance passed curiously over defensive arrangements which were new to her; a bulwark at the foot of the sheer Castle Cliff and, beyond the rising building estate of Paradise Pent, Archcliffe Fort, with many additional gun muzzles pointing menacingly towards the sea.

" Methinks, Martha," she mused audibly, " that howsoever we considered ourselves prepared to receive the invader when the Truce of Amiens brought temporary peace, we are now infinitely more ready to deal with any attempted descent on our shores."

" Let them descend," said Martha Teddiman. In themselves the words might have formed a challenge, but never that when delivered so miserably.

Impressions can be absorbed without immediately striking the responsive faculties. It was a little later that Caroline Rochefort, her attention drawn by the musical sound of water being poured into a flower-patterned wash-basin, coupled Martha's woebegone expression with that despairing remark.

" Martha," she asked anxiously, taking the older woman's hand, " something is troubling you ? Tell me what it is."

Promptly the housekeeper went off into a feverish refutal that anything ailed her, meantime displaying a fixed though not far from watery smile.

"There is something Martha, darling," her young mistress persisted gently. "Please let me help you if I can."

Martha, though blinking back her tears, was still determined. "No, you're mistook, Miss Caroline, quite . . . quite . . ." And then it all came with a rush. "'Tis Pepper, Miss Caroline," she gulped, "he's drinking, drinking terrible hard."

Since Caroline's mother died Martha Teddiman had been very close to her and, knowing her so well, Elizabeth Rochefort's daughter fully comprehended that Martha cherished a code of conduct a little more narrow than perhaps was wise. Maybe it was that same rigidity of outlook, she thought, which even now was causing Martha to be making a mountain out of a molehill.

"Oh, but Martha dear, men sometimes do——" she was beginning reassuringly.

"'Tis far more than that, Miss Caroline," Martha Teddiman interrupted tragically, relating the bestial bouts which had become the talk of the town. "And," her eyes were distracted, "he so fills himself with strong liquor that he can scarce stagger home, and once he gets there he lays in a stupor which lasts dunnamany days. 'Tis abominable, Miss Caroline, and . . . an' 'tis breaking my heart."

Miss Rochefort's air, as she comforted the sobbing woman, boded little good for Captain Pepper when she met him.

The night breeze, coming through the half-open window of the dining-room, was causing the yellow flames of the eight candles on the gleaming table to waver wildly and to give off black eddying smoke.

Supper had been a delightful meal, and both men, so long used to eating together, had reacted spontaneously to the presence of the gay young creature who looked so charming in her high-waisted India muslin gown. In particular, Henry Rochefort, with his girl changed into lovely womanhood, seemed nearer peace and happiness than since the dread day his beautiful wife had been taken from him.

"It is indeed a boon to have you back with us, my dear," he smiled, affectionately laying his hand over hers. "We've all missed you and——"

He had to desist, his speech drowned by the raucous, rum-charged voice of some powerful-lunged sot proceeding, no doubt uncertainly, on the near side of Snargate Street.

"Disgusting, in these days when the very life of the nation is in peril," the banker said angrily, rising to peer into the gloom without.

"There's few nowadays who don't realise the imminence of danger," Louis Rochefort began grimly. "But if I had my way with those few——"

Miss Rochefort decidedly informed them that so far they had had a delicious evening, and she was not going to have it spoilt because an addle-pated roysterer had chanced to pass the house.

"Nor shall it be, my dear," laughed her father, his quick flush of ill-humour gone.

The slight disturbance over, the threads of family relationship were gathered up and, from these exhausted, the daughter of the house, cracking nuts between her teeth in a most unladylike manner, demanded to know every single thing that had happened in the town during her absence.

"Jack Woodgate!" she exclaimed delightedly, the talk having come to Lou's romance with the young sailor. "Oh, I'm so pleased, Louis; I always liked Jack."

"They'll make a pleasant couple sure enough," her brother shrugged. "Though how they'll manage to keep house, I'm blest if I know. He hasn't a guinea of private money to call his own and . . ." He laughed off any further comment, not being wishful of involving himself in an awkwardness through any mention of the Faggs or of their declined income.

"And . . . and Charles?" asked his sister lightly.

"Charles . . . oh, Charles is quite well, I suppose," Louis replied a little uncomfortably. "In point of fact, m'dear, I don't see as much of him as of wont."

It was that queer reticence which she thought she discerned in his manner which caused Caroline Rochefort to glance curiously at her brother.

Indeed she would have questioned him further had not a peremptory summons on the knocker of the front door caused speculation as to whom the caller might be at this hour.

"Ralph Toke!" ejaculated Louis Rochefort, when an apple-cheeked girl had made known who waited. "What the deuce does he want?"

A look of the most acute dismay was on his father's face. Ever since he had learnt the gossip that it was Charles Fagg who was smuggling, Henry Rochefort had deeply regretted the call he had made at the Revenue Office. It wasn't that he approved of the young fool's goings-on—far from that—but he shrank from being the instrument which would force a conclusion, and deliberately he had refrained from pressing the matter any more.

"Evening, Toke," he pulled himself together. "You'll take a glass of wine . . . Louis, my boy."

The Revenue Officer, who was dressed in garments not likely to suffer much whatever the events of the night brought forth, was at such fever heat that, with scant courtesy, he waved aside the proffered hospitality, so eager was he to tell of the imminent settling of a score which was years old.

He opened by mentioning the undertaking he had given, on the occasion of the banker's call on him.

" You have information for to-night ? " Henry Rochefort inquired uneasily.

" For to-night, Mr. Rochefort," Mr. Toke retorted, his thin lips vicious. " Our boats are ready and we sail an hour after the turn."

The banker was warming his hands at a fire which had amply taken the evening chill off the room.

" And . . . er . . . who be the traders, Toke ? " he asked from that position.

By waiting, the Revenue Officer virtually compelled the master of the house to face him. There was also a minor account to settle here, and he was savagely convinced of Henry Rochefort's fears. The next minute would do something towards effacing the memory of a certain high-handed attitude.

" 'Tis young Mr. Charles Fagg, I fear," he smirked.

Caroline, lips parted and her breathing quick, was intently watching the speaker. She saw the malignancy in that smile and read more than the mere words into this evil creature's next remark.

"A wild young man forsooth," Ralph Toke proclaimed unctuously. " An'," he shook his head dubiously, " 'tis to be hoped we glimpse no gleam of a pistol in his hand."

Horror grew deeper in Caroline's eyes as, the covert threat made, he rapidly outlined elaborately conceived plans for the final and irrevocable adjustment of a bitter feud.

" I've been beaten before, Mr. Rochefort, but this time——" the Revenue Officer was saying when, burning with indignation, she grasped her father's arm.

" Papa, why are you concerned with this . . . this *gentleman* in such degrading business ? " she asked passionately, using the appellative witheringly.

Henry Rochefort, shifting his weight from one foot to the other, strove to gain her understanding by admitting freely, before the very Revenue Officer himself, that he saw no harm in this illicit traffic. But he had one proviso, a proviso which overruled the debt of gratitude he owed Charles for that daring rescue of Louis from France.

"And that is when the country is in parlous state, and it is to-day, my dear," he said sternly, dignity now replacing a more shamefaced manner as he recalled his public avowals. " Then I," his voice rang out, " and every public-spirited citizen along with me, will do my utmost to stamp out an evil which may sap our cause."

"Even if it means . . . But only God and this man know what it may mean, Papa," she reminded him desperately. "For when he speaks of Charles with a weapon in his hands I think only of a Folkestone smuggler who died on similar grounds. Even to this day 'tis said the poor fellow was no better than murdered."

Mr. Toke's expression, thunderous already, became envenomed.

"Young woman," he snarled, "because you were once sweethearting with Charles Fagg——"

"May I remind you that you are speaking to my sister, sir," Louis Rochefort interposed furiously, taking firm grasp of the Revenue Officer's shoulder.

"Sister or not I'll have my say," Mr. Toke shouted, jerking clear. "Whatever fate befalls either Fagg is only his proper due. They are proven smugglers and . . ." temper got the better of natural prudence, "maybe the younger one is more than that. I'll have you know that there's been strange leakages to the other side of the doings in this fortress of Dover."

Caroline Rochefort, her brown eyes sparkling, sprang to her feet.

"How dare you infer that Charles Fagg is a traitor?" she demanded. "How *dare* you?"

Mr. Toke, aware that in an incautious moment he had said far more than he could substantiate, wilted under her blazing regard. All the same he would not outright admit his error.

"There's been incidents albeit, Miss Rochefort," he was beginning, when the banker sharply cut him short. Mr. Rochefort made it evident that he took little notice of the Revenue Officer's wild statement.

"Nonsense, Toke," he said bitingly, "I'd not believe it of either father or son. And, knowing the Faggs, I'd advise you not to repeat this fantastic accusation."

Mr. Ralph Toke's reply was inaudible, but his plum-coloured face and the meanness of his mouth gave sound indication of his feelings. Snatching up his hat, he curtly bade them good-night.

With his going the three Rocheforts fell quiet, each apparently disinclined for speech. The harmony of the pleasant evening thus gone, it was perhaps with something of relief that they saw Martha Teddiman, sleepy-eyed with her journeyings, standing in the doorway pointing at the bracket clock.

"Axing your pardon, Mr. . . ." she yawned widely, ". . . Rochefort, but I think 'tis time Miss Caroline went to bed."

Louis half-heartedly essayed an attempt at humour. "Still the baby, Caroline," he laughed feebly.

A troubled smile came to his sister's face as she made a lukewarm rejoinder before kissing her father.

As Miss Caroline Rochefort went slowly up the stairs a party of soldiers, under the charge of a sergeant of Engineers, began to lower the boom across the harbour mouth.

Martha Teddiman, fatigued as she was, knew her duty, and no amount of dissuasion on the part of her young mistress could prevent her from completing the full round of her tasks. She *would* see Miss Caroline into bed before she left.

Though that young woman's heart was thumping inordinately, though she believed every minute to be precious, she considered it wisdom to permit the housekeeper her way.

But, when the door closed, Caroline Rochefort made amends for the delay. Lithely swinging from the four-poster, she hurried to the window.

It was not possible to see the mossy green line high on the timber and stone framework of the South Pier which would have told her the height of water but, screening her eyes, she succeeded in dimly perceiving the outlines of a few craft which, as yet, were swinging anyhow, sure indication that the tide was in that short intermediate space between flood and ebb.

This known, she began to speed, with quick fingers plaiting up her long tresses. Opening the *bombé*-fronted clothes press she chose a warm dress of neutral grey and a long dark cloak.

With the moment for action near, her breath came a little quicker between her parted lips. She tiptoed to the door, silently bolting it and, on her return, snuffed the candle which she had asked Martha to leave burning.

In the darkness she stood awhile until her sight was attuned.

The sash of the small window was cautiously raised, and soon she was lowering herself from the sill outside, her feet feeling for the sloping roof beneath. That safely gained, she shuffled down towards the gutter.

A tiny thud signalised that Miss Caroline Rochefort had reached the fire-alley at the side of her father's house.

2

There was no sign of life in Captain Pepper's shipshape cottage and, after again rapping the window, Caroline knew that this one hope had failed. The boatswain was in all probability with Charles and she was left to her own resources.

Her thoughts racing, she walked down the path, glad, despite her hurt through a nasty fall over an untidy pile of their squared paving-

M

stones, that the Paving Commissioners had not as yet lighted the town nearer than the New Bridge.

Outside the gate she paused, her purpose becoming clearer with every moment. Charles must be warned, somehow she must reach Jamaica Land.

Her sole idea now to obtain a boat, she turned away from Snargate Street-over-the-Wall and, immediately on the shingle bank, perforce trod as though walking barefoot on broken glass. Amherst's Battery was not more than eighty yards away, and had it not been that the breeze was down, blowing in her face, the crunching noise she made must have carried to the vigilant soldiers.

Foot by foot she stole towards the steps of the boat-dock and, so near, was beginning to hope that she was achieving the first part of her aim when a ghastly groan rooted her. Trembling a little she peered into the darkness. At first she could see nothing, but then she picked out a vague shape, low down.

Some agonisingly long seconds later, Caroline Rochefort was sure that the bravest thing she had ever done in her life was to cover the space between herself and the pitiable object she found to be the man who was bringing sorrow into Martha Teddiman's life.

" Captain Pepper ! " she said sharply, on her knees beside him.

He was in a sad state, dazed and shaken, with a great gash at the back of his head from which blood was oozing beneath his wig.

" Oh, Captain Pepper ! " she repeated, her tone far softer.

Swimming with dizziness he managed to sit up, to touch her wonderingly, to believe at last that, befuddled as he was, he had not mistaken the voice.

" Miss Caroline, or there ain't no niggers in Jamaicy " he muttered, realising that here was a true ally.

Whilst she, inexpressibly carefully, for the tearing of linen made frightening sound in the night, tore a strip from her petticoat for the bandaging of his ugly wound, he spoke to her of what was in train when an unseen rogue had battered him down.

" They're arter Mr. Charles, I suspex, an' if they catch 'im . . ." he said shakily, a tear of weakness beginning to fall.

" They won't . . . they *shan't* do that, Captain Pepper," she declared intensely, telling him of the decision she had made.

He was so disturbed that, with thought of scrambling up, he unthinkingly made himself wince by straightening up what had once been John Fagg's wig.

" You, Miss Caroline ! " he gasped, just stifling a groan. " You sail out to the North Goodwin ! Miss Caroline, you can't do it, 'twould perhaps mean your own life." As last resort he suggested that she should arouse Mr. Fagg but, hearing the state of the tide, admitted hollowly that that would be too late.

She was determined and, finding her to be so, he dismally gave her what advice he could, angrily brushing aside her worried suggestion that she should help him back to his house.

"I can git along middlin' well if I go steady. And," he added, chuckling weakly, " maybe I'll be able to draw attention to make it easier for you. They watch the 'arbour keen, Miss Caroline."

There were still one or two other things he had to tell her . . . if she was bent on . . .

" I am, so please say no more," she firmly silenced him.

Nor did he, with the exception of a few last hints. He knew for sure his own craft was too heavy for her and so she must take Mr. Charles's little sailing boat. It was in the boat-dock close by, ready almost . . .

" And God be with you, Miss Caroline," he said quiveringly.

She disappeared into the darkness, her first design the replacement of an article which had been broken in the assault on the boatswain.

It was the intention of the daughter of a highly respected banker to steal a lanthorn from the guard-house on the North Pier.

The Middle Battery, composed of one mortar, three thirty-two and four eighteen pounders, with many neat heaps of cannon balls piled in pyramid form, was disposed on the north pierhead, along which, with muskets at the slope, two sentries were patrolling, their beats so arranged that when one reached the extreme limit of the pier, the other, on the more landward berth, was halting close by the rectangle of light which marked the doorway of the wooden guard-house, a stoutly built hut erected for the purpose.

The theft of one of the gleaming lanterns which, already burning in preparedness for any emergency, stood upon a shelf behind the corporal of the guard, had been no easy matter. It was true that the corporal, his primary duty done with rounds completed, had nodded off, but it was an uneasy slumber and, even as Caroline slipped inside, her heart had nearly stopped when he had given vent to something between an exclamation and a snore.

Now, after escaping detection, after once again passing Amherst's Battery, the lamp hot beneath her cloak, she found her limbs quivering when she had clambered over half a dozen other boats to reach Charles's.

Shaking or no, she was aroused to quick action when she heard the murmur of many voices from Custom House Quay. Outlined against the yellow-illuminated windows of the Revenue Office were the tapering masts of two cutters, and it was very obvious that Mr.

Toke and his men would soon be proceeding in quest of their all-unconscious prey.

Urgently she set to work, slipping the painter and easing the rope softly into the water. As the skiff began to drift with the out-flowing tide she smiled mistily, simultaneously thanking God that the boat had recently been in service, that the sails would be easy to hoist and set.

Now she could do little more, save to seek concealment by steering close to the Basin's tall side, and ever to ensure that her cloak screened every ray from the lantern which lay on the bottom boards.

The lock-gates of the Tidal Harbour were drawing near, a leaden slit in the dense bulk of the Cross Wall. As the rate of close increased when in the fast stream which moved towards the narrow egress, a hail rang out from Custom House Quay.

" Name yourself," it demanded uncompromisingly. " Who's afloat at this hour ? "

The cry was repeated as, in the bows of the boat, Caroline Roche-fort clung to the slimy timber at the farther end of the lock, her purpose to keep the little craft within the impenetrable gloom at the edge of the Tidal Harbour, rather than have it taken directly into the middle by the main flow.

" Who moves there ? "

The shout was muted by the intervening wharf, but other calls were nearer to hand, and it was plain that those who defended 'The Key to the Kingdom' were alert and ready.

She heard voices overhead, and guessed that by now she must be level with the guard-house. But above all the hum of talk there arose another voice. It came from some distance and, though lacking its usual robustness, she knew beyond doubt to whom it belonged.

Captain Pepper's succession of bellows, realistically giving the impression that, single-handed, he was valiantly contesting the arrival of the French inch by inch, caused no small commotion. But even as men [began to run shoreward, the skiff was clearing the heads, to be taken seaward nearly half a cable's length where, the force of the ebb spent, she lay, tossed by the lop which tumbled in from the south-west. That quick motion was Caroline Rochefort's present undoing for, whilst her soft hands pulled desperately at chafing rope, the cloak slipped from the lantern and, as the boat canted in the trough, the light was seen by the sentries on both piers.

" Who goes there ? " came the martial hail.

" Answer . . . or I fire."

A sharp report, and the nearby sound not unlike that of a wasp in angry flight ; several dull plops in the water, and one which sent a splash of brine into her face.

Whilst stiff sail-cloth flapped, the alarm was sounded ashore; from both the Castle ramparts and the Western Heights drums began to beat the call to arms.

But now the tiny vessel would shortly cease to be a lifeless fabrication of oak and elm and canvas. Caroline grasped the wickedly flying tiller, thrusting it up. The bow started to pay off, and with the change the sails became lovely firm things.

It was still dark, though deep to the westward a single twinkling star showed that the great bank of low-lying cloud was passing.

Bobbing easterly, the skiff moved in a black void, the eyes of her helmswoman probing the hostile gloom. Ahead was a young man she hoped to save, and astern, closer on her heels than she knew, were those who wrought to mortally different ends.

The *Directions for Navigating throughout the English Channel* as compiled by Mr. Joseph Foss Dessiou, Master, of the Royal Navy, and approved by the Chart-Committee of the Admiralty, stated that the eastern stream was not done until two and three-quarter hours had elapsed from the time of high water at Dover Pier. And the much older *Coasting Pilot*, respectfully dedicated to the Right Honourable and Worshipful Master of the Trinity House of Deptford-Strond by his most humble Servant and Younger Brother, Greenville Collins, Captain of the Royal Navy and Hydrographer in Ordinary to the King's most excellent Majesty, gave courses for the avoiding of the Goodwin Sands and the dangers thereto.

But Caroline Rochefort, conceding her the skill to do so, had no desire to take advantage of the sound precepts expressed by these two gentlemen. Despite their solemn warnings, her resolve was to reach that vast and changing shoal on whose perils every cartographer wrote a noteworthy number of pages.

Since Dover had fallen behind she had been cudgelling her brains to recall the pilotage Charles had instilled into her. When, however, the ruined tower of the church of St. Margaret-at-Cliff, on the promontory of the South Foreland, became discernible in the growing starlight, she had determined her plan. It was perhaps based on rule of thumb, but then the hardy seamen of the Cinque Ports used no other method, and none knew the narrow waters better than they.

The temptation was to steer more to the right, straight for the three lights, triangularly set, which marked the position of the Goodwin Light Vessel on the weather bow. She knew the fat-bellied craft to be less than a mile beyond the North Sand Head, but to follow that shorter course might entail disaster on Bunt Head, the unseen westerly projecting finger of the North Sand.

Instead, she must make expressly towards the yellow gleam of the

North Foreland light. It was a track not without hazard if pursued too far, for beyond the centre of the Downs and the Over Falls were the Cress Ledge and the Brakes, the latter a 'sand four and a half miles long, one almost as treacherous as the Goodwins.

As the skiff danced past Kingsdown, running free, she began to recall those leading marks which Charles had taught her. It was one of these, she knew, which would tell her how nearly she might approach the Brakes before swinging round on a safe course towards her objective.

" The South Foreland light-houses in one." She shook her head— that was for standing clear of the South Sand Head.

" Ash Church on St. Peter's." No, that was for keeping wide of the South Brake black buoy, when bound for Sandwich and the Small Downs.

The breeze was freshening, and backing. A splather of spray damped her cloak, and her slim fingers tightened round the usage-smoothed end of the wooden tiller.

One by one, as she remembered them, she repeated directions as age-old as the churches and castles the Barons had built.

" Upper Deal Mill and Castle in one," she murmured slowly. That, she recollected, gave clearance one way of the shoal on which the *Minerva* had come to grief. But the other way . . .

" *Upper Deal Mill and Castle in one*," she said triumphantly, everything coming back to her.

She glanced over her shoulder. The South Foreland High light was still immediately astern, and dead ahead was the brightening gleam of the North Foreland. Satisfied on this, she shaded her eyes from the lantern and began to search the land, quickly picking up the windmill on an eminence at the back of the town, its sails distinctly outlined against the night sky. But the Castle of Deal, being lower down, was harder to find, and it was not until she chanced to espy the rambling King's Buildings that she knew the exact bearing in which she should look. Then she had both leading marks and, apart from occasionally checking her present course, never took her eyes off them.

" Upper Deal Mill and Castle in one," she murmured again.

Slowly they were coming into line, with the Castle, the nearer, moving more quickly than the other.

When, at last, the sails of the windmill were exactly above the tower of the old castle, she put the tiller down and the skiff, heeling, came round, to begin the run towards the trio of lights worn by the Goodwin Light Vessel.

It was then, with so much accomplished, that Caroline Rochefort received two devastating shocks. The first was when, too intent on further distances to see what was near, she crossed, within an oar's length, the bows of a frigate which was beating out from the man-of-war's anchorage.

"Boat ahoy," came the angry hail. "What the devil . . ."

She heard the sweet hiss of the phosphorescent bow wave and, in the faint light cast by the lantern, saw a figurehead—a warrior in tunic, bare of knee and arm, with helmet and shield, sword held as though he would strike her as she passed beneath.

There was another shout, and then one of the " eyes of the fleet " drew away to take up her share in a patrol which in sum now extended, through the despot's conquests, to the whole of the coastline of Europe.

The skiff was not behaving well. Ill-trimmed, she was carrying appreciable lee helm as she traversed the Gull Stream, the former blur of light ahead now changing rapidly into a clear-cut group of three. The Brakes was now on the lee quarter, and she was reaching to leeward of the broken water which surged over Bunt Head.

Caroline, so near the end of her quest, began to look about her, her heart dancing with excitement when she glimpsed a *coque* off Jamaica Land.

A singing joy permeated her as she put the tiller down.

It was when her little craft was gallantly swinging towards the wind that she thought she noticed, beyond Bunt Head, a boat approaching, with still another, cutter-rigged, further behind.

She supposed first vision had enabled her to see these, but later, strain as she would, she could not find them again. Then it was that she tried the way Charles had proved to her one night—the visualizing of an object by keeping the line of sight slightly to one side of its estimated position.

That trick worked, and with its working Caroline knew how sharp was to be the call.

Through her preoccupation, the skiff was in irons, the sails flapping aimlessly, so much up in the wind that she would not pay off on either tack.

A young woman, strengthened by the need for dispatch, fought with the inert thing.

Soon the little boat was cutting down the intervening waters to Jamaica Land, sailing full and bye, as near to the quickening wind as was possible, with eleven fathoms beneath her keel one moment and then, on the Sand proper, with the ground shoaling to little more than three feet.

On the remote side of that smooth expanse of dread repute two figures were standing, the one tall and the other short.

Caroline Rochefort, nearly at the end of her strength, raised and lowered the light three times.

In reply, reassuring answering signal came from ahead.

3

When men are engaged in a game in which one slip means a quick end, they do not leave the discussion of future plans until the last minute. Thus, when Charles Fagg set down the lantern, Jacques Perrier, immediately grasping its handle, began to drag his stiff leg through the shallow water.

" *Au 'voir, M. Charles,*" he said quietly. " And may the Blessed Virgin guard you."

He was showing the strain under which he was living. The agents of M. Fouché were everywhere in France and in those countries on which the Emperor's iron heel rested ; but nowhere were they so thickly stationed as on the northern coast, watching night and day for the spies of England, and for those amongst their own countrymen who dared outright to aid the enemies of the mighty conqueror.

" And you, Jacques," Charles Fagg replied sincerely, remembering these things as he shoved off the bow of the *coque* which had brought him so far.

" *Merci, M. Charles.*" Jacques, his face sombre, raised his hand in farewell.

Thinking sadly of this friend, Charles meditatively started to walk across the hard sandy surface of Jamaica Land.

It was the voice which aroused him, the thin cry which was snatched away by the wind. He started to run, spurting when he saw a slender figure floundering through the water, a woman in skirts he could swear it was.

" By all that is holy ! " he ejaculated.

They met on the edge, where rippling wavelets had ribbed the sand.

" Caroline ! " he said incredulously.

" Charles," she whispered.

In the silver starshine he could see the perfect oval of her face, and the curls which peeped from beneath the lace-edged hood she was wearing.

" Caroline," his breath caught, so deeply moved was he by the beauty of her.

She leaned weakly against him. " This is no time for explanations, Charles," she laughed shakily, spent with the reaction. " Mr. Toke means to take you, and I fear that he is devilish near."

His night-sight accustomed grey eyes, as he quickly scanned the horizon, saw more than the two craft at which she had pointed.

" And there, also, Caroline," he pointed out grimly, turning her gently about. A long and narrow boat, every inch of canvas on her, with topsail square and stuns'ls set, was rapidly approaching on the off-shore side of the Goodwins, and already had passed the swatchway which separated the North and South Sands.

" 'Tis another Revenue Cutter, Charles," Caroline remarked quietly. " Then they are nigh to being on both sides of us."

" True," he agreed imperturbably.

There was nothing consoling in that brief affirmation, but from then Caroline Rochefort became convinced that all would be well.

The spell of the fabled waste even began to replace her former disquiet, and she glanced curiously over the Sand, this space which, in gale, was the battle-ground of a consuming element that would allow nothing to live therein. Within a few minutes, she knew, it would be relentlessly flooded, covering the object close by her feet. The massive rudder, once part of a fine ship, was half-buried and, shuddering slightly, she was endeavouring to dismiss conjectures which made her flesh creep when . . .

" Charles ! " She all but shrieked, so unexpectedly did he act.

She was in his arms and he was striding through the water, carefully to place her in the skiff, vigorously pushing off before leaping in.

When a course was set, he did a strange thing. From the locker he pulled out a mending-piece of sailcloth, and deftly, using stout fishing-twine, secured it about the lantern, completely masking one side.

" Hold the lantern over the stern, Caroline," he said briefly. " Almost touching the water, and with the lighted side outboard."

Her eyes widened. " But, Charles," she protested, " they will be able to see us, and follow us, and——"

" So they will, Caroline," he observed calmly, eyeing the clouding sky.

More than ever her heart lightened. It was so like other days ; incidents of her childhood and girlhood came back, and with them the vivid recollection of Charles's ever unfailing resource.

Content, she held the lantern as he had told her, in no wise guessing his evasive design, only marking that, although the lantern threw a light astern, the sail-cloth which formed the mask wholly screened the boat. The pursuers, though they might follow that bright pointer, would see not so much as a spar of the craft in which the lantern was carried.

" Take the tiller as well, Caroline," Charles Fagg said quickly, as always assuming that here was no helpless female. " 'Twill be awkward for you, but keep her as she goes."

What he was doing in the darkness forward she did not know, but she heard the protesting splinter of timber, and heard the hard rap of a rope's end as he went about whatever that task might be.

She was in a strange position, half lying over the stern, but even so she once glimpsed the lights of the North and South Forelands, the one on the lee and the other on the weather beam. She shivered a little, recognizing at once that, being so far down, the perilous Brakes must be directly ahead.

" Chilly, m'dear?" Charles's even tone allayed her fears, made her fiercely glad that she had not spoken. " They say at Margate," he continued, " that these keen winds come straight from Spitzbergen, and that cheerless locality is nearly fourteen hundred miles away."

" No more than finger-cold, Charles," she replied gaily, her teeth beginning to chatter.

What happened next passed in a flash. To windward she perceived the sharp stem of a speedy craft bearing down, closing rapidly, and simultaneously she heard Charles's level command.

" The tiller up a fraction more, Caroline," he said, albeit still concerning himself with that bight of rope.

There was an alarmed tumult in the other vessel and a frenzy of action ; to her complete bewilderment she watched the hunter, when so near to effecting its capture, sheer off in sharp fright ; and saw also, not a score yards away, the unmistakable sheen of wet sand.

The keel of the skiff bumped twice before sliding into deeper water.

" You've . . . you've crossed the Brakes, Charles," she gasped.

He laughed. " And stolen an invaluable mile's start from our foulmouthed friends."

" As well as gaining the weather gauge, Charles," she glowed.

The first round was won, but he knew more must be done if the dice were not to be too heavily loaded against the little boat in the race of endurance back home.

Making light comment on the benefit she had acquired from the lessons he had taught her, meantime he directed her to the bringing of the skiff past the Cress Ledge towards those dangerous waters, eastward of Ramsgate, in which were dotted the Stone Bank, the Colborn Sand, and the Querns.

" And now for the worthy Mr. Toke's final discomfiture," Charles Fagg said succinctly, adding, with a flash of his old humour, " 'tis to be hoped."

She saw his contraption. Two oars lashed blade to loom, the turns taking in a flat stretcher, and the whole forming a floating platform on which the lantern was to be secured.

" Charles ! " she exclaimed delightedly.

Whilst rubbing an arm stiffened by her unrelaxing vigil with the light, she intently watched him as he worked dexterously over the side, shifting herself as far as she was able to offset the list of the skiff, over whose gunwale trickles of water were coming.

The last hitch tautened, he released the queer little raft. Gradually it fell astern, sometimes showing its gleam, sometimes not, depending on how the blanked side faced.

Off Sandwich Caroline once again saw its yellow glimmer, a pin-point in the distance.

" Methinks Mr. Toke has not yet seized the villain," she laughed joyously.

" Methinks Mr. Toke will consider those waters immoderately hazardous for his prized new craft," Charles observed dryly.

In that submission Charles was right. The Revenue Officer, fearing for his vessels, decided to place them in strategic position, an operation not easy to achieve immediately. Of his larger bottoms, one was ordered to take station on a line of bearing ' Ramsgate Mill upon the White Way,' cutting off retreat by Sandown and the Small Downs, and the other to patrol the northerly avenue of escape between the Brakes and the Colborn, himself having been put aboard the latter.

As two thin notes from the tower of St. Lawrence's at Ramsgate came faintly across the sea, Mr. Toke decided to send in the small boat. With due pomp, in accordance with the Commissioners' regulations covering both day and night, the signals prior to effecting a capture were made. The Customs pennant was hoisted to the masthead, and at the gaff was flown a blue ensign similarly marked with the castellated Customs badge. Finally a shotted gun boomed out its businesslike warning.

The humiliation of the discovery subsequently made was the real reason, so the Dover preventivemen declared later, which caused their senior officer to intercede with the Revenue Board for a transference from the town.

In this assumption, however, they were some distance from the mark.

4

The skiff was creeping towards the great bank of shingle which fronted Dover's waterways, its stem pointing to the one dark break in the length of the solid mass, the Canyon of youthful times.

Over Dungeness the vault of heaven still had all the blackness of full night, but the other way the pearly hue of morning was beginning to show. At that manifestation of approaching day, there was for the first time anxiety in Charles Fagg's expression, not even those few palpitating moments earlier having disturbed him unduly when, off the northernmost swamp of the South Foreland, an alert shore patrol had put a piece of lead into the boat's counter.

He glanced down at the fragrant hair so near, at the lovely face of the young woman who, for half an hour or more, had been sleeping with her head just below his shoulder ; involuntarily his arm tightened about her, as he thought of the effect upon her reputation should the news of this escapade become public property.

She moved slightly and her eyes opened.

" Yes, Charles ? " she smiled, blushing as soon as she found where she had been resting.

" We are nearly at the end of the journey, Caroline," he told her gently.

She straightened. " 'Twas delicious adventure, Charles," she said softly.

His tone deepened. " 'Twas a gallant act which I swear no other woman in this beleagured isle could have accomplished, Caroline. Nay, not another woman on——"

She sealed his lips with her finger, for she would hear no more such exaggerated talk, she said decidedly. She would not hear another word and . . .

.   The bow grated as the boat fetched up at the entrance to the solitary divide in that barrier of lofty-piled shingle.

Picking her up, Charles Fagg set her ashore. " Stay here, m'dear," he murmured ; " there is one thing I must do."

It was his purpose, within the limits of present possibilities, to destroy any link which, in the remotest degree, might connect her with the events of the night. Bending into the confined space of the skiff, he loosened the plug with short-travelling powerful blows, and, as the sea began to gurgle into the little boat, he took her out, the water in a few paces up to his waist on that steep-to beach.

" You're sinking her, Charles ? " Caroline's voice was horrified, indeed a little miserable when he rejoined her, for she had always loved the tiny craft, and loved it still more on this memorable dawn. " And you are soaking, Charles."

" Yes," he replied tersely.

To gain her father's house without being observed they must eschew all streets and thoroughfares, they must avoid every one of the fortifications and defences in which men watched.

Treading carefully they went up the Canyon, passing to the side of the erection now regularly called ' Rochefort's Folly,' and at the top fringed the Little Pent, where the aroma from Polly Fagg's cherished rosies and peonies was delightful. Thence they made along the Ropewalk towards Butchery Gate and the two branches of Dour which formed The Island. From there they curved wide, passing half-way between the Ordnance yards and the manned Battery adjacent to the New Bridge erected by subscription four years before.

From Mr. Beverley's rope-works Charles reconnoitred the Pent, Indian fashion. Luck was still with them, he mused, when he found the small wherry, a tidal-river craft which obviously had little business in a seaport.

"Here, Caroline," he said quietly, handing her in.

Relieved beyond measure, he began to hum a verse culled from the popular broadsheet, 'The Defence of Dover.'

"Thus shall the British Banners fly, boys,
On Albion's cliffs still raised on high, boys."

"That must be a new one, Charles," she whispered. "'Tis not one I've heard before."

Worn out by days and nights of immense jeopardy, his growing bitterness engulfed him before he was aware of it.

"You'll hear it on the morrow . . . and more to it," he declared harshly, and could have bitten his tongue off when he heard her dismay.

"What is wrong, Charles?" she asked, chilled, so quickly had he altered.

"Nothing," he said wearily. And then apologetically, "I suppose, Caroline, I'm overtired with . . . with various things."

Hurriedly he put an oar over the stern and, fisherman-like, sculled the sharp-pointed craft across the greying surface of the Pent, to bring it alongside the opposite wall, immediately in the rear of Henry Rochefort's house. After helping her ashore he secured the painter to a ring-bolt and then followed her into the familiar old fire-alley.

The eastern light was brightening, and now more clearly he was able to discern the change that an absence of nearly a year had wrought. He stared, struck of a heap by this girl who had become a beautiful young woman, whose blue stains of fatigue beneath a pair of soft eyes could not mar the enchanting loveliness of her.

"You'd . . . you'd not allow me to thank you before, Caroline——" he began lamely.

"Nor shall I now, Charles," she said firmly. "Besides, it has been a most diverting experience and . . ." she dimpled, "I vow that already I am in train to enlist as advance agent for free-trading ventures." That was her own explanation of his activities, for she had noticed that there had been no attempt at the transfer of dutiable goods.

All that bespeaking a young man drawn to a mortally captivating young lady died out of his face. He smiled—strangely too, she thought. "You have still much to learn, m'dear," he asserted lightly.

As she bade him farewell, she was wondering about the hard lines around his mouth, so troubled about the new Charles that she hardly took in his words.

" You have done something to-night I shall never forget," he said slowly. Taking her hand he kissed it. " And something, Caroline," he ended solemnly, " greater than you know."

For a reason she could not define, a lump came into her throat.

" Good-bye, Charles," she murmured, still watching him.

He stepped her up to the outbuilding, and waited until she had climbed into her room.

" Good-night, Charles," she whispered, her face framed in the window.

" Good-night, Caroline," he replied.

When she was gone he lost no time. The wherry was speedily back in the place where he had found it, and that done, he returned by the same route which so little before he and Caroline had traversed.

Entering Little Pent House, he immediately repaired upstairs.

It was full daylight, but in the elliptical-shaped bedroom a candle still burned on the mahogany bureau against which Charles Fagg was sitting, his quill flying over a sheet of paper.

The door opened and John Fagg, in nightshirt and nightcap, came in.

" You are safely back, m'lad," he said, sighing with relief.

Charles smiled outright. " As you see, Father," he laughed.

" You have important news from France ? "

Rounding off the careful report, his son nodded. " Vital . . . and ominous, I fear," he commented soberly, sanding the dispatch before speaking again, this time of Valentine Pepper's misfortune.

Within thirty minutes a specially detailed officer of the garrison cantered out of the Castle on a mettlesome roan mare. He galloped through the Market Place and turned up Biggin Street, in due course thundering over Buckland Bridge, with Barham Down and Canterbury ahead.

His ultimate destination was Downing Street, his errand to the gentleman in whom the country placed its full trust, the statesman who had become the Prime Minister of the land.

Thus Mr. Pitt received the latest information concerning that mighty and overwhelming body of seasoned veterans, the Emperor's *Armée de l' Angleterre*.

There was an immediate Cabinet Meeting, so serious were those rapidly-penned words held to be.

CHAPTER TWO

I

By reason of its 'nature, the news of the attack on Captain Pepper did not become common property.

Which explained why Martha Teddiman, on the second afternoon of her young mistress's return home, had the surprise of her life. Miss Caroline, prior to going to Little Pent House, invited her to a chair in the little drawing-room, and then told her of Valentine's hurt.

Though paling visibly, the housekeeper's mouth remained obstinate. Bestial drunkenness, she declared sharply, was a sin for which there could be little forgiveness, and she for one was not likely to relent.

" No, Martha dear," Caroline Rochefort said firmly. " 'Twas all pretence so that he could better aid Mr. Charles's smuggling ventures."

With humble respects, Martha Teddiman retorted that she didn't credit a word of it, affirming the belief that her young lady was being imposed on by a rascal.

" If 'twas so, why didn't Pepper tell me himself instead of causing me grievous mortification ? " she demanded triumphantly, if less surely.

" Was it his own secret, Martha ? " Caroline suggested gently, little dreaming how soon she herself was to be torn through similar cause.

By now there was uncertainty, even the dawn of some pride, in the housekeeper's expression. But not for all the King's Treasury would she have confessed that secretly she cherished the idea that Valentine was a romantic personality.

" Still, Miss Caroline, Pepper an' me are . . . *was* going to be married," she persisted aloofly.

Her mistress quite ignored the implied change of plan, immediately going on to speak of the care which was being given to Captain Pepper. Dr. Crouch was calling on him once a day, and Keziah Hart, by order of Mrs. Fagg, was visiting the cottage night and morning to perform those tasks best done by womanly hands.

The recital of these humane attentions may have had the result for which it was intended. Assuredly Martha straightway stiffened.

" Keziah Hart, Miss Caroline ? " she snapped.

Miss Rochefort smiled sweetly. " She's a wonderful nurse, I'm sure, Martha," she said consolingly. " So I swear you need have no fear."

No longer was Martha Teddiman's face pallid. Instead, it had taken on a dull, angry flush.

" Fear ! " she snorted. " My only fear, Miss Caroline, is that she won't be there when I goes along. I'll send her packing double quick."

Subsequently it was understood that, as Miss Caroline would be at Little Pent House until the early evening, Martha would have the opportunity of marching along to the end of Snargate Street-over-the-Wall.

And *marching* was the word which best described the housekeeper's progress when, after rounding off various domestic duties, she set forth.

Captain Pepper, three pillows stuffed against his back, was comfortably propped up in his high bunk, from which position he was able to see the Ropewalk and the sunlit sea. The ex-boatswain, head swathed in turban-like bandages, looked less rubicund than usual, but beyond that seemed remarkably cheerful as, stubby clay pipe stuck in his mouth, he puffed away contentedly, dividing his attention between an incoming East Indiaman and a company of boys striving to master the tattoo on the drum.

The minutes of the afternoon ticked away peacefully, the pleasant lullaby of the waves being broken only by a sharp word of command or other indication of martial practice—the distant roll of artillery, the roar of a volley, or the pop of a single musket.

But shortly after St. Mary the Virgin's had struck four the sick man, despite the injunctions he had received, sat bolt upright at the spectacle of a gentleman proceeding towards the Basin. As this unscrupulous individual passed from view there emerged from Captain Pepper's lips a stream of profane language.

" An' when I gets about agin," he rumbled on, eyes darkening, " I'll lace that slimmucks Toke summut terrible . . . an' 'is jackal Foxley. Lay into 'em an' no mistake, by God I will. I'll measure 'em for new jackets an'——"

A most disquieting thought vividly occurred to the enraged boatswain. Why was the Revenue Officer nosing around the boat-dock ? Had he discovered that Mr. Charles's little boat was missing, an' if so for why . . .

In the midst of these uneasy speculations, Martha Teddiman presented herself, and so pleased was he to see her that Valentine Pepper forgot his anxieties.

" Well, Martha, love," he beamed, " 'tis a joy for sore eyes to set 'em on you agin."

Miss Teddiman palpably sneered as she banged a basket on to the table. Within the wickerwork, covered by a snowy napkin, were appetising and beneficial dainties prepared by her own hands, but for the moment that was neither here nor there.

" Meaning, I suppose, that one woman's as good as another ? " she asked dangerously, arms akimbo, her face as though carved in stone.

Luckily the invalid's first impulse, that of passing a particularly bawdy jest, died at birth. Hastily muzzling a rollicking laugh, he inquired guilelessly as to what Martha meant, meantime avoiding her glance by assuming a vast curiosity in an erect figure who was walking briskly in the direction of Amherst's Battery. Mooseer Saval it was . . .

" There's been a female in this house, hasn't there ? " Martha demanded, pressing home the attack. " Morning an' *night* I understand."

Captain Pepper had lost all interest in the Frenchie's visit to friends in the small fort. Despite being self-righteously aware of the impeccability of his own position, he had the very deep conviction that a violent storm was in the offing, one which could be weathered only by the exercise of brilliant seamanship.

" Keziah 'as been along to tidy up," he observed guardedly. " Not . . ." he added ingratiatingly, " that she's the 'ousewife you be, love, as doubtless you can see for yourself."

Martha laughed disagreeably. " An' who axed her to come here ? " was her next threatening question. " Was it Mrs. Fagg or you, Pepper ? "

" Me ? " the boatswain demanded, outraged.

In no wise was there any sign of Miss Teddiman being moved a jot by his vigorous protest.

" You," she confirmed uncompromisingly. " An' I'm having the truth out of you, Pepper. Don't think that——"

A long shuddering breath escaped the occupant of the bunk, his eyes closed wearily, his trembling hand felt for his head.

Very much taken aback before barely having got into her stride, Martha showed no little discomfiture.

" Valentine," she said imperatively. " Be you ill ? "

Dramatically Captain Pepper's head fell back, his arm dropped lifelessly, a bubbling sigh spoke of the weakness of an exhausted body.

" Tedious bad, love," he moaned.

" Valentine ! " This time, as the housekeeper looked for water, the cry was really worried.

The patient feebly began to talk. He was capitulating, of that he felt sure, and if these were to be his last words before dropping anchor in Death's Haven, would his dear Martha heed to them. Never, sin' he had known her, had another woman so much as entered his mind, and . . .

Martha Teddiman, woefully agitated now, had snatched up a ewer. She was going to the pump, she said, and her dear Valentine . . .

" Geneva, love," Captain Pepper broke in hastily, his voice considerably stronger. Only spirits could save him, he added. An' if Martha would climb up and open the corner cupboard she'd find the draught which might stave off early decease.

The scrape of chair legs told him that the behest was being carried out. Cautiously he opened an eye and, after savouring to the limit of safety the sight of a shapely calf, he reclosed it, opening it again when he heard a gurgle not too long sustained.

" To the brim, love," he adjured her weakly.

In due course Captain Pepper recovered from the attack, but thereafter neither made further mention of Keziah Hart, the boatswain because he believed in letting well alone, and the housekeeper because she was conscious that her own deliberate contrariness had made something out of nothing.

Peace and the old understanding established, the pair had a most enjoyable time. Whilst watching Henry Rochefort's green-painted cutter go out to the East Indiaman, Captain Pepper was able, with Martha listening admiringly, to develop his own ideas on the current belief that Boney's next step, before attempting invasion, would be an effort to obtain local naval superiority in the Channel.

" Now don't you get too jawsy, Valentine," Martha said, overpatently anxious, this being after supper when he appeared about to propound again.

The boatswain did chuckle at this. Less than a minute before they had seen a young lady and a gentleman meet on the beach, Miss Caroline coming down the Ropewalk from Little Pent House and M. Saval returning from Amherst's Battery.

" An' what be you peeking at me like that for, love? " Captain Pepper grinned.

Amply was Martha Teddiman's change of heart demonstrated. She blushed, readily confessing she was aching to talk to him of Miss Caroline.

As, to her satisfaction, she did.

When Martha Teddiman's young mistress left Little Pent House she did so by the garden. For once Caroline Rochefort wanted to be alone, to have solitude in which to think out the strangeness she had noticed in Charles.

As she left the Folly behind and headed towards Mr. Beverley's Ropeworks—all unconscious either of the hopeful whistlings of several soldiers or of the smart young officer who, eyeing her admiringly, sought advantage for himself by rebuking his men more loudly than seemed necessary—she started to review the incidents of the early evening.

To begin with, Mr. Fagg had come home and, this being the first time he had seen her, promptly embraced her fondly and kissed her so heartily that Mrs. Fagg laughingly declared she was becoming powerfully jealous.

Then the shipowner, when his wife had gone into the dining-room, had detained her sufficiently just to whisper a few words.

" My thanks, my dear, for what you did for Charles t'other night," he had said, squeezing her elbow. " 'Twas the most courageous——"

Lou had been running down the stairs with a snipping of dress material but, at the sight of her father and Caroline, she halted to lean over the wrought-iron balustrade.

" So, Papa, I discover you in a shocking intrigue," she had declared severely, dancing eyes offsetting the effect of a sternly admonitory finger. " *Here*, in *Mamma's* house, I find you in a most compromising attitude. . . ."

There had been lots of fun about that, with herself boldly asserting that Mr. Fagg was her ideal of a man, and the shipowner, before he made a suitable exit, forthrightly blazoning, in a voice sufficiently strong to reach the ears of the mistress of the house, his regret at being already in the toils of matrimony.

Lou had reached the lowermost step as the front door opened but, at the sight of her brother, at once turned back, her most ridiculous excuse being that she had brought the wrong pattern. Charles's sister had always been a romantic creature but, in her happiness with Jack Woodgate, she was verily . . .

" Caroline," Charles had said.

" Charles," she had replied.

It should have been so wonderful, and yet how very different it was. In that so well-known hall, with its gilt chairs and tiled floor, its cream and white pedestals and urns, she and Charles had behaved as two acquaintances. Perhaps acquaintances friendly disposed to one another, but no more than that.

Only later, before Charles started back to Elizabeth Street, had there been any change. Then, in the gazebo, whilst Mrs. Fagg was excitedly calling the attention of Lou to a budding yellow rose, Charles had spoken of Charlton Fair, a month to that very day.

" 'Twould be nice to go there again, Caroline. Punch and Judy an' the shies, eh ? " For the first time he had grinned broadly, that horribly strained expression momentarily passing.

So glad had she been that he had become himself. "|Let's go then, Charles," she had said eagerly.

Caroline Rochefort bit her lip as she remembered that. He had replied, saying how immensely he would feel himself favoured if permitted to escort her there, but . . . but he was devilish busy nowadays, and being so preoccupied it was mortal difficult for him to make appointments in advance. He would hate to make an arrangement he might not be able to keep.

And then, positively, she had acted most childishly, so Henry Rochefort's daughter thought as she neared the Ordnance Yards. Why had she been so haughty with him, why had she so stupidly remarked that surely it was the lady's privilege to cut her engagements?

" 'Tis true, Caroline," he had instantly agreed.

So swiftly did he take her up, that she had the humiliating feeling he cared little about her proposal. Could it have been otherwise when his sole concern seemed to be the providing of an easy avenue of escape should she desire to take it?

He had smiled slightly, she remembered that, before going on.

" Then I shall expect to take you to Charlton if conditions afford and should it please you when the time comes," he had laughed lightly. " 'Tis a while yet, m'dear, and much water will run under old Buckland Bridge before then."

Puzzling over these incomprehensible things, Caroline turned across the shingle towards Snargate Street-over-the-Wall. It was then that she saw approaching a friend of her father and Louis.

M. Saval gallantly swept low his hat and made a most graceful obedience.

The interpreters attached to the Office of the Port-Agent for Prisoners of War worked in shifts, one week on duty and the next off.

M. Armand Saval, fortunately being possessed of private means, frequently left Dover for a spell during his turn of liberty. To the envy of a large circle of acquaintances in the Cinque Port, he would often announce his intention of spending a few days in London or elsewhere.

On that same afternoon, M. Saval returned to Dover after one such jaunt and, following a meal in his lodgings and a session at the Gaming Club in St. James's Street, decided to pay a visit to a crony, this being the young officer in command of Amherst's Battery.

The gentleman in question was delighted to have the tedium relieved and, in the company of the witty Frenchman, found the pleasant break all too quickly over.

" You flatter me, monsieur," M. Saval smiled easily. " To such degree that later I might perhaps inflict myself on you again."

" *Inflict*, my dear fellow," the artillery lieutenant objected reproachfully. " Damme, you'll be as welcome as the flowers in May."

One of the good-looking Frenchman's most attractive characteristics was to confer his company at an hour when it was most needed. Frequently, bearing with him a bottle of wine and maybe a cold collation, he would join grateful officers in their draughty war stations.

"No more, I beg of you, monsieur," Armand Saval observed deprecatingly, waving aside the compliment. "Expect me as usual around midnight, with all the necessities for a modest repast."

This arrangement made, the pair parted company on the most excellent terms, the artilleryman with a special twinkle in his eye. What that manifestation of amusement meant M. Saval learnt when he had trudged twenty yielding paces or more, about when the younger man started to guffaw heartily.

"Forgotten something, monsieur," he grinned. "Or is it that you think our sentries here are not over-zealous?"

The Frenchman turned, reflected a while, and then snapped his fingers, a rueful twist to the corner of his mouth.

"The password," he muttered. "Sometimes I recollect to ask for it, and sometimes, my frien'——"

"You forget, monsieur," chuckled the other, a ruddy-complexioned, open-faced young fellow.

Thereupon he made it known that a reply of ' *The Cloth of Gold* ' upon challenge would secure immunity, until dawn broke, for any prowler abroad within the liberties of Dover.

A little banter on the subject, and M. Saval proceeded, preoccupied with his thoughts, three parts to the boat-dock before his critical eye espied the female who was approaching.

"*Ma foi !* " he ejaculated, taking in a shapely figure. "Methinks here is one surely made for love."

A thin summer dress and a slight breeze moulding its fabric to her did truly make of Caroline Rochefort a sight to catch any roving male eye. The lines of her limbs, the swelling curves of her young breasts . . .

M. Saval's dark eyes narrowed in recognition. It was unbelievable, but none the less true that, within so short space, a pretty gel had changed into the most bewitching creature . . .

"Mademoiselle . . . Mees Caroline," he cried rapturously. " I saw you in the distance and I vow that, even so far away, I swore I had ne'er seen such dainty loveliness in my life. But now, when near to you . . . mademoiselle, words fail me."

It was a continental custom to kiss a lady's hand for such unconscionable time, so Caroline Rochefort mused, half enlivened and half confused.

"My dear mademoiselle," he murmured, relinquishing his hold.

Never before, she thought, had a man stared at her quite so, and she had a vague feeling of discomfort.

It chanced that M. Saval proposed calling at Snargate Street, and furthermore insisted on arming her over the deep shingle.

On the way thither, much of Caroline's embarrassment faded. M. Saval, it was true, protested too much as to how he was ravished by her, but she now put that down to a temperament strange in English idea. For the rest he proved a most charming conversationalist, apart from the one blunder he made after she had mentioned her visit to Lou.

"Ah, yes, mademoiselle," he said gravely. "'Twill be a mos' unhappy household, I should imagine."

"Unhappy, monsieur?" A pair of brown eyes revealed complete astonishment. "In heaven's name, why?"

It was apparent that her companion regretted an indiscretion, and they were close to her home before he permitted even a hint to escape him.

"You see, mademoiselle, I fear young Mr. Fagg is in disgrace," he allowed reluctantly.

"Charles *unpatriotic*!" Caroline repeated scornfully, when she had heard more of the tale.

The Frenchman shrugged. "After all, mademoiselle, you have an English saying, ' where there is smoke there is a fire.'"

Armand Saval then had his first foretaste of the metal of which Caroline Rochefort was made. Man of the world though he was, he found devastating sting in the snub she gave him.

"You will please remember, sir, that Charles is my friend," she said icily.

He bowed, to hide a face which had taken on an unusual coating of red.

"Your pardon, mademoiselle," he murmured, his voice nevertheless quite controlled and even.

Notwithstanding this setback, M. Saval recovered sufficiently facilely to congratulate Louis Rochefort on a most enchanting sister, and to felicitate Mr. Rochefort on the possession of a most adorable daughter.

Taking little heed of these meaningless protestations, Caroline went straight up to her room and there, standing in the window, looked for long at the Pent.

She was thinking over the last hour or so, little by little connecting Charles's queerness of manner, his many reservations, with the gossip M. Saval had passed on to her. Before Charlton Fair, she concluded, Charles must know she would hear the stupid charges which were being levelled at him.

The pucker of perplexity which had been on her forehead deepened into an unmistakable frown. Her eyes flashed, her foot was stamped.

" The nonny, the chivalrous addle-pate," she said furiously.

A young man was in for trouble. Miss Rochefort was in fine pet on realising the nature of his kindly forethought for her.

2

How the closely guarded secret seeped out it is impossible to say, but within a week of Caroline Rochefort's return home rumours were circulating in the town of Ralph Toke's recent murderous intent.

It was not, however, entirely on this account that John Fagg, on the day after Charles left for the Medway—on legitimate business this time—wrote to Mr. Pitt. There was another cause for the ship-owner's action, it being Charles's little boat.

This the preventivemen had found washed ashore near St. Margaret's Bay, the plug, damning fact, being missing. Moreover, the Revenue Officer had ascertained that the craft had been in the boat dock at nightfall on the same day Caroline had used it.

Ralph Toke, smarting under the most lacerating reverse of his life, was working with furious energy. So, unless a young woman's good name was to be fatally tarnished, unless one of the nation's most successful agents was to be placed under cruel handicap, steps must be taken at once.

The Prime Minister acted with promptitude. On the third day after the shipowner had set his quill to paper, he received an intimation instructing him to be at the Revenue Office at eleven o'clock the next morning.

" An' that, Valentine, will see the end of Toke in Dover," he commented grimly.

The boatswain, now doing light work at Elizabeth Street, was greatly interested. He desired to know whether the master thought that Foxley also would suffer the same fate and, receiving a reply in the affirmative, spoke movingly on the sad lot of those who find themselves out of employment.

John Fagg's shrewd eyes sought the face of his servant. The shipowner decided, nevertheless, that it might be impolitic to follow up a certain train of thought.

Evidently having no inkling of the matter which had brought to Dover two officers of his Service, one being a high official of the Board, Ralph Toke spoke with scant ceremony when John Fagg entered the outer office.

" Whatever your business may be," he began brusquely, " you can betake yourself off. An' speedily."

How this would have developed must be left to the imagination, the point being that at this stage the elderly gentleman from London poked his head from the inner room.

"Is this Mr. Fagg, Mr. Toke?" he asked sternly.

From then Ralph Toke knew himself to be in danger, knew that a noose was closing tight. His darting glances, the manner in which he occasionally would lick his lips, were implicit of that.

Within five minutes he had learnt that he was dismissed from the Revenue Service.

"But, sir, 'tis unjust," he stormed. "You accuse me of conniving at murder . . . and on what, sir? On this man's word, and what is he?"

He was permitted a fair amount of rein, and then the Board Member put a suave question.

"You say Mr. Fagg is a free-trader? How long have you known this, Mr. Toke?"

The Revenue Officer procrastinated, perceiving the drift and the trap beyond.

"How long, sir?" the demand was inexorably repeated.

"Eleven years," Ralph Toke replied sullenly.

The old gentleman testily rapped the table.

"Then why, Mr. Toke," he thundered, "have you not apprehended him if you knew that was the case?"

And that was the end of the feud between Ralph Toke and John Fagg. Two men looking at one another, their gazes so locked that neither saw the squat figure who, for the third time within as many minutes, shadowed the Strond Street window of the room. The shipowner's glance was hard and contemptuous, the eyes of the Revenue Officer, until they fell away, evil, venomous . . . and defeated.

"And now you, Foxley," the autocrat from London boomed.

Clement Foxley opened his mouth, said nothing, and nervously wiped moist hands down his thighs.

Then the torrent gushed forth. Whether or not the Assistant hoped to benefit by giving King's Evidence is a matter for conjecture. If so, never was an effort carried out so whole-heartedly. Not only was every cat let out of the bag but the canvas, as good measure, was turned inside out too. Beginning with his senior's "shoot at sight" order, he ended with a graphic description of the Revenue Officer firing a pistol in the cellar beneath their feet.

"Deplorable," the Member commented fiercely, on the high-pitched ending of the betrayal.

Thereupon Foxley was informed that he would share his senior's fate.

With the withdrawal of the crestfallen pair, John Fagg was introduced to the younger man. It appeared that this middle-aged gentleman was to succeed Mr. Toke. He had a pair of keen but very honest eyes and . . .

" Begging your pardon, sirs, but be the Revenue Officer about ? "

The voice came from Strond Street, with Valentine Pepper peering into the partly open window.

On this unexpected inquiry the august official, very human after all, made a hearty joke relative to an extraordinary speedy call on the new Revenue Officer's services, and Captain Pepper, before contentedly rolling out of sight, respectfully heard that the authority he sought was engaged for the nonce.

" Now, Mr. Fagg," the special choice of the Board opened up pleasantly.

His instructions were, he said, to further Mr. Charles Fagg's splendid work in any way possible. If young Mr. Fagg should ever need the service of the Revenue cutters or . . .

Still another interruption, this time from the next room. First a frightened shout and then a heavy thud on the wainscoting.

" Probably those two sorry rogues fighting, sir," John Fagg observed impassively, deeming it wise not to comment on the struggle now taking place in the sanded passage.

" Humph ! " the Board Member cleared his throat, and over the top of his spectacles glanced from one to the other of his companions.

" Shall we continue, gentlemen," he added blandly.

Conscientiously his suggestion was adhered to.

The folk on Custom House Quay, always a busy thoroughfare, witnessed a piece of the finest sport they could ever hope to see from the moment when Valentine Pepper thrust out of the Revenue Office doorway two men both taller than himself.

For the next two minutes you could hear nothing but feet scurrying along the cobblestones.

" Release me, Pepper," choked Ralph Toke, blood red, not with fury but with the powerful clutch on his neck.

Both he and the screaming Foxley were bent double, forced down by that relentless grasp. Kick as they might, grasp at the boatswain's oaken legs all they could, foot by foot they were taken to the edge of the wharf.

" Now I be going to larn you both," Valentine Pepper gloated.

They are strong men who live on the sea borders of Kent, but the laughter of that highly titillated assembly thinned into a whistle of amazement as they watched a prodigious feat of strength.

" Yes, I'll larn you," the boatswain muttered.

Arms out-thrust at either side, he held his victims away from him, and then, with all the force of a flying boom, he brought their heads together in a sickening crump.

The first impact burst the mighty Mr. Toke's nose and brought an angry bruise to Clement Foxley's forehead ; the second . . . but no more of that. Sufficient is it to say that thrice did flesh and bone meet flesh and bone, and by then these luckless creatures were limp and sorry sights.

" I think they've swooned," Captain Pepper remarked disappointedly.

He would have scratched his head had he not been supporting both gentlemen. As it was, fortunately, he remembered Martha's remedy of not so long before, and he grinned from ear to ear as he eyed the two foot or so of water in the Basin.

" Then we shall 'ave to bring 'em round," he announced gleefully.

He dipped a knee, ducked his shoulder, and Ralph Toke cartwheeled over his back, to come down with mighty splash into the shallow water beneath. Before the ex-Revenue Officer had stumbled to his feet, Clement Foxley had joined him below.

Valentine Pepper dusted his hands. " Settled that 'ere piece of business," he observed, no small satisfaction in him.

Great fists clenched, elbows out, he began to swagger down the quay.

3

It was a lovely day and every road led to the pretty village of Charlton. The fair itself, so said those who could remember similar events pre-war, was but a pale shadow of what it had been in time of peace, but still it was lively enough. There was a captivating hustle and bustle, and most merry makers, the news now being known that Boney's Toulon fleet had put back the same day it sailed, forgot that sharp thrill for the joys of the present.

Outside a large booth a hoarse-voiced barker was drawing a crowd for the next performance.

" Step inside, ladies an' gennelmen," he roared. " See the trickster Signior Napoleone exhibit 'is singular piece of activity, comprising of an 'op, step, an' jump from Italy to Egypt, from Egypt to Paris, from Paris to the coast of England. . . ."

A group consisting of three ladies, a gentleman, and a small boy had already sampled this entertainment, together with divertissements representing the Siege of Acre, ' Down Tyrant Down,' and The Cliffs of Dover, the last with full chorus of tars, soldiers and volunteers, accompanied by drums, trumpets, bassoons and continued discharges of musketry and cannon.

" Signiors Napoleone, Talleyrand and Berthier," howled the perspiring showman, " inform their customers that all the profits of the performance are for *their own sole benefit*."

During the ensuing roar of laughter Master Horatio Rochefort wheedlingly suggested to his ' Aunt ' Caroline that he would appreciate another visit to the monstrosities.

" No, no, dear," Mrs. George Rochefort interposed, shuddering at the recollection of a horribly stunted creature whose face was most hideously malformed.

" Why not, Mamma ? " the young gentleman demanded.

" Because Mamma has said no," Miss Rochefort told him firmly.

Master Horatio muttered some degree of defiance but, beyond that, made little to-do as the small party strolled towards lines of stalls displaying knick-knacks, novelties, draperies and pottery. Caroline was in front, the young man's sticky hand in hers, and behind, Charles Fagg with his sister and aunt. Both Mrs. George and Lou were holding on to Charles, and never so much as when they chanced upon any acquaintances. That was one way of showing their love and belief in him.

" Dancing ! " Horatio grumbled, when they reached the open space at the far end.

Charlton Green was a lovely spot. On its smooth turf many a lively measure was being trod to the airs of the fiddlers, with sparkling-eyed young women, screeching or dignified as varied their dispositions, partnered by brown-faced young men mostly in uniform.

" A shame that an evil man can cause war," the eldest lady said suddenly.

" 'Tis, Aunt Susan," Lou Fagg agreed warmly.

" When people want no more than their useful workaday lives with a few simple pleasures now and then, 'tis monstrous, Lou," Mrs. George went on passionately.

Lou, rather frightened by this unexpected outburst, later preened herself on the brilliant manner in which she had diverted her aunt. The deep sadness passed from Susan Rochefort's face when she heard that Lou thought Horatio, who was showing signs of weariness, should be taken home.

When the others were gone, Charles Fagg and Caroline Rochefort stood a while indecisively, each with lingering traces about them of a laugh Horatio's resentment had evoked.

" You know, Charles," Miss Rochefort said meditatively, nodding towards the houses which fringed the oval, " I think 'twould be most pleasant if you took me up the river."

" I'd love to, m'dear," Charles smiled.

" If you have no other calls upon you, Charles," she observed artlessly.

Charles eyed her but remarked nothing untoward in an expression which was of the most innocent.

For the moment little else passed between them. They reached the road at the edge of the green, and walked past the cottages set back from it, each with its flower-filled garden, every frontage a mass of creeper and rambler rose.

Gradually the hum of voices faded until at last, on Dourside, there was only the murmur of the limpid stream.

" 'Tis so beautiful here, Charles," Caroline said softly, slipping her arm into his with the somewhat unusual observation that, " 'twouldn't be so conspicuous now."

" Conspicuous ? " her companion asked sharply.

" We are hardly as like to be noticed," Miss Rochefort explained patiently.

In Charles Fagg's grey eyes a quick gleam showed. There was something in the wind, he'd be bound.

It was indeed picturesque up the river. Against a background of green trees there was the centuries-old mill, its wheel gently clicking ; a saffron-billed duck in the stream, proudly watching her vigorously paddling young, each of which, as fluffy down breasted the sluggish current, left two widening ripples ; here and there was the swift flash of silver beneath the water, and many a winged flight against the sheer blue of the sky.

Caroline paused at a bend. " 'Twould be nice to sit here, Charles," she suggested, lips pursed thoughtfully.

In that pleasantly shaded, sylvan retreat he spread a handkerchief for her, she meantime pulling off her bonnet, her heart-strings tugging when she glimpsed his face, so worn did it seem to her.

" That's delightful," she cried, in no wise revealing any of that emotion as she smoothed out her dress. On the contrary she forthwith embarked on a most gay recital of her stay in Worcestershire, one which, having seen him only twice in four weeks, she had not been able to favour him with before.

" And now, Charles," she turned to him on ending, her attitude nicely encouraging, " what about yourself ? "

He seemed in no hurry to begin. " I don't know, m'dear, that I have much to say to you," he eventually tried haltingly. " It has been very much the same as any other year, save . . ." he looked directly into her eyes, " that you have been away."

Praying that her cheeks were not as hot as they felt, Caroline Rochefort persisted with her purpose.

"I should have thought you would have had something to say to me to-day, Charles," she declared, her eyebrows moving quizzically.

So singular was this assertion, that he was perceptibly taken aback.

It seemed impossible she should tell him that she was aware of his love for her, so ran his thoughts, having quite forgotten that earlier warning of danger ahead.

"You see, Charles," she went on, apparently heedless of his involuntary start, "I have known you intimately for so long, and I have never thought you were one who would easily change."

Charles Fagg swallowed. "But, Caroline, m'dear," he ejaculated, restraining a single impulse to take her in his arms, an impulse which, in the circumstances about him, he must fight down at all cost.

Her voice was sugary. "So I'm waiting, Charles," she said demurely.

Seldom has a young man been more confounded when, to temporise, he hazarded a teasing question, lulled into false security by her wiles.

"Waiting for what, Caroline?" he smiled.

On her deathbed Elizabeth Rochefort had spoken, proudly and anxiously, of her little daughter's spirit. Never was a mother's judgment more proven. From calm, Caroline swept into a tempestuous little fury.

"For your apology, Charles," she said flamingly. "How dare you behave as you have done? How dare you infer that I might falter in my loyalty to my friends because . . . because a few horrid people——"

She sprang up, blinked once, and then averted her head.

He was by her now. "A few horrid people, Caroline?" he prompted her.

Blindly she shook her head. "Don't, don't, please, ask me that, Charles," she whispered, all yielding again.

His jaw tautened as he took her hand.

"I know," he said quietly. "But we'll not speak on that."

They were looking at one another, her heart beating so loudly she was sure he must hear it, he for her sake fighting off that desire which possessed him.

"Let me say something to you, m'dear." Slowly, reluctantly, he broke into that palpitating trance.

It was just as, for long now, she had imagined this divine moment might be. Soon, oh, so blessed soon, Charles would tell her of his love, and she, so gladly, so joyously, so unreservedly, would give herself to him, supremely confident that never could a woman have had greater bliss, utterly sure that she was passing within the portals of a paradise on earth.

" I'm sorry, mortal sorry, Caroline," he murmured. " But 'twasn't that I doubted your quality."

" No, Charles," she said breathlessly.

" I could never do so," he went on. " You believe that, m'dear? " She nodded. " Yes," she managed.

He began to smile. It wasn't Charles Fagg's old smile, and with its coming a dreadful pain began to steal into her.

" So are we friends again, Caroline ? " he rallied her.

Somehow she forced herself to respond, fiercely willing that never, be it in so little, would she betray herself.

" Of course, Charles," she laughed lightly. " 'Twas so silly of me when all's said and done."

He could not agree on that. " No," he said, his eyes longing, " I won't meet you there. I'd call it noble an' more, m'dear."

Caroline was quite amused by his persistence, but equally bent on not having a lovely afternoon spoiled by harping on such a tiresome subject.

No, she didn't want to go further up the river. It was rather dull after all, and a fair which came but one day a year was worth another round.

" Very well, m'dear," Charles smiled, beneath his playfulness a grim determination to fit himself in with her mood.

In this wise, each feeling constrained to deny every generous impulse of their natures, Caroline Rochefort and Charles Fagg sauntered back to the pleasures of curiosities and a blithsome crowd.

Nine days after Charlton Fair the townsfolk of Dover were ironically amused when they heard that Charles Fagg's name had been drawn for military service under the provisions of the Ballot Act, a measure enacted to scale down the vast numbers of eager volunteers to the insignificant quantity of equipment ready for them.

The following morning the scoundrel called upon the Mayor, and to His Worship tendered the sum of twenty pounds.

Under the provisions of the said Act, the payment of this sum enabled the rogue to go into the ballot again.

Jeremy Nethersole, Kit Crundall and Nicholas Stokes were so disturbed that they visited John Fagg.

Sparks did not fly from that. Nevertheless, the three gentlemen did not derive any satisfaction from the embarrassing meeting which took place at Little Pent House. In short, young Fagg was determined to go his own sorry way, notwithstanding what his father might have to say.

4

In France the preparations for invasion were approaching the peak, relentlessly forced to that conclusion by the unflagging energy of the short, deep-voiced, lined-faced man who meant to make himself master of the world.

Fittingly, to mark the vast progress made, the Emperor held gala on the fifteenth of August. On this day, his birthday, as part of the celebrations, he distributed crosses of the Legion of Honour to those men of the *Armée de l'Angleterre* who had merited the award.

On a plateau in the hills behind Boulogne, 80,000 men were drawn up, a part of the army which would, by the following summer, take the first stride towards the planting of the eagle on the Tower of London.

It was a most striking scene, one which Charles Fagg, some half-mile from the hummock on which was placed the throne of Dagobert, watched with a great deal of interest. The recipients marching up the dozen steps which led to the natural dais ; the two *aides-de-camp* respectively holding the helmet of Du Guesclin and the shield of Bayard, from which the crosses and the ribbons were taken ; the ten score or more banners which whipped in the rising wind, most of them showing dried patches of blood and many a shot-hole, stark emblems of a series of military victories the most dazzling the world had known.

Bonaparte would often pause to indulge in reminiscences with an old campaigner, and already two hours had elapsed since the ceremony began. Colourful as it was, with the passage of time the spectacle came to be rather monotonous, to such extent that the sole Britisher there—forgetting the few renegade Englishmen and a larger company of Irish, both contingents of whom, outwardly at least, were held in special favour by the French authorities—decided to return to the town.

One glance more at those far-ranging, unwavering lines of veterans, the unpalatable though honest concession to their superlative air of warlike efficiency, a final rough computation as to their numbers . . . and Charles carried out his intention.

From that height it was admirably possible to note the changes which so swiftly, considering the immensity of the task, had taken place. The camp of Boulogne sprawled ever wider, the stick and mud huts, divided by parallel avenues, extending beyond the encircling hills. Below, in such short while, the haven had altered unbelievably, now with its greater acreage of waterways, its hundreds of new jetties ready for the minute when regiment after regiment, cavalry, artillery, and foot, would embark for the conquest of a small but obstinately proud island.

There were boats everywhere, packed more tightly than the top layer in a cask of salted herrings. Barges, small brigs, gunboats, pinnaces—every one brand new.

Beyond these, lying outside the quays, though well within the cover of the powerful shore batteries, were larger vessels. Each of these was defended, such was the respect accorded to the cutting-out operations of the English Navy, by iron-spiked out-thrust poles, their decks protected by a canopy of netted cord to prevent any attacker gaining a foothold thereon, and, final proof of nervousness, each ship was secured to the shore by a heavy iron chain.

" Good God ! "   Charles Fagg couldn't resist a grin.   " The Frenchies don't mean them to be taken as prizes."

His gaze went over the sea, to the British squadron patrolling half-way to the horizon, to the frigate which, greatest impertinence of all, had cast anchor within a mile of the Tour d'Odre. Of the wooden walls of England were these, a part of those ever-faithful forces which, less than three weeks before, had compelled the Brest fleet to retreat, thus again foiling the concentration of those components whereby the despot sought to gain temporary superiority in the Channel whilst his enormous flotillas passed over in safety.

By now Charles was striding through the camp, along the Avenue Marengo, his hands negligently thrust into the wide pocket in his leathern blacksmith's apron.

Shortly he came into the little grey town and, as the rain started to fall, turned into a narrow passage in the old quarter, bursting into a snatch of the *Marseillaise* as he did so, his eyes watchful all the time.

The door of the low shed in the cul-de-sac at the end was, he saw, closed.

" *Marchons, marchons,*" he sang gaily, but from then continued the tune in a whistle, switching over with practised ease.

At that signal, as though caught by a gust, the door opened, disclosing Jacques Perrier intent on the paring down of the blade of an oar.

" Ho, Jacques," the lively artisan roared in the vilest Boulognese, " ever working even when you might for once have had an enjoyable afternoon ? "

Loudly Charles continued to talk, between whiles gulping lumps of meat which he had taken from the stewpot the Frenchman had silently indicated. Amidst the chaff that was exchanged the Englishman made known his future movements.

" I'll cross the night after the morrow, Jacques," he once whispered.

The fisherman, whilst scraping together with his feet the shavings which had fallen, nodded comprehensively.

" Methinks a couple of days around Ambleteuse might be worth while," Charles Fagg later said softly, wiping greasy fingers on the tattered coat he had donned.

A word or two more and he was facing the increasing rain.

There was still much to see in this great naval and military arsenal. The Emperor, as fitting *grande finale*, had arranged for the arrival of nearly 1,200 boats, those which had been built in the ports of Holland.

In due course they came, a veritable armada, but it was hardly quite as orderly a homecoming as might have been desired, and for that the impudent frigate could be held to blame. The French admiral-in-command of the first division, seeing the sea-tiger's manœuvres, gave the order to alter course further inshore, and from this instruction minor disaster followed, there being hidden newly erected defence works stretching out from the coast. A dozen craft came up all standing against the under-water barrier, a half-score more were swamped, and many a bobbing head began to make for the beach.

"Damme, that sight's worth many a wet night in a ditch," Charles chuckled.

It was a sentiment which was not, however, re-echoed in a most exalted quarter. The Emperor, violently thrusting aside the young officer who bore the treasured shield of a knight *sans peur et sans reproche*, did not smile. Instead he so fiercely snatched a telescope from the eye of the Minister of Marine that, failing to grasp it properly, it rolled step by step from the level of the ancient throne.

Against the whole gigantic scheme the misfortune to those French craft was trifling, but Napoleon Bonaparte behaved as though out of his senses.

The greatest project of his meteoric career lay before him—in that was the explanation of his frenzy. Every item, however inappreciable, must run to schedule. Then there could be no doubt of the utter subjugation of the nation which stood between him and his rightful destiny.

5

Towards the end of the summer the London Stock Exchange brightened on the intelligence that General Wellesley had routed the Mahratta hosts, the East India Company acquiring the North-West Province as result.

But Dover, within sight of the cliffs of France, had more to ponder over, and continued in that mood until autumn, when the uncertain weather made a descent less likely.

About this time the town was agape with the arrival of the American inventor of such strange devices as plunging boats. Mr.

Fulton, every soul in the district knew it, was staying at the Ship Inn. He had not, it appeared, been able to reach a satisfactory agreement with the French government, and therefore had decided to offer his services to their enemy.

There was much speculation on this, but such conjecture was quickly resolved following an influx of naval officers and high officials.

Mr. Fulton's latest invention was called a torpedo, a floating wooden coffer on which were stowed 40 barrels of powder and a quantity of inflammable material. This infernal engine, trailing a hawser at the end of which was a grapnel made buoyant by cork, was to be towed across the bows of the ship to be destroyed until the flukes of the grapnel engaged with her anchor cable. Thereupon, after a piece of clockwork mechanism had been started, the devastating raft was to be released.

It would swing alongside the doomed craft and then, so its designer deposed, would explode within five to ten minutes.

The Navy, it was rumoured, were bitterly hostile to the use of this contrivance, believing that, if successful, it would be a game two could play at, one which the greatest sea power in the world, for obvious reasons, should not inaugurate.

The townsfolk of Dover were immensely interested in the new weapon to be employed against the shipping off Boulogne.

Hundreds flocked to the Tidal Harbour, approaching the closely-guarded catamarans as near as prudence and the sentries permitted.

Sir Walter Plumbley and his party, of course, were not subjected to the same restrictions as lesser folk.

With the gentleman upon whom for so long had virtually devolved the affairs of the haven were Mr. Henry Rochefort, Miss Caroline Rochefort and M. Saval, all of whom had been moved to wonder when the lieutenant in charge had explained the workings of the deadly instrument.

The afternoon was crisp and bright and, on tendering thanks for the clear exposition, Sir Walter expressed the desire to stroll to the end of the North Pier.

" Eh, Rochefort ? " he grunted, jerking his thumb seaward.

" As you wish, Sir Walter," his host replied courteously.

The Harbour Commissioner, when in Dover nowadays, always stayed in the banker's Snargate Street mansion and, although he bore himself, constantly, as the competent man of affairs, there could be little doubt that, between these two, Mr. Rochefort was the dominant character.

M. Saval crooked his arm. " If you will allow me, mademoiselle," he suggested respectfully.

As though all her life she had been used thus to walking with a most debonair gentleman, Miss Rochefort serenely slipped her hand in.

"Thank you, monsieur," she smiled pleasantly.

From the end of the pier there was much to be seen. Below Archcliffe Point a naval auxiliary was being careened, and Mr. Crundall's premises were alive with workmen, three slips alone being used for the building of tenders to Admiralty order.

"Y'know, Rochefort," Sir Walter rumbled dogmatically, eyeing the strong eastward current which surged fiercely around the extremity of the opposite pier, "that fellow Fagg must be deluded to persist that anything could be made of the haven."

The banker laughed harshly. "A fanatic can oft persuade himself to anything, Sir Walter."

The elder gentleman digested that, and then winked broadly.

"Well, he ain't persuaded the Commissioners yet," he chuckled. "And I'd venture to assert that he never will. Especially nowadays when," he wheezed heartily, "he's rapidly losing the following he once looked like acquiring, if you take my meaning."

Mr. Rochefort did but, his daughter nearing, most adroitly tried to change the subject. Relieved though he had been that no harm had come to Charles Fagg through the former Revenue Officer, he remained sharply disgusted about the young man's unpatriotic attitude. Nevertheless, he felt that if Caroline should hear anything untoward, she was capable of speaking her mind very plainly. In view of the use which, sooner or later, he proposed to make of his companion, such an outcome would be most unfortunate.

"Quite, Sir Walter," he murmured. "An' speaking of the harbour——"

"Wants a damn horse-whipping, that's what the clever young buck needs," the baronet boomed cholerically.

Though not departing from his usual dignified bearing, the banker seized upon the Deal road as diversion, pointing to the turnpike where it curved over Castle Hill. There, in anticipation of what the future might bring, tools were being deposited in readiness for the breaking-up of the surface, and breastworks for defence, as was the case from the coast to London, were being thrown up at every advantageous point.

Sir Walter's bladder-like face sobered on the new thought.

"Aye," he reflected. " 'Tis seven years since the word 'invasion' came on to our tongues, but methinks that within another we shall be facing the actuality. And," he ended devoutly, "let's pray the Frenchies attempt it this time."

" 'Twill settle many accounts," Henry Rochefort agreed grimly.

"And I doubt me not that Bonaparte's trained hordes will be immoderately surprised when they encounter Englishmen on English soil."

"Them as live to tell the tale," the Harbour Commissioner added vehemently, not a semblance of bravado in his fruity voice.

In the rear the talk was of less stern issues. The assemblies at the Royal Oak Rooms had started again, and M. Saval was speaking of the ball which was billed for that day fortnight.

"So I beseech you to be kind to me, mademoiselle," he smiled. "Shall we say the first minuet and——" he shrugged ruefully, " unless it be, mademoiselle, as like it will, that the mos' delightful and charming creature in the ballroom is officially claimed for the opening by some elderly warrior of . . . of, how you say, dizzy rank."

Caroline's eyes danced. "I vow, M. Saval, that you are the most outrageous flatterer I ever, ever heard of."

He stopped, looked down at her, "Mademoiselle," he said earnestly, "I swear that——"

Firmly Miss Rochefort silenced his gallant protestations.

By now the quartet had reached the lock-gates dividing the Tidal Harbour from the Basin, where they passed over the narrow footbridge in single file. On the Cross Wall a special company of volunteers, those whose principles did not allow them to drill on the Sabbath, were being put through their paces, whilst along Crane Street, as further evidence of growing preparedness, a train of half a dozen wagons bumped along, their loads consisting of furze and barrels of tar for the building of more fire-beacons on suitable sites.

Arriving in Snargate Street Sir Walter, his glance lighting on the arched passage to the Grand Military Shaft, decided he would like to inspect the spiral staircase which had been driven vertically through the solid rock.

A few words with the sentry and permission was granted.

"But, hang it, Rochefort," Sir Walter chuckled later when they were entering his host's house, "plucky, maybe, but damned bad business albeit."

This referred to the remarkable feat of equestrian skill performed by Colonel Lord Poynte the previous week. His lordship, as result of a five pound wager with the Lieutenant of the Castle, had ridden a beast worth every penny of two hundred guineas from bottom to top of the echoing shaft.

Louis Rochefort was in the hall, bending over one of the Carolean chairs. His company, beginning that night, had been detailed for a three-day turn of duty, and he was meticulously checking over his pack; comb and brushes, flannel nightcap, silver brandy flask . . .

The Commissioner of Harbour guffawed as, picking up the latter, he unscrewed the stopper and appreciatively sniffed the spirits.

" An old soldier's tip," he roared. " Take a mouthful and rub an equal quantity over the feet when you get a soaking an' you'll be as fit as a fiddle the next morn."

Martha Teddiman came out to speak to Miss Caroline on domestic matters. It was nearly the hour for dinner but M. Saval, in response to Henry Rochefort's pleasantry on this, made a most expressive gesture of impatience, declaring an inability to stay for the meal.

" But I understood you would, my dear Armand," the banker expostulated.

The Frenchman made a long face. " So you did, monsieur," he laughed. " But now to my horror I recollect a promise to visit friends. I fear greatly . . ." his mouth took a humorous and deprecatory twist, " that already they will be looking for my arrival."

It seemed that the counter-attraction of Mr. Fulton's new-fangled torpedoes was responsible for this lapse of memory. By now M. Saval should have been a score miles from Dover and must, unless he was never to live down the discourtesy, make haste to tender his belated apologies.

Gracefully he excused himself, respectfully bidding adieu to Sir Walter and Mr. Rochefort, kissing mademoiselle's hand with the right shade of deference, clapping Louis as one bosom friend to another.

With an undisguised sigh of satisfaction Sir Walter Plumbley entered the dining-room.

As always nowadays, the talk dwelt on the growing shadow. There was disquieting news about the state of Lord Nelson's health. He was reported to be threatened with blindness and it was said he refused nevertheless to leave his post.

" Whilst we have men like him . . ." Henry Rochefort observed warmly.

" And Mr. Pitt, Papa," his daughter affirmed shiningly.

Sir Walter, mouth full, jaws champing, nodded complete agreement.

A toast was drunk to the sailor and statesman upon whose frail shoulders the hopes of their country rested.

A week later, on a pitch-dark night, launches and pinnaces took the torpedoes amidst the 160 larger craft which were anchored outside Boulogne Harbour. The new infernal device did not prove successful, though in some naval quarters the contraption was believed to possess possibilities. Certainly Mr. Fulton declared that a few minor adjustments would bring about the desired result.

Prior to this, Dover had had two nights of excitement, during both of which the drum beat the call to arms. On Louis Rochefort's first period of duty, round one o'clock in the morning, a small, unknown craft was sighted close in to the Castle Cliff. And three days later a French corvette, not long before dawn, loomed near the entrance to the haven, rousing the town with the thunder of her guns, sending her balls splashing into and ricochetting over the Tidal Harbour, one of the missiles, as so reported the commanding officer of Townshend's Battery, dropping within a hairbreadth of the magazine-like catamarans.

For some weeks past there had been anxious surmise as to the reason Napoleon was putting pressure on to Spain, but all that was forgotten in the new sensation.

The town buzzed with talk the following morning. A little more elevation by the Frenchy gunners, some had it, or a fathom more to the right, as others insisted, and most of the harbour would have been destroyed in a mammoth explosion.

A close escape it was, all were united in that belief.

6

In the last month of the year, Mr. Fulton's infernal machines were once more taken over to Boulogne. The attack on Fort Rouge failed dismally—" breaking the windows of the good citizens of Boulogne with English guineas " Bonaparte sarcastically termed the effort.

The Emperor had room for satisfaction in more than this. His ' representations ' to Spain had brought that country to his side, and now 25 sail-of-the-line and 11 frigates were added to the naval forces ranged against Britain.

At war with Spain, the English squadrons, already guarding the Empire and watching many thousands of miles of Europe's coastline, had to be further thinned out, it now being necessary to blockade Cadiz, Cartagena and Ferrol if a great plan of sea and land co-operation was to be thwarted.

The island race, squaring its shoulders, did not laugh so frequently as of yore, and nowhere was this more demonstrated than in the old Cinque Port of Dover.

There, about snowy Christmas time, a strange question began to be asked, a queer crop of rumours started to grow. How, it was demanded, did the gunners of the French corvette know so accurately the location of the American inventor's torpedoes.

How ?

Outside St. Mary the Virgin's after service ; in every parlour ; in every inn ; beneath the Guildhall ; everywhere—the mystery was burningly debated.

CHAPTER THREE

I

ON the eleventh day of January, 1805, the French fleet escaped from Rochefort, the first key move in that intricate strategical concept designed to give the Emperor the few hours' superiority he required in the narrow waters.

Wednesday of the following week, Charles Fagg was slowly riding down the London Road, his business call upon Mr. Stone at the Buckland paper mills completed. It was late afternoon and darkness had largely fallen over a bare wintry landscape on which patches of snow still remained. The thaw wind blew chill, and the rutted highway was deep in icy, brown-puddled mud.

" Come, boy," Charles muttered.

The Black Horse . . . the Maison Dieu and the bellows-forced blue-gold flames lighting up the forge opposite . . . Biggin Street . . . St. Mary the Virgin's, where Mr. Philip Virgile's raised lanthorn illuminated the corkcutter's ever worried face, the heavily-studded door and the Volunteer notice which was affixed to it.

Nearing the end of Bench Street the rider hesitated, but decided upon bedding-down his beast before proceeding to the warehouse. Often, when he had business as reasonable excuse, Charles would spend most of the evening in his father's room at Elizabeth Street. Dried driftwood generously thrown on to the fire, it was cosy there. Besides, it took him from his mother, who latterly had developed the habit of asking the most infernally awkward questions.

These gloomy preoccupations in mind, Charles turned along Town Wall Street.

After *Toke's Quality* had been tended, given his feed, and settled for the night, Charles Fagg crossed the street to enter his home.

About half-past six he set out again.

The wind was backing and, should it shift a point or so more, there were signs of further frost, with treacherous conditions underfoot by the morning.

Passing New Bridge, in the yellow light cast by the flickering oil-lamp on the corner of Bench Street, Charles encountered Mr. Thomas Bullack, but the tanner, in response to the " good-night " he received, did no more than glower in reply.

His mouth hard, the young man continued along Snargate Street, and had reached the drawing-room windows of Mr. Rochefort's residence when the front door of the mansion was opened.

"Howsomever, I don't think you should, Miss Caroline," he heard Martha Teddiman declare tartly. "An' if Mr. Louis or your papa was in I should fetch them to you."

Stepping from the lighted rectangle was the daughter of the house, well wrapped up, with the housekeeper evidently of the temper to pursue the argument on to the pavement and beyond.

Being thoroughly worked up, Martha, on recognising the passer-by, immediately gave him chapter and verse. It was all very well, she grumbled crossly, for Miss Caroline to say that someone would see her home from the glee party at Mr. Waade's, *but* she had to get there first.

"The place is that full of soldiers, Mr. Charles——"

Caroline laughed. "They wouldn't hurt me, frightened old silly."

"Oh, they're all right, Martha," Charles smiled on being appealed to. "Though I dare say when they've had a pot too much of our Kentish ale——"

"That isn't until much later, Charles," Caroline dimpled.

Despite her remonstrances he insisted upon escorting her to the Market Place, and the housekeeper, fears assuaged, thankfully closed the door when they started off.

"And where were you going, Charles?" Miss Rochefort asked.

He told her; she, in reply, teasingly charged him with being as assiduous a business man as was her own brother.

"My ambition, m'dear," he gravely informed her.

That was how Charles Fagg and Caroline Rochefort, meeting these days, conducted themselves. Two very good friends, perhaps not quite in the manner of old times, for reticences might be perceived here and there. But good friends always.

So on that January evening they continued, sometimes talking gaily, sometimes silent awhile, when there would be only the sounds of the moaning wind, the metallic chink of Caroline's pattens, and the squelchy crunch of the crisping slosh under Charles's heavy boots.

The house of the Clerk of the Cheque was on the eastern side of the Market Place, four doors from Mr. Adcock's Printing Office. It was Elizabethan, finely gabled, with a pleasant garden in the rear running down to the Dour, and a magnificent view, in daylight, of the Castle.

As Charles grasped the knocker he was remarking that, having discharged the cargo, he would now, being the industrious apprentice, betake himself off, when a young man joined them—or rather joined Miss Rochefort, for he treated her as though she were alone—on the shallow step.

" Caroline ! " he exclaimed delightedly. " I feared that from what Louis said you would not be here to-night."

This was one of the Town Clerk's sons, a gentleman who was an ensign in his father's company, the uniform of which rank he wore with patent satisfaction.

The door was opened by a girl and, in the shaft of light which came out, three things might have been seen. There was young Mr. Stratton's vaguely offensive half-smile, Miss Rochefort's rosy flush of temper, and the new set of Charles Fagg's firm jaw.

Young Mr. Stratton, a pretty female being there, was apparently of the persuasion to reveal himself as a most dashing fellow.

" You here, Fagg ? " he drawled, his manner immensely surprised. " *You're* not . . . er . . . joining us in the singing of *martial* songs ? "

Caroline Rochefort, feeling as though everything in the world had been stilled, saw the unspoken contest which followed. A blusterer uneasily striving to appear strong in the presence of one stronger— Charles steadily contemplating a young officer who soon failed to meet that hard, though mocking, challenge.

" I think," Charles said, smiling slightly as he turned to her, " that I must not leave you until I have ensured your safety indoors. These hell-for-leather macaronis . . ." Sadly he shook his head.

The face of the Town Clerk's son was the colour of his uniform coat.

" Damme, Fagg," he began furiously. " Either you'll——"

" No, Charles, there's no need for you to come in," Caroline whispered quickly, her gloved hand pressing on his sleeve. " And," she went on hurriedly, " thank you so, so much for——"

A glint had come into Charles's eyes. " I must do my full duty, m'dear," he rebuked her solemnly.

The servant closed the door behind them and, in the manner in which she had been carefully trained by her mistress, relieved two of the visitors of outer clothing. Her task done, she risked another glance at Mr. Charles Fagg and, once out of sight of the hall, ran into the kitchen with her news.

Around the drawing-room piano, on which the Waade girl was performing with a heavy hand, there was a tightly-packed crowd of young people.

" Once again," Miss Waade's brother shouted hoarsely. " And then . . ." The sideways jerk of his head undoubtedly referred to the lemonade and red and white negus on the table. " Ready . . . one, two, *three*——"

The pianist was nearly submerged as those in the rear, trying to read the words, pressed forward, and up to the beams went the resounding song, one which had been inspired by a French broadsheet of some time before.

> " For their officers and baggage in balloons are to come over,
> And Bonaparte drop in his camp just this side of Dover.
> Oh ! the Bugabos, how they will make us all to stare,
> Camps a swimming in the water and castles in the air.
>
> A hundred thousand men for him to lose is only a trifle,
> He is determined to invade old England for to rifle.
> Altho' the Kings of Europe crawl to him for alliance,
> Britannia's son alones bids the Corsican defiance ! "

The last line heroically dying, Captain Nethersole's one and only girl raised a wail. The daughter of one of the most important members of the Fellowship of the Passage was very much like her own irrational mother.

" 'Twould be terrible if the Bugabos came here," she chattered away, baby-eyeing the menfolk. " I mean what should we gels do ? "

There was a roar of laughter. Many novel suggestions were made for Miss Nethersole's well-being, most of which immensely agitated the distressed damsel, though it was noticeable that she invariably recovered in time for the next sally.

The fun might have lasted much longer had it not been for the remark made by young Mr. Elam. Every eye went to him, and the replenishing of a trayful of glasses was momentarily suspended.

" Wouldn't surprise me," the Master of Lodesmen's son observed pregnantly, " if a very proper refuge could be found at Little Pent House."

" *Little Pent House !* " one young woman gasped.

" At Lou Fagg's ? " another, wide-eyed, ejaculated.

Young Elam was avidly assailed for information.

" Well," he said airily, " in the first place, before Ralph Toke left the town——"

" Him ! " snorted ' Colonel ' Breton. " Forget that damn liar."

The cause of the sensation became slightly aggrieved.

" As you will, Breton," he exclaimed nastily. " But there's a parcel of incidents you can't so easily put aside."

Then, rapidly, he outlined the evidence. The day, he said, that Mr. Fulton's torpedoes were assembled in the harbour Charles Fagg left the town ostensibly on business, but that same night Fagg was recognised half-way round the Cliff beach, off which later an unknown craft was fired upon.

" And . . ." he snapped, " three nights after that the Frenchies made their attack. Putting two and two together——"

There was pandemonium, with hot partisanship from the few and, so is human nature, malicious glee from others.

" After this revelation," shouted young Mr. Waade, trying to quell the babel. " After . . . this . . . revelation . . ." he bawled.

Order came near to being restored, and Oliver Waade's son was able to suggest that a toast would be a fine mouth sweetener. Indeed, he was actually framing his first word when his near-sighted eyes chanced on the door. His jaw dropped, his Adam's apple moved spasmodically.

" Caroline," he said weakly.

Charles Fagg's bearing was admirably expressionless if he had gathered much whilst standing aside to allow first Caroline and then young Stratton to enter the suddenly hushed room. On the other hand, considering he was an uninvited guest, his subsequent conduct was assuredly strange.

Young Waade had a most sickly smile when, after two more glasses only had been filled, he raised his own.

" A toast, ladies and gentlemen," he began uncertainly.

Caroline Rochefort's amused, but perhaps just so slightly tremulous, laugh broke in on him.

" Oh, Charles," she smiled gaily, " do take my glass, an' Jim, as you're nearest, 'twill be mortal kind of you to bring me another."

" Most accommodating of you, m'dear," Charles thanked her courteously, accepting her offer and quite ignoring the really courteous thing to do.

' Colonel ' Breton had done as he was bade, and young Mr. Waade, too flummoxed to know how to act, carried out the intention he had announced.

" May . . . may Bonaparte and all his party meet the fate of Pharoah in the Red Sea," he proclaimed fervently.

Heads went back, with many pairs of eyes, intent on Charles Fagg, developing a squint rivalling that of Captain Pepper.

" 'Tis to be hoped so," Charles observed pleasantly enough.

To the amazement of them all, though to the gratification of a few unshaken friends, he sauntered up to the table, there calmly to pour another measure for himself.

" Help yourself, Fagg," the outraged young Waade said witheringly.

" Thanks, Waade," the unwelcome caller nodded.

Later, especially when Caroline Rochefort was not within hearing, the son of the Clerk of the Cheque was thoroughly abused. Why hadn't he, it was asked, ordered Fagg out of the house ? Why had he permitted him . . .

But, in the meantime, picking up the decanter, Charles made a round with the wine.

"Caroline, m'dear," he laughed, "I vow you are mighty unsteady of hand."

From her he continued. A polite word here, a light jest there, the company too stupefied to do little more than eye him dumbly whilst permitting their glasses to be filled.

"Damme, Fagg, what the devil . . ." young Mr. Wade succeeded in stuttering, a protest which was unheeded everywhere.

The decanter replaced, Charles Fagg turned, a tall, fair-haired young man who held himself more easily than they who gaped at him.

"A toast, ladies and gentlemen," his voice rang out. "I'll give you a toast."

He allowed a telling moment whilst taking up position in the centre of the room.

"My friends," he smiled, arm raised, his grey eyes quizzically ranging them, "I give you a toast. 'Tis this . . . May Britain never want for sons to volunteer their services." And, before the still discomfited Mr. Stratton could realise what was afoot, his glass made a silvery tinkle against that gentleman's.

There was an audible gasp. Miss Nethersole hardly knew what to do, swoon with the tenseness of the circumstances or speak admiringly to Charles on his doing.

Carefully setting down an emptied glass, Charles Fagg made a most commendable leg to the assembly.

Then the door closed.

2

Throughout dinner John Fagg acted as though in a daydream, and more and more did his wife's face grow troubled as, between increasingly toying with her food, she spooned out from the tureens when necessary. She wasn't imagining things, Polly Fagg thought miserably, for more than once she had seen her daughter and sister-in-law glance towards the top of the table. Even Horatio looked woebegone, and it took a great deal to get that young gentleman down.

"Uncle John," the small boy tried again as the shipowner pushed back his chair, "do you think Captain Pepper would make me a boat?"

John Fagg relaxed, smiled briefly, suggested that Horatio should put the question direct, and thereupon left the dining-room, going immediately into the parlour. Once there, he took out his keys and, unlocking the lower drawer of his writing-table, lifted out many papers and books—a mass of information which, through his careful study of them, had made him a real authority on the seaport of his birth.

" Mmmm," he muttered, beginning his search.

There were maps of Dover throughout the ages ; copies of plans with subject matter made by long-dead engineers ; and extracts from the ancient Customals of the Cinque Ports.

When Mrs. Fagg came in her husband did not hear her. He was flicking over the leaves of a volume, rapidly to begin with, but slowly when he neared the place likely to give him the line which had flashed into his mind as he was walking home.

" Ah, now here we are," he grunted. " The Court of Brotherhood and Guestling . . . part played in obtaining an increased portion of the Passing Tolls . . . see Rolls of——"

" John, dear," Polly Fagg opened urgently, " I'm sick of it too."

Her husband, licking his thumb in readiness whilst scanning the concluding paragraph of a page, was startled out of his concentration.

" Eh ! " he ejaculated.

She was still standing against the door, an attitude in itself unusual. Her hands were behind her, and from her worried expression, from the slight movement of her plump elbows, it was not difficult to deduce that she was nervously twisting a handkerchief.

" I know you're worrying about Charles, John," she said miserably.

Her husband stared. "About Charles ? " he repeated in some astonishment.

" Yes . . . yes," Polly Fagg nodded.

Then her story came, a long one. It wasn't that her friends said anything wrong about Charles, but rather that they most undeniably shunned any mention of him.

" An' . . . an', John, I sense there must be something happening that I don't know, that they wouldn't speak to me of. 'Tis queer, too, that such as Mrs. Stratton and Mrs. Braems constantly go out of their way to ask if Charles is away again. An' you know, John, he's been from here nearly three weeks this time, an' when you did the business at Rochester an' so on you *never* stayed away so long."

The shipowner tried to laugh it off. She was dreaming, she was having visions, she was fancying all this.

" No, John," she told him decidedly, her lips starting to quiver.

A half-lie spoken by one whose veracity is unquestioned can be most effective. John Fagg, his arm comfortingly round his wife, did his best to reassure her. Dover folk, he said, liked to be acquainted with everybody's affairs, and if they were baulked tended to be unpleasant about it. She mustn't give another thought to what the cats might hint or say. Charles was out of the town often, it was true, but he went on most important business, business which did not concern inquisitive people.

Mrs. Fagg was brightening, but she had still a shot in the locker.

" Then why have you been fretting about him all the dinner-time, John ? " she asked.

" I haven't, my dear," he retorted, twinkling.

On that, like a schoolboy, he explained the new move he had thought out for the harbour, one he considered of such consequence that, before going to the warehouse, he intended calling at the Antwerp, where he hoped to find Jeremy Nethersole and one or two more.

Such relief showed on Mrs. Fagg's face as she went with him to the fore-door.

" 'Twas better telling you than letting it grow on me, John," she said smilingly, the much-crumpled handkerchief out of sight.

" Much, Polly love," her husband chuckled, giving her an affectionate kiss.

The salutation repeated, John Fagg briskly set out to see those friends who equally embraced the haven to heart.

It was surprising how often Dover people, ladies and children included, now glanced at the sky. They, traditionally weather-wise, knew just the slant of wind which could bring the French flotillas over from Boulogne. Night and morning, throughout the day, times innumerable, the sign was sought which might indicate the coming of a trial to death.

Remarking the phenomenon, John Fagg crossed the Market Place towards the Antwerp.

In the broad passage of the inn two elderly gentlemen, one as mentor and the other as pupil, were practising drill.

" As you were," barked Mr. Jephrez Baker.

Smartly Mr. Matthew Adcock grounded the butt of his musket, thereupon smugly expressing the belief that in this exercise he would pass muster.

The tallow-chandler, who was parading with his weapon at the slope, halted himself with a smart click of his heels, then right-turned with a most martial one-two.

" Pass muster ! " he said sarcastically, running his glance sourly over the master-printer's generous mid-portion. " With a figger like yours, Matthew, you'll have to be puffect unless you want to call attention to yourself. Why, damme, when you're lining up with the company you'll have to take a full pace to the rear to make your belly level with the rest."

" Here, Jephrez," Mr. Adcock observed indignantly.

" No talking in the ranks, Adcock," Mr. Baker roared.

The next instruction consisted of ' Make Ready . . . Present . . . Fire,' and when John Fagg passed in to the parlour the old candle-maker had one knee on the sawdust-strewn stone floor. He was squinting ferociously along the sights, a bead drawn on the tall landing window.

" 'Afternoon, John," Mr. Breton greeted the shipowner.

" Just the man I want to see, Dick," John Fagg said eagerly, taking the Harbour-master's arm.

He saw that both Kit Crundall and Nicholas Stokes were near the fireplace, and that way he drew his companion.

The room was full and, with tongues wagging thirteen to the dozen, one large group were noisily grumbling about the state of trade and the increase in taxation ; though, contrarily, when the conversation came to Napoleon's recent overtures for peace, all were at one in agreeing that " Billy " Pitt had done well in refusing to be tricked into a position designed only to provide the despot with a refusal which, craftily shown to his war-weary people, might further goad them on.

" Aye, I think we can safely leave it to ' Billy,' " Mr. Crundall remarked warmly, shortly after John Fagg and Dick Breton had joined them on the settle.

" To be sure, Kit," agreed Nicholas Stokes.

For a time, leisurely savouring their Virginia tobacco and Rum Nantz, the four gentlemen debated the political and military situation. The Prime Minister had formed a Third Coalition with Russia, Austria and Sweden and, in a speech not many days old, had announced that the country had 600,000 men ready to take the field.

" Vastly different from the 30,000 we started out with," the Harbourmaster commented, " though Mr. Pitt sounded as if he reproached himself."

More talk on that, and then grave and anxious surmise on the naval position. Less than a month before Admiral Villeneuve's Toulon fleet had sailed and, although compelled to put back, the threat remained.

The Clerk of the Passage moved his head dubiously.

" Never has this land been in a more dangerous predicament than now," he remarked very seriously.

" No," affirmed Kit Crundall soberly.

None of them spoke awhile, each solemnly reflecting on the momentousness of the pending struggle which faced the nation.

" If we succumb 'tis vile slavery for us," Mr. Breton observed quietly. " But . . ." he quoted the line of a popular song, ". . . if we ' bear our father's virtues as our own ' I'll warrant we'll leave to our grandchildren a tale that will be worth the telling."

Nicholas Stokes's fist thumped on to the table, setting dancing the glasses of fine French brandy.

" Aye, an' we'll do that, I'm thinking, an' not alone about here. Half England's sleeping with a pistol or a cudgel under its pillow, and I swear they'll be used should the need arise."

" They will, Nick," John Fagg agreed heartily.

On this note of high endeavour, affairs of state were relinquished, Mr. Crundall nodding to the folio of papers which the shipowner, earlier, had stuffed into a side pocket.

" What have you got there, John ? " he laughed. " Plans for building a Folly on Pentside ? "

" Behind Henry Rochefort's house you're meaning, Kit ? " grinned the Clerk of the Passage.

Even whilst responding suitably, John Fagg made haste in shifting the glasses to one side.

" Listen to this," he began enthusiastically, flattening out the sheet he had opened.

When he had finished reading he recalled to them an earlier suggestion he had made, one relative to the Passing Tolls.

" You see for yourselves," he went on rapidly, " that it proves a majority of townsfolk can compel the Notary of the Court of Brother-hood and Guestling to act. And from that . . ."

They all were aware that the harbour, shortly after Christmas, had suffered further damage. It was known, too, that the Harbour Commissioners had declared their inability to provide additional funds.

" Unless money is spent at once, there is a risk we won't have a haven worth fighting for," John Fagg urged. " I'll admit our previous objection that even if we did succeed in obtaining a greater allocation from the Passing Tolls we should have no say in the spending of the extra income, but for the greater good we must suffer that."

Mr. Stokes glanced surreptitiously at Mr. Crundall before he spoke.

" 'Twould mean the summoning of a town meeting, John," he remarked guardedly.

The shipowner was ready for that. Already, he said ardently, he had thought out the procedure. He'd decided, if it met their approval, to call on Hugo Stratton in the Town Clerk's capacity of Notary to the Court of Brotherhood and Guestling, and request him . . .

Mr. Crundall, the slightest embarrassment on his face, was finger-ing his chin.

" I don't think I'd do that if I were you, John," he objected awkwardly. " What say you two ? "

The Harbour-master, shuffling uncomfortably, put forward the view that, with the state of the war being as it was, perhaps such an attempt would be inopportune.

The Clerk of the Passage, who could think of no excuse save the one he did not wish to bring forward, hastily agreed with Dick Breton. Hardly the time, he summed up obscurely, carefully avoiding the shipowner's searching glance.

" You think not ? " John Fagg said quietly.

Then, after slowly folding up his papers, he looked from one to the other of them.

" You three," he began evenly, " are old friends of mine and, for that reason, I'm entitled to plain speech from you. What's agin my thinking of calling a town meeting ? "

" Nay, John," Nicholas Stokes laughed weakly. " Why——"

" What's agin it ? " the shipowner repeated inexorably.

Afterwards, Kit Crundall told his wife he would not go through that five minutes again for five golden guineas. It was one of the most unpleasant experiences of his life.

" So 'tis Charles, is it ? " that young man's father murmured. " And am I to take it that I share the odium which I understand is falling on him."

The Harbour-master earnestly dissented.

" No, not that, John," he urged. " But there's dubious tales —as thick as hops they be—going about the lad, an' that's bound to cause mud-throwing elsewhere."

" I see, Dick," John Fagg remarked tonelessly. " Well . . ." he began to rise, " 'tis time for me to get along to Elizabeth Street."

Those three men, who had known him since boyhood, made attempt at parting consolation. They were clumsy, hopelessly so, but luckily for them there was diversion, a report in the inn which sounded as though the first of the French invaders had arrived.

A mass rush to the outer passage followed.

Mr. Jephrez Baker, a look of mixed confusion and surprise on his face, still knelt on the floor, wisps of smoke emerging from the barrel of his musket, the trigger of which he had pulled at the third full-scale demonstration.

" I'd forgotten as I'd just loaded it," he muttered, his previous whole-hearted exultation, when he had opened his powder-horn in exposition of the real thing, all vanished in the present deflation.

A hanging lantern was shattered beyond repair, a servant girl was in hysterics, and Mr. Matthew Adcock's toothless grin extended from ear to ear.

" Damn nice sojer you are, Jephrez," he rocked. " Not fit to be trusted with a dangerous weppin, I reckon.

Stepping over the glass which littered the place, pushing through the highly amused throng, John Fagg found the fresh air and the solitude he badly needed.

3

The moon was coming up, and the great military camp of Boulogne less than two leagues distant. Behind were many towns crammed with the armed forces of France—Cambrai, Peronne and Douay, packed with horse and foot ; Evreux and Havre, the troops they housed prepared for embarkation immediately the signal was given ; the thousands of veterans at Rouen ready for the word to move at thirty minutes' notice.

Every barn was occupied, and Charles Fagg, knowing this, perforce sought elsewhere for his night's rest, finding it in the damp undergrowth of a copse by the side of the road.

Wearily he sat down, too spent yet to ease his feet by loosening his boots.

" At least 'tis not raining for once," he muttered.

Shortly, he began to eat the remainder of the food he had bought two days before in Lille.

To the west, towards St. Omer, the blast from a furnace threw a light to the sky and nearer, taking advantage of the brightening night, hammer and saw began to be plied, ever adding to the already vast store of the Emperor's military equipment.

Refreshed by a few handscoops of water from a tiny rivulet, Charles returned to his resting-place and there, in the soft light which came through the tree-tops, peered at the Paris newspaper he had bought in the French capital.

Tired as he was, he could not resist a smile as he perused the sheet, so cunningly misleading were many of the articles. Assuredly the Minister of Police—for he had learnt that M. Fouché issued directions to the editors—knew how to indoctrinate the common people to continued war.

" We shall see, your Imperial Majesty," he mumbled, before stretching himself out to sleep.

Before the waning of the moon he was up, and was passing Pont-de-Briques, Napoleon's château and advanced headquarters, as full dawn arrived.

In another hiding-place he slept until midday. Then he started for the town of Boulogne, little more than a mile away.

From the lowly dwellings by the sea-verge a humble funeral procession was setting out—a crude wooden box on a two-wheeled fishmarket handcart, and a few tattered mourners.

Jacques Perrier, sentenced by summary court two days before, was being laid to rest. The charge brought against him had been that of trafficking with an unknown Englishman, and for that offence his thin breast had been pierced by the bullets of a firing-squad, his broken body left, as example, where it had fallen.

M. Fouché's secret police had added another victim to the toll they had taken through France and the countries which groaned beneath the Emperor's hordes.

No longer did Valentine Pepper sail out to Jamaica Land, the absences of his master's son being of too uncertain duration for any pre-arrangement to be made.

So Charles Fagg, in the boat he had so miraculously found, in the craft which, aided by good providence, he had seized so effortlessly, steered for Dover, his face marble-seeming in the moonlight, his eyes far away.

It was not of his escape that he was thinking, not even of a link with France which, breaking down so cruelly, might have brought a quick end for himself.

His thoughts were of Jacques—Jacques, to whom contentment would have meant the passing of his days in the simple pursuits which brought in an honest livelihood ; Jacques, who believed not in conquest ; Jacques, whose faith was that all men are free.

Charles, shivering slightly, stared at the great orb of the silver moon. His tightly compressed lips moved, he dashed the back of his hand across his eyes.

" You have not died in vain, Jacques," he murmured. " An' may God rest your soul, as I know He will."

The stars of the night winked in silent benediction.

4

The spring sun shone warmly on the front of Mr. Rochefort's bank in Snargate Street-over-the-Wall, but at the rear of the premises, in the senior partner's room, the crackling fire was welcome.

Henry Rochefort and his son had had a busy morning. There had been the checking of the specie for delivery to the China-bound merchantman which was expected in the bay during the course of the afternoon, and the examination of a consignment from the Bank of England of the new George III silver dollars whose usage, it was hoped, would prevent further forgeries.

These major activities completed, Louis glanced at his watch.

" Time for your drill, my boy," Mr. Rochefort observed, looking up gravely from a news dispatch.

" It is, Papa," his son replied grimly.

The information that morning was serious, its import and implication tremendous. Admiral Villeneuve, with eleven sail-of-the-line, had at last slipped out of Toulon and had successfully reached Cadiz, thus augmenting his forces by six more finely found Spanish vessels.

When the junior partner had gone, Matthew Godspenny, coming in with a sheaf of advices, ventured a word on the information which already was being posted through the land as fast as the endurance of man and his beast permitted.

" Methinks, sir, that we can place our confidence in Lord Nelson," the head clerk submitted respectfully.

" I'm sure on't, Mr. Godspenny," his employer concurred heart-eningly.

But when the banker was once more alone he began to pace the room. Within the next few months the crisis, he felt sure, would come, and although he had always had a keen nose for a profit, it was not to thoughts of gain that he was devoting himself. The country which had given shelter to his great-grandfather was in the direst peril— the solemnity of his expression revealed the extent of his belief that events of the days ahead would resolve whether mankind moved forward in darkness or light.

" Yes," he murmured.

Now he was standing at the window, staring at one of John Fagg's craft which was secured alongside Custom House Quay. From her, before the falling tide took her too low, whip and outhaul were being energetically employed in hoisting out 12 and 24-pounder guns for the miniature forts, Martello Towers it was rumoured they were to be called, the foundations for which had been dug in many places along the Kent coast.

Henry Rochefort started to smile, a look of pride in his fine eyes when, near the Cross Wall, he saw a slender young woman, shopping-basket on arm, walking towards Custom House Quay.

He fondly watched his daughter, delighting in the many salutations she received, following her progress to the moment when, near the Royal Victualling Yard, she encountered a tall young man.

After that the banker's demeanour changed. There was a concern about him as, leaving the pleasant view over the Basin, he took a slow turn along his room, arms behind his back and head bent thoughtfully.

He must speak to Caroline, he reflected heavily. There was

scandal surrounding Charles Fagg, perhaps more than that, for the word 'traitor' had been used in more than one quarter. The talk about John Fagg's son had reached ugly proportions, and he knew that the Mayor, Robert Spisour, and the Town Clerk had formed themselves into a deputation of two, their intention to interview the Officer Commanding the Castle Garrison.

" 'Twon't do," he muttered.

Impulsively he snatched up the spy-glass which, like most of Dover's well-to-do townsfolk, he generally kept near him in those days. Into the circle of the lens he brought the two young people, seeing the soft curve of Caroline's cheek and . . .

" No ! " he observed sternly, returning to his work.

That forenoon Mr. Rochefort had several business calls to make in the town. The last of these completed, he was leaving the Town Surveyor's office at the seaward end of Snargate Street-over-the-Wall when his attention was drawn to the firelock shooting taking place on the beach between the Ordnance Stores and Valentine Pepper's cottage.

Being professionally interested, the banker strolled on to the shingle, making for the rear of the group of marksmen. The range was a hundred yards, the target three feet in diameter, and the accuracy of the regulars evoked his unstinted admiration, two shots in every dozen finding one or other of the painted rings.

" I fear, sir," he smiled at the lieutenant in charge, " that we volunteers are some way removed from that perfection."

To that Mr. Rochefort received a most gratifying reply. The army, it seemed, was greatly pleased by the diligence of the parish soldiers of Britain.

The Ropewalk was an animated scene of martial manœuvre and instruction. Here was a leathery-faced Colonel with a group of juniors.

" Fire, gentlemen, is to be held until the enemy's boats ground, when each platoon will pour its fusillade into the enemy at the instant when they stand to jump ashore. . . ."

As might be expected this area was a paradise for children, and quite near the banker a most stubborn argument was in progress between a small boy and a diminutive servant girl.

" 'Tis time an' you be coming *now*, Master Horatio," she was saying shrilly, her temper fast fraying.

" I'm not," Mrs. George Rochefort's son replied doggedly.

As she tugged at him he stiffened his little body, resisted every inch, being dragged over the pebbles rather than walk of his own volition.

The nursemaid angrily brushed back a strand of hair. " Boney'll get you, Master Horatio," she threatened him. "An' do you know what he be like?"

"No," bellowed a very indignant child.

He looked slightly frightened when told that the ogre was as tall as Rouen steeple, a villain who supped every day on naughty boys.

"Don't care," he yelled, defiant albeit.

About now Henry Rochefort intervened. Always passionately fond of children, he firmly believed that the young respond to love and kindness, that fear should play no part in their training.

"Well, my boy, what's to do?" he asked smilingly.

Horatio's enraged cries ceased as though by a miracle, so surprised was he on being addressed by the tall sombrely clad gentleman.

"I want to watch the sojers," he said wonderingly.

"He be a mortal wicked boy, sir," Mrs. George's help declared sulkily.

Mr. Rochefort may not have heard her for he, strangely moved, was staring at his brother's child. He had seen his nephew before, of course, but this was the first time he had spoken to him.

"So you want to watch the soldiers, eh?" he laughed.

Subsequently the banker entered the low doorway of a shop beyond the lock-gates at the town end of Snargate Street-over-the-Wall and there, after glancing over the curtain at the back of the bow window, had made selection from the sweetmeats displayed.

Later young Horatio Rochefort, his cheeks bulging with sugary dainties, most contentedly trotted home. There he spoke in utterly approving terms of a new friend he had made.

It was Caroline's custom, when her father had acquaintances for the evening meal, to retire to the little drawing-room before the port appeared. But on the evening of the day on which Henry Rochefort had pondered often about his daughter, she and the banker were alone. Louis was dining at Armand Saval's lodgings, and so she stayed with her father and together, afterwards, they went into the room in which her mother had spent many happy hours.

For once Mr. Rochefort did not immediately shred tobacco for his pipe. Whilst fully resolved on the step he proposed taking, he intuitively felt it would prove to be a most unpleasant piece of business.

"Is anything worrying you, Papa dear?" Caroline asked anxiously.

She had noticed his abstraction and now, after drawing a satin-wood work-table nearer to her side, she voiced her thoughts.

"Worrying me, my dear?" Henry Rochefort retorted sharply.

He had meant to be gentle but succeeded only in sounding brusque

—which often is the result when the broaching of a delicate issue has been considered over long.

" You *are* troubled, Papa," she said solicitously.

Then, curtly, he told her. She must, he intimated abruptly, relinquish the acquaintance of Charles Fagg. It was for her own sake that he was speaking. Any young woman who deliberately allowed herself to be seen in the company of one widely reported to be selling his country . . .

" But 'tis not true," Caroline interposed beseechingly. " Papa, you can't believe it to be true of Charles."

Her cheeks were as devoid of colour as the piece of cambric which lay unheeded on her lap.

" 'Tis a cruel, evil lie," she added desperately.

Thereupon her father bluntly stated that, whether or not there were substance in the charge against the young man, it was most significant that he had not troubled to deny it.

" Why should he deny an enormity of which he is not capable, Papa ? " she persisted.

Henry Rochefort made it very clear that he was not prepared to argue the merits of the case. His will was, he said with finality, that in the future she dissociated herself entirely from Charles.

" And I expect you to obey me, Caroline," he ended harshly, steeling himself against her rising distress.

Some few hideous times in her life had Caroline Rochefort heard that same tone in her father's voice, but never before had he used it against herself. Always had he been her dear Papa, affectionate, considerate. . . .

" You hear me ? " he asked stormily.

She went to him, slipping to her knees by the side of the wing chair in which he was sitting.

" But, Papa," she begged, taking his hand, " do you realise the Faggs are my dear friends ? Would you have me condemn one of them on an accusation which is not proven ? "

The banker made an impatient gesture. " You'll do as I bid, girl, and let's have no more on't."

" Papa, dear——"

She might as well have appealed to a stone, with the one difference that that was lifeless, not a man whose blood could rise to fever heat when he felt himself opposed or thwarted.

" You will not speak to Charles Fagg again," he snapped.

There was flaming colour in Caroline Rochefort's cheeks when she rose ; her mouth was both girlishly mutinous and womanishly resolved ; her eyes, as she looked at her father, were sparkling and unflinching.

" Papa, dear," she said clearly, trembling a little, " I can't do that."

Fleetingly, perplexity and amazement effaced his fast-mounting fury.

" You'll go against your father's expressed desire ? " he shouted.

Dumbly she shook her dark head. " I . . . I only go as my conscience bids me, Papa," she whispered.

He flung to his feet, his manner so uncontrolled that one less spirited than his own girl would have cowered from him.

" Then . . ." he thundered, his face working.

" Papa, listen to me——"

" Though you're my own child——"

She clung to him, her fight for him as much as for herself, their dear relationship the prize that was at stake. With all the will she possessed she struggled, for she must not allow him to utter those words which later would bring him grief and despair.

" Listen, Papa," she implored. " Listen, listen, *listen*."

Perhaps it was the urgency of that appeal which stayed him.

" Well," he said, breathing deep.

" Listen, Papa," she repeated quietly.

It was a story she had to tell. Of a little girl who, waked out of her sleep by angry voices, tiptoed to the top of the stairs. . . .

A muffled exclamation escaped Henry Rochefort's lips.

" Yes, Papa," Caroline said softly, her eyes beginning to well, " I never quite knew what it was, but I always thought 'twas you and Uncle George had quarrelled bitterly. Then Martha took me to bed again, and Mamma came up to kiss me another good-night and to tell me to sleep well. But, Papa, I didn't. I was still frightened, and when everything was peaceful I got up again and I crept down to the hall. . . . And, Papa, I listened at the dining-room door."

Memories of childhood can linger long, and vividly did Caroline Rochefort remember her father's sorrow on that night long ago. So clearly could she yet recollect her mother's gentle voice repeating the catch-phrase which might have staved off disaster.

" And so, Papa, dear," she said tremulously, " now do I say to you Mamma's ' *one and two and three and* . . . ' "

Henry Rochefort's face was ashen.

" How dare you . . ." he choked. " 'Tis sacrilege to recall——"

His daughter shook her head. " No, Papa, 'tis love an' no more."

Without saying another word, a man who was feared by most of the townsfolk of Dover stumbled from the room.

Sick at heart, Caroline Rochefort sat down shakily. It was her impulse to run after her father, to comfort him all she could, but, instinctively, she knew it was wisdom to let him be.

It was very quiet that night, with few abroad in Snargate Street.

Necessarily, little late leave was being granted to the troops, and only an occasional passer-by or the dropping of the fire broke the silence.

Caroline began to think of Charles, of Charles she knew so well. Charles who could not possibly be doing the dreadful things that were said of him. Charles with whom she had sailed, Charles with whom she had ridden. . . .

She sat up sharply, her face intent.

A picture flashed into her mind, how she knew not. It was of Mr. Pitt when they had met him out riding on the Western Heights ; of Mr. Pitt's thoughtful eyes lingering on Charles, and the unexpected invitation for Charles to go to Walmer Castle.

Her eyes were shining, her thoughts racing.

" I wonder," she whispered.

The night at Jamaica Land—Charles had not brought back any dutiable goods. Charles's many absences . . .

" Oh, Charles," she murmured, the tears coming.

Now she knew beyond doubt. Whatever it was that Charles was doing it was honourable and . . .

The door opened and her father came in, saying nothing at first, only staring poignantly at her.

" My dear, don't cry," he began huskily.

She swallowed painfully. " Papa, dearest," she said softly, " 'tis only for joy."

" Joy, my love ? " he said in surprise.

" Joy, Papa," she told him simply.

He did not press her, for he had something more important to say, a confession which, as always, it would be hard for him to make.

" Caroline, my dear, you have saved me from myself this night and I want to thank you. Your dear . . . dear Mamma——"

Tenderly she turned to him, hands tightly clenched in her urgency.

" Don't, Papa, I understand. Please understand that I do understand, an' don't hurt yourself any more."

Henry Rochefort took her into his arms, his hand gently stroking her hair. She was weeping now, blessed tears of relief.

" I'm . . . I'm so happy, Papa," she said shakily.

" So am I, my dear," her father replied.

As hush follows wild storm, so peace flowed into Caroline's loving heart. Home was home again.

" I think, Papa," she smiled mistily, " that I must bathe my eyes. If Louis comes in he'll be prodigious annoyed if we won't tell him the why and wherefore."

She glanced at herself in the gilt mirror, the candles in the sconces at either side of which revealed all too plainly the tears which still stained her cheeks.

" Don't be too long, my love," the banker nodded affectionately, opening the door for her.

The name of Charles Fagg was not mentioned between them. But it was to think of him, rather than to remedy her toilette, that Caroline yearned for the privacy of her room.

" Oh, Charles," she said softly, when alone.

She was radiant, the radiance of young womanhood filled with love.

Suddenly, so suddenly, that effulgence sped. It was then that Caroline Rochefort, her breath catching, came near to imagining the description of deadly business upon which Charles was engaged.

5

The grime of travel removed, his hair tied afresh, and a pleasant repast disposed of, Armand Saval determined upon a stroll to the Gaming Rooms, a decision he communicated to the servant who had faithfully accompanied him from France two and a half years before.

" *Oui, monsieur*," François inclined respectfully, making haste to fetch his master's cane.

" A delightful meal, madame," M. Saval smiled, his landlady chancing to be removing the dishes.

She bridled at the compliment and, after delivering himself of further felicitations which brought her into an even greater good humour, her lodger set out for his amusement.

The Rooms were in St. James's Street and, reasonably commodious as they were, the abnormal influx of officers into the district filled them to capacity most hours of the afternoon and evening.

In the news-room Napoleon's unexpected departure from the French coast was the subject of much speculation. On the old battle-field of Marengo, *The Times* newspaper reported, the Emperor had been present at a pageant staged with all that theatre-like glitter which seems to be the prerogative of despots, and at Milan, when Genoa, Parma and Piacenza were added to his conquests, he had placed on his own head the iron crown of Lombardy with the words, " God has given it to me, woe to him who touches it."

" Ugh ! " snorted a captain of artillery. " A lunatic whose dis-ordered mind persuades himself implicitly to believe he is above common man."

" His journey is no more than to trick us into false security," scoffed a companion. " But neither his feints . . . nor, for that matter, his honied words——"

There was a laugh at that. Some day Napoleon might tell the

truth but never would it be credited by the people of Britain. Such is the coldly just reward of those whose lives have been a progress of deceit and chicanery.

Less serious affairs were being discussed in the coffee-room. One young officer, a silly fellow, was bitterly complaining that he had had to pay forty-eight guineas for a bearskin he could have bought for twelve pounds during the truce of Amiens.

" 'Tis monstrous," he cried indignantly.

Marking down this presumably affluent personage, a pigeon whom he must strive to meet when the green-topped tables were out, Armand Saval sought the long shooting gallery, not yet having seen any of his particular cronies.

Speak of the devil and he often appears. A group of the Frenchman's acquaintances, between wagering on their marksmanship, had his name on their tongues.

" Haven't seen the fella since his last duty-day ended," the commanding officer of Amherst's Battery observed easily. " Now . . ." he took careful aim, standing sideways to the target, left hand in the small of his back, right with pistol extended.

" We've a tale to tell him," chuckled a companion. " Damme, I nearly split my sides—sorry, sir."

The apology bringing the distraction to an end, a shot shortly rang out, a roar of laughter following when it was seen that the playing-card pinned to the wainscoting had escaped damage.

" Egad ! " the young man was saying ruefully, having spoken over-confidently about a steady hand and a good eye. To his relief, however, he descried the newcomer, to whom promptly he shifted the attention of the throng.

" Ah, monsieur," he bawled, " 'tis well you are here again. I hear that strange things have been happening in your absence."

There was a quick bleakness in Armand Saval's face, but he was smiling when he put the question.

" And they are, monsieur ? " he asked politely.

Another burst of glee before the story of François was related. M. Saval's servant, it appeared, had been heartily belaboured by a young woman in the Market Place the previous afternoon.

" It seems that your man met the girl once, and on the second time of meeting, despite her protests——"

" Or before she knew," was a grinning interruption.

" . . . had his way with her."

To the amusement of them all, the Frenchman clicked his tongue most gravely upon this. It was so crude, he declared solemnly, and en verité he must see that François had a few lessons towards a more suitable technique. . . .

" 'Tis so simple after all," he shrugged. " One first defers to the wench, an' then one takes a slight liberty. If she submits, or protests but little, then all is well and one proceeds further. But if she is violently resentful then one prostrates oneself, one for many days treats her as though she were a divinity . . . and then——"

" Yes, monsieur ? "

M. Saval smiled lightly. " Then one uses the method of François. Afterwards," he added cynically, " she will fall into your arms of very gladness."

Callous it was, but the worldly always gather sycophants about them, as a few appreciative sniggers demonstrated. Nevertheless, a young officer of the East Yorks. Volunteers, a homely and healthy-looking giant, bluntly declared that, if his sisters were in the neighbourhood, he'd take damn good care they didn't meet Moosoo.

The Frenchman still continued to smile.

" My dear fellow," he observed, his glance resting mockingly on a farmer-like face, " you need have no fear for the mademoiselles your sisters. My predilection, I frankly confess, is for the dainty and *petite*, despite the . . . er . . . substantial claims of the more, shall we say, Junoesque."

This piece of mordant wit was too well covered for the angry Yorkshireman to deal with, if his flush was any indication, as he would have liked. In any case shooting had been eagerly resumed, and that for a most cogent reason. Admiral Villeneuve, with his own and the Spanish fleet, had disappeared from Cadiz into the blue, and none knew how soon the fight would be on them.

So all practised assiduously, and all envied M. Saval his superb skill.

" Damme, monsieur," an infantryman ejaculated, bringing back to an awestruck company the ace, the heart of which, for the second time in succession, had been neatly drilled.

The Frenchman whimsically held out his hands.

" Gentlemen, 'tis easy," he explained. " I have three enjoyments in life : riding, drawing and shooting. Of the first I have sufficient, from the second I have been debarred since last autumn——"

There was another howl of glee, at the end of which M. Saval was besought to recount the farcical story of how, when doing a small sea-scape, he had chanced, innocently, to include the approach to Arch-cliffe Fort, for which offence the fiery-tempered colonel commanding, a gentleman of near fabled local renown, had threatened him with hanging, drawing, and quartering.

" *Eh voilá*, am I not compelled to devote many more hours to my pistol ? " he laughed.

With a will, until the room so reeked with fumes that retreat to a more salubrious atmosphere became necessary, the exercise of a tricky art was resumed.

CHAPTER FOUR

I

THE King's Birthday, always an occasion for loyal demonstration, but never with more fervour than on the fourth of June, 1805.

Fittingly was it celebrated in Dover, on the plain above Castle Hill, a mile out on the Deal turnpike. There the regiments guarding the Cinque Port, or such of them as could prudently be spared from duty, disposed in a Grand Review. The Light Dragoons were of the martial company, with militia regiments from Northampton, Hereford and Surrey ; the Royal Artillery and the Engineers were present, the ubiquitous Royal Miners, too, and Volunteers from nearly every county in the land—no longer, as centuries ago, did the Men of Kent watch alone.

It was well. Admiral Villeneuve's fleet was away, none knew whither ; and for weeks no news had come to indicate the whereabouts of Lord Nelson and his fleet—they, too, had disappeared into the far-flung spaces of the oceans.

Uneasiness was steadily growing.

The vast crowd of spectators cheered, and ladies everywhere waved handkerchiefs. Now 2,000 infantrymen, drawn up in a square, began stentoriously to sing their invasion ditty.

" Gaul may threaten invasion, by threats we're ne'er scar'd,
  Let them dream of the plunder, delighted,
  Let them float o'er their legions, they'll find us prepar'd,
  A phalanx bold, firm, and united ! "

And a tremendous ovation did their efforts receive.

Miss Caroline Rochefort contributed her generous measure of applause and then once again, surreptitiously, eyed her hand. This was the first time, publicly, she had worn the ruby ring George Rochefort had placed on her small finger the same evening he had given himself to the press gang.

Being guiltily conscious of her unbounded pleasure in the elegant trinket, she glanced at her companion, to find him gravely examining his watch. He appeared inordinately interested in the hour ; indeed, coming to think of it, Charles had pulled out his timepiece at least twice simultaneously with her own inspection of Uncle George's gift.

"Really, Charles," she chided him, firmly smothering a most horrid suspicion which had begun to rise, "One would think you were weary of—oh, Charles . . ." She blushed furiously.

Charles Fagg's grey eyes were on her. "I'm mortal proud of the turnip your father gave me, m'dear," he observed solemnly.

"You've been imitating me, Charles," she charged him indignantly.

He twinkled at that. It was the only time he was anything like himself that day.

Just how Charles Fagg came to escort Miss Rochefort to the review is easily explained. Lou hardly ever ailed anything except in hot summery weather, when she was prone to sharp feverish colds. When Caroline called at Little Pent House she found her friend had taken to bed.

"'Tis nothing, my dear," Mrs. Fagg had said when Caroline came downstairs. "But . . ." she nodded her head knowingly, "I always say that a little care in the beginning . . ."

Caroline couldn't slide a word in edgeways. Horatio and his mother had gone over to Maidstone to stay for a few days with Mrs. George's friend and her growing family, and Mrs. Fagg was revelling in this chance of a nice little tittle-tattle, more especially as she had had an acute difference with Keziah as to Miss Lou's treatment.

"Yes, Mrs. Fagg," Caroline murmured dutifully, having skilfully covered four steps to the front door, Lou's mother still in talkative attendance.

About then the older lady remembered herself. Most decidedly Caroline could not go to the review alone. Charles would gladly take her. He was in the garden and she would call for him through the parlour window.

"No . . . no, Mrs. Fagg," protested Miss Rochefort. "Really, 'twould be——"

But that was how she and Charles came to be together that afternoon. It wasn't pleasant, either. Charles seemed terribly fatigued and horribly bitter. So wretched did she feel, when there might have been such a contrast, she so joyously sharing the scowls he received. She knew now just how starkly ugly the talk about him had become ; she knew it was being said that if the military did not quickly show they knew their duty towards him the townsfolk would soon reveal they could act more directly.

"Greatly improved, Caroline," he broke into her thoughts, pointing to a company which, after swinging up in line, were now preparing to fire, an operation which, apart from commendably few exceptions, was carried out with noteworthy regularity.

She smiled gaily. " Papa is devilish proud of his company, Charles. His men, with Mr. Stratton's and Mr. Braems's, are giving a display on the Ropewalk after morning service on Sunday week. You *must* see it, Charles."

He made some sort of light and meaningless rejoinder whilst she, her heart thudding, gave him the second opportunity in that afternoon.

" But you're so oft away nowadays, Charles," she said breathlessly.

As before, he turned the subject, to leave her with an aching heart, perhaps the beginning of anger, too. Surely he trusted her, surely he could confide in her. It was intolerable to think . . .

Now the band was striking up a martial air. The corps manœuvred for the grand finale, with its waving of caps and three hearty huzzas.

" The divinest exposition, Charles," she remarked vivaciously.

And vivaciously she continued to talk, and was still doing so when M. Saval, a pretty compliment on her gown, broke into her forced chatter.

" I regret, monsieur," she smiled saucily, " that your extravagances are such that I must decline to believe a word you say."

Armand Saval's dark eyes never left her. " Then, mademoiselle," he bowed gravely, " I beg that you look in your mirror the moment you arrive home."

" Fie, sir," she laughed.

A group of friends awaited him. " You owe it to me, mademoiselle," he said earnestly ere he left.

To the road ; past the Castle with its massive keep, towers, and embattled wall ; down the steep hill to Tinker's Close and Eastbrook Gate, the huddled roofs of the ancient fishing quarter before them . . . Charles and Caroline walked.

" Thank you for escorting me this afternoon," she said on Town Wall Street, sounding, she felt acutely, so lifelessly formal.

" 'Tis to be hoped you don't suffer for it, Caroline," he replied curtly.

Little Pent House, Severus's Gate and the New Bridge ; Snargate Street and the green railings before Henry Rochefort's house.

" Good-bye, Caroline."

" Good-bye, Charles," she smiled miserably.

There could be no doubt that he was staring at her.

" What is't, Charles ? " she asked, sharply stirred.

He was on the pavement, the sun gleaming on his fair hair ; she beneath the wooden canopy, lilac spotted dress and herself darkly framed by the old doorway.

" I was thinking, m'dear, that never could I be in more complete agreement with a gentleman I mislike."

That said, he was abruptly gone, striding towards the Playhouse. She watched him go, slowly closed the door and then, quickly, ran upstairs.

Three weeks later the Emperor Napoleon, in considered elation, wrote the following words : " Give me mastery of the sea for six hours and England will have ceased to exist."

A fortnight from then blockships, laden with masonry, were anchored off Archcliffe Point. The subsequent attempt to render Boulogne Harbour unserviceable_was abortive, so the navy declared.

Six days after that, the frigate *Curieux*, one of the fastest eyes of the fleet, reached her home port. She brought the ominous news that Admiral Villeneuve's combined force, after ranging to Martinique, was in full sail for Europe.

Two nights following, when the last information became known in Dover, the windows of Little Pent House were smashed in on the Town Wall Street aspect.

The keel bullies of the Plain, in less decent terms, let it be known that that was the promise of what would happen to Charles Fagg when they got their hands on him.

2

The grey darkness of the summer night had come, and Polly Fagg, carrying a candle whose light clearly showed the red state of her eyes, was once more looking over the rooms in which she took such pride. First she had been upstairs, to her own bedroom where a jagged piece of stone had cruelly splintered the satinwood veneer of a lovely commode, then into the opposite room where a length of broadcloth, hastily tacked over the gaping window, warded risk of chill from Horatio, at last, fortunately, sleeping after all the excitement.

Now Mrs. Fagg, heart-broken indeed, was emerging from the dining-room where another missile, so wantonly thrown subsequent to every pane in the window being smashed, had ruined one of the graceful festoons of lovers' knots with which the lovely Adam mantelpiece had been decorated.

In the hall she met her sister-in-law, Mrs. George immoderately pale.

" Polly, dear," Susan said anxiously, " please don't look any more."

" Just the drawing-room," Mrs. Fagg replied dully.

In the room to which the mistress of the house always devoted most thought there was more damage. The gilt chimney-mirror was starred, and pieces of window glass littered the carpet and the sofas, even the top of the piano.

"Come, Polly," coaxed Mrs. George Rochefort, and succeeded at last in persuading her to the parlour.

John Fagg, all his movements expressive of anger, was marching to and fro, his daughter Lou, every bit as disturbed as her Aunt Susan, watching him with concern.

"But, Papa . . ." she was saying when her mother came in.

"I . . . I shall never want to put my head outside again," Mrs. Fagg blurted out.

Her husband put an end to any further nonsense. They would all, he declared resolutely, treat this dastardly outrage with the contempt it deserved. When there were Assemblies in the Royal Oak Rooms, when the Playhouse opened for the winter season, the Faggs would join in the entertainment whensoever it pleased them. In days to come the townsfolk of Dover would be bitterly ashamed of their attitude towards Charles, but meantime Charles's family were not going to behave as if he were doing wrong.

So forthright was the shipowner that Polly Fagg was roused from her despair, her woebegone face becoming just so slightly less frozen.

"What is Charles doing, John?" she asked.

"Nothing for us to disown him for," her husband observed briefly.

"I see," Mrs. Fagg said heavily, slowly turning towards the door.

Yes, John Fagg remarked briskly, it was full time they were all abed. Lou received marching orders, and Susan Rochefort was treated as though she, too, was little older than Jack Woodgate's sweetheart.

In their bedroom Polly Fagg quietly undressed, with her husband, between trying to maintain some attempt at conversation, now and then uneasily eyeing her. First thing in the morning, he grunted, he'd see a glazier, and after that he proposed to call upon Mr. Denne. The Clerk of the Paving Commissioners would be asked as to what the watchmen were doing whilst a crowd of hooligans rushed along the length of Snargate and Town Wall Streets . . .

"Yes, John," Mrs. Fagg said hollowly, climbing into bed.

The shipowner made up his mind. In giving a broad hint as to his son's activities he felt that, strictly speaking, he might be going against Mr. Pitt's instructions, but in the present circumstances he was convinced no other course was possible.

Polly Fagg was sitting upright—she looked terribly frightened.

"Then Charles is employed in mortally dangerous missions, John," she said.

"They're risky enough," John Fagg reluctantly agreed.

O

Charles's mother began to speak of him, her lips not too sure. Now she could understand why her boy's face had thinned, why his mouth had become so hard. In grievous peril night and day when he was away, scorned like a pariah dog when he was home. . . .

" 'Tis so, John," she quivered. " An' sooner or later he'll be trapped——"

" He's a cool head on him, Polly," her husband said consolingly, " an' we must hope for the best. . . ."

In the middle of the month, when every French churchyard within forty miles of the Channel was serving as an artillery park, when unending columns of troops and wagon trains were moving steadily towards the invasion ports, Mrs. Fagg's fears for her son and John Fagg's belief in his resourcefulness were both justified.

Charles was apprehended in the little village of Etienne, close by Boulogne . . . Boulogne; whose now extensive waterways were dense with craft not dissimilar from sailing barges, with pinnaces in their tens of hundreds, vessels which, under lug sails or by oars, would carry over the major part of the *Armée de l'Angleterre*.

Boulogne, where lay the *Prince de Galles*, the boat the Emperor had chosen for himself, on whose deck he would cross to England surrounded by a select company of his soldiers, with sailor veterans . . . Boulogne, where the *Corps de Guides-Interpretes*, renegades all, licked their lips whilst anticipating the spoils of the Kentish Weald.

The talkative loony yokel, who had provided so much entertainment for the detachment of light horse who had taken him, was almost good-naturedly thrown into one of the upper rooms of the house which had been appropriated for squadron headquarters.

" It is no good you carrying on, comrade," grinned the guard. " You haven't got papers——"

" Why should an honest Frenchman——" the captive shrieked, spittle trickling down his chin, his voice such that none in Dover would have recognised it.

" Now, now, now," guffawed the jailer. " It will be all right in the morning when you've seen the officer, but meantime——"

The door slammed and Charles Fagg, even whilst raising a bull-like uproar which caused the sergeant and his men to double up in mirth at the very idea of what the police officials would say when the half-wit was presented to them, rapidly scanned the place in which he was confined.

" Easy," he muttered, examining the window. " And as for that fellow . . ." He frowned slightly. In the alleyway below, a sentry was patrolling.

It was imperative for him to get away before morning, and no less essential, if he were to pass into Boulogne unmolested by those who cast a wide net in these days and hours prior to a great military venture, that he should provide himself with some form of safe conduct.

" Mmmm," he murmured thoughtfully.

Then, snapping his fingers delightedly, he had it.

Seldom could there have been a noisier and more refractory captive. He kicked the door, he howled for victuals ; he frenziedly banged a fist against the window, and with the other arm wrenched loose a bar which guarded the pane.

" That'll do now," the jailer said, not so amicably, putting down a bowl of broth and a crust of bread.

Sullenly the prisoner ate the food. Apart from an occasional outburst, he was reasonably quiet for the remainder of the evening.

Stars twinkled in the sky and summer darkness was over the land. Outside the window of the room in which he had been confined, Charles Fagg crouched on the sill, his glance intent below.

Once again came the measured tread, and this time, gauging the drop to a nicety, he let himself go, to alight on the shoulders of the sentry, to throttle the fellow before he could utter a word.

In a convenient wood-store Charles Fagg stripped the unconscious man of outer clothing, habiting himself in the red coat and green pantaloons.

Something like two hours later Mr. Pitt's agent was within sight of the hut on the Tour d'Odre which Napoleon Bonaparte, when now on the coast, used in preference to the château at Pont-de-Briques. Three days after that he crossed to England.

3

Melodiously old Peter Monin's clock chimed three times, the waves of sound spreading softly through the dark night.

Behind a curtained window in Trevanion Street, not far from the beach before old St. James's Church, the candles still burnt in a gentleman's lodgings.

" *Mon dieu*, how much longer will he be ? " Armand Saval muttered, impatiently tugging his ear.

It was more than an hour and a half since François had gone, nearly three hours since M. Saval had left his friends in Townshend's Battery close by Crundall's shipbuilding slips.

" *Sacré nom*," the Frenchman snapped, his nerves taut.

There was reason for the interpreter's unusual jumpiness. If he were right in his surmise—and the burglarous enterprise on which his servant was engaged might bring confirmation anytime—then under his very nose had an English agent been working in France. Should such bungling come to the ears of His Excellency the Minister of Police . . .

Again M. Saval's thoughts went back to that moment, a few minutes after midnight, when he had stood inshore of the Pilots Look-out, his ears attentive to the muffled noise he had heard seaward —a boat, he guessed at once, then the hushed murmur of voices, and at last the unmistakable sound of a man swimming.

So it was and, his brain alive to every possibility, Armand Saval had shadowed the fellow through the star-lighted obscurity . . . along Fisherman's Row, through the Plain, towards the southern corner of Paradise Pent where, as it chanced, the lanthorn carried by a roundsman leaving the guard-house at Archcliffe Fort had sent its thin rays over the reeds and rushes of that place.

" 'Tis impossible," the Frenchman ejaculated.

His mind was busy, to such extent that the wine he poured into a glass brimmed over unnoticed, leaving a red pool on the table. Could it have been the uniform of a soldier of France ? Assuredly it was Mr. Charles Fagg, he was definite on that. But, although he had secreted himself in an Elizabeth Street passage for over an hour, he had not seen the young man emerge. Maybe there was an alternative exit. . . .

The door opened silently, and with the appearance of the man Dover took to be a valet M. Saval abandoned speculation.

" Well ? " he asked quickly.

François reported. The damp clothing he had found after forcing a press in M. John Fagg's office. It bore the badge worn by the XXIIième *Corps d'Armée*. There were other interesting discoveries, strange either to a shipowner's or a smuggler's premises. A French artisan's tool-bag, the complete suit of a French naval officer, a cloak of a style of . . .

M. Saval's bout of foul language, for fear of arousing the good lady of the house, was almost inaudible. On that account it gained viciousness rather than lost that quality.

" In view of the Emperor's almost immediate intention, François," he checked himself, still breathing hard, " we must act quickly. It is necessary that the spy Fagg does not see France again."

François, a Marseillaise, suggested that the English agent's death might safely be entrusted to himself. A knife in the ribs made little sound, he observed thinly.

" My dear François," Armand Saval remarked deprecatingly.

The English, he added, had a strong detestation for murder, however they might execrate the young man. Then, too, those in higher places, the employers of Fagg, would be far from disinterested:

"No," he smiled, his dark eyes beginning to glitter. "I think I see a better way."

A deux, there was nothing resembling the relationship of master and servant.

"Let's have it then, Armand," François said flippantly.

His companion, recovering from the nigh paralysing disclosure, chose to tell the tale as it might seem through British eyes.

"I am a hot-tempered foreigner," he characterised himself, the smile now vulpine, "one passionately devoted to the *ancien régime*. I meet M. Charles, I designate him a knave . . . *et violà*. He replies as an Englishman would, and for the blow I call him out——"

"Then you put a bullet betwixt his eyes," François interposed sarcastically. "Damme, haven't you learnt that these barbarians don't think kindly of duelling?"

There was a suggestion of deadly triumph in Armand Saval's bearing.

"My dear François," he retorted softly, "'tis you who do not know these barbarians. Once their courage is impugned, whatever be the odds, they will risk themselves to any end."

Reluctant admiration came into the pseudo servant's expression. "Neat, Armand, hellishly neat," he commented. "So, after all, you will put a piece of lead between Fagg's eyes."

M. Saval shrugged. "There or thereabouts, my dear fellow. And afterwards, should the escapade reach the magistrate's ears——"

François did not need telling. "Hatred of the Emperor and of those who aid him," he grinned. "And the dense jurats of this desolate hole will scold you but, remembering that you have rid them of a sorry scoundrel——"

"Exactly, François," Armand Saval laughed harshly.

It was decided that the engagement must be forced at the earliest opportunity, the morrow—or rather the same day—if possible.

It was not, however, until later in the week that M. Saval met Charles Fagg in a place and setting suitable for his purpose.

* * * * * * * *

No longer was life leisurely in the old town of Dover. Clerks and shopkeepers, in the uniform of militia, volunteer or fencible, entered business premises whose doors opened at seven in the morning, and were leaving by eleven, when a full day's work had been accomplished.

Shortly after this last hour one hot morning in late July, Mr. Fagg's indoor staff, with the carters and wharfingers he also employed, had tramped out of the warehouse to relieve opposite numbers at the defence posts assigned to them. Their master remained behind, with him being his son and Captain Pepper.

" So you board the frigate to-night, Charles," John Fagg remarked quietly, meantime glancing over the tally of blocks of tin unloaded that morning from Cornwall.

On that, Valentine Pepper had to be smoothed down, not for the first time. He greatly resented the fact that Mr. Charles's journeyings to and from the Continent were now, on Mr. Pitt's instructions, the affair of the navy, touchily proud though he was of that service.

" Tarnation," he growled, " ain't I a 'sponsible person, Mr. Charles? Ain't I assisted you to-and-agin France many's the 'casion? "

Captain Pepper, to his ferocious squint there now being added a black eye, a split lip, and a puffed nose, looked the extremely formidable creature quite a number of husky labourers in the Plain district had latterly found him to be. In sober truth he had, for a week or more, been engaged in a series of fights, his opponents in each case being counted amongst those who had attacked Little Pent House.

" To be sure, Valentine," Charles Fagg declared heartily.

The ex-boatswain, who had no love for manning a trench, snorted dissatisfaction.

" A sailor standing in an 'ole in the ground," he said disconsolately.

" How long do you expect to be away, Charles? " the shipowner asked.

His son could not answer that. It might be a week, perhaps two or three. Napoleon was still reported to be in Italy, and it was most improbable that the descent would be made before the Emperor's return.

" Which is hardly like to be unduly delayed in view of the recent news," Charles added grimly.

Both John Fagg and Valentine Pepper nodded dourly. The squadron under Admiral Calder, hastily gathered together by the Admiralty, had fought, in a fog, a most indecisive action with Villeneuve's fleet off Cape Finisterre, and the French Admiral had put into Corunna, where his force had been strengthened by a further fourteen sail-of-the-line.

" I conclude as 'e'll now make for Brest," Captain Pepper growled. " He's a'ready got around thirty ships-of-the-line under 'is command, so he'll not dawther. He'll reinforce 'isself with the Brest fleet an' then the whole French armada'll swish along up-Channel. . . ."

" Aye," Mr. Fagg agreed gravely. " And not a word yet of Lord Nelson. Well . . ."

Day after day Britain breathlessly awaited advices from her great sea captain and the fleet under his command ; and night after night came without word. It was believed in London that Lord Nelson was still far away, whilst the French papers, their reports copied by *The Times* newspaper, openly asserted that Nelson and Collingwood were out of the immense battle pending.

"Aye," John Fagg repeated, starting to tie a red sash about his waist.

"Lord 'oratio'll be 'ere all right," Captain Pepper professed stoutly. "Anyways," he added, less certainly, "we'll scratch along if the Frenchies dares to show their ugly faces 'ereabouts."

It was turned a quarter after eleven and, realising the hour, the shipowner made haste in changing his old office coat for the volunteer one which went with the military pantaloons he was already wearing.

Outside the warehouse John Fagg and Valentine Pepper turned to the left, their objective the open space towards the South Pier where the shipowner's men would be exercising. Charles's destination was the Market Place, his purpose there the purchase of pills for *Toke's Quality*. Recently this very favoured animal had been off his feed through a mild ailment.

Briskly Charles walked through streets in which pedestrians were almost entirely aged or of the fair sex.

Captain Stratton's company, his being St. Mary's ward, were allowed to use the Market Place as a training ground. On this morning an exercise was being practised which, at close quarters, had made the British infantryman the most feared in the world—bayonet fighting.

"Naw naw, 'twilln't do," bawled the grizzled old Chelsea pensioner. "Gawd help me if you ain't all acting as 'twas a parlour game. Them's Frenchies, *Frenchies*, damn you. . . ."

Near the pillars of the Guildhall were four straw-stuffed figures, supported to the rear by a heavy wooden pedestal lest sharp impact should turn them over. The heads were daubed with a mouth, a nose, and a pair of eyes, the canvas bellies marked with a bright vermilion circle and, to give some verisimilitude to an enemy, each had a tattered military garment draped over the shoulders.

"Next four," bellowed the martinet, " an' for Gawd's sake let's see blood-lust in your e'en. You're larning to kill, not to play drop-handkerchief wi' a bevy of wenches. Nay rot me . . ."

Those who had passed the ordeal with credit found the proceedings highly amusing, but those whose turn had not come frankly sweated. Even Captain Stratton, ferociously charging a dozen paces alongside three of his volunteers, looked apprehensive before he started, and more so afterwards. The Town Clerk, unluckily catching his toe on a high-riding cobble-stone, came down heavily at the feet of the dummy through which he should have driven his gleaming bayonet.

"Nah kiss 'im, sir," grunted the instructor, no respecter of persons.

Mortified, winded, and discomfited though he was, the Town Clerk was game enough.

"Try again," he gasped, painfully rising.

"That's the spirrit, sir," the autocrat was pleased to say.

Bayonet drill was an exercise in which, perforce, the greater part of the company had to while away the time in idleness. So it was that Armand Saval, in pausing to talk with various of his friends—Strattons, Elams, Waades, Dennes—was not distracting them from their duties.

The younger Hexstall boy first saw who was approaching. Chancing to witness his senior officer's catastrophic fall, he had averted his head to hide a grin and, facing the end of King Street, sighted Charles Fagg coming round the Fountain Inn.

"Egad, look who's here," he nodded. "And, by heaven, from the interest the rogue is taking one would think his conscience as white as driven snow."

"Or that he purposed joining *us*," the eldest Denne commented wittily.

There was a laugh at that, with many an aside ranging from the salty to the labouredly dull.

M. Saval's eyes were darting bright. Here, at last, was the opportunity he sought. But for the moment he did not enter into the excited conversation about him.

"Mortally interested, ain't he?" another young man sniggered.

It was true that Charles Fagg, diagonally crossing the Market Place, did momentarily loiter near the corner of the Guildhall, there to inspect the dummies which were being stuck with such vim. But after that he resumed a normal pace, his path to Cannon Street taking him through the crowd of volunteers.

Armand Saval's voice rang out clear.

"M. Charles Fagg, being a Catiline who sells his own country," he said distinctly, the object of his attention being no more than five strides distant, "will no doubt earn a few pieces of silver for even the little he has seen this forenoon."

There was a sharp hush, with a score of enthralled faces turning from the Frenchman to the Englishman he had so blatantly, though deservedly, insulted.

Charles Fagg stopped. Beyond the normal sound of the exercises there was absolute silence as he walked towards the official interpreter.

"My ears may have deceived me, sir," he murmured, eyes steely.

" But I should feel myself obliged if you would be good enough to repeat your words."

M. Saval laughed scornfully. " With all pleasure, M. Fagg," he began. " I was merely expressing the belief to these gentlemen that a traitor such as yourself——"

When speaking to François, the Frenchman had observed that an Englishman, when outrageously affronted, retaliates in the manner natural to him. A blow he certainly expected, though it is doubtful whether he, powerfully built and a half-stone heavier than his antagonist, expected to be smashed to the ground as violently as he was. The flashing fist travelled little more than fifteen inches, but Armand Saval dropped as though a sledge hammer had hit him.

" And now, sir," Charles remarked coldly, " perhaps that will teach you not to express a belief so openly."

Spitting blood, the Frenchman found his knees and then, almost insane with rage, scrambled up unsteadily. A moment before, the quarrel he had forced on the young Englishman was an affair of high policy, the logical extermination of one who might cause hurt to the design of the Emperor—now it had become a closely personal issue.

" For this, M. Fagg," he spluttered, " you shall give me satisfaction. My friends, they shall wait on you——"

" I fear, monsieur, that we English do not settle our differences so," Charles Fagg retorted coolly.

" You . . . English," sneered the Frenchman, a wealth of implication in his tone.

He was rapidly gaining control of himself, for above all he knew that now he must keep a clear head. It was imperative that he should not alienate the sympathies of those about him, and no less vital that these fools, notwithstanding that duelling was against their prosy laws, should give him the necessary support, so shaming the shipowner's son into acquiescence. Craftily he went about it.

" You will agree, M. Fagg," he opened smoothly, " that many an honourable gentleman of your country has seen fit to defy the statutes . . ." He bowed courteously to the son of the Master of Lodesmen. " You, monsieur, will bear me out on that."

Young Elam admitted that disputes were occasionally settled by such means, provided secrecy was sworn on the part of all.

" But yes, monsieur, I am sure that no gentleman in the company——"

Charles Fagg smiled faintly. " But I gathered earlier, sir, that you would not apply such description to myself."

Involuntarily licking blood which tasted salty on his lips, Armand Saval hesitated little. Baulked on this lead, there still was left the one method which must bring response even from the spiritless. His hand lashed out, his fingers left their red imprint on Charles Fagg's cheek.

" Now will you meet me, M. Fagg ? " he said contemptuously. " Or am I to dub you craven as well as———"

For the second time a piston-like left shot out. Again he crashed to the dusty cobblestones, and there lay.

Charles Fagg stooped to the prostrate figure.

" Perhaps now, sir, you may appreciate that the engagement you propose does not appeal to me," he remarked curtly.

With that, apart from vouchsafing the brief advice that " 'twould be as well to hold the smell-powder's head under the market pump," he resumed the errand on which he had been bound, his tall figure followed by a hundred pairs of eyes.

Sympathisers helped the Frenchman to his feet, many a hand took honour in dusting him down.

" Thank you, messieurs," he groaned, his dark eyes pools of venom.

Possessed of a consuming vendetta, he did not leave for his lodgings at once. In the major matter he had failed, of that he was cognizant, but at least he could still further damage the man who had humiliated him. A subtle gentleman, M. Saval, and it was not long before he had his audience swearing that Charles Fagg, on another count, had disgraced the land of his birth.

A few minutes after noon Armand Saval, the greater problem unsolved, walked stiffly back to Trevanion Street.

4

It was that scandalmonger, the Chamberlain's daughter, the " Jellybag " of younger days, who first told Caroline Rochefort. Later, the same day it was, Miss Rochefort heard it in her own home when, coming down the stairs, her brother's voice distinctly carried to her.

" Dear God," she murmured, " will this nightmare never end ? "

For a few seconds, her face intensely pale, she stood on the half-landing, hands gripping the wood balustrade.

Her father, with her brother and M. Saval, were still in the dining-room when she entered, though the visitor was on the point of departure.

" Caroline, my dear," Louis called briskly, " if you'd furnish me with . . . let me see now . . . humph ! "

He consulted the list of his simple needs. Bread for four days, a couple of clean shirts, an extra pair of stockings . . .

"Of course, Louis," she nodded. On Martha's insistence she was beginning to conduct the affairs of the household, and her family, ever devoted to the housekeeper, loyally abided by Miss Teddiman's wishes.

Henry Rochefort smiled affectionately. "What think you of the mistress before whom we all quail, Armand?" he asked proudly.

The Frenchman opened his arms in wonderment.

"My dear M. Rochefort," he laughed—not too freely, for his lip still was far from healed, "if I told you what I thought of mademoiselle I vow that she, as always, would speak of me as a *flâneur*, one who embroiders——"

"As indeed you do, monsieur," the lady in question countered gaily, being not of the persuasion to wear her heart on her sleeve in another connection.

Armand Saval shrugged ruefully. "Monsieur, monsieur, *toujours* monsieur," he said whimsically. "Mademoiselle Caroline, after nearly three years do you not think you might name me as do your brother and monsieur your father?"

It was rather absurd. "Why yes, Armand," Caroline Rochefort laughed.

Louis might be fidgeting for his sister's services, but M. Saval, this gained, besought a greater favour.

"And if I, mademoiselle, could be privileged to call you——"

"Sorry, Armand, but really I have little time," Louis interposed impatiently. The hour of crisis was upon the nation, and from six o'clock that evening he, in common with virtually every other volunteer, was devoting his whole time to the cause.

"Of course, Armand," she laughed again, the Frenchman's fine eyes still being eloquently on her.

He bent over her hand. "You honour me more than I may convey . . . Caroline," he said simply.

Level-headed and dignified man of affairs though he was, Louis Rochefort would have lost his temper had there been more delay. Too observant not to notice this state of affairs, M. Saval gracefully made his *adieux* and, with his departure, Caroline obtained from the kitchen the bread her brother needed, and from a press the articles of clothing military regulations demanded he should carry.

One arm full, the other gathering up her skirts, she ran up to Louis's bedroom, not speaking at once on the matter which was nearly stifling her, but helping her brother to furnish his haversack to requirements.

"Louis," she said quietly, when he seemed about to pick up his musket and the sixty rounds of ammunition which had been served out that morning, "why is it being said that Charles is a coward?"

Brother and sister were greatly devoted, but Louis quite glared at at her. It was not an affair in which she should concern herself, he observed sharply. And would say no more.

"So now 'tis said Charles is that, too," she murmured.

"I definitely refuse to discuss the matter, my dear," Louis said, kindly but firmly.

Slowly she followed him down to the hall where, at the door, she and her father saw him off, all three instinctively glancing at the sky before he went.

"Still unfavourable for them," Henry Rochefort muttered. "You know, Caroline, my dear . . ."

He hesitated, for he did not doubt how she would receive his suggestion. Still, if the Frenchies landed, it might be tragic for any lovely young woman. . . .

"No, Papa." Decidedly she cut him short. She was convinced that the defenders of Britain would never permit the foot of an invader to besmirch the soil of England.

"Besides, Papa," she passionately urged, "'twould be shameful to run away, and those who seek safety elsewhere are to be utterly despised, for they do no less than deny their birthright. I should *hate* myself, Papa."

The banker patted her hand. "Very well, my dear, and now . . ." He had to set off for Snargate Street-over-the-Wall.

On the spur of the same moment his daughter decided to go to Little Pent House. The garrison of Dover, as thanks for the hospitality they had received in the Cinque Port, were shortly giving an assembly for the townsfolk. The gravity of the present crisis made it hardly likely that this social gathering would take place, but the possibility provided an excuse for the talk she proposed having with Lou.

It seemed unbelievable that excuse for a talk with her best friend should be needed, but Caroline Rochefort's world was rapidly turning topsy-turvy.

The call for supper was ringing from the Western Heights when Caroline put the question which had been on the tip of her tongue for two hours or more.

"Charles is away, Lou dear, isn't he?"

Lou Fagg was staring dreamily beyond the garden, over the deepening blue of the sea on which, somewhere, her loved Jack sailed. But at her friend's inquiry an expression of hurt, of fright, came into her soft eyes.

"Yes . . . yes, Caroline," she said breathlessly.

"When will he be back, Lou?"

Charles's sister didn't know. But . . . but . . .

Soon it all came. " I'm so miserable about him, Caroline," she confessed, her voice small. " I don't know what's to do, but I know there's something terrible."

Though it seemed as agonising as sticking a knife into herself, Caroline forced a teasing note.

" Silly Lou," she murmured affectionately. " But then," she added severely, " you always got the most ridiculous notions into your head. Well, m'dear, you must get them out for there's something I want you to do for me, an' 'tis a most delicate affair."

This sounded so uncommonly diverting that Lou forgot the gentle cross-examination in which she otherwise might have indulged.

" What is't, Caroline ? " she asked impetuously.

Miss Rochefort affected great mystery. When Charles came back Lou must inform him that a young lady he knew, Miss Caroline Rochefort to wit, requested his attendance upon her at the earliest opportunity. Miss Rochefort, she went on, would feel herself immoderately displeased if Mr. Fagg did not promptly obey the summons.

Ecstatically Lou clasped her hands, her vision at once conjuring up a romance as lovely as her own.

" Oh, Caroline dearest, I will," she cried joyously. " Immediately, the very moment Charles comes home."

Thereupon Miss Rochefort, smilingly owning that that, not stuffs and muslins, was the real reason for her visit, proclaimed that she must hurry home.

On the short walk to Snargate Street, Caroline Rochefort's heart started to beat faster as she reflected on the step she had taken.

But she must make Charles see that, whatever he might be doing, he could not permit his name to be trampled in the dirt any longer. He must . . .

Caroline shook her head, true to herself. No, that wasn't the real reason. It was that fiercely she wanted Charles to trust her, wanted nothing better than to walk with him whilst every soul in the town poured scorn. She longed to share his burden, desperately desired to show the very complete faith she had in him.

Thinking of these things, and of the moment when, leaving her on the day of the Grand Review, he had looked deep into her eyes, those same eyes, belonging to a proud and courageous young woman, perceptibly began to mist.

5

Relays of horsemen, speeding ahead of the Imperial vehicle, cleared the road from Southern Italy to the capital of France. In three days and nights the Emperor covered 500 miles, thence from Fontainebleau passed as swiftly to Boulogne, pausing only for scanty halts at the post stations. At these, groups of high military officers, who for hours had been waiting, received final instructions for the greatest assault of arms the ever-victorious forces of France had undertaken.

" *Vive l'Empereur* . . . *Vive l'Empereur*. . . ." From town, from village, from encampment, the exultant cheer rose to the sky.

On . . . on . . . on.

Midnight, the courtyard at Pont-de-Briques where, as Napoleon's large head and melancholy face were seen in the fitful light from the carriage lamps, a high-pitched howl of hysteria cleft the dark vault of heaven.

" *Vive l'Empereur, Vive l'Empereur*. . . ." The wave of emotionalism rolled over the surrounding hills, re-echoed for leagues by the sentries who watched over a sleeping host, men whose hot eyes testified to their knowledge that weeks of inactivity were at last ended.

Until daybreak the despot conferred with his Marshals, they who had won renown on many a battlefield in Europe ; his Admirals—strangely subordinated to lesser importance in this enterprise so largely maritime—throughout the night holding themselves ready to attend too.

Seven o'clock in the morning he reviewed an army whose frontage extended over nine miles.

*   *   *   *   *   *   *   *

The invasion fleet was, in the terms of the order of the day, " embarking everything," the port of Boulogne a scene of brilliantly ordered activity, as were also the havens of Etaples, Wimereux, Ambleteuse, Calais, Dunkirk, Ostend.

Nearly two and a half thousand boats were in course of loading. Provisions, firearms, and ammunition were being taken from private houses previously commandeered for storage. To the waterfront, wagon after wagon moved in regular stream, their massive artillery wheels supporting tubs of flints for firing mechanisms, boxes of cartridges, cases of ration biscuits, casks of brandy for medicinal purposes, sacks of bridles, high-piled bundled fodder, with oats, bran . . .

But it was not of these that Charles Fagg was thinking when, wearing the leathern blacksmith's apron which always brought him luck, he sat on a bollard midway along ' N ' jetty. Following the example of some hundreds more—journeymen, artisans, stevedores—whose legs dangled towards the shimmering water, he was devoting the fifteen minutes of stand-easy to eating. Though, so abstracted was he, his jaws champed merely mechanically.

" Armand *Chassepot*," he mused.

His thoughts went back three hours when, close by the Hotel de Dovres, his attention had been drawn to an officer in a long-tailed green coat and sharp-pointed half-boots.

" Humph ! Capitaine Chassepot," he cogitated.

He had had only a rear view of the gentleman in the corduroy pantaloons, but the manner in which the fellow had spoken to a companion had been vaguely familiar, something in the fashion he tugged his ear which struck a chord of memory.

Before noon Charles Fagg had ascertained that M. Armand Saval held two official positions, one as an interpreter in the Office of the Port-Agent for Prisoners-of-War at Dover, and the other on the staff of the French Minister of Police, in which latter capacity he doubtlessly passed under his own name.

" One of Fouché's agents in England," he meditated wryly.

Once a twinkle crept into his eyes as he reflected on the grim comedy of it.

" Methinks I now can guess why he was so infernally anxious to put me at the business end of his flintlock," he ruminated.

Until the drum beat for resumption of work he pondered the novel situation, wondering just how his secret had been penetrated. After that he abandoned fruitless speculation for more profitable activities to hand and, it not being difficult, once within the harbour proper, to lose his identity amongst the considerable number of workers brought to the coast at the last minute, went about his own devices.

There was much to note in the days following. Engineer officers, in preparation for the hour when it became known that Admiral Villeneuve's dispositions rendered a crossing safe, set up short wooden signposts, each painted with a white arrow indicating the route to their particular quay this or that regiment should take. Fully laden artillery wagons were manhandled aboard three-masted, lugger-rigged brigs, each of which vessels was provided with a stable containing stalls for two horses, and a 24-pounder and a howitzer in bow and stern respectively.

In the middle of the month the tempo increased. Droves of sheep were driven in from the neighbouring pasturage, the canteen women were allotted the craft in which they would serve, the *chaloupe canon-nières*, each to carry a company of infantry, had planking laid over them to give quick access to the outermost of their densely packed assembly.

The signal once given, a few hours would see the clearing for sea of the most powerful and handsomely equipped expeditionary force the world had known, an army strong enough to subdue a continent, let alone a small island race.

Charles Fagg, realising now that he must at any moment be ready to fly with news, was spending many hours in the vicinity of Pont-de-Briques. It was there, to Napoleon's headquarters, that messengers rode furiously night and day—from Paris, from Spain, from the Rhine, from Holland . . .

One evening in the third week of August, when dusk was falling over the countryside, one such horseman galloped up the winding drive to the château.

From the shelter of a creeper-covered summer-house to which he had penetrated, Charles peered with bloodshot, sleeplessness-tortured eyes. He saw the courier arrive, watched him enter the house.

Ten minutes afterwards there were unusual stirrings, many comings and goings, with groups of officers pacing the terrace in impassioned discussion, and aides-de-camp riding hard for the gates.

Finding a gap in the inner line of sentries, Charles cautiously started to crawl towards the rear of the house.

CHAPTER FIVE

I

THROUGHOUT those later days of August, when for four consecutive nights the 800,000 defenders of Britain stood to arms, the temper of the folk of Dover had progressively grown more obdurate. But on the fifth day, when it became known that Mr. Pitt had reached Walmer Castle and would drive over to the town early that summer evening, excitement temporarily replaced unflinching resolve, so dramatic did it seem that, in the hour of destiny, in this lovely corner of England closest of all to France, there should be amongst them the man who stood between Mr. Mounsieur and that egomaniac's dream of world domination.

The Prime Minister, it was said, would look in at the eve-of-battle ball which the Garrison of Dover were giving at the Royal Oak Rooms. This noteworthy event, eagerly anticipated for some weeks, was to take place after all, though in a strikingly new guise. It was to begin at the unheard-of time of five o'clock in the afternoon, with the band playing ' God Save the King ' at nine sharp.

To obtain permission even for this greatly restricted social gathering, the General Officer Commanding the Southern District of England, whose headquarters were at Canterbury, had had to be approached. Sir David Dundas, to this limited extent, had relaxed the rule whereby officers serving on the coast were not allowed to leave their posts for more than two hours. All, however, were reminded of the standing order, ' battle stations before dusk.'

Dover, heroically living in the dark shadow of the threat of invasion by Napoleon's invincible campaigners, seethed when it heard the news of the great statesman's visit—they would give ' Billy ' the reception of his life.

As so they did.

The Deal Road, after its steep descent of Castle Hill, entered the town at the extreme end of Town Wall Street, close by Eastbrooke. It was here that Mr. Pitt's calash was met by a wildly vociferous throng ; forthwith the horses were taken out, many a score of willing hands dragging the vehicle to its destination.

When the Prime Minister entered the Royal Oak Rooms, narrow, irregular-fronted Cannon Street, with its many inn-signs thrusting out across the thoroughfare, was choc-a-bloc with a crowd which, however uncomfortably tight they were pressed, howsoever long might be the wait, were determined to stay there until the Right Honourable gentleman emerged again.

Barely had they settled themselves when they found quick diversion under two heads.

The first was when a tall young gentleman in a fine satin coat and knee-breeches began to force through them with scant ceremony. Though his gait appeared unsure he was recognised at once, and with that recognition, with that sight of the flaunting of gay apparel when every other male of similar age wore the King's uniform, a growl of anger went up.

" Be you over to France to-night with the latest i'telligence of Billy's doings, Muster Charles Fagg ? " screeched a blowsy doxy from Heart's Row.

" Infamous, you treacherous Jerry Sneak," a precise, elderly man shouted hoarsely. " And may you burn in the fire of hell . . ."

There was a yowl of acclamation. A stone shattered the window of a pastrycook's behind Charles Fagg's head, but the sound of the tinkle of glass was lost in the rising uproar.

" Let's take the Frenchies' spy and——"

Tumult broke out, with noisy dispute on the bloody fate fitting for this miscreant. But long before the babel had subsided, long before unanimity had been reached, Charles Fagg acted, pulling himself together in time.

A powerful thrust with his right shoulder, a chop with his left fist, and he had cleared the space he needed. In the brief respite from clutching attentions, he slipped his sword from its scabbard and, behind the wickedly weaving blade, began to progress along the wall side, those before him tumbling back on the secondary lines at the steely approach.

The mob, throughout the ages, has been a terror to government, a terror to all against whom it directed its uncontrolled wrath. The animal howl which went up as Charles Fagg disappeared into the vestibule of the Rooms presaged what afterwards should befall the unpatriotic young buck.

But hardly had the roar faded when there came the second distraction.

From the Market Place an impatient horseman approached, his beast hard-ridden but the rider neither particularly sweat-streaked nor dust-powdered.

" Make way ! " he bellowed. " Damn you, make . . ."

Tongues were soon wagging . . . the messenger had brought important tidings for Mr. Pitt, it was being said.

2

The lay-out of the cream-and-gold decorated Royal Oak Rooms was passably simple. Leaving the outer vestibule behind, one entered the ante-room, beyond which was the ballroom, with card and supper rooms to the right. On the left the grand staircase curved majestically upwards, ending in a fine landing at the top. On the remote side of this was a pair of double doors, ivory-painted, which led to the foyer, a broad corridor at the right-hand side of which were pierced, at regular intervals, large horseshoe-shaped openings guarded by gilt-finished wrought-iron railings. The foyer, in effect, was a partially closed-in balcony confined by doors at each end, a promenade from which a fine perspective of the ballroom below could be obtained.

At the moment, minuet and cotillion were forgotten, the gleaming dance floor was empty, the fiddlers' chairs were unoccupied, and even the stately Master of Ceremonies, eager as the rest, had left his post.

Mr. Pitt, with whom were Lady Hester Stanhope and members of his staff, had been received in the vestibule by the Mayor and other dignitaries. Courtesies completed, the party had mounted the grand staircase, then passed along the foyer, finally descending another staircase, less ornate than the first, to the seldom-used private apartments at the rear of the building.

Meantime the ante-room had become jammed with a throng whose intention was to await the Prime Minister's reappearance. Some looked upwards, watching for any move amongst the company assembled on the landing outside the entrance to the foyer, whilst others, believing that Mr. Pitt would return by the more convenient ground-floor route through the now deserted ballroom, kept a sharp eye in that direction.

Amongst those who, at the head of the stairs, had such a magnificent view of the nodding plumes in the head-dresses of the ladies in the ante-room, was Caroline Rochefort.

To her, gradually, Lou Fagg found her way.

" Now I *can* join you, Caroline," she grimaced, wrinkling her nose in distaste.

Caroline laughed. " Oh, he abandoned me shortly after Mr. Pitt's arrival was known."

Charles's sister did not care for M. Saval, and no doubt her dislike had increased since she had heard rumours of the interpretation which the Frenchman had put on her brother's disinclination to accept an engagement of honour. But sweet Lou was not a young woman ever guilty of labouring a point.

" There's Mamma and Papa, Caroline," she smiled, forthwith waving over the balustrade to attract the attention of her parents.

Her mother, with whom were Mrs. Nethersole and Mrs. Stokes, was near the niche in which was placed a marble bust of His Majesty, and her father was just without the supper-room door. Mrs. Fagg did not look her usual cheerful self, and there was about her the air of one somewhat feeling her position.

On the other hand, Mr. Fagg was jesting with Mr. Adcock and Mr. Templeman as though quite unaware that he was held to be the man who had fathered a traitor. Only there was about the shipowner, so Caroline Rochefort noticed, a set of the mouth which rather indicated that an inquirer on the subject would find himself extremely unlucky.

Half speculating on this, Caroline was glancing down the grand staircase. Against the wall panels, on every level from top to bottom, stood officers in service uniforms and their gaily attired partners, young folk who were determined to see Mr. Pitt at close quarters should he return by the same route. . . .

" I protest you're not listening to me at all," Lou declared indignantly, an earlier piece of chatter having elicited no response.

It was true, too. Miss Rochefort, staring half unseeingly at the broad flight, had been daydreaming, wistfully wishing that Charles could miraculously appear. How it would be bliss to take his arm and walk by his side down those shallow steps, in this poor way showing a crowded assembly . . .

" Miss Rochefort . . . Miss Fagg . . . may we, your most humble servants . . ."

It was not likely that two attractive females could long remain unattended, and a couple of fresh-faced Artillery officers, seeing the girls, promptly seized the opportunity. Lou Fagg, however, decided upon going down to her mamma, who just then she thought seemed a little unhappy.

" Then, Miss Lou, 'twill be my pleasure to take you there," one young gentleman smiled.

The other suggested to Miss Caroline that a breather along the foyer would be mortal pleasant.

" We'll receive just as good intimation of Mr. Pitt's approach, Miss Rochefort," he urged eagerly.

So the two young ladies parted for the nonce, Caroline and her escort towards the double-doors on the right, Lou and a most pleasant young man the opposite way.

From his superior height Lou's Artilleryman nodded downwards as he crooked his arm.

" Methinks, Miss Fagg, that the lady coming up is in a devilish hurry," he laughed.

Ready for any fun, Lou, bright-eyed, strained on tiptoe, but one glimpse only dispersed her vivacity.

" 'Tis . . . 'tis my aunt, sir," she said quickly, frightened for no reason she knew.

Breathlessly Mrs. George Rochefort was mounting the grand staircase.

She was late, it was true, having been delayed at Little Pent House beyond the time her brother and sister-in-law left for the Rooms, but that could hardly account for her expression. Her face as ever most revealing, she looked distinctly troubled.

After confusedly apologising to her astonished convoy, Lou's sole coherent thought was that something must be amiss with Horatio.

The two women met in the thinning fringe of the company.

" Is anything wrong, Aunt Susan ? " her niece asked anxiously.

Mrs. George swallowed nervously. She loved her nephew dearly and, knowing the extent of the feeling against him, was terribly fearful lest he, in what she took to be his rash daring, should come to harm.

" Charles is back, Lou," she began worriedly. " And he is coming here . . . and I'm sure he's not well."

She spoke more of him. He appeared prodigiously weary, nay sick with exhaustion. " Notwithstanding," she added, her manner immensely surprised, " he scarcely seemed disposed to tarry at home at all . . . he was off on some personal matter or other . . . but when he heard that Mr. Pitt was to be present to-night . . ."

" Oh . . . oh, Aunt Susan." Mightily concerned was Charles's sister.

Mrs. George Rochefort nodded blindly. " An' . . . an' by now he'll be on his way here, Lou," she gulped.

For an instant they stared at one another and then, instinctively, both turned towards the staircase.

" John . . ." Mrs. George thought of her brother.

" Papa . . ." The one idea in Lou's mind.

They had reached the ante-room and were slowly progressing across the crowded floor when Charles Fagg passed in from Cannon Street.

There was the silence of stupefaction when it was seen who had dared to appear, to be followed by a hum of indignation when the impertinence and bravado of the scoundrel were remembered. Dover folk were not without tolerance, but there was too much about this rapscallion's name for him to be stomached. Then, too, though Britishers had little patience with duelling, they had their pride of race ; queer tales were circulating and it was felt that John Fagg's son, in the manner in which it was said he had refused a challenge, had further sadly besmirched the good name of an Englishman. On that alone he had let the old country down, and no one in those days could do that with impunity.

Only nice restraint held in check the throng in the ante-room. Had not all fervently desired that no unpleasant incident should mar the loving reception they desired to give the great statesman, there could have been little doubt that Charles Fagg, as he stumbled towards the marble staircase, would have been accosted by many an itching hand.

As it was, he was watched in scowling silence as he climbed upwards, the quietude of intense scorn continuing whilst he remained in view.

Then a chattering rose to the high roof.

Half a dozen couples were parading the foyer, with as many more sitting in the gilt-lacquered chairs arranged against the grilles overlooking the ballroom.

" Our fear, Miss Rochefort," the young Artilleryman harked back profoundly, " is more that the Frenchies *won't* make the attempt."

Caroline smiled absent-mindedly, lazily wafting her fan.

" You see, Miss Rochefort . . ." the young officer continued, delighted to have found a sympathetic listener to his shop, " we're infernally sure——"

Attracted by the sudden swell of voices which told that the doors to the left had been opened, Caroline glanced incuriously over her bare shoulder, to see the young man who had never been long absent from her thoughts that whole evening. Her breath caught, for a moment her limbs seemed to refuse action, then quickly, glowingly, she rose.

"You will please excuse me, sir," she murmured joyously.

Followed by her bereft companion's bewildered stare, she went to Charles Fagg, her head proud. In coming, Charles might be inviting obloquy or worse, but she was exquisitely glad he had obeyed her summons—for in the present thrill she was too excited to realise there might be other reason, too pent even to recollect that as yet he could not have seen Lou.

"Charles!" she cried, quite unconscious of couples who had begun to whisper together.

With a pang she saw his set face, grey beneath its deep layer of tan. His ruffles had been rumpled by dirty fingers, and his white silk stockings had been soiled by a filthied boot.

"There are abominable . . . cruel . . . things being said of you, Charles," she said passionately. "That is why I decided I must speak to you."

From fingering a small leaden shape, a cheap medal it appeared to be, automatically he began to toss it up.

"Let them be said," he muttered wearily.

"But I will not have them said," Caroline Rochefort retorted ardently. "To permit your name being associated with treasonable practices——"

For once an unerring hand faltered. The crownpiece-like circle struck the oaken floor and rolled to her feet. She picked it up, never remarking its nature, unceasingly attempting to persuade him to some action which should clear him for ever of such hideous charge.

"Why need I so do?" he asked harshly.

"Why need you . . ." she was beginning, horribly dismayed by his indifference. She bit her lip, hardly knowing what next to say and, looking down to conceal her distress, her eyes lit on the round object she still grasped. On it was an engraving of Hercules squeezing a Triton to death. . . .

"*Frappée à Londres*," she read along the rim. "Struck . . . in . . . London." She glanced up wonderingly, to meet a pair of blood-shot eyes. "What is't, Charles?" she asked slowly.

Courteously he suggested that elucidation might be found on the other side.

The strangeness of his attitude was causing a numbing chill to invade her, but she did as he said, to find on the reverse a bust of Napoleon, lauriated.

"'Tis Bonaparte," she said half inaudibly, so startled by his bearing.

It was not that she distrusted him, never that. But ever since Louis had rebuffed her she had been living on a rising note of exultation, and flights of heroic sacrifice should be carried to their appropriate end. Perhaps the new circumstances confused her momentarily, and maybe some trace of perplexity crossed her face. If so, then certainly his manner of presenting the tyrant's leaden image could be held as utterly contributing to that end.

"Bonaparte! Bonaparte, Charles?" Imperatively she grasped his wrist.

"The Emperor, please, my dear," Charles Fagg mockingly corrected her.

Had he not been overtaxed body and soul, he would have seen in her swimming brown eyes, not the suspicion he imagined, but all the love and affection she had for him, and a belief that would never waver.

"And that little trinket, my dear . . . " he bowed ironically, dazed misjudgment driving him on, "is one of the trial pieces for the medal which His Imperial Majesty will have struck immediately the Eagle flies over London. Being supremely confident, His Majesty, a year ago, ordered the dies to be prepared——"

"Charles!" She was deathly pale, wholly because of his abnormal behaviour, never on account of his words.

No appeal would stay him. Relentlessly he continued, a mirthless smile illuminating his worn face. The souvenir had been given him in Paris, the Minister of Police being highly pleased. . . .

"Charles!" she cried affrightedly. Taking his arm she drew him down the long corridor, her one thought to bring him nearer to himself before some dread tragedy ensued.

"I must speak to you out of earshot of all curious folk," she told him. "And as you are come because 'twas my wish you must hear me out."

He stared as though he hardly knew her, as though his brain was too fagged for any other than the one purpose upon which he was bent.

"I am not here to see you," he muttered, his voice thick with fatigue. "Nor have I time for you, Caroline."

She recoiled as though he had struck her, rich colour flooding her cheeks. Then she became what she was, the belle of the evening, the most sought-after young woman in Dover.

"How dare you speak thus to me?" she asked haughtily.

Though there was no feeling in his tone, and that spoke for much, he emphasised his offence by again making it brutally clear that he must dally no longer.

"Dare!" he grimaced. "I dare because I have business more important than your feelings——"

Insulted as she had been, Caroline Rochefort was now beyond kindly understanding. Her eyes blazed. " You monster . . ." she gasped.

" ——or mine," he had concluded, but his words were hidden beneath hers.

" . . . Then go to your business," she said furiously. " And never come near me again. I hate you, *hate* you."

His hand, feeling for his brow, dropped limply.

" You . . . you never want to see me again, Caroline ? " he asked dully.

Her eyes were brilliant. " *Never*," she feverishly vowed.

A spasm of pain crossed his face, his expression became more strained than ever.

He bowed stiffly. " You will gladly excuse me, then," he said haltingly.

Tempestuously she turned on her heel, her rustling draperies leaving in their train that scent of her he had always loved.

With the fragrant aroma lingering in his nostrils, Charles Fagg watched her go, waited until the dainty figure was gone from sight.

" So that is done," he muttered, infinitely sad.

The shock had roused him and he began to wonder how he might accomplish his duty. It was vital that he speak at the earliest to Mr. Pitt, and if he were to maintain in the future the façade of secrecy which he had built up at such cost to himself he must not, in this place filled with Dover folk, approach the Prime Minister. direct.

" Damme," he murmured.

He went to the nearest balcony and, leaning over, saw that Mr. Pitt had not come through, the crowd in the ante-room, seen beyond the ballroom doorway, still glancing hither and thither.

As luck had it, his dilemma was solved by the appearance of a middle-aged civil servant who had had reason to return from the private apartments at the rear. This keen-eyed gentleman had often seen Charles Fagg at Walmer Castle and, perceiving him now, most adroitly made for the same balcony, looking over the balustrade as if he, too, desired to know what was going on below.

" You are from over the way, Mr. Fagg ? " he asked beneath his breath. " Have you information as to when the French start ? "

Charles Fagg's terse reply nearly caused a highly sedate individual's eyes to jump out of his head. And right energetically did the gentleman overrule Charles's subsequent objection. Mr. Fagg must see the Prime Minister without a second's delay, and damn whether the whole of Dover knew of the meeting.

" Very good, sir," Charles commented.

Turning the knob, he opened and passed beyond the second set of ivory-painted doors.

Mr. Robert Spisour, Water Bailiff and Mayor of Dover, later handsomely confessed that he had never been so dumfounded in his life.

By virtue of his office as senior jurat, Mr. Spisour had led the Prime Minister's party towards the private room in which refreshments had been set out.

At the bottom of the further staircase Mr. Pitt, who had been in conversation with an officer of Engineers, expressed a wish to glimpse the new military road to the Western Heights which had been described to him. A portion of the winding track could be seen from a deep window embrasure in the big hallway, and to this viewpoint Mr. Pitt repaired, the less distinguished of the company awaiting his pleasure.

In due course the Prime Minister, after putting various searching questions, professed himself highly satisfied, and a move was made towards the buffet.

The Lieutenant of Dover Castle was bowing Lady Hester into the apartment when the attention of all was drawn by the sound of hurried feet.

Mr. Spisour's expression when, upon glancing up, he saw the renegade, drunk, too, he thought, was comical. With a fine sense of his own civic position and responsibilities, the Mayor placed his red-waistcoated generously-proportioned belly across the foot of the stairs.

" Hold there, Mr. Fagg," he sternly demanded, nobly barring with outstretched arms the bottom of the flight. " Is it not sufficient that you have the impudence to present yourself to public view without——"

" Enough, you old windbag," Charles Fagg retorted, brushing aside the restraining hand.

The Mayor's steel buttons looked in danger of parting, so visibly did he swell.

" Harkee, young fellow——" he shouted.

Mr. Spisour nearly choked with mortification when one of the private secretaries, unmistakably meaning him, the Mayor, shook his head in undisguised rebuke. And Mr. Spisour, too, running the gamut of all the emotions, goggled with stupefaction when he heard the Prime Minister warmly greet the spy in the pay of the Frenchies.

" Well, young man ? " Mr. Pitt asked pleasantly, the hint of a question in his greeting.

Charles Fagg nodded almost imperceptibly. " May I speak to you, sir ? " he said quickly.

Apologies were made by the Prime Minister to those around him, and shortly, when Mr. Pitt and his niece, with three or four more, had re-entered the room, the door was closed.

Outside, speaking in hushed voices, a dozen or more gentlemen and officers waited, amongst them the Mayor of Dover, a very puzzled man. Indeed Mr. Spisour was edging towards Mr. Ralph Jelly—the Chamberlain looked every whit as bewildered as himself—when the notice of all was drawn to the doorway communicating with the ballroom.

This time it was that same courier who had experienced no little difficulty in forcing his beast through the mob wedged in Cannon Street.

"Mr. Pitt?" he asked quickly, significantly touching the slim leathern case he was carrying.

A middle-aged gentleman, first nodding comprehension, gently tapped on the panelled door.

In the corner of the small room, Lady Hester Stanhope and two officers were quietly conversing. Meanwhile Mr. Pitt, his hands folded behind his back, was pacing to and fro.

"This is amazing news you bring, Mr. Fagg," he observed. "*Amazing.*"

Unobtrusively a colonel of horse refilled Charles Fagg's glass; the cavalryman had had too much experience not to feel quite sure that the young man, physically and mentally, was far spent.

The Prime Minister tweaked his long nose thoughtfully.

"Many reports have I had from you, Mr. Fagg," he remarked, "and never yet has their accuracy been subsequently disproved. But this time, in the closing hours before an attempt at invasion, you bring me the strangest intelligence of all."

Charles Fagg moved restlessly.

"You still avow that the *Armée de l'Angleterre* is shortly to be faced about, preparatory to being marched away towards the Rhine?" continued the statesman.

"I do, sir," Charles snapped.

Without a second's pause, ignoring the ill-humour of the reply, Mr. Pitt fired another searching question.

"Why do you so definitely name the Rhine, young man?" he asked keenly.

Charles Fagg's voice rasped. "Because," he replied savagely, "that was what I heard at eleven o'clock last night when I was gallantly *serving* my country with my ear close against the door to a cabinet."

This arrant piece of discourtesy caused one of the general officers to turn sharply, his intention to admonish the young gentleman who had dared to speak so ungraciously to one worshipped by his fellow countrymen.

"Young sir——" he began, fierce eyebrows beetling.

Mr. Pitt, whose thoughtful glance was on this agent who always had faithfully and devotedly served him, checked the interrupter by a quick signal. Indeed the others could plainly see how the young fellow regretted his boorishness.

"I ask your pardon, sir," Charles said wretchedly, behind the present remorse a greater and more personal sadness, the knowledge of what he had so recently lost.

"Mmmm," the Prime Minister murmured. "So Napoleon's grandiose plan of naval concentration has failed." Instinctively he knew that the French despot must have received wind of the Austro-Russian coalition he had been contriving, though that could not be the basic reason underlying Napoleon's astounding decision. The Emperor, he soliloquised, as second choice, intended crushing one of the partners, Austria, at once, abandoning at the peak of prepared-ness the most decisive test of all, that of invasion of England. With flaunting colours, Bonaparte would carry off his withdrawal, and the foxy Fouché would endeavour to persuade the world that the alternative plan had always been his master's scheme. But . . .

"A democracy," Mr. Pitt smiled wryly, "may survive many a hard knock, but a despot . . ." He began to stump across the room, concisely assessing the situation as he saw it. "Villeneuve prefers to take his ships southard to Cadiz, in the hope of still more Spanish reinforcements, rather than strike boldly across the Bay of Biscay to join the impatiently waiting French fleet at Brest. In short . . ." he spun sharply at the window, "M. Villeneuve has cold feet . . . but why, damme, why?"

Lady Hester anxiously began to beg that he should seat himself, and Charles Fagg, hearing Mr. Pitt's niece speaking so uneasily, was flooded with further regret. Too troubled by his own problem, hitherto he had not perceived how ill the Prime Minister looked. Very sick indeed seemed Mr. Pitt, a man whose face clearly revealed that here was one fighting two battles, the first heart and soul on behalf of his country, and the other to maintain a hold on life itself.

There was a light knock at the door. "A King's Messenger, sir," the incoming secretary said. "A dispatch from Portsmouth, via the Admiralty signal station and the Downs."

Mr. Pitt, unlocking with his own key the portfolio, unbuckled the twin straps and drew out the document within. He moved nearer the window and rapidly scanned the brief advice.

"Gentlemen," he said quietly, a vague hint of excitement in his tired voice.

His pale cheeks had coloured, there was about him a sense of relaxation, an easing after intolerable strain.

" *Lord Nelson has landed at Portsmouth,*" he informed them. " And I thank God for His goodness."

The silence which followed, so Charles thought, was measurelessly impressive. Not a word was spoken, not a comment made on the news and all that it implied.

William Pitt's voice deepened. " Now we have the explanation of much that appeared unfathomable."

Then a military officer spoke. " The Navy never fails us, sir," he observed a little dispiritedly.

The Prime Minister heartened the soldier. No one was more aware than he, he said wryly, that nearly a score of *small* military excursions had ended disastrously. But . . . Britain's army was growing.

" Be of good cheer, my dear fellow," he urged consolingly. " The day will come when we move to attack, a day when defence is not our sole consideration."

" Let's hope 'tis soon, sir."

A friendly clap on the shoulder ended that.

The Emperor's scheme for concentration of superior naval force against England had failed. Britain had allies ready to take up the fight . . . otherwise Napoleon might have risked the last desperate throw.

" But with Austria taking up arms . . ." Mr. Pitt's eye shone.

Now the Emperor was drawn off, with a war on more than one front to face.

With a warm smile, the Prime Minister turned to Charles Fagg.

" 'Tis a fine piece of work that you have done, Mr. Fagg, one for which your country is deeply indebted. The early knowledge of the exact doings of our relentless enemy enables us all the more easily to concert on future plans."

Charles Fagg reddened. " You praise me overmuch, sir."

None of them would have that, for more in that select company besides Mr. Pitt and his niece knew of the incredible risks which had been run.

" This means, sir," a Major-General observed pregnantly, " that there will be no immediate attempt at a descent on our shores."

" I suppose not," the Prime Minister murmured, apparently now occupied with other than affairs of state. He was again scrutinising the tired face of the young man.

" Mr. Fagg," he began deliberately, " I hardly think we shall need so much of your help in the future. And . . ." he continued gravely, " I believe I once made you a promise when you showed yourself rather . . . er . . . disgusted with the nature of the services you were rendering our land."

Involuntarily Charles rose. " You did, sir," he agreed longingly.

The Prime Minister said no more then. He had a brief colloquy with the principal private secretary, the upshot of which was that the younger man placed a writing-case conveniently and, after uncorking a bottle of ink, proceeded to select a sheet of suitable paper.

Meantime, after some little further cogent conversation, Mr. Pitt declared that, with this momentous news, he must forthwith return to Walmer, there to pen a number of dispatches. Sir David Dundas must be apprised at Canterbury. . . .

"For your signature, sir," the secretary, coming forward, said quietly.

Taking the quill, Mr. Pitt scrawled his name across the foot of the communication. Then, his mien inscrutable, he handed the missive to Charles Fagg with the request that it should be read.

The letter was addressed to Lieutenant-General Sir James Craig, its purport to the effect that the writer, William Pitt, would feel himself obliged if the bearer, Mr. Charles Fagg, could be appointed to an ensigncy in one of the regiments under Sir James's command.

"Sir . . ." Charles stammered, eyes faintly glistening.

Pleading urgency, Mr. Pitt made a show that he had no time for thanks. Additional details, he did say, were sailing the morrow evening for Malta, and though Mr. Fagg would not be able to join the transports, he had no doubt that in a week or so a passage in one of His Majesty's ships might be arranged.

"I'll sail with the reinforcements, if it please you, sir," Charles Fagg said expressionlessly.

"But your uniform . . . your gear, Mr. Fagg," the Prime Minister expostulated, not unkindly, for he was vaguely perturbed by this anxiety to be off. "I recollected your desire for an active appointment, but . . ."

One of the senior officers remarked that in Gib. there was a tailor fellow in Main Street who would surely be able to outfit Mr. Fagg with what he needed, even in the limited time of the call there.

"Nevertheless I should say the young man needs rest," the Prime Minister persisted. "And though I am not familiar with the Portsmouth tides . . . well, I'll warrant he must drive through the night if he continues with his determination."

"That would be my purpose, sir," Charles Fagg affirmed grimly.

Again Mr. Pitt eyed him sharply. "Then you must do as you will, Mr. Fagg," he observed, smiling a shade ruefully. "And now . . ."

A move was made towards the door, outside which Dover's Mayor and Chamberlain, hardly believing their eyes, saw the Prime Minister of war-torn England with his arm about the shoulders of one for whom, in Cannon Street, a mob was hungrily waiting.

The quickest way of returning to the ante-room was through the ballroom, by taking to the left. Mr. Pitt, signalling his entourage to proceed, stayed for a last word with the young man for whose resolute character he had a great deal of respect.

"I wish you all luck, Mr. Fagg, in your new profession of arms," he said, holding out his hand. Subsequently, before parting, he spoke a few words on the Rock, the citadel which Britain must for ever keep, and on Malta, an island-fortress she must ever hold.

"God bless you, sir," muttered Charles Fagg, deeply stirred by the white-hot courage of the ailing man.

"And you, my boy," Mr. Pitt smiled.

The Prime Minister, as though mourning his own inability to participate in active service, stood watching the young man hurry towards the side door beneath the curving flight of steps. Sighing a little, he was turning to the passage into the ballroom when, from the corner of his eye, he caught the flutter of petticoats.

Looking up, he saw a young woman, hands tensely gripping the balustrade, her lovely face as pale as death.

There was something familiar about her, and ere long he remembered once meeting her in the days of the Truce of Amiens, with her the young man whom then he recognised as a fine-wrought tool for his hand.

Their glances meeting, Mr. Pitt beckoned her down.

3

The double doors closed with a soft thud, largely cutting off the sounds made by the company which still waited at the head of the grand staircase. Caroline Rochefort began to walk along the foyer, passing the regularly spaced openings which were level with the magnificent chandeliers of the ballroom.

Why Charles had presented himself at the Rooms she now had guessed beyond doubt, but just why she was walking in the direction in which he had disappeared she hardly knew. Hazily, perhaps, she was aware that she must see him again, allowing him the opportunity to apologise for his abominable words.

"For . . . for abominable they were," she told herself, steeling her heart.

After covering the full length of the corridor and passing beyond the further doors, she reached a landing which was identical in design, though not so handsomely embellished, as that other near the front of the building. She had taken two or three steps towards the head of the stairs when, in the seclusion of a shallow though gloomy recess, she perceived a slight movement.

" Armand ! " she exclaimed in surprise.

M. Saval recovered the quicker. Laughingly he pointed down to the rear vestibule and, in amusing, conspirator fashion, bespoke her silence by touching his lips with a finger.

" You see, Caroline," he then whispered playfully, " you are not alone in being anxious as to what is detaining the renowned Mr. Pitt. I frankly confess I stole away . . . sssh . . ."

From below arose the sharp, metallic sound often heard when there is play in the mechanism of a door-catch. Caroline Rochefort, gazing down, had already seen a number of military and other gentlemen, together with the Mayor and Mr. Jelly, these last in restrained conversation, their unpowdered wigs almost touching. Now she witnessed them all straighten to attention, and watched also whilst three or four officers, with Lady Hester, left one of the apartments outside which the others had been waiting.

Following, there came the Prime Minister, his arm lightly about the shoulders of a young man.

Caroline knew nothing of the fury in her companion's face. She was conscious only of Charles, the man she loved, about whose strange conduct she had so rightly surmised ; the same gallant gentleman who was scorned by folk who had known him from his childhood, by people who should have known him better.

" Charles . . . Charles." Her lips tremblingly formed his name.

It was as if she had been turned into a statue and, when strength returned, Charles had gone. Then, unaware that M. Saval had discreetly slipped away, she found Mr. Pitt compassionately looking at her, found herself responding to the summons he gave.

Gathering up her skirts, she began to descend the broad steps, to curtsy when she reached the ground floor, and to hear the Prime Minister speak, at first quite unheeding of what he said.

Mr. Pitt, in those early moments, recalled their meeting on a former occasion ; meanwhile his shrewd judgment of men and women accurately told him the wherefore of this delightful young woman's despair.

" 'Twas then that I decided how best Mr. Fagg might render service to his country, my dear," he said gravely.

" Yes, sir," she murmured brokenly. " And . . . and he thinks that I also condemn him as do the rest." Mutely she opened her hand, to reveal the impression for the medal which the Corsican would have given his soul to distribute.

Comprehendingly Mr. Pitt nodded. " He has been held to ill account in the town ? "

" Yes, sir," she replied simply. " Despicable . . . outrageous things have been said of him."

One of the secretaries had returned and, being a man devoted to his master, dared to remind that master of time and its flying.

Mr. Pitt moved his head in acknowledgment. Then, taking Caroline's hand, he closed her fingers over Bonaparte's image, holding them so.

" I will do what I can towards rectifying that," he told her comfortingly. " And as for the other, I think you must be wrong, young lady "

Caroline Rochefort's brown eyes filled. " I vow not, sir," she said painfully.

" Why not, my dear," Mr. Pitt asked gently, " put the question to him yourself ? "

From that she changed, to become a spirited creature who would die rather than seek any man's favour.

" I would not do that, sir," she declared, all in arms.

When he left her, that, the last impression, was the one the Prime Minister retained : of a flushed and lovely young woman, soft and tender, but proud and unyielding.

* * * * * * * *

When daylight faded, the hundreds of wax candles in the Rooms were lighted and, for an hour, their mellow rays were thrown on the long and clinging muslin dresses of the ladies. The senior officer present, a Brigadier, had taken it upon himself, in view of the information confidentially received, thus to vary the instructions Sir David Dundas had given.

It had been a strange evening from the moment Mr. Pitt had reappeared. Tongues wagged and continued to wag, more especially those of the ladies and gentlemen of the neighbourhood, who knew more fully in what contumely the name of Fagg was vested. But, at the time when Mr. Pitt requested that Mr. John Fagg should be presented to him, they had truly been struck dumb. Nay, when they witnessed the spectacle of the Prime Minister strolling arm-in-arm with the shipowner, those townsfolk of Dover had been close to doubting their own vision.

From the foyer landing, from the varying heights of the stairs, in the ante-room—they had watched the unbelievable incident, keeping silent at first until, the real truth being revealed, a hum of sheer astonishment escaped them, one so sudden that there was danger that further amazing revelations might escape their eager ears.

But the Prime Minister, fortunately, spoke exceedingly clear all the while. Smiling genially, he had shaken Mr. Fagg's hand, and had promptly felicitated the shipper on being the father of such a son.

"A most courageous young man, Mr. Fagg," he commented admiringly.

John Fagg's face glowed with delight, and instinctively he glanced towards his wife and daughter. Lou and her mother were walking on either side of Lady Hester, and the pride and joy in their expressions were evidence enough that they, too, shared in his feelings.

"You speak most handsomely of Charles, sir," he replied a little huskily.

"As I should," Mr. Pitt retorted emphatically. "At imminent peril to himself he has done magnificent work, under conditions which could not have been the happiest for one of his temperament. You know, Mr. Fagg . . ." he ended whimsically, "we would all prefer a brave uniform when fighting for our beloved land. 'Tis only human nature."

"I suppose so, sir," agreed the shipper.

In their transit they had reached the entrance to the supper-room, and here Mr. Pitt and his companion turned, to walk back across the ante-room, through a human avenue which stretched towards the foot of the grand staircase.

"But, my dear sir," the Prime Minister's voice carried far, "when freedom is in peril there cannot be nice reservation, and this country of ours owes a brave gentleman. . . ."

A buzz of conversation broke out, heads were turned, and Charles Fagg was already in course of becoming a hero to his own folk. During the interval in which Mr. Pitt bade farewell to Mrs. Fagg and Lou, Lady Hester made herself most pleasant, and John Fagg, seeing in this unexpected encounter an opportunity for forwarding that project which his son's disgrace had halted, later begged the Prime Minister for a moment's private conversation.

Mr. Pitt hesitated. "You will be expeditious, Mr. Fagg?" he asked.

"I will, sir," the shipowner promised grimly.

A number of prominent Dover personages were now treated to the sight of Mr. Pitt and Mr. John Fagg sitting on a red plush sofa in the more deserted portion of the ante-room towards the outer door.

The two gentlemen were in close converse.

Concisely John Fagg outlined the history of the harbour of Dover, from the days of King Henry the Eighth's Foundation, which projection into the sea, it was said, was responsible for the trapping of the shingle which formed the Ropewalk before the little port. It was a tale of the townspeople's rising hopes and consequent disappointments.

"I venture to suggest that this, sir, is not entirely a matter for

P

the Barons of Dover," he observed significantly. " The Downs make an excellent anchorage, but when no more than a moderate gale blows anywhere from south-east to east-nor'-east, even His Majesty's ships-of-the-line have to make shift to stand out from an uneasy refuge."

Mr. Pitt took the point. He freely admitted to grave concern that on this battle-front of England there was no haven in which vessels of the Royal Navy, the first line of defence, might safely lie.

" But, Mr. Fagg," he added, " I understand that a natural phenomenon of silting-up would render abortive any attempt at improvement."

" What is your authority for saying that, sir ? " John Fagg asked bluntly.

The Prime Minister countered. " Is it not true that many attempts have been made—all equally unsuccessful ? "

" If you please, sir, I'll quickly relate such endeavours within the last ninety years or so," the shipowner retaliated dourly.

Keenly heard by Mr. Pitt, he began the melancholy recital.

In 1718, he said evenly, Captain Perry surveyed the port and advised the continuation of the South Pier for some 200 feet—the controlling party, as always throughout the ages with the evil example of the King's Foundation as frightful ogre, considered Captain Perry's reasoned views no more ; then there were Mr. Hammond's series of ingenious makeshifts carried out between 1727 and 1732—this, for once enthusiastic, Clerk of the Cheque had been financially blanketed by his sceptical Commissioners ; Mr. John Smeaton examined the haven in 1769—the report of the renowned builder of the Eddystone Lighthouse, because he advocated extension seaward, was summarily rejected ; Mr. Nickall's plan in 1783 was based on similar lines— this noted engineer's suggestions were pared down and mutilated until they became worthless ; and when, only three years before, the famous consultants Rennie and Walker had put forward a scheme— advocating a lengthening of the piers—their proposals had likewise been shelved.

" So the shadow of a Foundation nearly three hundred years old is more potent than the opinions of modern engineers ? " Mr. Pitt deliberated quietly.

" In the eyes of the Harbour Commissioners, yes," John Fagg confirmed.

For a space the Prime Minister continued thoughtful ; then, briskly, he told his companion that what he had heard had interested him vastly. If Dover could be made of service as a National harbour ...

" As you think it could, I take it, Mr. Fagg ? " he said most directly.

"Yes, sir," the shipowner proclaimed stoutly. "In my view it depends on the carrying out of the piers to the true tideway."

Mr. Pitt asked a few more pertinent questions. He was distinctly astounded to learn, concerning income, that the choked-up harbour of Rye received two-thirds of the Passing Tolls, with only one-third accruing to Dover.

"That should be rectified, Mr. Fagg," he remarked. "Without money . . . still . . ." The inference was plain, as John Fagg's beaming countenance showed. The government, if they made themselves responsible for the provision of a National harbour, would not hold up the proposal on the score of funds.

The Prime Minister began to rise.

"Mr. Fagg," he said soberly, "your submissions have made a deep impression on me, and I propose putting in train a new survey . . ." he smiled now, "an *independent* survey, one without recourse to the Commissioners of Harbour, notwithstanding that one of the offices I hold permits me to preside over that body."

"Sir !" ejaculated John Fagg, a wide grin breaking out.

Mr. Waade and Mr. Braems, who were at that moment staring at him, would have been hugely surprised could they have read the shipowner's thoughts. As indeed, it must be admitted, so would Mr. William Pitt.

John Fagg was brown-deep, reflecting on a far grander conception than a harbour into which medium-sized ships could enter at almost any state of the tide.

Another man of vision had had similar longings. Thomas Digges, an Elizabethan engineer called in to report on the haven in the 25th year of Queen Bess's reign, had proposed a scheme awe-inspiring in its magnificence, a design worthy of those days of England's daring and greatness.

On many a winter's night, Mr. Digges's plan before him, John Fagg had struggled in the deciphering of the unfamiliar script.

But now he, too, saw the Bay of Dover enclosed by a gigantic semicircular mole. Within such anchorage vast merchant fleets could swing at ease, with room enough left for all the maritime forces of the King.

That was John Fagg's dream.

* * * * * * * *

In the long room adjacent to the ballroom, the double-doors were being thrown open preparatory to the announcement of supper. Mr. Henry Rochefort, emerging from the card-room with Dr. Crouch, was wittily, though heavily, remarking that their game had come to its conclusion most opportunely, when he saw his daughter.

" My love," he said fondly, " methinks you look a little tired."

Her cheeks were slightly pale and her eyes a trifle shadowed. But then she had been notably gay the later part of the evening, and not for a second had she flagged.

She smiled brightly at the physician, and then made admission to her father.

" Yes, Papa," she agreed, professing to be horribly ashamed of herself, " I vow I'm most dreadfully wearied."

" You want to go home, my dear ? " the banker asked, scrutinising her again.

In reply she gave a quick little gesture of assent, one which passed unnoticed by Dr. Crouch.

" Very well, my love," Mr. Rochefort announced promptly.

They parted, Caroline to the retiring room to gather her cloak, and her father to the vestibule. Shortly they met again in the anteroom, where farewells had to be gone through with a crush of friends, and then they went out to the brief sweetness of the night air and to the stuffiness of the waiting coach.

" Well, my dear," Henry Rochefort remarked kindly, settling himself, " I was indeed pleased to hear the tidings concerning Charles. And ashamed that I ever should have misjudged him."

Caroline laughed. " Delightful, isn't it, Papa ? " she said lightly.

Cannon Street was now behind, and the carriage was screeching across the Market Place. Mr. Rochefort, troubled by a flippancy he had never noticed in his daughter before, glanced a shade anxiously within the brief light of a passing lamp. When King Street was reached he put a tentative question.

" No, Papa," she replied, seemingly distinctly amused. " Why should I be worried about anything ? "

This was even more than ever unlike his straightforward girl. " I thought you were, my dear," he observed quietly, being more unconvinced than ever.

For the whole length of that street she did not speak, intently occupying herself by smoothing out, again and again, the second pair of long gloves with which she always provided herself for the minuet. But suddenly, in Bench Street, near the Parsonage of St. Mary the Virgin's, she impulsively laid her hand on his.

" Papa," she said, her voice low, " I was not telling the truth."

Henry Rochefort's heart warmed. " Is it something in which I might assist you, my dear ? " he inquired gently. " Or Louis ? "

" Neither . . . neither of you, Papa," she whispered . . . and then was silent, very silent.

The only sound within the dark interior was the clop-clop of the horses' iron-shod feet, and once the fleeting deepening of noise as the coach passed within the loom of the old tower. It was then that Caroline spoke again, her words delivered as though she were keeping close watch and guard over herself.

" You see, Papa," she murmured painfully, " you might help me and within minutes bring me a happiness I have always wanted. But, Papa, explanations are oft queasy things, and you might cause me a humiliation I could never forget."

" As you please . . ." Henry Rochefort was saying tenderly when, from some distance ahead, dulled by intervening buildings, there came the echoes of a multitude of rough voices.

" Humph ! " The banker thrust his head out of the window and looked towards Severus's Gate.

It was twenty-seven years since the first Paving Act, and the farthermost outpost of the Paving Commissioners, in so far as street lighting was affected, had in that interval been advanced to the junction of Town Wall Street and Snargate Street. There, on the corner, a bracket lamp cast forth its flickering yellow rays.

" Most extraordinary," muttered Mr. Rochefort, for certainly no mob was visible, and nothing but a large crowd could make that uproar.

He was on the point of withdrawing as the coach was beginning to take the corner into Snargate Street ; then a shout from his own man, and an oath from the startled postilion of another conveyance swinging into narrow Bench Street, kept him where he was.

The vehicles collided obliquely, their wheels for an instant locking, their windows nearly touching. A young gentleman turned to look at the young lady so near.

4

The sentiments of the crowd in Cannon Street, who had blood-thirstily proclaimed an intention of whipping Charles Fagg until his mean soul yielded up the ghost, changed in a twinkling when the brave news of the doings of that young man percolated to them.

It was therefore not surprising that, after the tail-end of Mr. Pitt's calash had vanished and the storm of cheering had died, the suggestion of visiting Mr. John Fagg's mansion was bruited, it being already known that the gallant young fellow had slipped out of the Royal Oak Rooms, escaping attention by passing along the un-salubrious Black Ditch.

Immediately a move was made towards Town Wall Street, which quiet road, as night came, was enlivened by the hullaballoo of a throng which surged about the pleasant Georgian residence of the town's most prominent shipowner.

Noisily it was demanding that Mr. Charles Fagg should show himself, but it was a thunderous din which arose when the head ostler from the Antwerp Stables himself brought to the door a post-chaise.

With that indication of imminent departure, with diminutive Jim Page obviously prepared to do all he could to honour this hero of the town, excitement grew more intense.

Little Pent House was aglow with caressing light. The hall was bright, and the mirror behind the sconce in the corner of the staircase landing gave the illusion of a doubled cluster of lazily waving flames ; everywhere was the bustle attending the starting-out of the son of the house, with nearly all contributing towards the speeding of the traveller.

For the journey Charles Fagg now wore coat and breeches of dark stuff. He was sitting at the bureau in his bedroom where, after writing one short note, he was engaged upon another and most important letter, his brow knit with the perplexities of composing with a be-fuddled mind.

His sister Lou, who was dawdling over the very simple task of packing two fine cambric shirts into the valise not yet strapped, kept her hands busy a-doing nothing. All the while, however, half anxiously and half hopefully, she was watching her beloved brother.

" I have put those extra shirts in, Charles," she said eventually, for something to say.

He replied abstractedly. " Thanks, Lou, love . . . thanks," all the time his endeavour being towards the placing into precise form that matter of grave importance of which he had neglected to acquaint the Prime Minister.

" . . . this man," he wrote, " I saw in Boulogne during the employment from which I am just returned, and the enquiries I made then, though necessarily guarded, were sufficient . . ."

Lou could contain herself no longer. Quite intentionally she looked over his shoulder.

" Charles, dear," she then murmured, " you're not writing to Caroline and . . . and if you are not going to see her before you leave . . . well . . ." Her dismay showed plainly in her grey eyes.

Her brother tried to enforce some teasing element into his voice as he stretched up to grasp her ear, gently to pull the lobe.

" So you try to arrange the affairs of the universe, eh ? " he laughed.

" But, Charles . . ." she began again.

Smiling, he stayed her, and continued with his letter.

" . . . amply to establish to my satisfaction that M. Saval, or Captain Chassepot to name him rightly, is in the service of the Emperor's Chef de Police, Fouché.

" For your considerashun on the relative advantages to be gained either by cutting short his career forthwith or by permitting him to remain at liberty under discrete observation, the following details may serve. . . ."

A little more and he had done. After folding over the ends of the sheet, he found wax and, taking up a candle, dropped a blob of red, on it impressing the seal which Mr. Pitt's secretaries knew.

Then the final superscription, " *The Right Honourable W*ᵐ· *Pitt.*"

He propped the letter on the left-hand side of the bureau, a little apart from the other communication to Louis Rochefort in which, briefly, without any hidden sting, he expressed regret for the mis-understanding which had arisen between them. Louis was Charles's oldest friend, and he wanted the friendship to be resumed on his return.

His mother came in breathlessly. " The chaise is at the door, Charles," she said. " I think you have everything you need and——" She was carrying a basket covered with a snowy-white napkin. Inside, between well-buttered slices of darkish bread, were pieces of prime tongue which cook had thinly sliced, and a fruit tart of such dimensions that, had his journey been along Watling Street from Dover to Canterbury and thence to its most northerly limit, he would have been hard put to deal with the last crumb.

" Good God ! " Charles laughed. " And, by heaven," he roared, finding a cobwebby bottle, wrapped in a similar napkin, for which John Fagg a few minutes before had ransacked the cellar.

" Your father . . ." Mrs. Fagg was blinking, when that gentleman appeared.

" Here, my boy, put this in your pocket," he said genially, holding out a jingling leathern tie-bag. " 'Tis fifty yellow Georges and . . . and now damme, it's time you were off," he finished gruffly.

They found Susan outside the room, with the news that Horatio was awake ; at the same time Keziah Hart was panting up the stairs, her intention being, she declared, to take Mr. Charles's baggage down.

" I'll see to that, Keziah . . ." Charles was beginning to say.

Arms akimbo, his old nurse dealt with him. " *You'll* see to Master Horatio, Mr. Charles," she observed pugnaciously. " Ugh . . ." She then smiled, waddling off to carry out this one errand of love of which she was determined not to be robbed.

Whilst John Fagg and his wife returned downstairs, and Charles went off to see Susan's small son, Keziah, kneeling, strapped up that bag which was still unfastened.

She found the double burden more than she had bargained for, and just by the door of the bedroom, she hurriedly put down the two valises.

For years had she known of the loose floorboard, but never, so close had Charles been about it, had she had any idea of its connection with a secret hiding-place in the bureau about which, in his boyhood days, her favourite had been so proud.

There was a faint click, and with it disappeared that crimson-sealed denunciation of a spy.

Mrs. George Rochefort's room, now necessarily a larger one than that of her maidenhood, was on the Town Wall Street side of the house. The four-year-old Horatio had long before been aroused from slumber by the hubbub outside.

With rising indignation the young gentleman heard of his cousin going off to the wars. Sitting bolt-upright, black hair tumbling over his forehead, his dark eyes gleamed hotly.

" Why can't I go with you ? " he asked stormily.

Charles Fagg most effectively handled that query. Very deliberately, intently watched by a child too interested to think of giving vent to seething revolt, he picked up a toy musket and, most significantly, patted the tiny stock.

Horatio fidgeted. " I've drilled every day, Cousin Charles," he mumbled self-excusingly. " *Every* day," he added on a rising note.

" And seldom," the diplomat intervened hastily, " have I had report of a recruit who handles his weapon so well."

" Report, Cousin Charles ! " Young Horatio goggled.

Susan Rochefort, tender affection in her as she looked at both of them, listened to a tale which brought starry delight into her son's eyes. Following that, the two gentlemen gravely debated the perils of sending untrained men overseas, until Horatio freely admitted that, to take his place in the front line of England's battling soldiers, he perhaps required to give further attention to his warlike craft.

This decided, Charles bent beneath the canopy to kiss the warrior.

" Bye-bye, Horatio," he said. " And be a good soldier whilst I'm away, and promise you'll guard your dear mother always."

Master Horatio, realising that such solemn request merited an outstandingly staunch reply, proceeded to clear his throat in a most alarming fashion. Whilst his mother's blue eyes widened in horror, he spat on the floor, valiantly if not too professionally, for part of his effort still dribbled down his chin.

" Have my guts for a kerchief if I doesn't, Cousin Charles," he squealed with satisfaction.

" *Horatio !* " gasped Mrs. George.

Charles Fagg doubled with mirth, and his Aunt Susan herself was smiling when, after young Horatio, lost in one side of the great bed, had responded to his cousin with a salute no less smart, she and Charles were at the other side of the door.

" Valentine Pepper," she laughed. " *You* picked up the most awful sayings from him too, and . . ."

They turned downstairs. Now was the time for parting, and Charles was no believer in unduly protracting such ordeals. He fondly kissed the women, not forgetting Keziah, and wrung his father's hand whilst that gentleman vigorously used the other to thump his tall son's shoulder. John Fagg, though more than a little moved himself, did not intend a pack of females to sense it, being fully appreciative of the contagiousness of these feelings.

A last word, and Charles Fagg was off, to be greeted with a storm of cheering from the swollen crowd outside. He was stepping into the chaise when the recollection of one thing undone came to him, and he battled back a couple of paces.

Susan Rochefort was close by the doorpost, the nearest to him of his family. Against a deafening background of noise he tried to tell her of the letters to be delivered, and she, straining to hear him, gathered most, though not all, of what he was endeavouring to say.

" Valentine . . ." he shouted, and she knew it was Captain Pepper who should carry the missive. " On the bureau ? " she thought she heard him say, and, repeating that back to him, found confirmation in his nod.

A last wave and he was gone, with half the throng pursuing the chaise as it bumped along Town Wall Street. The door of the Fagg residence slowly closed, the gracious doorway became dark again, the glow in the fanlight gradually fading.

A lessening drone of the wheels told Charles Fagg that the chaise had passed over Butchery Gate, beneath which, before dividing to form the Island, old Dour ran ; and a change of direction, together with the faint illumination of the approach to New Bridge by the lamp opposite, was the indication that Severus's Gate and the corner of Bench Street had been reached.

He heard a sudden yell, and Jim Page's deeper oath ; almost simultaneously there was a shivering thud as the chaise jarred to a standstill.

For the merest infinity of time two young people looked at one another, until Caroline Rochefort, all too conscious of the revealing light and the glistening tear which was trickling down her cheek, turned away her head to hide this plainly evident distress ; whilst Charles

Fagg, vision-strained and desperate for rest, missed that first pathetic symbol and saw only a movement instinctive of recoil, as so, miserably, he thought.

Then the caps of the axle-trees freed. The chaise, bumping heavily over the narrow kerbstone, continued towards the Market Place, meantime Mr. Henry Rochefort's well-appointed coach entered the dark vault of Snargate Street, with the banker now fully cognizant of his girl's heartache.

"Caroline, my dearest," he ventured gently.

Fiercely she turned to him in the gloom, even as she went on with the dabbing of her eyes.

"Papa, you must pledge me this," she pleaded passionately. "Nobody must ever know of this present ridiculous weakness of mine. Throughout the whole evening at the Rooms not another soul beyond Mr. Pitt has had an inkling of how I have felt, and in the days to come I swear they shall not know either."

The banker, who had loved once and once only, squeezed her hand understandingly as the vehicle began to slow.

"And now, Papa," she said shakily, "if I am to deceive Martha I must sound as if I *had* been to a gay Assembly."

She achieved a laugh, a little tremulous albeit, when she entered the hall of her father's house.

Some fifteen minutes later the thoughts of three widely separated people were very near.

Caroline Rochefort was sitting beside her bedroom window, the soft night breeze gently disturbing the curly tendrils of her hair.

Charles Fagg, on the Folkestone post-road where it came perilously near to the verge of the high cliff, was looking back to Dover and thinking of what the little seaport held.

Susan Rochefort was in her nephew's bedroom and, not having heard Charles's directions over well, had been mightily relieved to find the letter. But it was not this note addressed to Louis which was causing her worried look, though instinctively she was aware that that could not contain anything likely to settle the misunderstanding she was utterly convinced had arisen between Charles and Caroline.

Inordinately fond of both, Mrs. George wretchedly pondered as to what could be amiss.

5

The battered *Victory*, bearing Lord Nelson's fragile form preserved in a cask of spirits, had sadly sailed by Dover. Trafalgar was past, with the land mourning the death of her great sailor rather than celebrating a sea victory which must, for years, make invasion impossible.

After living many months under conditions so tense, the townsfolk of Dover were left with a sense of flatness, and neither Mr. Fulton's very successful demonstration off Deal, where with one of his improved torpedoes he blew up a brig in the presence of Mr. Pitt and a distinguished company, nor the Master of Ordnance's new survey of the harbour, as promised to John Fagg by the Prime Minister, excited more than mild interest.

Elsewhere the news was bad. The French, following the battle of Ulm, had taken Vienna, and Austerlitz brought both the collapse of Austria and the break-up of Mr. Pitt's latest coalition. The dispatch of still another British Expedition had proved fruitless, the 6,000 troops sent to the Baltic for the purpose of retaking Hanover, and then freeing Holland, having to be brought home immediately the hopeless predicament of continental allies became known.

If the inhabitants of the Cinque Port were lethargic after years of strain they were contrastingly energetic concerning a grievous wrong they had done.

The Dover Volunteers made Charles Fagg an honorary captain of their company, and in further appreciation of his gallant doings, a special gold medal was ordered for presentation when he returned home. And Valentine Pepper, for his share in the young man's valiant deeds, received a purse of one hundred guineas, a handsome subscription indeed.

This was during that same week in which report was received that Admiral Villeneuve, released on parole to France, had mysteriously died, after getting no nearer to Paris than Rennes . . . still another well-known name to be added to the lengthening list of queer suicides of those from whom an Imperial Master had withdrawn favour.

Some few days after the delighted ex-boatswain publicly accepted the award, Miss Caroline Rochefort was taking tea by herself in the little drawing-room.

" I wonder," she murmured pensively, still worrying how to persuade the housekeeper into a happiness so richly deserved. " Mmmm, she *must* marry Captain Pepper."

When Martha came in for candle-lighting, a cunning little scheme was in readiness.

For a while the housekeeper found herself detained—a piece of gossip, a trifle of domestic interest. . . .

" 'Tis well you have brought me up so admirably, Martha dear," Caroline smiled. " For I declare you have made me into a veritable paragon, and I doubt . . . la, the conceit of me ! . . . that any other young woman in the town is less like to be cheated in the kitchen, or is more accomplished in the management of servants and such-like."

Martha tossed her greying head. " Not a one, I'll warrant, Miss Caroline."

Thereupon, most craftily, Miss Rochefort brought Captain Pepper into the conversation. When were he and Martha thinking of getting married ? As she herself was admitted by Martha to be a most competent creature, she supposed the banns would soon be up.

Martha Teddiman dithered. " But, Miss Caroline," she opened weakly.

Her surprise subsiding, her strength grew, and she brought forward all the objections in the world. Pepper and her would be wed when the proper time came, but it wasn't now. She'd made a promise to Miss Caroline's Mamma . . .

" You dear," Caroline cried affectionately, impetuously rising to give the housekeeper a cuddle and a kiss.

" So you see, Miss Caroline . . ." Martha sniffed, vigorously poking the fire to hide her face.

Emotion might be very right in such circumstances, but luckily the young mistress of the house recollected that it would not best serve her ends.

" I understand, Martha, dear," she sighed profoundly.

This being beyond her, Martha Teddiman straightened herself, poker still in hand, and remained rigidly so.

Caroline, staring steadfastly into the fire, spoke of the love the family had for Martha. Martha could always stay with them, gladly so, and when she became too old there would always be a pleasant little room for her and . . .

" You see, Martha, dear," she said, ineffably wise, " men are oft like that."

" Like what, Miss Caroline ? " The housekeeper stared open-mouthed.

Gently Miss Rochefort told her. Frequently, especially at a certain age, gentlemen became contented with their bachelor ways. They enjoyed a female with whom to spend part of their leisure, but as for matrimony . . . that was very different.

" Meaning Pepper's going to keep me dangling 'til I'm a tabby, Miss Caroline ? " Martha demanded fiercely.

Contrarily, Miss Rochefort vowed she had not been thinking of Captain Pepper, her protestations so urgent that the over-emphasis had quite the result intended.

" Oh ! " Martha Teddiman observed grimly, and betook herself off.

Perhaps being cruel to be kind was justifiable, but Caroline Rochefort felt horrible about it.

When Valentine Pepper, the following morning at Elizabeth Street, learnt that he had a lady caller, he was openly nonplussed. But speedily he limped to the lower floor.

" Miss Caroline," he beamed, seeing his visitor.

Miss Rochefort wasted no time. She told him the whole tale, and she firmly instructed him as to how he should act.

" Me 'esitate to wed her ? " he ejaculated.

He had to receive further instruction and, when it dawned on him, he gave vent to a great bull of a laugh.

" My, Miss Caroline," he roared, " you be a one, ben't you ? "

" You want to marry Martha, don't you ? " the young lady asked severely.

If Martha Teddiman could have seen her man's face then, she would have had no qualms. Rough and ready Valentine Pepper might be, but he never wavered towards those he loved.

" I wants nothing better, Miss Caroline," he declared eloquently.

The plan began to take hold of him. It was his custom, as Miss Caroline knew, to buy a couple of gallery tickets for the Playhouse of a Saturday night. Then he always went to Sunday evening service with Martha too . . .

" I'll give 'er a miss," he chuckled. " Nay," enthusiasm rising, " I'll do more. I'll make 'er think——"

Most decidedly his tutor put a stop to that. Did he want to lose Martha altogether ? No, he must do exactly as she told him.

" Act delicut, eh ? " he said dubiously.

" Yes," Miss Rochefort replied impressively.

" Act delicut," he muttered.

" And you can do it, Captain Pepper," he was informed.

Valentine Pepper scratched his poll, squinted fearsomely, shuffled, reflected, and finally squared his massive shoulders.

" I can, an' will, Miss Caroline," he observed resolutely.

" There ! " dimpled Miss Rochefort.

At the end of January, in the week after that in which the country was shaken by the news of Mr. Pitt's death, Martha Teddiman became Valentine Pepper's wife.

*　　*　　*　　*　　*　　*　　*　　*

The statute of 1338—whereby it was ordered that, in days of danger, one bell only should be rung in the churches of Kent within seven leagues of the sea, lest there should be confusion in case of attack—had been revived the year before. But, for Martha's marriage,

Mr. Henry Rochefort had persuaded the military authorities to relax the rule.

So a regular wedding it was, and never did a couple look more happy when emerging from St. Mary the Virgin's. Martha as bright and gay as you please, and her husband, face shining with soap and water, his grin extending from ear to ear.

" C'm on, love," he said fondly. " Get 'old of my fin, me moppet."

So the procession, in twos, began to follow the newly-weds. Through the Market Place they went, good wishes being called from every hand, towards Severus's Gate, where John Fagg and his wife turned up Town Wall Street. Behind the bride and bridegroom was M. Armand Saval, with Caroline Rochefort on his arm. Then came Mr. Henry Rochefort with Lou Fagg, Louis Rochefort . . .

And what a wedding feast it was, the banker doing all he could on this day for one, as his daughter had truly said, so loved by the family.

" 'Tis my pleasure . . ." Henry Rochefort toasted the bride.

A spread as fine as ever you saw, and a speech by Captain Pepper which drew howls of laughter from the throng and a sharp dig in the ribs from his blushing wife.

Before them all Valentine gave her a smacking kiss.

" Nay, you can scold me to-morrow, but you ain't a-going to shreap me on my wedding day," he guffawed.

" Of course she's not," Caroline Rochefort laughed.

" Methinks you are mortally well disposed towards the fellow, Caroline," Armand Saval grimaced. " I protest I mus' seek him out to discover the secret."

In the stir, however, the gallantry was lost, Mrs. Valentine Pepper, amidst tremendous acclamation, being engaged in putting her husband in his rightful place.

" Ain't she a peart 'un ? " roared the bridegroom, highly delighted with her.

" Valentine," Martha smiled tenderly.

Seeing how it was with them, Caroline Rochefort knew she had not done any wrong.

6

By early spring John Fagg realised that the Fox-Grenville ministry did not intend to proceed further in the matter of Dover Harbour.

With the same select number of cronies who, years before, had worked with him, the business was thrashed out. It was decided that steps must be taken towards acquiring for Dover a greater proportion of the Passing Tolls. Money was needed, and though the Harbour Commissioners would have the spending of any additional revenue, that objection had, of necessity, become a secondary consideration.

" 'Twill have to be done through the Court of Brotherhood and Guestling," Kit Crundall observed. " An' though Rye will be agin us, t'other Ports'll give us their support, I reckon."

" Aye, but remember that Hugo Stratton is the Court's Notary," Nicholas Stokes remarked significantly.

" But we've the town with us," Richard Breton commented succinctly.

" And them that's not we'll fight," Jeremy Nethersole said pugnaciously. " Though it won't do to forget that Stratton is to be numbered amongst 'em."

John Fagg was deputed to see the Town Clerk and received one of the surprises of his life when, braced for battle, he entered Mr. Stratton's room a few days later.

" In my . . . er . . . official capacity, you will appreciate I cannot . . . er . . . take sides, Mr. Fagg," the bewigged lawyer boomed.

The shipowner nodded. " No," he agreed guardedly.

Though the Town Clerk most skilfully shrouded his meaning in a flow of words both ambiguous and obscure, the impression survived that he was not without an element of disquietude as to the future of the town unless change came about.

" I have, admittedly, long opposed you, Mr. Fagg," he ranted on, " and . . ." he added acutely, wagging his podgy first finger sternly, " still do in some aspects, but 'tis now my considered opinion that more should be . . . er . . . done towards remedying the state of the haven."

John Fagg, knowing his man, expressed satisfaction at some length and then, still knowing his man, begged for guidance as to procedure.

This unspoken tribute brought a hint of gratification into Mr. Stratton's eyes. Leaning back in his chair he became quite expansive and subsequently, his hands meeting in an attitude of prayer, spoke most judicially to the smoked beam above his head.

" The Court of Brotherhood and Guestling, of which I am privileged, as you know, Mr. Fagg, to be the Notary . . ."

By June, that Court had decided upon a Petition to the Government and, when the document was finally prepared, John Fagg posted with it to London.

Thereafter was waiting, waiting, waiting . . . endless waiting.

Abroad, Napoleon had further secured himself as the Tyrant of

Europe. The Emperor's brother had been made King of Holland, Joseph Bonaparte received the crown of the Two Sicilies, and their benefactor formed petty German states into the Confederation of the Rhine, of which he proclaimed himself Protector.

These high-handed doings evoked immediate response, but Prussia's hasty alliance with Russia and England ended disastrously in October, when at Jena the Emperor captured the 100,000 men who formed the Prussian Army.

And still there was no news of the fate of the Petition.

" What with that and the war situation," the shipowner once groaned towards the end of the year.

More reverses for British arms had there been, mostly accountable to the crazily small forces employed.

In July, Sir John Stuart's five thousand men won a fine victory in Calabria, the bayonet being the weapon which brought the success. Had the bayonets been five times as many, the greater part of Southern Italy would have been cleared of the French. As it was, the British were compelled hastily to withdraw.

In November, Sir James Craig's landing at Naples suffered even worse fate, the retirement better described as flight.

Christmas . . . still no word of the Petition.

" Forgotten in a departmental pigeon-hole, damn me if it ain't," John Fagg growled.

But that precious piece of parchment, dusty though it might be, had not completely faded from the official mind. Some three months later, an easy-going Under-Secretary scrawled a marginal annotation on the document in which so many hopes rested.

Soon the real fight for Dover Harbour began.

Part IV

1807-1809

CHAPTER ONE

I

SHORTLY after noon one blustery March day in the year 1807, a young lady was leisurely riding past the frowning old Castle on her way home. Coming to the steeper part of the descent of the Deal Road, she adjured her beast to care, but lower down, near the gipsies' encampment at Tinker's Close, she reined in. From this still fine vantage point, before dropping down to Eastbrooke and Town Wall Street, she paused awhile to look over the nestling town and the sea beyond, giving especial attention to the escorting vessels of an outward-bound convoy led by an East Indian packet, itself a craft, save for the open waist, greatly ressembling a 64-gun man-of-war.

A very favourite view of Lou Fagg's was this, one which, when coming into Dover from that direction, she always savoured to the full.

"Steady, Tokey boy," she said soothingly, checking her mount's propensity to resume the journey.

A light swell was rolling in from the south-west, pigeons paraded on the lee side of the roofs, and the weather-beaten Cinque Port looked very much as ever. If difference there were since Trafalgar it was almost imperceptible, and that only in the defences of the place. These now seemed less hastily contrived, certainly more orderly, and positively of greater efficiency.

"Come, Tokey," Lou murmured.

And *Toke's Quality*, the most pampered and petted four-legged creature in the kingdom, as her father had it, moved off sedately. Charles Fagg, before leaving home nearly nineteen months before, had placed Lord Poynte's gift into the care of his sister, and right faithfully had she carried out the loving charge.

"Whoa, Tokey boy," Miss Fagg cried unexpectedly.

His comfortable stall awaiting him, *Toke's Quality* expressed mild disapproval on this departure from routine, but his mistress, having glimpsed a flag flying over the Council House, would have her way.

465

" 'Tis at half mast too," Lou mused, brushing off a strand of hair wind-driven across her eyes.

Wondering on this she completed her ride to Little Pent House. Perhaps Mr. Waade, the Clerk of the Cheque, had died suddenly. Or maybe fat Sir Walter Plumbley. . . .

Later, however, she forgot all about it and did not remember until nearly the end of dinner. Her mother was very much agog at the time.

" But if the Dutch do rise in rebellion, John ? " Mrs. Fagg was saying vivaciously.

Mainly through fishermen meeting whilst engaged upon their lawful business, the townsfolk of Dover often received news, of varying reliability, from the other side. At the moment a strong rumour was abroad that the cruelly subjugated people of Holland might soon break into revolt against their conqueror.

John Fagg shook his head warningly. " Shouldn't place too much hope on't, Polly," he commented. " Though . . ." he conceded this with a nod, " in my view it will occur some day or other in one of the countries where Bonaparte has set his iron hand."

On this Horatio peremptorily demanded complete details relative to iron hands, and what with his shrill chatter and his mother's subsequent insistence that he should eat the last spoonful on his plate, the affairs of unhappy peoples were forgotten.

Then it was that Lou recollected the flag which whipped over the Council House. Promptly she asked her father about it.

Blandly John Fagg eyed his girl. " Lord Hargill has passed away, my dear," he informed her solemnly.

" Lord Hargill, Papa ? " A pair of sweet grey eyes portrayed an utter ignorance of the deceased gentleman.

Her father's eyebrows went up in exaggerated astonishment.

" You don't know Lord Hargill, my love ? Lord Hargill of Hargill Park on the borders of Kent and Surrey ? " The shipowner clicked his tongue despairingly. " Here," he resumed, " is a noble lord who has had connection with this town since before you were born, and there you calmly sit——"

Lou's amazement might be growing but her mother decidedly was becoming cross at equal rate.

" Really, John," Mrs. Fagg protested, " how should the child know ? I protest I hardly do myself."

Her husband's reply to that might have been airily delivered, but the manner in which he pushed his plate from him was perhaps the better indication of his mood.

" True, 'tis no more than an affair which concerns her bread and butter, Polly," he agreed exasperatingly.

Not another word had been heard from London regarding the Petition which he had taken to the capital twelve months before. Mrs. Fagg was perfectly sensible of the cause of her husband's seething ill-humour, but she did not intend to allow him to vent his spleen on one quite innocent.

" She should know," the master of the house observed most unfairly.

Irritably he rose from the table. " Lou, my dear," he continued mirthlessly, " his lordship of Hargill Park was a Commissioner of Dover Harbour, an office which entitled him to have a say—but, damme, what's the use. . . ."

With that he impatiently left for the parlour, leaving the ladies looking at one another concernedly, and with Polly Fagg, in particular, heaving a deep sigh.

" I declare I can't imagine what we're coming to, I'm sure," she murmured hopelessly.

Having a fund of resilience, however, she soon brightened and, when Horatio rushed after his Uncle John, in prospect of being permitted a much desired puff at a pipe, she was able to join in discussing more general topics.

" A gala, too, Polly," Mrs. George Rochefort laughed delightedly.

Monday week, *The Maid of Bristol* was billed to open at the Playhouse, with a genuine London company, a special gala performance being advertised for the Thursday night.

" Caroline and her papa are going that evening too," Lou said excitedly. " Oh, 'twill be elegant, won't it ? "

But that diverting entertainment so eagerly anticipated was completely spoilt for the Fagg family. During that Thursday afternoon of delirious preparation, even whilst the hairdresser was attending at Little Pent House, sensational news was being passed about in the town.

After 201 years, for the first time since the day of King James the First's Charter, a Dover-born gentleman had been *appointed* to the company of the ' eleven discreet men ' who constituted the body corporate of the Commissioners of Harbour. He was recognised as an implacable personality who, for close on two decades, had strenuously put forth the conviction that any attempt to coerce one particular force of nature would be in vain.

Henry Rochefort, Esq., Banker, had succeeded Lord Hargill on the Harbour Board.

*　　*　　*　　*　　*　　*　　*　　*

A continuous storm of cheering rose to the elaborately decorated roof of the Playhouse. Mr. Marchbanks had spoken the Epilogue, but they *would* have him back. He bowed again and again, smilingly shook his head, but still the uproar continued, still they would not be denied.

Ultimately the wildly enthusiastic audience had its desire, and the actor who had won all hearts thrillingly declaimed his lines.

> " God ! must the mushroom Despot of the hour
>   The spacious world encircle with his power ?
>   Stretching his baneful feet from pole to pole,
>   Stride, Corsican-Colossus of the whole ?
>   Forbid it, Heaven !—and forbid it, Man !
>   Can Man forbid it ?—Yes ; *the English* can.
>   'Tis theirs, at length, to fight the world's great cause,
>   Defend their own, and rescue other's laws."

More thunderous applause—and then the end of an evening which all, apart from certain exceptions, had found most pleasurable.

With the final fall of the curtain a hum of conversation arose, the jabber and cackle more pronounced than usual. Friends and acquaintances exchanged far fewer smiles and nods of greeting, the interest of all being directed elsewhere. Heads were being turned, it was true, but the glances of their owners were equally divided between two well-known gentlemen of the town, the one being the new Harbour Commissioner, and the other a man who latterly had sworn that the years of dallying in respect to the haven should be brought to a speedy conclusion.

Captain Nethersole and his wife, behind neighbours too rapt to move anyhow but slowly, edged sideways along the fifth row of the ornate, red-plush seats in the pit, their intention to reach the Faggs, to whom Caroline Rochefort had already gone.

Lou was talking to her dear friend, and Mrs. Nethersole was delivering a non-stop stream of inconsequences to Mrs. Fagg and Mrs. George Rochefort when Jeremy Nethersole seized the opportunity for a quiet word with Mr. Fagg.

" This'll make our fight harder, John," he said gravely. " We know well enow what Rochefort's sentiments on the haven are."

There was a flickering glint in the shipowner's grey eyes, and a queer smile about his mouth.

" Aye, Jeremy," he agreed thoughtfully. " But methinks we might be able to offset his influence with the Commissioners."

" How so, John ? " puzzled the mail-packet captain.

John Fagg fingered his chin, his expression unfathomable. He spoke first of those who had long striven for the prosperity of the port. There was Jeremy himself, then Kit Crundall and Nicholas Stokes—

Dick Breton, because of his employment, could not be considered, of course.

" I have it in mind that we elect one amongst ourselves to the Harbour Board," he observed slowly.

Frankly, Captain Nethersole gaped. " Elect one of us ? " he ejaculated.

" 'Twould be a way of ensuring that the haven has a friend on the Board," the shipowner said calmly.

By now Jeremy Nethersole was on the way to being partially convinced that shock had unhinged John. But it was he who received the shock.

" Every September, Jeremy," John Fagg continued serenely, " a ceremony takes place in St. Mary's. Being Dover bred and born, I suppose you'll be knowing to what I'm alluding."

The packet captain was now quite sure about poor old John.

" Aye, I do, John," he agreed, humouring his companion. " Every year Mayor-making takes place there—— By God ! "

His jaw dropped, he gave the impression of being petrified despite the stinging rebuke he received from his wife. Mrs. Nethersole, in the very middle of a highly complicated story about her daughter's love affair, threw aside a reminder that he was in decent company and thereupon, wifely duty done, effortlessly resumed her galloping theme on the same note she had left off.

" By God, John ! " Captain Nethersole repeated, this time softly.

" Aye," the shipowner commented laconically.

Boisterously the seaman slapped him on the back. " We can do it too, John," Jeremy Nethersole said delightedly. " And whether or not Rochefort be as hostile as ever . . ."

In the centre aisle of the stalls that question was being answered. Mr. Henry Rochefort was accepting congratulations and had just parted from Mr. Paul Elam, Master of the Lodesmen, when old Mr. Jephrez Baker butted in.

" Still going to go agin the interests of the town, Rochefort ? " he asked testily.

From a height which was very superior the banker coldly eyed the inquirer.

" For countless years, Mr. Baker," he replied curtly, " I have never attempted to disguise the opinion I hold on the harbour question, and you may take it that those views remain unaltered. As a townsman I constantly opposed what I considered must necessarily involve a most wanton waste of money, and as a Commissioner I shall inflexibly continue to use what influence I have to the same end."

" You will, will you ? " growled the tallow-chandler.

Always choleric-tempered, there is no doubt that Mr. Baker

would have boiled over forthwith had not Caroline joined her father and M. Saval. As it was, the banker's daughter being a favourite of his, the candle manufacturer contented himself with a few explosive and highly fearsome noises.

The auditorium still showed no signs of clearing—supporters of port development were pressing round John Fagg, and a more limited stream continued to flow towards Henry Rochefort.

" Methinks Monsieur your father will for many minutes find himself engaged, Caroline," Armand Saval remarked considerately. " That being so, I suggest, if 'tis your pleasure, that you permit me to escort you home."

In other circumstances Caroline Rochefort would have been the last to leave any assembly, but this tragic cleavage terribly dismayed her.

" If you will, Armand," she said gratefully.

They proceeded towards the fine entrance hall in Snargate Street, their progress not entirely uninterrupted. Caroline had a host of friends, and her companion did not lack a measure of popularity in certain well-defined circles. Though M. Saval shook his head and smiled enigmatically when taxed, it was widely supposed that he often risked his life by slipping over to the Continent for information.

" A mos' unpleasant night after all, Caroline," the Frenchman remarked when they were outside, taking her arm the better to hold her whilst crossing the uneven road.

" A most unpleasant night," Caroline Rochefort sighed.

She felt unaccountably sad. Since she had been a child Charles's father and her own had been at bitter•variance, but now she had an awful presentiment that their differences were drawing to a dreadful climax.

Hardly conscious that Armand's arm touched lightly about her waist as she passed before him, she entered her home.

2

The government mills of departmental procedure grind slow, and not always surely, but a fortnight after a gathering of beaux in the Royal Oak Yard saw off the four coaches which carried away the young ladies of *The Maid of Bristol* company . . . Mr. Hugo Stratton, ' Captain ' Stratton in drill hours, received a most important communication from Whitehall.

Mr. John Fagg being absent on one of his periodical visits to Thames ports from which his larger vessels ran, the Town Clerk, in his capacity of Notary to the Court of Brotherhood and Guestling, summoned three gentlemen to his office.

Messrs. Nethersole, Stokes and Crundall, the 'inner cabinet' the Clerk of the Passage comically termed the quartet when John Fagg was with them, duly presented themselves.

After fit and proper preliminaries, Mr. Stratton imparted the contents of an impressive folio.

" All the Passing Tolls say you ? " Captain Nethersole jumped up

" *All ?* " Mr. Crundall demanded, no less overwrought.

" The *whole* of 'em ? " Nicholas Stokes spluttered.

Mr. Stratton most tolerantly took pity on them and, whilst they, with a meekness most suspicious had he been shrewder, listened respectfully to him, he reduced the pitfalls of legal phraseology into simple English.

" In short, the sum total of revenue accruing from the Passing Tolls is now placed at the disposal of the Commissioners of Dover Harbour," he concluded obligingly.

A little afterwards, expressing fulsome thanks, the three gentlemen withdrew, their intention to go into immediate conclave at Mr. Stokes's house.

Pipes evenly burning and glasses not too remote, a long-prepared and cunning scheme was reviewed, one to which, of course, John Fagg was privy.

" So 'tis to-night we'd better call the full cabinet," Mr. Stokes winked.

This body, which was kept in blissful ignorance of the actual powers behind the throne, met in Mr. Jephrez Baker's evil-smelling candle manufactory, a gesture, considering the character of its owner, not without a measure of guile.

In addition to the 'inner cabinet' there were present Mr. Baker, Mr. Richard Breton, Mr. Francis Stone, Mr. William Beverley, Mr. Henry Templeman, Mr. Philip Virgile, Mr. Thomas Bullack, Mr. Matthew Adcock and Mr. Jonathan Dawkes.

Full report on the interview with Mr. Stratton was made by Mr. Crundall ; thereupon Mr. Stokes submitted for consideration the next step—the calling of a meeting of the Freemen.

" For why ? " demanded Mr. Jephrez Baker, snapping back the lid of the snuff-box he had just opened.

" To express public appreciation to John Fagg for his never-relaxing exertions on behalf of the haven," the Clerk of the Passage replied patly.

Mr. Baker snorted violently, but the commotion he made was but the prelude to a most unexpected tribute.

" Agreed," the tallow chandler rapped. " An' if anybody questions that 'tis me they'll answer to. 'Twill be my pleasure to point out to 'em that John Fagg was worrying his soul long before the rest of us were ' waken ' ! ''

This redoubtable ally gained, this invariable raiser of objections firmly on the right side, Captain Nethersole's relieved smile betrayed a belief that his own proposition would have a smooth voyage.

" To extend him an invitation to stand at the Mayor-making in September," the packet-captain declared stoutly.

That was acclaimed.

But Christopher Crundall's explanation of the motive behind John Fagg's potential elevation to the rank of senior jurat was the crux of the matter. The boatbuilder delivered his astonishing state-ment in such matter-of-fact manner that it passed over many of them. Assuredly Mr. Virgile was far from grasping it at once.

" To ensure," Kit Crundall murmured, striving to repress a smile, " that when September comes, Henry Rochefort will find John is facing him over the Council House table."

Before long there was a whistle of awe—of course, damme, if John Fagg became Mayor he would also obtain a seat on the Board of Harbour Commissioners during his term of office.

" And he'll not be a milk-and-water Mayor like Joseph Denne," Mr. Adcock shouted.

" Nor will he hope to line his pockets if the haven chokes to the pier-heads, like Robert Spisour," growled William Beverley.

" Nor be looking for more building sites like Edward Hexstall," grunted Harry Templeman.

It was the hard-drinking though tight-fisted Mr. Francis Stone of Buckland, however, who best summed up the meeting of John Fagg and Henry Rochefort when both were Commissioners of Harbour.

" I'd give ten guineas to be there," he ejaculated.

That adequately expressed the sentiments of the ' full cabinet ' when, business completed, they repaired in a lively body to the Antwerp.

*   *   *   *   *   *   *   *

During those four days which remained before John Fagg returned to Dover, interest grew apace in the town. Even the fine news from Eylau, where Napoleon's vaunted army had, for the first time in its encounters with the Russians, sustained a sharp check at the hands of those stubborn foes, failed to be hailed with all the encomiums it deserved.

The real purpose of the Guildhall meeting of Freemen was on every lip ; and each and all, save three gentlemen better posted, were asking the question : " Would the shipowner stand for Mayor ? "

He should do so, it was asserted on every side ; but it was also freely conceded that hitherto he had taken little part in local politics.

The upshot, however, after many a public demur and much deliberation, was that John Fagg signified a willingness to permit his name to go forward when nomination day came.

Captain Nethersole, in the privacy of the parlour of Little Pent House, laughed himself sore on the evening the news of his friend's acceptance was bruited abroad.

" Rot me, John," he guffawed, " but you're a sly 'un."

Nicholas Stokes grinned agreement. " For we've got to allow that, as well as the official clique, there were a few waverers on't."

" But now John's seeming hesitation has done the trick," Kit Crundall gasped. " 'Tis choice, by heaven ! "

The four gentlemen, their dark machinations showing such rosy promise, settled themselves to chuckle over an artful course of action which had brought them thus far.

Eventually a number of indignant ladies, wearied of being deserted so long, came from the drawing-room to bring sense into male heads.

There was no need whatever to ring the fire-bell over the Guildhall to recall to the Freemen of Dover the meeting due to take place.

The nautical men attended in full force, with corn-millers, hay and straw dealers, and merchants of every description, all of whom were becoming more apprehensive that, if peace with its forced economies ever came, the cost of lightering goods in and out of the harbour would place their commercial affairs on a hopelessly non-competitive basis.

All the ' linen-drapers ' were there. Bell-hangers, wheelwrights, innkeepers, coachbuilders, gilders and carvers, watchmakers, blacksmiths, grocers, bakers, drapers, and all other shades of work-a-day life—every one clearly perceiving the disaster which further silting of the haven would bring to them.

The proceedings went strictly according to plan. A motion that Mr. John Fagg should receive the thanks of the community for the predominant part he had played in obtaining the Passing Tolls for Dover was passed in a roar of approbation.

And a forest of upheld hands, and a cheer which went re-echoing round the gables of the Market Place, were indeed evidence of the support Mr. Fagg would receive when Mayor-making came at the end of the summer.

The following morning, Mr. Henry Rochefort, subsequent to calling upon the Clerk of the Cheque at the Council House, decided that a consultation in connection with a mortgage necessitated a visit to Mr. Jeffrey Braems.

The events of the previous day naturally came up for discussion when business matters were completed. It would have been strange if they hadn't, for the town still hummed.

" But even if Fagg should become Mayor, what can he do, Braems ? " Henry Rochefort observed contemptuously.

The wrinkled, parchment-like face of the Notary to the Harbour Commissioners remained unsmiling.

" No more than any other Mayor," he replied sourly, " save, perhaps, to make himself unpleasant."

The banker laughed harshly. " And that, I warrant, will not get him very far."

" Nowhere," the Register sniffed.

" 'Tis only mass hysteria which persuades his supporters that he can hope to best the Commissioners," Mr. Rochefort said bitingly.

Mr. Braems was occupied with a piece of dirty tape and a bundle of stiff documents.

" Votes are the tokens which are counted, Rochefort," the lawyer said dryly.

This arid commentary in memory, the man who truly believed that the haven could never be made permanently serviceable, or no more so than would allow a lugger or news-cutter to slip over the bar, left the gloomy room for the spring sunshine outside.

3

Again more discouraging intelligence : the Treaty of Tilsit— Prussia utterly crushed and Russia compelled for the future to support the French against England, thus reversing her alliance.

A gentleman and a young lady, strolling past the venerable buildings of the Almshouse Hospital in Market Lane, were discussing the general situation.

" 'Tis my opinion, Caroline, that this country should invade the Continent on a large scale," Armand Saval observed seriously. " In short, no more petty excursions but an operation conducted in the grand style."

That was not her father's opinion, Caroline Rochefort frowned prettily. England might be the greatest sea-power in the world, but she was no match on land for a mighty continental despot.

" Papa thinks that when conditions become more opportune, and our army is bigger and still better equipped, we might advantageously endeavour to take up the offensive, but at the moment he swears 'twould be monstrous rash."

But such weighty preoccupations are not for a charming young woman, as the Frenchman pointed out that scorching July morning.

"My dear Caroline," he smiled, "infinitely would I prefer to speak of your sparkling eyes, the bewitching dimple——"

Quite decidedly, she turned to him, her glance very direct.

"And I, Armand, would infinitely rather you did not speak of them," she said earnestly.

"And why, Caroline?" he asked quizzically.

"Because I care not for it," she declared plainly.

So unmistakably forthright was her manner that he appeared fleetingly disconcerted. That much, too, was apparent in the fretfulness of his retort. Although a most experienced and successful gentleman, M. Saval was beginning to realise that this cool miss had, for a year or more, kept him at arm's length. It was a departure from the usually smooth progress of his affairs of the heart which he did not at all relish.

"Methinks you are out of humour this morning, Caroline," he said, rather shortly.

To his intense annoyance she laughed delightedly.

"You find me amusing, Caroline?" he asked icily.

Her eyes were dancing as she confessed. "'Tis your discovering a fault in me, Armand. And . . ." there was a twinkle now, "'tis a devilish pleasant change after all t'other flattery."

They were beyond the top of Cowgate, near the fringe of the Western Heights, before M. Saval was quite recovered. By then he had decided that it was full time to bring this attractive little piece to heel.

"The divinest day, Armand," she was rejoicing, "an' 'twill be glorious up at the Bowling Green."

"A thousand thanks for *that* at least, my dear Caroline," he said so gravely that she had to laugh.

Miss Rochefort, relieved that he was not making a fuss, and perhaps thinking, too, that she might have been over severe on one who could know little of English reserve, started to tell him a most endearing story about Lou.

"Nevertheless a mos' annoying little creature," Armand Saval commented when she had finished. "Damme, I swear that if she were a degree more frigid with me I should freeze. After all," he gesticulated freely, "I have since made it clear that I do not impute any lack of courage in her brother through his failure to meet me in an engagement of . . . a certain engagement."

"He was already pledged in a deeper affair, Armand," his companion said lightly.

Close by was the sheltered fold of ground above the Bredenstone where the gentlemen of the garrison found pleasant recreation in a game of bowls.

" Perhaps so," the Frenchman smiled, shrugging delicately before he opened the wrought-iron gate which gained the club through a narrow, hedge-lined path. " Though I venture to assert that a man of more mettle . . . still, let's not speak on these disagreeable outcomes, my dear."

Immediately within the secluded track Caroline Rochefort turned, putting away the hand which he had slipped beneath her elbow. She was rather pale, but there were tendencies in Armand Saval which she had long noticed and which she was determined to stop.

" Armand," she began earnestly, " I once told you that the Faggs were my friends . . . they still are. I detest to say it, but I must declare that your attitude towards Charles is . . . is churlish. Far too oft do you hint at his supposed deficiencies, and I shall feel obliged if for the future you refrain from doing so in my presence."

He darted a quick though calculating glance at her, but then, to her intense annoyance, he appeared to be vastly amused ; indeed, admiration in his bold eyes, he drawled a compliment.

" Those tantalising spots of anger in the cheeks," he soliloquised maddeningly.

" Armand ! " Caroline said stormily.

Before she had realised what he was about, he had taken her hands in a hard grip, and slowly, as if enjoying to the full the anticipation of what he was about to take, began to draw her towards him.

" Release me, Armand," she demanded flamingly.

He laughed softly. " Come, my dear, you have led me a pretty chase for too long, and now you must understand that I am putting a term to it. I assure you that in my arms you will find——"

Struggle all she could, inexorably he had pulled her to him, his mouth within a few inches of her lips, his intention obvious.

" Monsieur ! " she gasped passionately.

The Bowling Green was deserted, there could have been one end only to the unequal combat. But, even as Armand Saval, after releasing her hands to snatch her slimness into the circle of his arms, bent down to her, there was a silvery jingling from the military road as a solitary rider trotted his beast towards the town.

" You damned little vixen," Armand Saval swore, his face made livid by her imperative call.

Recoiling as he let her go, Caroline stumbled backwards against the dense greenery of the hawthorns ; her breasts were heaving, her lovely eyes pools of fiery fury.

" You unspeakable blackguard," she said shakily.

The major of cavalry saw the rest from over the top of the gate. The anger and chagrin on the Frenchman's face, and the lovely young woman who, as if she had been contaminated with something foul and evil, was scrubbing her lips with a handkerchief.

" Egad, 'tis Miss Rochefort ! " he ejaculated.

Within a brace of shakes he dismounted and was down the path, his brown mare left cropping the sweet grass outside.

" This fellow been worrying you, Miss Caroline ? " he asked sternly, most suggestively causing a length of plaited leather to whistle through the air.

Henry Rochefort's daughter achieved a tiny smile.

" I no longer have the gentleman's acquaintance, Major Stanton," she said disdainfully, " so 'twould hardly be worth soiling a whip on him."

The cavalryman, eventually being dissuaded from a course of action he most certainly itched to take, saw her to the confines of the town.

Still too angry for mere words, Caroline decided she would call at the bank. Her father was engaged in his room but her brother was amongst the specie cases, and to him she went.

Louis Rochefort was most unprofessionally diverted by the news from the Baltic, Lord Cathcart's expedition having taken as prize from the Danes eighteen sail-of-the-line and fifteen frigates, thereby contributing no little towards the frustration of Bonaparte's dream of restoring his disastrously broken naval strength by annexing the fleets of the Continental Powers.

" Great news, ain't it, Caroline ? " he grinned.

His sister clapped her hands. " 'Tis wonderful, Louis," she said delightedly. " Where was it ? "

His expression sobered—he knew Caroline's great affection for her Uncle George.

" The action took place at Copenhagen, my dear. Where Uncle George received his mortal wound."

They said little more on that. Later, Louis cursorily asked her what she had been doing during the morning, and she passed the question off.

" 'Tis only the Town Clerk in there, so go in if you wish," Louis remarked on seeing her hesitation when, starting towards her father's room, she stopped on hearing the sounds of conversation.

His sister smiled acknowledgment and opened the door, a baize door still beyond.

Her father's voice came through plainly.

" My dear Stratton," he laughed, a hard edge to his laugh howbeit. " Need I tell you again that I am merely diverted by the reason behind Fagg's candidature ? "

" Then why press me so infernally hard as to how the town is disposed towards him ? "

Mr. Stratton's tone was palpably ruffled, thought Henry Rochefort's daughter as, turning back, she relinquished her purpose.

The Town Clerk was assuredly on his dignity. He, the most important and responsible official in the town's administration, had been addressed as though he were of little consequence.

" Because," the banker intimated sharply, " I wish to ascertain whether 'tis worth while opposing him, though not, mark you, because he could have any influence with the Commissioners. On the contrary, my sole object would be to prevent the townsfolk from having their hopes falsely raised. The haven is useless, and I know it."

" Maybe," Mr. Stratton laughed shortly, " but an overwhelming majority of the freemen are behind Fagg in demanding action on't."

" I take it you may be included amongst such ? "

" I am strictly impartial," growled the Town Clerk.

Henry Rochefort smiled sourly. " The attitude one would expect from a split-cause, the somewhat vulgar though remarkably accurate definition given to members of your profession."

That affront ended the discussion. Mr. Stratton, flabby face as red as a turkey cock, grabbed his hat and slammed the door so violently that the impact sent reverberations throughout the old building.

It could safely be asserted that no longer was the Town Clerk quite neutral.

When Caroline Rochefort and her disappointed escort had disappeared down the military road, Armand Saval took the steeply descending track past the plague graveyard and, reaching Archcliffe Fort, turned towards Limekiln Street, on either side of him a long row of houses which Henry Rochefort had added to those he had previously built on Paradise Pent.

The Frenchman's expression was not pleasant, nor had it been since he had become aware of the deplorable mistake he had made with Louis Rochefort's sister. But, despite that error, he remained convinced of eventual success. In his experience a woman will often resist once but, handled with *finesse* meantime, inevitably succumbs at the second attempt if such attempt is pressed far enough home.

" In short," he was cynically reflecting, " a female is attracted by two extremes embodied in the same person, the tender and submissive and the brutal and domineering. Well, in that order . . ." he smiled faintly.

It was a philosophy of love which he had once complained François lacked.

In the midst of these abstractions, at the corner of Snargate Street and Snargate Street-over-the-Wall, he all but collided with the young woman who, he was rapidly coming to know, had the trick of bringing his blood to fever heat. She was returning from the bank, on her way home.

Remorse in every line of him, a proud gentleman humbled for her to see, he bared his head before her.

" I pray you stay, Caroline," he petitioned fervently, " and I beg you to allow me to speak. 'Twill detain you little, for no more than will enable me to crave of you the one boon, an' 'tis this. Believe me when I swear that I am mos' deeply sorry, believe me when I say that I would lose my pistol hand rather than you should think ill of me."

She eyed him cuttingly. " Your protestations, monsieur, would seem more convincing had you not sought to treat me like a wench in a house of call."

He seized her hand and, regardless of passers-by, burningly pressed his lips to it.

" Caroline," he pleaded.

Miss Rochefort made no bones about what she would do if he did not permit her passage. She had not told her father and brother of his despicable conduct but . . .

" If Papa learnt of it, monsieur," she said scornfully, " I promise he would thrash you through the length of the streets to your lodgings."

He tried to tell her that it was her beauty which had gone to his head. That if she would pardon him he would take oath by the Virgin that never again would he offend.

His words fell on the perfumed air she left in her wake.

" So . . ." Armand Saval murmured softly, staring after her.

Entreaty and contrition remained no longer in his expression ; his eyes were hot and his lips cruel as he resumed his way.

4

On Hornblowing Morning John Fagg was early at the warehouse. The day chanced also to be the one when his *Dover and London Hoy* left for her weekly trip, and this often meant last-minute bookings of passengers and the acceptance of small parcels of goods for which arrangements had not been previously made.

" That's done then, Valentine," he said briskly.

" About these 'ere shipments of corn and malt to Deptford, sir ? " Captain Pepper reminded him reprovingly, being taskmaster for once.

With a good half-hour left before the horn was blown at nine o'clock for Mayor-making, the shipowner was able to deal with this query and several others.

A quarter before the hour he and his henchman set out for St. Mary-the-Virgin's.

The same space after the hour the election was over, Mr. Joseph Denne, the Clerk to the Paving Commissioners and an aforetime Mayor, receiving a paltry eleven votes, a humiliation which, even in the special circumstances as they were known, was so crushing as to be visibly reflected in his discomfited face.

The name of John Fagg, Esq., Shipowner and Merchant, would that day, before nightfall, be brush-writ on to the ancient Roll of the Mayors of Dover.

With the announcement of the poll there was an odd silence in musty St. Mary's, not the usual cheer which, a decision having been made, whole-heartedly expressed goodwill to the new Mayor from supporters and opponents alike.

In that brief interval, during which nobody seemed to know quite what to do, Mr. Henry Rochefort courteously suggested to Mr. Edward Hexstall that now the function was concluded there was little point in tarrying further.

"And, Denne," he condoled, holding out his hand, "think no more of this lamentable exhibition. Rest assured that it represents no conceivable discredit to yourself, none whatever."

With this the banker, his face a mask of indifference, stepped erectly past the pulpit.

From now a certain disorder came into proceedings which hitherto had been conducted with perfect propriety.

"Call it exhibition if 'twill gratify you, Rochefort," Mr. Thomas Bullack angrily interposed. "But remember that you and your money-bags can be uprooted any time, whereas Bullacks have been tanning in the same building in Stembrooke sin' the days of William the Red. When you do business with London you dips a quill and writes a draft on a sheet o' paper, but maybe soon I willn't be able to do business there at all. As 'tis, I'm paying out an extra crown-piece on every three packs o' leather because there ain't enow depth of water between the pier-heads to 'low any respectable-sized craft to come in."

A number of other prominent gentlemen spoke on very much the same lines; and the owner of the Ship Inn put a conundrum to the banker. How would he, he stuttered, be able to live after the war if the packets didn't bring lucrative custom?

Henry Rochefort unflinchingly faced his antagonists. "How do you imagine the new Mayor will make difference to these natural drawbacks?" he asked sarcastically.

It was the well-meaning though stupid Mr. Jonathan Dawkes who laughed slyly. A reputation for scholarship, most falsely founded, had given him an influence amongst the ignorant, and for this reason he was included in Mr. Stokes's ' full cabinet.'

" On that, Mr. Rochefort, I would venture to asserverate," he observed oracularly, " we shall, in due course, be powerfully instructed."

" You almighty fool," the banker retorted angrily. " How do you suppose Fagg can do more than other Mayors ? "

" We shall see," snapped the incensed Postmaster.

It was this very attitude which John Fagg and his more intimate friends deprecated. Whereas the shallow-pated assumed that the presence of a fighter on the Board of Harbour Commission would work wonders, *they* knew the inherent difficulties of the situation.

" We must check this tendency, Jeremy," the shipowner declared emphatically.

" Aye," Captain Nethersole nodded soberly. " 'Tis a case of a long pull and a strong pull."

Cannon Street was filling with the freemen who streamed out of the church, and their ways being together, John Fagg and his close associates set off for their respective places of employment.

" To-day is only the first gradual step," Nicholas Stokes propounded sagaciously. " The Commissioners are deeply entrenched and it may take years to move 'em."

" We've made a start anyway," Mr. Crundall remarked cheerfully. " An' everything's got to have a beginning."

" Has it ? " Mr. Breton complained gloomily.

A steam-pump had recently been installed under his charge, with the result that the Harbour-master's outdoor staff were highly suspicious that in due course men might be displaced through usage of the new power. Extraordinary and highly dubious mishaps were regularly happening to this piece of machinery.

" The pump, Dick ? " Kit Crundall guffawed.

Getting a laugh out of their companion's disgust, the group began to lessen as progress was made towards the commercial quarter in Lower Snargate Street and beyond.

Whatever illusions a number of exuberant but short-sighted freemen might be capable of, John Fagg did not delude himself on the formidable nature of the mission before him. Nevertheless, on Hornblowing Day, he went home to dinner half an hour before his customary time, proof positive that he was appreciably affected by the outcome of the morning.

Sped by Captain Pepper's ostentatious " Good-morning, your

Worship," he walked smartly towards Severus's Gate and Town Wall Street, kept busy replying to the many genial salutes he received.

" John ! " Polly Fagg came gaily into the hall to greet him.

Little Pent House was in a rare state of flurry. The result of the election in St. Mary-the-Virgin's had, of course, reached the family long before, but John Fagg discovered, slightly to his chagrin, that the honour bestowed upon him was not solely the cause of the stir.

" Yes, my dear, practically unanimous," the shipowner reported easily, his studied casualness unfortunately counterbalanced by the fact that he had stepped inside with just so little of an air. " A matter of eleven votes cast against me to be precise."

" *Only* eleven, dear ? Goodness gracious ! *Fancy !* "

Mrs. Fagg expressed gratification for the Freemen's soundness of judgment by cocking a marvelling eye and forming her mouth into impressive shapes, but otherwise did not dwell on the subject quite as long as would have given her husband the most complete satisfaction.

" And who do you think is here, John ? " she switched animatedly.

The appearance of Lou, flying out of the dining-room with a young man in tow, saved any response to that question.

" Oh, Papa," she cried joyously. " Oh, Mr. Mayor."

Jack Woodgate was the cause of all the pother. The sailor had arrived from Plymouth that morning and forthwith had given his sweetheart the most delicious surprise of her life.

" Jack, my lad," the shipowner beamed on a gallant young fellow he had not seen for three and a half years. " And how are you, my boy ? "

Mr. John Woodgate, Lieutenant of the Royal Navy, an officer who had fought at Trafalgar and in a dozen minor engagements, looked excessively smart in a uniform which had had little wear.

" And, Papa," Lou was dancing on her lover's arm, " Jack wants to ask you something."

Mr. Fagg, relinquishing the young man's hand, comically proposed a retirement to the dining-room lest misfortune befall the mistress of the house's pet urns and pedestals.

" Then, Lou love," he smiled, " Jack can put his question, whatever 'tis."

There was trouble with Horatio, that young gentleman being in no little disgrace with his mother. To begin with, he had arrived home with his mouth full of sweets, a sticky bag was also in his pocket, and from where he had obtained these confections—apart from the fact that a gentleman had bought him them—could not be ascertained.

" *He* was a *kind* gennelman," Horatio was roaring, his face red with outrage, the deduction being that his probing mamma was the most cruel-hearted creature in the world.

" Who can it be, Susan ? " Polly Fagg wondered.

Midst all this, Jack Woodgate was making his request. The matter of which he spoke was, by ordinary standards, of a most personal nature, but being the same Jack Woodgate he was not deterred through the presence of a few people.

" You want to wed Lou, eh, Jack ? " Mr. Fagg observed when a direct reply had been asked of him.

" As soon as 'tis possible, sir. Before my absence-leave expires."

" Mmmm . . ." murmured Lou's father.

" Mmmm . . ." Lou mimicked indignantly.

Jack continued tersely. He was not, he announced with self-satisfaction, without means.

" 'Tis good to hear that in these days," John Fagg smiled ruefully, frankly puzzled until the solution dawned on him. " Prize money, my boy ? "

The young naval officer nodded before proceeding to give precise details. These were somewhat less ambitious than Mr. Fagg had expected, he knowing that, in one such case, a ship's company had shared a million pounds betwixt themselves.

Meantime, there was a further commotion for which Horatio was responsible, it being his steely and immediate resolve to attach himself faithfully to an officer in the Navy.

" No, Mamma," he howled.

" You will, you naughty boy," Mrs. George Rochefort said crossly.

" No ! " bellowed her son. " 'Tis silly . . . an' I want to go to Jack."

His mother would have no more nonsense. " And was it silly of your dear papa to like poetry ? " she asked severely. " Well, Horatio ? " she inquired, her final tone awful.

Never had a small boy possessed a father as noble and heroic as was Horatio's, and young Horatio glorified in his papa's great deeds. And never could he fall below his papa's great example.

He began his lines as Jack Woodgate rounded off his talk with Mr. Fagg.

" Yes, sir," Lou's very dearest said momentously. " One hundred and fourteen pounds. Very handsome, I call it."

With an equal gravity John Fagg answered. " 'Tis a very considerable sum indeed, Jack."

" Then we can, Papa ? " Lou jumped, anticipatively.

Her father fondly embraced her. " Yes, my dear, you may," he said affectionately.

There were kisses all round . . . Lou in her lover's arms, Jack kissing Mrs. Fagg and Susan, Horatio, wide-eyed, staring at them all.

Before dinner was over it had been decided that the wedding should take place at the beginning of October.

5

Little Pent House, for once in its dignified though ever-homely existence, was fearsomely quiet. Cook and the maids were already in their seats at St. Mary-the-Virgin's, and Mrs. Fagg and her sister-in-law, with Horatio, were gone too.

Keziah Hart was hurriedly seeking a prayer-book in her own room, preparatory to taking a short-cut through St. James's Passage to the Market Place, and Mr. John Fagg, in his finest attire, was pacing the hall awaiting the moment when he could hand his daughter into the second of the two coaches which were drawn up at the door.

In Lou's bedroom Caroline Rochefort was thinking that she, too, must hasten, with Shep melancholily thumping his tail on the floor, the sheepdog being completely bewildered by a state of affairs he had never known before.

"You look lovely, Lou dear," said Miss Rochefort. "'Tis the most elegant material I have ever seen, I do declare, an' Jack's the luckiest man alive, I do swear. Now will that do, madame?"

"Oh, Caroline," Lou gurgled.

Miss Fagg, her face framed in a pretty blue silk bonnet, looked as happy as she felt and that meant, as she had confessed a few seconds before, she thought she might burst with joy. She had but one regret that day—if only her dear Charles had been there.

"Malta . . . then Sicily . . . and now, from what he writes, on some ill-considered expedition to Egypt," she said wistfully. "Oh, Caroline, 'twould have been quite perfect had he been here."

Miss Rochefort was much preoccupied in reproving the quite innocent Shep. Shep must not suddenly paw his mistress, Shep must remain the good dog he had been. . . .

"Wouldn't it, Caroline?" Lou repeated, her grey eyes watchful on her friend.

"Isn't it perfect as 'tis," Caroline smiled. "Jack waiting for you an'——"

"Yes, Caroline," Lou breathed, glory in her eyes.

"Very well, then," Miss Rochefort scolded her severely.

Now she must be off, as off she was, flying past Mr. Fagg at the bottom of the stairs, and bundling the surprised Keziah into the coach with her before that stout party knew what was what.

As bonny a wedding as you could ever hope to be privileged to see, with Mr. and Mrs. John Woodgate—he wearing a full suit of uniform, sword, and gold-laced hat—driving back in state and Keziah and the servants, all breathless with the run back, greeting them when they arrived.

Little Pent House packed to overflowing, speechifying and, later, the Rev. Nathaniel Woodgate's eyes gleaming when he saw the preparations on a side table—a bowl, a bottle, a jug, a fruit dish and a basin.

" Better make it yourself, Doctor," twinkled John Fagg.

The Rector of St. Mary's predilection for punch and his claim to performing the best mix in East Kent were well known.

" *Contradiction*, it should be named," proclaimed the parson, meantime arising with alacrity, with every one nearly bursting whilst awaiting the familiar lines he would quote as though they were brand new to all.

He ran true to form on that day of his son's marriage, his actions suited to his words.

" Spirits to make it strong," he said zestfully, and up went the bottle.
" Water to make it weak,"—now the carafe.
" Lemon juice to make it sour,"—and here he made a wry face.
" And sugar to make it sweet."—on this he referred to the ladies.

Glancing round his pent audience, he explained carefully, " *Contradiction*, you see. They all *contradict* one another."

A roar of glee, a stream of badinage, with Jack's father not the least offended, bless you.

The pleasant minutes ticking away. And a chaise coming to the door, and Lou changing in her room, and at last a mass surge to the pavement outside.

Lou waving out of the window the length of Town Wall Street, bliss and Lord Poynte's Dower House ahead. " Saw the lad into the Navy, and I'll see that mine's the first roof he and his sweetheart have over their heads," his lordship had declared. " And, damme," he had generously added, " I'll see I'm godfather to the first boy, rot me if I don't."

In Little Pent House the celebrations continuing. Games for all until it was time for the small 'uns to be taken home to bed. Then dancing for the young people in the drawing-room, with the ladies gathering in the parlour, and the gentlemen making a fug in the dining-room—fun and laughter in the one, gossip in the other, and some grave talk in the third.

" 'Tis serious, albeit, tarnally serious," Mr. Matthew Adcock persisted.

The Emperor's Berlin Decrees instituted a vigorous blockade of

English goods throughout that part of Europe he controlled, which meant the entire Continent saving Sweden, Turkey and Portugal. It was a body blow at England's carrying trade. . . .

"This is a day of rejoicing, Matthew," old Jephrez Baker growled.

Doctor Woodgate laughed until tears came into his eyes, until he nearly rocked off his chair—all of which, at a rough estimate, caused four score or more winks to be exchanged.

The party continued with unabated enthusiasm until the early hours of the morning.

6

That same November day on which Jack Woodgate kissed his sweet Lou good-bye before returning to sea, the Clerk of the Cheque of Dover Harbour, instructed by Sir Walter Plumbley, went through the formality of notifying the Commissioners as to when a meeting of the Board would be held.

By evening it was as if the bellman had been through the port and liberties.

CHAPTER TWO

I

THE water in the Pent was ruffled, and in the sea beyond the Rope-walk a few scattered white horses were beginning to show themselves. It was a grey and gloomy morning, with a heavily overcast sky in which sombre Folkestone Girls rolled along from the south-west.

Louis Rochefort, wiping his mouth, pushed back his chair and, from the breakfast-room window, glanced out doubtfully. On this day, more especially so because of his father's absence at the meeting of the Harbour Commissioners, he was to be particularly busy, and a most important transaction in which he would be occupied was directly concerned with those natural elements at which he was now looking.

"No sight of the *Melianda* yet, Caroline," he remarked, taking out his watch.

This was a frigate which, *en route* from Chatham to the Mediterranean, was to call at Dover, lying off there whilst a large consignment of specie was put aboard her.

"She'll come all right," his sister smiled. "The Navy is always on time."

"Wind and weather permitting," Louis laughed. "Though 'tis sure that Jack Woodgate wouldn't agree even to that."

Smiling about Jack's whole-hearted enthusiasm for his Service, Caroline peered into the coffee-pot. Most unusually, for Mr. Rochefort was a gentleman who believed in regularity, brother and sister had breakfasted alone. But the truth was that the banker, turning and tossing over thoughts of the struggle he was sure the morrow would bring, had not slept until the early hours, and then had fallen into that deep slumber which often follows wakeful hours.

"Papa is late. I wonder——" she had started to say when that gentleman, a trifle shadowed under the eyes, opened the breakfast-room door and, after giving her his customary affectionate salutation, sat down to his meal.

"Well, my love," he said, over-heartily for him. He would have gone to any length rather than have shown he was singularly keyed-up for his meeting with the new Mayor in the Council House.

Louis was at the window again, his eye close against the pane which would allow him a sight of Dungeness.

"I fear the weather hardly promises to be propitious, Papa," he observed astutely. "You know, if the wind freshens, I think 'twould be advisable to put the gold aboard in two trips."

The banker himself looked out. A pale shaft of sunlight was striking down on to the sea beyond the Ordnance Yard, creating a circular patch, sharply delineated from the sullen dark water about it, in which the frothy white tips on the wave crests were beginning to join together to make one continuous line.

"Nonsense, Louis," he said testily. "Conditions could be better, but you know perfectly well that on a day like this the currents often vary immensely, and you might not be able to get back in time to do a second trip."

Surreptitiously, Caroline shook her head in warning and her brother, despite his pique, gave her a little nod when the opportunity provided. Certainly Henry Rochefort was in an edgy mood that morning, as was evinced when, after trifling with his plate a few minutes more, he declared he was ready to go.

So Mr. Henry Rochefort and his son, as was their habit, walked together to the House's premises in Snargate Street-over-the-Wall.

*   *   *   *   *   *   *   *

In the Basin a miniature sea was slapping and splashing against the green-slimed stone steps which gained the solitary door at the rear of the bank.

Standing at the top of these, his hat crammed down incongruously over his ears, was Mr. Godspenny. He was holding a wildly fluttering piece of paper on which, each time a couple of apoplectic-faced clerks staggered past him with a small iron-bound box, he added a mark to the growing list of tallies.

"Hurry up with you," he said sharply, when the sixteenth had been safely stowed in the smart green-painted cutter below.

The *Elizabeth Rochefort,* broadside on to the diminutive waves, was having an uncomfortable time despite the rope fenders which sought to ward off damage from her gracious-running clinker-built sides. She moaned and wailed, her securing hemp groaning as the backwash from the steps took her away, shuddering whenever coming in again too hard.

Her skipper, waving his hand inquiringly, called out an inquiry which was lost in a quick howl of wind.

Matthew Godspenny, knowing the meaning of that action below, screened his mouth. "No," he shouted down, "Mr. Rochefort says the lot . . . *the lot,*" he yelled, seeing he had not been heard the first time.

Meantime, in the general room behind the bank proper, the owner of the boat, the minute hand climbing to the hour, gave final instructions to his son.

"And get the captain of the *Melianda's* signature, Louis," he snapped. "Though . . ." being acutely conscious that since rising he had been no other than cantankerous, he forced a laugh and strove in some degree to make amends, "there's little need for me to tell you how to conduct this piece of business."

"I'll see to it, Papa," Louis Rochefort said tersely.

"I know you will, my boy," Henry Rochefort agreed handsomely. "And now . . ." a flicker of nervous irritation came into his voice, "I suppose I had better betake myself to this meeting."

About that time another gentleman of the town bethought himself that he must leave his supporters and friends and make for the same destination the banker had in mind.

Draining off the measure of rum, Nicholas Stokes, slapping his chest pleasurably, set down the glass, and then thumped the Mayor's back.

"Right, John," he roared. "If 'tis time for you to be off, then 'tis time for you to be off. And when you get there, give Henry Rochefort and that sly fellow Waade . . ."

The gathering had taken place in Mr. Crundall's snug little office above the shed in which, during the winter months, he kept his men working indoors in the making of smaller boats. The atmosphere was reeking with the eddying fumes of Virginia tobacco, along with an aroma of fine French brandy and potent rum.

" They'll hear my views all right," John Fagg promised grimly.

But he was not replying to the Clerk of the Passage. Rather his words covered them all, for all, in this minute of his departure for the Council House, were hotly engaged in giving him parting advice on similar lines.

" I'm sure on't, John," Kit Crundall remarked emphatically.

Mr. Philip Virgile nodded gravely, and hiccoughed. The cork-manufacturer had not a very strong head.

" My 'pinion is . . ." he began vaguely.

They were all a little restless on this, the morning of the culmination of their efforts. Harry Templeman was lighting a spill at the glowing oak-wood fire but, thinking he was missing something, came forward and, between pulling vigorously at his pipe, emphasised his particular point by dangerous waves of his brand.

" I'm off then, gentlemen," grunted John Fagg.

William Beverley and Francis Stone both gave him an encouraging clap, and Tom Bullack and Matthew Adcock proceeded to escort him to the door, the opening of which sent Mr. Crundall's office papers flying, and brought down a gust of smoke which nearly suffocated old Mr. Baker close by the fireplace.

" Shut . . . that . . . door," bawled the tallow-chandler.

" Looks like we're in for a tumultuous blow," remarked Jonathan Dawkes.

" A blow ? " bellowed Captain Nethersole, highly tickled by the Postmaster's landlubber-like definition. " If I'm any judge we're in for one o' the biggest gales we've had for many a winter. Eh, William ? "

He and the rope-maker were exchanging storm reminiscences as John Fagg went out.

Behind the shipowner the door slammed violently, and now he was alone on the top of the rough flight of outer stairs. One moment he found himself forced against the wooden side of the building, and the next, when the wind pressure unexpectedly eased, in danger, through bracing himself against something which was not there, of reeling heavily against the flimsy hand-rail which was sole guard to the steps.

These negotiated, he jarred deeper than he anticipated into the shingle at the bottom and then, the following wind pressing him on faster than his feet, sinking at every stride, would easily permit, he made direct for Fisherman's Row and Red Pump Square, his eyes narrowed against the stinging particles of sand which were now beginning to lift.

An uncomfortable journey, but a short one. Soon, his face tingling, the noise was behind and he was in the contrasting quietude of the entrance to the Council House.

2

The Board Room of the Commissioners for Dover Harbour was a long and low-timbered apartment on the seaward side of the Council House. It was panelled, mullion-windowed and, save for an enormous fireplace from which leaping flames cast their shimmering reflection on the polished floor, the only appointments were a massively proportioned table and the intricately carved but equally ponderous chairs which were about it.

It was significant that, on this day, six Kentish gentlemen, none of whom had attended more than two meetings of the Board since the time when each respectively had been elected, were present.

For that there was a very simple explanation. Sir Walter Plumbley was an upstart, one whose code would permit him to curry favour from those above him even if it was at the expense of another whose bed and board he would condescendingly accept when it suited his convenience. In short, Sir Walter Plumbley had passed the word that there might be sport worth witnessing.

" Terrible strong-minded individual, this fellow Fagg," he was saying. " Eh, Waade ? "

The Clerk of the Cheque hastened to declare his agreement.

" Unquestionably, Sir Walter," he laughed. " And . . ." he added slyly, " not the only one if I might say so."

Given the opening the baronet decided to make the most of it.

" No, by Jupiter," he started to guffaw. " No, by——"

" This the banker fella that you're meaning ? " eagerly interposed a Commissioner whose previous attendance had occurred at that immediately following his election, seventeen years before. " Tell us something more of him."

Sir Walter's legs were stretched comfortably towards the warmth, his thumbs ensconsed in the armholes of his waistcoat. One hand he now removed and, with the inward feeling that socially he was rising fast, waggled a finger in the direction of the questioner.

" You'll shortly see for yourself, y'lordship," he chuckled. " And, from what I understand, when Fagg and Rochefort get together——"

He suddenly and very clumsily went off into a bout of coughing, artistically continuing for some little while after the newcomer had entered.

" Good-day, Sir Walter," Henry Rochefort observed coldly.

" Er . . . good-day, good-day, Mr. Rochefort," that Commissioner said flurriedly. " Delightful weather . . . no, damme, I must be bemused or . . ."

What he might have proceeded to inform the company about

himself was not to be revealed, for he, just then, had the far better idea of presenting himself as the keen and competent man of affairs. Brusquely he demanded to know the time, and explosively asserted, on hearing the hour lacked two minutes, that the matters in hand would open promptly whether or not the Mayor had arrived.

" This Fagg used to run his free-trading ventures to a hair's breath," he observed trenchantly, " and rot me if I don't learn him that other business . . ."

The small interval was amply sufficient for John Fagg. Already he was in the lobby ; there three gentlemen were in attendance, their presence essential should the Commissioners require a specialist opinion upon any subject regarding the haven and its accompanying estate.

The Harbour-master discreetly gave the shipowner a warm wink, a greeting far more cordial than either the Register of the Harbour, Mr. Braems, or the Land Surveyor to the Commissioners, Edward Hexstall, evidently cared to bestow. Both of these contented them-themselves with a cool nod.

" Day, Dick," said John Fagg.

An odd word or two between them, and then he passed into the big Board Room.

" The Mayor, Sir Walter," the Clerk of the Cheque announced blandly.

" The Mayor, Mr. Waade . . . ah, to be sure, the Mayor," said Sir Walter Plumbley, grimacing at a neighbour.

The Commissioners of Dover Harbour began to seat themselves at the substantial Stuart table.

With the passage of twenty minutes, six country gentlemen began to feel themselves considerably aggrieved. The Clerk of the Cheque had reported on various items of routine, and on none of these had either Mr. Rochefort or Mr. Fagg evinced the least indication of coming to loggerheads. Indeed, the banker, as was reputed of him, had shown his very complete grasp of financial matters, and the shipowner a most comprehensive knowledge of maritime concerns. Already it had entered the heads of more than one of those half-dozen disgruntled Commissioners that a tiresome journey had been made in vain, and that the banker and his sworn enemy, the Mayor, together could admirably have conducted the affairs of the Board, more especially so if Sir Walter, with his prosiness, and Mr. Waade, with his attention eternally on procedure, had been removed from it.

" So that little matter . . . er . . . completes our . . . er . . ." wavered Sir Walter, glancing for confirmation to the Clerk of the Cheque.

Oliver Waade cleared his throat, meantime neatly tying up a bundle of documents.

"Exactly, Sir Walter," he said courteously. "Everything, sir, has been . . ." The concluding part of his sentence was lost in a squall of wind which set the windows rattling.

But even at that late hour some faint hope began to displace disappointment in the breasts of a number of gentlemen. They saw the Mayor rise.

"May I ask," John Fagg demanded, "for a definition as to what is the function of this Board?"

"Mr. Fagg, sir . . ." began the Clerk of the Cheque, much scandalised.

"Really, my dear sir," Sir Walter Plumbley grunted.

The shipowner continued quite unperturbed. "As I seem to receive no adequate reply, may I take it that the statutes of the Charter by which the townsfolk of Dover were compelled to relinquish the direction of the haven to a body of non-freemen have in no wise been abrogated or changed?"

Three men started to speak at once. They were Henry Rochefort, the Clerk of the Cheque and Sir Walter Plumbley. And six gentlemen simultaneously settled themselves joyously.

It was the banker, however, who came best out of the minor conflict.

"The charge of the Commissioners, Mr. Mayor," he said cuttingly, "concerns the estate and property of the Board."

John Fagg's face was perfectly impassive, and remained so even when a gentleman, whose mansion was on the London side of Maidstone, roared with glee at the question he put.

"Is the haven of Dover considered to be within that duty?"

"That, Mr. Mayor," Henry Rochefort rejoined sarcastically, "is a lunatic question."

"That, Mr. Rochefort, is nevertheless the question I am putting," John Fagg said levelly.

A Commissioner at the lower end of the board nudged his neighbour.

"Now we have it all clear, Will," he said, mock gravely. "*That* is the question which the worthy Mayor is putting to——"

Undoubtedly difference there was between a merchant and one who was a landed proprietor. But Dover's spokesman cared not for that, assuredly cared not for any of them. His blistering retort brought the witty one to his feet in outraged protest, and seemed likely to cause the noise within to rival the increasing tumult without.

"That's why, gentlemen, levity is out of place in this assembly,"

John Fagg ended vehemently. "The haven of Dover has been in your care, and you have entirely failed it. . . ."

" 'Twas not worth attempting, for how can one foil the forces which work against it ? " shouted Henry Rochefort.

" You have failed the townsfolk whose livelihood depended on the harbour," John Fagg continued inexorably.

" They should have had better sense than to have depended on what could never have been more than a broken reed," retorted the banker.

" You have failed the men who from time to time have lost their lives as result of your neglect of the haven," the shipper went on bitingly.

Eyes blazing, Henry Rochefort leaned far over the table which separated him from his adversary.

" They should have had more intelligence than to have risked——"

" Cruel words," said John Fagg scathingly, " to use of fellow creatures so wantonly compelled to face disaster. Cruel words, I tell you, Henry Rochefort. . . ."

It was as though the struggle were between two men only, the one waxing hotter, and the other more deadly, with each passing minute, their voices carrying throughout the old building, certainly to the ears of the two clerks in the room adjoining Mr. Waade's.

" That's Mr. Fagg," one of them chuckled. " I knew when him and Mr. Rochefort met there'd be fireworks."

" Aye," the other replied casually. He was looking over Red Pump Square to the Tidal Harbour beyond. " Aye," he repeated himself, but there was now in his tone an increasing interest, not in what his companion said, but in what he could see.

The frigate off Archcliffe Point had men heaving on the capstan, with more nimbly springing up the rigging. Others were battening down, securing gear liable to come adrift in heavy weather.

" Methinks the *Melianda* is shoving off, an' quick," he commented. " Well, I don't blame her by the look downward."

His fellow clerk had joined him but, after briefly glancing to the southard, continued to watch the top of a mast moving outward above the nearer pier. The vessel to which it belonged, as yet hidden, was still snug in the shelter of the low timber and masonry structure.

" Damme, there's a craft a-going out," he ejaculated. " 'Tis a nice day for a sail, eh ? "

Both young men gave their attention to that slowly moving mast which, steady at first, swayed more and more as it approached the Lookout station at the extremity of the South Pier.

" Why, 'tis the *Elizabeth* . . ." the first clerk exclaimed, as a

green-painted cutter came into sight in the tumultuous waste of water
beyond the pier-heads.

The other laughed. "And methinks her skipper will be hearing
his owner's voice if Mr. Rochefort shouts just a little. . . ."

Savage gusts whistled past the eaves of the building, drowning half
of what they were saying. In a comparative lull, the banker's angrily
pitched denunciation continued as savage as ever in the Board
Room.

"You may have persuaded the town to support you, Fagg," he
said mordantly. "But, as you have so eloquently pointed out to us, the
townsfolk have no authority concerning the haven, whether or not
that is on what they depend."

John Fagg dryly retorted that harbour revenues belonged solely to
the province of the Commissioners, yet it was the Court of Brotherhood
and Guestling which had secured for Dover the full receipts of the
Passing Tolls.

"And," he added, his eyes suddenly dangerous, "we propose
ensuring that you use this additional income for its rightful purpose.
Always have you failed before. . . ."

The gentleman from Maidstone smiled whimsically as he broke
into the duel.

"Yes, I've . . . er . . . gathered 'tis your view that we've failed,
Mr. Mayor," he laughed.

The shipowner turned on him, too. "And you, sir, think differently," he challenged pugnaciously.

The thoughtful-looking gentleman raised his eyebrow fancifully.

"On the contrary, Mr. Mayor," he retorted pleasantly.

It appeared that the Commissioner, this stranger to the affairs of
the haven, had been decidedly impressed to learn from the lips of
John Fagg that Mr. Pitt had, shortly before his death, been sufficiently
interested in the port as to send down Major-General Ford of the
Royal Engineers to survey and report.

"If Mr. Pitt was of opinion . . ." he was resuming when Sir
Walter Plumbley, Malmsey nose an even richer ruby, and plaguey
resentful of any course likely to suggest that he, Sir Walter Plumbley,
upon whom for so long virtually had devolved the affairs of the Commission, had not carried out his duties with supreme sagacity.

"Sir !" he began explosively, "do I understand you to infer . . ."

"Merely that I have no little respect for the late Mr. Pitt's acumen,
my dear Sir Walter," the gentleman from Maidstone interposed gently.
"And that being so, I, for my part, would on that ground alone venture
to propose that we look further into the Mayor's various complaints."

If ever a man looked thunderstruck, it was John Fagg. Here
was an ally from a quarter in which he had not expected to gain one.

"Your hand, sir," he bellowed delightedly. "Damme, sir, I never dreamt——"

Henry Rochefort, face white with the intensity of his feelings, made an impassioned appeal for reason, his finger quivering as he pointed at his opponent.

"I beg you, gentlemen, not to heed this man," he said frenziedly. "He falsely allies patriotism with the sad, though inevitable, state of the haven, and he plays on your sympathies with his talk of the travails of the townsfolk. Instead of balanced judgment he advances sentimental account of lost lives——"

The door crashed open, the sound heard even in that room where powerfully delivered utterance was muted by the snarling undertone of the rising storm.

One of the Clerk of the Cheque's young men stood there, all fear of the consequence of his unceremonious entrance forgotten in the emotion which gripped him.

"Mr. Waade, sir . . . Sir Walter . . ." he said hurriedly. "Mr. Rochefort's news-cutter . . . Look!"

The *Elizabeth Rochefort* was half a cable's length out of the haven, that distance past the welter of dangerous waters which, from every angle it seemed, surged and eddied round the pier-heads. She appeared infinitely safer now, stemming the lines of great rollers which, in unbroken sequence, raced in from the west. Curling, white-topped rollers, creating by their very speed the illusion that it was the green-painted cutter, not they, which was flying along.

But a line of bearing told the truth more clearly. Despite the heroic efforts of two men, the one pulling and the other backing the oars, the craft was slowly dropping astern towards the pyramidical confusion of dark water and light spume.

"My God!" gasped the gentleman from Maidstone.

John Fagg, from that awesome sight, turned to glance at the banker who, ashen of face, was watching all.

"The Lord help you, Rochefort," he said devoutly.

Throttling back a heart-rending cry, Henry Rochefort, forgetful of his hat and coat, rushed pell-mell from the Board Room.

The news was travelling fast through the town, and those hardy seamen who dared risk the violent wind were running along the piers.

By now the *Elizabeth Rochefort* was little more than the length of the Charlton Green cricket pitch from the seething cauldron behind her. In spite of superhuman effort, she was drifting more rapidly, and her crew, obviously beginning to tire.

The seas were crashing against the weather side of the South

Pier, with regularly, here and there, solid fountains of water thrown high aloft. Above the low barricade, the spray was snatched madly by the fierce beam wind and, with the speed of a cannon discharge, shot into the Tidal Harbour beyond, creating the image of torrential rain.

" 'Tis Mr. Rochefort a-coming," bawled a Loadmanage man, one of a group crouching in the lee of the Pilot's Look-out.

Heedless that he was soaked to the skin, the banker ran erratically, his tall figure sported with by wind and water. He rounded the dog-leg bend towards the end of the pier, making queer, choked sounds which bore witness to the fear and impotence which possessed him ; then stood, gulping great breaths, both feet on the low baulk which formed the brink of the jetty, as near to his son as he was able.

" Come back, Mr. Rochefort," a rough voice called out im-peratively.

" Leave me alone, leave——" Henry Rochefort muttered strickenly, warding off the hand which would have drawn him back, his eyes never wavering from the life-and-death struggle taking place before him.

Willy-nilly, two pilots pulled him from that hazardous perch.

What poor preparation there could be to succour the men aboard the *Elizabeth Rochefort* had been made. Heaving-lines were ready, but all knew that the hemp, as soon as thrown, would be flying down to leeward. And all knew that only a miracle could save those poor souls.

" Dear God," prayed Henry Rochefort, his lips moving. " Save him, save him, give him back to me, oh thou giver of life. Give him again to me and I will . . ."

There was a roar of apprehension. The green-painted cutter, which by fine seamanship had been kept bows-on to the charging seas, had received a vicious cross-slap on her counter which threw her sharply round. For a moment she was lost to sight in a deep valley of the ravening water and then, half-way to broadside on, she came into view, tilted crazily on the steep bank of a racing sea which relentlessly was taking her towards the hell's-brew of the boiling water on the shallow harbour bar.

" Louis ! " screamed the banker.

He looked as though he would have gone to his beloved son. But they held him tight.

" God *save* him, I beg of you in your mercy . . ."

And the Almighty, in the instant of that anguished appeal, was of mind to be merciful. One of the great seas striking the North Pier-head came back obliquely to punch the bow of the *Elizabeth Rochefort*, facing her stemways to the moving mounds which sought to encompass her ruin.

"My boy . . ." Henry Rochefort murmured brokenly, tears now streaming down his cheeks.

Louis Rochefort and the crew laboured as men, spent in every respect, can labour only when they have been embraced by the cold hand of death. One clung to the demoniacal tiller, two others wrought with the oars, and . . .

"My boy . . ." wept the banker, all unconscious of the peril in which he and those lodesmen around were in.

The wind was shrieking in its intensity, and the grey waters of the wide-spaced further ocean were piling together between the converging shores of the Channel, a concentrated fury both majestic and awesome to behold. The South Pier was shuddering and trembling, and the Look-out station was a-quiver with every hammer blow. Between that knot of helpless men and the shore, a pulsating torrent was pouring across the pier, smashing away the low barricade which was in its path.

"We'll never get back if . . ." one of the pilots shouted.

"If it breaches the pier . . ." another finished grimly.

Despite the precariousness of their position, the group continued to watch the *Elizabeth Rochefort*. Shipping so much water she had lost her former buoyancy and was floating sluggishly, her wearied crew, gallant as ever, still fighting on.

"Here's Dick Breton," bawled a Loadmanage man.

The Harbour-master, water dripping from him, his fingers lacerated and bleeding through a struggle to preserve himself when caught by a sea which swept his feet from under him, reached them from the shore.

"The lot of you back," he thundered authoritatively. "You can't do anything for them poor devils and . . ."

"I will not go," shouted Henry Rochefort, frantically fending off the hands which tried to drag him to safety. "I will not go, I will not . . ."

And then, dispute was cruelly futile as the concluding act of the poignant tragedy took place before their helpless eyes.

The *Elizabeth Rochefort's* mast broke with a thin snap, the falling spar smashing the weather oar close by the rowlock, the tangle of line and canvas causing the bow to pay off, leaving the news-cutter defenceless, broadside on, inclined steeply from a mountainous over-curling sea which, speeding, would soon clutch her.

"Louis !" shrieked the banker.

Now the *Elizabeth Rochefort* was canted madly on the side of that sheer watery slope, a white-capped lather hanging over her. Irresistably, in one pitiless surge, she was borne sideways towards the harbour bar. Striking the fringe of the wild maelstrom she seemed to stop dead,.

as though she had bottomed, and then, as if there were all the evil malice of a giant behind the throw, she was hurled bodily against the North Pier, just a dull crump announcing the disintegration of her sweet frame.

" Louis," moaned Henry Rochefort.

Once a white face appeared above the surface, and once, else-where, an arm emerged from the welter, the first finger of which, by some strange freak, pointed steadily to the lowering heavens above.

That was all they saw then of Louis Rochefort and his companions.

" Come, Mr. Rochefort," said the Harbour-master, his tone gentle, though any other would have been equally unheard.

The banker, his face benumbed, made no reply.

With each gust the violence of the storm increased and, with every inch a fight for life, Richard Breton and the lodesmen started cautiously to move shorewards, sometimes gauging a short run, sometimes clinging desperately to ring-bolts whilst a wicked torrent tore at them, always buffeted and half-drowned.

Supported in the midst of them was the bereaved father, a man old of face within the hour.

3

The storm continued without abate and, after nightfall, the moon's light, greyly diffused through the scudding clouds, revealed a merciless seascape even more awe-inspiring in its dreadful magnificence. Throughout the evening, when occasionally thin and melancholy signals of distress were heard from ships in sad plight, the high velocity of the wind never slackened, with every while an overriding squall of such ungovernable fury that it seemed impossible any roof in the town should remain whole. Great stone tiles crashed down into the streets, and in all three waterways of the port vessels were torn from their moorings, man quite impotent to prevent their fouling and subsequent damage or destruction.

Altogether a night when only those compelled were abroad.

Of such was the Mayor's Sergeant, whose business took him to Little Pent House.

" So you've taken him to lie in the Guildhall ? " said the Mayor.

His Sergeant nodded gravely. " Shocking disfigured he be, Mr. Fagg," he observed expertly. " When I saw 'is face . . . begging your pardon to be sure, ma'am."

Mrs. Fagg, very pallid, was showing her abhorrence and distaste for the gruesome details which, had she not risen so impulsively, she would no doubt have heard.

" 'Tis horrible . . . horrible," she cried, her eyes swimming. " A nice boy Louis always was . . . and to think of him cold and . . ." her shoulders began to heave.

" Come, my love," John Fagg said comfortingly.

" I . . . I . . . I can't help it," sobbed his wife, giving way altogether.

" So . . . so awful," Susan Rochefort grieved.

Both she and Lou were red-rimmed and swollen of eye, and not a mouthful of food had any of the ladies taken since they had received the sad news.

The Mayor's Sergeant, greatly abashed by the disturbance his matter-of-fact details had caused, tried to make amends.

" I must ax your pardon, Mrs. Fagg and ladies, for the——"

John Fagg, silencing him curtly, perchance further clumsiness should provoke greater distress, asked for a short report.

The body, taken by a freak under-eddy towards the Cross Wall, had been found trapped at the base of the sluice gate leading to the Tidal Harbour. Many of the cases of gold had already been recovered, two indeed in the *Elizabeth Rochefort's* forepart which, in some miraculous fashion, had survived.

" Very good," commented Mr. Fagg. " Now," he considered thoughtfully, " you'd better inform Mr. Rochefort that——"

Afar off there was a muffled roar and then, ever increasing in volume, ever seeming to grow nearer, a deafening thunder which filled the air, subduing all other distinctive noises of that torn night.

" Papa ! " Mrs. Jack Woodgate gasped.

Every bit as much alarm was depicted on the faces of her aunt and mother. Mrs. George had gone to Polly, both women standing as though doom were on them, as indeed it sounded.

John Fagg had stepped to the centre window, where he was shading his eyes. Versed in weather-lore as it affected Dover's haven, he instantly guessed the calamity which had occurred.

" I fear the pier is breached," he shouted. " And . . ."

The stupefied officer commanding Amherst's Battery saw most, but not all, of what happened. Attack after attack had the sea made on the pier inshore of which his guns were mounted, tearing off the stout timber facings as though they were straw. But it was the onslaught from a mountain range of water which, in its stride, cut the North Pier into two parts, the ravening fiend which had made the broad gap flying on and beyond, alongside the high shingle bank of the Ropewalk, its hissing flank far advanced up the steep slope.

At the one depression in the ridge the frothy crest divided, the seaward part continuing along the shore, the other leaping menacingly up the Canyon, annihilating in its passage a flimsy and contemptible memorial of a man's spite.

A narrow crack showed across the face of Rochefort's Folly as the gigantic wave struck its face ; beneath the fabric, shingle and sand were sucked from the foundation. It lurched drunkenly and, as the man whose pleasure it had spoilt saw, collapsed like a tower of playing-cards, a splash the last sight before it was lost beneath the swirl.

John Fagg turned away slowly. "Your garden will have suffered sad misfortune, Polly," he muttered inconsequently.

They wanted to know just what he had seen, wanted to know whether he thought he was right in his supposition about the pier.

Briefly the shipowner responded and, as rain began to crack against the panes, he completed his instructions to the Mayor's Sergeant, a tight little smile about his lips.

"You will inform Mr. Rochefort that I shall sit at ten o'clock in the morning," he said crisply. "And . . ." he added grimly, his wife's glance now anxiously intent on him, "you had better advise Mr. Rochefort to have his attorney with him. At the inquest I propose putting a number of questions——"

"No, John !" Mrs. Fagg, her face blotchy but her mouth more determined than ever her husband had seen in his life, again rose to her feet. "No, no, John, you can't do it, and I won't 'low you. I won't, I won't."

John Fagg, perhaps intently preoccupied with the weapon the disaster had placed in his hands, was not as skilful in placating her as he might have been.

"Polly, my dear," he began cajolingly, "ladies are all very well in their place, but when it comes to interfering in matters beyond their ken, well . . ."

Polly Fagg faced him resolutely. "John," she said, her tone controlled but high, "I won't have it, and if you carry out this cruel purpose——"

"Polly !" her husband exclaimed sharply.

"We'll . . . we'll talk of it later, John," Mrs. Fagg told him with quiet dignity.

The Mayor, resolute as ever but nevertheless dismayed by the whiteness of her face, let it go at that.

Shortly his Sergeant, blaspheming freely, proceeded to Snargate Street. With not a scrap of shelter from the fiercely driving rain until he reached the houses beyond Severus's Gate, his head was bent low. He was like a drowned rat when he reached Henry Rochefort's door, barely seeing that a gentleman stood there on the step by his side. Grasping the knocker he rapped out a summons for both.

*   *   *   *   *   *   *   *

The Rochefort mansion, despite the noise without, had that peculiar atmosphere so often found when death has visited a habitation. The servants seemed to creep about, and this had nothing to do with the presence, in her old sitting-room, of the disciplinarian before whom they had all shivered.

Captain and Mrs. Pepper were in the small room from which, ever since her loved mistress had died, Martha had conducted the affairs of the household until Miss Rochefort took certain matters into her own hands.

"Now you go to Miss Caroline if she be ready for you, love," Valentine Pepper said soothingly. "An' bear up, an' don't cry no more, an' if there's anything I can do, whatever 'tis, well you know your Valentine'll do it."

Doing her best to be brave, his wife wiped her handkerchief over a face distorted with grief.

"You 'ave been a comfort to me, Valentine," she murmured thankfully. "I don't know what I should have done without you."

This caused Valentine Pepper to expand visibly. He was sitting on a small wheel-back chair before the fire, his fat hams hanging over the edges.

"As soon as I 'ears the sad news," he roared, "I says to myself 'tis my duty to break to my little gal . . ."

"Sssh . . . I'm not death," Mrs. Pepper warned him. "But, Valentine," she added softly, "I'm glad as you thought of me first of all."

Captain Pepper turned to face her more directly, in this process settling his haunches more comfortably. His eyes shone as he saw, not only a woman with grey hair, but the fetching creature of younger days.

"As if I should think of anybody else, Martha," he beamed affectionately.

Cheered a little, Martha went about her affairs.

The fire in the dining-room, unattended for so long, had sunk low, giving out but a small glow to supplement the meagre light from a single candle burning in the right-hand wall-light by the fireplace.

Staring unceasingly into the dying embers, Henry Rochefort failed to hear the door open, failed indeed to know his daughter was there until gently she touched his shoulder.

"Papa, dear," she said tenderly, "the Mayor's Sergeant is here to see you."

The hunched figure moved a little. "Request him to come in here," her father replied tonelessly.

" Papa, don't," she begged him.

Slowly he turned, a man who appeared living-dead. " I will see him," he muttered, still in that flat voice.

Agonisingly wanting to break through his defences, Caroline stayed awhile with him until, shortly, she came to realise how hopeless would be any such attempt.

At the door again, she beckoned to the waiting official and then, when the Mayor's Sergeant had gone in to her father, went back to that other who waited in the hall.

" No, monsieur, 'tis kind of you to come, but there's nothing you can do."

M. Saval nodded compassionately. " I hardly expected you would have any call for me, Caroline," he said wistfully. " But my heart it so bled for you."

" Thank you, monsieur," she replied simply.

Her eyes were bright with unshed tears, and her mouth not too sure of itself. For two aching years now her face, little by little, had thinned down, and on this desolate eve it seemed that the hollows beneath her cheek-bones had become accentuated. It was a change which, adding to the delicacy of her features, had given her a beauty greater than she had ever possessed.

" If I, who have so rashly forfeited the sound of my name on your sweet lips, can be of service in whatever fashion, Caroline," the Frenchman persisted.

She shook her head, her hand slipping from the carved back of a Carolean chair. " No, monsieur," she told him wearily. " But I and my father will think kindly of your desire."

" 'Tis not on account of your father, Caroline," he urged passionately. " For you I would——"

" I would remind you, M. Saval," she said, dismissing him, " that this is the day of my brother's death."

He bit his lip, bowed, and soon was gone.

With the door closed against the wind which whistled along Snargate Street, Caroline glanced first at the broad staircase and secondly at the door from behind which came the rough voice of the Mayor's Sergeant. She hesitated, but then decided to continue with the sad task on which she had been engaged.

Joined by Martha in her brother's bedroom, the two women, in the wavering candle-light, prepared the chamber for the reception of the dead. Whilst the gale howled, the finest of linen was placed on the bed, and a new cambric night-shirt laid out in readiness. And knick-knacks and gew-gaws which stood on the bow-fronted chest of drawers were removed and decently hidden in the seclusion of a cupboard.

" 'Tis heartache sad for us all, Miss Caroline," Martha Pepper blurted out when the sorrowful task was nearly done.

Her eyes at last suffusing, Caroline nodded dumbly before she spoke.

" Poor Papa," she said miserably. " He . . . he frights me, Martha. Nothing moves him at all, and not even the advent of the Mayor's Sergeant caused him to throw off that terrible apathy."

" He loved Master Louis so." Mrs. Pepper sniffed hard, tears again beginning to stream down her cheeks. " And was so proud of him. But then . . . Master Louis was a son any one could have been proud of . . . I . . . I . . . I was so proud of him too."

" Martha, dear." Caroline hurried round the foot of the bed to give what comfort she could.

The business which the Mayor's Sergeant had in that house was swiftly accomplished.

" At ten o'clock in the morning, you say ? " Henry Rochefort said quietly, his thoughts still far away.

" Yes, sir. That is the time as Mr. Fagg instructed me to inform you he would open the court."

It was as though the name of his former friend and present adversary pierced into the banker's insensibility.

" Mr. Fagg . . . Mr. Fagg ? " he reiterated sharply. " What business is it of that gentleman . . . my notary with me ? Why——" He stopped abruptly, in this new emotion taking a quick breath as the full purport reached him.

The Mayor's Sergeant looked vaguely perplexed. Mr. Rochefort, afflicted though he was, must surely know that the Mayor of Dover, from time immemorial, had also been the Coroner of the town. He was about to point out the patent fact when the banker smiled unnaturally.

" So 'tis John Fagg who will hold inquest on my son," Henry Rochefort muttered, half inaudibly.

A representation of that Court began to be pictured in his distraught mind. He saw standing there a once-dignified man, every eye upon him, whilst John Fagg probed deep with exacerbating examination. He could hear the excited buzz as the Mayor plied searching question after searching . . .

" Being Mayor, Mr. Rochefort, Mr. Fagg nacherally——" the Sergeant mumbled bewilderedly.

Somehow Henry Rochefort told the fellow to go and, alone again, sank back into his bitter, self-accusing reverie. But soon, as if compelled to it by a latent urge, he rose and listlessly made sure a key was in the tail-pocket of his coat. Picking up a silver candlestick he held the wick to the wall-light and, his shadow deep behind him, walked steadily into the hall whence, grasping the smooth handrail of the staircase, he pulled himself up each painful step.

Through the open doorway of Louis' room, two crying women saw the tall figure walk past the tallboy on the landing, the spare and anguished face so nearly illuminated by the candle's waving yellow flame.

Caroline shook her head. " No, Martha," she whispered, " 'twill be well to let him be."

And Martha Pepper, knowing, too, that there was only one place in which her former master might find some measure of comfort, nodded her head soberly in agreement.

So Henry Rochefort, as a vicious and frightening blast of wind, the last of the storm, struck the house, unlocked the door of the room in which his wife had died.

He held the candle aloft, its rays bringing shining reflection from the pigment of Elizabeth Rochefort's portrait. His lips began to frame words, and soon from them came a torrent of haunting regret.

" Why had you to leave me, my love ? " he asked piteously. " Why, my dearest, had you to go ? "

His mouth began to tremble, its first relaxation since he had beheld his son's death.

" I . . . I am not fitting that you should look down on me with your soft and candid eyes, Elizabeth," he whispered. " For . . . through my pride and arrogance, I am the murderer of our loved son."

He was changed now, unbelievably changed. And, standing there, he confessed to her those many things he would not previously have told any man.

" For years I have opposed John Fagg, my beloved. And this night our first-born lies on a cold slab. Our little boy, our Louis, lies . . . lies stiff and dead."

Now tears came. " Oh, Elizabeth, my loved one," he said brokenly.

Sinking to his knees, he buried his face in the bed. That vigil he kept until the thick wax candle began to gut, until its last flicker left darkness in the thickly dusted room.

*   *   *   *   *   *   *   *

When that ferocious squall came which eventually proved to be the last throw of the elements, little Horatio Rochefort was shifting restlessly in bed. In his dream he was seeing himself as the captain of a ship, and her sole surviving officer. He was standing undauntedly on the high poop, and in the well of the ship he could see, looming ever larger and larger, the brutal faces of the mutineers. They were swarming towards him, thousands of the ruffians, when the window of his room banged violently.

"Mamma," he screamed, "Mamma... Mamma... Mamma..."

Keziah Hart reached him first, but soon came Susan Rochefort too.

"Lovey," she said soothingly, hurrying in anxiously.

"Mamma," he began shrilly. "There was a lot of nasty men with blooded kerchiefs round their heads, and they was going to kill me an'——"

"Master Horatio!" Keziah reproved him sternly.

"An' then a big cannon went off . . ."

As Susan fondled him her heart-strings tugged, so much did he, with his tumbled hair and dark eyes, resemble her dead husband.

"Hush, darling," she crooned tenderly.

Horatio was continuing non-stop with his nightmare when Keziah tried another method, an act which she and his mother had often found efficacious.

"Horatio's father wouldn't 'ave been such a baby, would he, Miss Susan?" she jeered.

Mrs. George, conferring alone with the old nurse, shook her head slowly.

"But then, Keziah," she explained brightly, "Horatio's father was a Hero."

Keziah recalled a most stirring adventure in which Seaman George Rochefort had participated.

"They cut out the Frenchies' ship in the dead o' night," she announced admiringly.

"With muffled oars," the small boy's mother added importantly.

As if by some magic charm, the tears stopped. Insistently Horatio clamoured to hear the full story of this incident in a romantic life.

"An' what are muffled oars, Mamma?" he asked eagerly.

Susan Rochefort's pretty brow creased a little.

"Muffled oars . . . muffled oars are . . ."

Blinking perceptibly, Keziah left the room, thinking as she went that never had she seen a sight more touching in her life. Miss Susan sitting on the bed, her arm about the fatherless child nestling against her. . . .

So Mrs. George related the tale of glory at full length, for she hardly wanted to go downstairs yet. Sensitive herself, she knew that Polly, quiet all the evening, wanted to speak to John as soon as they were alone.

Nor was she wrong in this estimation.

For perhaps the sixth time that evening, John Fagg came back from the parlour window, an expression of exultation on his face.

"Well, the Folly's gone all right," he said, rubbing his hands.

Whilst he was delving into his tobacco jar, Mrs. Fagg put away her needlework and then closed her workbox.

"John," she pleaded, "'tis unheard of for you to do this thing. You can't use Louis' death as a weapon forged for your hand."

The shipowner, standing before the fireplace, pressing down the tobacco in the bowl of a long clay pipe, turned to look at her. Something in the direct gaze, something in her very demeanour, told him that for the first time in their lives he and his wife were in danger of having a major difference.

"Polly," he urged, "don't misunderstand me, my dear. Don't think that I'm not deeply shocked by Louis' sad passing. He was a good lad, and I mourn for him as much as you do."

Mrs. Fagg did not depart one jot from her point. "Then you can't in decency utilize him as something through which you can castigate Henry Rochefort for his opposition to any improvement ever suggested for the harbour."

Very carefully John Fagg set down his unlighted pipe. "Henry Rochefort is a Harbour Commissioner," he began unyieldingly. "He is one——"

"Henry Rochefort is a father bereft of a beloved son. He has been punished enough, John."

"Punished enough?" her husband retorted harshly.

"More than enough, John," Mrs. Fagg said steadfastly, high spots of colour in her swollen cheeks.

Her husband's mouth and jaw were ruthless as he outlined the vengeance he would extract from the banker in the morning.

"I've got him now," he said intractably. "And before I allow him to pass out of the Coroner's Court I'll secure from him every admission I want. Publicly I'll make him concede——"

"If you do, I'll never forgive you, John."

At this opposition, at the complete lack of understanding, John Fagg lost his temper.

"Then you'll never forgive me, Polly," he snapped. "For I mean to do what I have said." Violently he went on to declare that the tragedy of Louis Rochefort's death was but a small part in the greater tragedy of Dover Harbour's decline.

"And I'm fighting for the haven, and to-morrow morning I shall still be fighting for it when I have Henry Rochefort before me. And . . ." his voice dropped, "God help him, too."

Mrs. Fagg gathered up her things, put into its proper place the adjustable fire-screen which had been keeping the heat of the fire from her face, shook out a cushion, and then walked to the door. She neither bade him good-night, nor did she later refer again to the matter on which they had so deeply divided.

4

Apart from the warning, to be passed on to the banker by the Mayor's Sergeant, no one in the town could have anticipated what John Fagg was contemplating. Nevertheless, it was not to be remarked upon as extraordinary that, on the bright morning succeeding the storm, when the Mayor sat in inquest on the banker's son, the Guildhall should be a-jostle with curious folk. The circumstances, it must be admitted, were dramatic.

The proceedings began in the routine manner. Attestation, as to the finding of the body, the identification of it, and so forth, was given with proper decorum.

Only when the Mayor's Sergeant called out a name did a quick stir of excitement pass through the crowded assembly.

" Henry Rochefort," was the stentorian cry.

Apart from the noise of his own movement, there was not a sound in the Coroner's Court as the banker took up the position of witness, all eyes now on him and the Mayor.

John Fagg took his time in scrutinising the notes of previous evidence. Then, his grey eyes on the tall figure so near him, he quietly began to put his questions.

" The deceased, Mr. Rochefort, was a partner in your banking business ? " he asked.

" He was," Henry Rochefort nodded slightly.

" An equal partner with yourself, or a junior partner, sir ? "

" A junior partner, Mr. Mayor."

John Fagg inclined his head gravely.

" Then," he inquired with extreme deliberation, " can I take it that you could, had you so wished, have forbidden your son to make the perilous trip ? "

Henry Rochefort moistened his lips. " You can," he replied, almost unheard.

There was a slight movement in the Court amongst those who were beginning to perceive the line the Mayor was taking. Mr. Stratton, his expression clearly admiring, was whispering to Oliver Waade, and Captain Nethersole was nudging Christopher Crundall.

The Mayor's papers rustled as he turned over the sheet, to scan the folio following. Now he looked up again.

" Mr. Rochefort," he resumed gravely, " already you have

heard Matthew Godspenny testify that the deceased expressed considerable anxiety about embarking the full cargo of specie in the *Elizabeth Rochefort*. Is that correct ? "

" That is correct, Mr. Mayor," said the banker, some further horror coming into his eyes.

" But a full cargo nevertheless was embarked in your cutter, sir," John Fagg observed courteously.

" It was," Henry Rochefort agreed throatily.

A pin could have been heard drop. All were positive as to what the next damning query would be, all were certain that the Coroner would presently extricate an admission that it was upon the banker's bidding that the *Elizabeth Rochefort* carried the whole burden.

To the astonishment, however, of such gentlemen as Mr. Braems and Mr. Edward Hexstall, John Fagg allowed the present issue to rest.

On the other hand the Clerk of the Passage glanced knowingly at Richard Breton.

" He's keeping it back for a grand finale, Dick," he whispered.

The Mayor was dealing now with the precious freight itself. He congratulated the banker on its safe recovery. Forty thousand guineas, he said, was a very appreciable item.

" Indeed, Mr. Rochefort, a very large sum."

The lean figure, as the Mayor made this comment, swayed visibly, thereupon the Coroner, with nice consideration, suggested that the banker, if it so pleased him, might sit.

" No . . . no . . . I am quite well," Henry Rochefort replied.

The chief magistrate assuredly allowed him sufficient time for recovery, and then took up, not the causes leading to the disaster, but the basic root of the pitiful event.

" We have heard evidence from many expert quarters," John Fagg said, his voice plainly becoming exacting, "which leaves room for no doubt as to where the blame lies. All, whether the Loadmanage men, Fellows of the Passage, or our worthy Harbour-master, have expressed agreement that the shallowness of the water on the bar ensured the loss of the *Elizabeth Rochefort*."

Apart from the general throng packed in the railed-off enclosure at the back of the room, the company might have been described as being divided into two cliques. To the right of the Coroner were such as Jeremy Nethersole, old Jephrez Baker, and others of his numerous partisans and friends ; to his left was a smaller coterie, headed by Jeffrey Braems, Oliver Waade and Paul Elam.

It was to the left, to that small and ever-obstinate group, that John Fagg was now sternly looking.

" Most of those who have had the well-being of the town foremost in their minds have long struggled for the improvement of our harbour," he resumed decisively. "But always the controlling authority has ignored our appeal."

His glance came back to the bereaved father.

"There is nothing, save one thing, that I can do in this place," he continued grimly. "And that one thing is to close these lamentable proceedings after first placing on record my view, as Coroner, concerning the tragic accident on which we are gathered . . . Henry Rochefort."

His voice rang out, implacable challenge in its timbre.

"Henry Rochefort, you are a Commissioner of Harbour ? " he demanded harshly.

The banker's head, sunk at first, was raised. "I am a Commissioner of Harbour, Mr. Mayor," he said simply.

With all trace of his proud bearing gone, Henry Rochefort looked steadily at his old friend. It truly seemed that here was one who, realising his error, was fully prepared to do penance for every wrong ; one who would welcome crucifixion in the hope that the pain, gladly undergone, would contribute towards setting a tortured soul at rest.

"Yes, Mr. Coroner, 'tis true I am a Commissioner of Harbour," he repeated.

The shipowner was staring searchingly at the haggard face, sharply and painfully sick in his own heart at the sight of a once haughty spirit whose defences were so utterly down.

"Then, Mr. Rochefort," he began . . . and hesitated ; meantime heads began to be turned in amazement.

Abruptly and resolutely John Fagg put down the papers he was holding, and turned to face them all, his quick glance ranging from right to left, taking in the stupefaction he could see everywhere.

"Henry Rochefort," he said, his voice strong, his shoulders squared, " 'tis no part of my present duty to demand of you what office you may hold. All that I may rightly do is to declare my verdict in accordance with the known facts. And that is what I propose to do. But first——"

He held up his hand to quell the rising undertone of speculation and disbelief before continuing.

"But first, Mr. Rochefort, on behalf of myself and, I am sure, of those here assembled, permit me to express to you our deep regret. Your son, sir, was a fine young man and one whom Britain, in these days still full of peril, can ill afford to lose. And we, sir, sorrow for him, whilst to you and yours we extend our deepest sympathy."

For a while he was thoughtfully silent, but then expanded his theme.

The family to which Louis Rochefort belonged had previously suffered noble loss, he reminded them. More than six years before,

George Rochefort had died gloriously, and now another member of the family, in the service of freedom, had been taken.

Through the southerly windows of the room wintry sunshine came in, the beams palely flooding the faces of Dover worthies who never stirred, so gripped were they by the telling oration.

John Fagg, the attention of an absorbed audience riveted on him, drove home measured sentence after measured sentence.

" Yes, gentlemen, the deceased was a painstaking and hardworking member of the Dover Volunteers, in whose uniform he might have died whilst confronting the French despot's invading host, as we on this coast had it sharply brought home to us not so long ago. But, though he did not die resisting those who would put us into eternal chains, I say without fear of contradiction that Louis Rochefort, whilst in the round of his daily duty striving to place chests of guineas aboard one of His Majesty's frigates, contributed his share towards the fulfilment of that end to which we, as a nation, have set ourselves. Louis Rochefort was doing his duty and *He did his duty* shall be his epitaph."

Henry Rochefort's eyes were brimming. " Mr. Coroner, I . . . I thank you," he said huskily. " After the manner in which I have . . . I ill-deserve your generous——"

The Coroner interposed by brusquely intimating that there were certain official matters it was necessary to complete.

" My verdict, gentlemen, is one of accidental death," he announced more gruffly than ever. " With the rider that young Mr. Rochefort died in the performance of honourable duty to his country. And that . . ."

Blindly Henry Rochefort moved down the aisle separating those who held opposing views, and blindly he stumbled out into the bright light of day.

John Fagg penned his name and office across the foot of the document his Sergeant presented. From that he looked up to see Captain Nethersole eyeing him. For a man of such tough exterior, Jeremy Nethersole was considerably swayed by emotion.

" 'Twasn't the outcome I expected, John," the seaman grunted. " But, damme . . ." he blew his nose violently, " 'twas right and proper moving."

Astoundingly, too, both the Register of the Harbour and the Master of Lodesmen came and expressed similar sentiments.

" I could do no less, Mr. Braems," John Fagg commented dourly.

There were knots of people in the street outside, avidly discussing the unexpected course of the inquest. The Mayor, when he came out, would not add to his last words when they importuned him.

The sky was watery blue, seagulls floated in the fresh wind, and

the day was fair. Sadly and yet light-heartedly John Fagg walked to
Elizabeth Street.

5

The inquest on Louis Rochefort and the probable effects of Bonaparte's Berlin Decrees against British trade, in that order at first, but
within a month reversed in importance, were the subjects which kept
Dover speechifying.

Thereafter, until far into the new year, the latest method by which
the Emperor hoped to subdue an undaunted enemy, by destroying
her national credit, held the field everywhere, in drawing-room,
counting-house, and inn.

The British Government's reply to the Berlin Decrees had been
' The Orders in Council,' a measure which, crudely interpreted,
pronounced that if the commerce on which the country's prosperity
depended were to be brought to a summary end, then there should
be no trade elsewhere either.

To this, in December, the Corsican responded with the Milan
Decrees. Any neutral vessel, it gave notice, which touched at a
British port should be legitimate prize of war. In essence this ensured
that almost every port in Europe was closed, that the commercial
activities of a large part of the world had been brought to a standstill.

With the passing months such outcome was decidedly a topic
momentous enough to reduce to small proportions the memory of
Louis Rochefort's death. There was prospect of war with America
through the arbitrary restrictions on her trade, and a consequent
enormous rise in the price of tobacco and cotton, the last a heavy
blow to the rapidly expanding Lancashire cotton trade whose export
business had contributed outstandingly towards financing the paralyz-
ing cost of the war.

During those despairing days, while the fleets of England held
the seas and her swollen army kicked its heels idly at home, Caroline
Rochefort struggled with all her heart and strength in the most uphill
mission of consolation and mercy a young woman could be called
upon to face. Sad and wretched though she was through the loss of
her dear brother, her own feelings had to be subordinated if her
father were to be saved from himself.

No longer with a son to succeed him in the banking house of which
he was so proud, Henry Rochefort was a lifeless husk, all virtue gone
out of him.

CHAPTER THREE

I

On the afternoon of the third Sunday in January, Caroline Rochefort left for Little Pent House with a vague sense of reluctance. She did not at all like the look of her father who, since dinner, had been behaving in a queer, jumpy fashion. He would be brooding over the fire when abruptly, very much as always when conscience refused him rest, he would get up and pace quickly, hands characteristically clasped behind his back.

"No, no," he had dissented impatiently when she most tactfully said that, after all perhaps, she would not go on to Lou's.

So Caroline, her cheeks tingling rosily with the keenness of the air, had walked briskly along to Town Wall Street and subsequently, in company with Lou and Minnie, had taken a walk as far as the Maison Dieu.

Lou's elder sister, with her husband and three children—the baby having been left with her mother-in-law—had come down to Kent the week before Christmas and were not to return to Wales until the middle of February.

In temperament, though assuredly not in appearance, Minnie had not changed an iota. Half way up Biggin Street, not far from the Ladywell Spring and the forge beyond, she proved that most effectively.

" 'Tis strange to think that me an' Lou are wed and dear Caroline isn't," she puzzled, honey-mouthed. "And I vow," she added, finely indignant, "that the gentlemen hereabouts can't have eyes in their heads."

"Every unattached officer 'twixt here and Barham Down——" Lou burst out in hot protest.

Miss Rochefort, however, sighed dismally. " 'Tis not for lack of endeavour on my part, Minnie," she admitted wanly.

Sharp enough in her way, Mrs. Morgan Davies tartly declared that there was no need for Caroline to act so cleverly.

"Don't you want to be married?" she demanded. "Wouldn't it please you to have a husband?"

"Not having experienced the state how can I say?" Caroline laughed carelessly.

Thereupon an over-ripe young married woman giggled most suggestively, her eyes darting to her sister.

"Lou," she tittered, "how think you she will like the state?"

Mrs. Jack Woodgate flushed to the roots of her fair hair. "You always were nasty and horrid, Minnie," she said furiously. "An' if you don't stop I shall turn back."

"Really, you scold me as if I . . ." Mrs. Morgan, up in arms, was beginning, when her victim took a turn.

"Yes, you always were nasty and horrid, Minnie," Caroline Rochefort said very distinctly.

For the remainder of the walk Minnie most conspicuously withdrew into an aloof silence.

Back at Severus's Gate, where Caroline, still anxious about her father, simply refused to be persuaded into returning to Little Pent House for tea, they met Mrs. George Rochefort. With Susan were three children, Horatio and Minnie's two swarthy boys.

"We've been to the North Pier to see how the repairs are progressing," Susan explained as they stood against the parapet of the New Bridge.

Whilst the ladies talked, Horatio continued to put his companions into their proper places, being especially proud of a knowledge of the beginning part of the *Loyalists' Illustrated Alphabet* which his mother had bought him at the Albion Library. It was a volume from which, in his usual wild flush of enthusiasm when presented with anything really taking his fancy, he had never allowed himself to be parted during the four days he had possessed it.

"What's 'A', Gwyn?" he demanded intimidatingly.

"Albion's Isle," was the prompt response.

Equally satisfactory replies were obtained down to 'E', but thereafter the rejoinders became less forthright.

"Don't know what 'J' is?" the mentor said scornfully, glibly reeling off the answer.

Not long after that a fight started, sequent upon Idwal Davies' stumping Horatio with a question on 'Z', a dilemma which Susan's son solved by making pretext of fastening his shoe behind the Battery, in which seclusion he rapidly turned the pages of the book on whose yellow back was a picture of Emperor Nappy flourishing a cruel-looking cat-o'-nine tails.

"'Z' is the Englishman's zeal to humble the . . . the zany of France," he loftily instructed his pupils when the chance arose, unluckily being unaware that the thin-faced Idwal had spied upon the preparations for an intellectual falsehood.

Hostilities immediately broke out between two very small but berserk Welshmen and one slightly larger Englishman who had realised that only an outstanding success in fisticuffs could leave him with a shred of honour.

"Horatio!" shrieked Mrs. George Rochefort.

Mrs. Morgan Davies indiscriminately cuffed her boys whilst

R

Susan, on discovering her son's sharp-practice, gave Horatio a whipping he was not likely to forget. With that the two mothers, pushing their howling offspring before them, set off along Town Wall Street.

"You're sure you won't come, Caroline dear?" asked Mrs. John Woodgate.

Her friend explained and Lou nodded understandingly.

"Then I'll expect you to-night, Caroline," she smiled.

Miss Caroline Rochefort duly appeared that evening at Little Pent House. But she was breathless and terrified when she arrived there.

* * * * * * * *

The solitary bell of St. Mary-the-Virgin's, calling worshipers to evening service, had not yet begun to ring. It wasn't late, so it may be that the sight of an unused cup and saucer was the reminder which brought Caroline Rochefort's apprehension about her father to a head.

At the same time, as it happened, she thought she heard a slight noise in the hall and, going there from the little drawing-room, caught a fresh-faced maid whose beribboned Sunday dress proved that, one small duty done, she would not be long in scurrying upstairs for outdoor coat and bonnet.

"Oh, Miss Caroline," she began confusedly.

Her young mistress apologised for her thoughtlessness. Yes, of course, the tea-things could be taken out.

"But I think you'll be in time for church, Clara," Miss Rochefort smiled.

On a thought, she went to the front door and looked right and left along the darkness of Snargate Street. No, she couldn't hear the familiar footsteps either.

Half an hour later Caroline went out in search of her father, drawing a blank at place after place.

The bank was shuttered and barred; nor had he called in to see Martha; here and there she hurried, but never a word of him did she obtain.

Hardly knowing what to do, she ran and walked to Little Pent House.

"Oh, Caroline." Lou excitedly came to meet her. "Why didn't you come sooner, silly, instead of sitting by yourself all alone? Morgan was just on the point of bringing me along to see whatever 'twas you were doing!"

Despite her uneasiness Caroline's attention was captured. "*Alone*, Lou? How did you know?"

Lou Woodgate, her grey eyes shining, pointed to a hat and cane which lay on one of the gilt chairs.

"Because," she thrilled, "your papa has been here this last hour, and he's with Mamma and Papa in the parlour. Aunt Susan and Minnie and Morgan are in the dining-room so we'll go in there until——"

"Lou, dear, you won't mind if I go in to Papa, will you?" Caroline asked impulsively.

"Course not, Caroline dear."

Her limbs a little shaky, Caroline Rochefort walked towards the door of an elliptical-shaped room she had known since childhood.

From leaving home, Henry Rochefort had walked fiercely until long after darkness had fallen, hardly knowing where he was going, hardly caring. He was cognizant that he had decided upon a course of action from which he shrank, a self-abasement to which he must brutally force himself.

In due course, long after the last worshippers had crept into St. Mary-the-Virgin's, he found himself standing on a step where his feet had last trod twelve years before. With all the constrained energy of nervous irritability, he grasped the heavy knocker on the green-painted door of Little Pent House.

Keziah Hart, awe and emotion, everything save belief, in the expression on her face, waddled into the dining-room to announce the caller.

"Mr. Rochefort, Keziah . . . *Mr. Rochefort*?" Polly Fagg went as white as one of her own spotless linen sheets. Then she began to tremble.

"Steady, my dear," John Fagg said reassuringly, before instructing Keziah to show Mr. Rochefort into the parlour.

There the two gentlemen met ; John Fagg, impassive but somehow watchful, hardly through the doorway before the banker, holding himself as proud as Lucifer, clothed his repentance in sackcloth and ashes.

"I have come, Fagg, to tender you my regrets for many years of bitter opposition to any suggestion that the haven might be improved. As to whether 'tis possible to better it I know not even now, but I do know that I have been in wicked error in taking up an unyielding stand on a question which I dismissed without competently informing myself. I deplore that more deeply than I can say. I am bitterly ashamed, too, of the childishness and malice which caused me to build before your very windows and, had I my time to go over again, I should not erect dwellings on Paradise Pent."

His gaunt face ashen with the strain, his dark eyes tortured, he bowed stiffly, turned, and had a hand on the door-knob when John Fagg's even voice recalled him.

"Henry," the shipowner said quietly, "sit down a minute or two, will you?"

Mr. Rochefort wheeled, instantly on his guard, but saw no more than his former friend busily, most matter-of-factly, opening a knife with which to scrape out a damp dottle from the bowl of a pipe.

"You . . ." His lips and tongue formed the word, but at first attempt no sound came from a dry throat. "'Tis your wish to prolong a situation which, no doubt, gives you some satisfaction?" The words came out with contrasting loudness.

John Fagg might have been picking up a conversation a dozen years old, meantime his cheeks were distended as vigorously he tried the draught of the pipe.

"'Tis my wish," he said, between blowing again, "that you sit down, Henry."

As though he was at the end of his resources, both mental and physical, the banker took a chair.

What took place between the three people in the parlour of Little Pent House Caroline Rochefort never properly learned. She only saw that there were dried streaks on her father's face, that Mrs. Fagg was still weepy, that Mr. Fagg was energetically puffing away at a pipe whilst taking documents and plans from the Chippendale writing-table which, since the great storm, had been moved back into its old place near the window.

"Papa," she cried.

"Yes, my love," her father nodded, and there was no need for him to say more than that.

Polly Fagg's expressive face, at the sight of a girl of whom she thought the world, portrayed the most vivid relief. Whilst John had been interminably turning over his wretched papers, as in her embarrassment and anger she termed the two or three minutes of her husband's quest, she had been undergoing agonies trying to keep a conversation going with a deathly silent man who was largely a stranger to her, and a man, to make it worse, who had been at terrible enmity with John.

"Sit here, Caroline dear," she chattered. "'Tis not too far away from the fire . . . and 'tis not too near. I always say that though a fire is one of the most enjoyable things to sit around on a winter's night . . ."

To what extent she would have continued to dilate on the subject before recovering from her ordeal is not easily determinable. In any case her husband, completing his selection and coming briskly on to the hearthrug, probably spared her the realisation that she was talking quite foolishly, as assuredly she would have known when her words trailed off into nothingness.

"Now examine these at your leisure, Henry," the shipowner rumbled, proffering a small package of papers. "I'll hazard you'll find 'em interesting when you've got into them, an' I'll warrant they give every salient point in connection with the haven for hundreds of years."

The banker was rising. "I will, John . . . an' willingly," he muttered.

No, he would not stay for supper and, being wise, they did not press him, for it was evident how near to breakdown he was.

The shipowner was in the hall lighting up a lanthorn for their return, Caroline not having brought one. Meantime Mrs. Fagg, left with Henry Rochefort, started to palpitate again and, to carry it off, talked of anything she could think of. Yes, it was pleasant to have Minnie with them, but three grandchildren *and* Horatio in the house could be too much of a good thing. Oh, and yes, Charles was now at Gibraltar. And wasn't it extraordinary that he had been transferred to the 5th Foot, a regiment recruited in the Northumberland of his maternal side?

"I understand he has seen a deal of fighting, Polly," the banker commented limply.

"Yes . . ." Mrs. Fagg gulped at the fence before her ". . . Henry," she managed somehow.

The mention brought further remorse to Henry Rochefort. "I was unjust to him, Polly," he said miserably. "Mortal unfair 'twas to——"

"That'll do, Henry," John Fagg interposed firmly. "Now 'tis lighted, and as you won't stay . . ."

So Henry Rochefort and his daughter walked home through the crisp night.

Along Snargate Street, nearby where the lanthorn threw its rays as far as the gaitered legs of the sentry guarding the arched passageway to the Grand Military Shaft, Caroline gently squeezed her father's arm.

"I'm glad, Papa," she said simply.

"Yes, my dear," Henry Rochefort replied quietly, more at peace than for many weeks.

They found a visitor awaiting their return. M. Saval, since the tragedy, had spent several evenings with the older man.

The Interpreter stayed for supper, towards the end of which Caroline left them sitting at the dining-room table. From the little drawing-room she collected her book before going upstairs to the small sewing-room in which a fire was kept burning.

She heard her father and his guest cross the hall and then, their quest fruitless, return to the dining-room ; she later heard M. Saval bid her father good night.

A little afterwards, Henry Rochefort came in and put the question she feared.

" My love," he began, his manner slightly brighter, " I have noticed that you never sit with us when Armand is here. He speaks most respectfully of you always, but I fear that you do not feel quite so well disposed towards him."

Caroline laughed it off. " Oh, Papa, 'tis hardly that, though I confess I do not greatly like him."

Once in the mood for self-sacrifice, the banker did not spare himself. He was grateful for the Frenchman's companionship, he admitted, but if that meant he was to be deprived of the society of his girl then M. Saval would have to stay away.

" No, no, Papa," Caroline said anxiously, " you must not think of such a thing. To-night there . . . there was a chapter I wanted to finish, but 'twill not always be the same."

" You are sure, my dear, that you do not find his presence in the house objectionable ? "

She could have burst into tears at his humility, his tender regard for her.

" Of *course* not, Papa," she insisted.

" 'Tis an easement to hear that, my love," her father said sombrely, " for he has oft done me good when I felt not far from despair."

She made herself smile gaily. " Then the next time he comes, Papa, I must make myself prodigious agreeable."

As she brushed her hair that night Caroline Rochefort reflected that, in her desire that no comfort should be denied her dear Papa, she must be monstrous careful how she behaved lest she place herself in a horribly false position.

*   *   *   *   *   *   *   *

In Dover it was incumbent, between six o'clock in the morning and two o'clock in the afternoon of Friday each week, for the occupiers of all business premises, shops, and dwelling-houses, to sweep their frontages from pavement to the centre gutter of the street, in readiness for the scavenger's cart.

Caroline Rochefort, in common with other young ladies of the town, made a regular practice of distributing patriotic pamphlets, and on one such morning in February, when progress along the narrow streets was often hampered by the brooms which were being vigorously wielded, she was engaged in this self-imposed task, carrying a basket in which were various stirring addresses—' *Who is Bonaparte?* ' ' *Important Considerations for the People of the Kingdom,*' and so forth.

Her calls completed at the seven houses on Crane Street, overlooking the Tidal Harbour, she was turning down the alleyway alongside the King's Head when she met Armand Saval. Making a leg quite too grand for that fairly noisome spot, the Frenchman respectfully inquired as to where she was going, a question not as impertinent as it might sound.

" To Red Pump Square, then into the Plain, along Heart's Row and back by Round Tower Street, monsieur," she told him, all these being localities which were, to say the least of it, of not too fine repute.

" Then, Caroline, I insist on accompanying you," he declared decidedly.

Which he did, his behaviour as pleasant and deferential as could be wished, with never a glance or a word to cause her to bewail that she had conceded much to him for her father's sake.

As for conversation, mainly they discussed the latest news from the Continent, where it would appear that many oppressed nations were starting to experience faint stirrings of life.

" Little Portugal refusing to confirm, or at least evading the Berlin and Milan Decrees, monsieur," Caroline remarked delightedly.

" And the French under Marechal Junot occupying Lisbon as result," M. Saval reminded her pointedly.

Her brown eyes clouded. " Yes," she agreed, rather dashed. " But 'twas courageous of the Portuguese, forsooth," she picked up admiringly, " for, like the rest of the civilised world, they must have known that Bonaparte has grown so arrogant that he conceives it desecration to depart from his slightest word."

More on this, meantime passing through the unsalubrious Plain district. Then along the easterly marge of Paradise Pent, and finally on to the Cross Wall, where a big catch of sprats was being landed, part being salted for delivery to Canterbury and London, one group of men filling the small tubs, another covering the ends with pieces of canvas over which wooden rings were thrust before nailing down.

" 'Tis more pleasant here, monsieur." Miss Rochefort took in a deep breath of the invigorating sea air.

" T'other is no place for you, Caroline," her companion observed earnestly.

They parted outside the old Snargate Street residence—Caroline to attend to various household duties before dinner and M. Saval to call in for a session at the Gaming Club.

" Thank you, monsieur," she smiled ere he left.

" 'Tis I who have to thank you, Caroline—for the only moments worth remembering for . . . twenty-nine weeks and three days."

There was a profound homage in his bearing, and nothing could have been more exquisitely deferential than the glance he gave her.

He bowed low. " Your ver' faithful servant, ma'am."

With no more than that, a restraint which did not serve him ill, he went his way.

3

Once again, in St. Mary's, the families of Rochefort and Fagg held memorial service for their gallant dead.

That April Fool's Day, the twenty-fifth anniversary of the tragic passing of fine young men, Captain and Mrs. Pepper decided to do a special piece of shopping when the observance was over.

The selection of the cloth for Valentine's new coat being settled to Martha's satisfaction, the tailor's door-bell was dancing merrily behind them at the same time as a far-extending column of foot swung through the Market Place towards Biggin Street.

" Methinks here's another regiment leaving the town, Valentine," Mrs. Pepper remarked, taking her husband's invitingly-open arm. " An' 'twill be the fifth or sixth within the month."

Captain Pepper screwed his face into an alarming wink. " An' not one of 'em replaced as allus used to be the case, my love," he propounded sagaciously.

" You'd better tell me afore your features set," Martha Pepper said, unmoved.

Her husband laughed heartily. He was very partial to Martha's sharp answers, providing they were not too piercingly directed.

" In my 'pinion 'tis this, love," he explained carefully. " I thinks that shortly we be going to do some fighting instead o' sending gold to our allies to do it. Moreover, I shouldn't drop dead, dang me if I should, if I was told that the govinment was a-preparing to send a 'uge army into Portugal to 'elp the Portugeeses."

A very considerable part of this passed over his wife. " Portugal," she murmured vaguely.

Valentine grinned indulgently. " Portugal, my dear . . ." he started off expansively.

Martha was smiling. Miss Caroline, she said, breaking rudely into her husband's proposed lesson in geography, had told her so many officers had left Dover latterly that the young ladies of the town were complaining bitterly.

" Only a paltry four of 'em to every young female," she scoffed good-humouredly. " Now what do you think of young people these days ? "

Captain Pepper was red to his cauliflower ears. " I think," he said explosively, " that they 'as better manners than some wot's a bit older."

Properly astonished was his wife. " Whatever be the matter with you, Valentine ? " she exclaimed.

" Nuthin'," the boatswain replied distantly.

" Nothing ? "

" Nuthin' ! " he repeated, this time airily.

It was not until she was passing her old home that enlightenment came to Martha. And then she giggled outrageously.

" An' whatever's come over you ? " her husband asked sullenly.

His spouse looked at him with streaming eyes. " Portugal," she tittered. " Come on, Valentine, 'twas Portugal, wasn't it ? "

" Pre'aps an' pre'aps not," Captain Pepper retorted, a little unhappy, thinking now that it was all a fuss about nothing.

He was not one to bear a grudge and, before they had crossed the sluice-gates in Snargate Street-over-the-Wall he was in his usual sunny temper.

Two doors this side of Mr. Rochefort's bank they encountered the proprietor who, after pausing to pass the time of day, stepped more briskly homeward than he had done for many a week.

" He's a mortal sad gentleman yet," Mrs. Pepper murmured lugubriously. " But Miss Caroline says as how he's improved a dollop albeit. Of course, Valentine, with him being friendly with Mr. Fagg again, an' having something to specially interest him——"

" Interest 'im ? "

Captain Pepper, before he had heard her out, slapped his thigh forcibly. That were it, were it, he roared. He'd seen Mr. Rochefort more nor once around the harbour, an' many the time a-talking to Mr. Breton down the same way.

" I thought 'twas because 'e were a Commissioner, love," he explained. " But now I sees as there be more in it than that. Maybe——"

The boatswain stopped dead at the very door of his cottage. " I wonder, Martha ? " he ejaculated.

His wife couldn't make much out of that, but she was not long before she extracted the cause of his perplexity. It appeared that, first thing that morning, Matthew Godspenny had been round to the warehouse with a note for Mr. Fagg. " Axing him to 'tend at the bank at four this afternoon, Martha."

" But why didn't he ax him at the church instead of going to that trouble ? " Mrs. Pepper asked shrewdly.

" Dunno, excepting . . ."

It was some time later that Valentine Pepper solved the mystery to his own satisfaction. Indeed he called out so loudly that Martha, frightened out of her wits, nearly dropped the stewpan into which she was sniffing.

" I 'ave it, love," he declared, ignoring her rebuke. " Mark my words, Martha, there's going to be some sort of a meeting at the bank 'safternoon, an' few that's going'll know the reason why until they gets there."

Mrs. Pepper looked her scorn. " How be it you make all that out ? "

Her husband grimaced widely. He'd also seen, he chuckled, Matthew Godspenny delivering similar communications elsewhere—at the Custom House, to the Clerk of the Cheque, at the Harbour-master's. . . .

" A very speshul meeting, Martha, I'll be bound."

Captain Pepper, putting two and two together most accurately, hit the nail right on the head.

That afternoon, as it happened, John Fagg left Little Pent House early, his intention to call in Stembrooke. Their business with each other being completed, Mr. Bullack, picking up his hat, observed that he'd better be getting along too.

" I've got to go down the harbour way, John," the tanner remarked.

On the Antwerp corner the two gentlemen were joined by Matthew Adcock, who was " going along the same road seemingly." Mr. Ralph Jelly and Mr. Robert Spisour with " Where be you three a-going ? " swelled the company at the junction of Bench Street and King Street, and by Severus's Gate ten gentlemen were walking down Snargate Street.

" I think 'tis that you're all following me," Mr. Harry Templeman announced humorously when the party, as one man, wheeled into the first fire-alley which entered Pent-side.

Suspicions might be growing, but only outside Rochefort's Bank was the truth fully known.

Apart from Mr. Jeffrey Braems, every Dover notability was in the crowded bank that afternoon. There were the men who had fought alongside John Fagg for the future of the haven ; there were also those who, with Henry Rochefort earlier, had derided the possibility of improvement in the port's facilities.

The proceedings were opened by Mr. Rochefort. Bluntly he declared that he had requested the attendance of each and all to discuss the question of the harbour.

" 'Tis incumbent upon me, however, frankly to state that in

taking this step I do so with no intention of going over the head of the man who for years has fought for the rest of us. I refer, of course . . ."

Cheers drowned the remainder of his utterance. Thereafter he tersely reviewed the position. The town, till recently, had been divided on the merits of the case.

"That does not represent the circumstances to-day, though. Once we had two warring cliques, and even of late there has been a small, but influential, body determined to resist the general desire. Of these I was one. . . ."

Now Henry Rochefort came to that which made John Fagg's eyes gleam. Assuredly, he thought warmly and thankfully, Henry may have been doing secretive work, but damme he's done it to some tune.

" . . . and with your permission, gentlemen," the banker wound up, " I will ask a number of highly respected officials to give us their considered views on the general aspect. Perhaps you, Mr. Warren . . ."

The Collector of Customs made known the extent to which, for twenty years past, the receipts of the Custom House had been falling.

The Chamberlain, Mr. Ralph Jelly, provided figures proving that the revenue of the town was slowly, though none the less regularly, diminishing.

Mr. Denne, the Clerk to the Paving Commissioners, readily admitted that Dover had fallen far behind other towns in pursuing development. But, he added, the lighting, paving and watching of the streets cost money, and the returns from the toll-gates and dues on coal entering the port were dropping little by little. The cause, he concluded, was not far to seek.

The Town Surveyor, Mr. Edward Hexstall, affirmed positively that the price of building land was declining, an ominous sign.

Mr. Elam, the Master of Lodesmen, pronounced that unless improvement shortly came about, pilot cutters would experience difficulty in using the haven. The Court of Loadmanage, he further said, was vastly perturbed.

"Not a very satisfactory state of affairs, gentlemen," Henry Rochefort remarked dryly. " But now for other aspects. Perhaps you, Mr. Breton ! "

The Harbour-master, plunging at the risk of his livelihood, firmly placed on record his belief that the harbour, within five years, would be little better than that of Rye unless measures were taken.

Captain Nethersole recalled the warning of Mr. Elam, the Master of Lodesmen. How, he asked, could even such small craft as mail-packets use the haven if the pilot cutters found it impossible.

Mr. Stone of Buckland, coldly angry, and Mr. Jephrez Baker, fierily furious, both spoke from the point of view of traders whose capital investment would be completely lost if the port became useless.

"Thank you, gentlemen," Henry Rochefort said gravely. "You have starkly brought to our notice a condition of affairs which should bring solemn warning to all, and one which, for my part, makes me feel deeply ashamed. But first . . ." his glance wandered, "perhaps you, Mr. Stratton, will kindly favour us with your appreciation of what we have heard."

The Town Clerk, at some length, did so most pontifically. But, despite his wealth of florid delivery, his terminal sentence might have been filched from the gospel preached by John Fagg for years.

"In short, gentlemen, we may be sure that the prosperity of Dover, and of its townsfolk, depends entirely on the well-being of the port," Mr. Stratton declared.

Upon this, Henry Rochefort put a motion to the company. "That the freemen of Dover, in common front, should strive together towards the preservation and betterment of the haven, and that plans for so doing to the utmost shall be concerted with the minimum of delay."

Save for one dissenting vote the motion was passed unanimously.

The objector was Mr. Oliver Waade, who whiningly complained that he could have no part in the creation of a body whose avowed design it was to set itself against the Commissioners of Harbour. Asked, by way of interruption, where the office of Clerk of the Cheque would be if there were no haven, the Clerk of the Cheque made no reply.

Mr. Rochefort summed up. Amongst the responsible dignitaries of Dover two only opposed constructive change.

"But I venture to say that neither the Clerk of the Cheque nor Jeffrey Braems, the Register of the Harbour, can for ever thwart the wishes of the town."

Thereupon he called on John Fagg.

The low room of the bank thundered with applause. Cheer after cheer greeted the shipowner, who appeared perceptibly affected by both the spontaneous ovation and what had already taken place. He said very little, just three articles of his creed.

"Gentlemen," he opened huskily, "I believe the haven could be made one of the best in the kingdom. I believe the fight against entrenched authority will be long and mortal hard. I believe that if we stand shoulder to shoulder we can beat the one and do the other."

More cheering, more talk, the election of a committee, and at last a dispersal by two's and three's.

In time they were all gone, the bank silent, with John Fagg and Henry Rochefort left alone there.

"John," Henry Rochefort remarked quietly, "perhaps you may think my conversion has been over-quick, but it has been slower than you know. For long now I, and more with me, have been realising how far things were from being well. Only, I suppose, we lacked the courage to discard sentiments we had sworn to for years and——"

" I don't give a damn, Henry, now that Dover is ready to fight the battle for what was once its own," John Fagg said movingly.

" I'm sure on't, John," Henry Rochefort nodded unhesitatingly.

The door of the bank was locked again and, arm-in-arm, the banker and the shipowner walked down Snargate Street-over-the-Wall as lights began to peep in the windows of the town.

4

Before the middle of the year a feeling of relief, even of optimism, started to permeate the land. There was little that was tangible, it is true, to explain the lightening of heart which spread through a war-weary nation but, nevertheless, the change was quite apparent. It was as though the people of Britain had decided that the years of desperate defence, and the dreary spell of inactivity which followed Trafalgar, were coming to an end. Rumours and speculation relating to troop movements were heard everywhere, and officers and men of a great army, kept at home through no fault of their own, began to hold up their heads.

But it was an intelligence of quite another character which, in June, sent wild enthusiasm flooding through town and countryside.

Spain had broken out into armed revolt against Napoleon.

It was the first national insurrection against the tyrant who held dictatorial sway over Europe.

From Margate it was a pleasant afternoon drive to Broadstairs and the North Foreland Light, one which Mr. Henry Rochefort, in consultation with his daughter and Mrs. Jack Woodgate, decided to enjoy at the beginning of their second week at the seaside resort. When they left their elegant lodgings the watering-place was very much as usual—by their return it was beflagged, with the church-bells, despite any regulations to the contrary, setting the belfry a-shaking with the reverberations of their joyous peal.

" What is't all about, Papa ? " Caroline wondered.

" Do you think 'tis peace, Mr. Rochefort ? " Lou demanded, her eyes filled with longing.

Shortly after the banker had handed down from the carriage two young women whose acquaintance, when parading in the Assembly Rooms, several gentlemen had made the most impudent attempts to obtain, he was able to give them the news of Spain. It was very important, he said.

The two young ladies were enjoying a special holiday at Margate, because the death of her brother made impossible the celebration of Caroline's twenty-first birthday in the usual grand manner.

So one sunny morning in early June the banker's roomy old barouche stood in Snargate Street, the luggage aboard and his daughter comfortably seated awaiting him.

" I shall miss you, Caroline," M. Saval, bareheaded on the pavement, told her earnestly. " 'Twill be a different place without you."

Miss Rochefort, it must be confessed, laughed at him.

" Oh, monsieur, you will persist——"

" May it not again be Armand, Caroline ? " he asked wistfully.

The sky was clear, the day beautiful and, excepting one dull ache which never left her, she was thrilled about the month before her ; to fuss under such marvellous conditions about a mere trifle would be truly foolish.

" I suppose so, Armand," she smiled agreeably.

With her father's coming they were off ; past Severus's Gate to Little Pent House, where Miss Fagg's corded box was carefully stowed. Then came Lou in new bonnet, new dress, new everything of a surety, she so intoxicated she hardly knew what she was doing.

" Oh, Caroline," she gloated ecstatically, taking the seat alongside her friend.

There was a last-minute talk before parting. Mrs. Fagg and Mrs. George were chattering away to Caroline and Lou, and John Fagg and Henry Rochefort, with Horatio butting in all he could, were in companionable conversation.

" Well, I suppose 'tis time we were off," the banker remarked as St. Mary's struck the quarter.

Just then Lou, chancing to look down, let out a most despairing shriek and, without so much as by your leave, flew out of the carriage. Into the house she rushed, through the tiled hall, and up the stairs, her skirts fluttering wildly around her.

" Bless my soul ! " ejaculated John Fagg.

Caroline was rocking with mirth. " She found she was wearing her oldest pair of house slippers," she explained, rather incoherently.

In the ensuing laughter Horatio entered into further negotiations with " the kind gennelman " who latterly he had learnt was his Uncle Henry. Could he go to the bank whilst Uncle Henry was away ? Would Mr. Godspenny give him a bag of money to count ? Could he sit on a high stool at the desk ? Could . . .

" You mustn't worry your Uncle Henry, Horatio," Mrs. George chided him gently.

Henry Rochefort smiled fondly at the boy. " He's not doing that, Susan, my dear," he said pleasantly.

Hearing this, Polly Fagg succeeded in catching her husband's eye. They had the feeling that Henry, though no other could replace Louis in his heart, had only just made the discovery that Horatio was a Rochefort after all, a Rochefort who might carry on a business maintained always at a standard of high repute.

Lou was coming out of the house nearly as quickly as she had gone in.

" Well, Lou," chuckled her father.

More teasing all round and then the travellers were off, dispatched by a frenzy of waving and Horatio's shrill voice.

Up the Deal Road, climbing the steep hill past the Castle. Then into the more level portion of the turnpike, with a long halt above St. Margaret's Bay, where they had to pull to the side to allow the passage of what seemed to be an entire army of cavalry and foot.

" A big troop movement, I should say," Mr. Henry Rochefort remarked.

Infantrymen swinging by winked at the young ladies, their officers smartly saluted ; column after column moved along of the finely equipped army which the people of Britain had raised by their unceasing exertions.

" Magnificent," the banker added appreciatively. " Very different from what 'twas."

Bread wagons and ammunition wagons, forge carts for the artillery, and horses bearing surgeons' chests ; battalion guns and carts with entrenching tools—billhooks, pick-axes, spades, axes, and shovels. The camp kettles carried by the men sometimes ringing out unmusically against their accoutrements, whips cracking now and then, and a squealing wheel which brought a stern rebuke to a driver.

" 'Tis, Papa," Caroline murmured, her thoughts far away from the tramp of these dust-raising feet.

Then on to Margate, where the two young ladies enjoyed themselves hugely. They took excursions into the neighbouring country, they ' drank the water,' and on the single wet afternoon of their stay spent a delightful hour or so in the circulating libraries and toy shops. Several times, too, Miss Rochefort and Mrs. Woodgate hired a bathing-machine and, whilst beginning to undress in the tiny cabin, took turns to peep through the small window in the front, watching the deepening sea rise up the horse's massive legs.

" Oh, Caroline," Lou gasped on the first occasion, half apprehensively and half delightedly.

The horse, driver on its broad back, had splashed towards the beach and, ready now, the young ladies cautiously opened the door.

Soon, beneath the screening canvas umbrella, they were descending the short ladder.

"Ugh . . . ooough!" screamed Miss Rochefort.

"I daren't!" shrieked Mrs. Jack Woodgate.

But eventually, one careful step at a time, they ventured lower until beneath their feet were ribs of sand.

Holding hands, they bobbed and ducked to their shoulders in the prodigiously cold sea.

How they revelled in the dissipations of that month of summer days.

By the beginning of August it was known that a British army had been landed in Portugal. It wasn't, by European ideas, a large army, but the 20,000 men of which it was composed was enormous by comparison with the absurdly small expeditionary forces which hitherto had suffered ignominy at the hands of enemies counting ten to each of their own one.

The end of the month heard the eight bells of St. Mary-the-Virgin's likewise defying all regulations.

"*Vimiero . . . Vimiero.*" In the Antwerp, in the Fountain, everywhere, the crushing defeat which General Sir Arthur Wellesley had inflicted on Junot was refought.

The first time the Frenchies had come against British infantry in reasonable force it had cost them dear. Marching recklessly against his adversaries, his intention to hurl them into the sea, the renowned Marshal had been signally discomfited, forced indeed by subsequent agreement to yield up the whole of Portugal.

Again the clanging of the bells of St. Mary-the-Virgin's spoke of the wonderful news.

"We've started now," the hot-heads crowed. "'Twon't be long 'fore [we've got Nappy on the run from end to end of the Continent."

"Don't count your chickens," the wise retorted. "'Tis mightily encouraging, but the greatest military power on earth ain't likely to throw in his hand because an odd battle has gone agin' him."

The excitement of new and brave times had not subsided in Dover by Hornblowing Day, when John Fagg, by common consent of the freemen assembled, was appointed to a second term as Mayor.

That evening, Mr. Henry Rochefort gave a quiet supper party in Snargate Street, his sole guests being the Faggs.

"I . . . I shall really have to pull myself together," Mrs. Fagg confessed ruefully, fanning her face with a handkerchief.

She was so proud and so much of a-dither that she couldn't eat. No, it was Charles's letter which she had brought with her, not the honour done to her husband which caused all her stress, though, as she indignantly retorted when charged by him, "Naturally, John,

I'm greatly delighted by the honour the Common Councilmen have done to you. Of all the things to say, I declare."

Yes, it was Charles—Charles who had fought at Vimiero, Charles who had received another promotion, Charles who now was with General Sir John Moore in the Peninsula.

" 'Twill be the General John Moore who used to be at Shorncliffe," Lou said knowingly, her face glowing about her brother.

And Henry Rochefort had risen to propose a toast, no, hang it, two toasts. It was a pretty scene, the banker standing at one end of the table whose lovely grain was brought out by the candles on it, opposite him his daughter, her bare shoulders enchanting against the gloom outside the light.

" To the Mayor of Dover," Henry Rochefort called warmly.

" The Mayor of Dover," Caroline echoed gaily, making them all laugh by representing that but for one certain obstacle she might have been the Mayoress herself.

" Caroline ! " laughed Mrs. Fagg. " And just look at them, Henry ! "

" Papa ! " giggled Mrs. Jack Woodgate, as much as ever diverted by an age-old joke.

When the Mayor and the lady who might have shared his distinction had finished clinking their glasses, when the last smile had died at their interpretation of a love-lorn pair, Mr. Rochefort rose again.

" I give you . . . Captain Charles Fagg," he offered distinctly. " A very gallant soldier and gentleman."

From then, somehow, the atmosphere seemed to change. The banker became quiet and preoccupied, and Caroline, seeing how it was, promptly caught Mrs. Fagg's eye and the ladies retired to the drawing-room.

John Fagg, moving up the table nearer to his host, briefly grasped Henry Rochefort's shoulder.

" I know, Henry," he said, his voice deep with sympathy. " He was a gallant soldier and gentleman too."

" I miss him, John," the banker replied simply.

A sorrow shared may be a sorrow halved. Perhaps it was not in quite that proportion, but Henry Rochefort found true comfort in the society of his friend.

Enraged by Vimiero, the Emperor was by October at the head of the *Grande Armée* of 250,000 veterans which marched across Spain for the purpose, as the despot said, " of carrying the victorious eagles to the Pillars of Hercules and to drive the British leopard into the sea."

Prior to this, England formed a new coalition with Austria and, as ever, continued her unrelenting watch over the sea.

It was in a minor engagement, one too insignificant even to creep into the history books, that Jack Woodgate received his hurt and paid his contribution to the price of Admiralty.

To Susan Rochefort, as at the post office she took the letter addressed to Lou, it was all too fearful a reminder of a day long before when she, too, had dreadful intelligence of one she loved from the hand of the Postmaster.

"Thank you, Mr. Dawkes," she whispered, nearly as pale as she had been seven years before.

A dozen times did Mrs. George look at the superscription, "Mrs. John Woodgate," penned in a queer and unformed writing; and a dozen times, thinking that the tidings could be more gently broken to dearest Lou, she was on the point of opening the letter.

Lou, laughing over some foolishness with her mother, was in the parlour, and never so quickly did a smile pass from a girl's face as when she saw Aunt Susan looking at her so miserably.

"Aunt Susan !" she cried in alarm.

"'Tis a letter for you, Lou," Mrs. George said faintly.

Fear spreads like a fire of straw, and her niece's hands were trembling when she tore the wafer. Her grey eyes dilated as she scanned the lines, her mouth puckered up into a tremulous shape.

"'Tis Jack," she sobbed. "He's . . . he's——"

"Lou, dearest." Her mother sprang to her.

Because she never afterwards remembered, Mrs. George Rochefort was never able to reproach herself that, in snatching from Lou the fluttering sheet, she was doing an unconscionable thing. She was only aware that she must know what it was.

"Jack's . . ." Lou was whimpering.

Mrs. George Rochefort's breath came in a burst of relief. Jack's left hand had traced awkward-looking words which said that he had lost his right arm, that he was doing very well, that his *dere* Lou must not fret about him, and that he would be with her by Christmas or shortly afterwards.

"Oh dear," Mrs. Fagg said tragically when she knew.

Lou remained inconsolable, and it was only when her mother was running upstairs for smelling-salts that Susan Rochefort brought her back from a state bordering on hysteria.

"Lou, dear," she began firmly, now more colour in her own cheeks, "I once had a letter which seemed as this."

"Jack's lost his arm, Aunt Susan," Jack's wife raved.

It was strange how Susan Rochefort, so frail and yielding, could always find strength when the need came. She found it now, using it to smack her niece's hands until they were pink.

Lou shivered. "Aunt Susan . . . *Aunt Susan !* "

"My dear," Mrs. George said affectionately, " 'twas for your own good."

Tears might still be trickling, but now there was horror and incredulity in Lou's expression.

"You . . . you were hitting me, Aunt Susan," she muttered plaintively.

More naturally, Mrs. Jack Woodgate began to cry, her head cradled on the breast of her widowed aunt. Dim-eyed she still was when at the end of the evening she went to bed, but she saw the misfortune more truly in its proper perspective.

"Thank you, Aunt Susan," she said shyly from the door.

And then, of all things, Mrs. George Rochefort herself started to weep when her niece was gone.

Towards the close of the year Sir John Moore and his gallant band of 25,000 men fell upon the lines of communication of the great conqueror's immense army.

The Emperor, compelled hastily to leave Madrid, detached 100,000 men under Soult to deal with this audacious but no less serious threat. Skilfully inveigled by the British Commander-in-Chief, the French Marshal's overwhelming force was drawn step by step further into the rugged hills of Galicia.

Off Ferrol and Corunna frigates and sail-of-the-line of the Royal Navy began to rendezvous. It had often been their task to take off the army in the teeth of the enemy—it might be so again.

5

Far-reaching exercises were taking place in the South-Eastern Command, and on the ranging grass-land behind the cliffs from Dover to Shorncliffe many military movements were in course that mild January day. Here would be the chaise of a general officer, there cavalrymen each carrying two days supply of corn, and elsewhere bât horses bearing poles, tents, and blankets.

Some five miles from Dover, where the high cliffs began to dip steeply, three riders, two gentlemen and a lady, were on the point of parting company after a most entertaining conversation.

"Well, 'tis most disagreeable to have to leave you, Miss Rochefort," the Major of Dragoons grunted. " But military necessity, y'know."

M. Saval laughed. " Speaking of military necessity, monsieur, there's a mos' amusing story going of our mutual friend Willie Donald-son. It appears that before leaving for Colchester, he——"

" Colchester, monsieur ? He's not at Colchester."

The Frenchman smiled sweetly. " I regret you are not well informed, monsieur."

" But he ain't," the Major observed testily. " Damme, as if I shouldn't know, man."

" In that case, monsieur," was the rather insolent reply he received, " your sense of omnipotence is the root of your error."

At this stage Miss Rochefort intervened. Very decidedly she in-formed both gentlemen that the issue was too insignificant to become heated about.

" True, Caroline," Armand Saval laughed unpleasantly. " Though I confess I mislike my word being doubted. Colonel Donaldson's brigade are gone to Colchester and there's no possible dispute on't."

The Dragoon's face was brick-red. " Colonel Donaldson's brigade is at Bristol with orders for overseas," he roared.

This time Caroline stopped any further nonsense, and subsequently, when a furious-faced Major had galloped off, she most severely re-buked her companion.

" 'Twas your fault, too, Armand," she added vigorously. " You almost forced a difference on him."

M. Saval shrugged, conceded that perhaps he had gone too far, and suggested that they should put aside what was, after all, no more than a minor affair.

" I fear," he smiled, dismissing the whole business, " that the clock prohibits our visit to the Royal Military Canal. 'Tis a pity, but perhaps another day, when the ground is something better than hock-deep, 'twould be more suitable to ride there."

It had been their intention to visit this defence against invasion, but as an attractive alternative the Frenchman, pointing below to three brick fortifications not dissimilar in shape from sand-pies, suggested that his fair companion might find it amusing to look over a Martello Tower. The centre one was deserted by the army, he knew, the bomb-proof top being proved to be sadly lacking.

" The usual rascally contractor, I suppose," he ended.

" 'Twould be most interesting, Armand," Caroline Rochefort de-clared eagerly.

The path downwards was narrow and there was on Armand Saval's lips, as he allowed her to pass before him, the hint of an exultant smile.

Breaking into a trot on the bottom, they speedily reached the small fort, and there the beasts were tethered to a convenient tree.

" Such thickness, Armand," Caroline marvelled as she passed

through the low doorway. " I protest the walls must be nearly three yards wide."

On that the Frenchman made no response. Indeed he seemed more content to watch her in the half-light whilst, in an interior pierced by no more than a couple of ridiculously small windows, she examined the powder magazine and the storehouse.

" How may we gain the upper story, Armand ? "

In a few words, his tone exactly reminiscent of that he had used at the Bowling Green months before, she was informed that her curiosity must remain unsatisfied.

" Methinks I care not for your manner, Armand," she turned haughtily.

" An' methinks I am more interested to hear that you care for me, my sweet but tantalising little intriguer," he laughed softly.

" Intriguer, sir ? " she asked, bewilderment waging war with anger.

" Even so, my lovely coquette," he bowed sardonically.

Soon she learnt his preposterous meaning, and how her apparent change of heart towards him had been fantastically misinterpreted ; she understood that, in pleasantly welcoming him for her father's sake, she was now being charged with raising him up only to cast him down again, deliberately for her own amusement.

Their voices sounded strange in a compartment which was un-believably smaller than the outside circumference of the building.

" 'Tis untrue," she quivered angrily, contempt for him in her eyes. " And, sir, you will please stand aside or you will answer to my father this time."

He took a step towards her, then another.

" I have warned you, monsieur," she said fearlessly.

" So . . . you have warned me, eh ? " he asked dangerously.

She had moved a little, and what light there was touched directly upon a face which, if pale, was proudly resolute. Perhaps it was her unflinching bearing which brought realisation to Armand Saval that he was in the presence of a woman who might bend, but who would never break, a woman far more likely to be moved by declared passion than any threat.

" Caroline, I love you," he told her fervently. " If you will exalt me by becoming my wife I swear that——"

" Monsieur Saval," she broke into his frenzy, " please, I beg of you, say no more. I thank you for the . . . the honour you have done me, but I must tell you it cannot be."

" Why ? " he demanded hoarsely.

" I do not love you, monsieur," she replied simply.

" 'Twill come, Caroline."

She shook her head. "No, monsieur," she answered quietly and very finally.

It was that very finality in her which persuaded him that, entreat or threaten as he might, he would not move her, which told him, most lacerating of all to his pride, that she was utterly indifferent to him. From then he had but one urge, to hurt her as cruelly as he could.

"You do not love me, eh, Caroline?" he laughed harshly. "You prefer to waste your bloom awaiting one who went away without a word to you, one——"

"Monsieur!"

He laughed again. "Oh yes, Caroline, long have I realised that Charles Fagg was the man for whom you were repining."

"How dare you . . . how *dare* you speak thus," Caroline Rochefort said furiously, her fingers tightening. "Stand aside or——"

The Frenchman sneered with the full force of his rage.

"The man who preferred to put his native town behind the same night, rather than be called upon to meet an engagement any man claiming to be a——"

There was a quick whistle through the air and an involuntary sob from him as the whip left its vicious weal across his face.

Trembling, and yet with eyes blazing, Miss Rochefort of Dover stayed long enough to apply a scorching title to a man whose head was buried in his hands.

"That, you infamous knave, is for your insult to me. 'Tis also your reward for a foul slander against one who is not here to speak for himself."

She was gone before he recovered from the agony of that blow, nor did Armand Saval make any attempt to overtake her.

His eyes vengeful, he watched her ride up the winding track.

"You shall pay, my dear, for that," he whispered. "Yes . . ." his finger-tips were gingerly exploring the uplift of flesh which scored him from chin to temple, "yes, you shall pay . . . and dearly."

When the feeling of sickness was past, he mounted his horse and slowly rode back to Dover.

Afterwards, the ostler in the yard of the Royal Oak stables avowed that the Frenchy looked like a lunatic.

"An' behaved like one, Jim," he told his crony, the head ostler at the Antwerp Stables. "He'd brought in the beast he allus hires, an' there he were, with a scar on his hat-carrier you could light a cannel with, standing afore the notice for the next Assembly, and staring at it as though 'twere the answer to 'is prayers. And I says to 'im, respectful enow, 'Bin in the wars seemingly, moosoo!' an' he

rounds on me an' begod I'll swear if he'd 'ad a pistol in 'is hand he'd
have shot me dead on the spot. His face, Jim . . . well, seeing's
believing, 'tis true, but . . ."

M. Saval's servant François had worse experience than that when
his ' master ' returned home. Jocularly remarking on Armand's lack
of success with a certain young lady, the man whom Dover knew as a
valet was seized by the throat and so held until nearly throttled.

" You will now listen to my instructions," M. Saval said viciously.
And François listened.

" First, I have intelligence of embarkation movements to Bristol.
Shortly I will work out the combination of lights and you will see
they are displayed to-night."

" Yes," François nodded painfully, seeing reply was expected of
him.

" Next . . ." Armand Saval's eyes were glittering.

His orders were quite simple. On the morrow François was to
take the London stage and journey as far as Canterbury . . . no,
that was too near . . . as far as Faversham. From there he was to strike
out into the country towards Newnham.

" There or thereabouts you will find a lonely house to which a
gentleman may bring his wife, alas a beautiful though disordered
creature . . . "

François, his nerve recovered and his breathing less difficult, did
venture one impudence towards the conclusion of his instructions.

" Assuredly you take considerable risk, Armand," he grinned.
" For I warrant that never again will you dare to show yourself here."

M. Saval reflectively pulled an ear. " On the contrary, you stupid
fool," he smiled gently, " I shall return with my dear wife. 'Tis merely
my purpose to break her first—after which I dare assert she will not
be unfavourably disposed towards a ring."

Thereupon François actually sniggered. " Indeed are the mighty
fallen, for now I'd swear that Mademoiselle has possessed you.
The gay Capitaine Armand Chassepot in the toils of matrimony
. . . 'tis too——"

His ' master's ' cold-blooded smile vanished. There was that about
Armand Saval which caused the speaker to decide that unspoken
words may be best.

The insolent raillery died in a sorely-bruised throat.

Two days before Assembly Night in the Royal Oak Rooms, the
church bells of England expressed their joy for the great victory of
Corunna.

The fleet was bringing home the tired but valiant army.

Their countrymen prepared to do them all honour.

CHAPTER FOUR

I

THE Assemblies in the Royal Oak Rooms were social occasions much
appreciated. In grim days of the ebb and flow of conflict, less grim it
was perhaps true than in the anxious years when England could do
little more than await attack, they were indeed a welcome relaxation
from present cares and a foretaste of the better times to come, when
the shadow of a hateful oligarchy should be for ever removed from
the lives of free people.

The older gentlemen liked the card-room ; their wives the opportunity for dressing-up and a round of gossip in pleasant surroundings ;
the young men, whether they were macaronis from the garrison or
irregulars from the county regiments stationed on the Heights, turned
up in full force ; and as for the young women of Dover and district,
outnumbered by clamant partners, these events were pure joy.

So, on this evening in January, the news of the victory of Corunna
bringing a specially large and jolly throng, carriages and horsemen
in droves came to the Royal Oak Rooms, some baiting there in the
inn's cobbled yard, with the overflow proceeding into the Market
Place and thence under the lamplit arch to the Antwerp Stables.

In the card-room, games were in full play. There were three
tables at loo, one at quinze, another at vingt-et-un, and a number
more at which whist was held to be the best of all hazards.

Mr. John Fagg and Mr. Henry Rochefort, after disposing of their
females, devoted themselves to whist. Supper would not come until
midnight, and even then was rather a makeshift replacing the rich
spread for which, in peace days now almost forgotten, the Royal
Oak Assemblies were renowned.

" Aye, Henry," sighed John Fagg, " well, perhaps some day . . ."
In mime he gave an exhibition of the gourmet's finicky selection from
a board groaning with luscious victuals. " And, forsooth," he added,
brightening, " we've had news which will go towards hastening the
day."

" I'm positive on't, John," Henry Rochefort asserted. " But in
the interval . . . eh ? "

" Aye, smile and keep cheerful," the shipowner nodded grimly.

Both Captain Nethersole and Mr. Stratton signified confirmation
of these sentiments to such an extent that the boisterous acclamation
brought a *sssh* of expostulation from neighbouring tables. Indeed,

Mrs. Fagg, who had wearied of watching the younger folk in the ballroom, raised an admonitory finger as she came in with Mrs. Stokes and Mrs. Crundall.

"John," she taxed him severely, "I suppose 'tis you who is responsible for the uproar?"

Her husband unwinkingly stared back. "Nay, 'tis Henry an' not me," he declared virtuously. "He's been expressing the view that we ought to compromise with the Frenchies."

There was a roar of laughter. It spoke much for the relations now existing between John Fagg and Henry Rochefort that the latter joined in the jest as heartily as the others.

In the ballroom the orchestra was tuning up preparatory to the third minuet of the evening, with a crowd of suppliants in the foyer beseeching their claims on the delightful Miss Caroline Rochefort.

"But really, Miss Rochefort, won't you go down a dance with me?" miserably remonstrated a sapper captain, a very dashing fellow.

"Miss Rochefort, *please*," laughed a cornet of Light Horse. "Rank is surely forgotten . . ."

Jack Woodgate was home at last, his wife clinging adoringly to his remaining arm. There was something disturbingly poignant about the right sleeve neatly tied off near the broad shoulder, something grand too.

"Caroline *is* really so lovely, dearest," said young Mrs. Woodgate softly. "Small wonder that she always has a bevy of beaux."

Her husband stared reflectively as they turned down the grand staircase.

"She's lovely enough, sweetheart," he agreed slowly. "I think even more beautiful than she was when I last saw her. Somehow she's . . . she's . . ."

The difference in Caroline Rochefort was hard to define. Perhaps in the main it was spiritual rather than physical, though even in this last, some change might have been discerned. There was maybe a reminder of suffering in the brilliant dark eyes, perhaps less fullness in the cheeks.

But all this those young soldiers besieging her were not likely to see. They saw a charming young woman, oval-faced, with sweeping eyelashes; one who could, as she pleased, be either provocative or demure; a dazzling young female whose clinging white muslin gown could not but reveal the enchanting lines of her.

"Oh come, Miss Rochefort, can't I have the honour of your hand?" an officer of the Royal Miners asked dismally.

The alluring creature, dimpling roguishly, said it was her purpose to fetch a clean pair of gloves, after which it was her intent to seek her father.

So a play proceeded which was really delightful to all, with a tall figure at the extreme end of the foyer seeing much that was going on, his eyes angry, his bearing that of a man charged with a need he is determined to fulfil.

Many of the older ladies, ostensibly watching the dancing whilst sitting on the gilt chairs arranged in the small balconies, had remarked on M. Saval's queer attitude during the seven or eight minutes he stood there. There was much speculation about him, and no few asides when the direction of the Frenchman's quick glances was revealed. His supposed discomfiture at the hands of Mr. Rochefort's daughter had been the cause of much conjecture, and there was no disputing the livid mark he carried. Now they could see him, obviously taut, obviously indeed waiting.

When old Peter Monin's clock struck the first quarter after eleven, the ivory-painted doors to the staircase luckily having been latched back, they witnessed something which for years they continued to recall.

M. Saval, inactivity behind him and the inward certainty of eventual submission before him, caught up to Caroline Rochefort on the wide landing at the top.

"Mademoiselle," he opened intensely, "may I speak with you . . . alone? You will not be detained unduly," he added icily. " 'Tis merely that I am commissioned to convey to you a matter of the utmos' import."

Even had he been wavering, the dislike in her eyes would have goaded him on.

"Strange words, sir," Caroline declared bitingly.

At this his voice altered, to become charged with the pregnant unknown, so vitally that even gross impertinence might be forgotten in a curiosity thus aroused.

"Of that, mademoiselle," he said gravely, "you shall, if you will, judge for yourself. And . . ." a faint smile, mocking, came to his lips, "I would remind you that this is a public place, so if 'tis fear which restrains you, well . . ." he shrugged carelessly.

Impressed despite her aversion, and furious at the inference he had made, Miss Rochefort nevertheless succeeded in concealing both these emotions.

"Fear, sir," she laughed lightly. "Fie, monsieur, you have a pretty conceit of yourself, so extravagantly so that I pray you lead me where 'tis you will."

He bowed and, after indicating the way she should go, the pair proceeded along the foyer, watched by a score or more of curious eyes. Thence they descended the less ornate staircase at the further end, passing that same banister-post near which William Pitt had talked to a horribly distressed young lady.

In the vestibule the Frenchman glanced at the range of doors and, as if it were of little moment, chose a room which abutted on to the Black Ditch. It was quiet in that part of the building and there could be heard, quite clearly, the uneasy movements of horses and the muffled admonition of a rough-voiced coachman to his refractory animals.

" Well, sir ? " Caroline Rochefort asked. " You will oblige me by being expeditious in informing me of whatever tidings you bring."

He smiled, just smiled. Standing with his back to the closed door, fingering a button on his brocade waistcoat—he smiled. Perhaps her stinging tone may have brought him directly instead of guilefully to the matter which concerned him alone.

" Tidings, Caroline," he said softly. " No, my dear, let's talk of other things. Rather let me tell you that I love you, Mistress Spitfire, for all your waywardness. Though you have treated my advances with contumely——"

" Your message, sir ? " she interposed disdainfully.

Gently he confessed the truth. " You see, my angel, I am determined to have you. You shall be mine whosoever shall dare to stand in the way. And——"

Fury burned in Caroline Rochefort's eyes. " So you are a liar, too, monsieur," she said scornfully.

" My sweet Caroline," he murmured reproachfully, " come, be reasonable. I have a chaise awaiting and, ere dawn, you will be far away. Accept the situation, and I swear—— Now, now, my dear."

With all a man's strength he thwarted her plucky attempt to escape, his hand tightly over her mouth.

" Now will you come willingly, you obstinate little hellcat ? " he demanded viciously.

Her answer he read in her undaunted eyes. " So . . ." he growled. The back of her head forced against the hollow of his locked arms, his fingers sinking deeper into her cheeks as he increased the pressure on her mouth, he partly lifted and partly dragged her towards a corner of the room. There, even as one of her frantic kicks, catching him squarely on the shin, brought a grunt of pain to his lips, he stopped, bending her with him, to grasp the heavy, hooded cloak he had secreted in readiness.

St. Mary-the-Virgin's began to chime the half-hour.

2

The frosty moon, bringing silver sheen to the sleeping countryside, gleamed on the pyramid-capped church tower which helped to give the semblance of a Flemish town to the old and irregular buildings of Rye, a conception which, considering the number of those from over the narrow seas who had found refuge there, throughout the ages, was not quite of the most fanciful.

A post-chaise was hurrying through the narrow High Street and, once clear of the town, began to speed along the winding turnpike, but never flew quickly enough for the impatience of the solitary traveller. Ahead was the county of his love and birth, doubly dear in an absence of some months over three years ; behind was the glorious battlefield of Corunna and the many tedious leagues of travel which now separated him from Portsmouth, with its frigates and ships-of-the-line which had brought home an outnumbered but victorious army.

Charles Fagg watched intently, first to one and then to the other side. There was the lighthouse at Dungeness, its flashing Argand lamps throwing a glittering beam almost to his feet ; New Romney, where the watchman's swinging lantern showed clearly the chevron-patterned brickwork of the pavement on which the old fellow walked ; then Dymchurch Wall and, pointing seaward, menacing muzzles in a great circular redoubt. All about were the signs of efficient preparations for the reception of an enemy, a perceptible improvement upon what the traveller last saw when on that same coast.

At these sure indications of the progress of a nation upon whose tongues the fear-impelling word 'invasion' had once so heavily rested, Charles smiled faintly. Above his mouth his head was in gloom, but below, where moonlight impinged upon tan, his firm lips curved in satisfaction at this proof of change in old England. Crazy attempt might still be made on her shores, but such rash effort would be brushed ruthlessly aside, being recognised by the defenders of those shores as Napoleon's last vain effort to distract the growing legions who had even now begun to take the fight to him.

On the post-chaise lurched, to the left Romney Marsh stretching back until it vanished into the low blue line of distant hills. Its green surface was star-speckled with frozen pools, and its famed sheep, as always in winter, had been driven on to the drier ground of the higher lands.

So into the narrow, black-and-white shadowed streets of Hythe, where the lower windows of the White Hart made a welcoming line of mellow light. The excitement of the news of victory, so seldom received, was still keeping a number of townsfolk from warm beds.

Briskly stamping his chilled feet, Charles Fagg walked into the hostelry whilst the change was made, there to take a pot of nicely mulled Kentish ale.

There was a hum of conversation from the parlour, where a group of men of vastly differing degree were declaring that which expressed Britain's heart and soul.

"That cunning Mounseer," growled a red-faced fellow, "can think 'ow he pleases, but we'll lick him howsomedever long the fight goes on. We've been at it fifteen years now, apart from the two years break of——"

A precise, thin-faced gentleman in fine, though sombre, clothing nodded even as he interrupted.

"Bonaparte . . . I will call him none other," he said austerely, "desired the Treaty of Amiens for the one reason that the people of France, impoverished an' deadly weary of a state of perpetual warfare, were showing signs of restlessness. The same may happen again, but I affirm that never again will we accept Bonaparte's word. Time without end he has broken faith in the past——"

Another, who had vainly attempted to stop the flow when that ill-famed Treaty was mentioned, now took a turn.

"The Corsican wanted breathing space to build up his navy to match ours," he grunted. "Meantime, he plotted every sly and dastardly thing agin us——"

The red-faced man, his bearing revealed it, was of the type who believes in sticking to the immediate and vital point.

"Aye, fifteen year," he rumbled, "and for the most part of that our belts have been drawn so tight that the buckle has been shoving against the backbone. But even if 'twere for another fifteen year . . . eh, my lads?"

There was a roar of acclamation, and the call, by the attorney-like gentleman, for the host and another round of rumbo.

Charles Fagg, at this slight diversion, drew back. That day, as to his cost he had already learnt on the journey, Army officers from overseas were in danger of receiving attentions such as tended to become distinctly embarrassing.

Now that he stood in the light, it was possible to see what change had been wrought in him during the years of his absence. The bitterness which had been in his face had gone, to be replaced by an impressive authority ; here, it could be said, was a most decisive gentlemen, well-favoured, too.

"Ready, sir," the ostler called out cheerfully.

Charles, drawing his high military collar about his neck, entered the vehicle for the last stage to his home.

With every mile the landscape grew more familiar. The ribbon of the Military Canal, and the stubborn-looking Martello Towers, objects which were new to him, received a professional glance of approval from the young officer. The camp at Shorncliffe, greatly extended, and with its buildings less makeshift, stood up on the high ground to the left, whilst on the right, the argentine sea lapped gently against the very foundation of the road.

Then came the steep hill of Sandgate, from the top of which was view magnificent towards the coast of France, and further along, in the ill-paved and narrow streets of Folkestone, a glimpse of a square-towered church on a bluff to the westward of the town.

At last, after another long climb slowly taken, the six-hundred feet height of the Dover turnpike, and chalky white cliffs curving in a long arc towards the place where the passenger was born.

From here the road bent and twisted, sometimes giving an en-chanting prospect of Dover at the fringe of shimmering waters, with the distant horizon richly and darkly lined against the deep blue of the night sky. But soon the road wound away from the sea, dipping gradually as it progressed down the valley, to either side sparkling pastures and picturesque farmhouses nestling here and there.

Then the old town ; the Maison Dieu and Biggin Street ; the tower of St. Mary's with its many stages ; and, passing the Royal Oak Rooms, the throbbing strains of stringed instruments in the minuet drowned suddenly as Peter Monin's clock began to boom the first stroke of eleven.

Charles, with that childhood's loved reverberation in his ears, saw the Market Place bathed in moonlight, each window beyond the Guildhall reflecting the fairy glow. He blinked slightly, saw little of King Street or of the old tower in Bench Street beneath which, in a crypt, George Rochefort had mistakenly plotted eleven years before. But, with Severus's Gate, the high bank of shingle beyond, and Town Wall Street, the Castle heaven flood-lit on the heights ahead, he had to control his emotion, growing excitement possessing him as the post-chaise, at his signal, came to a halt before the family mansion he had for so long not known.

The valises were carried to the panelled door, the driver received his charge and a gleaming guinea for good measure. Only after the clip-clop of hoofs faded away did Charles Fagg, who had for these moments stood drinking in the very essence of his surroundings, grasp· the knocker, to send a sharp summons through the dark house.

Before long there came simultaneously the sound of shuffling feet and a growing gleam in the fanlight ; then a fumbling and a muttering behind the door, which at last opened to disclose Keziah, the candle she carried causing high light and alternate shade in her homely face.

" At your service, Mrs. Hart," the caller said solemnly.

There was a sudden gasp, a mixture of belief and disbelief. The candle-stick went up arms-length over her head, to cast its rays on the erect figure standing at the door.

" Master . . . Master Charles ! " she ejaculated. Still unrealisingly, and then, as full truth came, she found tongue. " Master Charles ! " she shrieked joyously, covering the intervening distance in a half-run, there to draw him to her ample bosom, with arms about his neck. Meantime the candle, tilting madly, steadily dripped hot wax to the tiled floor.

" And my mother and father, how are they, Keziah ? " Charles asked laughingly, when all these transports were over, when Keziah tearfully had satisfied herself that no harm had come to him, and when she had feigned wrath about his teasing of her, and had given him an old-time buffet about the head. " I won't disturb them to-night, and I'll leave the surprise for the breakfast table in the morning."

" They're still at the Assembly Rooms, Master Charles," said old Keziah, rather abstractedly, her face wreathed in pride as she stood off to view the soiled uniform now displayed by the relinquishing of a greatcoat.

It seemed, too, that the young man himself became suddenly thoughtful, even though, to disguise it, he carried on some sort of conversation when they reached the parlour.

" You say the Royal Oak Rooms, eh, Keziah ? " he at length murmured carelessly. " Methinks I might saunter over there, and here and now let them have the surprise."

Keziah, it appeared, had no liking for the suggestion. Mr. Charles, she objected, was too fatigued after so long a journey. He would need food, too, she insisted on that. It would be far better if he sat down comfortably whilst she ministered to his requirements. And, too, she ended triumphantly and conclusively, poking the banked-down fire, it would be far more suitable if he met his family in the privacy of their home.

To all this Charles listened smilingly. But it seemed his mind was made up.

" I can always stay abed in the morn, Keziah," he cajoled her. " And I swear I won't touch a taste of breakfast until you have brought me a cup of chocolate earlier on."

She brightened, putting aside her disappointment. And, she said, if Master Charles wanted to flaunt his handsome person she at least would ensure he did it properly. She would also make assurance doubly sure, she added ominously, by seeing to his linen.

" If you needs clean-changes——"

" Nay, Keziah," he grinned, " surely I'm old enough——"

There was some more badinage, and another kiss and a squeeze around a substantial waist. Then at length Keziah happily rolled off to the kitchen, her quest hot water for a young gentleman who had never been far from her thoughts.

The bedroom was redolent with shaving soap, discarded clothes were scattered, whilst on the bed, freshly unpacked, lay a creased though moderately new gosling-green faced uniform coat of a captain in the 'Shiners'. Its owner, whistling gaily, was standing before a mirror tying up his hair, the nether portion of his attire complete, the upper part clad in a clean shirt which as yet had not been tucked into his white kerseymere breeches.

It was about then that Charles Fagg made the discovery which cut short his blithesome song. He started immoderately at that amazing sight of his own hand, a writing which brought back the memory of another night long ago, a night which had been the dividing-line between the bitterness of distasteful tasks done and the glories of honourable service ahead.

" My God ! " he ejaculated sharply.

Almost as if in a trance he took a candlestick from the adjacent tallboy and, with the improved illumination, scrutinised the endorsement on the note which he must have missed in the bureau drawer when, just for curiosity, he had opened that old-time hiding-place a few minutes before.

" *The Right Honourable William Pitt*," he read slowly.

There was no need to look further, but look further he did, running along those lines he had once hurriedly penned.

" Sir,
　　In the discharge to you this evening of the vital news concerning affairs on the Continent, and in my following flush consequent upon your graciousness in securing for me the military appointment you wrote of, I fear me that I failed to report a fact of some disquietude and moment.

　　To be brief, sir, there is at present in this town a French emigré living under the name of Saval. . . ."

Charles Fagg was hurrying, his eyes rapidly scanning the missive which should have disposed of a spy. Now he threw the condemnatory letter back into the drawer and, no longer dressing with the dalliance which could be allowed one who had long been absent from soft surroundings, he made ready with all the celerity of the seasoned campaigner.

" Perhaps before dawn, pray God," he muttered grimly, searching for his pistols, " both a matter of honour to myself and another of service to the state may have been discharged . . . if 'tis that he is still here."

Rapidly he completed his preparations. The candles were snuffed, and quickly he passed down the length of the shallow stairs.

Keziah was awaiting him in the hall, but he had little time even for her. Only when the door was closing behind him did he have that afterthought.

"You remember a M. Saval, Keziah?" he asked quickly. "Is he hereabouts yet?"

She was well primed. Yes, the French gentleman was still in the town, though he had moved to superior lodgings in St. James's Street. Since Master Charles had left he had become exceedingly popular with both the local bigwigs and the neighbouring gentry, especially since Trafalgar, from when it had become widely reported that the monsieur had often risked his neck by stealing across to France to obtain information.

"He did, did he?" Charles commented impassively.

It seemed, too, that all the young ladies of the district were captivated by M. Saval. It was the one, however, upon whom the French gentleman lavished most of his attention who appeared the least likely to respond to his suit.

"But Miss Caroline was always a madame, Mr. Charles," Keziah laughed.

"Miss Caroline!"

The mob-cap of the figure silhouetted in the doorway nodded.

"'Tis rumoured, too, that 'twas she who cut him across the face with a whip."

"Cut him . . . an' what does gossip say is the reason for Miss Caroline having to do that, Keziah?" Charles Fagg inquired, his tone deadly.

"Well . . ." Mrs. Hart reflected leisurely, "'tis said—— Mr. Charles . . . why, for goodness' sake——"

He had spun round, and was off at a raking pace down the street. Dumfounded by this abrupt departure Keziah, eyes widened in wonderment, craned round the jamb of the doorway, there to remain gaping until Mr. Charles's disappearance, coupled with a shiver caused by the penetrating chill, brought her to her senses.

"Lawkes a me!" she gasped, shutting out the cold.

It was about the time when Charles Fagg, set of face, was crossing the Market Place, that sharp illumination replaced bewilderment.

"Lawkes a me!" she repeated, this time profoundly.

Old Peter Monin's clock began to strike the half-hour.

3

As was usual at most routs and assemblies, the rhythm of the gathering slackened during the half-hour before midnight. In that period young men bespoke supper partners, young ladies carried out whatever repairs might be necessary, and even in the card-room the former air of concentration was replaced by some inattention and a growing buzz of small talk.

Thus it was that the ante-room, rather than the ballroom, was the scene of most interest as the minute hand of the clock moved slowly upwards. Jack Woodgate was amongst a group of friends but, though he appeared one of them, there could be no doubt whatever that he was continually on the look-out for the entry of his pretty wife, Lou having disappeared for one of those touchings-up beloved of her sex.

A lively conversation was brought to a standstill by the piercing scream of a young lady who chanced to see the vestibule door swing open.

" Look ! " she shrieked.

" *Charles !* " yelled a young man.

The latecomer found himself in the midst of a milling crowd of people all of whom, whether it was by wringing his hand or thumping his back, whether by a sincerely worded little apology or a neat ambiguous phrase, expressed regret for the wrong they had done him.

In the end he got clear of these and, accompanied by his brother-in-law, went off to find his parents, still with numbers of folk scampering down the grand staircase in pursuit.

" I'm mortal grieved to see that, Jack," he said feelingly, nodding to the tied-up sleeve.

" 'Tis bad, Charles," Jack Woodgate agreed outright. " But it could be worse, an' I've been posted to a good shore billet, so let's have no more on't."

All the time, even as Charles bowed or smiled to those who eagerly sought the opportunity to salute him, his keen grey eyes searched the throng. He knew it would be useless looking for Caroline beyond the ballroom but . . . Before entering the card-room he voiced his other thought.

" That fellow Saval, Jack," he asked carelessly, " is he here to-night ? He was ever one for bright lights and the ladies."

The sailor chuckled. " He's here all right, and 'pon my word——" Suddenly to Jack Woodgate's face there flashed an air of great concern. He almost stuttered, so confused was he. " My oath," he muttered awkwardly, " I'd long forgotten that proposed affair with the Frenchy. I wasn't at home at the time but I tell you, Charles, everybody afterwards admired you for not being deviated from your purpose by the slights a refusal would bring."

Charles Fagg thwacked his brother-in-law's sound shoulder. "Thankee, Jack," he twinkled. "And we'll not have any more on that either."

"But——" Jack Woodgate protested, his mind not eased by the steely eyes of Lou's brother.

"No more," Charles laughed.

Some of the green baize-covered tables in the card-room had already been vacated when the two young men entered. At others desultory conversation was taking place, and only the fanatics continued to play.

Mrs. John Fagg, it might be said, was talking, and talking *thirteen* to the dozen. But in the very midst of an involved account in which Minnie's baby now and then figured, she caught sight of her son. In the middle of a word she stopped, stared incredulously, and then, her progress so rapid that her draperies set flying the cards on every table in her path, she went to him, to hug him, and kiss him.

"Charles, my dear," she cried. "Oh, Charles, Charles!"

To the delight of the room, deeply pleased to see this homecoming, he picked her up, and held her with face level with his own.

"Mother," he said fondly.

"Your father——" Mrs. Fagg squealed excitedly.

That gentleman was now thumping his son, roaring, joking and, in general, making a thorough exhibition of himself.

"Good God!" he grunted at last, belatedly having remembered that the language he had been using was hardly suitable for present company. "And when did you arrive, and where did you come from?"

Charles looked slightly discomfited. "Er . . . from Portsmouth, Father."

Mr. Henry Rochefort, who had been vigorously pump-handling the new arrival's hand, glanced at him, his dark eyes shrewd.

"Portsmouth, Charles?" he enquired sharply.

Through his letters, Charles was aware of the reconciliation which had taken place between the two gentlemen. He winked cautiously at his father's friend.

"Yes, Mr. Rochefort," he said. "And a deuced long journey 'twas . . ." he was rapidly going on to say when the banker, definitely deciding to ignore that warning signal, revealed his thoughts.

"The fleet brought you back from Corunna?" he asked.

"Yes," Charles Fagg remarked hastily. "But——"

Growling "modesty be demned," Henry Rochefort turned and, holding up his hand to gain attention, informed the company that they had amongst them a hero of the battlefield of Corunna. It would be fitting, he suggested, that Captain Fagg should be escorted into the supper-room and there toasted. . . .

A cheering crowd was now pressed into the doorway of the card-room. Through it, forcing her way, came young Mrs. Woodgate. Her husband it was, running to meet her, who knew that something was wrong.

"Jack, darling . . . Mr. Rochefort !" she said breathlessly. "I can't find Caroline and I'm frightened. I've—— *Charles !* Charles, dearest."

"Lou, love," smiled her brother, briefly kissing her and removing the arms which she had flung round his neck. "What's this about Caroline ? "

"She's gone, Charles. I can't find her and I've looked *everywhere.*"

"When did you last see her, my dear ? " John Fagg asked.

"In the foyer, Papa," she replied. "Since then not a glimpse of her."

There was more up-to-date news than that. Three or four ladies simultaneously vouchsafed a description of the scene in the foyer.

"And has any one seen M. Saval since then ? " asked Henry Rochefort, his face anxious.

No one had. A heavy silence came over the room, and then the roar of action. It was resolved to comb the building from cellars to attics, and a score of young officers deliberately loosened swords from scabbards.

Some few minutes later the third search party made a discovery in that quiet room of the establishment, in a dark corner behind a small overturned table.

Mrs. John Woodgate was requested to present herself with all dispatch.

When she came, Lou gave a sudden despondent cry as she shakily examined a piece of soft muslin, that confirmation of sinister happenings already suspected.

"'Tis Caroline's," she gasped. "From her waistband, I know it. To think . . ." she seemed on the edge of swooning as her young husband tenderly supported her to an old chair.

"Steady, m'love," Jack Woodgate said consolingly.

The first shock over the tumult began.

"I fear me that poor Miss Caroline . . ." Mr. Virgile began despondently, mournfully shaking his head.

"Men of St. Mary's ward," roared 'Captain' Stratton.

"We want no Jonahs here, Virgile," snapped Jephrez Baker.

Charles Fagg had gone through the outer doorway, taking a candle with him. Methodically and quickly he was prepared to search, but at the outset found the one sign which was sufficient. In that narrow, ill-paved yard communicating with the Black Ditch he found horse droppings not yet frozen despite the rigour of the night.

He hurried back, beckoning to his father and Mr. Rochefort.

"Abduction," he announced crisply. "And of a surety in a wheeled vehicle. Have every man with a horse scour the neighbourhood, with others, the hardest riders, to take the turnpikes to Folkestone, Canterbury and Deal."

Coolly, accepted as leader by those gathering about him, he was considering the probable route. Deal was a coastal journey, least likely of all, he thought; Folkestone, speed being essential, would serve, but the highway beyond it, across Romney Marsh, widely deviating and ill-founded, would be difficult to negotiate when the moon waned. . . .

"Yes," he said briskly. "Put that into train."

"And yourself, Charles?" asked John Fagg. "You'll . . . mmmm," he nodded."

"God speed you, my boy," Henry Rochefort, also perceiving who would be in the van, said frantically, his face ghastly.

Lou Woodgate, vainly comforted by her mother, was crying miserably.

She raised blotchy eyes to her brother. "Bring Caroline back, Charles," she implored. "Oh, do bring her back. I can't abide to . . . to think of her with that horrible wretch. I *never*, *never* liked him."

There was a steadfastness about Charles Fagg, something, too, far more forbidding and iron-willed than that.

"I'll bring her back, Lou love," he reassured her.

He did not waste another precious minute. Hastening out, he threw off his sword in the cloakroom, flung on his greatcoat, felt for his pistols and, in an atmosphere which hummed, brusquely warded off the inquiries of those who would have delayed him.

There were many stalls in the Antwerp Stables, to which he had run down Cannon Street and along the north side of the Market Place. He made quick, though careful selection, a light grey mare built for speed.

"Saddle her," he rapped, his voice ringing down the lengthy interior.

The ostler, a bow-legged, self-important little fellow who, carrying a lanthorn, had come post-haste after this imperious-sounding gentleman, put down the light the better to argue out the matter. The beast, he was beginning to declaim eloquently, before he caught full view of the young officer, was the property of Lord Poynte and what his lordship would be likely to say when he found that his favourite *Rosy* had been taken . . .

" Mr. Charles ! " he jumped.

" Me, Jim," Charles Fagg retorted. " And now get ready with all the speed you can muster, you tarnal old sea-lawyer."

There was no further dallying. Jim Page, between hissing and biting off his tongue with curiosity, soon had the lovely creature prepared.

Charles swung up, *Rosy* curvetted, and just for fun kicked out wildly, and then did another special trick or two.

" Steady, old girl," her rider said consolingly.

With a rush she went through the arched passage, her progress thunderous in the restricted space, sharp right into Cannon Street, now lively with young bucks themselves eager to join in the chase.

Lord Poynte's valuable piece of bloodstock was galloping freely now. Both she and her rider, passing the Royal Oak Rooms, were greeted with a hearty huzza from the military men and others pouring out of there.

Luckily, at the top of Biggin Street, the breaking of a gig's near-side scroll spring had caused the blacksmith to be called from his bed. Charles, succeeding in curbing a mount made even more spirited by the darting gleams of the forge fire, made pithy inquiries concerning the recent passage of vehicles past a point which commanded both the London Road and the Folkestone turnpike.

He received intelligence. Some short time before, a post-chaise, hard-driven, had taken the London Road.

4

The Agent-Victualler's beautiful red-brick Elizabethan house and the squat Maison Dieu were behind. Charles Fagg, on the back of a flier renowned in East Kent, flew along the Canterbury Road, with *Rosy*'s iron-shod feet ringing out a quick tune from the ice-bound surface.

To the right was a glimpse of slumbering Charlton village, its church clearly showing beyond the huddle of moon-lit roofs, and its old mill, as ever since Domesday Book, casting a sable shadow on Dour's bubbling waters.

" Good girl," said the rider soothingly, checking a dangerous slip. " And now, my girl . . ." he continued, preparing her for the pending throw with fortune.

At that furious pace the wind was intense, and Charles's eyes were streaming. He picked up the Black Horse Tavern and the tattered relics swinging gently from the gibbet before it. The barred toll-gate stood out across the path and with it the figure of the gate-keeper who, roused by the drumming hoofs of the fleeting horse, was emerging grumblingly from his cosy parlour, wig awry, to fee the night-rider to the extent of a penny.

The man's hand went up in signal to stop, but there was no delaying Charles Fagg on this errand.

" Steady . . . steady, old girl," he told her. " Now . . . *whoop*," he shouted, lifting her well over the barrier, and catching in his flight a lightning impression of the frightened gate-keeper diving for safety, hearing the fellow's scream of mixed rage and fear die suddenly as he fell far behind.

On, on, on, up the London Road, passing the sixty-ninth mile-stone and then the sixty-eighth ; to either side, in their ranging parks, the noble residences of many of those gentry who had been glad to have a share in his father's free-trading ventures. The little hamlet of Lyddon came next, echoes of his swift passage dying as he cleared the last house, the noises of startled poultry and the far-carrying barks of dogs persisting for long after he had gone.

Three miles farther on was the half-timbered Halfway House, and beyond that Denn Hill, with its approach to Barham Down. On the summit, Charles reined in. From that vantage point the view, to every point of the compass, was bewitching. Far to the eastward, in a long curve, was the sea, a dove-grey moulding to the sweet picture of the silent English land ; to the west and southward, blue-black, the rolling hills of Kent ; and all about were sleeping villages, farms, and nestling churches, all that which was the glorious essence of the soil of his upbringing.

Charles Fagg drew in a deep breath, but it was not solely this charming landscape which aroused him.

" *Rosy*, girl," he whispered joyously, giving her a quick caress.

His eyes were narrowed, his mouth was both gay and grim at the nearing of the quarry. The pursuit would soon be over for, towards the end of the Down, he could see a post-chaise negotiating the extraordinarily deep ruts caused by heavy military traffic.

His heart was singing. " Come, my beauty," he laughed blithely.

In the further distance Canterbury showed up clear, the tower of her famed cathedral dominating all beneath, the medieval buildings and gabled houses, a quaintly irregular architectural pattern softly gleaming with starshine.

On the stretch of the Downs, in rows and orderly squares, was laid out an enormous camp, within it men who jealously guarded their birthright. Sentries gaped at the flying rider, and once a challenge thundered out. But shortly the pickets began to thin, soon all proof of martial preparedness was left behind, ere long the country began to be desolate again.

And soon, too, Charles Fagg was approaching the big rear wheels of a vehicle which, the turnpike improving, had gone into its aforetime frenzied pace.

His face was tense as he took in the situation. To the left of the road was a bank whose steepness precluded any possibility of passing on that side ; close up to the chaise on the right was a hedge and, immediately beyond that, its white-painted posts standing out bold, the broad track of Barham Down Race-course.

Taking this in, Charles, an odd smile transfiguring his determined features, decided on his plan. Easing down, he took a dark kerchief from the flapped pocket of his greatcoat and, tucking two of the corners beneath his cocked hat, pulled down the bight of silken material between, improvising a mask revealing nothing more than his forehead and grey eyes.

Thus prepared, he put *Rosy* at the bare hedge, and a moment later was in the stretch where once, on *Toke's Quality*, he had taken such advantage of the slope of the ground.

Silently, over the scintillating turf, the strange jockey galloped until, where the dividing hedge fell away, he was alongside a jolting chaise neither whose driver nor postillion, as yet, had perceived anything untoward.

When they did, the fellows' reactions were swift. Indeed, what they saw was assuredly enough to bring paralysing fear into the stoutest of hearts, let alone those who would certainly never willingly have any truck with the supernatural.

The grey-coated mare, phantom-like in the moonlight, twin jets of vapour puffing from her nostrils, for backcloth the silent course on which the death-rider from hell was madly tearing. A partly masked face, from which a pair of eyes stared unwavering and maniacal, and a kerchief once lifted over those eyes to disclose teeth bared in a diabolical grin.

M. Saval's driver gave a strangled yell of terror and, without more ado, took a panic-striken vault, fortunately to fall into the bracken at the side of the road, there speedily to be joined by his scared subordinate.

Charles, with an agility which would have done credit to any acrobatic performer, left *Rosy's* back to swing on to the off-leader, quickly gathering up the dangerously slipping reins.

Adroitly, with little disturbance, he persuaded the team of four to relinquish the turnpike.

A ghostly chaise, so it would seem, continued to fly along the round turn of Barham Down Race-course.

＊　　＊　　＊　　＊　　＊　　＊　　＊　　＊

By the time the vehicle in which she had been carried off reached

Buckland Bridge, Caroline Rochefort was largely recovered from the rough handling she had received. From then M. Saval began, first with persuasions and then with threats.

" After all,. my angel," he was saying when the wheels set up the scream which showed the vehicle was passing over the rough-cobbled street of little Lyddon, " an elopement is surely mos' romantic, so why not accept the position, my dear Caroline ? "

At the Halfway House, not having elicited a single word of response from the ashen-faced young woman who, if she looked at him at all, regarded him with horror and loathing, he was speaking in very different terms.

" I'll break that obstinate spirit of yours, young lady," he promised her viciously. " By the time . . ."

But, anon, even M. Saval had reached the conclusion that neither coaxing nor threat would move this slim and beautiful creature of ice. From then, his mouth cruel, he seldom offered more than an ill-tempered oath, itself lost in the creakings and groanings of a conveyance travelling at high speed over a wickedly broken-up road.

" Yes, by the Virgin——" he was beginning.

The last word was perfectly audible. It was as if they had entered upon some carpet which not only largely nullified the outraged protests of the ' C ' springs, but also muffled to fairy-like proportions the still fast tread of the rapidly moving horses.

" Sacré nom . . ." Armand Saval shouted.

The fore-window had, by his orders, been securely shuttered, and he sprang to the leathern side curtains, securely fastened against any rash attempt which might have been made by his unwilling passenger. By the time he had unloosened them the carriage was slowing and, as he thrust his head through the window, the wheels stopped. M. Saval craned round to see what the driver was about and, seeing nothing but the two pairs, his hand went outside, violently to wrench open the door.

" You damn fools ! " he stormed, jumping down.

To the amazed eyes of his fair victim the scene disclosed through that rectangle of light was indeed strange ; the course stretching dimly into the distance, and looming above her the tiers of the familiar stand of Barham Race-course. But the mettlesome Miss Caroline Rochefort's glance dwelt but momentarily on these things, as feverishly, resolved to defend herself to whatever end, she seized the pistol case resting on the opposite seat. Even as she did so a shadow fleetingly darkened the interior, the shadow thrown by a tall man who, after hitching the reins, leapt down and then skirted the back of the chaise, appearing a few paces to the rear of the cursing Frenchman.

Caroline's movements, imperative as they were, were stilled at the sight of this masked newcomer who held himself so easily. Then she heard his voice, a voice deliberately thickened, and one certainly distorted by the piece of material hanging over his mouth.

" Sir," it rasped, " if you please, you will face me.".

M. Saval gave a muffled exclamation, and spun as sharply as a man shot through the shoulder.

" What in hell——" he was beginning, and then recoiled involuntarily when he perceived the weapon directed on him. " What is the meaning of this, *cochon* ? " he continued wildly. " A new trick of a Knight-of-the-Road, or a footpad aspiring . . . now come, my frien'," he altered his tactics, " you interfere with an affair of the heart, and no man of sentiment does that as I'll warrant you'll agree."

Charles Fagg tossed up the pistol, neatly catching it again.

" Then you are not alone, sir," he commented, his delivery still coarsened, his tone full of disappointment. " Ah, I see not."

He bowed to the young woman whose head and shoulders were framed in the chaise window and persuaded himself it was the most un-English obedience as could be imagined.

" What the devil does it concern you ? " M. Saval shouted, his smouldering eyes gauging the space between them, ever watching for a slip on the part of a fellow who handled a weapon so carelessly. " Have I not told you . . . and if what few guineas I possess . . ."

The interloper elaborately shrugged that aside. " My business with you, sir, is not of the nature you appear to conceive. But first, before dealing with a rather wearisome matter, permit me to express my regrets to your charming companion. And allow me, madame."

The door handle was stiff, and Caroline Rochefort had not found it easy to turn. Charles, his grey eyes watchful about him, handed her down.

" Regrets, sir ? " Miss Rochefort took him up witheringly.

The masked man bowed again. " That I have interrupted what was no doubt a romantic journey, madame."

" Sir," she said distinctly, " you have done me the greatest service a man may do a woman, and one for which I thank you with all my heart and soul."

" So, so," he nodded thoughtfully. " Then I assume, madame, that you are in no mind to continue with the adventure."

" I would die first," Caroline Rochefort declared passionately, " rather than——"

Her breath caught, her eyes never left a wrist whose deft twist had sent a pistol curving in the air. She saw the chased barrel gleaming as it turned in the moonlight, and the shining silver-figured butt as it dropped into the sure and waiting hand.

" Rather than . . . ? " Charles Fagg asked courteously.

It seemed that her high courage, salvation at hand, had faltered a little. With this sharp reaction she swayed, and was steadied by her saviour's firm arm.

" I . . . I can only thank you, sir," she said faintly, yet always searching him as she spoke.

" Your servant, ma'am," Charles Fagg replied gruffly, bowing a third time.

Then he became brutally decisive. His eyes, trained in guerrilla warfare, had already espied the shape of one whom he believed to be the chaise-driver. Peremptorily the creature was called up, and forthwith told what to do.

" You will carefully drive this lady back to Dover, you scurvy rogue. And after that, if you are wise, you and your fellow knave will make yourselves scarce." He went on to speak of the penalties for conspiracy and abduction, until the wretched individual began to see himself swinging in the chains—if he lived so long.

" I'll guard the lady, your honour," he said tremblingly. " And for Gawd's sake be werry careful with that 'ere barking iron, y'lordship."

M. Saval, shaking with bafflement and rage, now took a hand.

" You'll stay here, fellow," he stormed. " If you dare to dis-obey my orders . . . and *damn* you."

His effort to accomplish the intervening distance between himself and the tall figure was utterly foiled. Little more than an arm's length away he affrightedly checked himself, not entirely subduing the cry of fear and chagrin which came to his lips as that unerring hand once again caught the pistol butt to leave the dark muzzle steadily sighted at point-blank range.

The unknown laughed. " I fancy the charge will long have been scattered, sir, but methinks 'twould seem such risk as remains you care not to stomach. Now, sir," he rapped out, laughter gone, " you will please withdraw to a more comfortable distance. . . ."

So it was. And so it happened, too, that Charles Fagg gravely handed into the carriage a young woman who was valiantly trying to conceal the radiance she felt must be in her face.

" But your name, sir ? " she asked softly. " My father would wish to express his gratitude . . . as again I would myself."

He was examining one of the pistols he had taken from the case and, within earshot of the quivering chaise-driver, was instructing her as to how the fellow might best be shot if she found he diverted one inch from the Dover Road.

Always endeavouring to keep his face in shadow, his back was to the moon as he shook his head. " I would not wish to receive thanks for an act any man would be pleased to do," he responded briefly.

" But, sir," she protested from the chaise window.

The erect figure, glancing upwards, then jerked his head sternly in signal for the rascal to take towards the road.

" But, sir," she repeated, a trifle desperately as the now-returned postilion climbed on to the leader.

He said little more. But such as it was struck a chill into her, made her lips surprisingly tremulous.

" I have a certain business to transact with this gentleman," he remarked curtly. " You will please not argue."

She flushed deeply at his abruptness. Her mouth went mutinous in that moment, and for a few seconds it looked as though she might revert to her girlhood, to become for a spell the madcap Caroline Rochefort of more youthful days.

But no. " I bid you good-night then, sir," she recollected herself haughtily.

He made a stiff inclination. " Good-night, ma'am."

Her shoulder had been turned away from him, and all he faintly could see within the poorly lighted interior was an entrancing profile.

Whips cracked, and the chaise began to move. As the white posts of the race-course started to come and go more quickly, Miss Rochefort, dignity soon forgotten, peered back.

Behind, still standing as if in some suspended action of a play, she could see two figures.

At that spectacle her hand involuntarily went to her thudding heart.

She sat rigidly, until at length a swaying of the chaise gave notice that the turnpike was reached.

But a short way up the road her hand grasped tighter on the pistol. Impulsively but decidedly she proceeded to attract the driver's attention.

They walked five paces apart, Charles Fagg to the rear, his own pistol trained steadily, and a second tucked under his arm in readiness.

The new stand was receding rapidly and the walk, amidst the *tumuli* of the Down, was growing increasingly rough underfoot. The trickiness of that moonlighted heath, the circumstances and the silence previously imposed on him, had caused drops of sweat to form upon Armand Saval's forehead. Now he could suffer it no longer.

" Not a *metre* farther." He turned passionately, his voice just a little shrill. " Who are you, and what want you of me? I demand——"

His captor made an expressive gesture. " Keep moving, sir . . . or . . ."

" You will murder me even before we reach the privacy you have already chosen for that fell design," the Frenchman gasped. "Oh yes, I know it, but I tell you——"

"To the right, sir, and no more than a few steps," came that falsified but inexorable voice.

The dell was secluded even in that expanse where few habitations were in sight. To one side, L-shaped, was a copse, and bounding the square of level turf to the other sides was low broom.

"The end of our journey, sir," Charles Fagg announced grimly.

"Who the devil are you?"

M. Saval did not receive answer just then. Unequivocally instructed to seat himself on an outcrop of rock, he watched his captor prepare two pistols, the first his own, and the second that which, through its tumblings, prudence would suggest was in need of re-priming.

"I, sir?" The tone was whimsical—and new. "Well, maybe 'twould be fitting to satisfy your curiosity."

Charles Fagg tossed aside his hat, and the released kerchief fell to the ground.

Indescribably taken aback, the Frenchman half rose. "*You!*" he marvelled, a mixture of profound relief and astonishment in him, the one because the dread Fouché had many ways of putting an end to those agents found displeasing, the other because the voice of the stranger had fully persuaded him that, at least, he had to deal with no man he knew.

Then M. Saval, softly at the beginning but more loudly later, began to laugh.

"La, la," he chuckled sardonically, "so am I to gather that you stage-managed my progress here merely to complete a small matter you conveniently overlooked erstwhile? A duel, eh?"

This quixotic action provided a heaven-sent opportunity to settle an outstanding debt, and arrogance was in the Frenchman again.

"No, sir," was the quiet reply.

Now, at the sober denial, M. Saval came to be a little uneasy.

"How, sir?" he asked quickly. "What mean you? Why the brace of pistols if 'tis your purpose to shoot an unarmed man?"

Faintly amused by this swift change, Charles eyed him levelly. "On the contrary, sir, it is my intention, in due course, to place one of these weapons in your hand."

"Then why——"

In M. Saval's adversary there was a new steeliness which silenced that gentleman. Yet for some moments Charles Fagg stared composedly over the neighbouring land before he spoke.

"These Downs, sir, are steeped in English history," he began reflectively; and went on to relate of Kentishmen rallying to the banner of King John when danger threatened from without, and how, down the ages, past Philip of Spain's Armada days to the present, it had ever been so.

"With just a single difference, monsieur," he continued. "The men of Kent are here as always, but now close at their shoulders are the men of England, and of Scotland, and of Ireland and Wales. And with them, in spirit, are the stalwarts of the colonies overseas, their cause as one, their only variance who shall deal the first blow at a puffed and bloody tyrant."

M. Saval sneered. "You speak most patriotically, my worthy friend," he said slightingly. "But if 'tis not your plan to put a bullet into my back, then let us without delay seek a suitable duelling——"

"There is to be no duel, sir," was the blunt interruption.

"Then what do you call it, damn you?" shouted the French-man.

Charles Fagg smiled. "I propose calling it the Battle of Barham Down," he observed impassively. "You see, sir, though true English-men throughout the ages have drilled and exercised in readiness on these old acres, never have they here drawn up in battle line, for as yet no foreign adversary has dared put a foot on this soil. But to-night, methinks, you and I may take the place . . . indeed, as an officer of His Majesty, I would not dare contravene the strict rule against duelling, if that were our purpose here. But as matters stand, it is with an easy conscience——"

M. Saval had passed through many humours that night; from excitement to exasperation, from soft supplication to brutal anger, from rage to a gripping fear. But now the greatest apprehension of all began to germinate in him.

"Explain, hell blast you!" he said viciously.

Charles Fagg still had that unfathomable smile as he sternly replied. "Think you that is necessary, Capitaine *Chassepot*?"

A tiny breeze, an icy breeze, was beginning to stir, and it may be its chill caused M. Saval to shiver. But simultaneously, at the mention of that name, with the knowledge of all it implied, his cheeks blanched, the drained colour almost immediately replaced by the dull flush of a more controlled anger.

"So we fight no duel, monsieur," said Charles Fagg dryly.

"We fight nevertheless," Fouché's agent retorted, a laugh up his sleeve.

The outcome of the episode with the Rochefort wench, he realised, would for months prevent his return to Dover. But that was a mere trifle. Now he had to deal with a man whose death alone could give him security.

Thus it came about that M. Saval, who could snap-fire a hole through the head of the Jack from the full length of the practice gallery in St. James's Street, was moved by inward mirth, confident that his own supreme ability and, of course, a certain little design he had in mind, provided him with an overwhelming assurance that all would be well.

" The conditions," Charles Fagg said briefly.

Twelve paces . . . the time to fire being when the rim of the moon was touched by a flossy piece of cloud now approaching it . . . the adversaries to stand facing that signal which sailed serenely in the sky . . . then to turn inward to shoot.

" You may choose your weapon, monsieur," he ended coolly, laying across his arm the two pistols, butts outward, the barrels, directed away from his own body, being firmly grasped lest there should be any attempt at foul play.

" Enchanté, my heroic friend," smiled the Frenchman. " Seldom—"

" You have little time, Chassepot," Charles said curtly, glancing at that narrowing distance.

The selection was made and, stringently instructed, Armand Saval backed step by step with the weapon extended high in his out-stretched arm, meantime his opponent held him covered. Then the Englishman took up his own position, his arm in fairness reaching loftily, too.

" No more than a few seconds now," Charles Fagg, steadily facing ahead, remarked quietly. " And then——"

Had he not been trained to the battlefield, to the demands of guerrilla warfare, he would have been lost. But the faintest of sounds warned him of danger, the slightest rustle alone told him that treachery was afoot. He twisted quickly, dipping one knee, the report of his own pistol merely fractionally behind that of the other.

There was the thud of a body falling, then only one of two remained upright.

For a moment, shaken by this close call, Charles waited before he moved those few paces, there to kneel down to see what had befallen a spy whose last miscreant blow had failed.

He tried his finger against the tissue of one staring eye, he looked at the neat puncture from which surprisingly little blood flowed.

Armand Saval was dead. No more would messages of his cross the narrow waters.

Charles Fagg straightened, his thoughts far away from the thing which lay at his feet.

Then, his face less implacable but sadder, he picked up his hat and began to retrace his steps across the Down.

In the distance a twig cracked and the sound, wind-borne, brought

Charles from his reverie. The light was deceptive but ahead, in a depression beyond a clump of high grasses, he perceived the gallant creature who had carried him so well.

" *Rosy*," he called invitingly.

The mare, it appeared, was both frisky and shy. She lured him on, sometimes withdrawing daintily, at others swinging away in a mad gallop which, after a great semicircle of the heath had been covered, brought her back to him.

" Flighty girl, eh ? " laughed Charles Fagg, when at last he caught her, close to the New Stand.

She whinneyed, allowed a few more familiarities, and then sedately moved with him alongside the low wooden barrier from behind which, in more happy August days, the ladies of East Kent and their escorts watched the races.

" And now, my beauty . . . steady . . . *steady*, girl."

Lord Poynte's lovely grey mare had become temperamental. Wildly she plunged until, when mastered, she stood tremblingly, her melting glance suspiciously bent on the gloom within the stand.

Charles Fagg gave a sharp exclamation as his own gaze followed that pointer. Sitting on the lowermost bench he saw a young woman, whose garb was a prodigiously large cloak which nigh upon smothered her, who rose as he came near.

Beneath the twinkling star canopy he was able to see her distinctly.

" Caroline ! " he muttered, half unbelievingly.

" Charles," she said softly, no surprise in her, only a lilting gladness.

" So you knew me then, Caroline ? "

She smiled a little wistfully. " You have a trick, a habit, Charles, not easily forgotten."

" But what are you doing here ? " he demanded sternly. " What would have been the case if it had been t'other, not I, who had found you ? "

From the other side of the grey head which separated them, she began to stroke *Rosy*.

" Because . . . because," she said, utterly sure, " I knew whatever might be the affray afoot, you would emerge the victor. Remember 'tis a long time that I have known you, Charles."

" Oh damme, no, Caroline," her playmate of youth mumbled deprecatingly, flushing deeply.

Miss Rochefort impetuously stamped her small foot. " Oh damme, yes, Charles," she declared imperiously.

Charles Fagg, looking at her then, swore he had never beheld anything so beautiful in his life. The exquisite face and the little ringlets which escaped from beneath her hood, the lines of her slim body revealed as she gathered the folds of that outrageous garment close about her.

"You stare mortal hard, Charles," she laughed, a tiny catch in her voice.

He had taken her arm and easily, with *Rosy* at his side, the three were making up the gradual rise which led to the post highway.

"Yes, I was staring mortal hard, Caroline," he agreed slowly. "You see, m'dear, oft in these long three years and more have I pictured you, but 'tis only now that I know how the splendour of my dreams fell so short of the perfection of living reality."

"Charles," she said tremulously. "I . . . I . . ."

There was an intimate silence for some moments, a silence too precious for words, a silence too wonderful for either to break it by explanations or any such everyday things.

"That is how it is with me, Caroline," he let fall tenderly.

From the distance, clear cut in the frosty air, came the quick noises of horses speeding, a drumming tune which seemed, to Caroline Rochefort, far more muffled than the pounding of her own heart.

"Oh, Charles," she murmured.

As if he must know one thing beyond any shadow of doubt, he gently held her elbow and turned her towards the moon, his intent grey eyes never leaving her face. "And 'twill always be the same with me, Caroline," he ended, so gravely.

A shuddering breath of happiness escaped her. "As so 'twill be with me, Charles," she whispered.

"Caroline, darling," he said huskily.

"Charles, my dearest," she smiled, her eyes starry.

She was in his arms, her lips crushed against his.

And so, in close embrace, they remained awhile, with *Rosy*, a part of the scene, portraying a lively curiosity, until she started to prick her ears at the nearing tattoo from her own kind.

"And now I suppose I must convey you back to your father," Charles said reluctantly, adding teasingly : "Well, m'dear, at least you will always be able to say that you were once the principal in an abduction."

He was busily looking over *Rosy*'s gear for the double burden, so she was not able clearly to see his face. Nor was he, for that matter, in good position to witness her mischievousness consequent upon his next few words.

"'Twould only require," he continued casually, vastly preoccupied in his task, "your participation in an elopement for you to boast a most unique record."

She sighed gently. "I fear, Charles, that Papa thinks too well of you for it to be necessary."

At that, he did briefly glance at her before resuming whatever he might be doing with the girth.

" If my memory serves me faithfully, my sweetheart," he observed thoughtfully, " you were ever one who detested to miss anything. There was Jamaica Land, and the night you climbed out of your window to hear of Louis's escape, and your insistence to be taught the handling of a boat. . . ."

Miss Caroline Rochefort made every effort to control her throbbing self.

" 'Tis true, Charles, that I am a mortal curious creature," she laughed.

Charles Fagg, his hands quicker, started to soliloquise aloud. Nodding across the heath, he remarked that it would be necessary to outdistance those fellows. That, of course, would definitely add savour. . . ."

" Charles ! "

He continued tranquilly. A post-chaise could be obtained in Canterbury, he said, and there, too, various short notes of explanation might be entrusted to a horseman for delivery to Dover. And there, also, the faithful *Rosy* could be given the feed of her life and left behind with instructions for her dispatch to Lord Poynte in the morning.

" Charles, Charles, what mean you ? " Miss Rochefort asked, her senses pulsating.

His grey eyes were on her, her brown eyes on him. Unheeding of all the world they stood, their coming glory shining in their eyes.

" Need I explain, Caroline, my sweet ? " he asked quietly.

No defences, nor need of defences had Caroline Rochefort then. She came to him, in his arms finding all that she had longed for in this world.

" Charles, my dear one," she said softly, lifting her head from his shoulder again to give him her lips.

Thirty and three fire-eating riders were nearing the encampment of Barham Down, giving much tongue when their leaders perceived an ambling chaise.

And so, with all the rich future ahead, Charles Fagg and Caroline Rochefort were carried by the gallant *Rosy* to the turnpike, and thence towards the great tower of the cathedral church of Canterbury.

In that ancient city, whose history figures in every page of English pageantry, the lovers lingered little. The notes were speedily penned, and a post-chaise ordered to the hostelry door.

" See extra rugs and hot bricks are put in, and a guinea for every minute you save under seven," Captain Fagg of His Majesty's 5th Regiment of Foot shouted to the ostler.

" 'Twill save explanations if we are gone, Charles," his lovely lady laughed afterwards, heavenly colour of happiness and excitement still staining her cheeks as their vehicle, after thundering between the lofty, machicolated, drum towers of West Gate, soon put a solitary, yellow-lighted upper window in the Falstaff Inn far behind.

A chaise once again sped through the quiet night.

" Oh, Charles," Caroline cried rapturously, nestling against him.

His arms tightened about her. " My very sweet," Charles Fagg said solemnly.

The moon sprinkled silver on the road, and the overtaking chimes of Canterbury blessed them on their way.

CHAPTER FIVE

I

' MARCH many weathers ' it might be, but work was proceeding apace in Dover Harbour. A crumbling portion of the Crosswall was being refaced with new stone, and masons and their labourers were busily occupied on the scaffolding which had been erected against it. On the South Pier, measuring instruments set up, Mr. Edward Hexstall and an assistant were jotting down distances and angles for the projected sluicing canal which, in its last course running within the framework of the pier itself, was to bring the scouring water of the Pent directly on to the accumulation of shingle which so often collected between the pier-heads. In mighty stream would the current come, with none of that wastage of effort as hitherto when the flood released from the Pent first wandered over the broad width of the Tidal Harbour before narrowing into ineffectual force between the piers.

Yes, the Commissioners of Dover Harbour, two of whom were on the North Pier on that morning bright with the promise of spring, had begun to move at last, and to some purpose. More than fifty men were engaged in deepening the Pent to provide a greater head of water, and cart after cart filled with the mud excavated, seams trickling as result of their wet burden, moved on the seaward side towards the New Bridge, the loads destined as manure for the farm lands behind the town.

" Well, I suppose 'tis a start, John," Mr. Henry Rochefort remarked to his companion in a most dissatisfied tone.

" I suppose it is, Henry," smiled John Fagg. " Yes," he looked about him and then grinned widely, " I think we may say that much, Henry."

Perceptibly his friend frowned. " But no more than that, John," he persisted ill-humouredly.

Truth to tell, Henry Rochefort had developed all the ardour of the zealot and, despite the Commissioners' decision to undertake a scheme of harbour improvement more comprehensive than any other since the days of King Hal, he was far removed from being content. In point of fact the grandeur of the proposals made by an Elizabethan engineer had also seized *his* imagination, and he was a rabid supporter of the long-dead Mr. Thomas Digges' conception of the entire enclosure of Dover's Bay, an idea which by now he was in danger of forgetting he had purloined out-and-out from his friend.

" I say no more than a start, John," he repeated sharply.

The banker might repine, even deride, but John Fagg's grey eyes were shining as, amidst the baulks of timber and the neatly arranged piles of stone which gave the pier the semblance of a builder's yard, he looked about him. It was low water and the period was one of neap tides. The Tidal Harbour was dried out almost to the end of the two piers, and from below came the squeal of shovels as a gang of workmen cut into the shingle which formed the bar between the heads. Below, too, were more carts which, when loaded, were each dragged by three horses up the steep slope of the obstruction and thence, the beasts splashing through the verge of the sea and the water up to the axles, round the tip of the North Pier, their destination the far end of the Ropewalk beyond St. James's churchyard, where disposal could safely be made, ' eastward drift ' ensuring that the shingle thus deposited would never work back to foul the entrance to the haven.

Their backs to the sun, Mr. Rochefort and Mr. Fagg started to stroll homeward, towards Amherst's Battery, the shipowner still immensely interested in everything about—stone masons at work in wooden shelters, iron-shod fir piles being driven deep into the chalk rocks on the seaward side of the pier ; here a musical ring as a binding bolt was tapped through one of the new mainposts of the quay, and there a sweet thudding as wooden keys and wedges were forced home.

" No more than a start you say," the shipowner murmured glowingly, thinking of a dream about to come true.

The banker did not make any comment and, save for a few desultory words, the pair continued in silence towards the boat-dock and then, rounding Captain Pepper's cottage, entered Snargate Street-over-the-Wall where, notwithstanding that the thoroughfare was as busy as usual, they were almost immediately seen by a very young gentleman.

" Uncle Henry . . . and Uncle John," Horatio shouted, leaving his mother's side to rush ahead.

" My boy," laughed the banker, all his vexatiousness gone at the sight of his nephew. " And Susan, my dear."

John Fagg nodded to the very lovely posy of primroses and violets which his sister was carrying.

" And where did you get those, my love ? " he smiled.

Of course Horatio answered that for her. He and his mamma, he said, had started up Charlton Back Lane and there, from shady banks and in the woods further up the valley of the Dour, they had collected the fragrant flowers.

" An' then, Uncle John and Uncle Henry," he chattered on excitedly, " we walked right round by Buckland Bridge. . . ."

This very ordinary piece of news caused Mrs. George to grimace amusedly at both her brother and brother-in-law.

" Buckland Bridge," she laughed ruefully. " I wonder if he'll ever forget it ? I swear that all the way back he's done nothing else but talk his head off about Charles's and Caroline's homecoming."

That day, two months ago it was now, when his Cousin Charles had brought back to Dover his Cousin Caroline, still remained Horatio's great topic of conversation. Buckland Bridge, on the boundary line of the Liberties of the Port, had always been the place at which the townsfolk gathered to meet distinguished people, and it was there that Horatio had been in the very forefront of the tremendous crowd which assembled to meet Charles Fagg and his bride. An enormous cheer had gone up when the newly-married's chaise-and-four was seen bowling down the London Road, with applause far longer sustained when Captain Stratton, after felicitating the happy pair, presented Captain Fagg with the gold medal which had been specially struck for him in 1805.

The speeches over, and there were many of them, a procession had been formed, with Charles and Caroline changing over into the spacious open carriage which had been arranged for them if the weather held fine, they being joined in the vehicle by the members of their respective families.

It was hardly likely that Horatio would quickly allow to escape from memory the thrilling spectacle he had witnessed as, standing on the leather cushions of the rearward seat between his two big cousins, he had craned this way and that all the pompous journey to Town Wall Street. The drum and fife band immediately in front of the carriage, with Volunteers marching in fours still farther beyond ; jurats and freemen behind the carriage, with more Volunteers, their muskets at the slope ; lines of waving banners to either side and, entering the precincts of the town, wildly agitated handkerchiefs from the upper stories of houses welcoming back the hero and his wife. For it was with such honour, and in such state, that Captain Charles Fagg and his bride were drawn to Little Pent House.

Susan's blue eyes were a little dim. " 'Tis grievous to think that

Charles and dear Caroline have to separate in the morning," she said quietly.

"Aye, 'tis," agreed her brother soberly.

"Yes," Henry Rochefort remarked simply.

Now, as Horatio was racing a curricle along Snargate Street, the three adults, Mrs. George between the two gentlemen, could speak more plainly on the pending parting and the reason for it. The government had decided, and the country echoed their resolve, not to abandon Portugal and Spain, and it was apparent that Britain, beginning to feel her strength, intended soon to intervene in force on the Continent, there fighting it out face to face with Napoleon's armies.

"'Tis the only choice we can make, Susan love," John Fagg commented grimly. "The only one indeed if such as Horatio may look forward to a decent life."

"No doubt on that, John," Mr. Rochefort observed earnestly.

Mrs. George nodded, glanced at the cliff which overhung the street, bit her lip and nodded again.

"I know," she murmured. "But 'tis touching all the same."

General Moore's regiments, which had been reforming after their brilliant victory, were to be sent out to Lisbon, there to come under the command of General Sir Arthur Wellesley.

Her nephew Charles, ten days of special embarkment furlough drawing to a close, left early on the morrow to rejoin his comrades. His regiment was under orders to proceed at once to the Peninsula.

2

The collection of primroses and violets which Mrs. George Rochefort had gathered from so many dewy folds were for her husband's grave, and these she was taking that afternoon to the burial ground on Castle Hill where her dear one rested in sight of the sea.

Charles and Caroline had had dinner with Mr. Rochefort that day and so Little Pent House was rather quiet when, after John had returned to Elizabeth Street, Susan sought her sister-in-law.

Always a lover of flowers, Polly Fagg made a great to-do about them when Mrs. George, before starting out, at last found her in her bedroom.

"So, so lovely, Susan," she smiled waterily, burying her nose in the delightful smelling offering. "I always say, and I always did say, that there is nothing . . . nothing like freshly gathered . . . wild . . ."

"Polly, dear," Susan Rochefort said gently, "please don't worry so much about Charles."

Thereupon, looking as misty-eyed as she might, the mistress of the house emphatically denied the charge.

"I'm not doing," she declaimed indignantly, patently blinking back a tear. "Really, Susan, you do get some nonsensical notions into that head of yours. I . . . I may be a little distressed because Charles has to leave Caroline so soon . . . and . . . and perhaps for so long, but I should never dream of—— Now, *what* was I saying, Susan? I vow, girl, you've got me so mixed up. . . ."

Seeing how it was, Mrs. George did no more than squeeze her sister-in-law's arm consolingly, though perhaps it was as well that an interruption from below prevented the sympathetic little action from having an effect quite contrary to that intended.

"Whatever is't?" gasped Mrs. Fagg, knuckling her eyes and rushing to the head of the stairs at the sound of Keziah's screech of joy.

And what a tremendous surprise it was to see a certain young lady and gentleman in the hall. Lou had received Caroline's letter, and she and her husband, quite reckless of the stage money, had firmly decided they must see Charles off. Upon which Mrs. John Woodgate had begun to pack, and her husband, with his usual tenacity of purpose, had obtained the necessary absence-leave from his duties in Chatham Dockyard.

"Lou, my love," shrieked Mrs. Fagg. Down the steps she flew, nearly to smother a daughter whom she had not seen for close on eleven weeks.

"Jack," smiled Mrs. George from the half-landing, she coming down a little less precipitously.

Mr. Woodgate, having put down the valise he had carried from the Royal Oak yard, was able to take off his hat, after which he heartily kissed his Aunt Susan and then his mother-in-law.

Her shock over, Mrs. Fagg began to hurry about. They must be famished, she declared, and startlingly soon a most handsome cold collation was laid out on the dining-room table. It was a meal which the sailor disposed of in a very neat style, having evolved a most business-like method of eating with one hand.

"And Charles and Caroline?" Lou asked a shade breathlessly, coming to the end of a non-stop account of her own and her husband's doings in Chatham naval society.

She learnt that her brother and very dear friend would not be back until later. They had a round of visits to make during the afternoon and then a most tremendously important tea engagement with Captain and Mrs. Pepper, one of such consequence that Valentine had plainly indicated to his employer that, with old Peter Monin's clock striking three, the warehouse would see him no more that day.

" Then we're coming with you, Aunt Susan," Mrs. John Woodgate announced with determination. In the stir created by the new arrivals Mrs. George had not yet departed on her loving errand.

Horatio, who was grubbing about in the Little Pent, was called in from the parlour window and, when the commotion he raised on seeing " Jack " had subsided to some small extent, his extremely dirty face was washed before his mamma would allow him to go out in her company.

So, in due course, a party of four entered the sloping graveyard which overlooked the sea, and there George Rochefort's widow arranged the gift she had brought against the base of an oblong slab of shining Bethersden marble.

" He would have loved them," she said softly, still busy with slim fingers, on one of which was the fine diamond ring her lover had given her in the gazebo of Little Pent House one dreadful night. " Flowers, birds, the green fields . . ." Her blue eyes started to fill.

" I know, Aunt Susan," Lou comforted her.

" Here, Aunt Susan," Lou's husband said helpfully, proffering a positively enormous white linen handkerchief.

Just then Horatio, who on and off had been staring seaward, utterly lost interest in his Uncle John's *Martha*, a craft which, as he had advanced three times in as many minutes, was carrying lime from Beachy Head to London River.

" My papa died for his country," he observed importantly. " He was a Hero, Jack."

" He truly was, Horatio," Lou agreed solemnly. " Like Lord Nelson, who also fell in the very midst of battle."

An officer who had seen active service being present, the young gentleman was having no truck with womenfolk, though his cousin's reminder provided him with the next line.

" Lord Nelson commanded the fleet in which my papa received his mortal hurt, Jack," he vouchsafed impressively.

For this rudeness to Cousin Lou, he received a severe scolding from his mamma. But, never downcast long, he was chattering away as gaily as ever when the little group, on their way back, paused for a moment at the edge of the Castle cliff before dropping down to East-brooke.

" Charles and Caroline ain't arrived at Captain Pepper's yet," Mr. Woodgate chanced to say, pointing down towards the further end of the Ropewalk.

His wife started to laugh. It seemed that Lou's eyes were keener, or her perceptions greater, than those of her sailor husband.

" Methinks, too," she giggled, " that Captain Pepper is behaving as though he was signally discomfited."

" 'Twill be Martha," smiled Mrs. George Rochefort.

From that position it was just possible to see the boatswain's weather-boarded cottage. Its owner, after sharply closing the door, was rapidly crossing the plot of turf.

From his bearing, to those who knew him well, it would hardly have appeared likely that Mrs. John Woodgate was wrong in her judgment.

As though outraged beyond endurance, Valentine Pepper, wearing his best mulberry coat, stumped along, limping quickly towards the white-painted flagstaff at the head of which was flying his very largest ensign, freshly washed the previous day.

" Dunnamany times as 'ow she's straightened up sin' dinner," he grumbled. "An 'appy ship should be clean, true enow, but slit my gizzard if it ain't being carried to 'stremes."

He squinted up at the battle flag, gave an extra turn or two of the halliard about the cleat and then, making for his little gate, glanced along the street. No, Mr. Charles and Miss Caroline hadn't hove in sight yet.

" 'Course Martha wants it to look speshul tidy for 'em," he soliloquised, gradually forgetting an exasperation consequent upon being ordered out whilst his wife completed her preparations.

Indeed, when the visitors arrived he was very much enjoying himself, being in animated conversation with five great friends, three small boys and two small girls who, glimpsing him, had promptly abandoned their game to scurry in his direction.

"You ain't ever seed a sea serpint?" he was saying, looking pityingly from one to the other of his wide-eyed audience. "*None* o' you?"

A hushed chorus was informing him of their ignorance when there was a scrunch of shingle. Hastily Captain Pepper dismissed a company who, harsh-sounding though his words seemed, withdrew but little and still lingered on hopefully.

"Miss Caroline, Mr. Charles," he roared.

The gate was ceremoniously thrown open and from then, after bowing them into the little garden, their host acquired a grin which he did not lose for the first quarter of an hour.

Mrs. Charles was taken to the best bedroom so that she might lay off her coat and bonnet, whilst her husband warmly congratulated a very faithful friend on the happy conditions in which he found him.

"Not another 'ome in Dover better than this, Mr. Charles," Captain Pepper thundered.

Charles Fagg looked about him. The singing brass kettle, and the plump black cat curled up on the hearthrug; the snowy-white tablecloth, the delightful china on it ; the panelling from the saloon of an East Indiaman, the beams fashioned from the oaken ribs of a once-lovely craft, and the line of small windows from the stern of an old flagship, all fitted with consummate craft.

He was heartily assuring the boatswain on that when the ladies returned, whereupon Martha, following any amount of further fussing, invited them to sit down to the spread.

" Oh, how divine," Mrs. Charles Fagg gloated, frankly peering at plates on which was the evidence of Martha's deft hand with pastries.

Trying to hide how much she was overwhelmed with delight, Mrs. Pepper was doing the honours with the teapot.

" Miss Caroline," she murmured. " Mr. Charles . . . and . . ."

Gravely Captain Fagg handed on the cup poured for the master of the house.

" Partial as ever to tea, Valentine ? " he asked courteously.

Now there had been on Captain Pepper's face a distinct expression of disgust as he eyed the steaming beverage but, at the question, he smartly pulled himself together.

" Nuthin' I likes better'n a dish o' scandalbroth," he announced loudly.

During the meal the conversation continued general, but afterwards the ladies talked clothes, Miss Caroline having bought a most elegant wardrobe in London after she was married there. Meantime, the two gentlemen, over a bottle of Bristol Milk, debated the war situation until the lengthening shadows and old Peter Monin's clock reminded them all of the passage of time. To round off a most enjoyable afternoon Mrs. Charles Fagg accepted, and Martha was coaxed into having, a glass of that same fine Spanish sherry, and with this the social function which, for two whole days, had disjointed the Pepper household, came to a glorious end.

" It's been lovely, Martha," Caroline Fagg said warmly, kissing her hostess.

Mrs. Pepper sniffed suspiciously. " 'T'as been . . . been lovely to have you both, Miss Caroline," she remarked over-brightly.

But when they were gone Martha had recovered sufficiently to wave to them with unabated vigour until they passed from sight.

Despite the fact that he and his wife were seeing Mr. Charles off on the Chichester ' Express,' which pulled out of the Royal Oak yard at six o'clock on the following morning, Valentine had proclaimed he would keep station abeam the visitors for half-way along Snargate Street-over-the-Wall, but he did not part·company until they reached the sluice gates. Here, in view of the Basin where, the incoming tide sweeping over mud and sand, the masts of shipping would shortly be moving towards the vertical, he bade them farewell.

" Well, I'll 'ave to be a-going back ," he mumbled. " An . . .
an'——"

Captain Pepper's affectionate glance embraced them as sharp
change came over him. Cauliflower ears seemed to waggle with
emotion, a squint showed signs of moistness, and tanned cheeks
acquired queer wrinkles.

" An' God bless you both," he muttered huskily.

As Charles Fagg and his bride turned into Snargate Street they
looked back. Nearing the Bank there walked a squat figure beloved
since their childhood. Elbows out, clenched fists swinging, a man who
had many small faults and many noble virtues limped home to his
wife.

Mr. Henry Rochefort, his daughter and son-in-law calling for him,
walked along with them to Little Pent House, where he and John
Fagg immediately closeted themselves in the parlour.

Finding Lou and Jack, Caroline and Charles had a wonderful
surprise, with Mrs. John Woodgate at once taking her sister-in-law
and dearest friend upstairs.

The two young ladies gossiped away, with Lou portraying
the very able wife of some standing, giving an impressive display
whilst shaking out the creases in her husband's best uniform coat.

" Ah," she sighed wisely, " 'tis most difficult in lodgings to——"

" How I envy your competence, Lou, dearest," Mrs. Charles
murmured respectfully, so reverential and admiring.

Mrs. Woodgate's grey-eyed glance came round, and it was two very
gigglesome young married women who went down to the drawing-
room.

There, Mrs. George Rochefort was turning over some music,
Charles and Jack were yarning, Horatio was stretched out on the
floor, busying himself with a tiny ship exquisitely carved from a beef-
bone by one of the French sailors made prisoner-of-war, and Mrs.
Fagg, during a brief respite from her many journeyings between the
dining-room and the kitchen, was pleasurably musing over the grand
supper she had arranged, to which, of course, Doctor and Mrs.
Woodgate were coming.

On his wife's arrival, Captain Fagg bowed most elegantly before
her. He would, he declared, feel himself forever favoured if she
would honour him with her sweet company for half an hour on the
Western Heights before the evening meal.

" Then," she answered demurely, " I'll put on my cloak an'
prepare myself."

" Meantime I'll look into the parlour, m'dear," he smiled.

Their hands slipped away and, when from the hall he had seen

her to the top of the stairs, Charles cautiously opened the door of a
room which would have been more appropriate to the Surveyor to
the Harbour Commissioners than to a shipper and banker. There
were charts which curled open on the turkey-red carpet, maps laid
over convenient furniture, with two chairs drawn close together and
two heads bending over a plan of Dover Harbour which was so large
that it covered the entire top of a moderate-sized table.

" By extending the South Pier into the true tideway . . ." John
Fagg was saying when his companion interrupted.

" Yes, yes," the banker remarked rather testily. " Most admirable, I warrant, but I still contend that 'tis a paltry method of dealing
with the problem."

The shipowner scratched his chin. " Aye, maybe so, Henry," he
agreed. " But much as I'd like to see the Bay enclosed, I fear we must
walk before we can run."

Henry Rochefort laughed shortly. " Hardly an attitude of mind
likely to carry through a great project."

At this stage Charles gently closed the door upon two men who
had been far too preoccupied to notice his entrance.

The waiting for his wife he whiled away by crossing Town Wall
Street with a gift of sugar for *Toke's Quality*, Shep in faithful attendance.
On his return to the house, wondering if Caroline had come down,
he glanced into the drawing-room.

Mrs. George's blue eyes lit up at the sight of her nephew.

" No, not here, Charles," she smiled over the piano, anticipating
his question.

It was a very happy domestic scene. Jack and his wife holding
hands whilst sitting on the striped sofa ; Aunt Susan idly resting her
fingers on the ivory keys ; Horatio seizing upon the good-humoured
Shep and straddling the sheep-dog for a ride ; and the pleasant-faced
mistress of the house complacently sunk into a reverie wherein figured
prime sirloin, butter sauce for the potatoes, baked tart, cream, table
decorations, gleaming cutlery and such-like.

Nevertheless, Mrs. Fagg was not too intent to miss her son.

" I think she went upstairs, Charles," she smiled affectionately,
gaily twiddling her fingers at him. " 'Twas only a few minutes ago
but—Lou, you did say Caroline had gone upstairs, didn't you ? "
Reassured on this, she continued: " But if she isn't upstairs——"

" She'll be down," grinned her soldier son.

" Really, Charles," Polly Fagg was protesting when that gentleman, expansively winking at her, put himself on the other side of
the door.

In the tiled hall, with its gilt chairs and side-table and urns on
cream-and-white fluted pedestals, Charles was kicking his heels, when

from the parlour there came sounds which caused him to make hastily
for that oval-shaped room.

It certainly appeared as if a considerable difference of opinion had
arisen between two gentlemen.

No longer were the shipper and the banker seated. John Fagg,
slightly flushed, was dividing his attention between his friend and
the pier-heads, lovely in the red richness of the afterglow. And Henry
Rochefort, pausing only to fling a few more heated words, was pacing
furiously between the writing-table and the fine fireplace, hands
tightly clasped behind his back.

" Now come, Henry," Charles's father grunted. " The idea is all
right, but 'twould cost a mint of money there ain't any possibility of
raising."

" The funds can be found if we boldly state our objective, and then
fight hard enough to attain it," Mr. Rochefort snapped.

The shipowner shook his head, a simple reply which immeasurably
increased the ire of the banker.

" I tell you they can," he stormed.

" An' I tell you they can't," growled his friend. " 'Tis true I
used to dream of Mr. Digges' scheme myself an' still do, but for the
moment I believe it quite impracticable. Damme, we don't even
know what 'twould cost, but you can take your oath on't that if we
did an' mentioned the sum the other Commissioners 'ud have fits.
No, we're doing very well, Henry, so let's move one step at a time
an' ensure that the hour will come when we can safely broach t'other,
as come it will."

Henry Rochefort's dark eyes were fiery as he wheeled abruptly,
and so pent-up was he that his son-in-law's entry passed unperceived.

" 'Tis a magnificent concept," he shouted. " 'Twould mean that
the facilities here would be large enough to harbour as big a fleet as
ever we should need on this coast, an' 'twould mean that merchant
ships of any tonnage could enter the haven. Do you comprehend all
this ? "

" Do I comprehend all this ? " Mr. Fagg stuttered.

In other circumstances his ludicrous expression, as the sentiments
he himself had preached for over two decades were thrown back in his
teeth, would not have been without comedy. He was so dumfounded
that, when his reply came, it was certainly lame.

" I say, do you understand what I have been telling you ? "
Henry Rochefort demanded passionately, his fist crashing on to the
map on that moderate-sized table.

" Surely I do, Henry," John Fagg muttered feebly. " But——"

The banker, drawing himself up to his full height, was obviously prepared to denounce the fellow for what he was—one who talked a great deal, but one who would not actively give himself heart and soul towards the gaining of that upon which the future prosperity of the townsfolk depended.

" Then . . ." he thundered.

Intervening dryly, Charles Fagg inquired whether they would prefer pistols or swords. As a sally it was decidedly cheap, but notwithstanding that drawback, it effectively crumpled his father-in-law.

The denunciation died in Henry Rochefort's throat as the colour drained from his cheeks. He stood there, a tall, sparsely built man, his shamed glance going from father to son.

" Methinks, John," he murmured sadly. " I shall never improve."

" Well, I confess I prefer a fighter any time," John Fagg remarked huffily. " For rightly or wrongly 'tis only through such that Dover's haven will be placed in the state it should be. But when it comes to——"

Suddenly the banker buried his face in his hands.

" No need for you to say it, John," he muttered.

Nor did John Fagg say it. Instead he stared out of the window. What his first thoughts were no one knew; maybe he was thinking of how much the present improvements were due to this self-willed man, or possibly he was reflecting that personal annoyance must be forgotten towards the greater good. Perhaps, simply, he was pondering over the insensate rages of one who was, after all, his friend.

Slowly he picked up and begun to suck at a cold pipe.

" Methinks, Henry," he said quietly, " that so long as our aim, in its broadest sense, remains the same, there ain't very much to worry about. And," he smiled a little, " seemingly there ain't much doubt on that."

A sweet voice was calling from the hall and, believing implicitly that these two men were best alone, Charles Fagg went out to his wife, leaving his father and father-in-law peacefully resuming their seats before the large scale plan, John Fagg's arm momentarily resting on his friend's shoulder.

With that sight, a rear view of two gentlemen proceeding with their important business, the one wearing a fine curled wig, unpowdered, and the other with his hair tied plain, Captain Fagg closed the door on them.

" So you're there, Charles," smiled Caroline.

He took in the picture she made. " I'm here, m'dear," he said fondly.

Her arm in his, they went along Town Wall Street, past Butchery Gate and the Island, where stood two derelict houses ; then by

Severus's Gate and into the cliff-shadowed shade of Snargate Street.

They reached their chosen destination by the Grand Military Shaft, first receiving a smart salute from the sentry outside the arched approach, and once on the edge of the cliff walked over the rough turf towards the Bredenstone, quietly talking in these closing hours before they parted.

" I feel horribly sad, Charles," Caroline confessed shortly before they began to retrace their steps for home and supper.

He looked at her. " But you would not have me stay, my sweet ? " he asked her gently.

" No, Charles," she shook her head. " No, Charles dearest, I would not have you stay."

The light of day was steadily fading, and from the low vault of Snargate Street the bugle-horn of the London mail echoed as the vehicle left the post office.

" We are fighting for no evil cause, Caroline," Charles Fagg said quietly. " Our struggle is not to place other men under a cruel yoke. We go forth not for conquest, but to seek out and destroy an insatiable beast. 'Tis not for ourselves alone either, my dear, but for the sake of our children and our children's children."

She took tighter hold of his arm. " 'Twill be a long road, Charles, for even now, after so many heart-grievous years, we are but at the beginning."

His outstretched hand pointed towards Dungeness and then moved round the greying sea to Boulogne and beyond. It was as if he, a soldier who had fought in the Peninsula, possessed strange foresight of a six-year fight which, stubborn step by stubborn step, should take the British standards from the lines of Torres Vedras over the Pyrenees to Waterloo.

" But we *are* at the beginning, m'dear," he smiled. " After an age of dreary waiting we now take the fight to them. And soon, pray God, they shall know what that means."

Charles Fagg was drinking in a loved scene it would be long before he saw again. The old town between the chalky precipices at the foot of the valley, the darkening line of the French coast and the proud fortress which faced it so undauntedly, the ' key and gate to England ' as it was called. The fortifications, from Archcliffe to the base of the Castle cliff, to which at that moment were marching files of men whose duty it would be to hold them inviolate for the night. The Harbour . . .

" Yes, Charles," his wife said softly, following his glance, " I'm exquisitely glad that Papa feels the same way now. 'Tis hard to struggle alone."

His arm was about her shoulders as he stared down at the tiny haven. The South Pier which ran out so modest a distance from the beach near Townshend's Battery, and the North Pier which was, in effect, no more than a reinforced spit of shingle shooting off from the Ropewalk.

" Father has fought a long time, Caroline," he said thoughtfully. " Whether he will ever see what he dreams of I don't know, but I'll swear he'll never give up the contest until his dying day, and at that he'll leave an example behind him which may serve as an inspiration to others, for 'twill to more than me."

For a while, silhouetted on the Heights, stood Captain Charles Fagg and his wife, a most handsome young gentleman and a most lovely young lady.

" *Satisfied*, Charles ? " she asked impertinently, for he was steadily eyeing her.

Grey eyes surveyed her coolly. " Quite, m'dear," he said.

" Oh, Charles," she blushed divinely.

" And you, m'dear ? " he inquired courteously.

She hesitated perceptibly.] " Mmm-mmm, Charles," she murmured, tantalisingly.

Still in that place, within sight of half Dover should it be turning that way, Charles Fagg's grip increased as he kissed his wife.

" *Satisfied*, Caroline ? " he asked with just the same shade of impertinence.

" Yes . . . Charles," she said breathlessly.

For another moment they looked deeply at one another, and then, arm-in-arm, her elbow pressed against his side, his hand tightly grasping hers, Captain and Mrs. Fagg of Dover moved into the growing dusk.

Soon full darkness would spread its concealing canopy over the old Cinque Port of Dover, over its Castle and Harbour, over men who, in the name of liberty, would ever faithfully defend their priceless heritage.

THE END